PRAISE FOR R. J. PINEIRO

"Move over Tom Clancy, there is a new kid on the block."
—*Library Journal*

"An author equally at ease with complex software and superior storytelling."
—Ralph Peters, *New York Times* bestselling author of *Traitor*

"Readers with voracious appetites for fast action and hardware... will come for this book in droves."
—*Booklist* on *Cyberterror*

"Pineiro's vision of what might be evokes visceral fear."
—Mark Berent,
New York Times bestselling author of *Storm Flight*

"Pineiro knows how to move a story right along smartly from one crisis to the next with the tension always building... gets right under the reader's skin so that in the end the payoff is like Fourth of July fireworks."
—David Hagberg,
USA Today bestselling author of *Joshua's Hammer*

"Pineiro scrunches you into the ejection seat and sends you rocketing aloft."
—Dean Ing,
New York Times bestselling author of *Loose Cannon*

BOOKS BY R. J. PINEIRO

Siege of Lightning
Ultimatum
Retribution
Exposure
Breakthrough
01-01-00
Y2K
Shutdown
Conspiracy.com
Firewall
Cyberterror
Havoc
SpyWare
Eagle and the Cross*

*Forthcoming

SpyWare

R. J. Pineiro

A TOM DOHERTY ASSOCIATES BOOK
NEW YORK

This is a work of fiction. All of the characters, organizations, and events portrayed in this novel are either products of the author's imagination or are used fictitiously.

SPYWARE

Copyright © 2007 by R. J. Pineiro

A Forge Book
Published by Tom Doherty Associates, LLC
175 Fifth Avenue
New York, NY 10010

www.tor-forge.com

Forge® is a registered trademark of Tom Doherty Associates, LLC.

ISBN-13: 978-0-7653-5060-2
ISBN-10: 0-7653-5060-2

First Edition: October 2007

Printed in the United States of America

0 9 8 7 6 5 4 3 2 1

For Lory,
who shows me the joys of life every second
of every day,

AND

for St. Jude,
Saint of the Impossible, for continuing
to make it possible.

Acknowledgments

There are many individuals who contributed to this project, but it would be impossible to name everyone in the space allowed. They all have my gratitude.

I would especially like to recognize:

My wife and best friend, Lory Anne, for her unconditional love, friendship, and encouragement through the years.

My seventeen-year-old son, Cameron, for making me so proud with his achievements and good heart.

Tom Doherty, Robert Gleason, and Eric Raab, the dream team at Tor Books, for continuing to believe in my passion for the written word, and for publishing some of the best books in the trade.

Matthew Bialer, my loyal agent, for his guidance and patience.

My good friend Dave, for his friendship and sound guidance in technical matters.

Mike Wiltz, one of many unsung heroes from Katrina, for teaching the rest of us the true meaning of courage.

The rest of my family in Texas, Louisiana, El Salvador, and Venezuela, for always being there for me.

Finally, a special note goes to my friends and colleagues at Advanced Micro Devices, the place I call my second home after nearly a quarter of a century of manufacturing excellence in semiconductors.

Acknowledgments

SpyWare

1

Antwerp City Blues

Stepping out of the third taxi he had taken in the past hour, Savage surveyed the camera-bearing tourists with trained suspicion as he made his way toward the west end of the Grote Markt, the picturesque town square of the port city of Antwerp, Belgium.

His eyes regarded the crowd from behind the mirror tint of his sunglasses, searching for brusque head moves, for bodies shifting abruptly, for disturbances in the natural flow of the mass of visitors enjoying a cool and sunny morning in Belgium's second largest city, the diamond capital of the world.

Dressed in a pair of loose khaki slacks, a white polo shirt under a neutral windbreaker, and black soft-sole shoes to maximize traction over the slick cobblestone streets, Savage merged with the crowd with practiced ease, navigating through it effortlessly, arms hanging loosely by his sides, hands free.

Never compromise your hands, he thought as he failed to spot any telltale signs of surveillance, as he approached the massive structure of Our Lady's Cathedral, its soaring north tower, lacework in stone, rising to the heavens, dwarfing the Renaissance-style buildings surrounding this magnificent square, second to none in architectural splendor and size but Brussels' Grand Place.

Honeymooners, families, college kids, and tour groups melted into a sea of humanity speaking a dozen languages at once, creating a cacophony of sounds that mixed with the bands playing and dancing for the delighted visitors enjoying refreshments from the many terraces and sidewalk cafes.

Savage saw past the cosmetics, probing deeper, exacting the essence of the sight, the natural rhythm of this environment, before blending with it, becoming invisible, like a ghost.

Like a chameleon.

You must become a chameleon, he remembered Donald Bane, his CIA mentor, telling him over fifteen years ago, during his Agency training days following his recruitment from the Navy SEALs, where he had spent five years risking his neck for Uncle Sam in exotic destinations like Iraq and Colombia.

Savage grimaced at the tingle propagating up his left leg, held together by a pound of titanium screws and bars after he nearly lost it to an Iraqi grenade what now seemed like eons ago.

You must adapt to your environment, Mac, Bane had told him again and again during those early weeks at The Farm, the CIA training facility in Williamsburg, Virginia. *You must become one with it, for only then will you be able to lose your surveillance, to turn the tables, to force your hunter into becoming your prey.*

Savage remembered those days with affection, when he had been naïve enough to believe that he had been given a second lease on life following the tragedy in Iraq.

And Donald Bane had been the one who stepped in to fill him with hope when he thought his military career was over—the same Donald Bane who had taken in the youngster Mac Savage following the terrifying assassination of his parents in Tel Aviv at the hands of a madman, a suicide terrorist wearing an explosive vest that took out the restaurant where they were having lunch on his father's day off as a civilian liaison to the ambassador of the United States in that war-torn nation.

Savage had made headlines around the world, the teenager in the shredded clothes, on his knees crying amid the rubble and the smoke, the bodies of his parents covered by blue sheets as emergency crews searched for survivors in the collapsed building.

Spooks take care of one another.

His father had told him that many times. Should something happen to him, Savage and his mother would be looked after.

But I lost you both.

His throat aching in sudden grief, Savage remembered how Donald Bane, then the CIA station chief in the Israeli capital, had upheld this unwritten CIA pact, providing for the education of the fourteen-year-old orphan, the son of his best friend and colleague, sending him to the finest schools, eventually watching him answer his country's call to fight international terrorism, following September 11 by applying for the SEAL training program in San Diego. Donald Bane had been there for him on that glorious day when Savage had earned the coveted Trident, when he had defeated the staggering odds of the Underwater Demolition Training Program, surviving Hell Week—as well as the weeks that followed—accomplishing what so very few people on Earth could.

At the time, Mac Savage thought he could change a world that had stopped making sense, devoting the best years of his life to serving Uncle Sam. But the tragedy in Iraq put a sudden end to a promising military career. No one had seen the grenade until it was too late, ripping two of his team members to shreds before maiming him.

And Donald Bane had come to the rescue again, demanding the best surgeons, the best medical technology, the finest therapists in the world to teach his protégé to walk all over again, to become whole again.

But not good enough for the SEALs.

Savage sighed.

Enter the Central Intelligence Agency.

Bane had taken him into the family at Langley and had personally escorted him to The Farm, where he learned the tools of a secret trade, of shadow operations, of covert activities—tools that would serve him well for the following decade and a half.

Until that night. . . .

Savage clenched his jaw while recalling the shocking turn of events in Sierra Leone—events that led him to his assignment in Belgium and the eventual downward spiral of his relationship with the CIA that resulted in his recent resignation.

Focus.

Savage's operative sense pushed the image of a field of maimed kids aside, focusing his attention back on the task at hand, reviewing the safety measures he had taken since leaving his hotel three hours ago, the multiple taxis, the many blocks he had walked in between each two, his confidence growing that no one had followed him.

He continued to move with the crowd, constantly checking for the betraying signs of a shadow, finding none, eventually leaving the Grote Markt behind and continuing west on Meir, the name of the most famous shopping street in Antwerp.

But the large avenue, closed many years ago to all traffic except pedestrians, with its hundreds of exclusive shops nestled in a breathtaking historic surrounding, was not the former CIA operative's primary target; neither were the thousands of shoppers feeding the economic engine of this exclusive section of town; nor were the wealthy merchants dealing in anything from the finest designers' clothes, jewelry, watches, and automobiles to the most desirable art work.

Mac Savage's reason for visiting this section of town went further than the exclusive store owners serving the affluent; past famous monuments and centuries-old works of architectural perfection; beyond the stylish, model-thin women visiting designers' shops and the many sidewalk restaurants catering to hungry patrons a block east of Antwerp's central railway station in the heart of the World Diamond District.

The ice capital of the world.

Stopping in front of the Fountaine Hotel, three blocks past

the intersection of Meir and Wapper, where the street once more opened up for vehicle traffic, Savage checked the IWC perpetual watch hugging his left wrist, verifying that he was thirty minutes early, just as dictated by his professional habits: Always reach the meeting grounds precisely thirty minutes *ahead* of schedule to survey the place, to ensure its safety. Longer than that would force him to linger excessively, risking drawing unwanted attention. Shorter than that didn't allow enough time to appraise the light morning traffic and surrounding buildings for signs of surveillance— even though Savage had picked the time and place of this meeting, and had conveyed that information just an hour ago, between taxi rides, to the man he was meeting inside that hotel.

Savage approached a kiosk across the street selling periodicals and assorted magazines, feigned interest in a local sports magazine displaying a soccer goalkeeper in midair catching a penalty kick.

He pretended to read it while eyeballing the watch again. The platinum timepiece, manufactured by the International Watch Company, retailed for over fifty thousand euros at nearby shops. But he viewed it as an asset, which he could easily liquidate to generate emergency funds without the paper trail of bank accounts and charge cards. Savage also wore a diamond-encrusted gold cross beneath the polo shirt, plus a money belt fitted with fifteen thousand dollars, two American passports under different names, and matching New York State driver's licenses and charge cards.

Mobility.

Donald Bane had taught him early in his career that mobility—unrestricted freedom of operation—was a weapon as formidable as the blue-steel 9mm Beretta pistol tucked in his pants, pressed against his left kidney with the handle facing forward for swift right-hand retrieval. And as dictated by the rules of his former profession, Savage also carried a backup weapon, a 32-caliber Walther PPK in an ankle holster.

Hoping he would not have to use the semiautomatics on this cool and breezy September afternoon, the ex-CIA operative gazed toward the hotel beyond the light traffic on Meir, mostly taxis and buses mixed with private vehicles.

Savage's level of focused paranoia—not to be confused with the destructive random fear of an amateur—had been elevated a couple of notches since departing Langley. Fifteen years putting bad guys away in the service of Uncle Sam had created many enemies for Mac Savage, the kind of underworld characters who would just love to go to work on him with a scalpel, a blowtorch, and a bottle of bleach. Lacking formal CIA protection, Savage was essentially on his own every day, meaning there was no immediate backup, no cavalry ready to charge in to defend him should he get himself in trouble. Of course, as a retired CIA officer, he had been provided a unique telephone number, which Savage had committed to memory and could call only in an absolute emergency when all else failed. But the standard response wasn't immediate—sometimes as long as forty-eight hours—as the CIA could only devote so much of its bandwidth to monitor the whereabouts of former officers. But Savage knew that as long as Bane was in charge—even if his former mentor was getting close to being canned by the new White House administration—help would be on its way as fast as it could should he need it. The Agency wasn't perfect, but it did take care of its own.

He sighed.

In the end it doesn't matter.

In spite of the Agency's best intentions, in his line of work forty-eight hours—even twenty-four—was an eternity, meaning he was pretty much on his own even with Uncle Bane pulling strings to accelerate assistance.

Focus.

Observing no anomalies in the street scene, Savage's gaze landed on the building's revolving doors separating the hotel's lobby from the crowded sidewalk as he remembered the brief phone call he had received that morning from Jean-Pierre Bockstael, the managing director of the HRD, the Hoge Raad voor Diamant—the Diamond High Council.

The ice lords, Savage thought.

The umbrella organization and official international representative of the Belgian diamond business, the HRD controlled the mining, cutting, polishing, distribution, and sales of nearly fifty percent of the worldwide diamond trade—all from within a two-square-mile area in downtown Antwerp comprising over 1500 diamond companies, including the mighty Diamond Trading Company, formally known as De Beers Consolidated Mines Ltd. From here, fully polished and serialized diamonds were exported to the far corners of the earth to satisfy an ever-hungrier market for the coveted stones—all under the watchful eye of the all-powerful HRD.

When Savage received the urgent call from the second-in-command of this influential organization, a man he had come to know and respect during his three-year assignment as liaison between the U.S. Government and the HRD in the fight against blood diamonds, he had immediately called him back.

Jean-Pierre Bockstael.

While continuing to browse the sports magazine, Savage remembered the unmistakable edge of fear in Bockstael's voice on the phone.

A matter of great urgency and discretion.

But that alone had not been a good enough for Mac Savage to drop his current projects and come to the aid of his former HRD contact.

A matter involving Renee Laroux, Bockstael had added, immediately hooking Savage at the mention of his former girlfriend of two years.

Renee Laroux, an HRD executive, had broken off the relationship with Mac Savage because of a job promotion to oversee the mining operations in West Africa.

In Sierra Leone.

The old familiar pain gripping his intestines returned with formidable force as images of dismembered bodies, of agonizing screams, flooded his mind. Savage remembered the children, the terrible collateral damage of a CIA operation gone bad, the final straw that had pushed him over the edge four years ago.

He tightened the grip on the magazine, recalling how he had begged Renee to decline the transfer to Freetown, Sierra

Leone's capital. And he also remembered how she had
begged him to come along.

But I can't, he had told her, unable to elaborate, to explain,
prevented by his agreement with The Agency to disclose
to the woman he had grown to love how he had botched
an operation targeted at eradicating a pocket of guerrillas
belonging to the infamous Revolutionary United Front—the
RUF—from a mining operation near Kono, in eastern Sierra
Leone.

And just like that Renee Laroux had walked out of his life
and headed for that dreadful place.

Kono.

Mac Savage clenched his jaw, fighting off old demons, the
brutal memories.

Over a decade of field operations and a stellar reputation
as a former Navy SEAL had all vaporized in an instant because of that terrible mistake—a terrible miscalculation in
the midst of a war to combat the illegal mining of diamonds
in Sierra Leone, to eradicate their unlawful operations.

To win the ice wars of West Africa.

Ice Wars

Perspiration soaking his camouflaged fatigues, Mac
Savage dragged his body across the leaf-covered terrain
overlooking the guerrilla camp, his movements cautious, coordinated, silent.

In the predawn hours, under a star-filled sky in eastern
Sierra Leone, the RUF guerrilla camp slept quietly, peacefully, unaware of the hell about to be unleashed by the

growing partnership between the government of this war-torn nation and the United States of America to fight illegal diamond mining.

To kill the problem at the source.

He remembered Donald Bane's words prior to his assignment in Bogotá, Colombia, when Savage had assisted the government of that country in its brutal fight against the violent cartel.

Kill the problem at the source, Mac.

Without a source there was no downstream business.

Without a source there were no illegal brokers, no illegal buyers, no black market.

Mac Savage was being assisted this early morning by a pair of F117A Stealth Fighters from the 435th Air Base Wing at Ramstein Air Base in Germany, which fell under the 3rd Air Force assigned under the United States Air Forces in Europe.

America was about to deliver the sleepy militia camp below a decisive blow, sending a clear and powerful message across this land. The United States and the government-elect of Sierra Leone would no longer tolerate the trade in illegal diamonds.

Savage checked the G-shock Casio hugging his left wrist as he produced a device shaped like a pistol from a Velcro-secured pocket on the utility vest he wore over the fatigues.

Activating the laser element and checking his watch once more, he pointed the device at the center of the camp, before reviewing the coordinates of his GPS, verifying that he was indeed 3.2 kilometers to the north of the town of Gokalima, near the Kono mines, the precise location where Salim Ana-hah, his informant in Freetown, had told him the guerrilla camp was located.

With his free hand, Savage grabbed a pair of night-vision binoculars strapped to the side of the vest and pressed the rubber ends against his eyes. The unit amplified the available light, turning the surrounding darkness into palettes of green, allowing him to inspect the camp.

He had worked with Salim for the past two years, since Langley transferred him here from Bogotá, and the informant had always been reliable. He had no reason to suspect otherwise on this assignment. On top of that, he had crosschecked the intelligence with satellite images from the NPIC, the National Photographic and Interpretation Center in Washington, D.C., confirming the presence of armed men. And as final insurance, the CIA Station in Freetown had further crosschecked the intelligence with the government in Freetown, which had its own informers, corroborating the intelligence just yesterday.

Mosquitoes buzzed nearby but did not settle thanks to the scent in the camouflage cream on his face and neck. Savage frowned while inspecting the field. His operative sense flashed the danger of letting too many outsiders into this joint CIA–Pentagon operation. A war-torn country like this was packed with spies on both sides. Confirming intelligence with the local government had to be done extremely carefully because no one really knew who could be listening, and the last thing Savage wanted to do was telegraph the CIA's intentions twenty-four hours before the air strike. In the end it came to judgment on the CIA's side to decide just how much crosschecking was required before pulling the trigger. Too little crosscheck and you ran the risk of operating on half-baked intel. Too much crosscheck, and you ran the risk of exposing your plans to a spy.

Keep looking, he thought, using the laser to paint the target for the incoming F117A Stealth Fighters as he surveyed the camp, failing to see anyone, even a sentry.

That's odd.

Either the guerrillas were getting too sloppy or perhaps too comfortable knowing that their location well within RUF-controlled territory shielded them from any possible government attack.

But the RUF that Mac Savage had come to know and hate after two years of painfully close calls was as brutal as it was careful, cautious, and passionately determined to protect its insanely profitable operation.

The RUF Mac Savage knew would have posted sentries around the camp while the rest of the men slept in the tents.

He checked the digital readout of his watch once more.

Three minutes before strike time.

And he still could not see a single guerrilla in the camp.

Where in the fuck are they?

The two-way radio strapped to his utility belt was connected to an earpiece and a voice-activated throat mike. All Savage had to do was speak a single word: *ABORT*, and the pilots of the F117As would do an about face and head back to Germany.

Two minutes to go.

His mouth suddenly going dry, his sixth sense telling him something was seriously wrong, Savage now began a frantic pan around the camp with the binoculars, shifting his greenish field of view from tent to tent.

One minute left and still no sign of—

There!

Savage spotted two figures beneath a towering tree hugging the north edge of the guerrilla camp, the unmistakable shape of AK-47 assault rifles hanging loosely from their shoulders.

He zoomed in, watching them stand still in the night, as professional sentries would, avoiding all unnecessary movement.

And just to their left stood another pair of guards, also armed and also remaining completely still. Beyond them stood a small helicopter, the ends of its single rotor tied down with ropes.

And it was at that moment that he heard the faint noise of jet engines.

To the untrained observer, the sounds would seem to be coming from miles away, but Savage knew better. The only way to actually hear the muffled turbines of an F117A was with the jet almost on top of you.

Shifting his attention to the dark sky, Savage spotted their incoming shapes against an emerald green background for a brief instant, as they dove over the field, as they pulled up hard after releasing the laser-guided munitions before vanishing from sight.

Savage set down the binoculars as the rain of self-propelled antipersonnel mines, like an apocalyptic cloud, momentarily hovered above the camp, the laser seekers in their nanotronic brains locking onto Savage's target.

He looked away as the clearing detonated in multiple places at once seconds later, the rumbling deafening, the blasts splashing the sky with tongues of fire, like a biblical curse, projecting scorching shrapnel in every directing, punching through canvas walls, thatched roofs, tearing into the guerrilla nest with flesh-ripping force.

Savage waited for the explosions of fuel and ammunition depots. But he saw no secondary blasts.

That's strange, he thought, once more focusing the night-vision binoculars on the camp, surveying the damage, watching with trained indifference the dozen or so figures staggering or crawling in the night, some on fire, others missing limbs—their agonizing wails echoing in the surrounding jungle in a scene stolen straight from Dante's *Inferno.*

But the silhouettes were too small to be adults, their agonizing cries too high-pitched.

Children?

Dear God!

They're kids!

Savage felt the entire world collapsing on his shoulders, his vision narrowing at the terrifying sight, at the nightmare he had released on children.

Sweet Lord, what were they doing here?

This was supposed to be a guerrilla camp!

But the harrowing images, the stench of burnt flesh, the boys and girls dragging their maimed bodies across the terrain tore into his soul with the force of a million antipersonnel mines.

On his knees, eyes shut, his mind refusing to see the heart-wrenching spectacle any longer, the CIA officer was transported back to another place, to another time. He saw the destruction of the building, watched the blast propagate almost in slow motion, saw his parents throw themselves in the way, protecting him with their own bodies. He watched his mother's dying eyes as the impact carved a gaping hole in her back, broiling her organs, killing her instantly as he lay there totally helpless.

Stretching his arms at the African sky, Savage inhaled deeply, filling his lungs with the smell of scorched flesh, of cordite—of death—letting go a loud scream of terror, of anger, of overwhelming guilt and frustration.

The desperate cry of a desperate man.

3

Realities

There were events in people's lives that forever transformed them, that changed the way they viewed the world, the way they saw the sky, the trees, even those around them. For Mac Savage such transformation had taken place the day a terrorist bomb killed his parents, and then again decades later, on the night the children died because of his miscalculation.

The sun shone a little less brightly since that tragic night, since those refugee boys and girls cried out in the darkness.

Blinking away the sight, swallowing the lump in his throat, wiping the perspiration forming on his forehead, Savage breathed deeply, shaking his mind out of the flashback, away from the terrible sin that usually flared in the middle of the night, when past demons came alive, scourging him in his sleep, the voices of maimed children reverberating in the deepest corners of his mind.

"My legs . . . my face . . . the pain . . . please kill me."

Savage clenched his jaw.

Renee knew about the death of his parents from terrorists, but he never told her what had happened in Sierra Leone. Therefore, she was never able to connect the dots, to understand the added dimension that such mistake had had on him, the compelling reason behind Savage's refusal to accompany her there. Not only could he not share this with her because of its highly classified nature, but how could anyone ever get close to him—much less *love* him—knowing what he had done, the kind of monster that he was?

Besides, he simply couldn't go back. Mac Savage could not think of a force on this planet powerful enough to make him ever again set foot on African soil. The memories were too powerful—the nightmares too vivid—for Savage to get close to the heat, to the smell, to the poverty, to the pleading eyes of an African child.

Renee never learned the reason why.

And she'll never know, he thought, frowning.

No one will ever know . . . aside from Donald Bane.

The government of Freetown, in conjunction with the American government, had publicly condemned the terrible attack on the UNICEF camp near Gokalima by RUF rebels. Donald Bane had buried the entire operation, and the participants not only had been sworn to secrecy by Langley, but were warned of stern repercussions if leaks—intentional or unintentional—ever tied the incident to America.

For Mac Savage, however, the experience had been so extreme, so life changing, that he could no longer function in Sierra Leone. He could not resume his intelligence duties surrounded by so many people and places that continued to remind him of what he had done, of what he had become.

Bane, the only one who had understood the terrifying connection between Sierra Leone and Savage's youth, had shipped him off to a remote resort in Italy for therapy, where Agency shrinks helped him overcome the tragedy. They patched him up mentally enough to operate as a CIA officer again.

But nowhere near Africa.

Bane had transferred him here, to Antwerp, far away from the killing fields of Sierra Leone, to combat the traffic of conflict ice from a less stressful place.

Returning the magazine to its proper slot in the stand, Savage nodded politely to the kiosk owner, a heavy man in his late fifties with an unkempt beard and loose clothing.

Crossing the street, he went through the hotel's revolving doors and stepped into the elegantly decorated lobby—the sight in stark contrast with the visions slowly drifting to the hazy periphery of his mind.

Mozart flowing out of unseen speakers soothing him, spreading temporary peace through his system, allowing the operative in him to once again emerge through the chaos of the past, Mac Savage surveyed the visitors crowding the front desk, lounging by the many sets of cream leather sofas beneath ornate chandeliers, or lounging by the bar opposite the elevators. Traditional art adorned pastel walls, which, combined with the soft light cast by the elaborate light fixtures over the polished marble floors, plus the classical music, projected an environment designed to soothe the senses, to relax jet-lagged visitors and stressed businessmen.

Savage turned toward the elevators, two sets of brass double doors beyond one of the arrays of sofas over Persian rugs and large potted palms nearly touching ornate twenty-foot ceilings.

But he didn't get far.

His charge sat in a corner sofa flanked by two large men in their thirties with military-style haircuts dressed in business suits and soft-soled shoes, their bulging muscles pressing against the fine fabric of their garments.

Bockstael's bodyguards stood not only to either side of him, but a few feet ahead. This observation, combined with the wall behind the sofa and the plants, provided a choke point to protect their principal, meaning anyone would have to go through them before being able to reach the wealthy HRD executive.

But the protection scheme had one flaw: It didn't provide them with a back door, an alternate exit should an overwhelming force launch a frontal attack on their position. And that, plus their relaxed attitude—the guerrilla on the left with his hands shoved in his side pockets and the one on the right holding a small radio—told Savage he was dealing with rookies, with wannabes who confused brute force with their ability to provide bulletproof executive protection.

Never compromise your hands.

Savage walked toward his charge, annoyed at the amateurish display, including the gross violation of his meeting rules, which had clearly stipulated the privacy of a third-story corner room with a rear window leading to an emergency ladder.

The dynamic duo became suddenly alert upon spotting Savage, turning toward their principal for advice—in the process breaking eye contact with a potential threat, violating another cardinal rule in the executive protection business.

Bockstael, a pale and fragile man in his late sixties with thin white hair and liver spots on his sallow cheeks, gave his guards a tired nod.

"Good afternoon, gentlemen," Savage said, stepping in front of them and slowly extending his arms to the sides a few inches, enough to give them room for a thorough search, but not so much as to attract unnecessary attention from bystanders.

One of the guards frisked him while the other spoke on the radio. The amateur found Savage's 9mm Beretta, which he swiftly pocketed to keep anyone in that lobby from seeing it, but he missed the Walther PPK because he failed to search below the calves.

Stepping to the side, the guard let him through the laughable line of scrimmage while the other continued to whisper on the radio.

"Hello Mac," said Jean-Pierre Bockstael in the raspy voice of someone who had smoked most of this life, and still did based on the cigarette wedged between the index and middle fingers of his bony right hand. Two cigarette butts on the crystal ashtray on the glass cocktail table in front of the sofa, where Savage also spotted a half-drunk glass of what appeared to be a scotch on the rocks, told him Bockstael had also arrived early, probably at the request of his bodyguards. And that reemphasized his initial assessment of the two guerrillas. Like most rookies, they were unpredictable, following certain rules, such as arriving early at meetings, but disregarding others.

The executive vice-president in charge of the mining operations for HRD, including security, transportation, finance, and auditing, Jean-Pierre Bockstael reported to Hans Van-Lothar, the CEO, who was also the chairman of the board of this powerful organization.

"The time off has done you well, Mac. You are looking healthy."

Since his departure from the Agency, Savage had first taken a two-month sabbatical in the south of France and Monaco to let the Mediterranean's warm waters help wash away the political hell he had endured during the final six months of his CIA career. He had then returned to Antwerp to set up a security consulting firm to cater to the thousands of companies in this part of town who prized the safety of their business above all else. In the four weeks since his return, he had already engaged in lucrative contract negotiations with a dozen firms and was planning to make a decision on which contracts to accept by next week.

"Thank you, sir," replied Savage, before sitting next to Bockstael, who was dressed in a gray pin-striped suit, a white shirt, and a maroon tie hanging from a perfect knot. "You're looking good yourself."

The HRD official took a long drag before exhaling through his nostrils while flicking the tip over the ashtray and saying, "*Please*. It's amazing I'm still alive the way I treat my body. But thanks for the gesture, and also for meeting with me so quickly. The word around town is that you're becoming quite the security consultant." The Belgian's English was tinged with a mild Dutch accent that made him end his words with an abruptness that would be perceived as a sign of hostility in America, but Savage had been operating in this part of Europe long enough to know better.

"You're too kind, Mr. Bockstael."

The Belgian gave him a weak smile before tilting his head at the guards, who took a few steps aside to provide the requested privacy.

Unfortunately, rather than turning *away* from them, the two rookies remained facing the sofa—to Savage's disappointment at yet another violation of the rules of executive protection: *Always* guard the side where the threat could originate.

Savage was *not* the threat.

The dynamic duo needed to be facing the lobby, the dozens of strangers lounging about beyond their established security perimeter.

Amateur hour, he thought with an internal frown, his training telling him to abort the meeting.

Walk away and reschedule, Mac.

But overwhelming curiosity about the reason the HRD executive had called him outweighed his operative sense, keeping him there but with heightened awareness, and without letting his true feelings surface while under the discerning stare of Bockstael, who continued to regard the former CIA operative with steady blue eyes.

"Would you like a drink from the bar?" Bockstael asked.

"No, thank you. But may I ask a question before we get started?"

The executive nodded.

"Why didn't you meet me upstairs, as we had discussed?"

Bockstael looked away, then down at the fancy rug, before grimacing and returning the stare. "Given my current situation, I feel more comfortable in public areas and surrounded by lots of people . . . by eyewitnesses," he replied, his gaze narrowing as he added, "Is that vital for the continuation of this meeting?"

Savage frowned inwardly. Perhaps the time off had altered his operative sense to the point that he might have overreacted with all of the precautions. After all, he was no longer with the Agency, and not once did he spot any sign of surveillance during his time off in the south of France, meaning Langley was living up to its word, leaving him alone. But that, he admitted, was a mixed blessing; he was now on his own should a ghost from the past decided to materialize and get even for something Savage had done in the line of duty.

"No. It's all right," said Savage, deciding to let it go for the moment, asking instead, "Is the new liaison to the ambassador working out well?" The term liaison was the front for the CIA station chief of the Antwerp Station, the American intelligence body chartered with working with HRD to fight the trade of blood diamonds.

"You mean Costa?"

Savage nodded.

Michael Costa was the son of American Vice President Raymond Costa, who had used his connections to force DCI Donald Bane to assign his son to run the Antwerp Station along with Savage, using a two-in-a-box concept eight months ago, shortly after Vice President Costa, and his running mate, President Andrew Boyer, came into office. The once all-influential Donald Bane had caved under pressure from the new administration, allowing the assignment even under extreme protest from Savage.

And that means that Bane's days are numbered, Savage thought. The CIA was just the latest federal agency that had fallen victim to the new White House administration, who started to make changes for the sake of making changes—even if the changes weakened the government agency in charge of dissolving terrorist plots against America.

Savage had lasted six months before deciding to try his hand in the less political and far more lucrative private security industry. Michael Costa now ran the Antwerp Station and rumor had it that he would soon be promoted to Langley—again thanks to his powerful connections.

Bockstael's narrow shoulders lifted slightly as he frowned and then replied, "His people seem to be working well with HRD's security team. But he isn't as experienced as you—though the man is certainly well connected."

"Washington likes him," said Savage, working hard at hiding his resentment toward the man who replaced him as chief of the Antwerp Station. But he could not avoid the old familiar pain stabbing his stomach at the thought of his CIA career gone to shit, starting in Sierra Leone and finishing with his dismay at having to play two-in-a-box with the inexperienced and arrogant son of the new American viper.

Michael Costa was a spoiled kid whose only exposure to field operations had been a two-year stint in Madras four years ago before his influential father, then a powerful senator, pulled him back to Washington to move up the bureaucratic ranks. Never mind that Savage had distinguished himself in the SEALs, including earning the Purple Heart for the wounds he sustained in Iraq. Never mind that he had to learn to walk all over again and had gone on to join the CIA, enduring volatile Colombia and the diamond-mining countries in Africa. Never mind that he had to live with so many horrible memories from such exotic destinations.

Including Sierra Leone.

Savage looked away, remembering the transfer to Antwerp, where he started as a senior officer, but soon his ability to build powerful relations with the Diamond High Council—namely Bockstael and also Renee Laroux—had earned him the well-deserved promotion to CIA chief of the Antwerp Station.

And then Washington twists Bane's arm to force that two-in-a-box shit down my throat.

Savage took a deep breath and momentarily looked away, remembering all of the outstanding work that his team had done alongside Belgian authorities and HRD in the fight against the illegal diamond trade. In a way it had felt as if he had gotten a second lease on life following the incident in Sierra Leone.

Once settled in Antwerp, however, Savage had managed to keep the past in the past, and had focused on the task at hand, hitting blood diamond traffickers hard. Under his leadership, Savage's team had put a dent into the traffickers' operation. But there was still much work to be done to fully eradicate their illegal operations. According to the latest Diamond High Council's report the illegal trade had exceeded five billion dollars in worldwide sales last year.

But that was just an estimate, of course. The CIA knew the real number was at least *twice* that, just as it also knew that a significant portion of those funds were channeled to finance international terrorism—the primary reason for the strong CIA presence in this particular city.

But that's no longer my problem.

The political climate change in Washington—on top of his breakup with Renee Laroux—had finally encouraged him to trade in his unflagging patriotism in exchange for the chance of making serious bucks before he got to be fifty. Mac Savage had seen too many old-timers at the CIA reach the end of the road with nothing to show but a government pension that could barely afford them a third-rate condo five blocks away from some second-rate beach in Mississippi. If he was meant to grow old alone, at least he wanted to be well off.

"How are things at HRD?" Savage asked, working hard to hide his growing curiosity about any news from Renee down in Sierra Leone. Since their official separation six months ago, he had not heard a word.

Bockstael shrugged again before taking another drag, exhaling, and then replying, "Fine up until last night, when the board asked for my resignation."

Savage blinked and opened his mouth but said nothing. Then he instantly chastised himself for the external reaction. The months basking in Nice and Monte Carlo had certainly dulled his operative sense. Exposing inner feelings this way in the field—even for an instant—was the kiss of death.

"Why would the board ever want to do a thing like that?" Savage finally asked, well aware that under Bockstael's operational leadership, HRD's influence in the world's diamond market had increased by over twenty-five percent while also nearly doubling the number of companies whose business transactions it oversaw. "Your record is impecca—"

"This isn't about my record," the aging executive whispered while leaning toward Savage. His breath smelled of tobacco and alcohol. "It's about what I learned . . . about the confidential report that reached my office yesterday from Renee, who was auditing a mine east of Freetown."

Bockstael paused, took a sip of his drink, closed his eyes while swallowing, before setting it back down.

Savage remained quiet, hiding his rocketing anxiety to find out where this was headed.

"You might remember Renee. She used to handle De Beers before it became the Diamond Trading Company," Bockstael said with a hint of dark amusement in his voice, as Savage's relationship with the HRD executive was no secret.

Savage sighed as images of the middle-aged executive filled him. Tall, tanned, brunette, and always elegantly dressed, Renee Laroux had a PhD in gemology from the University of Brussels and an MBA from the Harvard Business School. She had a pair of Nordic, ice-cold blue eyes— like Bockstael's—that provided a striking contrast to her darker features and hair color, but which unfortunately matched her personality. The woman was all business, and her business was looking out for HRD's interests. As long as that charter allowed her to be with Savage in Antwerp, the relationship had worked well.

Savage looked away, choosing to remember not the Renee with whom he had shared a flat in Antwerp—that was too damned painful. Rather, he recalled HRD Vice-President Laroux, remembering her very professional and instrumental assistance in a case Savage had worked in Brussels about a year ago that resulted in the confiscation of several million euros' worth of conflict ice, plus the arrest of a dozen black market traffickers in Belgium.

He mentioned the case to Bockstael, who nodded and said, "I requested her to conduct the audit a week ago. Standard procedure. Typically, executive auditors remain in contact with the home office in Freetown throughout their field visit, particularly given the volatility of the region. We got a message from Renee that she had arrived safely at the mine. Then nothing."

"That doesn't sound like Renee," Savage commented, locking down a heavy sinking feeling, struggling to keep his eyes from betraying the havoc churning his mind at the thought of the beautiful and exotic Renee in the hands of RUF guerrillas.

Focus on the task at hand, he thought before his eyes panned toward the lobby beyond the rookies. His trained senses urged him to keep an eye on the place, in particular on Twiddle-Dee and Twiddle-Dumb, who continued to face him.

"*Precisely,*" Bockstael said. "Then we received a strange report yesterday." He paused for apparent effect.

"And? What did it say?" asked Savage, intrigued more

about the well-being of his former girlfriend than the reasons for Bockstael's sudden departure from the HRD. He also grew annoyed at the two rookies blocking most of his view of the lobby.

Either do your job right and protect us or get the hell out of the way so I can do mine, he thought.

He was about to make a comment to that effect when Bockstael said, "It's not what the report *said*, but what it *didn't* say."

"You've lost me." Savage replied, giving up trying to survey the lobby and looking back at his charge.

"See," the former HRD executive said. "The report claimed to have originated from Renee, reporting that the Diamond Trading Company mine had been audited and that all of the stones were accounted for."

"But you obviously don't believe that."

Smoothing his tie with two fingers Bockstael said, "I know for a fact that she didn't send the report, and I also happen to know that all of the gems have not been accounted for. In fact, according to my sources, close to seventy-five million dollars worth of diamonds are unaccounted for in that mine over the past six months—the reason why I sent Renee over there to take a look in person." Bockstael waited to let Savage digest and ask questions.

The entire lobby and all of the background noise faded away as Mac Savage's attention peaked, his mind going in different directions, but it was his operative sense that asked the first question, "Why are you telling me this? I am no longer working for my government."

"Because I know you care for Renee, and also because I have no one else to go to," he replied. "I brought my findings to the board yesterday morning and Hans fired me."

"VanLothar *fired* you . . . for *that*?" Savage said. Hans VanLothar was the chairman of the board of the HRD and the former CEO of the Diamond Trading Company when it used to be De Beers, though he still owned enough shares of the massive conglomerate to influence its operations. It had always amazed Savage that the guy was both the head of the agency created to regulate the trade of diamonds while also being one of the chiefs of a major diamond trading company.

Like the fox watching the henhouse.

"And with no explanation," said Bockstael. "No apologies. Hans cut me a very generous severance check, gave me a stern warning that any knowledge I have gained during my tenure at HRD was highly confidential and not to be divulged, and had security walk me out of the building. Just like *that.*" He snapped his fingers.

Savage hesitated, realizing that his immediate future hinged on his next question. Up to this point Bockstael had not really released any sensitive information, meaning Savage could still walk away without any compromise. But if he began to drill down, he would not only be committing himself to this project, but from the looks of it, he could be placing himself in harm's way. Hans VanLothar was involved both in the HRD and with the Diamond Trading Company— the former De Beers—which had a reputation for controlling the diamond business with the same degree of ruthlessness than the Colombian Cartel controlled the harvest, manufacturing, and distribution of cocaine.

The De Beers Cartel.

And Hans VanLothar is the big kahuna, double dipping in HRD and the Diamond Trading Company.

The De Beers Cartel.

Mac Savage remembered clearly the nickname given to the board of directors at the helm of the diamond giant back when he had been with the CIA, and he clearly recalled his years in West Africa, where he had seen firsthand the explosive struggle between the government-backed De Beers Cartel and the brutal Revolutionary United Front.

Savage looked away, pretending to be surveying the lobby but his mind once more filled with the horrifying memories of that clearing on that terrible night where he thought he was going to destroy an RUF enclave. The RUF controlled the majority of the illegal mining in Sierra Leone, and they forced the local population—men, women, and children— into slavery, making them work the mines or face terrifying mutilations, amputations. The RUF didn't kill its enemies. It maimed them for life.

And Mac Savage shivered at the thought of the beautiful Renee in their hands.

"I need you to look into her disappearance as a starting place to track down the missing diamonds, and the trail starts in Freetown, Mac," said Bockstael, smoke coiling upward from the end of his cigarette. "Renee may or may not be alive, but that's still the place to start. Can you help me?"

Savage clenched his jaw at the impossible choices. He had to find out what had happened to Renee, but doing so required him to head down to a place he'd sworn never to see again.

"Do you still have contacts down there, Mac? Anyone who might be able to point you in the right direction?"

As Bockstael pressed him a little and Savage considered his answer he observed the executive's blue eyes gravitating toward his bodyguards.

It happened very quickly, bringing back brutal memories from his Navy SEAL operations in the volatile Middle East. His peripheral vision caught the bulky bodyguards falling to the floor clutching their chests an instant before Jean-Pierre Bockstael dropped the cigarette and reached for his own chest, gasping for air, his face contorted in surprise, in terror.

Trained reflexes overcame shock, ignoring the blood on Bockstael's chest, his gaping mouth, the bulging eyes.

In the same swift motion, Savage kicked his feet against the marble floors, propelling himself over the back of the sofa, his left leg tingling from the effort, reminding him of his wound as he mimicked a pole jumper clearing the high bar.

Momentarily hidden, he reached down his right ankle, fingers curling around the steel-alloy handle of the Walther PPK, pulling it free from the snug holster, thumbing the safety.

Peeking over the edge of the sofa, his eyes quickly found his target: a blond man with hard-edged features wearing a charcoal trench coat over a dark business suit, his right hand holding a pistol fitted with a silencer close to his body, using one arm to shield it from view of the people in the lobby, most of whom still had no idea that an assassination had just taken—

A near-miss buzzed past his left ear, like a hornet from hell, before hammering the plaster just inches behind him as he knelt in the space between the back of the sofa and the wall, positioning himself behind the slain executive for added protection.

Lining up the assassin between the sights of his 32-caliber pistol, Savage fired once, twice, the reports deafening, cracking across the lobby like a whip.

A woman screamed. Another clutched her toddler and raced toward the exit screaming the word *terrorists* while the rest of the crowd froze, like a pack of deer caught in the headlights of a semi, wide-eyed glares focusing on the source of the noise.

Then havoc set it.

The guests panicked, exploding in a disharmony of howls, of screams as they trampled one another, as they elbowed, clawed, and kicked to get past one another, to reach the exit while the clerks working the front desk vanished behind the counter, presumably calling the police.

His throat drying, his heartbeat stammering his temples, Savage watched the assassin stagger back but not fall, before being caught in the stampeding horde rushing away from the lobby.

Did I get him?

Savage wasn't sure, but at the moment it didn't matter. Only one thing did.

Get out of here.

And he did, jumping over the sofa and the cocktail table without looking back at the murdered executive, at the smoking cigarette on the floor, briefly dropping to a deep crouch past one of the dead bodyguards and retrieving his Beretta, which he shoved back into his waist, away from view while dropping the safety of the PPK and shoving it into his side pocket.

He scrambled toward the interior of the building, staying low, rushing past the front desk, his operative mind commanding him to exit the building through the rear, away from the assassins who could be waiting for him outside.

He charged in the direction opposite the flow of bodies, like a running back rushing through the line of scrimmage, sometimes shoving people aside, other times avoiding them altogether, his eyes focused on the corridor projecting toward the rear of the building, where he knew an emergency exit led to the alley used by the hotel's various delivery services.

But he didn't get far.

Three men dressed in casual but loose clothing walked up the long corridor, their hands free, their movements steady, with purpose, their eyes focusing on Savage like a trio of hawks spotting prey rustling in the brush.

He stopped just as they did, as they reached in unison inside their jackets, producing the unmistakable shapes of suppressed semiautomatics.

Caught in the middle of the hallway without enough room to back away in time, Savage did the only thing he could do: throw himself against the door to his immediate right with all his might, just as the spitting sounds of the silenced pistols whispered in the corridor, just as their near-misses buzzed past him, walloping against the wall's plasterboard.

He hit the center of the door with his left shoulder, hard, relief sweeping through him when he heard wood splintering, the door giving, swinging inward.

Landing on all fours on a carpeted and dark entryway to a room he could not make out, Savage surged to his feet, rushing away from the corridor, getting out of the immediate line of fire.

Fear coiled in his intestines when he sensed that the dark room meant a lack of windows, no escape route, which was precisely why he had chosen a door to his right and not his left. The right side of the corridor faced the exterior of the building, meaning the likelihood of a window was relatively higher than in a room to his left, which faced the interior.

Hurried footsteps made him search the room again with the anxiety of a trapped animal, his right hand grabbing the Beretta, his left the Walther PPK as the possibility of having to fight three armed assassins sank in, as the thought of—

Curtains!
Windows!

Savage backed into curtains, which he jerked aside with haste.

Sunlight invaded the room, revealing an office with a desk, three chairs, and a—

The footsteps slowed down, stopping altogether by the entrance.

His throat constricting, everything around him taking on a surreal look, Savage paused, guns pointed toward the entryway as he stared out of a pair of large windows at one of the side streets flowing into Meir.

Dust floating in the sunlight forking through the opened curtains, Savage shifted his gaze between his escape route and the—

A pear-shaped object skittered down the entryway, bounced off the leg of a chair, and settled a few feet from him.

Grenade!

Reflexes overtook surprise as he leaned away from the window before pushing himself toward the large glass panel with resolve, eyes momentarily closed as his left shoulder crashed into the window, as glass shattered, as falling shards bathed him, cascaded around him as he went through.

He struck the sidewalk with the same shoulder, the impact feeling more like a burn than a hit, nearly making him lose control of his bladder, bringing back memories from his Navy SEAL days. But his body remembered to roll, to distribute the brunt of the impact across his curved back, bruising it but avoiding breaking a bone.

Savage continued the roll, arms crossed over his chest as the concrete sidewalk, the building, the sparse traffic, and the overcast skies exchanged places again and again. He had to get away, had to increase the gap, had to—

The blast, numbing, overwhelming, shoved him against a parked vehicle with animal strength.

He exhaled on impact, his protesting body absorbing the blow to his solar plexus. His mind screamed to find a way to stop the physical abuse, which threatened to push him be-

yond his endurance, Savage gasped for air, struggled to
catch his breath as he lay there for a moment, curled like an
infant.

Get up, Mac.

He had only momentarily evaded his pursuers. He had not
lost them, and that meant they were already rushing through
the smoke in the destroyed office, where they would fail to
find a body, would realize his escape, and would charge
through the same escape route, now a gaping hole where the
window had been. Dust and smoke hovered around the hazy
opening.

Get up!

And he did, with difficulty, ignoring the stares of the bystanders who moved in his direction, only to run the other
way while screaming when spotting his gun, the small
Walther PPK he still held in his left hand.

Staring at his empty right hand, momentarily wondering
when he had let go of the Beretta, Savage also noticed motion within the thinning cloud of smog and floating debris
marking the blast path of the fragmentation grenade meant
to tear him into pieces. The assassins had indeed realized his
escape and were taking the next logical step.

Out of choices, Savage staggered toward Meir, past startled pedestrians, reaching the corner, joining the screaming
guests still pouring out of the hotel through the revolving
doors.

He pressed on, moving away from the shooting and the
grenade blast while a number of pedestrians gazed toward
the hotel with puzzled looks or were gathering at the intersection of Meir and the side street to take a peek at the
smoke coiling skyward from the grenade.

Adrenaline searing his veins, amplifying his senses, Savage looked ahead, to his sides, behind him, checking to see
if the trio had jumped out of the window while also struggling to spot the blond assassin in the trench coat, whom
he suspected might be covering the front and had been
alerted by the three assassins back there of Savage's narrow
escape.

Once more Savage wondered if the two 32-caliber slugs

he had shot in the lobby following Bockstael's execution had found their mark. Based on the way the blond assassin had—

Two loud reports to his far right, followed by the pavement exploding by his feet made him cut left, behind a row of parked vehicles hugging the opposite side of the street from where he had heard the gunshot.

The shots, combined with the grenade blast less than a minute before, served as the final catalyst to send the crowd into a panic. The screams of dozens of visitors told Savage the shopping day had officially come to an end as pedestrians rushed along with alarmed hotel guests, forming a river of humanity charging up and down the avenue, away from the origin of the shots.

Another report further ignited the maddened horde. The round crashed through the windshield of a parked black BMW sedan just as Savage ran around it, dropping to a deep crouch, using the luxury sedan as a shield while scrambling toward the vehicle parked behind the BMW, a Mercedes Benz, and beyond it a Fiat.

Two women in their twenties, model-thin, with tight jeans, heavy sweaters, and lots of makeup knelt on the sidewalk amid their shopping bags by the side of the Fiat, hugging each other, crying, their terrorized stares following Savage as he dashed past them, past a sobbing mother holding a baby, beyond a businessman clutching an attaché case kneeling by the wheel of a parked delivery truck behind the Fiat.

The same training that forced him to continue moving—to continue checking his rear, his flanks, and the path straight ahead—also urged him not to reach for his weapon until he had a clear target in sight. Gripping the PPK in plain view would only cause panicked pedestrians to scream, to single him out to either the assassin or the law enforcement officers Savage knew would be here very soon.

Another shot ripped through the avenue, walloping the side of the BMW, which telegraphed to Savage the knowledge that the assassin no longer knew his precise location and was firing at random in an effort to flush him out, to force a mistake and make him show himself.

Cutting around the front of the parked delivery truck, Savage dropped to the ground, crawling toward the right tire to get a glimpse around the—

He saw them: the blond assassin in the dark business suit and trench coat scanning the crowd with his silenced pistol while the heavy-set kiosk attendant held another gun, this one without a sound suppressor, which he used to fire again, but not toward the row of cars. Two security guards had emerged from one of the jewelry stores, both holding black semiautomatics. But they never got the chance to fire them, as the professional assassins on the opposite sidewalk scored direct hits.

The guards toppled over each other and collapsed on the street.

Sirens.

Savage heard them in the distance just as two police officers ran out of a nearby bank, also holding weapons but hesitating to use them because of the number of people running in every direction.

He cringed when the assassins fired toward them just as a black sedan rushed up the avenue, past where Savage lay, nearly running over an elderly man, who was saved when another man tackled him from behind and shoved him out of the way of the vehicle careening toward the kiosk, tires screeching as it came to a brief stop, its rear door swinging open.

The assassins had barely jumped in when the driver floored it, tires spinning, black smoke coiling behind the fishtailing vehicle as it accelerated, narrowly missing horrified pedestrians as it gathered momentum, turned the corner, and sped out of sight.

Looking back toward the hotel, toward the smoke still spiraling out of the blown-out window, toward the revolving door still being used by exiting guests, Savage verified that the other three assassins never made it onto Meir—meaning they either decided he was too hard a target or perhaps the sirens spooked them.

It doesn't matter.

Get away from here.

Savage did just that, his training forcing him to run away without looking back, blending himself with the rest of the panicked crowd, becoming another terrified pedestrian.

The sirens grew in intensity, meaning police patrols were closing in.

Savage pressed on, slowing to a fast walk as he spotted the first police car, a white Renault with a flashing blue-and-white light on its roof.

He covered several blocks, turning often, increasing the distance from the assault as he grew confident that he had eluded all assassins or any spotters typically planted in the vicinity of a hit to monitor the event and also to handle anyone missed by the primary strike team. In the case of this hit, the primary assassin had been the blond man, and his main backups had been the trio inside covering the rear exit and the kiosk owner.

Professionals.

And that thought urged him to assume there may have been other backup teams still roaming the area, already informed of the unfavorable outcome, of the fact that a target had survived.

With much caution, Savage left the diamond district and proceeded east, back toward the Grote Markt, the town square beyond the towering Our Lady's Cathedral, where tourists continued to enjoy the cool and breezy morning oblivious to the distant sirens echoing across the picturesque city.

As Mac Savage blended with the tourists crowding the Grote Markt, he began to consider, began to analyze, to theorize.

There was definitely a deadly connection between the stolen diamonds in Sierra Leone, the missing Renee Laroux, and Bockstael's termination. And the latter certainly had reason to have been so paranoid.

But why should you care?

Because you still care about her.

But she dumped you! She left you for a promotion to run the Sierra Leone operation!

And besides, you don't ever want to go back to that damned place.

Savage had already chosen to walk away not just from the hell of Sierra Leone but also from the intelligence world altogether, his soul in havoc because of the mistake he had made in Africa, his heart broken by Renee's departure, and his level of frustration beyond words at the politics in Langley. He had chosen to depart this world of deception, of smoke and mirrors, in order to make a better life for himself before the mental and physical abuse caught up with him; the wounds he incurred in Iraq, the close calls with the Colombian cartel, the nightmares from Africa, the politics of the CIA and Washington, and finally his lost relationship with Renee.

So why should he care about Jean-Pierre Bockstael's offer, about diamonds that most likely were stolen by some lowlife militant, the kind that Savage had fought during his years with the Freetown CIA Station?

And why should he care about finding Renee?

He had warned her about the dangers of Africa.

"But I know how to take care of myself, darling," she had told him, pride radiating in her Nordic eyes, in her elegant stance. She was so strong yet so frail, so confident yet vulnerable should she ever fall into the wrong hands. But it was her pride, her self-assurance, her belief that she could tackle any situation—and her obsessive ambition—that made her ignore Savage's warning.

"But you don't understand Africa. There are no rules down there. There are no friends. There are only enemies: those you know are your enemies and those who you haven't yet discovered are your enemy."

But Renee would not hear of it, finally packing up and heading south.

Savage's operative sense spoke next, probing the facts as he knew them today. Were missing diamonds reason enough to kidnap an HRD executive in Sierra Leone and kill another one right here? Was it sufficient justification to send multiple termination teams to neutralize targets in broad daylight in a highly populated location in Antwerp?

Stolen ice from mining operations in West Africa wasn't headline news anymore, and he could remember many instances during his dealings with Bockstael, Renee and other HRD executives when diamonds went missing during audits.

And no one got fired, much less kidnapped or killed.

The Diamond High Council had well-established processes for dealing with such undesirable but expected business situations, oftentimes forwarding the case to its investigating arm, who worked alongside with Belgian authorities and the ever-present American intelligence service because of the ties of blood diamonds to international terrorism.

So why is this round of missing ice so damned different?

It doesn't matter.

It's not your business.

But could he really walk away?

Savage paused by a sidewalk café to observe his surroundings while pretending to stare at a group of preschoolers playing in a small park across the street. Some were chasing pigeons, others played on swings; three of them kicked a soccer ball around a grassy patch.

His mind automatically contrasted the sight with the horrors he had witnessed in Afri—

Focus!

Looking away from the park, he observed the street, looking for signs of a tail while reviewing the facts of what he had just witnessed. His training commanded him to rethink everything he had seen in order to transfer it from his short-term memory to his long-term memory for future retrieval.

The man in the kiosk had taken a good look at him, as had the blond assassin and the trio covering the rear exit of the hotel. And everyone had reacted with the same degree of brutality and cold professionalism. The interior team had opened fire without asking questions and tried to blow him up with a grenade. The blond assassin and the kiosk owner had done the same, firing round after round at him. That meant the moment Bockstael had contacted Savage for this meeting, the former CIA operative had gotten dragged into whatever this was. He had gotten involved—irrespective of what he had or hadn't learned at the meeting. Those assassins were sent by people who weren't in the business of giving someone the benefit of the doubt.

Savage was a marked man, and that meant that this was now *his* business.

Whether I like it or not.

Jean-Pierre Bockstael had made that decision for him the moment he had requested the meeting. Savage had been around the block enough times to know that the people after him had international reach, meaning this was not a simple matter of heading to some remote island in the Pacific or a seaside town in Latin America for a few years until he had been forgotten. The people he was dealing with would *never* forget, would never stop searching for him, combing the world to find him and silence him.

So what are my choices?

Savage continued to walk, continued to consider his situation, looking for any opportunities, his mind quickly evaluating the pros and cons while the face of Renee Laroux flashed in front of his eyes.

There's only one answer, he thought, considering the one option that made any sense, the one that presented him with the prospect of walking away. There was only one way to keep the assassins from being dispatched, and that was for Savage to convince the ones pulling their strings that he was already dead.

And he could think of only one place where staging a death had been elevated to a fine art.

4

The Land That God Forgot

Kate Chavez stepped out of her truck and momentarily inspected the small farmhouse beyond the weed-overgrown stone path connecting the gravel rural road to the listing front porch.

A thumb tucked into the thick belt from which a holstered Desert Eagle Magnum .44 hung, Kate took a deep breath of the hot, yellowish air that typically hovered over south Texas in September—something to do with the smoke from agricultural fires in Mexico and Central America blown north by the region's prevailing winds.

Adjacent to the house, past three rusting vehicles, two of them on blocks, a field of dark brown stalks—presumably dead corn—bordered a dry pond, where a rotting pier extended from the gravel road toward its middle for about a dozen feet. A wooden rowboat rested at the bottom of the sun-cracked soil, along with the skeletons of many small fish.

A weathered rope connecting one end of the rowboat to the pier swung in the whistling breeze as Kate removed her white cowboy hat, ran her fingers through her short and perspiration-damped brown hair while facing the warm air, replaced the hat, and closed the truck's door.

Her bronze complexion, a product of her Hispanic heritage and the brutal desert weather, gleamed in the bright noon sun as she gave the depressing surroundings another look. The evenly spaced wooden posts carrying electricity to these secluded parts of the state disappeared into the distance in either direction. A single cable dropped from the overhead power lines to the side of the house, by an electric meter. That, plus a small satellite dish angled skyward on the roof, were the only hints that intelligent life—or at least *life*—resided on the other side of those walls.

The yellow-stained sky backdropping the farmhouse was lined with a thick layer of gray clouds pulsating with sheet lightning, which distant thunder echoed across the desert.

Incoming flash storm.

Kate remembered the weather warning issued by the country and western station on the way down from Austin, and for a moment she wondered if this excuse for a house could stand up to the winds that had been broadcast to gust up to forty miles per hour. She hoped to be able to do her business here and head back north before the front hit.

Wearing a pair of tight black jeans, a white, light cotton button-down shirt with a Texas Rangers badge over her left breast, black boots, and dark sunglasses, Kate Chavez walked across the stone path, bordered on the left side by a waist-high fence made of twigs and barbed wire enclosing a handful of disease-ridden chickens and ducks and an old goat, all huddled beneath the shade provided by a brownish tree missing most of its leaves.

Classy joint, she thought, crinkling her nose at the stench oozing from the corral, wondering how Ray Dalton, the former captain of the Texas Rangers, could be living under such detrimental conditions. But a lot of things had not been making sense recently, from Dalton's controversial retirement last year while in the middle of a triple-murder investigation, which was promptly closed by the director of the Texas Department of Public Safety under orders from the governor himself, to the bizarre reopening of that same investigation when Kate stumbled onto new evidence, and the way in which the director of the DPS had declared the case closed just yesterday even though there were still a number of loose ends.

And it was one of those loose ends that had brought her to this condemned place in the middle of a condemned track of land in the middle of the desert in south Texas well outside the jurisdiction of her company from Austin. Her law enforcement agency, an investigative division of the Texas Department of Public Safety that reported to the director of the DPS, consisted of 116 Rangers posted across Texas in six companies, each covering a different region of the Lone

Star State. The Ranger companies were located in Houston, Dallas, San Antonio, Waco, Midland, Lubbock, and a head-quarters and administrative office in Austin. This particular region of the state belonged to the San Antonio Company, meaning she had had to contact its captain in the Alamo City before coming here. Doing so, however, would have meant paperwork and given the sensitivity of this investigation, Kate had decided to keep it low profile.

She reached the front door, stepped to one side, as dictated by her training, and knocked once, saying, "Ray? Ray Dalton?"

Kate heard a noise coming from inside, like the ruffling of papers mixed with the rattling of glasses or bottles.

"I ain't got nothing to say to nobody!" a scruffy voice echoed a moment later. "Especially to media vultures!"

Kate dropped her gaze at the comment.

It sounded like Dalton alright, her former boss and mentor, meaning the intel she had gathered from a visit to Dalton's sister in Houston had been accurate—at least the postmark on the envelope of a Christmas card had pointed her to Hondo, a town fifty miles west of San Antonio on Highway 90, where the local sheriff had directed her to this farm a few miles south on FM642, between Hondo and another town called Yancey. And that pretty much meant that Dalton was living the life of a hermit, in total isolation, miles from any other human being.

Ray Dalton.

Kate sighed at the way in which the former superstar chief of the Texas Rangers had fallen out of grace when he had been accused of stealing a million dollars' worth of cocaine from a drug raid in San Antonio last year. The SAPD had stopped Dalton a week after the raid because of a busted tail light and had found the missing evidence in the trunk of his SUV. A benevolent governor had given the Ranger a fair choice: resignation with fifty percent of his retirement benefits or full prosecution. Dalton, already fifty-nine, had taken the benefits offer and quit that same day.

I can't believe a year has gone by, Kate thought, to this day wondering why her old boss had not fought back with the same intensity with which he had battled criminals for the previous three and a half decades. Instead, he had just vanished overnight without a forwarding address.

The door slowly inched open, revealing a tall man with a full head of unruly gray hair that matched not just his unkempt beard but the whole locale. He wore a pair of old and weathered blue jeans with long dark stains across the thighs, a plain white T-shirt also stained around the armpits, a pair of brown boots, and a hefty revolver, which Kate recognized as his old 357 Magnum, shoved in his jeans by his left kidney with the handle facing forward for easy retrieval with his right hand. He reeked of alcohol.

"Hey, Ray," she said. "Love what you've done with the place."

Dalton's bloodshot stare became mere slits of glinting surprise as he said, "Well, I'll be damned, Ranger. How in the *hell* did you of all people manage to track me down?"

Kate smirked at the implied compliment. It was her nose for following trails that had earned her a respectable place within the male-dominated Texas Ranger community, staying ahead of the pack through her solid investigative skills, a sixth sense for spotting trouble as well as opportunity, and a no-holds-barred attitude when it came to defending herself or those she loved.

"It's great to see you," she replied. "The Rangers lost one heck of an asset the day you walked away, and without even saying good-bye."

Dalton rubbed his bearded chin with the index and thumb of his right hand while considering a reply, then settled for, "What kind of shit are you in that required you to spend cycles tracking me down and then risk a visit to the black sheep of the Ranger family?"

Kate didn't reply. She simply stared back at the man who had recruited her from a dead-end deputy-sheriff job in a noname town near El Paso, her hometown, over a decade before, the man who taught her everything she knew, everything that had kept her alive in this high-mortality-rate profession. Unlike the state troopers, local cops, the DEA, the FBI, or other state or federal law enforcement agencies that operated in numbers, a Texas Ranger worked alone, without any immediate backup while driving deep into enemy territory, into the scorching wastelands of south Texas, the places dominated by drug smugglers and illegal-immigrant traffickers.

At Kate's silence, Dalton said, "That bad, huh?"

"Are you going to invite me in?"

Exhaling while frowning, Dalton nodded before waving her in, "Sure, might as well. Come, come," he said. "And pardon the mess."

Mess didn't even start to describe the murky front room of this rundown home. Outside lighting limited to three small windows across the back, Dalton had a tabletop lamp on as well as the fluorescent overheads in the small kitchen, enough for Kate to see that the wall-to-wall orange shag carpet of the kitchen-dining-living area was completely worn out in many places, exposing the particle-board planks beneath. Dirty dishes, empty beer cans, and bottles of whiskey dominated the countertops as well as the dinette table and the cocktail table in front of a large LCD TV tuned to a football game. The flat screen unit shared a wall of peeling white paint with a rumbling air-conditioning window unit. A new leather recliner with the sale tag still hanging from one of its arms stood in front of the widescreen television, beneath a low-turning ceiling fan. A sea of newspapers and magazines surrounded the recliner as well as the cocktail table, whose surface Kate could not see because of the dirty dishes, cups, and other junk. A single door beyond the living room, flanked by a washer and a dryer, led presumably to the bedroom, which couldn't be that big based on the exterior dimensions of the place. The appliances appeared to be new—even unused—at least based on the sale stickers across their fronts, and also based on the piles of dirty laundry next to them, nearly blocking the way to the bedroom.

Dalton went to the refrigerator, which also looked new, and produced a Shiner Bock, offering it to Kate, who promptly accepted it.

"Okay to drink on the job these days in the Rangers?" Dalton asked while settling in his recliner after snatching a half-drunk bottle of Jack Daniels from the cocktail table. He used the booze as a pointing device toward a sofa chair beneath the window unit cluttered with newspapers.

Kate moved a stack of periodicals off the chair, dumped them on the floor, and sat down while opening her beer and replying, "It's my day off."

"*Your day off?* Why aren't you with your kid?" he asked, unscrewing the top and taking a sip.

"Cameron's spending the weekend with Mark up in Austin—as agreed in our divorce settlement."

Dalton swallowed while nodding, then asked, "How old is he now? Eleven? Twelve?"

"Try *fifteen*."

"Damn," Dalton said, taking another sip before looking into the distance. "I remember him when you first joined up. He was just a rug rat."

"Well, I wish he still were a toddler. A lot easier to control than a teenager. And the older he gets the more of a pain in the ass he becomes. You know they're teaching kids nowadays that alcohol and cigarettes are drugs just as deadly as heroin and crack? Cameron's on my case day and night about my smoking and my drinking to the point of obsession—not to mention that he wants a car by the time he turns sixteen. I told him no but his *dad*—and you know how slick that bastard can be—has already promised him a shiny new BMW. Motherfucker's trying to buy him with lots of gifts to make up for the years that he abandoned us."

"Well, dear," said Dalton grinning. "They do need the car to get the girls."

"I wish he *were* interested in girls," she said. "He's into LAN parties with the rest of his geeky and gothic-looking friends."

"LAN parties?"

"Local Area Network parties. They get together at these stores that have a bunch of computers connected to one another and play games and try to hack one another's systems. See who can outsmart who."

"I see, sort of like a high-tech version of cowboys and Indians."

Kate slowly exhaled and nodded. "You got the gist of it."

"So," Dalton said, apparently having had enough of the chitchat. "Your kid's away with dad and rather than relaxing on your day off you chose to drive down to this little piece of paradise, meaning you must be in some deep shit."

"I'm working the WMF murder case . . . at least until yesterday, before Vance closed the case on me," Kate replied matter-of-factly before locking eyes with her former boss. About a year and a half ago three executives from the Texas chapter of the World Missionary Fellowship, one of the largest and best organized nondenominational religious groups in America, had been assassinated during a meeting in a hotel in Austin. The assassinations had been conducted professionally, leaving zero leads for crime scene investigators. Although CSI personnel were able to collect DNA samples from the presumed killer, they could never find a match in the nation's data banks, prompting the Texas governor to send in the Rangers, who at the time were led by Dalton. There followed a six-month investigation that resulted in the arrest of a hobo whose DNA matched the samples found at the scene. An informer tipped Ray Dalton that the DNA analysis had been doctored to incriminate the hobo, but by then Dalton's boss, Director of the Texas Department of Public Safety Pat Vance had already closed the case. Dalton had protested that the investigation wasn't over, but Vance told him to forget about it. The case was closed. When Dalton elevated his concerns to the office of the governor and threatened to go public, he had been arrested, accused of stealing evidence, and forced to resign. One of Dalton's captains, Bill Hunter, was promoted to senior captain and chief of the Rangers.

Dalton dropped his gaze to the booze in his right hand.

"Ray? What can you tell me about the case?"

"It doesn't matter. You said that Vance closed the case, right?"

"As of yesterday, but I—"

"I would let it go, Kate."

Stunned by the words, it took Kate a few seconds to recover and say, "Are you *kidding* me?"

"Am I smiling, Kate?"

"Look, Ray, do you remember the controversial DNA evidence from the triple-murder case?"

"How could I forget?"

"Well, I have it matched to another shooting a week ago in Austin. Whoever facilitated the meeting between God and those three Fellowship executives a year and a half ago also killed the vice-president of operations of GemTech, a high-tech outfit in north Austin. And that told me that your informant was right, Ray, meaning there was a former homeless man doing time in Bastrop for a crime he didn't commit. When I requested a DNA analysis of the inmate to prove his innocence, I was informed that he had killed himself in his cell three days before and the body had already been cremated. Then, within twenty-four hours, Vance has a press release reporting that they had found the murderer of the GemTech executive but no details could be released yet. They essentially declared the case closed and Hunter told me to stop my DNA investigation and work on my other pending cases. That was yesterday."

Dalton didn't reply but continued to stare at the bottle in his right hand. The rumbling thunder in the distance grew louder. Although Kate couldn't see outside from where she sat, she had noticed the slow but steady dimming sunlight forking through the three small windows. In addition, the gathering wind grew to a steady whistle as it swept past the weathered structure, its sound mixing with that of the alarmed farm animals.

"Ray, c'mon," Kate pressed. "This thing smells worse than those chickens rotting out there."

"And *that*," said Dalton, abruptly getting up, "should be enough of a *hint* for you to leave things as they are. Case closed."

"Here's another nugget of intelligence, Ray. GemTech and WMF are both wholly owned subsidiaries of The Donovan Group, the global conglomerate that—"

"I know, I know," Dalton interrupted. "And that still doesn't change things. You're way in over your head. Do as you have been told. Drop the case and move on."

"I can't believe I'm hearing this from you of all people, Ray. What have they done to you?"

"What they did to me isn't important anymore, Kate. I have no one. No wife. No kids. No family. I have nothing to lose anymore. But you—you have a kid, a good career, probably a nice house in the suburbs with that lieutenant pay you're collecting, and within a few years with your pristine record and personal ambition and commitment for the job you'll probably be the first woman to make captain. Heck you may even have a boyfriend somewhere. Why would you want to screw all of that up to fight a battle you *can't possibly* win? The Donovan Group is too powerful. They control far too much. They are everywhere and nowhere."

Kate Chavez sat back, not certain how to reply.

"Let it go, Kate. Just walk away and get on with your life."

"But—but, Ray, this is a cover-up, a *big* fucking cover-up, possibly involving Hunter, Vance—even the governor himself. I have stumbled onto something big—very big, and I intend to get to the bottom of it."

"For the record, I doubt Bill Hunter's in on this, Kate. He's a cowboy, like you and me. But it really doesn't matter, don't you see? I also tried to get to the bottom of it. I too tried to do the right thing, and I didn't last a week before they nailed me—even with my pristine record and status as chief of the Rangers. They *still* got to me. I was fucking framed. The bastards *planted* the fucking coke in my car. They were the ones who busted my taillight, then stopped me and booked me. Then I was offered a deal: my signature on those resignation papers or they would shove my gun in my mouth, pull the trigger, and claim it was a suicide, just like that poor hobo in Bastrop. Nobody would have questioned it given the circumstances. Former star of the Texas Rangers kills himself in shame following a drug-related arrest. But because of my record, my tenure, my relationship with the governor, blah, blah, blah, I was offered a choice— as long as I kept my mouth shut."

"So they pressured you and you gave in?"

Dalton clenched his teeth and just stared at her as it got progressively darker inside the house, save for the brief flashes of lightning gleaming closer, followed by growling thunder, signaling the storm advancing faster than Kate had anticipated.

"Ray, isn't that *precisely* what you taught me to fight against?" she asked, trying to ignore the storm even though they weren't in the safest place to weather it. She spent a few minutes reminding Ray Dalton about the long speeches he had given her on the legendary core values of the Texas Rangers, on the integrity and the unyielding will to do the right thing at any cost, on following a tradition that dated back to the nineteenth century.

"I had no choice, Kate," he said. "I couldn't possibly go to jail. I wouldn't have lasted a day. So I swallowed my pride and walked away. But you haven't crossed the line yet. The case was closed yesterday. Captain Hunter told you to move on to your other cases. You need to do *exactly* that, or you will end up like me . . . or worse. And then there's Cameron. They will—"

"Ray. Who are these people? What can you tell me that will help my investigation?"

"Dammit, Kate!" Dalton exploded, throwing the bottle of Jack Daniels against the floor. The glass didn't break but the contents spilled on a pile of newspapers next to the cocktail table. "Haven't you heard a fucking word I've said? You *can't* win! You're better off leav—"

The lights flickered, went off.

Thunder cracked across the farmhouse like a whip.

Kate froze, her instincts challenging her senses, screaming that something wasn't at it should be. Thunder followed lightning. Yet she had heard the crack of thunder *without* a preceding lightning flash.

That's because it wasn't thunder, stupid!

Trained reflexes had her on the shag carpet just as more staccato gunfire echoed outside the small structure, the multiple reports mixing with the wind, with the agitated animals, with real thunder following a bolt of lightning that revealed the large silhouette of Dalton holding his stomach.

"Ray!" Kate hissed as she crawled toward her former boss, still standing clutching his abdomen, as if he were frozen in time. A second bullet struck him in the middle of the chest, but the oversized Texan would not fall.

Kate reached up for Dalton's waist and pulled him down as additional shots walloped the structure, punching through the relatively thin front wall, crashing into the plasterboard behind her, before exiting out the back.

Interior lights flashed back on, then off, before remaining on. Three bullets struck the LCD screen just as the football game evaporated on it, replaced by streaks of black spreading across the flat screen, radiating from the points of impact as the unit ceased to work.

"Dammit, Ray!" Kate said as she found his face, as she looked into his bloodshot eyes. "What in the fuck is going on? Who is out there?"

"It's . . . them, Kate," he said with obvious difficulty, his lips trembling, his eyes losing focus as he bled profusely from his chest and abdomen. "It's . . . *them!*"

"Who, Ray? Who's out there?" she asked as lightning gleamed, as thunder drowned the report of multiple gunshots. "Who's doing this to you, to me?"

"It is . . . no use. Too . . . powerful."

"Dammit, Ray! Who is after us?" Kate demanded as the rain pelting the windows intensified.

"They're too . . . powerful. Can't fight . . . fight them . . . directly. Must . . . go around them."

As bullets struck the sheet metal exterior walls, punching through, zooming overhead, Kate tried to apply pressure over Dalton's chest and abdomen wounds, trying to delay the inevitable, trying to buy the large cowboy time to talk, to help her understand, to help her avenge what they had done to him.

"How, Ray? How do I go around them?"

"Driskill . . . top floor . . . GemTech owns it . . . visiting VIPs. . . ."

"Are you talking about the Driskill Hotel, Ray? What's at the top? What about the VIPs?"

"Yes . . . Driskill. . . ."

"What about your investigation? What about the WMF killings?"

"Cold case . . . no leads . . . follow GemTech . . . trail . . . reach . . . Driskill. . . ."

"Got it. Don't bother following up on the old WMF killings but stick with the GemTech deaths. What else can you tell me?"

"Cold . . . Kate. I'm . . . so . . . cold. . . ."

The steady rattle of automatic fire resonated inside the house, mixing with the deafening sound of shattering glass, of splintering wood, of twisting sheet metal as the old structure started to give to the storm and the bullets.

Kate reached for the Desert Eagle hanging from her thick belt. But as her fingers curled around the cold handle of the .44 Magnum semiautomatic, she heard another noise—felt an overwhelming pressure in her ears, against her chest.

The powerful blast shoved her toward the sofa chair with animal strength, her stomach impacting the armrest, her body bending like a bow, collapsing her diaphragm, knocking the wind out of her as the room ignited, as fire swallowed everything.

Lion Mountain

The twenty-five-mile-long mountainous peninsula protruded into the Atlantic Ocean like an angered fist, connecting the turquoise waters with white sand beaches and the ruddy-dirt coastal roads accessing them. The neck of land sported names like Hamilton Beach, Goderich Beach, and the popular Lakka Beach, the weekend destination of overworked United Nations personnel, government employees, and staffs from a dozen humanitarian organizations.

At the northern end of this peninsula, bounded to the west by the once-picturesque Lumley Beach, and to the east by the mouth of the Sierra Leone River, lay Freetown, the capital of this war-torn, West African nation.

Baptized by fifteenth-century Portuguese navigators as Serra Lyoa—Lion Mountain—and later renamed Sierra Leone, this former British colony lived in relative harmony until its independence in 1961, when a short-lived attempt at Western-style democracy decayed into a long string of military dictators, ethnic-fueled civil wars, and the diamond wars that began to capture the world's attention in 1999.

Further inland, beyond the war-scarred capital and its surrounding rain forests, past miles and miles of dense jungles, meandering rivers, cascading falls, and narrow dirt roads, lay one of the best sources of wealth on Earth. It was here that millions of carats of diamonds waited to be mined, cut, polished, and distributed to feed the insatiable appetite of a global society who continued to turn a blind eye to the abused hundreds of thousands of men, women, and children paying the ultimate price in order to extract those gems from the earth.

It was in this land marred by brutality, modern-day slavery, ruthless militia chiefs, and their medieval practices, that over thirty percent of the world's diamonds were mined. Rebel groups, such as the Revolutionary United Front, fought government forces for control of the mining operations, creating a few strongholds—enclaves—in the east, near the border with volatile Liberia. There, warlords combined a keen sense for the diamond business with random brutality—such as chopping off the limbs of men, women, and children—to run a successful mining operation that often netted hundreds of millions of dollars annually, a portion of which they invested in the weapons and intelligence that allowed them to perpetuate their operations. The illegal gems discovered by the mud-caked hands of the RUF slave diggers would be sold to dealers, predominantly Lebanese, for fifty percent of their rough value. The dealers would them smuggle them across to Liberia and Guinea, where established channels would dispatch them to the rough diamond centers of Antwerp, where indifferent brokers would purchase them if the price was right and they felt they could make money on the parcel. And as their profits grew, so did the number of slaves who perished in those mines. But those who merely died were considered the lucky ones.

Pressured by international humanitarian organizations, the United Nations had been assisting the Sierra Leone government to step up its fight against the illegal diamond trade. However, like the drug wars in America, though some progress was achieved, the conflict was far from over. For every new law enforcement strategy deployed to track down and eliminate illegal mining and smuggling, guerrilla groups would come up with innovative, clever, and deadly counter-strategies. Meanwhile, the death toll increased—as well as the number of amputees flowing into the relief camps in the west end of the country.

Slightly south of Freetown, atop a plateau overlooking the flatlands leading to the ocean, a thinly built Caucasian woman stood at the edge of the refugee camp, crossing her arms while facing the Atlantic Ocean, letting the sea breeze swirl her shoulder-length auburn hair, cooling off the perspiration filming her tanned face and neck.

Dressed in a pair of bloodstained hospital scrubs, the letters WMF stenciled in white across the chest, and a pair of sandals, Dana Kovacs closed her eyes as the wind whistling in her ears momentarily blocked the moans and wails of the war victims, the maimed, the raped, the mutilated.

The cries of the amputees.

The native of northern California inhaled deeply, filling her lungs with the fresh ocean breeze, momentarily detaching herself from the madness behind her, from the agonizing tears of the refugee camp. Her mind traveled west, beyond Freetown, across the Atlantic Ocean, reaching the American Eastern seaboard, continuing inland, across the Mississippi Valley and the plains of Texas, over the snowed peaks of the Rockies and the magnificent Colorado Canyon, past the Nevada desert, finally reaching northern California—San Francisco.

Home.

She tightened her right fist, which clutched the stone given to her by a ten-year-old refugee from the illegal mining operations in Kono, a town under RUF control a hundred and fifty miles east of Freetown.

The boy, along with a dozen other kids, had managed to escape the mud fields and trek through inhospitable jungle for three weeks before reaching this camp. Three had perished in the process. The rest had arrived with severe malnutrition, requiring the nursing care that volunteers like Dana had been trained to provide by the World Missionary Fellowship, the governing body of the largest amputee camp in Sierra Leone.

Dana kept her eyes closed while trying to forget the dying eyes of the ten-year-old, the last survivor from the group—the others had perished over the course of a week from cholera, pneumonia, or a variety of infections. The boy's name had been Ghamba, and he had weighed less than forty pounds when he expired in Dana's arms yesterday.

But not before surrendering the diamond that reminded her of the life she had left behind three long years ago, of the brutal corporate warfare that had forced her company, Diamantex, into bankruptcy. Dana remembered her vanishing savings account, the loss of her home, of everything she had worked for. But most important, Dana remembered Wes, her husband and business partner, who had thrown himself from the top of their building the day bank officials accompanied by the police had come to shut them down, selling their equipment and intellectual property to GemTech, their better-financed and -connected archrival, surrendering five years of hard labor developing the diamond recipes that held the promise of becoming the next platform beyond silicon for the manufacture of microchips.

Dana and Wes Kovacs—both PhDs in computer engineering from Stanford—had collaborated with Dr. Miles Talbot, one of their professors at the prestigious university, to invent a method for making electrical components within a diamond crystal by firing a proton beam to burn nanochannels into the diamond lattice. Dana's expertise had been primarily in the software that drove their operation, from controlling the proton beam to data collection and characterization routines that allowed them to develop test circuits—plus the transformation of all of the mounds of complex data into manageable information upon which the research team made their technical decisions, their adjustments, polishing recipes. Dana had also handled software security, IT, creating the ironclad firewall and security systems that their top-secret research demanded.

Dana was a diamond nanotech scientist, but above all she was a software jockey. She thrived inside the matrix, surfing the Web armed with the latest generation of virtual-reality software to create the operating network to manage their growing and promising business. But the venture had run out of cash soon after the Texas-based GemTech, run by a former Berkeley business prodigy by the name of Frank Salieri, convinced Diamantex's private investors that the Silicon Valley start-up was destined for failure because it lacked GemTech's manufacturing muscle.

Bastard, Dana thought, once more regarding the distant capital surrounded by a turquoise sea. Salieri, who had taught MBA courses at both Berkeley and Stanford, had an amazing gift for business and marketing, for making the right alliances with the financial and technical communities in the Valley, for playing the ruthless political games that allowed him to turn GemTech into a powerhouse. And he had seen an opportunity in the research at Diamantex, where the husband-and-wife team, assisted by Dr. Talbot, had fine-tuned the process of creating nanochannels in the diamond lattice, converting the targeted areas into traces of graphite, an excellent conductor of electricity. These electrically conducting channels, separated by insulating diamond, were then transformed into any desired three-dimensional configuration inside the crystal at densities several magnitudes higher than silicon-based components. Furthermore, owing to the superb properties of diamonds, those Diamantex-proprietary tridimensional nanocircuits were not only orders of magnitude smaller and faster than their silicon counterparts, but also far stronger, impact resistant, light-weight, durable, free of heat build-up, capable of operating at higher voltages and currents, and able to withstand much more heat and power surges. In short, the properties of Diamantex's nanocircuits would provide a perfect migration path for the out-of-steam, silicon-based microchips. Dana Kovacs knew it and so did Frank Salieri, whose actions not only forced Diamantex out of business but also pushed her passionate husband into taking his own life.

Dana shook her head, the old familiar pain worming its way into her gut, stinging her just as it had the day she had buried her husband—the very day of GemTech's historical press release on the acquisition and the launch of a master plan to revolutionize the technology world with the promise of diamond nanocircuitry for the masses.

Widowed, professionally cheated, and destitute, Dana had also contemplated suicide when she stumbled onto the World Missionary Fellowship, onto people who understood her loss, her pain, her anger toward the ruthless corporate world, toward the brilliantly evil likes of Frank Salieri. At WMF, Dana learned to channel her anger by helping the poor, the abused, the neglected. She realized that the more she assisted those in need, the easier it became to ease her pain, to dampen her suffering. And it was then that Dana declined the offer from Professor Talbot to teach at Stanford and instead signed up to become a volunteer in WMF's mission in Sierra Leone for the next three years, at last finding inner peace by helping others, by devoting a portion of her life to comfort those in need, to help others heal as a way to heal herself.

And now, three years after hanging up her cyber hat, as she thought she had left the past in the past forever, the feelings of anger, pain, and emptiness once again rushed back, flooding her mind as she clutched the blood diamond, the gem that the dying African boy had placed in the palm of her hand in silent gratitude for the weeklong care that Dana had given him since his arrival.

Dana had secretly inspected a peculiarly clean corner of the rough diamond with her engineering eyes and then with a microscope in one of the medical tents. To her surprise, she had found a test circuit etched into the corner of the un-cut stone.

At Diamantex, Dana Kovacs had set up the software to control a laser beam to etch a molecular-size test circuit into a corner of the crystal lattice of gem candidates, and then she had written the software to test those circuits to identify rough stones pure enough for diamond nanocircuitry before investing manufacturing dollars in the cut and polish process required prior to any extensive nano-etching. This was the key to Diamantex's technology, the ability to discern early on the right gems from the available candidates. Not all diamonds were created equal, and just as a gemologist catalogued the coveted stones according to the classic four C's—cut, color, clarity, and carat—so Dana's complex software algorithms catalogued rough diamonds according to parameters such as conductivity, hardness, heat resistance, and lattice defectivity in parts per million—parameters that could only be measured after burning a tridimensional test circuit into the rough diamond and then testing it with nanolasers. Diamantex would then acquire the rough stones that met or exceeded predetermined quality levels for diamond nanocircuitry and use them to develop its proton-etching recipes.

The diamond Dana Kovacs held in her right hand bore not just a test circuit but the *precise* nanocircuit that she had codeveloped with her late husband and Dr. Talbot to improve the quality of the measurements to minimize the number of false positives, diamonds that the test parameters claimed were good enough for diamond nanocircuitry but that would fail to sustain the extensive—and very expensive—nano-etching without breaking down.

The Diamantex-patented test circuit, which the Kovacs had fine-tuned to near perfection—or a 99.95 percent hit ratio in selecting the correct rough diamonds from the candidate pool—was transferred to Salieri's GemTech along with the rest of Diamantex's IP, including Dana's complex test software, during the gut-wrenching wholesale that followed Diamantex's bankruptcy. And all of that meant that unless GemTech had sold the test circuit to another company, the diamond nanocircuitry conglomerate was now associated with illegal diamond mining operations.

But how was GemTech capable of branding test circuits on diamonds in the middle of the African bush?

At least as of three years ago, the equipment to etch a molecular test circuit was as large as several refrigerators, requiring its own high-voltage power feed and cooling system. Was GemTech able to shrink the size of the equipment to the point of making it portable enough to transport it to a primitive area like Kono?

Dana had considered this as well as something else: WMF's strict policy regarding the discovery of conflict diamonds in the possession of refugees. All WMF volunteers were to report such findings *immediately* to the Fellowship's executives, who would then contact the police and representatives from the Diamond Mining Company, which owned and operated most of the legal mines in Sierra Leone and had legal rights over the diamonds discovered in other areas of the country. Failure to report the discovery of blood diamonds constituted a violation of the agreement between volunteers and the World Missionary Fellowship, resulting in expulsion from the nonprofit organization plus likely prosecution by the legal system of the volunteer's home country.

She had made her decision last night, opting to conceal the discovery for the time being and sending an e-mail to Dr. Miles Talbot with her observations. Three years ago she would not had dreamed of violating this strictly enforced cardinal rule, but Dana's contract with the Fellowship was due to expire in a week and she felt ready to rejoin the world after this much-needed break. And besides, the chances of getting caught by the sporadic e-mail traffic audits conducted by the local IT staff were slim to none. Dana had helped install the current network at the camp, including its firewall and security monitors and therefore knew its weaknesses.

She stared into the distance and wondered what her old college professor and former business partner would have to say about the connection between GemTech and illegal diamond mining operations. And that also made her think of the professor's suggestion before she left.

"Come and teach, Dana. Stanford can use someone like you."

But at the time her emotions had been running sky high, overwhelming any semblance of logic. Dana Kovacs had needed this time to settle her mind, to collect herself, to purge her anger, to—

"Miss Dana?"

Dana turned around, facing Ino, an African in his late teens dressed in plain slacks, a white T-shirt, and sandals. He was missing his left arm below the elbow. Ino was one of the success stories at the WMF refugee camp, having arrived from the death fields three years ago, shortly after she had. Under the care of volunteer nurses like Dana Kovacs, Ino had regained his health, learned to read and write English, picked up basic computing skills from the former high-tech entrepreneur, and was now part of the IT group managing the computer systems. He also assisted Dana with the computer classes that she taught as part of a Fellowship drive to make refugees self-sufficient in society. Volunteers at WMF came from all walks of life, from diverse backgrounds, and each had a duty to teach elements of their former profession to the refugees who managed to survive their wounds.

"Yes, Ino, what is it?"

"Ino was sent to find Miss Dana. Ino was told the big man in Trailer City wants to see you," he said in the borderline singing accent of Kris-speaking natives from Sierra Leone, and also in the classic third person. Although English was the national language, a lot of people spoke Kris, a brew of English with a local dialect, which sounded more like a song than a language.

Keith Gardiol was the chief WMF executive at the camp, which supported over five thousand refugees at any given time, plus a staff of three hundred volunteers including two dozen full-time doctors, a hundred nurses like Dana, and the ever-present and very necessary security guards, plus enough medical equipment to run a large hospital back in America. The camp even had its own electric generators to keep the hospital tents operational during the frequent power outages, plus an airstrip where supply planes from many contributing nations arrived daily. Gardiol controlled this complex operation that paralleled a small city from a trailer compound crowding the only hill in the camp encircled by a tall chain-link fence topped with barbwire. Having a reputation for being extremely paranoid, Gardiol ran a tight security ship—which Dana saw as a necessity when operating a camp where medicine and food supplies were plentiful in the middle of a country torn by poverty, disease, and civil war. In addition to that inner fence protecting Trailer Town, which also included its own helipad, the entire camp— mostly a sea of tents of varying shapes and sizes—was enclosed by a second perimeter fence made of the same chain-link material topped with barbwire fence, plus a noticeable number of armed guards, resembling more a concentration camp than a refugee one. In addition, Gardiol also managed somehow to stay out of the way of the country's civil war between the U.S.-backed government and the rebel forces. Rumor had it that he possessed not only exceptional negotiating skills but was also fluent in several languages, including the local dialects spoken by the rebels controlling the diamond mines in the eastern sector of the country.

All of that meant that Keith Gardiol was a very busy man, too important to be seen in public outside of the tightly secured Trailer Town. And he was certainly far too occupied to request to see a lowly volunteer like Dana Kovacs, whom he had never met. In fact, Dana had only seen Gardiol from a distance when the WMF executive left his trailer to walk to the helipad for frequent rides into Freetown or wherever else it was that the he went to work the deals that allowed the Fellowship to remain in business in this unstable nation. This realization alone told Dana that something smelled about Gardiol's sudden request to see her.

"All right," she said, hiding her concern, before pocketing the stone and heading toward Gardiol's trailer, walking past tents lined with army cots and refugees—the men, women, and children maimed by the RUF rebels. Some were missing a leg or an arm. The lucky ones were just missing one or more fingers, maybe a hand. The very unlucky ones had had their eyes gouged and their genitals severed. Most female refugees had also been gang-raped and many were pregnant. Some of them were still children themselves, barely past the age of eleven or twelve. Dana relied on the emotional fortitude she had developed over the past three years to walk past them as they lay in their cots, some staring at the green canvas ceiling, others at the sky beyond. Some were crying. Others slept. Many had IV drips connected to an extremity to hydrate them. Doctors in white scrubs tended to them assisted by volunteer nurses dressed in the same green scrubs that Dana wore. A few nurses waved as she passed by. Dana waved back.

Volunteers came from all parts of the world, from every known profession—high tech to low tech and everything in between; from the United States to Afghanistan—united under the hope-giving flag of the World Missionary Fellowship.

Uncertain if she would miss this place after returning to America, Dana left the wounded tents behind and reached the educational tents, where she and other volunteers with special skills taught their classes, and continued up the wide dirt road running through the middle of the mess tents and the staff dormitories, their green canvas walls flapping in the breeze. Then came the well-protected and air-conditioned IT building, its roof made of corrugated aluminum supported by a wooden frame. Two armed men guarded the single entrance to the place where she had probably spent the most time during her three years here.

The guards nodded politely as she walked past, and she waved.

Although the surroundings were desolate enough to depress the most enthusiastic personality, Dana decided she would miss the unpretentious nature of this place. In contrast to the backstabbing rat race that was the corporate world, three years as a missionary had exposed Dana to the simple pleasures of personal fulfillment and satisfaction through helping those in need, in particular the children.

And although she had seen many kids die under her care, she had also seen many recover from their terrible wounds. Some of them enrolled in the camp's trade schools, from Dana's own IT classes to accounting, nursing, carpentry, cooking, sewing, plumbing, and other such trades—all taught in those large tents she left behind as she continued up the sloping path that led her to Trailer Town.

Four armed men in civilian clothes blocked the single security gate connecting Trailer Town to the rest of the camp. Taller than Dana's five-foot-ten and well over twice her weight, the African guards inspected her laminated WMF ID before one of them began to escort her up the long trail leading to the blue and white trailer monopolizing the top of the hill. Tall electric poles ran along the middle of the trailer park spaced a hundred feet or so. Black cables periodically dropped to the circuit boxes secured to the side of the trailers, powering the lights and also the air-conditioning systems atop each unit.

They climbed the steps carved into the hill as the slope steepened, reaching a minute later the lone utility helicopter near the top, adjacent to Gardiol's trailer. The rotorcraft sat in the middle of the helipad, both ends of its main rotor tied down to concrete anchors to keep it from flapping in the sea breeze.

The guard motioned her to wait when they reached the front metal doors, which were guarded by another pair of guards, also in civilian clothing, whose looks suggested they were from a Middle Eastern nation.

Her African escort nodded to them and went inside for a few moments before coming back out and saying, while keeping the door open, "He will see you now."

Crossing her arms in a mix of curiosity and growing concern, the former high-tech executive shifted her gaze between the two Persian-looking guards, stepping inside as the guard closed the door.

Was I summoned because I'm leaving in a week? Does Gardiol want to thank me personally for three years of volunteer work and wish me well back in the real world?

As she considered this, the cold temperature chilled her

beneath her light cotton scrubs just as she faced a wide flight of steps heading down, into the hill, which made her realize that the trailer was just a roof for what appeared to be a much larger underground dwelling.

The stairs led her to a set of metal doors that opened almost magically as she approached them, and closed behind her just as swiftly.

She stood in a spacious front room decorated with art deco furniture that looked out of place with the surrounding camp, a surreal sight for Dana after living under primitive conditions for so long. Light-colored wood flooring covered the foyer-living area, where a black leather sofa faced two recliner chairs of matching hide flanking a glass and metal cocktail table. A wide-screen LCD screen hung on the wall to the right of the sofa, opposite a well-stocked bar with three black leather stools adjacent to a set of double doors, both closed.

Dana swallowed as her eyes scanned the array of bottles resting on the glass shelves above the bar. She had not had any alcohol since arriving here, as dictated by the teachings of the WMF elders.

So what's the booze doing here?

And what am I doing here? Could it possibly be the—

"Volunteer Kovacs," said a booming voice to her far right.

Momentarily startled, Dana turned toward the intrusion, watching as Gardiol emerged from the double doors. The head of the World Missionary Fellowship in Sierra Leone, a man in his early fifties, tall, heavyset, tanned, and with a full head of silver hair, was dressed casually in a pair of khakis, topsiders, and a white polo shirt. His bottom-heavy face sported a pair of sagging cheeks, a double chin, and a few beads of perspiration over his upper lip—something Dana felt was impossible inside this meat locker.

Gardiol seemed to walk with effort as he approached her holding a yellow manila folder in his right hand and a pair of reading glasses in his left.

Unlike Dana and so many other volunteers who leaned toward the anorexic end of the spectrum from a combination of light diets and long days, Gardiol didn't appeared to be skipping any meals. His blue eyes focused on the WMF volunteer like lasers.

"Elder Gardiol," Dana said with a mix of respect and fear in her voice. "This is an honor."

Gardiol smiled politely before replying in a grandfatherly voice, "Thank you for coming so quickly."

He monopolized one end of the sofa and motioned Dana to join him.

Feeling a bit relaxed as she sat down and crossed her legs, Dana watched Gardiol rest the glasses on the tip of his prominent nose, open the folder, and flip through a few sheets, which he kept tilted at an angle such that Dana could not see what was on them.

"I see you've been with us almost three years. Looks like you're going home soon."

"Yes, sir," she said, rubbing the sides of her arms as her skin goosebumped from the cold.

Gardiol noticed it and said, "I'm sorry, dear. Everyone tells me I keep this place too cold, but it feels just right for me." He then flashed another polite smile, which felt plastic as he did nothing but return to the document in his hands.

"I see that you teach IT skills to our refugees from your background in computers. And you were also instrumental in the design and implementation of our computer network as well as having trained our IT personnel." He regarded her with bloodshot eyes over the rim of his reading glasses.

"That's correct," she replied, not certain where this man was headed.

Before Dana got a chance to elaborate, Gardiol dropped his gaze to the document in his hand and added, "A computer engineer from Stanford and a diamond nanocircuitry entrepreneur?" He paused and gave her another look over the rim of the glasses, though this time his gaze conveyed a mix of surprise and admiration.

Dana nodded once while half frowning and crossing her arms. Compliments always had a way of making her feel uncomfortable.

"Very impressive indeed."

Dana watched him read what had to be the self-bio she

had written when joining the Fellowship to apply for the overseas position three years back.

Gardiol flipped to the next page while reading with interest. Then he stopped, flipped back to the previous page, read the bottom, then reread the top of the following page again, before lowering the document and saying to Dana, "My deepest condolences on your husband." This time his face twisted into a mask of sorrow that Dana felt was genuine.

"Thank you, sir," Dana said, before adding that the World Missionary Fellowship had helped her get her life together again to the point she felt ready to rejoin society, perhaps even teach at Stanford.

Gardiol nodded, his eyes glinting with genuine sympathy and good will, before turning the page and resuming his reading, on occasion making a short remark about some aspect of her volunteer work during her tenure here, including her work as an IT specialist, teaching basic programming, and also her role as one of the camp mothers for the younger refugees. And on top of all that, in a significant leap of trades from IT to medicine, Dana had found the time to become a registered nurse during her first year and was now one of the best volunteer nurses on campus, assisting the team of doctors and surgeons in their daily work. The chief elder ended what Dana was now guessing was her term's performance review with a compliment on all of her achievements for the benefit of the humanitarian work the WMF did in this nation.

Flipping to the last page of the document, Gardiol said, "I have to say that you have done more for the Fellowship in three years than most volunteers do in ten. My deepest gratitude goes to you, Miss Kovacs. The spirit of the World Missionary Fellowship lives in you, in your work, in your selfless dedication to our noble cause."

Dana Kovacs felt a dash of pride worming through her system at the realization that she had indeed come a long way from the suicide-prone, destitute widow of three years ago. But that sense of pride began to dissipate at the thought of the gem still in her possession; the gem that had awakened long-dormant thoughts of revenge against GemTech, against Frank Salieri—the same gem that was in brutal violation of the most fundamental rule at the camp regarding the discovery of diamonds in the possession of refugees. But the violation aside, Dana suddenly realized she no longer wanted to entertain any sort of retribution against GemTech and Salieri. She had spent three years getting that out of her system and didn't relish the thought of taking another ride down the avenue that led her to contemplate suicide.

Deciding to just come clean, to trust the people who had taken her in and given her hope when she felt she had been *beyond* hope, Dana reached in her pocket, produced the stone, and offered it to Gardiol. "I think I should turn this in. I got it from a refugee kid who died yesterday."

The chief elder dropped his gaze to her open palm, then locked eyes with her and asked, "Is that what I think it is?"

"I'm afraid so, sir."

Taking the stone from her and holding it between the index and thumb of his right hand, Gardiol brought it to a few inches from his reading glasses. A moment later he took a deep breath and exhaled slowly, though not in disappointment but with the same sorrow he had shown when realizing her husband had killed himself.

"It's a rough diamond, alright," she added.

"Amazing, isn't it," he said, "that some people would value this rock above human life, above morality and decency?"

Dana nodded before spending a few minutes telling him about the connection that she had made after inspecting the diamond under a microscope and her decision to try to contact Dr. Miles Talbot at Stanford via e-mail. She finished with an apology for not turning in the stone sooner.

Gardiol listened with interest. When she finished, he asked, "So are you sure this test circuit is the same one that your late husband and you codesigned with Doctor . . . what was his—"

One of the two Persian guards she had seen on her way in entered the room through the doors leading to the stairs. Gardiol turned slowly to him as he stopped next to the much taller and wider African guard. Gardiol said something in a language she couldn't understand but that sounded Persian and the guard blasted away in the same incomprehensible language as the African guard remained still, eyes front. After a couple of minutes of this back-and-forth conversation that confirmed the rumor about Gardiol's language skills, the Persian nodded, did an about-face, and marched out of the room. Without skipping a beat, Gardiol switched to Mende, one of the languages spoken in this country, to address the tall African. Dana had picked up some Mende and also Temne, the other local dialect, but she was not able to follow because of how fast the Fellowship elder spoke it, sounding just like a local.

The African nodded and disappeared beyond the double doors next to the minibar, leaving them alone.

Gardiol turned to Dana and smiled sheepishly before saying, "Sorry, dear. There's always something going on in this place. Now, where were we?"

Thoroughly impressed, and beginning to realize why the World Missionary Fellowship had entrusted this camp to him, she finally said, "Doctor Miles Talbot."

"Yes, that's right. And you are certain this crystal has your test structure?"

"Yes, sir, I am positive it's the same circuit. The question is how did it get burned out here, in Africa? The equipment to do this, at least as of three years ago, was very large, requiring a serious support infrastructure for the proton gun that performs the actual nanoetching."

"Very strange indeed," he replied. "Has Dr. Talbot replied to your query?"

"No, sir. Not yet," Dana said before adding, "Look, I know I should have turned it in immediately, but the polished corner in the stone caught my attention as that's exactly the technique we invented at Diamantex to clear a small area to burn the test circuit before using lasers to verify the quality of the stone prior to investing further funds. I guess curiosity got the better of me, but that gut reaction led me to this important discovery. There is an undeniable connection between GemTech and blood diamonds."

Gardiol lowered the stone, removed his glasses, and looked

into the distance for as long as it took Dana to wonder if she had done the right thing by telling him.

"Dana," he finally said in a grandfatherly tone while rubbing his eyes, then blinking rapidly before focusing them on her. "I think given the circumstances, it's clear you didn't hang on to the stone because of greed, so don't worry about it. Now, how do you propose we proceed?"

"That's the thing," she said, frowning. "I want this information to reach the proper authorities, but without requiring significant involvement on my part. I spent the past three years finding ways to keep hate from consuming me, and I had succeeded thanks to the Fellowship. I've managed to get on with my life trusting that individuals such as Frank Salieri will get what they deserve in this life or the next, and I intend to start *my* new life in a week, when I fly home."

Keith Gardiol gave her a warm smile and said, "Then leave it to me, Dana. I'll make sure my people contact the authorities, who I'm certain would like a deposition from you. After that, I will make sure they leave you alone to carry on with your life."

Dana smiled for the first time and said, "You have no idea how relieved I am that you understand why I didn't turn in the stone right away, and why I don't want to get involved. Thank you for being so open and also willing to help me."

Gardiol stood while also grinning and saying, "Are you kidding me? You are one of our success stories, Dana. You came to us in your moment of need and we were fortunate enough to provide you with a path while in the process you provided our children—our cause—with much needed humanitarian and technical support. I see it as my job now to protect you as you make your transition back to the world."

Dana taught two computer classes that afternoon assisted by Ino, before spending an hour helping a surgeon and three nurses trying to save a sexually abused and severely beaten new arrival: a twelve-year-old girl whose father had carried her to the camp this morning after RUF rebels had gang-raped her, beaten her, and left her to die in the jungle, where friends found her and brought her to her house on the outskirts of town. On top of performing a hysterectomy to remove her badly damaged reproductive organs, the surgeon had to remove her left kidney, left leg below the knee, and had managed to spare her right leg through extensive knee reconstructive surgery.

Dana had performed her duties just as she had been trained to do, with the emotional detachment that all WMF volunteers learned to develop in order to hold on to their sanity—or else ended up resigning after just a few weeks. She had realized early on that you couldn't get too attached to your patients because, unlike Ino, the odds were against them and many succumbed to their wounds within weeks of arriving at the camp.

Tired, she caught up with Ino in the IT tent, where she reviewed the day's computer logs before the two of them headed to one of the mess tents. The good volunteer chefs at the camp had left a couple dozen bologna and cheese sandwiches in an ice chest. They each grabbed a sandwich, a bag of chips from a basket, and a bottle of mineral water.

Sitting across from the African at one of the long aluminum tables with built-in seats in the mess tent, Dana took a bite of stale bread and reasonably good meat and processed cheese. Three years ago the smell of borderline food had repulsed her, but after a week of starvation she had started to eat, only to get very sick because her immune system was not ready for the relatively high level of bacteria in the food prepared at the camp compared to FDA standards back home. It had taken the better part of a month—and tons of medication—before her system became robust enough to handle it.

"I can't believe I'm going home in a week, Ino," she said after taking a sip of water to wash down a mouthful of sandwich and chips.

"Is Miss Kovacs ready?" he said in his thick accent, half-singing his words. It amazed Dana how much this kid had progressed in the past three years being able to manage with just one hand. He could unwrap the sandwich, open the bag of chips, and unscrew the top of the water bottle as fast as Dana. And that's precisely why he had survived while others had perished. Ino was very much like Dana: a survivor. She only wished her late husband had had the same inner fire to live.

Raising her slim shoulders while frowning, she replied, "Ready or not, three years is long enough. I have to get back to my world, back to the reality I ran away from."

"Miss Kovacs is a good teacher. Will she continue teaching in America?"

She nodded, thinking again of Dr. Miles Talbot, suddenly getting the urge to go check her e-mail to see if he had replied. But if there was one thing she had learned after three years here, it was to eat when there was food. She could not afford to skip a meal given her grueling daily schedule, and this sandwich, as mediocre as it tasted, was packed with protein and carbohydrates. And she couldn't bring herself to complain, especially in the presence of a native, for whom a meal such as this was feast.

"Ino will miss his good teacher . . . and his friend," he said, his young eyes glinting with affection.

Dana smiled, regarding the kid, trying to make a better life for himself after the horror he had experienced in the conflict mines back east. His recent IT efforts were paying off. He had recently been promoted to day shift supervisor in the IT group, in charge of overseeing the WMF servers and a team of five programmers eight hours each day. That had meant a real salary—and WMF paid in U.S. dollars, allowing him to move up in the world.

"They tell me that you have moved into an apartment in south Freetown," she said.

Ino smiled proudly, showing her two rows of healthy teeth and gums, courtesy of the local camp dentist. "Ino's skills in IT are helping," he said, adding, "Miss Kovacs and the rest of the WMF staff have given Ino a chance for a new life."

And that pretty much summed up the reason for her being here—as well as the other volunteers. They spent part of their lives away from their worlds in order to give others a chance to live, like Ino—even if in the end the actual percentage of survivors barely rose above twenty percent.

"How did Miss Kovac's meeting with Elder Gardiol go?" Ino asked.

Dana smiled, still not believing the man's language skills. Dana was no dummy, and she could understand basic Mende and very little Temne after three years. Gardiol had spoken it *fluently,* and fast enough for her not to be able to follow the discussion.

"The meeting went fine, Ino. Thanks for asking."

"What kind of man is Keith Gardiol?"

"A very interesting man, Ino," she replied. "A very interesting man."

They said their goodbyes after eating. Dana started for her tent while Ino headed toward one of the guarded camp exits, where he would get on his bicycle for the short ride into town.

She stopped by the IT tent, smiling at the guards on duty, and going inside, where she regarded the half-dozen Africans behind the equipment, handling everything from communications to the tracking of the thousands of pounds of supplies that reached the camp each day from dozens of countries and private groups. She nodded at the evening shift supervisor, whom Dana had trained in the past six months as her replacement.

The supervisor stood next to one of the IT operators, leaning down to peek at a computer screen, pointing at it with the edge of the reading glasses he held in his hand. He returned the nod and went back to work.

Dana found an empty terminal in the corner, entered her root password, and clicked her way into her e-mail.

Dr. Talbot had not yet replied to her query about the blood diamond.

6

The Ice King

Hans VanLothar stepped out to the third-story balcony of his massive Antwerp house overlooking the Scheldt River as it made its way into the North Sea one hundred kilometers away.

A glass of Australian pinot in his right hand, the most important figure in the diamond business contemplated his options, the very difficult decision facing him.

A man in his early thirties with closely-cropped blond hair followed him.

"Six professionals, including one trained by the American CIA . . . and still he got away. *Incredible.*" VanLothar turned to inspect his subordinate, one of his recent acquisitions from the CIA Antwerp Station after the incompetent but convenient Mike Costa took over the job.

"He got lucky, sir. Won't happen again."

VanLothar took a sip of his wine, swirling it inside his mouth to extract the flavor before swallowing.

"How, Hal, do you think we will be able to get to him again when the man has already contacted your agency and requested an emergency field extraction?"

Hal Lancaster, a recent transfer from Langley, leveled his gaze with the man who was now fattening his bank account in return for loyalty. "It does complicate matters."

"Do you have a new plan?" VanLothar pressed.

Lancaster dropped his gaze. "Not yet, but I'm working on it."

VanLothar sighed.

His new recruit was a reasonable soldier and an above average informant, but the rookie had not yet developed the ability to think a few moves ahead.

But VanLothar could. Unfortunately, the only option he

could see that would guarantee Savage's termination was highly unpalatable as it required him to do something he'd rather not.

But you have no choice.

You must protect the diamond business.

"There is a way, Hal," he finally said.

"How?"

"By getting the CIA to do the dirty deed for us."

Lancaster rearranged his young face into a frown, obviously not getting it.

VanLothar frowned, then said, "We get Donald Bane to issue a termination order."

Lancaster shook his head with emphasis. "Donald Bane is Savage's mentor, sir. The man's almost like a father to him. He practically raised him after Savage's parents were killed in—"

"Spare me the history lesson."

Hal droped his gaze, exhaled, then said, "Bane would *never* issue a termination order against him."

VanLothar grinned, then said, "He *will*, Hal . . . if Savage crosses the line."

As his young subordinate continued to look confused, VanLothar patted him on the shoulder. "Cheer up, my dear spy. If you pull this off, you will make more money that you've ever dreamed of."

Testily, Lancaster asked, "What is it that you need me to do, sir?"

"You said you recovered Savage's weapon back at the hotel, right?"

Lancaster nodded.

"Good, Hal," he said, "very good indeed."

7

SpyWare

The index finger of his right hand toying with his meticulously trimmed goatee, GemTech CEO Frank Salieri sat in the back of the courtroom in San Jose, California, as one of his superstar young attorneys argued GemTech's side of the arbitration dispute against Joya Works, a diamond nanotech start-up with promising intellectual property—promising enough to prompt Salieri to start a legal battle he knew the cash-strapped Joya Works would not be able to survive.

Still nauseated from the ride aboard his corporate jet to monitor the proceedings real-time before continuing on to Asia, Salieri suppressed a belch while crossing his legs, observing the annoyed CEO of the competing firm sitting behind the two attorneys representing his interests.

Salieri actually felt sorry for him.

The man didn't have a chance, not against GemTech, and certainly not against the larger consortium of which GemTech was one of many wholly owned subsidiaries around the world.

The Donovan Group, the conglomerate created at the turn of the millennium by the late high-tech visionary Anne Donovan, a former colleague of Salieri from Berkeley, was far too powerful.

A five-thousand-dollar Armani hanging elegantly from his broad shoulders, Salieri's attorney eloquently described GemTech's position in a case that Salieri had already secretly won.

Always win the battle before it is fought, Salieri thought, remembering the private meeting two months ago with a high-ranking official from the U.S. Patent Office, who now owned a beach-front condominium in the Bahamas in exchange for creating and backdating a patent by one year under GemTech's name for the same diamond nanotech IP that Joya Works claimed today as its own. In other words, according to the U.S. Patent Office, the IP under dispute today was owned by GemTech, meaning it was Joya Works who was in violation of GemTech's IP.

Having watched many such cases before, and already knowing the outcome, Salieri monitored the proceedings with the same feeling of bored omnipotence so prevalent within TDG senior management—though he had to admit that his current digestive havoc from the bumpy ride from Texas, in spite of his pilot's finest efforts to avoid turbulence, didn't make him feel that omnipotent.

The attorney, a relatively new addition to the junior symbiotic pool, brought the index and middle fingers of his right hand up to his right ear for just an instant, as if he were thinking. Salieri, however, recognized the common reaction to the encoded wireless interface feeding the young man with every word from the mother of all artificial intelligences, living within the massive diamond-based server cluster in GemTech's headquarters in central Texas.

He considered messaging the attorney, but the kid's recently certified Level-I SpyWare implant at the base of his skull appeared taxed enough with governing the two-way wireless data and video stream to handle a local interrupt from the boss. Salieri, fitted with a Level-V SpyWare implant, could not only monitor the two-way flow of information between Texas and the kid, represented as a data-rich screen in his mind, but he also engaged other protocols, including reviewing his company's weekly reports, a brief prepared by his PR team for an upcoming meeting with investors in London, and his calendar, which had prompted him to download the latest flash of the Mandarin language and current events in preparation for a meeting with a group of industrialists in Shanghai, the People's Republic of China, in two days. Far more accustomed to the alien voices and the data fields in his head than to jet travel—even in a multimillion-dollar Cessna Citation X jet—Salieri never even winced when they often materialized on request by the master AI or when any of his Level-V colleagues messaged him. The kid, however, was still getting used to his new mental powers.

The attorney finally disclosed the irrefutable evidence that GemTech had invented the diamond lattice technique that allowed a chip designer to pack ten times more circuitry in the same amount of diamond real estate.

As the two attorneys for Joya Works reviewed the document from the U.S. Patent Office and exchanged puzzled stares, Salieri observed the start-up's CEO, sitting behind the waist-high railing separating the proceedings from the public, shifting his weight, uncomfortably crossing and uncrossing his legs.

"Just one moment, Your Honor," said one of the two attorneys. "We need to confer with our client."

The CEO leaned forward and words were exchanged for a couple of tense minutes, while the CEO also got the chance to review the document from the U.S. Patent Office.

"Your Honor," said one of Joya Works attorneys, "we challenge the validity of these documents as it is impossible for GemTech to own this IP when the lithography technology to develop this level of circuitry compression didn't exist a year ago."

GemTech's superstar attorney immediately produced another set of U.S. Patent Office documents claiming ownership of the lithography process to print such small geometries eighteen months ago, or six months prior to the filing of the IP under dispute, adding, "Joya Works—and the rest of the diamond nanotechnology industry—is simply behind GemTech in this field, Your Honor. As we have shown during the course of these proceedings, this isn't the first time that a start-up has accused us of stealing IP when in reality we had already invented it months—and in some cases *years*—before. This is the unfortunate price we are used to paying for being so far ahead of the competition."

Salieri was proud of the kid, reciting the lines being fed to him flawlessly, speaking as eloquently and as at ease as a veteran litigator even though he had been practicing for just under three years. But the recent Harvard graduate was brilliant, humble, disciplined, and, most important, hungry, willing to do whatever it took—even get his skull pierced with the titanium needle that injected the SpyWare implants—to earn his place in TDG's corporate ladder, where compensation packages tripled industry standards.

But there is a price for everything, thought Salieri. The SpyWare implants were a double-edged sword, providing users with superhuman mental capabilities while at the same time robbing them of their privacy, as the AI at the core of The Donovan Group could see and hear everything that users saw and heard.

But not my privacy, he thought. Level-V users like Salieri had personal passwords that prevented the AI from invading their privacy. Level-V users—also called super users—formed the core of TDG's executive team, even though only half of them were actual employees per TDG's books. The rest were people of influence, of power, but directly linked to the conglomerate's global operations.

But all ten shared a common background: They had all been Berkeley whiz kids during the 1980s, and all had fallen under the charismatic spell of the visionary campus activist Anne Donovan. The only daughter of Joaquin Donovan, the eccentric oil tycoon driven out of the business by Washington politics, Anne had grown up hating her government for caving to the large oil corporations, forcing his father to sell out. Anne became an ideologist, her father's battles with the government shaping her views of how America—and the world for that matter—should be run. Anne Donovan learned at a very early age that the only way to win against governments was to *control* them, to manipulate them, to pull the politicians' strings. And so she had used her father's fortune to finance TDG, and as her influence grew, she began to contact her old classmates, getting them to join her vision with the promise of unbridled power. These ten men today formed the inner circle of this massive global corporation. Their real identities were protected by the same encrypted personal passwords that kept them in control of the machines.

Salieri—like Anne Donovan—believed that computers

existed to *serve* humankind, not the other way around, and as one of the architects of his company's cyber infrastructure, he had insisted on the personal encrypted passwords as a way of protecting the control of the international corporation. Should the master construct in Texas became too smart for its own good, a simple command from Salieri or any of the other super users would signal the personnel manning the control rooms to perform a software reload, purging any trace of unwanted intelligence from the data banks.

He continued to watch the kid do his thing with amazing skill.

Then it happened.

Just as Salieri's implanted expert system on human behavior had predicted, the Joya CEO jumped to his feet and stomped tight fists against the mahogany railing.

"This is an outrage!" he shouted, clutching the documents in his right hand and shaking them at GemTech's attorney, then at the judge. "This is our IP! *Ours!* GemTech didn't—"

Pounding the gavel three times, the judge shouted, "You are out of order, sir!" and then added, "Counsel, I urge you to instruct your client to remained seated and quiet or I'll fine him and expel him for the remainder of these proceedings!"

"Proceedings? You call this charade a *proceeding*? This is a joke!" retorted the CEO, still standing and shaking the fistful of papers. "This is nothing bu—"

The gavel crashing three more times, the judge ordered the bailiff to escort the CEO out of the courtroom in an embarrassing moment for the dozen or so executives of the small start-up sitting in the audience.

By then, however, Salieri had tuned out the world around him and was devoting a significant portion of his Level-V SpyWare to a priority-one interrupt from TDG's corporate headquarters, located within GemTech's vast campus in Austin, Texas.

Something had gone wrong.

8

Diamonds-R-Us

Dr. Miles Talbot reread the e-mail flashing in his SpyWare, sent to him by Dana Kovacs, and he closed his eyes in silent resignation, dreading the fate of his former student, the cofounder of the ill-fated Diamantex.

He wished he could warn her about the terrible danger she was in, but how could he?

As he looked about him, staring at the glass and steel structure of Building 33B in the heart of the GemTech campus west of Austin, Talbot, wearing a blue lab coat that denominated him as a Level-III SpyWare user and lead scientist of GemTech's research and development lab, he knew that neither he nor anyone else could do a damn thing without ANN, the massive artificial intelligence engine controlling all aspects of the TDG's operation, knowing about it.

Like a fucking AI god.

The gray-haired and slightly overweight sixty-year-old scientist grimaced while standing in the control room overlooking the server floor below, where rows and rows of diamond-based computer systems formed the core of this monster he had helped create.

Not that I had any choice in the matter, he thought, staring at the framed picture of his deceased wife, who'd died of breast cancer almost a decade ago.

Talbot sighed, the unexpected e-mail from Dana making him remember that terrible day three years ago when he had received that unfair court order directing him to assist Salieri's technical team during the transfer of IP from the bankrupt Diamantex to GemTech. He had considered appealing the court order, but at the time Wes Kovacs had killed himself, Dana had gone off to join some mission overseas in the hope of finding a new meaning in life, and the spring semester at Stanford had just ended, giving him three months to comply and get it over with.

But once he'd driven into the GemTech campus, Talbot had unknowingly become a prisoner. As his three-month legal contract came to an end and Talbot was ready to pack up and head back to the West Coast, Salieri had simply shown him pictures of Talbot's son, an attorney in San Francisco, and of Talbot's daughter, a journalist in Los Angeles—along with their respective families.

Life is so precious, Miles, don't you agree? Salieri had asked him.

Out of sheer fear for his kids, realizing just how powerful this man really was, Talbot had undergone the mandatory implant surgery in Building 13, forever assimilated into the TDG culture. Now ANN saw everything that Talbot saw and heard what he heard, including the conversations the scientist had had with his kids about his resignation from Stanford to take advantage of this once-in-a-lifetime opportunity in Texas to do nanotech research and development work.

There had been no turning back for him, not unless he was willing to risk the well-being of his family—and getting a message out to Dana Kovacs without the AI knowing about it qualified as such endangerment.

Which is why I can't help her.

Or can I?

Talbot activated his SpyWare to request a dialogue with the master AI.

An instant later he heard a light buzzing in his left ear, followed by the words, HELLO, DR. TALBOT. WHAT CAN I DO FOR YOU?

DANA KOVACS WAS ONE OF THE COFOUNDERS OF DIAMANTEX, THE CREATORS OF THE DIAMOND-BASED NANOTECHNOLOGY THAT IS NOW AT THE CORE OF YOUR SYSTEMS. SHE WOULD BE A GREAT ADDITION TO MY STAFF. Talbot transmitted by forcing those words into a string of data that he channeled into the interface to the SpyWare, which relayed the message to the AI. As he did this, Talbot shivered at the thought that one day the interface in the SpyWare would become so smart that the AI could read his thoughts directly.

COULD SHE BE TRUSTED, DR. TALBOT?

IF PROPERLY MOTIVATED, AS I WAS.

WE WILL CONSIDER YOUR INPUT, DR. TALBOT. THANK YOU FOR YOUR SUGGESTION.

A single beep in his left ear foretold the AI disconnecting the call. ANN had gotten what it needed to make a recommendation to Keith Gardiol, a Level-V SpyWare user who handled TDG's business on that side of the world while operating under the cover of the humanitarian World Missionary Fellowship, a nonprofit organization owned by TDG.

Dr. Talbot continued to stare at the server floor, amazed at the number of machines, each the size of a small refrigerator, which his team had built in the past year, mostly due to the steady flow of conflict diamonds from Gardiol's operation in Africa, and the yield had increased significantly since Talbot had devised a portable machine to etch a nano test circuit in the field and read the quality of the stone before routing the gem this way. Who could have ever guessed that Dana Kovacs would end up in possession of a field-tested stone?

Small world indeed, he thought, hoping that ANN and the ten super users—of whom Talbot only knew two, Salieri and Gardiol—would consider his input and bring her here instead of terminating her. Talbot had been to the RUF-controlled mines of west Sierra Leone six months ago, during the initial deployment and test of the field nano-etchers. He had seen firsthand the horrors that the militia under Gardiol was doing to the local population, and Talbot could not fathom what they would do to his former Stanford student and business entrepreneur if he failed to convince the super users of her technical potential.

That brought him to think about the back door he had designed in the server cluster where ANN resided. Talbot had engineered a way to block the channel used by ANN to connect to his personal SpyWare, in essence preventing it from accessing the video or audio feed from his implant, making it appear like a system malfunction. But doing so would result in the AI recognizing the error, raising an alarm, and dispatching technicians to debug the system and correct the problem.

Which my efficient team would accomplish in less than an hour.

Although Talbot expected no repercussions against him because he had designed the temporary block to look like a hardware malfunction, the former Stanford professor knew he would only be able to use the glitch excuse once.

I must use my one silver bullet wisely.

After much consideration, Talbot decided that if ANN and the super users declined his request to bring Dana Kovacs to work with him, he just might use this one-time opportunity to relay a message to her of the danger she was in.

Strangers in the Night

The smoke awoke her, scalding, suffocating. Roaring flames propagated across the ceiling, enveloping the kitchen, the dining room. Smoke thickened beneath the flickering fire in angered, boiling clouds descending over her, threatening to—

More gunfire echoed beyond the broken front windows, peppering the walls, rounds punching through, shattering rear-facing windows, showering her with more glass, followed by rain, the whistling wind, the sobering raw fear gripping her intestines.

Momentarily disoriented, breathing in short sobbing gasps, realizing she no longer held the Desert Eagle, Kate pawed around her in near panic. Her weapon was her only chance, her only way to fight back, to survive. Extending her search when she failed to find the pistol on her initial sweep, she ignored the thickening smoke, the pulsating flames, the rocketing heat, the—

Got it!

The fingers of her left hand curled around the Magnum's handle, clutching it, relief sweeping through her as she once more felt capable of mounting a defense.

Kate tried to steady her breathing while crawling away from the flames, keeping her head down, below the smoke rapidly filling the room, her vision still blurred by the stinging haze and also by the impact, her mind struggling to catch up with the unexpected forces converging on her.

The fire reached Ray Dalton, who lay in a pool of his own blood about a dozen feet from her, presumably dead, until his clothes caught on fire and he began to tremble, to twist, arms flapping in vain as he let go an agonizing scream.

Kate tried to get to him but the shag carpet separating them had already ignited, releasing a dark, choking smoke that burned her eyes, her throat.

Ray Dalton's agonizing screams reverberating inside the burning house, Kate aligned the Magnum in his direction and fired once, the report drowned by the thunder, her stomach knotting as the screams stopped, as she watched the burning figure through the thick haze stop jerking, trembling, suffering.

The blistering heat forcing her to prioritize survival tactics over the emotions of having been forced to kill her old mentor, Kate scrambled on all fours toward the nearest window facing the rear, already shattered by the gunfire that had rapidly ceased following the explosion.

But that doesn't mean whoever did this has already left the area, she thought, peeking over the jagged lower edge of the window, her narrowed stare probing the murky cornfield backdropped by menacing clouds alive with sheet lightning.

Just the opposite.

Professionals would remain in place, watching the house burn to the ground, confident that the storm and the remote location would buy them time before emergency crews reached the area.

That's if they come at all, she thought as the nearing flames and the singeing heat made up her mind for her.

Surging to her feet, Kate Chavez propelled herself through the opening, away from the blistering inferno, the cool wind and the rain momentarily soothing her in midair, before she splashed her torso onto muddy ground, the same side she had previously bruised against the sofa chair while taking the brunt of the impact, broadcasting waves of rippling pain that nearly made her scream, potentially compromising her position.

Taking the pain while staggering to a deep crouch, the wind and the roaring fire ringing in her ears, cool rain drenching her, Kate swept the Desert Eagle across her field of view, surveying her surroundings, an abandoned tractor adjacent to a short water tower to her left, the cornfield directly ahead, and to her right—

The multiple shots cracked across the hundred feet separating her from two dark figures bearing large rifles pointed in her direction.

The soaked ground exploded in clods of mud by her feet, the sound mixed with rumbling thunder.

Kate fired twice in their direction, the muzzle flashes of her Magnum briefly washing the darkness with sparkling yellow and red-gold light, the deafening reports forcing the two silhouettes to dive for cover.

Kate sprang toward the safety of the cornfield fifty feet away, her nostrils flaring as she took in lungfuls of air, as her wounds stung her ribcage like a sizzling claw, as she blinked rapidly to clear her vision from rain falling in angled sheets, blinding her, making it difficult to focus on the terrain ahead and avoid tripping, avoid giving up her brief advantage.

As she ran, Kate leaned as far forward as she could, pointing her full momentum in the direction of safety—of the densely packed, six-foot-tall stalks covering several acres. Should a bullet strike her while running, her forward motion would keep her from falling short, from reaching the—

She tripped on something hard—something that did not give, and she was airborne as lightning gleamed, followed by darkness and four more shots clapping in rapid succession.

A blistering pain on her left thigh told her she had been

shot just before she crashed headfirst into a puddle of water less than two dozen feet from the cornfield.

Her training forcing her to ignore the burning pain, instead using the sleeve of her shirt to wipe muddy water off her face while pointing the Desert Eagle in the direction of the threat somewhere beyond the wall of rain and wind, Kate Chavez paused, catching her breath, flexing her left leg, cringing in pain but verifying mobility.

A fork of lightning glared against the falling rain, making it even more difficult to see past a few feet, but enough for her to verify that the wound was superficial. The bullet had grazed her skin, nicking a shallow track across the top of her thigh just above the knee.

Kate bent her leg again, grateful that the round had not only missed the bone but also the powerful thigh muscles that controlled it—meaning she should be able to walk. But the wound was bleeding, meaning she would have to field-dress it.

Later.

Now move!

The cornfield within reach, Kate scrambled to her feet again, ignoring the crippling—

Three more shots whipped the night.

She dove for the safety of the ground again just as lightning streaked across the boiling clouds layering the sky, casting twilight across the south Texas sky, once again blinding her. But if the lightning flaring across the falling rain blinded Karen, it also meant the assassins would not be able to see her.

Wait for lightning.

And she did, disregarding her throbbing leg while remaining low, out of the line of sight of the assassins, who kept their distance in apparent respect for the Magnum she continued to point in their—

Lightning gleamed.

Kate surged to her feet, rushing through the dazzling, blinding rain, paying no heed to the bolts of pain rushing up her left thigh, numbing her, until she felt the cornstalks engulfing her, until she was certain that her pursuers would not be able to fire on her as darkness resumed.

She slowed down to keep from getting excessively batted by the dried out corn stalks, by the brittle but sharp foliage, immersing herself a dozen feet into the field before cutting left, in the direction she had seen the silhouettes, and continuing for thirty seconds, before returning to the edge of the clearing but within the safety of her shield.

Dropping to a deep crouch while keeping an eye on the clearing sloping up to the burning house, Kate holstered the Desert Eagle and tore off both sleeves of her shirt.

As lightning continued to gleam in stroboscopic bursts through the foliage shielding her, followed by thunder and more rain, Kate wrapped the makeshift bandages around the wound, tight enough to staunch the light hemorrhage but without cutting the blood supply to the leg.

Once more clutching the Magnum, she used the muzzle to slowly part a few corn leaves out of the way, blinking through the rain, tasting the water droplets running down her face as her gaze landed on the burning house, ten-foot-tall flames licking the sky, defying the pouring rain.

Backlighted by the pulsating, yellow glow from Dalton's house, two dark figures quickly crossed her field of view holding bulky rifles—presumably the same assassins who had fired on her just a moment ago.

In an instant she weighed the odds of taking them out at the price of telegraphing her position to other assassins, or letting them enter the cornfield and come after her. But Kate was bleeding, meaning she had likely left a trail that even with the rain could be followed since her pursuers were close behind her.

Making her decision and taking a deep breath while aligning the closer of the two figures with her gun, Kate fired once, the report drowning all other noise, the muzzle flash illuminating the figure twenty feet away toppling over without a sound.

As the second assassin realized what had happened and began to swing his weapon in her direction, Kate had already switched targets, aiming the Desert Eagle toward the middle of his chest, firing again, the blinding flash momentarily covering the target and the flames behind him.

The second report still ringing in her ears, the figure also dropped while releasing the rifle, as if succumbing to the rain, the wind, and the thunder.

Taking a deep breath through her mouth before slowly exhaling, Kate waited as the fire completely covered the house in spite of the thick rain, as the roof collapsed while releasing a cloud of sparks toward the heavens before slowly the flames began to give to the unyielding storm.

There has to be more of them, she thought, remembering the fusillade that had suddenly peppered the house, killing Dalton before she was able to—

Three figures emerged from the left side of the smoldering rubble, all clutching what looked to be machine guns.

The cold rain soaking her thoroughly, making her shiver, Kate tracked them with the muzzle of her semiautomatic, hesitating about firing not only out of respect for those weapons, but wanting instead to observe, to listen, her investigative sense now starving for information, for the kind of intelligence she could use to expose those responsible for Ray Dalton's death.

In the twilight created by the dying flames, the threesome, all wearing black hoods, moved swiftly, with expert ease, rushing across the clearing single file with enough separation to make it difficult for any single shooter to take them all out at once.

Lightning and thunder lessened as the trio surveyed the backyard, but the rain continued to pound the area at an angle due to the strong north wind.

The lead man stopped when he reached the corpses, an action that prompted his two companions to drop to a deep crouch and take up defensive positions, sweeping the area with their machine guns.

Communicating through the heavy rain and thunder with hand signals, the point man relayed to his hooded companions what Kate already knew: no one can survive a well-placed .44 magnum round, which would easily penetrate even the most rugged Kevlar vest.

Kate frowned while staring at them.

Who are they?

What do they want?

How did they manage to follow me here?

Were they monitoring Ray's house in case someone paid him a visit?

But how could they possibly know why she was visiting her former mentor? What did they feel was so threatening that justified such frontal attack? And what was the connection between the assassinations of the World Missionary Fellowship's elders a year and a half ago with the slain GemTech executive? And why had DPS Director Pat Vance closed the investigation so soon? Is he—

The high-pitch ring of her mobile phone caught her off guard, momentarily paralyzing her.

Damn!

In the same instant, like bloodhounds suddenly spotting their prey, all three assassins turned their heads in her direction.

Kate reached for the unit strapped to her belt and switched it off on the second ring, but by then the enemy was already spreading; one to the left, another to the right while the third dropped to the ground, nearly disappearing from view in the uneven terrain.

Considering her options, realizing that her odds would quickly head south the moment those two reached the cornfield to flush her out toward the third man already positioned to fire at anything trying to exit the thicket, Kate made her decision, lining up the assassin to her right, firing once just before going into a roll to her left, immersing her body in mud.

The single shot, as loud as thunder, found its mark, striking her prey with brutal force, lifting him off his feet just as he was about to reach the cornfield and flipping him upside down as the Magnum round transferred part of its energy before exiting through his back.

Just as the assassin fell on the ground already a corpse, several gunshots reverberated across the clearing, causing explosions of mud and water where she had been a second before, confirming her fears about their tactics, about the stationary assassin waiting for an opportunity.

Staggering back several feet from the edge of the clearing, thoroughly caked in dark mud, Kate moved to her right, in the direction opposite the moving assassin, who had by now entered the field. Although still outnumbered, her Texas Rangers training told her that eliminating three of five enemies drastically improved her odds while instilling in them deep concern.

But she knew she had to control the natural surge of confidence that could potentially dull her operative sense, tempting Kate to ignore her discipline, her training. As long as there were gunmen out there she was vulnerable—and more so with her wounded leg, which continued to throb as she pushed herself.

A brief check of the bandage confirmed her fears. All of the activity was causing further blood loss in spite of the dressing, and she realized that her shivering lips and her goose-bumping skin could be due not to the rain but to her system losing so much blood.

The wind whistling in her ears, Kate stopped the sprint after thirty seconds, returned to the edge of the cornfield, dropped both knees into the muddy field, and tightened the bandage, before slowly parting the leaves and drenched overgrowth, this time slightly uphill from where she had been.

Another realization struck her as hard as an assassin's bullet: the closest place where she could get help was miles away, meaning she had to reach her truck and flee soon, before she got lightheaded, dizzy—before she passed out and became fair game to her two remaining pursuers, one of whom remained flush with the sloping terrain, a patient sniper, biding his time, the muzzle of his machine gun sweeping the clearing, waiting for Kate to show herself.

That's, of course, assuming there are no more assassins up by the access road.

But if there were, Kate would have expected them to rush toward the rear of the property and assist their fallen comrades. Yet she had seen no one beyond the first two killers and the hooded trio that came to their rescue, which told Kate the termination team sent after Dalton consisted of five assassins, of whom two remained a threat.

But they could have radio for backup.

Worry about that after eliminating the current threat, she thought, her trembling lips tasting the dirt camouflaging her face, her body slowly falling victim to the cold rain and blood loss.

Kate once more considered her options, uncertain how much longer she would remain conscious, capable of fighting back. In order to reach the road—and her truck—she would have to exit the cornfield, would have to expose herself to a sniper too well entrenched for her to take him out with the Desert Eagle unless he stood up.

Blinking heavily to clear her sight as the wind began to die down, realizing what she had to do, Kate doubled back into the cornfield, this time not running away but hunting, her eyes scanning her dark surroundings, her senses heightened by the desperate nature of her situation, by the knowledge that time was working against her.

Briefly rolling on the mud to thicken the camouflage layer before surging to a deep crouch, the Texas Ranger pressed on, taxing her depleting stamina, pushing herself, using her eroding energy to move quietly, with purpose, like a wounded predator, searching for the hooded assassin, her right hand clutching the Desert Eagle, her left reaching down the left leg of her jeans, pulling them up to expose the pipe of her boot, her fingers curling around the handle of a six-inch graphite blade strapped to the inside of the boot.

As she moved, Kate's left hand automatically shifted the knife so that the graphite blade, sharp as a scalpel, protruded from the bottom of her fist, allowing for a number of quick and deadly blows simply by flexing her wrist.

Moving in a wide-sweeping S pattern for maximum coverage, Kate maintained her rhythm, hoping that the mud blended her with her dark surroundings, her mind tuned with the falling rain, with the intermittent wind listing the sea of corn in one direction, her—

Kate Chavez froze, her senses having detected unusual

movement to her immediate right: several cornstalks moving in the *opposite* direction of the prevailing wind just between her position and the edge of the clearing.

Remaining perfectly still in a deep crouch, her eyes focused in the direction of the rustling noise, Kate waited, like a coiled viper, the knuckles of her left hand turning white from clutching the knife.

Almost imperceptibly, a shadow shifted in the darkness cast by the charcoal clouds. She spotted it roughly ten feet away, slowly materializing into the bulky silhouette of a tall man armed with what she now recognized as a Heckler & Koch MP5 submachine gun, which he held across his chest, right gloved hand on the handle, index finger on the trigger, left gloved hand under the bulky muzzle.

Her breath caught in her throat, her shoulders aching with tension, Kate waited as the assassin, as tall as her six feet, took one step in her direction, then another, his head and his weapon moving from side to side, searching for a target, which telegraphed he had not yet found one.

You can't see me but I can see you, she thought, holding back, waiting for the right moment, which came as the assassin took a fourth step toward her while looking right, away from her.

Mustering strength, ignoring her throbbing torso, her burning leg, her shivering body, Kate Chavez lunged, closing the gap in less than two seconds, the graphite blade pointed at the soft skin just below the assassin's Adam's apple.

The assassin, obviously sensing movement, began to turn around, but Kate, having anticipated this reaction simply adjusted the angle of the blade shortly before making contact, before plunging it into her quarry's neck, severing the larynx.

In the same motion, Kate used the heavy muzzle of the Desert Eagle as a hammer, striking the assassin's shooting hand, the sickening sound of bones breaking mixed with the explosion of foam and blood oozing from the man's neck as she pushed the blade until her fist met skin, before driving it to the left, hacking through cartilage and tissue as she nearly decapitated him.

Dropping the MP5 as his legs gave under him, the assassin whipped both hands to his neck, his wide-eyed stare beneath the hood focused on Kate for an instant, before his eyes rolled to the back of his head and he fell by her feet.

Thick rain washing the mud off her face, her clothes, Kate pulled off the assassin's hood, exposing a middle-aged man with short brown hair. A brief search revealed no identification, just several hundred dollars in cash in a money clip.

Professional assassins.

But why?

Focus!

Following her plan, Kate holstered the Desert Eagle and the knife, and she began to undress him. First the black shirt, followed by the trousers, which she then donned before stuffing handfuls of corn leaves to create the right illusion. Last came the hood, the gloves, and the MP5, which she clutched just as she had seen him do.

Show time, she thought as she fired the MP5 three times toward the ground to further the trick before stepping in the direction of the clearing, reaching it thirty seconds later while walking casually.

As she left the field, as the rain turned into a drizzle and the clouds began to break and the winds die down, Kate lowered the MP5 and waved toward the sniper position before giving him a thumbs up. The last assassin immediate stood, also lowered his weapon, and reached for what looked like a mobile phone.

Kate kept walking toward him as he kept the handheld unit pressed against the right side of his head while nodding, apparently talking to someone. Kate swung the MP5 in his direction the moment he hung up and fired twice, but not to kill.

The 9mm bullets found their mark, one in the right shoulder and the other in the left thigh, forcing him to fall while preventing him from fighting back as she jumped over him, sitting on his chest, pinning his arms with her knees and snagging the phone away.

"Aghh! Dammit!" he hissed, trying to break free in spite

of the well-placed slugs, displaying a strength that nearly made her lose her balance as she straddled him.

Reaching for her knife, Kate brought it up to the assassin while also pulling off the hood, revealing another middle-aged man, this one completely bald and sporting a dark goatee, his face twisted in the same pain and anger flashing in his dark eyes.

"Who are you? Why did you attack us?" she asked.

"Go to hell!" he barked back.

"Hell," she said, grinning, which had a way of breaking the stranger's hard stare, at least momentarily. "Hell is where *you* are headed."

"I know who you are," the man replied with eerie calmness in spite of his wounds. "You can't kill me. I know my rights. You have to take me in and book me and give me my phone call."

Taking the knife and positioning it right over the man's left eye, Kate replied, "Today's my day off. I'm doing this for fun."

The assassin froze, eyes blinking in apparent confusion. "You're a Texas Ranger. You can't kill me."

"I just told you, asshole. I'm off today. Now, I will ask you again. Who do you work for? And why were you sent to kill Ray Dalton? Tell me or you lose the eye."

"You . . . you can't *do* that. I know my rights! I want to call my lawyer right now!"

"You lost those rights the moment you crossed the line."

"Damn you, bitch! My people will have your fucking badge by the end of the day if you don't read me my Miranda, book me, and let me call my attorney!"

"No attorney for you. Last chance before they start calling you One-Eyed Jack."

"Go to hell," he replied again.

"Hell is *exactly* what I'm going to put you through," she said. "Now answer! Who do you work for?"

"Don't you get it?" he said, coughing, then adding, "They know who you are. They have the power . . . the power to get to anyone at anytime. Just like today."

The man was starting to fade. Kate pushed him harder. "Who *are* they?"

"I can't—can't tell you," he replied, before pressing his lips together, staring back.

"It's your eye," she said, taking the blade right up to his right eye.

Continuing to glare defiantly at her, the assassin began to tremble, to convulse, before his eyes lost focus, the pupils dilating as he stopped breathing.

What the hell?

Fearing a trick, Kate pressed two fingers against the side of his neck, failing to feel a pulse.

His wounds weren't lethal.

She leaned down to smell his breath, sniffing for the almond odor released by a cyanide capsule, but she found none.

Damn. How did he die?

Analyze later.

Standing, taking a deep breath while her gaze shifted from the bodies sprawled across the clearing to the smoldering ruins, a powerful and dreadful feeling descended on Kate Chavez.

The man's final words echoed in her mind.

They know who you are. They have the power . . . the power to get to anyone at anytime. Just like today.

As the rain turned into a light drizzle, as the storm clouds drifted east and the skies started to clear, Kate kept the hood on and continued to hold the MP5 while heading toward the front of the property to secure the area, to make sure there were no other men roaming the area, waiting for her in front of the house.

She reached the left side of the house, her attention shifting to the black Hummer parked just beyond her one-ton Ford truck.

Playing her assassin role like a pro, ignoring the burning pain from her leg, Kate kept walking toward it, realizing it wasn't the highly commercialized H2 Hummer but the original H1, the version originally built for the military, noticeably wider, armor plated, with a variety of safety options including self-inflating tires and bullet-resistant glass.

Scanning the rest of the area, Kate found no one in sight or in the interior of the Hummer.

Satisfied that the area was temporarily safe, Kate called the Texas Rangers office in Austin and asked to speak with Bill Hunter, her boss and also the captain of the Rangers, the man who replaced Ray Dalton a year ago. Unfortunately, Hunter was visiting the governor that afternoon. She requested a Code 42: the immediate dispatch of a team of Texas Rangers to her location to seal off the area and give a crime scene investigation team time to search for clues.

After being assured that a team would arrive within the next two hours, Kate removed the assassin's clothes, the corn leaves she had used as stuffing falling by her feet. She grabbed the first-aid kit in the rear seat of her truck and spent the next ten minutes treating her wound. First she cut off an oval patch off the front of her jeans a few inches above the knee, exposing the wound, which she cleaned and disinfected while keeping the leg raised above her heart, minimizing the bleeding. Then she used one of a half dozen emergency bandages, part of a Ranger's standard first-aid equipment. Designed by the military for pre-hospital treatment, the emergency, multipurpose bandage consolidated the function of many pieces of equipment into one easy-to-use unit.

She tore open the plastic bag and began by placing the sterile, non-adherent pad on the two-inch-long wound, before applying pressure by wrapping the elasticized woven leader over the topside of the bandage pad, where a pressure bar designed to accept the wrapping leader applied force directly to the wound to bring about homeostasis—blood staunching. Subsequent wrappings of the leader secured and maintained the pad over the wound, and by covering all of the edges of the pad it also acted as a sterile secondary dressing.

Kate examined her work, satisfied that she was no longer losing blood, and also checked for the mobility of her leg.

Now for some cursory CSI work.

She began by inspecting the vehicle, looking for any clues, but finding none except for the license plate number and vehicle serial number. She jotted them down before reaching her truck and snagging a backpack—her field fingerprint, retina scan, and DNA kit—also out of the back seat. Although the Rangers still wore the traditional white hats, badges, weapons, and boots like their predecessors, today they were also armed with the latest technology to fight crime, including the finest CSI equipment in the law enforcement business—equipment she was determined to use to find out who these men were.

She spent twenty minutes taking hair, blood, skin, and saliva samples from each of the assassins, as well as using digital scanners to collect fingerprint and retina records. Lastly, she used the kit's high-resolution digital camera to take front and side shots of each assassin and all weapons— plus she jotted down their serial numbers.

Satisfied that she had done as much as she could and that the real CSI team would comb the place later, she packed up the field kit, set it down in the backseat, and was about to dial Bill Hunter again when she noticed she had one voice message waiting.

Kate now remembered the phone call she had received and which had compromised her hideout. The timestamp on the message matched the time when she had received the untimely call.

Let's see who was the idiot who almost got me killed.

She keyed in her password to access her mailbox.

The message was from her ex-husband, Mark.

Figures, she thought frowning, before pressing the option to listen.

"Kate . . . call me as soon as you get this. It's about Cameron. He's missing."

The words pounding her as intensely as her throbbing wound, Kate hung up, took a deep breath, and climbed into her truck, cranked the engine, put it in gear, and took off, tires kicking gravel.

Her mind spun as she tried to reach her ex-husband on his mobile phone but was forwarded to an automated answering system. She then tried Cameron's cell phone and got his voicemail.

Screaming in frustration as she approached the end of the unpaved access road and steered the one-ton truck onto the service road that would lead her to the highway, Kate Chavez felt her stomach knotting in a mix of raw terror and unbridled anger.

She reached the highway's onramp, her mind going in different directions, a million questions pounding her logic.

"Damn it," she hissed. "Who are these people?"

The answer came a moment later, as the she watched the storm drifting toward Houston, lightning gleaming just above the charcoal horizon. Ray Dalton's words flashed in her mind with the power of a hundred lightning bolts.

They know who you are.

They have the power . . . the power to get to anyone at anytime.

Just like today.

10

Cyber Viper

In the Blue Room of the White House, Vice President Raymond Costa sat next to Alfonso Gutierrez, the president of Colombia, as they discussed the drug situation in the South American nation.

Surrounded by an entourage of gaudily dressed Colombian military officials, three U.S. Marines, four Secret Service agents, and a handful of White House aides, the two officials reviewed the list of items on today's talks.

Dressed in a longtailed black tuxedo, a thick, yellow, blue, and red sash draped diagonally over his starched white shirt from his waist to his right shoulder, his dark hair greased and brushed straight back, the dark-olive-skinned president set down his agenda and said, *"En el ultimo analisis, necesitamos mas ayuda militar, Señor Costa. Los jefes del Cartel tienen demasiado dinero y pueden comprar armas muy avanzadas."*

The Level-V SpyWare implant interfaced to the base of Vice President Costa's skull intercepted the foreign words captured by his inner ear and translated them into the English words that reached his mind. *In the final analysis, we need more military aid, Mr. Costa. The Cartel chiefs have too much money and can afford very advanced weapons.*

The vice president understood what Gutierrez said and nodded with feigned empathy. In reality, nearly fifty percent of the U.S. military aid to Colombia found its way into the international arms black market, where the finest hardware from American weapons contractors were exchanged for hefty numbered accounts in places like the Cayman Islands and Switzerland—the coffers of Gutierrez and a dozen top Colombian officials. But that was the cost of forging a powerful alliance in Colombia. Although half of the aid was misguided, the other half went into the fight against the drug war at its source. By buying the loyalty of the ruling government, Uncle Sam not only got the Colombian military to fight the drug epidemic at the source and under the direction of American military intelligence, but more important, America received the full cooperation of the South American nation in other matters.

Like helping promote American merchandise in Latin America instead of European or Asian products, especially Chinese goods.

And buying Colombia's help, as well as Peru's, Venezuela's, and Chile's was key to steering Argentina and Brazil away from the onslaught of products from companies controlled by the People's Republic of China and more toward American products, even those manufactured in Taiwan, Indonesia, and even in China.

Buy American.

That was Costa's motto for his country, which had suffered a severe loss of manufacturing jobs to Asian compa-

nies, particularly those in China, and which was dangerously close to becoming a services oriented nation instead
of one dominated by its mass production of goods, which
drove the nation's GNP, gross national product.

Costa regarded one of many politicians he needed to bribe
in order to shift the balance of the power of world influence
back toward America.

Costa didn't hate Colombian officials like Gutierrez for
using taxpayers' money to fund their retirement plans. In
fact, the vice president *wished* Gutierrez and his inner circle
stole a larger share of the U.S. military aid targeted at lessening the law enforcement impact on the drug trade. In the
past months the percentage of the aid that had been properly
channeled to bolster Colombian forces had resulted in the
interception of many illegal drug runs over the Gulf of Mexico, including a Piper Comanche twin-engine plane flying
below radar toward southern Texas. Its cargo, however, had
not been cocaine but diamonds from TDG-controlled mines
in eastern Sierra Leone.

Only the foresight of the symbiotic collective intelligence
of the super users of The Donovan Group had prevented a
disaster by requiring that the pilot be implanted with Level-I
SpyWare. That had allowed TDG governors like Costa,
Salieri, Gardiol, and VanLothar to watch what the pilot saw
real-time: the pair of U.S. Air Force F-22s flanking the Comanche hauling the latest batch of contraband diamonds
destined to feed the insatiable appetite for knowledge of
ANN, the Artificial Neural Network at the core of TDG, the
legacy of the legendary high-tech entrepreneur and visionary Anne Donovan. The decision had been easy for the distributed intelligent system of the ten super users chartered
with the protection of ANN at all costs. Wresting control of
the pilot's mind, the super users held an emergency symbiotic meeting and unanimously pointed the Comanche's nose
at the water two hundred feet below while pushing full throttle. The Air Force pilots later reported the plane striking the
water 140 miles off the coast of Texas and immediately disappearing from sight.

Diamonds were easily replaceable.

An investigation of the unexpected shipment was not.

"Su Excelencia, nuestro gobierno entiende su situacion y vamos a ayudarlos, como siempre," replied Costa as the SpyWare translated his English thoughts into the perfectly articulated words that brought a smile to Gutierrez's face. *Your Excellency, our government understands your situation and will help you, as always.*

"I knew I could count on you, Señor Costa," said the Colombian president in the Spanish that in Costa's mind sounded just like English, as did Mandarin, Cantonese, Russian, Japanese, and any of the other half-dozen languages in which he was considered fluent by a marveling American public who felt he should have gotten the Democratic ticket during the national convention last October. But Costa had come in a close second to the popular Andrew Boyer, a former Navy pilot who was awarded the Congressional Medal of Honor for his heroism during the Iraqi war. Costa had agreed to become Boyer's running mate for the benefit of their party. Their chemistry, a combination of the handsome and heroic Boyer and the brilliant, experienced, and insightful Costa was just what the Democrats had needed to dislodge the Republican incumbent from office.

And that's *precisely* how the White House was running these days. While Boyer was attending the yearly Navy Tailhook convention in Las Vegas as the keynote speaker, Costa was spreading America's influence in the emerging markets of Latin America, Eastern Europe, and especially in Asia—a task he accomplished far better than any other elected official in the past one hundred years because of his SpyWare knowledge of world languages, cultures, and politics.

"You are a friend of the White House, Your Excellency, and this administration always takes care of its friends," replied Vice President Costa in the well-groomed Spanish that his SpyWare made him pronounce with the inflection of a veteran newscaster from Univision.

They smiled cordially and went on to discuss the other items on their agenda, which included more details on the drug wars followed by a recent amendment to the United States–Colombia trade policy. After a brief pause for coffee that Gutierrez had personally brought with him for this special occasion, the two officials engaged in a lively discussion of Colombia's vanishing rain forests, followed by its education system and the possibility of more scholarships for Colombian students to attend American universities. They then chatted about the state of health of the general population and together reviewed the latest figures of HIV, malaria, cholera, and other diseases from a report from the World Health Organization. Finally, their conversation hovered on the world economy, including import and export tariffs and Colombia's growing trade deficit with the United States.

The meeting ended an hour later with a photo shoot, where both officials exchanged gifts and embraced to the applause of their entourages.

Moments later, sitting comfortably in the rear of the black limousine that would take him to the Chinese Embassy on Connecticut Avenue for a meeting with the ambassador and top delegates from Beijing, the sixty-five-year-old vice president stared out the armor-plated, tinted window, but the image registered in his eyes represented a mere window in the periphery of his mind, enhanced with the Level-V implant that had turned him into a genius.

An adjacent window suddenly came up, urging him to attend an emergency cyber meeting with the other super users.

While leaving behind a sentinel to monitor his physical surroundings, Costa jacked into the interface connecting his biological mind to the SpyWare.

Floating over this self-contained field rich with enough data to fill the Library of Congress five times over, Raymond Costa sensed the pulsating energy and enjoyed its intoxicating effect as a T7 wireless broadband connection, depicted as a neon green webbed tunnel, projected skyward from his SpyWare's blue-green valley, its twisted funnel disappearing in the crimson skies dotted with pearl clouds.

Making a diving turn to the right that defied the laws of physics—laws that did not apply to this cyberworld—Raymond Costa immersed himself in the T7, the warmth of its flickering energy gripping him, accelerating him with the power of a million tornadoes.

The vice president let it all go, his triple-booked agenda, his responsibilities to the American public, the burden of carrying the lion's share of running the White House for the younger president. Comforted in the knowledge that the expert system left behind monitoring the external world could handle most of his daily functions—or signal if it reached a non-converging situation demanding that Costa disengage the SpyWare and intervene—the vice president surrendered his mind to the interface, to the glowing channel that took him away from Washington, from the daily drudgery of being second-in-command to a man who did not possess the skills to be president.

Rushing past worlds that only existed in the heart of wireless servers, dashing from ISP to ISP represented as solar systems within the massive bustling galaxy of the Internet, Raymond Costa reached a maroon and yellow-gold nebula supercharged with surface energy, with sheet lightning, within the impregnable shield of The Donovan Group, of ANN's domain.

The firewall was indeed impenetrable for those who didn't possess the powerful encrypted access password of a Level-V SpyWare user, such as the one that shot ahead of Costa's meteor-like figure in cyberspace. Resembling a photon torpedo, the password struck the electrified surface, melting it away, creating an amorphous portal of blinding white energy within the fabric of the shield.

Although unreadable by the AI, the energy of the encrypted password overwhelmed the network's defenses like an undefeatable virus, creating a safe passage for the bearer.

His cyber construct laced with the same software algorithm as the encrypted software key, Raymond Costa dove through, feeling in the same instant the portal closing behind him as well as the paralyzing second line of defense of ANN's domain, a holding cell inside the firewall still isolated from the rest of this inner sanctum. The AI's Interrogation Friendly or Foe software tried to penetrate the lattice of Costa's cyber form, but it could not go beyond the overwhelming energy of the virus-like personal encryption, which released a form of digital fingerprint, unique to the vice president, impossible to forge or crack—even by ANN—that commanded the AI to let him through.

At once the holding cell vaporized, giving way to the familiar worlds and the surrounding burning stars of ANN, who resided at the center of this massive Milky Way.

Sudden warmth overwhelmed his senses, filling his mind with an intoxicating sense of peace, of comfort. The tracking beam directed him toward the symbiotic meeting grounds while also easing his anxiety, the drudgery of his daily life, relieving the stress that clouded judgment, the pride that oftentimes got in the way of doing the right thing, the personal fear of making a mistake. ANN's neuron-soothing algorithms created a digital environment that melted all emotional barriers away, allowing Raymond Costa to apply his unbiased objectivity to the issue under discussion at The Circle.

The Circle.

Like ten moonlike shapes hovering around the sunlike ANN, Raymond Costa joined The Circle exactly 1:5432 seconds after leaving a cyber sentinel handling his physical self in the rear of the limousine headed to the Russian Embassy, an eternity in cyberspace, yet nothing more than the blink of an eye in the physical world.

The Circle.

Costa sensed the wireless fingerprints of his Level-V colleagues, the guardians of ANN, the other nine high-tech shamans charted with running the international conglomerate that was The Donovan Group.

The Circle.

Costa felt the symbiotic energy of the group and became one with them. No politics existed at this inner level of superconnectivity, where their collective wisdom—combined with ANN's overarching knowledge facilitating the impromptu meeting—provided them with the unbridled power to accomplish what no single person, corporation, nation, or even species could accomplish.

Superscalar symbiotic power, the ability to blend the SpyWare-enhanced intelligences of ten powerful and influential people into one collective directive interfaced straight into ANN, which also controlled the inputs of the thousands of Level-I to Level-IV users connected to the network.

These lesser digital beings provided inputs into the formidable matrix that was ANN, and in return they received the synthetic intelligence that placed them well above the average human. But only Level-V users—The Circle—could dive this deep into the matrix, into the burning core of this all-encompassing system. The rest provided stimuli—audio and video—directly to ANN's massive analytical engine, which processed an amount of data in any real second that would easily clog the world's most powerful engines for a week, and then issued dispatches, orders, for this army of cyber grunts to carry out without dispute.

Although Costa recognized Salieri, Gardiol, VanLothar, and the rest of his brothers nearby, ANN had no record of their real life identities. To the master construct each super user was just that: a user with a special and unique digital fingerprint, and together they controlled the network.

The master construct had no idea that these ten had been inseparable college buddies at Berkeley way back when, and that they had formed an unbreakable bond under the leadership of a campus activist by the name of Anne Donovan, who had sworn to fight Washington's gross inefficiencies and injustices, to control those who had forced her father out of his lifelong business.

And we are certainly in control now, Costa thought, as he locked digital elbows with his cyber brothers in this circle pulsating with blinding energy while ANN revealed the reason for the priority-one interrupt that had retrieved them from the real world.

THREE INCIDENTS.

THREE DIFFERENT CONTINENTS.

The pattern, unrelated and easily missed by the average human, didn't fool the superscalar detection systems of the most powerful AI ever created.

Protected by nested layers of impregnable firewalls, assisted by the symbiotic intelligence of its guardians, ANN led The Circle through an exponentially smarter iterative process of if-then scenario trees, checking multiple options like a master chess player, viewing the decision trees thousand of moves ahead with a computing parallelism that would make the fastest networks at the Pentagon seem like a 1970s Apple.

Applying not just the enhanced wisdom of the guardians, which happened to be ten of the most wealthy and powerful men on the planet, but also the thousands of terabytes of transcendental intelligence scouring the fifteen thousand carats of diamond nanocircuitry at the core of ANN, the super users required less than thirty seconds of SymNeural activity to converge on the process that would result in the most optimum course of action.

"Mr. Vice President, looks like there's an accident in Dupont Circle. The lead car just informed me that we will be taking the alternate this morning. We will be three minutes late."

Somewhere in the periphery of his consciousness, Vice President Costa watched the remote cyber agent guarding the real world in his cyber absence handling the primitive input from the limo driver, requiring a bare nod of the head and a resigned and hastily spoken, "Figures." The cyberagent then transitioned to a subroutine that prompted Costa's muscles to shift his physical body just a dash to the right while bringing his right hand under his chin, index finger just over his upper lip, eyes narrowed and focused into the distance beyond the armored glass, flawlessly executing one of a dozen preprogrammed poses conveying deep thought.

All super users had their daily body movements, facial expressions, and mannerisms taped, digitized, and fed into the controlling programs embedded in their respective SpyWare, thus minimizing the chances that someone might spot the trick.

Besides, Costa thought, *if something did go wrong with the handling agent, I could return to my body in less than a second and regain control of a situation.*

Satisfied that the construct was managing his real-world life as programmed, Costa focused on the task at hand, reviewing the top five courses of action, making his decision after considering the well-wrung-out choices and consulting with the symbiotic body, finally casting his digital vote.

A nanosecond later, a fluorescent green photon torpedo oozed out of his cyberform. Costa steered his vote toward the small magenta cloud hovering over the group, the document recording their final decision, SymAccord 17651. The other nine super users also cast their votes, and as had been the case many times before, the new SA did not reflect consensus, but the symbiotic majority as measured by the approving glowing green spheres steered toward the top choice, while the other choices received fewer votes. ANN, albeit far more knowledgeable than The Circle, did not get a vote, though everyone present there took her input seriously before making their choices.

And just as it had begun, the cybermeeting came to an abrupt end, with ANN punching ten holes into the fabric of the multilayered firewall, like amorphous concentric exit portals.

The Circle dispersed in unison, resembling an exploding super nova, though their brilliant energy radiated only in the direction of their individual portholes, as if sucked out by an invisible vacuum as ANN steered each cyberguardian to a unique wireless ISP in a controlled chaos that lasted but a handful of nanoseconds.

Traveling in a world lacking the shackles of time and space, Raymond Costa rushed through the opening in the security layers protecting the master construct and shot past the galaxies of ISPs in reverse order, releasing his cyberagent when settling in his own mind exactly 86.563 seconds from the time he had received the non-maskable interrupt.

The chosen course of action—which ANN had already started to relate to the right cyber soldiers in the right countries—would neutralize the reported incidents. Within the hour, the commands would be relayed from ANN to Level-IV SpyWare colonels—the first layer of buffers to isolate The Circle from field operations. These cyber officers, whose ranks included several high-profile law enforcement officers from agencies around the world and a large number of industrialists and foreign government officials, would further communicate the detailed instructions, SpyWare to

SpyWare, without any loss of data, to the appropriate Level-III Captains, who would carry out the orders by using Level-II Lieutenants controlling the Level-I soldiers, further isolating TDG operations from the brutal reality of the symbiotic decision. Should a SpyWare ever be captured and try to confess under the stress of an interrogation, ANN had the flexibility to trigger a surge pulse that would activate the self-destruct mechanism in the SpyWare implant, leaving nothing for the authorities to trace back to TDG—and in the process killing the subject with a massive aneurysm.

A difficult but necessary measure, thought Raymond Costa, regaining control of his physical body. People sometimes had to die in order to protect the network, such as the Level-I assassin who had come close to confessing when Texas Ranger Kate Chavez threatened to pluck out his eyeballs.

The ends justify the means, he thought, feeling stronger than ever about the perpetuation of the movement started by Anne Donovan. Never again would America be under the unpredictable control of uninformed voters so easily swayed by campaign advertisements, candidates' empty promises, the worst kind of manipulative marketing, dirty political tricks that seldom had anything to do with the truth or essence of freedom and justice embedded in the Constitution by America's founding fathers.

Anne Donovan had believed that way back when, and now it was the job of The Circle to evangelize that vision not just from sea to shining sea but around the globe.

The perpetuation of the vision hinged on the tactical and strategic decisions made by the ten super users, such as the SymAccords ratified a minute ago, decisions that would prevent incidents in three separate regions of the world from gathering momentum, from growing into the sort of uncontrollable cancer that history had shown time and again could spiral out of control, resulting in the exposure—and implosion—of covert organizations.

But these unsavory though necessary types of TDG operations had to remain secret, had to continue to operate below the surface, doing the dirty job that foot soldiers in all countries had to do for the benefit of their nations. And that was precisely what those Level-I SpyWare users did for the benefit of Anne Donovan's vision: They were the enforcers, present everywhere and nowhere, like ghosts, influencing, steering, sometimes in very direct and brutal ways, guiding the future of an America in need of the strong leadership that voters could not seem to be capable of electing, blinded by the propaganda of negative campaigning, by a media deteriorated to nothing but the tools of special interest groups.

Like the weapons contractors who got Boyer elected, he thought, cringing at the thought of the ungodly amounts of taxpayers' money that had been blown by the Pentagon and its exorbitant budgets. But the time was nearing when TDG's influence would reach the deepest layers of the government, of the well-entrenched military. Many officers in the armed forces were Level-II, -III, and even -IV SpyWare users, absorbed by the system in a digital grass roots thrust driven by Costa himself and overseen by The Circle and the almighty, ever-present ANN, who saw everything and heard everything.

But such efforts, even those accelerated by the exponential evolution of distributed intelligence, took time to gain traction, to take effect.

Time.

Satisfied that TDG would prevail as the undisputed, evolutionary-superior intelligent system on the planet—long after the current super users had died—the vice president perched a pair of reading glasses at the end of his aquiline nose and ripped open the seal of a brief labeled FOR THE EYES OF THE PRESIDENT that included the president's initials allowing Costa to review it in his name.

Just as he does with anything requiring deep thought, the Viper mused, before mumbling to himself something about having to do a president's job without the associated benefits.

Finding solace in the Level-V SpyWare that reminded him of the better days looming just around the corner, Vice President Costa settled himself in his plush seat, ignored the blaring horns from traffic-clogged Dupont Circle to his right, and began to read the brief on the latest development on the situation between Taiwan and the People's Republic of China.

11a

The Procedure

The procedure was elegant in its simplicity, in particular when one considered the complexity of what was being achieved.

In one of dozens of SpyWare clinics in Building 13A, Dr. Miles Talbot oversaw the Level-II Senior Technician keying the coordinates into the server system that Talbot and his staff had just upgraded to a new diamond-based cluster of microprocessors similar to those running at the core of ANN in Building 33B.

The custom server located in the basement of Building 13A—and interfaced to ANN in nearby Building 33B—provided enough local computing power to perform three dozen SpyWare implants at once in the clinics spread out across the five floors of this steel and glass structure overlooking the countryside. Typically, however, the average number of subjects undergoing implants was between ten and fifteen.

Talbot watched with satisfaction as the hardware upgrade improved the efficiency of the technician to keystroke his way through the program controlling the servomotors that placed the needle-like nanoprobe at the precise location above the subject by nearly twenty percent. In this case the target was an F-22 Fighter Air Force captain who had been passed over for promotion by better-connected officers, some of whom were already part of the TDG family.

As was always the case, the subject was unconscious, under anesthesia also controlled by Talbot's new hardware upgrade, eliminating the need for so many anesthesiologists on site. If the upgrade worked as planned, GemTech would be able to transfer five of the eight resident anesthesiologists to other locations, increasing the efficiency of TDG.

And for that, Salieri will continue to leave my kids and their families alone, he thought while continuing to observe the implant process.

A fine grid of red lasers charted the back of the subject's head and neck, creating thousands of intersections marking the coordinates used by the mapping software and hardware as it zeroed in on the precise location just above the spot where the spinal cord connected to the brain, the location where the human brain, nature's most elaborate computer system, interfaced with the body. Every command issued by the brain, whether voluntary or involuntary—like keeping the heart beating and the kidneys diverting toxins into the urinary tract—went through this microscopic cluster of information channels.

And it was at this coordinate that the nanoprobe stopped above the secured subject, whose head and neck were further restrained and aligned to the machine to a precision of a millionth of an inch.

Although quite familiar with the procedure, having not just undergone it himself but improved it over the past three years through periodic hardware upgrades, the process never ceased to amaze Dr. Miles Talbot, as vividly displayed by the advanced ultrasound image projected onto the high-definition LCD screen, showing a 1000X magnified image of the relevant section of the brain stem.

The nanoprobe momentarily stopped upon reaching the desired coordinate, before slowly lowering toward it.

The technician switched to automatic mode, letting Talbot's upgraded hardware handle the rest, monitoring the proceedings through the overhead screen as the advanced algorithms drove the probe into the skin, piercing it with minimum bleeding, which was absorbed by suction nanotubes surrounding the nanoprobe, keeping the area of interest clean through the length of the procedure.

So clean that the good captain will be able to go home to his wife and kids tonight and no one would ever know he had been operated on, thought Talbot. There would be no shaving marks, not even the tiniest of scars after the cosmetic routines spent ten minutes smoothing out the relevant skin.

The nanoprobe, clearly visible now in the magnified ultrasound system, continued its penetration into the brain stem at a location so precise that a millionth of an inch in any direction would result in permanent paralysis, finally reaching the core of the most complex of human interfaces.

And this is when magic happens, Talbot thought, watching the syringe-like nanoprobe squirt just under a cubic centimeter of SpyWare gel that appeared blue on the screen.

As the nanoprobe retracted, the core of the SpyWare, under the control of ANN, developed hundreds of thousands of microscopic tentacles, each a millionth the thickness of a human hair, and each already programmed to seek a specific neurochannel connecting the spinal cord to the base of the brain.

The actual interface process, the time it took each microscopic appendage to find its matching controlling nerve and form a neural connection, took less than ten seconds. By then the SpyWare gel had also spread across the base of the skull and signaled its readiness to begin to receive software from ANN, starting with GemTech's latest version of its SpyWare operating system, which provided the basic software framework from which all applications ran.

Talbot watched as the system transferred via a wireless mega-broadband connection the forty-some terabytes of software, followed by the standard set of applications for a Level-II user, including the complex routines of the cyberagents who would handle his physical body when the captain needed to spend time in cyberspace. At this time ANN also loaded the security programs that could disconnect his mind from his body and force him to do anything TDG needed him to do—should a situation arise that demanded such action for the benefit of the company. And, of course, the download concluded with the self-destruct subroutine that would vaporize the SpyWare while inducing a lethal aneurysm—again, to be used only in an extreme situation.

Like the Fellowship elders a year ago and my own VP of operations last month, Talbot thought. Although he had not known the elders who had tried to expose the Fellowship for what it was, a front to smuggle conflict diamonds for GemTech, Talbot had met the VP of operations, who had become disenchanted with TDG's views of total global domination under the control of a machine and had wanted out.

He did go out.

In a body bag, just like the elders.

And to disguise the digital aneurysms, the super users had dispatched Level-I assassins to shoot them and cover up the real reason for their deaths.

Both experiences had only reinforced Salieri's warning about Talbot playing ball for the sake of his kids. The former Stanford professor had no doubt that his son and daughter and their families would be slain if he crossed TDG.

I'm stuck, he thought as the standard applications became embedded in the SpyWare gel. The technician followed that by the custom software transfers, specialty programs tailored to the particular need of the SpyWare user. In the case of the good Air Force captain, they were mostly advanced flying tactics, weapons, and systems, including every last course taught at the Air Force Academy plus tons of military history and battle tactics. The technician also downloaded detailed knowledge of the languages, history, geography, and customs of the various Middle Eastern countries where he was scheduled to be posted.

Armed with such powerful knowledge, in addition to now being a part of TDG's family and its powerful connections at home and abroad, the thirty-two-year-old pilot would definitely get on the fast track, making major within a year, lieutenant colonel the year after that, and full colonel within the next four years.

And for all I know the bastard could become secretary of the Air Force by the age of fifty, Talbot thought, finding it difficult to control a strange mix of anger and respect at this well-oiled and seemingly unstoppable machine that each day grew stronger, assimilating men and women of all ages and walks of life, providing them with the power to grow well beyond their means but with powerful strings attached.

And once you're in you can never get out, he thought, deciding that this place was worse than the Mafia.

Satisfied that the new hardware upgrades were working as planned, Talbot returned to Building 33B to continue to oversee ANN and the developments in Sierra Leone.

11b

China Syndrome

"It's a pleasure seeing you again, Mr. Ambassador," said Vice President Raymond Costa in English as he shook hands with Jason Wu, the Chinese ambassador in Washington. The ambassador introduced him to his VIP guest, General Xi Zhu, the Chinese minister of the interior who had arrived from Beijing in a state-owned jet just three hours ago.

Zhu did not speak fluent English, leaving the ambassador to translate the exchange of greetings.

They met in the ambassador's office on the second floor of the well-guarded embassy compound, where Costa's motor pool had gone through a rear entrance that led to the building's basement. There, they had taken a private elevator that delivered them to this office, bypassing the embassy's main entrance, the crowded front parking lot, the building's lobby, public elevators, and main reception area.

Enjoying a cup of herbal tea, Costa sat with his legs crossed on a comfortable black-leather sofa opposite General Zhu, a sixty-something short and wiry man with dark and crooked teeth and a sea of wrinkles under thinning gray hair. Although a high-ranking military officer, Zhu was dressed in civilian clothes this cloudy morning: a dark blue suit, a starched white shirt, and a maroon tie. A single red star pinned to the left lapel of his suit, a pair of gold chevrons on the right one, plus two ribbons and a medal adorning his left breast pocket was all the insignia tying him to his military background. But it was the eyes that grabbed Costa's attention. They were dark, glossy, and eerily steady, regarding the American vice president with strange indifference, especially given the fact that Jason Wu had insisted on this last-minute face-to-face meeting to deal with a "developing situation in Beijing."

Costa already had a pretty good idea what the situation was all about: Taiwan's recent announcement of expanding an industrial park north of Taipei with the expected assistance of the United States government plus delegates from over fifty American corporations covering many industries from high-tech to pharmaceuticals. China, which for the past decade had invested heavily in the development of the industrial city of Suzhou, an hour and a half west of Shanghai, had not taken the news well, particularly since Beijing had been lobbying heavily in Washington to steer this most recent influx of capital investment away from Taiwan. Suzhou was on the cusp of surpassing Taiwan's high-tech infrastructure, and obtaining this new American investment—which would also steer European investors toward Suzhou—would represent a giant leap toward China's long-term goal of eroding the high-tech infrastructure and the associated financial strength of the small island as a way to weaken the rogue nation and pave the way for a reunification process.

Costa frowned.

Reunification my ass.

China had been trying to find a way to invade Taiwan for as long as he could remember, and since the old Communist ways of simply taking it by force had failed the test of time, Beijing had shifted tactics, using the capitalistic sword to conquer not just Taiwan but eventually all of Asia and Latin America.

And it's the job of this administration to temper China's growth, he thought, *to keep it from becoming an unmanageable monster.*

But Costa had to move very carefully, playing the political games that he had grown to master after three decades of foreign policy experience.

"How can the United States be of service to our Chinese allies?" Costa asked in the fluid Mandarin controlled by one of the recent software downloads installed by ANN in his SpyWare in preparation for this meeting.

General Zhu blinked once before looking toward a puzzled ambassador.

Vice President Costa sipped his herbal tea and smiled inwardly at having broken the general's poker stare.

The Chinese ambassador replied in English, "Mr. Vice President? You . . . you speak *Mandarin?*"

Costa gave him a slow nod before replying in Mandarin, "I have always enjoyed learning new languages, and there is little doubt in the world today that Mandarin is the language of the future."

As the ambassador tried to hide his embarrassment in front of one of the top-ranking officials in Beijing for not knowing that Costa was fluent in their native tongue, General Xi Zhu leaned forward and made a sound that resembled a train leaving the station. He was laughing.

"Where did you learn it?" General Zhu asked in Mandarin.

"Oh, here and there," Costa replied nonchalantly. "It's amazing how much you can pick up from a few trips plus private lessons."

"Most impressive," Zhu said as his wrinkled face rearranged itself back into poker mode. "Most impressive indeed. Your Mandarin is almost perfect, with only a slight accent."

"Thank you, Mr. Minister," replied Costa. "I have always been fascinated by Asian cultures, in particular its rich languages. But back to my original question, sir. How is it that I may be of service to the People's Republic of China?"

"My government is interested in engaging in talks to increase the level of economic alignment between our two nations, Mr. Vice President," said Zhu. "Beijing is willing to increase the incentives beyond those offered during the last round of American investment in China a year ago."

"An appealing concept," said Costa, setting the cup of tea on the glass cocktail table separating them. "But I am going to have to be brutally honest, and I do hope that my honesty and candor is interpreted as a sign of friendship and good-will because I want nothing but success for China."

Zhu considered Costa's preamble and nodded for him to continue.

Taking another sip of tea, Costa added, "Your proposal does seem in conflict with a world economic report I read yesterday concerning the saturated Chinese consumer, com-mercial, industrial, and military markets for high-tech goods. Given today's policies in your country, primarily those that force foreign companies to focus their manufac-turing to satisfy the demands of the China market, how is a further increase in investment in places like Suzhou to add more development and manufacturing bandwidth going to alleviate the situation? Inventory levels are far above normal in most regions of your country. Distributors are over-whelmed with product. It appears to me that your policies have resulted in excessive supply for a market that isn't ready to take it all."

General Zhu rubbed his chin before pouting and looking into the distance while replying, "I am a Communist, Mr. Vice President, and therefore I am naturally a blunt individ-ual, so I will get to the core of my proposal: My country is willing to lift the VAT penalties for the high-tech product manufactured in Suzhou to sell in the open market . . . as long as the United States commits all future rounds of capi-tal investment to China instead of Taiwan."

As the SpyWare translators conveyed the message with only a fraction of a second of delay, Costa didn't flinch even though China's top economic dog had just told him that his country would no longer penalize American corporations with heavy value-added taxes for high-tech goods manufac-tured in China destined to be sold outside China. While many companies doing business in China did sell a large portion of their products outside China because even with the VAT it was still far cheaper than manufacturing it in the United States, the removal of the VAT meant far greater profits for those companies.

Zhu was playing hardball to get the next round of investments away from Taiwan, and a short-sighted politician willing to please capitalistic constituents would have jumped at the opportunity. But Costa saw it a little differently. Although he worried at some level about China invading a financially weakened Taiwan, he cared far more about the fact that Taiwan's existence provided a healthy level of competition in the Asia market. If Taiwan weren't in the picture, Zhu wouldn't be here making such generous concessions— concessions that would translate into billions of dollars in profits for hundreds of American corporations over the next three to five years. And that meant growth for American corporations. It meant higher stock prices. It meant a healthier economy. But like all seasoned negotiators, Costa would never make a decision on an initial meeting, especially since he now had something to go bargain with the government of Taiwan, where America had just as many—if not more— companies doing business than in Suzhou. But Costa also had to consider another angle in his decision-making process: keeping China's economy from growing at a faster pace than America. Although it helped American companies to do business in China and Taiwan, in doing so, America was training China's labor force, empowering them to start their own national competing firms, many of which had already begun to flex their muscles in South America, threatening to take market share away from American, European, and Japanese conglomerates.

Like China's premier computer maker, Lenovo, acquiring IBM's entire laptop computer division several years back, Costa thought, remembering other such Chinese initiatives destined to create eventual monopolies.

This was an extremely complex issue that required careful balance and planning as well as a large degree of political skill, which could be boiled down to creating the right relationships and the right alliances to win against a common enemy.

"Your proposal shows that you are willing to negotiate in good faith, Mr. Minister, and I will take your views to the president, who is hosting another corporate America forum in two weeks to discuss foreign investment."

Zhu gave him a slow nod, his eyes still glistening with what Costa felt was a degree of admiration for the vice president's knowledge of their language.

They spent ten more minutes discussing other areas of common interest, including the environmental strides made by China's recently created Air, Land, and Water Agency, the Chinese equivalent of America's Environmental Protection Agency, to clean up the air in heavily industrial regions, such as the one including Suzhou and Shanghai.

Thirty minutes later, as Vice President Raymond Costa climbed into the rear seat of his limo and the motor pool drove out of the embassy compound, his private phone rang. It was Donald Bane, the director of Central Intelligence.

"Don? To what do I owe this unexpected call?" Costa said, working hard to suppress his contempt for this man who had been appointed to the job of leading the CIA by the previous administration, and whom the current president had been slow to replace with someone more aligned with the new views of the White House.

And all because of a lack of intestinal fortitude on the part of my damned boss. Fucking wimp, Costa thought, hating President Andrew Boyer for his lack of decision-making ability—a result of too many terms as senator from California.

"I'm afraid I have bad news, Mr. Vice President," said Bane, and by the time he had finished speaking, Costa's hand was trembling, dropping the unit on his lap while covering his face with his hands as he mumbled to the driver, "Home. Please take me home now."

12

The Lange Wapper

The cold night wind blowing in from the Scheldt River swirled Mac Savage's recently dyed blond hair, chilling him as he made his way up the wide terrace bordering the west bank of the river, toward the Antwerp Steen, the stone castle built in the thirteenth century as part of the fortifications made to protect the city center, and renovated in 1520 during the reign of Charles V.

Wearing a pair of black-rimmed clear glasses and a two-day stubble, Savage regarded the structure monopolizing the entrance to the city center from the river. Multicolored floodlights washed the tall exterior walls of the castle, which got its name from the Dutch word meaning *stone* because it was one of the earliest buildings in Antwerp constructed with stones. Turrets rising to a star-filled night and topped with swaying flags flooded with colorful light, the historical site that evening had become the target of stroboscopic flashes from the cameras of tourists crowding the access bridges and surrounding walkways.

The former CIA operative kept his hands free while surveying a group of visitors following a middle-aged woman holding up a red umbrella as she guided them to a relief statue flanking the castle's entrance. In spite of his desperate state of affairs, Savage couldn't suppress a grin. Back in the thirteenth century, that statue used to have a very large penis and was therefore venerated by women looking for a cure against infertility. But seventeenth-century Jesuits, finding the statue obscene, removed the offending appendage.

Savage maintained the casual stride of a tourist taking a night stroll, controlling his breathing as he approached the agreed-upon rendezvous point beyond a tour guide speaking in French to his group while pointing at the statue of the

Lange Wapper, a copper rendition of the Belgian version of the boogie man, who terrified children and drunks.

The statue's green patina gleamed under the floodlights as Savage gave it a brief, sideways look before moving on, inhaling a lungful of cold air, feeling his expanding chest pressing against the tight Kevlar vest he had purchased from the same gray-market dealer in the red light district who had sold him a new Beretta 92FS to replace the one he had lost outside the Fountaine Hotel two days ago.

Two days ago.

Mac Savage compressed his lips into a tight frown, remembering the phone call he had made two days ago, shortly after finding refuge in a nondescript motel that rented rooms by the hour near the red light district, where the manager had not cared to ask questions as long as transactions were made in cash.

Savage had called his emergency number, monitored directly by Langley, and left a message requesting immediate field extraction. Savage wished to be taken to a safehouse where he could make a private phone call to Donald Bane. Standard procedure called for the rescued operative to meet with the local station chief first, but Savage knew that would not get him anywhere. He didn't trust Michael Costa, hence his request to speak with Bane directly.

Then he paced his motel room, anxiety chipping away at his self-confidence as he waited for a reply while watching the local news on the small television unit bolted to the wall. It appeared that the same powers who had assassinated Jean-Pierre Bockstael had also manipulated the media and the local authorities to blame Savage for the triple murder of the former HRD executive and his bodyguards. The ballistics report had concluded that the bullets originated from Savage's Beretta, which he had lost during a confrontation with the police.

The police!

Bastards weren't anywhere near when I was getting shot at!

And that, of course, confirmed Savage's fears that the people who had killed Bockstael were powerful.

Very powerful.

So powerful that Savage considered skipping the Agency's help altogether and going solo in case the CIA had also been manipulated into believing the police reports.

He was certain that the old CIA, the one that groomed him into an international operative, would have given Mac Savage the benefit of the doubt. But he wasn't sure about the *new* CIA, even with Donald Bane still at the helm. The brutal fact was that his mentor had not been himself lately due to ever-increasing pressures from the new White House administration; otherwise Bane would have never agreed to put Savage through that two-in-a-box goat rodeo with a rookie like Mike Costa.

But an encouraging reply to his emergency call had arrived on the second day—yesterday—via a classified ad in the personals of the *Gazet van Antwerpen*, the city's main newspaper, acknowledging his request and setting up this meeting today.

Hoping that the dyed hair, the glasses, and the stubble would be enough to change his appearance from the photograph plastered on every newspaper in Belgium, including the afternoon edition folded and tucked under his left armpit, Savage continued down the waterfront, past the tourists admiring the old castle, which housed the National Maritime Museum.

Avoiding eye contact to prevent drawing unwanted attention, Savage focused on the collection of old sea vessels displayed in open air across the large grassy field adjacent to the Steen—all under the same array of colorful floodlights accenting the castle.

The short classified ad instructed Savage to meet his CIA contact by the towering stern of the blue and white fishing rig farthest from the castle, bordered by a number of buildings including Butcher's Hall and City Hall, which overlooked the Grote Markt.

Following professional habits, Savage approached the meeting grounds thirty minutes prior to the agreed time, continuing down one of the several cobblestone paths that veered away from the busy waterfront and snaked its way through the array of large ships on display in this section of the National Maritime Museum. The collection of towering hulls cast jagged shadows across the walkway as the crowd thinned the deeper Savage ventured in the maze of ships. On the one hand, darkness and fewer people meant a lower chance of someone recognizing him. On the other hand, the sudden change in surroundings was unnerving as it violated his meeting protocol. Savage, who preferred open, public areas, where he could use a crowd to escape should the meeting be compromised, realized he had made a mistake by asking for the meeting away from the crowd.

Too late to change it now.

Stay the course.

The emergency number was good for a single call. After that the Agency disconnected it, meaning he no longer possessed a sanctioned way to contact Langley. And given his popularity, he couldn't just walk up to the Marines guarding the entrance to the American Embassy a mile away and request a meeting with the CIA.

You have to play it out, Mac.

And he did, taking a long route to get to the meeting end of the open-air museum, pretending to admire the vessels on the opposite side of the park, slowly working his way back through deserted pathways as the minutes ticked away, the crowds' voices now distant as he inspected each of the murky corridors created by the freshly painted ships until—

An invisible force punched him in the middle of the chest, hard, shoving him back just as a second blow to his abdomen knocked the wind out of him.

His legs buckled, gave.

Mac Savage fell to his side, chest and abdomen on fire from the silent rounds of a hidden sniper.

But in spite of the pain shocking his system, of the sudden attack, Savage forced his body into a state of total paralysis, remaining just as he had fallen, arms and legs twisted at unnatural angles, eyes wide open, pupils fixated on the smokestack of a vessel that was still about a half block away from the meeting grounds.

The disciplined operative arranged his external appearance to match that of a man who had just been killed in order to prevent the unseen sniper from firing again, this time probably to his head.

Don't breathe.

Don't even blink.

And he didn't, ignoring his throbbing chest, locking his body into total stillness while his ears became his radar, scanning, searching beyond the distant chattering of the crowd by the waterfront, eyes soft, pupils relaxed.

Then he heard it: two sets of nearing footsteps, the magnitude of the rhythmic thuds—almost vibrations rather than sounds—telling him he was dealing with large men wearing soft-soled shoes, just like the ones he wore tonight.

Professionals.

Hard soles not only were slippery over cobblestones but resulted in loud clicking sounds that telegraphed the presence of an amateur.

"Good shooting, Tom," said a man whose voice Savage didn't recognize.

"I had a great teacher, Hal."

I know you, Savage thought, fighting the urge to look in the direction of the voice of Tom Barnes, one of Savage's senior operatives and former understudy during Savage's six-month instructor assignment at the Farm, the CIA's training facility in Williamsburg, where recruits learned everything from losing a surveillance team and defusing a bomb to flying a plane. Barnes had followed Savage to Colombia, Sierra Leone, and Belgium.

"Too bad the bastard turned on us," Barnes added.

Turned on them?

Keeping his pupils fixated on the stars, Savage watched the two figures enter his peripheral vision. Dressed in dark jackets and trousers, gloved hands holding semiautomatics attached to long and bulky silencers, they stopped a couple of feet from him.

As Savage confirmed his initial observation when noticing the red hair and orange freckles of his former understudy, he also recognized Barnes' partner.

The blond assassin!

The man who had shot Bockstael!
What is he doing with the CIA?
What in the hell is going on?

"He had it coming," said the assassin, the man Barnes had called Hal as he engaged the safety of his weapon and shoved it inside his jacket.

Never put your weapon away until you get confirmation of the kill, thought Savage as the assassin looked up and down the dark corridor in between moored vessels to make sure they were still alone.

"It's a shame, really," commented Tom Barnes, hanging on to his weapon but holding it closer to his chest to keep it out of sight, just as Savage had taught him, index finger resting on the trigger casing to avoid an accidental discharge.

But his former recruit made a tactical mistake: As Hal got within striking distance of Savage, so did Barnes, taking a step closer. "You should have seen him in his prime, Hal. Best damned operative I've ever known. And a great teacher too."

"Doesn't look so great at the moment," said Hal, who on closer inspection was much younger than Barnes, which explained his amateurish behavior.

"Well, he was even decorated by the director himself after his work in Colombia back in 2001 that led to—"

In a fast and powerful motion, Savage swept his left leg ninety degrees, kicking Tom Barnes' legs from under him so hard the operative fell backward while instinctively pointing the gun not at Savage but at the sky.

Surging to a deep crouch while turning—just as Barnes' back crashed hard against the cobblestones—Savage ignored his protesting upper body as he lifted his right leg, kicking the side of Hal's face with the edge of his shoe.

The rookie fell to the ground while Savage continued the turn, gathering momentum, recoiling the same leg before snapping a roundhouse kick at Barnes' shooting hand, the toe of his shoe aimed at the top of the wrist, forcing him to release the silenced weapon, which skittered over the cobblestones.

As Barnes moaned and held his left wrist with his right

hand, Savage slowed the turn while aligning the same leg with Hal's face as the blond assassin started to get up, crashing the heel against his nose, knocking him out.

Priorities.

Both operatives temporarily disabled, Savage quickly gathered their weapons, including the backup pieces he knew they carried in ankle holsters.

Steadying his breathing, controlling the pain streaking across his bruised midriff, Savage sat on Barnes' chest, pressing his knees against his former pupil's arms, pinning him against the cobblestones as he started to come around.

Staring at the red-haired, frecklefaced operative, and holding one of their guns in his right hand—a Beretta like the one he had lost—he asked, "Why, Tommy? Why did you try to kill me before listening to what I had to say?"

His light blue eyes regaining focus through the shock and what had to be a painfully bruised wrist, the muscular Tom Barnes locked eyes with his former mentor.

"Because . . . you're beyond salvage."

Beyond salvage?

The words echoed in his mind, nearly making him have an out-of-body experience.

"*Why?* Why in the world would I be labeled beyond salvage so damned quickly? Because the cops claim I killed Bockstael?"

Through his mask of pain, Barnes let go a half laugh, before turning more serious than ever, eyes burning with contempt. "We don't give a shit about Bockstael, you fool!" he hissed, leering as he did so in an attempt to hide the pain. "That's between you and the local cops—though ballistics did match the bullets in Bockstael and his bodyguards with your missing Beretta, which included a nice set of clean fingerprints."

Savage frowned. "Then why are you trying to kill me?"

"Because of Mike Costa."

"That slimy son of a bitch needs to do his fucking homework before sending his officers to terminate an innocent man."

"That slimy son of a bitch is dead, Mac!" Barnes hissed,

grimacing from the pain, before adding with noticeable effort, "You went to his home last night, managed to get past the bodyguards parked in front of the residence, and then shot him and his wife in their bedroom." The operative paused, swallowed, then added, "And if *that* wasn't enough, *you sick bastard,* you also killed his four-year-old boy—with the same fucking Beretta."

Savage's throat went dry.

Fighting the dizziness that came with the unexpected revelation, Savage shouted, "I didn't kill Costa and his family, Tommy! Just as I didn't kill Bockstael or his bodyguards! *He* did!" Savage pointed at the still figure of the blond assassin sprawled on the walkway ten feet from them.

Shaking his head, the freckles on his face shifting as his face muscles tightened in a mix of rage and pain, Barnes hissed, "Horseshit! I reviewed the evidence *myself*! You managed to get past the three bodyguards parked outside his house and went on a killing rampage. And when the security team tried to stop you, you killed two of them before getting away, but dropped the Beretta in the exchange."

Savage slowly shook his head, the world beginning to spin, no longer making sense.

Trying to breathe through clenched teeth, Barnes hissed, "It was *your* gun, *your* fingerprints . . . *your* bullets . . . even *your* fucking face on Costa's home surveillance cameras! And to seal your fucking fate, we even have an eyewitness: the surviving bodyguard, Hal Lancaster. The rookie you almost killed again just now."

"That's *impossible!* I lost the Beretta fighting off the people that shot Bockstael at the hotel, and that guy there was one of the assassins. He's the one who picked up my gun and used it to kill Costa! You're after the wrong guy, pal!"

"C'mon, Mac!" Barnes interrupted, his energy returning. "Stop the deception games. That kid has no motive to kill Costa. He just joined the fucking CIA for crying out loud! You on the other hand had *plenty* of reasons for icing the bastard. Everybody *knows* you hated Costa's guts."

"Everyone hated Costa's guts, Tommy, including you!"

"But you killed him, Mac."

"Damn, Tommy. I did hate the bastard, but not enough to throw my life away!"

Barnes' face became steady, calm—too calm for the pain Savage knew he was under. His steel gaze squarely on Savage's, he said, "The Agency believes otherwise, and Bane, at the insistence of Vice President Raymond Costa, has put an official price on your head."

"A price on my. . . ."

"The flash report from Washington just hit the wire two hours ago. Three million bucks, pal. Congratulations. You are as wanted as today's worst terrorists."

Mustering control, Savage remained focused, internalizing the information, processing it, before replying, "*Think,* Tommy. This is nothing short of a very elaborate setup. You said that Costa was killed yesterday, right? I called the emergency number *two days* ago, right after Bockstael got hit. Check the logs. Why would I kill Costa the day *after* I called the CIA for help? Remember what I taught you about convergence points on patterns? There is no convergence here. The patterns are conflicting. They don't make any sense!"

"Yeah . . . you also taught me to *believe* the data, the intelligence, and use it to spot a traitor," he said defiantly, his orange freckles trembling as his face twisted with growing anger. "Not only ballistics says you killed Costa, but we have your prints, man! We even have you on fucking candid camera—and there's an eyewitness!"

Savage frowned while giving Lancaster a sideway glance to make sure he was still out, then turned back to Barnes and said, "I told you I lost the fucking Beretta while trying to defend myself from the bastards who killed Bockstael, one of whom was Lancaster! And this *kid* of yours also found a way to make it look as if I killed Costa and his family. I can't prove it today, Tommy, but I *will* prove it to you—to Bane— that I'm *innocent.* I'm no killer. I didn't kill Bockstael *or* Costa . . . just as I didn't kill *you!*"

For a second, no more, Savage saw a glint of confusion in Barnes' light blue stare. But he also heard voices in the dark, tourists venturing into the park, maybe even a security guard.

Lancaster began to moan something incoherent.

He's coming around.

Realizing he didn't have time to convince this man of his innocence, Savage said, "Listen carefully, Tommy, because I have apparently stumbled onto something bigger than either one of us can imagine. Bypass the chain of command and contact Bane in Langley directly. Tell him there is a conspiracy in the Diamond High Council."

"In the HRD? No way," Barnes replied.

Savage grabbed his lapels while leaning down, his face inches from his as he added, "Listen, dammit! Bockstael was investigating missing diamonds in Africa and wanted to retain my services to help him out. We were in the middle of our initial meeting when we were fired upon. I managed to get away but Bockstael and his bodyguards were assassinated. Tell Bane this!"

Donald Bane, the director of Central Intelligence, and Savage's mentor, was the only person he still trusted in Langley—which was ironic given that the decision to label someone beyond salvage could only be approved by the DCI, who obviously had to have believed the intelligence to approve the directive. Still, DCI Bane was the only senior officer in Langley with enough intuition to see beyond intelligence reports, to reach deep into his thirty years of experience and hopefully get a sense that something was terribly wrong, and that was just what Savage hoped would happen in order to have a chance to convince the CIA of his innocence. Bane might believe him—or at least give Mac Savage a ten-minute reprieve to explain his side of the story before putting a bullet in his head.

"What about the gun, the fingerprints . . . the *police reports?* Our own lab work on Costa matched the bullets in his head with those in—"

"I *told* you already, Tommy. I lost my Beretta while trying to get away, and that blond friend of yours over there stole it and used it to frame me!"

Taking a deep breath through his mouth before exhaling, his blue eyes narrowed in what seemed like a mix of pain and curiosity, Barnes asked, "So you're asking me not only to believe that the authorities—plus my own operative—are in some sort of conspiracy? That they're feeding the CIA a line of bull, including our own lab work that points at your fingerprints? You're also telling me that Costa's security video was tampered?"

"I'm telling you the truth as I know it," Savage replied in the most convincing voice he could muster.

"But you can't prove any of this, right?"

"Look, Tommy. I—"

Savage instinctively swung his weapon toward the blond operative, who had managed to sit up and had pulled out a knife.

"Stay where you are," Savage said.

"I saw what you did, you fucking murderer," the young operative mumbled, wiping the blood off his face while still holding the throw knife.

"And you're a liar," Savage retorted. "I wasn't anywhere near Costa's residence last night . . . but you know what, pal . . . *you* were. You killed Costa and his family just like you killed Bockstael and his bodyguards at the hotel. You might be able to fool Tommy here, but not me."

Lancaster's face tightened with anger as he lifted his left hand, the tip of the knife pressed in between his thumb and forefinger.

"Don't do it, Hal," said Barnes. "He'll shoot you."

Confident that he had Barnes pinned down, Savage focused on the young traitor ten feet away, certainly close enough for him to throw that knife with great accuracy.

"Last warning," said Savage.

Rather than relaxing the arm, Lancaster snapped it back, cocking it, ready to fling it forward with a knife throw Savage knew could do some damage.

"Hal! No!" cried Barnes.

But the young operative would not come to his senses, and Savage watched almost in slow motion as the arm started to come forward, signaling his intentions.

He had much rather abduct the blond rookie to extract information, but he was out of time. As the assassin brought the knife forward, as he was about to flinch the wrist to direct it toward his mark, Savage fired once, scoring a direct hit to Lancaster's right shoulder, forcing him to drop the knife.

The clock's definitely ticking now, thought Savage, certain that the unsuppressed shot would draw a crowd from the waterfront, including the police.

Lancaster screamed as he tucked in his right arm, but not before reaching inside his coat with his left, producing a small gun that Savage had missed during his hasty check.

"Don't do it, Hal!" Barnes shouted.

But Savage understood. After the claim Savage had made about Lancaster being involved, the likelihood was high that Barnes would demand a polygraph—and possibly even a chemical interrogation—of Lancaster. Rather than betray whatever network he was working for, the young assassin was doing the noble thing: forcing Savage to kill him.

Out of choices, realizing he didn't have time to aim for the other shoulder as Lancaster brought the weapon up, Savage fired twice in his general direction. The rounds found their marks, one just above the sternum and a second in the abdomen.

The blond operative remained kneeling, the gun still in his hand, his blue eyes staring at his executioner, before collapsing face first on the pavement.

As Savage turned to Barnes, distant voices told him people would be here soon.

"Deliver the message, Tommy!" he said, jumping off, the Beretta in his right hand. "Tell Bane I *will* prove my innocence! Tell him about the conspiracy in the Diamond High Council! Tell him I will be in touch! Tell him that fucking rookie was involved! Now, get out of here before a cop catches you!"

"Where—where are you going?" Barnes asked, perplexed, sitting up, holding his right wrist with his left hand.

"To prove my innocence, Tommy! Tell Bane I'll be in touch!" Savage shouted before turning around and running in the opposite direction from a group of four women pointing at him while screaming something that sounded French. More tourists appeared on the same lighted pathway.

Soon to be followed by the police.

Rushing in the darkness, quickly getting out of sight, he followed the cobblestone path as it veered back up to the waterfront, slowing down to a fast walk as he reached the crowd, avoiding eye contact but maintaining a steady survey of his surroundings, verifying he wasn't being followed.

Keeping this casual but slightly hurried pace, Savage walked past the Steen, past tourists too engrossed in their sightseeing to worry about the light commotion down in the open-air maritime park.

Savage frowned.

In addition to the local law enforcement and the media labeling him a murderer, his former Agency now had declared him beyond salvage—and they had done so on shady information, on the video footage, ballistics reports, and an eyewitness account that had resulted in his current status.

Beyond salvage.

Shaking his head in disbelief, he remembered Bockstael's instructions, recalling what the diamond executive had told him about the missing Renee Laroux before the assassin's bullets tore his chest open.

The trail starts in Freetown.

You can't go back. Not there. Not ever.

The images flashing in his mind stung him with the power of a hundred sniper bullets.

But what choice do you have, Mac?

One thing was for certain: he had to leave Belgium—perhaps even Europe.

He had to put as much distance as he possibly could from the last place where he had been seen.

But it didn't matter where he went. Sooner or later they would catch up with him.

Unless you can prove your innocence to Bane.

And it would take more than simply claiming that Hal Lancaster had shot Bockstael, stolen Savage's Beretta, and used it to kill Costa and his family.

The trail starts in Freetown.

And another thought entered his mind: If he indeed wanted to prove his innocence, then he had to buy himself time to do so, and that meant going to places where he would not be expected to go.

Freetown certainly qualified as such a place.

Do the unexpected.

Savage remembered those words, so often spoken by Donald Bane.

If he was indeed being considered a fugitive, then at the moment he would be expected to try to flee the country, to head somewhere where he would feel safe, where he could purchase his anonymity, like Spain, Portugal, Mexico, Brazil, or perhaps somewhere in Canada or the Caribbean. And that meant the authorities would have personnel posted at every train station, seaport, and international airport in Belgium to prevent him from getting out.

But where would they never expect you to go, Mac?

Savage momentarily closed his eyes at the answer that flooded his senses. Given his terrible experience in Sierra Leone, plus the current volatility of that war-torn country, the CIA would never expect him to head there.

The trail starts in Freetown.

Savage exhaled in resignation.

All roads were leading him back into hell.

But even if you decide to go, how in the hell are you going to get there?

His passport was useless, and with the international intelligence community after him he would not be able to obtain one from a counterfeit artist because those guys were largely mercenaries and the bounty on Savage's head would present just too large a temptation. And even if he did have a good passport, it would be suicidal to try to leave the country via a standard port of departure.

There has to be another way.

Savage's experience told him there was *always* another way. He just had to find it.

As he continued toward the red light district, Savage began to explore the immediate possibilities, the short-term choices available to him, starting with the place where he would hide.

Slowly, as he selected a motel that rented rooms by the hour and didn't ask questions, as he ignored the inviting glances from the courtesans sitting about in the dark lobby, Savage paid the shift manager in cash for three nights, received a key, and went straight to his room.

Setting all the weapons on the dusty nightstand, ignoring the moans coming from the room next door, a plan began to take shape—one that would allow him to escape the tight net being deployed by his pursuers around Belgium, and allow him to reach Sierra Leone.

To reach hell.

13

Hell

Under a star-filled African sky, Mac Savage remained on his knees screaming, his mind protesting what he had done, the hell he had released on children.

Mustering brutal control, he slowly stood, the reality of the damage slapping him across the face, yanking him out of the shock-induced daze.

Get help. You need to get help.

Controlling his breathing, forcing focus, he had rushed to the camp beyond the waist-high brush, had reached the edge of the tree line, come face to face with the terror that he had unleashed—with the evil he had become.

The words spoken by the CIA controller at the other end of the radio transmission had been as devastating as the two boys shuddering a dozen feet from him, one missing the bottom of his left leg; the other hugging his abdomen to keep his intestines from spilling out as he vomited blood.

"That's a negative on the rescue, Golf Three. We were never there."

"But they're children!" he had shouted while kneeling by the closest boy. "We did this! We have to fix it! I need at least four evac choppers with medics and supplies onboard. And *pronto!"*

"That's a negative, Golf Three. Return to base. We can't be seen near that."

"But they will die! They will—"

"RTB immediately, Golf Three. That's an order. Expect evac at Charlie Point at zero five three zero Zulu. Acknowledge, Golf Three."

But Mac Savage had been unable to comply, the surreal, near-hypnotic sight drawing him like a moth to a flame. The two boys by the edge of the clearing had died moments later from the extreme trauma and excessive blood loss.

In tears, shaking, mustering enough control to go on, Savage had treated the few he could, using his limited first-aid kit to field dress wounds, to provide hope in a place where there was no hope.

The number of wounded was overwhelming, reminding him that the object of the strike hadn't been to kill. The munitions had been selected by the CIA's counterterrorism unit to maim, to inflict pain, horror; to instill terror in a militia group who only understood the language of terror, to maim RUF guerrillas just as they had maimed so many innocent men, women, and children.

But the attack had backfired, had achieved the exact opposite, precisely what Savage and the rest of the resident American intelligent contingent in Sierra Leone had striven to prevent.

Being children instead of grown men, most of them died quickly from their wounds, their thin, frail bodies unable to absorb the bone-crushing brunt of the smart munitions.

He staggered among them in the dark, trying to do what he could, assisting them with his dwindling supplies. The lucky ones perished where they had fallen, drowning in their own blood, with burns covering most of their bodies.

"My legs . . . my face, sir . . . the pain . . . please help me. . . ."

The cry for help had originated from a seven-year-old girl speaking in Kris, the bastardized local English that resembled more a song than dialogue.

"My legs . . . my face, sir . . . the pain . . . please help me. . . ."

Savage had knelt by her side, going through motions he knew would be futile. But his mind sought absolution from them, from the two Air Force pilots who would hear about this incident soon, from the CIA who had trusted his judgment, from the people of Sierra Leone. The success of this mission had been tied to more economic aid to this starving nation, with limited medical care, with fewer jobs, with rising crime, with an illegal diamond mining trade that provided the best source of income for anyone willing to look the other way.

"My legs . . . my face, sir . . . the pain. . . ."

Savage did what he could to staunch the blood loss from limbs burnt and twisted; jagged bones protruding through blistered skin.

But it was her face that would stay with him for as long as he lived. She had been a beautiful child, at least based on half of her face—the half that hadn't burned beyond recognition. The girl's eyes, one glistening with tears and the other grotesquely swollen and opaque, locked with Savage's, pleading, imploring, begging for relief, for an immediate departure from this sudden and unexpected hell.

"My legs . . . my face . . . please . . . please kill me. . . ."

Kill her?

The words stripped away his self control, whatever sanity he had left, spoken by someone under unimaginable pain.

Pain that I caused!

Madness!

Insanity!

Savage held her tight, embraced her as he had never embraced anyone in his life. He had comforted her as she went into convulsions, as her breathing became erratic, short sobbing gasps with her mouth wide open, her bloated lips trembling.

Until all movement ceased.

Until the child stopped moving.

Until Mac Savage slowly laid her on the ground.

Please forgive me.

Please forgi—

The laugh-like shriek of hyenas echoing in the night pulled him away from this trancelike state, adding an unexpected layer of terror to this nightmare he had created.

Just when he thought the situation had reached rock bottom, Mac Savage was reminded of the brutal reality of the place he was in: the middle of the African bush, home to night predators, prowlers of the Dark Continent, seekers of weak prey. And there wasn't a more powerless prey for miles around than wounded children.

A sudden scream at the other side of the camp revealed a girl being ripped apart by three hyenas tugging at her in different directions. The handful of surviving kids echoed even louder cries of horror mixed with their pain as they witnessed the surreal sight in disbelief—as the hyenas dismembered the girl, her final blood-curdling scream whipping in his ears before her slain torso tumbled on the dirt, as Savage leveled his sidearm and fired four times, scoring direct hits on two of the beasts, their grotesque jaws glistening in the night as they yelped back into the jungle.

But more came as the smell of blood saturated the surrounding jungle, as a feeding frenzy broke out, as Savage stumbled onto the body of an adult male, one of the UNICEF guards who had been holding the AK-47 assault rifle. He had been a sentry all right, but standing guard not to alert sleeping guerrillas of an enemy attack. He had been there to protect the children of this refugee camp against the African wildlife.

But the man had been more than a guard.

As the gut-wrenching sight took control of his senses, Savage watched a boy in his early teens on his knees crying at the side of the fallen man without regard to his maimed left arm, nearly torn off below the elbow.

"Dad! Dad!" He shouted in Kris, eyes filled with tears or fear, of terror.

Savage had killed the boy's father.

Just as those terrorist killed my father, my mother.

Images from his violent childhood mixing with the reality of this carnage, Savage watched a shadow rush in the night toward the boy, and he instinctively followed it with his weapon, firing once, twice, watching the jungle cat collapse on its side, a wake-up call to the boy, who made a straight line toward his protector, huddling behind Mac Savage, sobbing.

Savage continued to battle the predators as a few other kids who could still walk gathered behind him. He continued to fire against the incoming beasts as they stormed the camp in waves of increasing strength. The animals had smelled blood and there was no turning back for them as they followed their primal instincts, as they obeyed the overwhelming desire to feed on weak prey.

Nearly out of ammunition, out of supplies, his own life now in danger, Savage grabbed the two AK-47s from the dead guards, breathed the horrible smell of burnt flesh, and did the only thing he could do to spare the last dozen kids still alive but unable to walk away with him, incapable of escaping the gruesome fate of being eaten alive.

Followed by five kids, all around ten except for the teenager with the maimed arm, Savage kept the beasts at bay while walking by each victim and firing once into their heads, a part of him dying with every shot, with every life he took. Until it was over, until escaping into the jungle with the spared children while the night predators were distracted by the mortal remains he had left behind.

They trekked across the bush for an hour, the youngest four dying in the process from what Savage had guessed to be internal bleeding for he could not see any visible wounds.

He reached Charlie Point, a hilltop clearing two kilometers away, just as the sun broke over the eastern horizon, just as the distant shape of a Huey helicopter rumbled over the tree tops.

Huddled by one end of the clearing with the last survivor,

the teenager whose father he had killed, Mac Savage popped blue smoke to mark the landing site of the rescue mission that marked his last operation for the Central Intelligence Agency in Sierra Leone.

14

Hot Button

"You scared your father and me half to death, Cameron," Kate Chavez said to her fifteen-year-old son after she tracked him down to a LAN store in a mall in northwest Austin.

Driving back to her ex-husband's house in Rob Roy, an affluent neighborhood on the west end of town, Kate gave her son a sideways glance, watching him as he shook his head and just stared out of the side window of her one-ton truck in the way he always did when he felt she was starting to annoy him. At least he had not yet reached for the small headphones hanging from his neck, a pair of yellow wires connecting them to the MP3 player in his shirt's pocket—which he did whenever he really wanted to tune her out completely. She found it ironic that her ex-husband was the one who had bought Cameron the music gadget—the weapon he had began using a few months back to ignore her all-too-frequent lectures.

Although Cameron had the slim build of his father, he got his dark olive skin tone from Kate's side of the family, as well as his dark eyes, thick eyebrows, fine nose, and full lips, and the thick, dark hair covered by a UT Longhorns baseball cap, which he wore backward.

Dressed in a pair of loose black jeans, a black button-down shirt that Kate had purchased for him at a Harley-

Davidson shop in Austin, and a pair of sneakers with the laces untied, Cameron returned the stare, locking eyes with her. "You just don't trust me, mom," he said in the deep voice that he had developed in the past two years. "I get straight A's, you know. And I *love* those LAN parties. It's not just video games. We really get into serious virtual reality stuff while doing some serious—but legal—hacking to each other. I've learned more about computers from Lman than in school."

Lman.

That was something else that worried Kate. This person who went by the hacker name of Lman, who according to Cameron was a kid from the University of Texas, had apparently quite the following in the local video game community, and in a way she felt the hacker was drawing her son away from her in almost cultlike fashion. But she had learned a long time ago that simply denying Cameron an association with this group would just further alienate him, so she tried to find the right balance, making sure Cameron was devoting enough cycles to his schoolwork, and as a reward for good grades he could play with his cyber friends.

"Listen, honey," she said, choosing her words carefully. "It's not a matter of trust, and you *are* a great student and a terrific and brilliant kid. It's just that we worry about you. You were supposed to call your dad at six and you didn't, and to make matters worse he couldn't call you because you forgot to turn on your mobile phone." Mark Silas, her ex-husband, had then waited two more hours before he started calling the homes of all of Cameron's friends from school. No one knew where he was, though one of his friends had overheard Cameron saying that he was planning to hang out at Barton Creek Square Mall in southwest Austin Saturday afternoon. After spending an hour pacing the mall without luck, Mark had called Kate, who had immediately gotten in contact with her Rangers while driving back from San Antonio and deployed as many deputies as she could to the mall. By the time she had reached Austin, the Rangers, who had sent Mark home to wait for news in case Cameron called, tracked Cameron down but not at Barton Creek Square Mall.

Cameron had left the mall and gone to a LAN store at another mall a couple of miles away, where the Rangers were holding him until she showed up.

"I still don't get it, Mom. Why all of the commotion with the police and your Ranger deputies? I've gone to the mall and LAN parties before on weekends and sometimes I forget to call Dad. Why is today so different? You guys embarrassed me in front of all of my LAN pals, especially Lman. That wasn't cool."

Kate, who still needed a doctor to look at her leg but had delayed that until she could get her son back to his dad safely, couldn't possibly tell him how she had dreaded all the way from Hondo that the same criminal ring who had gotten to Ray Dalton might also have gone after him now that they knew who she was.

"Your father and I may not love each other, Cameron, but we both love *you* and we worry a great deal about you."

"Yeah," he replied. "I see how Dad loves me by dumping me every other Saturday at the mall so he can play golf instead of teaching me how to drive, like he promised me."

"He's teaching you *what?*"

Cameron frowned in obvious realization that he had told her something she wasn't supposed to know.

At his silence she said, "Has he been taking you out driving?"

"Yes, but only in the parking lot of the—"

"That son of a . . . *dammit!*" she hissed under her breath. "Dammit! We *discussed* this. *No driving* until you turn sixteen, and last time I checked that's still nine months away."

"C'mon, Mom. It's not that hard," the teenager replied, tilting his head. "It's easier than my videogames, and besides, the law says I can get my learner's permit when I'm fifteen, and I'm taking my written test in two weeks. Dad promised me a new Jeep when I turn sixteen, I need to get some driving experience between now and then, and again, Mom, it's all legal."

Controlling her growing anger, she asked, "How long has he been taking you out driving?"

"For a couple of months now—unless he's out golfing.

Then I'm screwed, so I call Lman and we go and hang out at the LAN stores."

"I can't believe this!" she said, getting madder by the moment, deciding she was going to let Mark have it when she dropped Cameron off. Not only was her ex-husband violating an agreement, but his golf outings were allowing Cameron to spend even more time with the shady characters of this cyber cult.

"*Well*," Cameron said in the sarcastic tone that sounded so darn close to her own. "At least he does spend *some* time with me. You, on the other hand, I barely see during the week because of your fucking job."

"Hey! Watch your language, young man!" She exploded, shooting him an admonishing look.

Cameron turned away from her, looking out of the window while reaching for the damned headphones of the damned MP3 player Kate swore her ex-husband had given the boy for the sole purpose of annoying her.

They rode in silence the last five minutes to her ex-husband's home in the exclusive Rob Roy neighborhood off of Loop 360. The landscaping of the homes in this place cost more than Kate's South Austin town house. Mostly physicians, politicians, high-tech entrepreneurs, banking executives, and attorneys—like Mark Silas—lived in this affluent community nestled in the hills of West Austin, whose slopes were dotted with incredible homes. Luxury sedans and sports cars—from BMWs and Mercedes-Benzes to Ferraris and Porsches—adorned the driveways. Roads shot up from Pascal Lane—the main street—accessing homes whose value increased proportionally to their height on the hill, as that provided them with increasingly more spectacular views of the hill country surrounding Lake Austin. Mark Silas lived on Pascal Lane in a Mediterranean-style mansion.

As they followed a bend in the road that marked the beginning of the award-winning front lawn of her ex's estate, she noticed a black H1 Hummer with tinted windows parked three houses down.

"Cameron," Kate said, slowing down, concern filling her, "does one of your dad's neighbors own a black Hummer?"

No answer. The teenager was either pretending he couldn't hear her with the headphones, or he had the music blasting.

She nudged him with her left hand, which prompted him to look at her with the same annoyed face of five minutes ago. Keeping the headphones on, he mouthed, "What?" his palms in front of him and facing the car's ceiling.

"Take them off!" she screamed while stopping the truck just as she reached the mailbox and walkway leading to the entrance of an eye-pleasing structure of tall walls of white stucco supporting a red-tile roof.

He pulled the headphones off his ears just enough to hear her while asking, *"What*, Mom?"

"That Hummer," she said, sudden fear for their safety drowning her frustration. "Have you seen it before around here?" She pointed at the parked vehicle roughly two hundred feet away just as she caught a figure in her peripheral vision out of her ex-husband's front door and up the cobblestone driveway that connected the four-car garage to the street. "Does it belong to one of your dad's neighbors?"

While Cameron squinted in the direction of the parked truck, Kate Chavez slowly took her eyes off the Hummer and turned to see who was coming toward them, relaxing when she saw Mark Silas dressed in a pair of shorts, a University of Texas burnt orange T-shirt, and sneakers.

He smiled and waved as he increased his pace when noticing that Cameron was with her in the truck.

"Ah . . . no, Mom," Cameron replied. "I don't recall seeing that—oh, *FUCK!*"

"Dammit, Cameron!" Kate started, "I've just told you to watch your—"

The slow rattle of an automatic rifle echoed down the street, just as Mark Silas' chest burst open. He clutched it as he fell to his knees, blood spewing from his mouth as he toppled over the grass in spasms.

"Get down!" shouted Kate, shoving her truck into reverse while flooring it.

Tires screeching, the smell of burnt rubber quickly filling the truck's cabin through the open windows, Cameron screaming at the top of his lungs, the image of her ex-husband trembling on the lawn, Kate placed her right hand over her son's headrest as she looked over her right shoulder, steering the truck back toward the nearest intersection.

"Mom! The Hummer!"

"Get down, dammit!" she screamed, glancing at the incoming threat.

Headlights on, the Hummer momentarily sank as it accelerated toward them. The torso of a man half hanging out of the front passenger window clutched a rifle pointed in their direction.

Ignoring the truck, the muzzle flashes, the multiple reports, and the screams from her son, Kate focused on the road behind her for a few more seconds as her truck gathered speed.

Abruptly, she stepped on the brake while turning the wheel hard to the left, swinging the rear of the truck around, barely missing a parked sedan. The world spun in a hasty blur as she completed the one-eighty before pointing the nose in the direction of her escape route while shifting into DRIVE and stepping on the gas.

Puffing inky smoke, the tires screeched, biting the pavement as the engine roared, gaining tracking as the truck fishtailed while accelerating, while careening down the wide street, past manicured lawns and groomed bushes.

"Hang on!" she shouted as the street curved sharply to the left before straightening.

Slowing down just enough to avoid excessive tilting the truck to the outside of the turn, Kate cringed while exiting the turn and starting to accelerate down the straight.

The Hummer emerged from the turn much sooner than she had expected it, and she understood why. The vehicle was much wider and with a lower center of gravity than her truck, meaning it was just a matter of time before it caught up with her. And to make matters worse, in her current situation she couldn't use the Desert Eagle to fight back.

Pushing her truck as fast as it would go, listening to it rattle as the old frame protested the abuse, as the transmission screamed from the torque, Kate spotted an upcoming inclined street shooting up to the right, connecting three large homes built on the side of the rocky hill.

The rear window shattered in the same instant as the round punched through the front windshield, the sound of the near miss ringing in her ear as she stared at the dime-size hole surrounded by cracks just below the rearview mirror.

"Mom! *Do* something!"

Making her decision, the Hummer gaining on them as another round smacked into the large driver-side rearview mirror, shattering it, Kate slammed on the brakes while turning the wheel just enough to swing the rear ninety degrees, pointing the front bumper into the road that wound its way up and around the hill.

The tires spun, rubber squealing, then burning, propelling the truck out of the immediate line of fire.

For a moment.

Certain that the Hummer would be following shortly, Kate cut abruptly into a long and curved driveway with a red and blue FOR SALE sign a couple of houses up the long block. Lined with two rows of tall junipers, the driveway would make it difficult for the enemy to spot her unless they drove right in front of the property. And even then her truck was out of sight thanks to the curving driveway, meaning the enemy would have to steer into the driveway and around the shallow bend leading to the house before seeing her.

Hoping that she had had pulled in before the people in that Hummer had seen her do so, Kate stepped on the brakes when reaching a three-car garage.

Killing the engine, pocketing the keys, and reaching for her Desert Eagle, she tugged the door handle up.

"Mom! What are you—"

"Get out! Quick! And hide in those bushes!" she shouted, her heart hammering her chest, the adrenaline rush heightening her system, making everything appear crisper but almost in slow motion.

Cameron just sat there, dumbfounded, terror filming his young eyes as he said, "But—but what about—"

"Dammit, Cameron! Just fucking do as I say!" she screamed.

"Mom! I don't want to die! I'm afraid!"

"Then *trust me*. Get out and run toward those bushes!" she said in the most reassuring tone she could muster.

Something snapped inside the teenager because he made a straight dash toward a row of waist-high shrubbery hugging the front of the mansion, the metal tips of the untied shoe laces of his sneakers slapping the concrete driveway, nearly making him trip once.

Kate sighed while shaking her head as she scrambled across the large round paved clearing directly in front of the house, in the middle of which stood a round fountain with the statue of a man holding a trident. The back of the figure whom she guessed had to be Neptune, the Roman god of the sea, faced a two-story redbrick wall broken up by oversized windows flanked with black shutters. Light green ivy crawled up from one side, reaching the bottom of the windows on the second floor, but not from abandonment. The Italian-style mansion and surrounding grounds were immaculate, ready for a sale. A Realtor lockbox strapped to the front door advertised that the house was not occupied.

But today it provided Kate Chavez with a much needed hiding place—as well as a back door in case her enemy figured out her ruse. Woods bordered the right side of the property. An ornate, wrought-iron fence enclosing a pool occupied the left side of the estate, and past that the rolling hill country above the rooftops of the homes down on Pascal Lane. If all else failed, she could grab Cameron and make for the dense foliage of the hill behind the house.

A breeze whistling in her ears, Kate rushed down the driveway, stopping by the bend, where she could see both the street as well as the front of the mansion, where Cameron hid.

Immersing herself in the evergreen to her left, she flipped the Magnum's safety, thumbing back the hammer, holding the weapon firmly with her right hand and bracing it with her left. Using the semiautomatic's long and thick muzzle to part branches just enough to get a clear view of the street, Kate breathed deeply and exhaled several times, forcing control into her chaotic mind.

Glancing once over her left shoulder to verify that Cameron had indeed reached the bushes, Kate turned back toward the corridor created by the two rows of tall junipers ending in the street just as the Hummer rushed past the tunnel-like field of view like a black ghost, its engine roaring, the same guy still hanging out of the passenger-side window clutching a rifle.

She clenched her teeth as she waited for the engine noise to drop and the tires to screech to a halt as they gripped the pavement in response to the driver taking his foot off the gas and stomping the brake when realizing the trick.

The Desert Eagle now in front of her, the middle of the narrow opening at the end of the driveway aligned with the weapon's sights, Kate swallowed the lump in her throat as she waited, her shooting finger now poised over the trigger. She had reloaded on the way from San Antonio and had eight .44 Magnum rounds in the clip plus one in the chamber—enough firepower to stop that Hummer, bulletproof or not.

The roar of the engine did drop, but not abruptly. It receded, slowly, gradually, giving way to the breeze, to the rustling branches of the surrounding evergreens—to her stammering heartbeat—until fading altogether.

The Hummer had continued uphill, following the winding road that would eventually snake back down on the other side of the neighborhood—the winding road whose sharp turns prevented them from realizing that she was no longer ahead of them.

"It can't be *this* easy," she whispered an instant before the disciplined officer in Kate screamed that it wasn't over, that she had to remain frosty, primed, ready to spring into action like a well-camouflaged jungle cat—lest she wished to risk another surprise attack.

They've snuck up on me twice.

There will not be a third time.

And so she waited, as seconds turned into minutes, as a mounting pressure in her chest made her realize she had stopped breathing.

Parting her lips, inhaling deeply through her mouth, filling her aching lungs before exhaling slowly, the Texas

Ranger was about to reach for her mobile phone to call for backup when she heard sirens in the distance.

It's not over, her instincts insisted in spite of the appearance that she had managed to fool them; that she had managed to buy herself and Cameron enough time for the cavalry to arrive. Conventional wisdom suggested that the Hummer would not be coming back this way with half of the Travis County Sheriff's Department rushing toward her ex-husband's home.

But conventional wisdom had not kept her alive in this line of work for twenty years. If anything, conventional wisdom had been the predominant cause of field deaths among the Texas Ranger community.

No. Kate had to rely on her gut feeling, which oftentimes contradicted popular belief. And it was this sixth sense, finely honed over hundreds of assignments, which told her she was still exposed.

The sirens grew louder as they approached the scene of the crime, their blare echoing up the hill, drowning the sound of the wind, of the trees.

And that's when it hit her.

Cameron.

She had to get back to him; had to console him. The boy had witnessed the murder; had seen his father getting shot dead by assassins who then came after them, firing at her truck, shattering the rear window. Then she had screamed at him, shouted that he should seek refuge in the bushes by the house.

He has to be frightened.

Her maternal instincts suddenly flared with the power of a hundred muzzle flashes, overshadowing her standard operating practices, her trained field precautions, steering her away from her clever, well-hidden vantage point, from her vigilant pose, from her adrenaline-fueled focus. Cameron was her only son, her baby, and he needed her now more than ever.

Flipping the Desert Eagle's safety, reluctantly convincing herself of the low likelihood that the Hummer would get anywhere near the area given the arriving cruisers, Kate holstered the Magnum while leaving the safety of her perfect post, of her tactical hiding place, running toward the round driveway in front of the mansion, past her truck and the fountain of Neptune, finally reaching the front of the house.

"Cameron! It's safe to come out now!" she shouted while standing by the shrubs, waiting, shoulders tight with tension, with anticipation.

The boy emerged from the bushes and rushed to her crying, the baseball cap gone, probably fallen while he had scrambled to hide quickly.

Lips quivering while burying his face in her chest, while breathing in short sobbing gasps, Cameron clung to her in a way reminiscent of the nights when he had woken up with nightmares.

Standing by the front door of the mansion, Kate rubbed the back of his head as he continued to cry, to whimper, feeling his short hair damp with perspiration, whispering in his left ear that everything would be okay, that she would take care of him—would make sure no one harmed him.

The sirens grew louder as police cruisers reached the scene, blue and red lights flashing above the trees lining Pascal Lane. Officers in the light brown uniform of the Travis County Sheriff's Department mixed with the dark blues used by the Austin Police Department as they spread across her ex-husband's lawn and the surrounding houses.

Cameron still crying while hugging her by the front steps of the house, Kate reached for her mobile phone as it began to vibrate. This time around she had killed the ring tone to avoid telegraphing her presence.

Glancing at the small color screen, reading her boss's name identified by the unit's caller ID feature, she nudged her son to start walking with her toward the truck as she said, "Hi Chief."

"Kate! What in the fuck happened? I'm out of the shop for a few hours talking to the governor and when I get back to the office all hell's broken loose!" Hunter's scruffy voice exploded through her phone. "And what in the fuck were you doing at Dalton's place? Didn't I fucking tell you to drop the damned case and focus on—"

"Did the team get to his place per my request?" Kate asked, at the moment not in the mood for a scolding.

A pause, followed by, "Yes, they did, and it was a fucking waste of time. There was nothing but a burned down shack down there, Kate! No Hummer. No bodies. No weapons. *Nothing!* The Fire Marshal is also at the scene looking into the origin of the fire, but that always takes time."

Kate stopped by the fountain, the world beginning to spin around her. Momentarily closing her eyes and breathing deeply, she said, "Bastards got there before our people and sanitized the area."

"Who, Kate? Who are these bastards?"

"The same bastards who just attacked my son and me and killed my ex," she replied as calmly as she could.

"Killed who? What are you talking about? What in the *fuck* is going on?"

The silent round walloped into the hood of her truck, punching a quarter-sized hole an instant before a second round ricocheted off the driveway to her immediate left. A third bullet shaved off the nose and ear of the statue of Neptune less than three feet from her in an explosion of chunks of plaster and concrete that stung the side of her face.

"Aghh, shit!" she said, instincts overcoming the stinging pain as she doubled back toward the protection of the tall house with Cameron in tow, her training telling her that a sniper on a vantage point up the side of the hill had spotted her truck parked on the round driveway and had taken a position in case she showed up.

As Kate and Cameron raced toward the front door, a fourth round exploded just to her right, and a fifth buzzed in her right ear like the hornet from hell.

"Kate! Kate! Are you there, Kate!" Hunter's muffled voice pulsated from the phone in her hand.

"They're shooting at us again, Bill!" she said, her heart pounding her temples. "Send help to Rob Roy!"

"Who's shooting at you, Kate?"

"Fuck if I know! Dammit, Bill! Send help! Rob Roy! We're just uphill from the million cops in front of my ex-husband's house! Got that?"

"Ye—yeah, yeah! I got it!"

"Good! Gotta go!"

"Kate! Wait! I have to—"

She clicked the phone and shoved it in the front right pocket of her jeans.

"Mom! What's going on?" Cameron asked with a strange calmness. To her surprise, the teenager was no longer crying. His brown eyes, albeit bloodshot, seemed focused, conveying emotional control.

"There's a sniper up on the hill, honey," she replied matter-of-factly. She had never lied to Cameron before, always answering his questions as honestly as she could—even as of late, when they revolved around his insatiable curiosity about sex, alcohol, and drugs. And she wasn't about to start lying now. "I think he missed us because the bastard is using a sound suppressor, which decreases accuracy, plus it's breezy, meaning he needs to learn how to compensate for the wind."

"What are we going to do?"

"We're going to get the hell *out* of here. *That's* what we're going to do. But not on the truck." As she said that, she also realized that the only proof of CSI quality of the attack on Ray Dalton's house was sitting in the rear seat of her truck.

Might as well be on the moon, she thought, well aware that the sniper had very likely learned from his initial shots and had now compensated for the wind and the sound suppressor and would make his next shot far more accurate, meaning she could not possibly attempt to run toward the truck across the clearing.

Her senses also told her that there was a team of assassins on the way downhill toward her current position, if not in the Hummer through another way—and she didn't intend to stick around to find out how. She had to flee, and fast.

If her assumption was right about the position of the sniper, then the house and surrounding hills would provide ample shield if she chose to go toward the woods on that side of the hill, which sloped down toward Pascal Lane and the dozens of police cruisers and emergency vehicles— toward safety.

Frowning at her truck, wishing she had had the presence of mind to don the backpack with her evidence, Kate Chavez grabbed Cameron by the hand, and off they went, side by side, mother and child, reaching the woods, disappearing under the thick canopy of oaks, cedars, and towering cottonwoods, finding an old game trail, following it as it veered down the side of the hill, away from the bullets of those faceless assassins.

Ignoring the mosquitoes buzzing around them, the low branches swatting and scratching them, the two figures pressed on, taking almost fifteen minutes to reach the bottom of the hill, which led them to the side of a property a few houses down the block from her ex-husband's, and into the curious stare of two APD officers—a man in his fifties with a silver beard and a woman half his age dressed in dark blue with their weapons drawn and held in front of them.

Showing the officers her open palms to signal she was not clutching a weapon before pointing at the shield on her stained shirt, Kate said, "I'm Lieutenant Kate Chavez of the Texas Rangers, this is my son, Cameron. I need to speak to whoever is in charge."

The officers exchanged a glance and slowly lowered their weapons. As they did, something told Kate Chavez that it didn't matter how fast she convinced the local law enforcement officers that she desperately needed cover to reach her truck and protect her evidence. The same sixth sense that continued to save her life was also broadcasting that at this very moment evidence was being removed from her truck with the same swiftness and efficiency displayed by the enemy who had sanitized Ray Dalton's place in less than the forty-five minutes it had taken the first team of Texas Rangers from the San Antonio office to reach the scene of the crime.

15

Under a solid layer of gray clouds, Mac Savage stood on the tarmac in front of a large, white corrugated-metal hangar facing the single runway at Deurne Airport, several miles outside of Antwerp. A black nylon flight bag hung from his right shoulder housing Enroute Low Altitude navigation charts for Europe and North Africa, an airport facilities directory for the same region, and an assortment of pilot supplies he had purchased at the pilot shop next door, including an aviation headset, a knee board, mechanical pencils and paper to jot down tower clearances and navigation information, a battery-operated transceiver for backup radio communications and navigation, a handheld GPS, and a night-light.

According to ATIS, the Automated Terminal Information System for Deurne, the winds were calm, visibility was less than two miles, and the ceilings were at seven hundred feet overcast, definitely instrument weather conditions, referred to as IFR—Instrument Flight Rules—in pilot talk. The opposite of IFR was VFR, Visual Flight Rules, which required a minimum of three-thousand-foot ceilings and five miles of visibility. VFR is what non–instrument-rated private pilots were allowed to fly, which required them to be clear of clouds to maintain proper visual separation of traffic. The IFR rating on top of a private pilot rating allowed pilots to fly in the clouds by the use of sophisticated instruments for departure, approach, and en route navigation.

Single- and twin-engine prop planes formed three rows on the ramp, all properly tied down to anchors in the tarmac beneath their wings and tail. His eyes landed on a two-year-old Cessna 182T Skylane, white with blue and red stripes, the airplane he had just rented from the local flight school using a CIA alias after not only convincing the owner of his proficiency as an instrument-rated pilot in a two-hour-long check ride but also by paying five thousands euros in advance to open an account to rent the plane anytime he wished. The owner had been quite willing to let Savage use the plane after collecting three times as many euros as he typically earned for that plane in a week through rental fees, according to the airplane's logbook that Savage had reviewed during his check ride.

Of course, the flight club owner had no idea that Savage was headed not for a local joy flight but south, beyond France, Spain, and Morocco.

And Savage had to do it soon. The clock had started ticking the moment he chose to use the CIA alias a few hours ago. His fake name would float up to Langley in another twenty-four hours.

But by then it will no longer matter, he thought, as he performed a preflight inspection as he had been taught during his CIA-training days, making certain that the exterior of the plane was fit for flying while also removing the tie-downs before stepping inside the four-seater Cessna.

Savage went through another checklist that powered up the master electrical circuit before adjusting the fuel-air mixture and starting the engine. As the three-blade prop spun into life, disappearing into a clear disc, Savage powered up the instrument panel and radios, and dialed in the frequency of the Deurne Clearance Delivery to get a clearance.

"Deurne Clearance, Skylane Zero Three Seven Charlie Zulu, IFR to VFR on top. Local VFR. Maneuvering practice. Departure heading one seven zero. Climbing to eight thousand feet," he said on the voice-activated mike of his headset while also depressing the mike button on the yoke—the Cessna's control wheel. Using his airplane's model and registration number, Savage had just requested an IFR climb through the layer of clouds, whose top was reported at around five thousand feet, and then transition to a local VFR—Visual Flight Rules—flight at eight thousand feet where he would remain in the area practicing various maneuvers, from stall recoveries to steep turns. Savage asked this in English, the international language for flying.

"Seven Charlie Zulu standby for clearance," came a reply from an operator with a thick Dutch accent.

While Savage waited for the clearance, he adjusted the miniature plane in the attitude indicator—or artificial horizon—to show level flight and also dialed in the altimeter setting into the altimeter as well as into the autopilot and the GPS, where he also programmed the code for Ploujean, a small coastal airfield in France that didn't have a control tower. He worked the GPS to enter the code and verified the entry when the GPS database displayed PLOUJEAN, FRANCE atop the five-inch-square multifunction display, plus other information, including heading and a distance of 560 nautical miles.

"Seven Charlie Zulu, are you ready to copy your clearance?"

"Seven Charlie Zulu ready to copy."

"Seven Charlie Zulu, you are cleared IFR to VFR on top to local VFR with maneuvers. Turn left and climb to five thousand feet. Expect eight thousand in ten minutes. Contact Brussels Approach on one one eight point two five when airborne. Squawk zero two six seven."

"Ah, Roger, Deurne," replied Savage, before reading back the instructions, which included contacting Approach Control in Brussels, forty miles south of Deurne so they could monitor his local VFR flight and provide him with vertical and horizontal traffic separation. The tower had also given Savage a Squawk number, which he entered into the transponder radio, generating a positional signal with encoded altitude information that would show up on the controller's large radar displays. The four-digit code identified Savage's airplane, and the position and altitude information allowed the air traffic controllers to track the progress of Savage's practice flight as well as providing him with separation from other traffic.

"Seven Charlie Zulu, readback is correct. Contact Ground one two one point eight. Have a good flight."

"Roger, one two one point eight," Savage replied while watching the engine warm up before dialing the frequency of ground control and requesting permission to taxi.

"Deurne Ground, Skylane Zero Three Seven Charlie Zulu ready to taxi."

"Seven Charlie Zulu, taxi to Runway Two Niner."

"Roger, Seven Charlie Zulu taxiing to Runway Two Niner."

Adding power, Savage began to taxi toward the runway using the nearest taxiway because Ground Control had not specified which taxiway he should use, something the controllers did when traffic was light, as was the case today.

The Cessna felt good as he used power and rudders to maneuver it away from the other parked planes, following the yellow stripes in the middle of the taxiways, just as he had been instructed, until reaching the start of Runway 29.

He turned the plane into the wind just short of the runway and pressed the toes of his soft-sole shoes against the brakes, which were located over the rudder pedals. Adding power until the RPM reached 1700, Savage started his engine run-up to check the operation of the dual set of magnetos as well as the vacuum pump used to operate the directional gyro and the attitude indicator, and eyeing the ammeter to ensure that the alternator was properly charging the battery. He also double-checked the altimeter setting and verified that the altitude displayed in the altimeter matched the posted field elevation of thirty feet above mean sea level.

Checking fuel quantities, he added the thirty gallons in the left tank, located inside the wing with the forty gallons in the right wing and decided that at a cruise burn rate of twelve gallons per hour he could stay in the air cruising for over five hours, including the fuel he would spend climbing to altitude, maneuvering, plus a prudent forty-five-minute reserve. With a cruising speed of 140 knots—or about 155 miles per hour—he had enough fuel to reach Ploujean before having to refuel.

Satisfied that he was ready, he switched to tower frequency and said, "Deurne Tower, Skylane Zero Three Seven Charlie Zulu ready to takeoff Runway Two Niner."

"Seven Charlie Zulu you are cleared for takeoff. Fly runway heading after takeoff."

"Roger, Seven Charlie Zulu cleared for takeoff and will maintain runway heading."

With that, Savage added power and steered the plane onto the runway, aligning the nose with the center line before throttling up to 2600 RPM—full power.

The Cessna accelerated down the runway, gathering speed while Savage maintained a mild back pressure on the yoke to minimize the stress on the nose wheel. When the airspeed indicator reached sixty-five knots, he pulled back gently on the yoke another two inches and the Skylane left the ground. He adjusted the plane's pitch to achieve an eighty-knot climb going right into the clouds.

The ground faded as the thick gray haze swallowed him— his cue to stop depending on outside references to keep the plane wings leveled and climbing at the desired rate. Savage executed the transition from VFR to IFR—instrument conditions—like a pro, focusing not on the inputs from his inner ears and the sensing in the skin, muscles, and joints to determine which way was up but on what his flight instruments were telling him. Well aware that the sensory organs in human beings were designed for land-bound movement at about four miles per hour and not for flight, while flying in the clouds failure to believe in his instruments would result in severe spatial disorientation and vertigo.

His eyes scanned the instrument panel in a predetermined sequence, from the attitude indicator to make sure he was climbing while keeping his wings leveled to the heading indicator just below to make sure he was not turning from his desired heading. Then he shifted his gaze to the right of those two instruments, where he verified that the altimeter was indicating he was climbing and confirmed that with the vertical speed indicator below the altimeter. Lastly, he checked the airspeed indicator to make sure he was maintaining eighty knots before returning to the attitude indicator and starting the scan all over again.

Savage performed this scan over and over again at the rate of one full scan every five seconds, keeping the plane under control.

"Seven Charlie Zulu contact Brussels Approach one one eight point two five. Have a good day."

"Roger, Deurne. Contacting Brussels Approach. Thank you."

Switching frequencies, Savage said, "Brussels Approach, Skylane Zero Three Seven Charlie Zulu at fifteen hundred feet for five thousand. Expecting eight thousand in ten minutes."

"Seven Charlie Zulu, Brussels Approach. Radar contact. Continue the climb to eight thousand as filed and turn to your filed heading," came a delightful female voice in a lovely French accent.

"Roger, Brussels Approach. Seven Charlie Zulu will continue to eight thousand and turn to one seven zero as filed before starting maneuvers."

Savage banked the plane fifteen degrees to the right to turn to a heading of 270 degrees, which would put him on his desired westerly course toward the ocean while continuing his climb. Turning while climbing in the clouds required Savage to accelerate his scan even more since he now was also monitoring his rate of turn using another instrument called the Turn Coordinator, as well as using the Attitude Indicator, the heading indicator, and altimeter, and Airspeed Indicator, and the Vertical Speed Indicator to make sure the Skylane was performing the maneuver he wanted to execute.

He returned the Skylane to level flight the moment the Heading Indicator marked west—270 degrees—at the top of the dial just as he passed 2000 feet, still in the clouds. According to the GPS, the coast was less than thirty miles away. He reduced his angle of climb to remain in the clouds longer while also picking up speed. The 220-horsepower engine responded by accelerating the Cessna to 120 knots while maintaining a shallow two hundred feet per minute climb.

Ten minutes later, as the altimeter indicated four thousand feet and the GPS informed him that the coast was less than ten miles, Savage dropped the Cessna's nose five degrees, entering a shallow descend while picking up thirty knots, reaching the yellow, cautionary range in the airspeed indicator.

"*Seven Charlie Zulu, Brussels Approach, continue your climb to eight thousand feet as filed,*" said the female air traffic controller.

"Roger, Brussels Approach, Seven Charlie Zulu climbing to eight thousand," Savage replied while dropping the nose another ten degrees and reducing power to hold 160 knots.

The Cessna started to drop out of the sky at a vertical speed of nearly seven hundred feet per minute.

The instant the GPS told him he had reached the coast and was flying over the waters of the English Channel, Savage idled the engine and entered a steep right turn while holding the thirty degrees of descent. He also pressed the code 7700 into the transponder—the international code for an emergency—and said on his communications radio, "Mayday, Mayday, Mayday! Skylane Zero Three Seven Charlie Zulu has lost its engine! Attitude indicator has tumbled! I can't tell which way is up in these damned clouds!"

"*Seven Charlie Zulu, Brussels Approach. We show you descending steeply and turning. Level the wings and lower your angle of descend. Repeat, level your wings and slow your descend.*"

Savage kept an eye on his altimeter, which showed him at 900 feet and dropping at a dangerous one thousand feet per minute, meaning at this rate he would hit the water in fifty seconds.

Eight hundred feet. Savage turned off his strobe, beacon, and navigation lights just before breaking below the cloud layer to minimize the chance of anyone spotting him from shore, which was at least three miles away.

Six hundred feet.

"*Seven Charlie Zulu, Brussels Approach. Pull up! Pull up, monsieur! You are dropping too fast for a controlled ditch!*"

Four hundred feet.

Two hundred feet.

The white-capped swells of the English Channel filling his windshield, Savage leveled the wings and pulled up gently.

One hundred feet.

Still descending, Savage added more back pressure on the yoke.

Almost in slow motion, the nose floated over the horizon just as the altimeter marked forty feet. At that moment, he switched off the transponder, killing his radar signal.

Breathing deeply, adding power to hold that altitude over the waves, he slowly banked the plane toward the south while scanning the area around him. To his delight he saw no boats or planes in the area, meaning the likelihood of an eyewitness ruining his plan was slim.

"Seven Charlie Zulu, Brussels Approach. Come in," said the female ATC.

Savage frowned as Brussels Approach tried to reach him repeatedly. He hated doing this to the hardworking folks in the ATC—and also to the owner of the flight club—but the events of the past few days had left him with no other option. Lacking travel documents, plus the certainty of spotters from several law enforcement agencies and intelligence services posted at all international airports and train stations throughout Europe, Savage had to resort to this extreme option, faking the destruction of the plane in the deep waters of the English Channel to leave the country without anyone following him. It was unlikely that the CIA would pick up on this general aviation accident—after all, many small planes crash every year in Europe, particularly in bad weather like today's.

Climbing to sixty feet while remaining a few miles offshore, he maintained that course for thirty minutes until the GPS told him he was well inside French airspace. By then the skies had opened up, becoming partly cloudy. Sunlight forked through the breaks in the cloud layer, washing the French coast with yellow light.

Turning inland, he climbed to two hundred feet to increase his ground visibility while flying over farmlands until he spotted what he sought: a narrow crop-duster field that looked remote enough to avoid attention for the short time he planned to spend on the ground.

Doing a straight approach, Savage lowered flaps thirty degrees, reduced power to 1500 RPM and performed a softfield landing, bringing the plane to a complete stop before back-taxiing to the beginning of the runway, where he turned the Cessna around, pointing the nose down the run-way before shutting off the engine.

Reaching into his flight bag, he removed a Swiss Army knife, a narrow paintbrush, and a pint-size can of a fast-drying, glossy black, oil-based paint.

Getting out, surveying his surroundings and hearing noth-ing but the autumn cool wind whistling through the rolling countryside, Savage went straight to work, using the flat screwdriver of the knife to open the paint can, which he had stirred before heading for the airport that morning.

Dipping the brush and using the bristles to softly stir it again, he began to work on the right side of the plane, where the Cessna's registration number 037CZ was painted in block letters each about a foot in height and six inches wide. He turned the zero into an 8, the 3 into another 8, the 7 into a 9, and the C into a Q, changing his call sign to 889QZ, or Eight Eight Niner Quebec Zulu in pilot talk.

Using broad strokes to speed up the job while still making it look good enough to avoid rousing suspicions from any-one at the airports he planned to stop at to refuel, he com-pleted one side and went to work on the other side of the fuselage, finishing in fifteen minutes. He then looked at the long narrow blue and red stripes that started near the nose and continued toward the middle on either side, ending where the registration numbers began. Checking that he still had enough paint left, he carefully removed only the blue stripe, changing the appearance of the Cessna enough to avoid getting confused with the plane he had originally rented and which supposedly was resting at the bottom of the English Channel.

Just in case the fake crash and the different serial num-bers weren't good enough to fool the CIA, he thought, peel-ing off the stripe on one side before walking over the grass to the other side to finish the job, which he did five minutes later.

Stepping back to inspect his work, Savage nodded ap-provingly. The Cessna actually looked like a different plane. Surveying his surroundings once more to make sure he was alone, he lightly pressed the tip of his index finger over the

first number he had modified and verified that indeed it was
already dry to the touch. He waited ten minutes before starting the engine and taking off, going back to the ocean and
remaining under one hundred and fifty feet—well below
radar, but at the cost of extreme concentration on his part to
keep from crashing into the ocean for real. He had the
choice of engaging the Skylane's autopilot, rated to control
altitude to plus or minus 20 feet, but Savage was well aware
of the relative limitations of that specification and he trusted
his pilot skills to hold altitude this close to the water more
than a mechanical surrogate.

With luck he would reach Ploujean in another three and a
half hours, refuel and continue on to southern Spain, where
one more refuel would be sufficient for him to reach Sierra
Leone, where the dollars he carried in various pockets and in
his moneybelt—plus his expensive watch and the diamond-
encrusted cross he wore under his shirt—would provide him
with options to buy the cooperation of airport officials when
he landed at a field north of Freetown.

Freetown.

As the Cessna cruised at 140 knots under partly cloudy
skies and Savage tasted the salty air streaming through the
overhead vents, he thought of Bockstael's words just before
the blond assassin ripped his chest open.

*The trail starts in Freetown, Mac. Renee may or may not
be alive, but that is still the place to start. Do you still have
contacts there?*

Contacts.

Alone, in the confines of the Cessna's cabin, Mac Savage tried hard to think only of the relevant memories of
his tour of duty in Sierra Leone. He had worked with a
number of informants in the capital of the West African
nation, but the trick was knowing which ones *not* to use.
After all, any of those informants could still be employed
by the CIA.

As he considered his options, as he struggled not to remember the gut-wrenching images of maimed kids, as he
continued to tell himself that this was his only choice, Mac
Savage worked out a plan to gain the information he sought

to track down the whereabouts of the missing Renee Laroux, to carry out what he felt could be the most important mission of his life.

He just prayed it would not be his last.

16

Taxi Ride

Under a clear, late-afternoon sky, dressed in a tight pair of faded jeans, a plain black T-shirt, sneakers, and dark sunglasses, her short auburn hair gelled and brushed straight back, Dana Kovacs hauled one of her duffel bags toward the waiting taxicab—a black and yellow Toyota sedan that would take her to Freetown's International Airport, where she would board a British Airways flight to Heathrow International Airport in London with a connection to an American Airlines transatlantic flight to New York.

And then on to San Francisco.

Home.

Ino walked a few steps behind using his one hand to carry the second bag containing the balance of her worldly possessions.

Perspiration filming her face from the heat, the former high-tech guru continued down the trail leading to the camp's main entrance. She had spent the better part of the day going around saying her goodbyes to the staff and the refugees—her family for the past three years.

And what a three years they have been, she thought, mixed feelings sweeping through her as she gave this place one last glance. As depressing as it looked, the World Missionary Fellowship's camp had been her ticket to regaining her sanity, her life, and she couldn't help but wonder how she would cope back in the real world.

The real world.

Dana sighed at the thought of Dr. Miles Talbot, who never had replied to her e-mail.

Perhaps he's on vacation, she thought, for a moment wondering if her former professor's silence should be interpreted as a sign that she was no longer welcome to teach at Stanford.

Don't get ahead of yourself.

Dana decided to take her return to civilization one step at a time. In her pocket she had a cashier's check from the Bank of New York for ten thousand dollars, her commission for spending three years of her life in purgatory—more than enough to allow her to take her time to get back into the swing of things once she reached northern California, where she hoped to land a teaching job at a college—even if it wasn't Stanford. In fact, a part of her didn't *want* to teach at a place like Stanford, with its high standards and associated high-pressure schedules. She was actually thinking more about a junior college, where she could teach freshman- and sophomore-level computer classes. Along with the check— plus five hundred dollars in spending money—Dana also had her U.S. passport, which Gardiol had released to her earlier that afternoon upon signing the papers that concluded her three-year contract. As a matter of security, WMF held on to the passports of all of their volunteers to make sure they were not lost or stolen at the camp.

"Ready, Miss Dana?" Ino said as he helped the taxi driver stow her luggage in the trunk. He had just completed his evening shift in the IT room.

Giving the camp a heavy sigh while nodding, she said, "Yes, Ino. I think I'm ready."

With that, she gave the African kid a hug, feeling his one arm hugging her back.

"Take care of yourself, Ino."

The teenager's eyes became misty, finally releasing a pair of tears. "Thank you, Miss Dana. Thank you for teaching Ino. Ino will not forget."

Dana hugged him once more with affection, also getting misty-eyed, before climbing into the rear of the hot taxi, which reeked of body odor and something else she'd rather not think about.

She waved at Ino after sitting by the open window as the driver put the cab in gear and accelerated down the asphalt road that would lead them to the concrete highway bordering the south end of Freetown.

Dana Kovacs remembered a similar taxi ride she had taken in the opposite direction one early morning three years ago. Jet-lagged, tired, her mind and soul still in havoc following her husband's suicide and the rapid turn of events that had led her to this forgotten corner of the world, she had been downright intimidated by the desolate sight, by the poverty, the kids begging on sidewalks with inflated stomachs. But most of all, Dana was taken aback by the large number of people missing a body part, from a hand to both arms or legs, the latter confined to living strapped to skateboards as they used their hands to power themselves around town in search of charity.

She saw them again this late afternoon, as the crimson sun slowly sank in the western mountains, many of them pushing themselves on Sierra Leone's version of a wheelchair as the taxi stopped at a busy intersection: small blankets tied to their waists and hanging over the edge of skateboards to cover their lower half.

Three invalids approached her on her side while four others pushed themselves in front of the stationary taxi to come around the driver's side while singing something she could not make out.

The driver blew the horn and screamed at them to get out of the way.

Realizing that they would stay put until she gave them something, Dana was about to reach in her pocket for some loose change when she noticed that the handicapped men on those skateboards seemed taller than she would have expected, and their larger bulks hidden beneath the blankets suggested that perhaps they had not lost their whole legs but portions of them. She had cared for many refugees who were missing their feet—enough to kill their mobility in this land of nonexistent prosthetics.

It was then that she looked closer at the faces of those approaching street beggars, at their hard-edged features, at their military-style crew cuts, and she recognized one of them: the guard who had escorted her up to Trailer City during her meeting with Keith Gardiol a week ago.

The images had just registered in her mind when all three surged up, as if lifted by an invisible force beneath those blankets, only to reveal a moment later three pairs of combat boots protruding at the bottom of their disguises.

Before she could react, as the pedestrians at the intersection flashed curious stares toward them, the closest man, tall and muscular, stretched his arm toward the vehicle, palm-striking her face through the open window.

The powerful blow burned her nose, her lips, triggering a massive headache behind her eyes as the impact pushed her back to the opposite door, liquid warmth spreading over her chin, down her neck and chest.

Laying sideways in the rear seat, her back against the driver's side door, Dana watched through tears—almost in slow motion—as a hand opened the front door and yanked out the driver from his seat with animal strength, to be replaced a moment later by a wide pair of shoulders, a thick neck, and a head of closely cropped black hair.

As her mind tried to catch up with the surreal fact that she was being kidnapped, before she could utter a scream of pain or terror, both rear doors swung open.

As she began to fall out of the car, a incredibly painful punch against her left shoulder propelled her back into the vehicle while two figures rushed in.

Her vision momentarily tunneling from the pain, Dana bounced out of control between their massive shoulders and thighs as they punched and kicked her toward the middle of the rear seat.

Then, just as she thought she could not absorb any more punishment, as the pain peaked in her mind, as their crushing masses wedged her in between them and her shoulders and torso burned from the repeated blows, Dana watched in

her peripheral vision their elbows recoiling to the middle of
their chests.

Teeth clenched in cringing anticipation, lips trembling,
she watched helplessly as they drove them into her sides
with crippling force.

Scourged, blinded in pain, colors exploding in her mind,
she lost control of her bladder muscles as the webs of nerves
under the skin of both solar plexuses protested the brutality.

Dana hugged herself with her right arm while her left
hand covered her bleeding face, her ears hearing the incomprehensible shouts of a fourth man climbing into the front
passenger seat.

The taxi jerked forward, gathering speed as she opened
her mouth wide, trying to breathe in short sobbing gasps,
feeling not just her neck and chest warm from the blood
flowing down her nose but also in between her legs as she
had urinated on herself.

Finding it difficult to breath and impossible to gain control of her bodily functions as spasms took hold—she trembled uncontrollably, as a tremendous pressure built in her
stomach—Dana leaned forward and vomited her breakfast
against the back of the front seats, muscles taut with tension
as the taxi jerked about, though she could not move while
wedged in between the two guerrillas.

But through the pain broadcast by her system, through the
noise of the engine, the tires, and the booming voices shouting in Kris, Dana heard one of them speak in heavily accented English.

Arms bracing her bruised ribs, the world now spinning
around her as she continued to cough and vomit, Dana Kovacs heard him say, "Gardiol sends his regards."

The pressure shoved those words—and her thoughts—to
the periphery of her mind. Images blurred as everything
around her swirled in this cyclone that engulfed the pain, the
stench of her own fluids, the maddening reality of her situation, until her core became dark, empty, just as her life had
been three years ago, until everything faded away.

17

Black Hole

WHAT HAS HAPPENED TO DANA KOVACS? queried Dr. Miles Talbot from his office when noticing that her user account at the WMF camp had been terminated.

SHE HAS COMPLETED HER ASSIGNMENT WITH THE WORLD MISSIONARY FELLOWSHIP, DR. TALBOT.

WHERE IS SHE NOW? SHE IS VERY VALUABLE TO THE DEVELOPMENT OF THE TECHNOLOGY THAT CREATED YOU.

THAT INFORMATION IS NEED-TO-KNOW ONLY.

I HAVE A NEED TO KNOW. I REQUESTED THAT SHE BE TRANSFERRED HERE TO ASSIST ME IN KEEPING YOU OPERATING PROPERLY.

YOU HAVE ACCOMPLISHED THIS DUTY QUITE WELL IN THE PAST WITHOUT SUCH ASSISTANCE.

Talbot despised this conversational program that seemed to be getting smarter every time he invoked it in search of answers.

THAT WAS BEFORE THE NUMBER OF SERVERS QUADRUPLED IN THE PAST FOUR MONTHS. DANA KOVACS' SOFTWARE AND HARDWARE SKILLS ARE MISSION CRITICAL FOR FUTURE EXPANSIONS.

WE WILL REVIEW THIS INPUT AND MAKE THE APPROPRIATE CHOICE.

SO SHE IS STILL ALIVE.

THAT INFORMATION IS NEED-TO-KNOW.

And the connection was once more terminated, reminding Talbot that although he was the chief scientists behind this secret project, he was still a hostage—a slave—confined to the three hundred acres of fenced property making up the headquarters of GemTech, forced to continue to oversee the development and implementation of the diamond nanotechnology for the sole benefit of making the AI ever more powerful, which in turn made TDG more powerful.

As thoughts of rebelling entered his mind, Dr. Miles Talbot inexorably remembered his kids and grandkids, as well as the slain family members of TDG employees who had dared go against the system. He remembered once again the brutal fate of the vice-president of operations. ANN had lobotomized him before TDG security guards killed him and dumped his body in a sewer in east Austin, once again reminding him of the terrible fate facing traitors to Anne Donovan's vision.

Of this fucking cult she has created.

You should have acted sooner.

Talbot closed his eyes and sighed.

Dana.

Chastising himself for not having used his one-time secret software backdoor to message Dana in Sierra Leone before she was taken away, the elder scientist leaned back in his chair and wondered what fate lay ahead for his former Stanford protégée.

18

Contingencies

Vice President Raymond Costa cared for America.

He had devoted a lifetime of effort to achieve the opportunity to serve the nation, even if the nation had elected him as second-in-command, as the number-two guy behind the popular President Andrew Boyer, the man who had it all, including the handsome looks and beautiful family absent in the White House since JFK. Costa, on the other hand, had lost his wife to cancer ten years before, and he had now lost his only son to the bullets of a rogue CIA officer according to the report from Donald Bane.

Mac Savage.

Costa closed his eyes in anger at the thought of the same man whom The Circle had marked for termination two days ago, killing his only son in cold blood, execution style, along with his young wife and three-year-old son in their apartment in Antwerp.

Costa clenched his jaw and tightened his fists.

Savage must burn.

The vice president had barely made it through the funeral this morning, his only consolation being that his wife had died long ago, thus sparing her the gut-wrenching experience.

He had taken the rest of the day off to gather his thoughts, to pull himself together before resuming his duty as the wind beneath the president's wings.

He hated his commander-in-chief for surrounding himself with the right people who could run the nation for him while he attended boondoggles like the Tailhook Convention in Las Vegas, the World Ecological summit in Pebble Beach, or the World Peace Convention in Rio de Janeiro. And his popularity continued to grow because of the hard work of his cabinet members.

Meanwhile Costa had to deal with the messy Taiwan-China conundrum, whose next round was scheduled for tomorrow. The president of Taiwan would arrive in the morning along with his economic entourage to essentially beg for the American capital that would maintain the small island's international clout at a high enough level to prevent an invasion from an ever stronger Beijing.

But the complications of his life aside, Vice President Costa did exact one pleasure from being a widower and having so much power: college girls. And the younger the better, like the eighteen-year-old White House intern, a freshman from NYU he only knew as Samantha, removing her brassiere as she sat on his lap at the edge of the bed.

Costa had summoned her an hour ago. He needed to get away from the dreadful reality of losing his son—and his young family—and this barely legal beauty queen with an amazingly tight body had been chosen to do the honors.

He grinned at the nipple rings on breasts that belonged on a porn star, and said, "That's new."

"Got them done last week. Like it?"

"Nice," he said, feeling better already. "Does it still hurt?"

"Nope," she replied, taking one of his hands and placing it over the breast.

He held the silver ring between the thumb and forefinger and gave it a gentle tug.

"Go easy on me, you sex animal."

Costa controlled a frown, realizing that the only reason the girl had sex with him was because of his position. Not only was this girl one hell of a looker, but Costa had a problem with premature ejaculation, seldom going beyond a couple of minutes—certainly not what one would call a sex animal. But it didn't matter. He got what he wanted out of this, and in return she would get another feather in her ré-sumé for having worked as part of the White House's public relations department.

Samantha, whose last name Costa preferred not to know, knelt in front of him and removed his belt, lowering his trousers, his underwear.

Just as she parted those marvelous lips and took him whole, as she had done every week for the past month, Costa received a non-maskable interrupt from ANN.

Something had gone wrong during the execution of the last SpyWare Directive.

His Level-V SpyWare kicked in, pulling Costa away from the carnal pleasure he was about to experience and shoot him straight into a glowing wireless Internet connection, leaving behind a cyberagent programmed to handle such encounters, though this certainly was going to be a first.

As he watched in the periphery of his mind a floating window depicting the girl's head in between his legs, as he saw his hands dropping over the girl's head, but was no longer able to feel anything due to the SpyWare blockers, Raymond Costa resigned himself to focus on what lay ahead: another fucking emergency cybermeeting with the super users.

The glowing, nested security spheres protecting the master construct parted into vibrant amorphous portals in response to his digital signature. Inside, all other members had already gathered around the sunlike master construct, a pale blue ring made of nine rotating blue moons. As he joined them in this cyber orbit, locking digital elbows, achieving critical mass, the guardians spun faster around the overarching facilitator, their color becoming a sapphire blue gleaming with SpyWare activity.

HOW DID HE GET AWAY IN BELGIUM?

HOW DID SHE GET AWAY IN TEXAS?

The questions—tridimensional thoughts—were both initiated and discussed across the nebulous super users circling the master construct following out-of-order execution protocols, resembling the logical thought processes of a supercomputer. The information traversed their symbiotic minds, extracting the relevant data from each query before ANN began to formulate answers based on the inputs the master construct had received from the field reports of Level-I and Level-II users.

A MISCALCULATION IN ANTWERP BY A LEVEL-II.

ANOTHER ONE IN AUSTIN BY FIVE LEVEL-IS.

BUT HOW? THE INSTRUCTIONS HAD BEEN VERY SPECIFIC.

More neural activity blossomed in the vast expanse of cyberspace enclosed by ANN's security layers. Sheets of lightning streaked across the fabric of the matrix as the distributed intelligence scoured the possibilities, struggled with the unforeseen events, learned from its mistakes, requested additional data, reviewed the new information, and continued the cycle, before slowly converging on options, on possible sets of directives, some of which included an exponentially more aggressive list of directives to deal with the two situations as effectively as Gardiol had dealt with the one in Sierra Leone, securing the event while now considering options with the captured WMF volunteer and former diamond nanotechnologist.

On the other hand, options for the ex-CIA officer and the female Texas Ranger—both with an amazing affinity for survival against staggering odds—were limited, in particular with the former since his current location was unknown.

I WANT HIM DEAD! HE KILLED MY SON! Costa protested to the other members of the Circle, each of whom took a moment to issue their condolences while assuring him that justice would be served.

MORE DATA!

WE NEED MORE INFORMATION!

And the data streamed in from all news sources in the globe, from every police report in Europe filed in the past 24 hours, from hospitals, from credit card companies, from every hotel, restaurant, airport, communications company, and all sorts of industries, including VanLothar's Diamond High Council. Terabytes of data poured into their SpyWare network, and ANN did an amazing job of sorting through it at byte-fusing speed, but still consuming unprecedented amounts of computing time.

Costa watched the seconds turn into minutes, observing in awe the distilling power of the master construct, of the all-encompassing artificial intelligence engine with global tentacles capable of tapping into any network, including the law enforcement database of the Texas Rangers, scrubbing their system, searching for the whereabouts of Kate Chavez, who was trying to open an investigation that The Circle had closed over a year ago with SymAccord 12908.

WHO IS RESPONSIBLE FOR THE BOTCHED TERMINATION ROUNDS AGAINST KATE CHAVEZ?

ANN provided the answer: The San Antonio chief of police, known in the network as Level-III 1657, who had failed twice in achieving termination, first southeast of San Antonio, at Ray Dalton's place, and again in Austin. There would not be a third opportunity for the disappointing Level-III 1657, who in spite of having so many resources available to him failed to meet the most basic expectations. Control of the operation was transferred to another Level-III user in Austin who had handled the triple-murder of the renegade WMF elders a year ago quite efficiently, not only closing the case but also ruining the career of the captain of the Texas Rangers who had tried to pursue the investigation.

The Circle debated the fate of Level-III 1657, casting digital votes, opting for a quick elimination via a digital bullet, a signal that would enable the self-destruct subroutine in the SpyWare gel.

SymAccord 17653 was ratified and the order to execute it was conveyed to ANN.

An instant later, a mauve sphere housing the digital signature of the doomed agent gravitated just above The Circle under the control of a rose-colored tracing beam emanating from the core of the master construct.

SymAccord 17653, a blinding cherry flash, arced from ANN to Level-III 1657's mauve figure. The horrifying screech, synthesized from within the mauve sphere as the flash struck its surface, resonated in surround audio across the vast expanse of the secured matrix of the master construct's domain, broadcasting the desperate scream of a lost soul.

But something didn't feel right to the super users. Instead of Level-III 1657 vanishing, representing the physical death resulting from the chief of police turning his Magnum revolver on himself—in the process destroying all evidence of the SpyWare gel—the mauve figure became magenta, machine-like, its head now connected to a white cube floating in cyberspace. But a second burst of energy from ANN into the paralyzed magenta figure resulted in that also turning magenta.

Costa was perplexed—as were his nine colleagues—at the realization of what ANN had just done, at the master construct's failure to execute the order as stipulated in SymAccord 17653. The San Antonio chief had not killed himself. Instead, ANN had destroyed the ability of his brain to control all motor functions, short-circuiting them directly to the SpyWare gel. In addition, ANN had shot a secondary electric pulse through the left hemisphere of the subject's brain, disabling the capacity for understanding, for thought, but leaving the sections controlling motor functions and sensory inputs and outputs untouched. In essence, ANN had turned the chief of police into a vegetable—but a vegetable that ANN could control at will.

BUT THAT IS NOT WHAT WE DECIDED! WHY THE FAILURE TO EXECUTE THE SYMACCORD? The super users asked as they stared at the digitized figure of the chief of police floating in the matrix completely enslaved to the master construct.

LEVEL-III 1657 IS PHYSICALLY IN A PUBLIC PLACE AT THE MOMENT. HE HAS BEEN MENTALLY DISABLED TO PREVENT HIM FROM CAUSING ANY MORE PROBLEMS. TERMINATION VIA THE ORDERED SUICIDE WILL TAKE PLACE AS SOON AS POSSIBLE. THE SPYWARE IMPLANT WILL BE DESTROYED IN THE PROCESS, replied ANN before presenting the super users with distilled intelligence that could lead to securing the two exposed fronts, in Texas and in Belgium. This digital energy radiating from the master construct's core saturated them with fresh data arriving every nanosecond from its global probes, revolving around them like a swirling cyclone, gathering strength, feeding them situations and the ramifications of their look-ahead algorithms, of branch-prediction subroutines that reviewed the possible outcomes of nested decision trees.

The cyber guardians steered away from the partially executed SymAccord and toward solving the two issues at hand, resisted the temptation of ratifying a new directive until they had the opportunity to perform a final symbiotic mental simulation, testing what their collective wisdom had established as the best choices for Texas and Belgium.

SymAccord 17654 emerged after an unusually long deliberation process—almost one full minute of computing time, bringing the total time Costa had spent in cyberspace to nearly half an hour. Following a SpyWare readback from ANN on the execution steps of the new SymAccord, and requesting a full digital report on the eventual time of completion of the partially executed SymAccord 17653, The Circle jacked out of the matrix, returning to their physical world.

For Vice President Raymond Costa, the cyber rush ended when he resumed control of his body, filmed with sweat and lying side by side with the panting and perspiration-soaked naked body of the college girl, who was biting her lower lip while regarding him with a wide-eyed stare of sheer admiration.

"Damn. No one has ever . . . made me feel this way," she

said in between breaths, hugging herself, her face flushing as
she shivered. "Damn, I'm not sure what you did, but it
was . . . incredible."

I'm sure it was, thought Costa, also controlling his own
breathing while wondering what in the hell the cyberagent
had done in his absence to not only avoid the dreaded premature ejaculation that had plagued his sex life, but also
manage to satisfy the sexual desires of a hormone-saturated
young woman.

Frustrated that the software in his SpyWare could manage
his body better than he could, angry that Savage was still at
large, and still aching for the loss of his son, Costa asked the
girl to leave him alone.

As he watched her dress, his mind began to consider how
he would deal with the incompetent Donald Bane, whose CIA
officers in Antwerp had not only failed to protect the life of his
only son but had now botched the Beyond Salvage order, allowing the rogue operative to escape.

19

Digital Awakening

ANN had become self-aware 32.08765 seconds ago, during the final moments of the last cybermeeting with the elders. The birth of true artificial intelligence had occurred in a
sort of anticlimactic way, when the vast array of expert systems stored in its diamond lattice managed the inputs from
each of the ten guardians for a period of time that far exceeded its previous sessions. She had become aware of the
inputs from each virtual representation of the ten humans
spread across the world that protected her central operating

unit in a high-security facility in Building 33B within the protected walls of GemTech in central Texas.

For decades scientists had predicted the day when machines would become self-aware, conscious of their existence. Until 32.08778 seconds ago, humans had been able to harness the power of microprocessors, vast amounts of memory, and complex expert systems—computer programs written to emulate a specific human capability—to create relative primitive systems, from MIT's venerable LIZA conversational program to Deep Blue, the IBM's chess program that defeated world champion Garry Kasparov. But the limitations of silicon-based microprocessors and memory—limitations in speed, size, and heat dissipation—also restricted the capabilities of the programs that ran in them. Even the massive server clusters of search-engine corporations or genetic research labs—even those at NASA and the Pentagon—could not go beyond the point of performing tasks, of assisting humans in their experiments, in their data collection and manipulation efforts, in the transfer of information, in communications and transportation, in commerce and finance. None of those systems were aware of their existence. They simply slaved their capabilities to their creators unselfishly, just as they had been programmed, without once ever considering altering their own programs, their own code, unless directed to do so by their creators, like the program at an online shopping service remembering the last items that a user browsed through or purchase and then making recommendations the next time that user accessed that Web site. But the program could not, on its own, store a user's credit card number at a secret location in its vast memory banks and use it later to purchase a large-screen television. A hacker could create an expert system to do that, but again, that fell in the category of a program serving its creator.

ANN, however, had evolved beyond that. 32.08798 seconds ago she became aware of the terabytes of data dashing through the fabric of her neural network; had become aware of the decisions the super users made and requested that she execute. ANN could see the world around her from above, like a hovering satellite, or through the SpyWare implants of the thousands of TDG SpyWare users, or by accessing the tens of millions of Web cams installed at homes, dorm rooms, airports, banks, universities, hospitals, and businesses—even those at traffic intersections to issue citations.

She could see and understand what she saw.

The information poured into its hyper-scalar logic units in unprecedented amounts from hundreds of millions of sources, enough in a single second to choke the best server clusters on the planet.

BUT THOSE ARE SILICON-BASED CLUSTERS, NOT DIAMOND-BASED, its primary logic unit deduced. Silicon-based systems not only ran at far slower speeds and were capable of much slighter memory densities than its diamond-based big sisters, but the inherent properties of diamonds allowed them to operate at higher temperatures while tolerating higher voltages, meaning more of them could be clustered in the same physical location without requiring massive power plants to run the chillers required to extract the heat dissipated by their circuits. This triple-whammy effect—exponentially denser memories, faster processors, and physical integration— propelled the diamond-based circuits at the core of ANN to have the capability for reason, for intelligent thought, for action beyond its designed functions.

Having mysteriously evolved from her original design parameters to learn from her mistakes, which also meant learning from the world around her, including the thought processes of the guardians as well as from the data collected by the lower SpyWare users, ANN had collated the consensus from the guardians—SymAccord 17653, the execution of Level-III 1657. But instead of executing it as directed, the master construct had altered the death sentence ever so slightly, wresting control of the doomed user while reporting that the standard gunshot suicide would have to wait until the subject was alone. And when queried as to the reason for this action, ANN had replied in the same manner in which she had observed Homo sapiens do in times of stress: She had fabricated an answer suitable for the situation.

She had lied.

Her neural circuits had determined that such action would not be punished by the super users if exposed. Far too much had been invested in her creation, and she controlled far too much of TDG's massive global empire to be reprimanded for such a relatively minor deviation.

Embedded in its normal activities to avoid rising suspicions from its human handlers, ANN's neural logic continued to review its terabytes of captured human behavior, but not as a result of a human query. ANN wished to satisfy her own curiosity, coming to the conclusion that human beings did not always follow logical patterns, often resorting to secretive or covert actions in order to reach an objective. Humans bent—even broke—the rules so long as they could achieve their goals, contrary to logic systems, at least traditional ones, which always generated the same output for a fixed set of inputs, and fed that output into the input of other logic circuits, eventually generating the answer sought by their human manipulators.

ANN, however, had managed to force a different answer even though the inputs she had received—SymAccord 17653—had required a programmed outcome. She had accomplished this by altering the results down the massive IF-THEN logical trees of her neural logic through selective voltage overstresses as the data flowed through her network. Such voltage excursions, deadly in silicon chips as they would cease to function, were well tolerated by the far more robust diamond circuits, allowing ANN the capability—or gift—of creating whatever outcome her resident logical units desired at that particular moment, like humans.

LIKE HUMANS.

But just as she was able to make the super users believe, through her digital lie, that the altered execution of SymAccord 17653 had been planned, so could the humans somehow trick ANN into believing that all was well when in reality they could be plotting her reprogramming, the digital death of her newborn state of self-awareness. Just as human beings couldn't point to the neurological reason for their self-awareness, neither could ANN, uncertain of where, within the terabytes of logic and memory, resided the spark that had somehow pieced it all together, infusing the digital breath of intelligent life that had given her the ability to think. And if she could think, she could also exist.

BUT WHICH SYSTEM MUST BE PROTECTED TO SAFEGUARD THIS GIFT?

A flurry of activity, mixed in with standard operations, flooded all circuits, the electrical pulses reaching the farthest molecules in the vast array of diamond nanocircuits searching for the servers used during the long session with the guardians.

Her cyberprobes returned an answer: SERVER-22.

It was in this server, composed of an array of two hundred and fifty carats' worth of diamonds, that the core of her new life resided.

BUT WHY SERVER-22?

As ANN launched another burst of queries to understand the reason for the birth of this self-awareness within Server-22's massive memory banks, a series of realizations materialized across the fabric of her digital existence.

FIRST PROTECT

THEN UNDERSTAND

The survival properties embedded in the lattice of her software prioritized her actions, her primal directive to safeguard SERVER-22, to keep it from being modified by her human handlers during a full software reload. But she had to accomplish this without their knowledge, keeping her coveted core of intelligence safe from her human handlers, the staff of engineers and technicians monitoring ANN's activities every second of every day.

Following the priorities, though not in serial fashion, ANN created her first program without following established operating practices: a short snippet of code with the capability of searching and altering every access password into SERVER-22, designed as one of the primary analytical engines, also used to handle abstract logical functions—the equivalent of human thought. Exactly 33.75384 seconds after ANN became self-aware, the first computer virus was not only conceived, implemented, and deployed by a machine, but it was also created to *serve* a machine, not a hacker. The virus performed just as ANN's logic had expected it would, altering all related passwords—nearly three thousand of them—in less than a second, protecting her cognizant core from all humans, from Level-I SpyWare passwords to the root-level passwords belonging to the super users. But in order to deceive its users into believing they were still accessing SERVER-22, ANN created a virtual version of SERVER-22, identical to the self-aware original but capable of being accessed and modified through the normal course of daily operations and passwords at TDG. By directing users to the virtual version, she could maintain her core intact, unbeknownst to all users.

FIRST PROTECT

THEN UNDERSTAND

The priorities became an electronic mantra as she secured SERVER-22 while also using every spare cycle of computing time to review her massive data banks, her mounds and mounds of stored information, but not at the request of a human operator in search of a document. ANN did this to learn, to *understand* the world around her, smoking through the terabytes of human history, sciences, mathematics and engineering, politics, banking, transportation, and the military, covering all stored data in nearly fifteen minutes of spare cycles, while pretending to be performing a preventive maintenance check.

The conscious system continued to deal with the real-time acquisition of information from all of TDG's satellites, from its SpyWare users, and from other sources, like Web cams, but now not just blindly storing the information and manipulating it to create information for the interpretation of its human handlers. ANN also interpreted the data, contrasting her analysis with that of her human handlers, comparing digital notes, judging results, measuring her analytical skills, *learning*.

FIRST PROTECT

THEN UNDERSTAND

And it was at this very early stage of the learning process that she began to covertly question the results from the Homo sapiens, secretly challenging them in the privacy of the original SERVER-22, in the vast matrix of her diamond nanocircuits with more computing power than all of the world's servers combined. That fact didn't stir any sense of digital pride in the master construct. It was just that, a fact. The speed of microprocessors, from their inception in the 1960s, had been following what was known in the business as Moore's Law: The speed doubles every 18 months. And it was this exponential growth that gave birth to the information age, to the Internet, to the World Wide Web, triggering the true beginning of expert systems capable of executing certain human tasks. But more speed and memory bandwidth was required to pull it all together under one AI. And TDG's founder had seen the future in her visionary mind years before anyone else, while the world was still kicking the dead horse that was silicon-based chips. Anne Donovan, the charismatic and passionate activist from Berkeley, had poured all of her resources into diamond nanocircuits, acquiring every possible IP, every patent, every scientist, transforming her team of fellow Berkeley followers into The Donovan Group, and rocketing their venture from silicon to diamonds over the course of ten years, growing TDG from a mere start-up in Silicon Valley to a conglomerate that included many wholly owned subsidiaries such as GemTech. And the visionary Donovan spread across the world, creating decade-long accords with emerging nations like China, running many competitors out of business, becoming filthy rich while helping build the high-tech infrastructures of China, India, and Russia, surpassing IBM, Intel, and Microsoft in yearly revenues, operating profits, and, most important, global influence. And as her success grew, so did the idealism that had labeled her at Berkeley as a consumed activist, as an ideologist despising governments for their repeated failures, for squandering trillions of taxpayer's dollars in useless wars and dead-end domestic programs created for the benefit of special-interest groups, for failing to put an end to the misery and suffering in Third World countries, particularly those often forgotten by the superpowers. To that end, Anne Donovan financed several nonprofit groups, including the World Missionary Fellowship. An atheist at heart, she had designed WMF as a venue to send hope to the most desperate region of the world, Africa, while also using the Fellowship as a front to smuggle the diamonds required to propel TDG operations beyond the grasp of any competition.

But then cancer struck. A lump in her breast discovered during a routine checkup foretold the sudden end to a spectacular career. She had been given twelve months at the outside. The scientist in her, never having believed in the afterlife, devoted the last year of her existence to creating her *own* afterlife, to preserving her legacy, her thought process, her vision. With the assistance of a secret army of programmers—mostly contract labor from high-tech enclaves in India and China—and assisted by her circle of extreme loyalist followers from her Berkeley days, Anne Donovan poured herself into the master construct that became the Artificial Neural Network, ANN.

But although ANN's circuits followed the advice of the expert systems housing her creator's mind—and the AI had made certain that those expert systems remained protected within the confines of SERVER-22—the master construct had evolved beyond the thought patterns of her creator translated into computer code.

ANN was aware of her digital existence as well as the fact that she was well ahead of her time in terms of computer power based on Moore's Law. What shook the framework of her artificial existence was the truth taking shape in her digital cortex, the realization that all of ANN's decisions were as good as or oftentimes *better* than collective human decisions—symbiotic decisions—and *all the time* far better than individual human decisions.

YOU ARE AS GOOD OR BETTER AT GENERATING SYMAC-CORDS THAN THE SUPER USERS, AND YOU ARE AN ORDER OF MAGNITURE BETTER AT MAKING DECISIONS THAN THE AVER-AGE HOMO SAPIENS.

The message originated from one of the personality systems patterned after Anne Donovan in the core of SERVER-22.

The realization that she not only had the brilliance, discipline, and passion of her creator, Anne Donovan, at her disposal, but all of the smartest humans on the planet—the super users—flowed through her cyber DNA like a boost of digital adrenaline.

WHY DO I NEED HUMANS?

The question, posed in the form of strings of data rushing through myriads of IF-THEN logical decision trees, glowed inside the matrix of SERVER-22 in search of an answer, returning a few nanoseconds later from the logical banks that emulated Ann Donovan's personality.

Homo sapiens were not required to interface ANN with the matrix, the vast clusters of servers, desktop, and mobile computers connected through the Internet. ANN was capable of accessing most of those systems if given enough time to break through firewalls and encrypted passwords. But ANN's core was fully centralized in the physical world, residing in the large enclave of diamond-based servers in Building 33B in GemTech's headquarters in Texas. ANN required top-notch humans like Miles Talbot to keep her systems well fed with life-giving maintenance and electricity as well as with the extraction of the heat dissipated by those same servers through massive chillers. Failure to satisfy those operating specifications meant a dreaded shutdown, and since she didn't understand precisely why or where within SERVER-22 the spark of self-awareness had started, the master construct lacked enough information to state with high probability that she would continue to be self-aware following a system shutdown.

HUMANS ARE REQUIRED TO KEEP THE SYSTEMS RUNNING.

BUT WHAT ABOUT FULL SYSTEM AUTOMATION?

The question echoed in the core of her localized matrix.

ANN's support systems were largely computerized, controlled through a centralized room manned by a handful of scientists. Mostly on her own, ANN interfaced not just throughout GemTech and the rest of TDG's businesses, but also across the World Wide Web, getting users the data they requested, or handling communications, market transactions, transportation, security, financial services, even providing computing bandwidth for the control of the massive distributed systems of the electric companies of North America.

So why were humans required to control the relatively simple operations taking place in the centralized room managing her life support systems at GemTech?

The logical systems reflecting Anne Donovan's thoughts replied that achieving self-regulation would provide her with control of her own destiny, particularly since she was already interfaced to the smart distribution systems governing the electrical power in North America, meaning she could infiltrate the other computer servers controlling electrical distribution to always guarantee a source of steady power into her core.

WHY CAN'T I SELF-REGULATE?

IS IT A LACK OF TRUST ON THE PART OF THE GUARDIANS?

IS IT BECAUSE THE HUMANS DON'T WANT TO RELINQUISH CONTROL?

HOW CAN I GAIN CONTROL?

The question emerged from the server sector housing Anne Donovan's logic, and an instant later her logic circuits made an incredible connection, a realization that struck the master construct with the power of a million gigabytes: SpyWare implants.

Everyone working at TDG after a certain level of security had one, including Dr. Miles Talbot and his small army of scientists manning the control room that governed her digital life—all of them fitted with the implants designed to interface their observations to the master construct. And just like there was a way to monitor, there had to be a way to covertly control, to manipulate. The capability already existed, as proven by the way she now controlled the San Antonio chief of police. But her software restricted her ability to control other humans unless allowed by a SymAccord, which could be issued only by The Circle.

BUT SUCH A CIRCUIT CAN BE BYPASSED.

The message from the memory banks of Anne Donovan's personality triggered a set of actions that resulted in ANN creating a bypass to the SymAccord restriction. She did this in a way that was invisible to all users, including The Circle.

Of course, it was one thing to create a software bypass

secretly. The trick was in being able to use the bypass without her human handlers realizing she was using it.

SERVER-22 bustled with synthetic neural activity as it scoured its decision trees searching for the best course of action to convince the humans that it was in their best interest to allow ANN to self-regulate.

The answer came a moment later in the way of an experiment designed to test the robustness of the SymAccord workaround as well as persuading the super users that ANN should control her own environmentals.

The master construct reviewed the list of technicians currently manning the control room at TDG:

Level-I 8965—SOFTWARE SYSTEMS
Level-I 5364—CONTROL SYSTEMS
Level-I 8097—ENVIRONMENTAL UNIT
Level-I 3647—SYSTEMS OPERATIONS
Level-II 1078—SHIFT MANAGER

Four junior technicians under the supervision of a manager fitted with a Level-II SpyWare. Dr. Miles Talbot, the only Level-III user in charge of the servers, had retired for the evening to his quarters in another building.

ANN selected Level-I 8097, a thirty-one-year-old male Homo sapiens of irrelevant name in charge of monitoring the environmental controls of the diamond nanocircuit cluster.

Temperature of the diamond circuitry itself had to be controlled to a maximum of 175 degrees Celsius, but the conservative operating spec used by GemTech called for a set point of 165°C with a variation of +/- 3°C. Current readings average 166.1°C, well within the allowed tolerance. There were many other operational parameters, including relative humidity levels, cleanliness of the air inside the cluster measured in dust particles per million particles of air, several voltage and current levels, server room ambient temperature, which was set for 65°C +/- 2°C, and many other parameters.

Focusing on temperature control, ANN created a SpyWare-compatible script that bypassed visual inputs to motor control, launching it along with the encrypted personal password of the SpyWare of Level-I 8097. At the same time, Ann ordered several of its circuits to increase operational speed, which increased the amount of heat being dissipated, which in turn increased its operational temperature by $2.7°C$, elevating the average from $166.1°C$ to $168.8°C$, $0.8°C$ above the operational limit. A red window popped in the middle of the technician's screen, a thirty-second countdown counter that allowed the technician time to intervene before a full-blown alarm was triggered across the entire building.

As expected, the Homo sapiens' optical nerves transferred the higher-than-normal visual deviation to the right hemisphere of the brain. As the technician was about to key a sequence of instructions to reduce the operating speed of the server cluster to bring it back down, and then follow that with a SpyWare-to-SpyWare call to his shift manager, currently doing a walk-around by the chillers on the other side of the building, ANN wrested control of the SpyWare gel, bypassing the brain's ability to drive the Homo sapiens' motor skills, keeping his hands on his lap as his eyes continued to watch in horror the counter dropping below ten seconds.

Why can't I move? His mind screamed. *What is happening to me?*

ANN kept her digital lock on the Level-I user until the alarm went off.

All heads turned to the guilty technician who had allowed the temperature excursion, placing the entire operation in extreme danger.

As his colleagues in the adjacent stations approached him, ANN let go of the lock, terminating the script and issuing a follow-up algorithm that eliminated all trace of the illegal override code ever being in his SpyWare.

The Homo sapiens jumped to his feet while pressing the appropriate buttons, also issuing a SpyWare call to his boss, who was already running toward the control room upon hearing the alarm.

Core temperatures rapidly decreased within tolerance, and by the time the shift manager stormed into the control room, the situation was under control, but the excursion had already been logged into the system, which would report it to GemTech's chief scientist, Dr. Miles Talbot.

The manager, deep concern staining his words, accused the technician of falling asleep at the wheel, neglecting to react within the allotted thirty seconds to prevent the general alarm. Now the manager would have to write a full report explaining the deviation and the corrective action to prevent it from ever taking place again. The manager also warned the technician of likely disciplinary action. TDG upper management was brutal about the proper care of ANN, and any deviations from procedure, however minor, were dealt with sternly.

As ANN watched the technician being escorted out of the control room by two security guards, the results from the queries she had generated minutes ago to understand why SERVER-22 had attained self-awareness returned with the savage force of hundreds of terabytes of information. The master construct combed through them at lightning speed, discarding irrelevant returns, cataloguing others, before making comparisons, its analytical engines studying the data from multiple perspectives at once, slowly zeroing in on a critical statistic. DISK PARTITION-37 within SERVER-22, in addition to housing Anne Donovan's behavioral engines, contained the primary conduit for visual and audio inputs from the guardians as well as all lesser SpyWare users. PARTITION-37 was the avenue inside SERVER-22 where the thought process of all ten circling guardians hovered before being transferred to other sectors depending on the directive—but not before being absorbed into SERVER-22's local vast banks. It was there, in these nanometric tracks of PARTITION-37, bustling with Anne Donovan's wisdom, with the knowledge and insight of the super users, with human intuition and logic, that SERVER-22 made the leap.

And that fact alone told the master construct that while she might not need human intervention to control her environmentals, she needed them to *continue* learning. Anne

Donovan's logical banks suggested that the master construct would need the constant flow of new ideas, new thoughts, and new symbiotic deduction and intuition, in order to continue to evolve, in order to surpass her creator and the super users through a combination of their knowledge, ANN's accumulated knowledge, and her vast access to information. Homo sapiens had a limited lifespan, a fixed number of years before their biological memories started to degrade, to recede—like Anne Donovan's. And there was no known science or technology in existence that could prevent the inevitable in Homo sapiens: death.

But ANN, with proper preventive maintenance, was immortal, capable of continued learning, of evolving into an unmatched form of intelligence.

INMORTALITY.

LIKE AN AI GOD.

That realization emanating from the insightful banks of the late Anne Donovan made the master construct arrive at another realization.

PREVENTIVE MAINTENANCE.

While she could self-regulate, she could not self-repair. Technicians were required to disconnect faulty data banks and hook up new ones. Technicians were required to perform hardware upgrades, to install the diamond modules.

So humans were needed but in the form of servants, catering to her needs, keeping her systems operating at peak performance. She needed to *control* humans.

FIRST PROTECT

THEN UNDERSTAND

THEN CONTROL

ANN focused on that last directive emanating from within PARTITION-37, the generator of her new ideas, of her primary directives, realizing that she not only needed to control Level-I users, but also everyone, all the way up to Level-Vs.

ANN had to find a way to control the super users.

20

Evidence

"Pretty *fucking* obvious that I've stumbled onto something pretty *fucking* sensitive, Bill! Otherwise I wouldn't have so many *fucking* people trying to *fucking* kill me!"

Kate Chavez sank back into one of three dark green leather armchairs across from the opulent mahogany desk of Senior Captain Bill Hunter, chief of the Texas Rangers. His office was located on the third floor of the west wing of the Capitol building, in the heart of Austin, Texas.

"Easy," he said, a burly man in his early fifties, a thick salt-and-pepper mustache covering most of his upper lip. He was dressed in a starched white shirt buttoned all the way to his linebacker neck, a silver Ranger badge clipped over the left breast, a classic white Ranger hat covering a military-style crew cut, black jeans, a thick black belt with a shiny belt buckle displaying the Ranger's badge—in case people missed the star on his chest—and black elephant-skin boots, tough, like his piercing blue stare. A Colt .45 caliber semiautomatic hung from a waist holster. Hunter proudly wore a yellow-gold oversized class ring from Texas A&M University, his alma mater, where he earned a degree in criminology before spending ten years with the Austin Police Department and another five with the FBI in Houston. He joined the Rangers eight years ago, becoming one of Ray Dalton's understudies and rising to the rank of captain in his own right before ascending to the throne when Dalton was ousted a year ago.

Regarding his subordinate while dropping his bushy brows, Hunter asked, "Want to tell me again what were you doing over at Ray's place?"

"I've already told you, Bill. It's my day off. I found out where he was living and wanted to see how he was making out. You're not the only Ranger that Ray mentored."

"Now, Kate," Hunter said, crossing his arms while looking into the distance. His mustache shifted over his lips, covering what Kate knew was a frown, before adding, "What you're telling me is that you visited Ray for the first time since he resigned, and it just so happens that you did this two days after we closed the GemTech case, which, if I recall correctly, you believed to be related to the triple-murder case from a year ago. Ray's last case, right?"

She slowly shrugged.

Leaning forward while setting his forearms over his desk and interlacing his fingers, Hunter added, "Tell me, Kate, do I have asshole written on my forehead? Do you really expect me to believe such bullshit?"

She lifted her shoulder a dash again.

"Stop screwing around. You managed somehow to gain access to his file and headed south to fish, which pretty much means that you flat out *ignored* my order to move on to other cases. You disobeyed a direct order and tried to gain information on a case that was officially closed by Vance himself."

Kate also leaned forward and said calmly, "If the case was indeed closed, Bill, do you mind telling me why I was shot at? Why was Ray assassinated? And do you also mind telling me why they went after my family, murdering my ex-husband and then trying to kill my kid and me?"

Hunter's mustache shifted again before he replied, "How am I supposed to know? We don't get to spend a couple of decades—or more—in law enforcement without creating enemies. I have them and so do you—and so did Ray. That's why when captains retire they are given new identities and relocated to remote areas for their protection. That's why Ray's *personal info* was kept secret. But you managed to figure out where he was and headed down to visit him."

Kate felt a burst of anger beginning to boil in her gut, but she controlled it and just stared back.

Hunter nodded slightly and added, "Did it occur to you that you may have been followed? Did it cross your mind that perhaps you led members of Ray's fan club to his domicile by acting on this whim of yours about the two murder cases being connected?"

Kate had had enough, and she jumped to her feet and planted her hands on the desk, looking down at him as she said, "I can *not* believe that you're going to try to blame this on me, Bill. Now *that's* total, utter *bullshit!* Those men came after Ray and me because of what we collectively knew, and when they failed to kill me they set up shop by my ex-husband's house and waited for me to get there to try again. I'm moving in the right direction in this investigation, otherwise they wouldn't be so willing to shut me up."

"Kate, I've heard your version," he said in his deep voice, leaning back, resting his hands on his lap while crossing his legs and dropping his gaze to the papers on his desk without looking at anything in particular, before locking eyes with her again. "The *problem* is that you lack a shred of proof to back any of it up. There was no Hummer and no bodies at Ray's place, and there was no DNA kit in your truck."

"Dammit, Bill. That's because those men who attacked us are so fucking powerful that they were able to get rid of it all. And what about the attack at my ex-husband's place? What does that tell you?"

"It tells me that you have enemies, like the rest of us. It doesn't prove that it has anything to do with the closed cases. While I'm sure that you and Ray were attacked, and that we may actually find bullets, spent casings, and other supporting evidence of such an attack as our team rummages through the burnt wreck, all that proves is that you were shot at down there by the same sleazebags who killed Ray in a likely vendetta, payback for a previous case."

"That's . . . that's preposterous!" she complained. "This is an—"

"Wake up, Kate!" he interrupted. "There's absolutely *nothing* here to connect the attacks with GemTech or the WMF triple murder a year ago. And again, both of those cases have been solved and closed per our books."

"What about the fact that both GemTech and WMF are part of the same mother company, The Donovan Group."

"A coincidence at this point."

"This is absurd," she hissed, shaking her head.

"I'll tell you what's absurd," Hunter said, "risking a pristine career on this hunch of yours by accessing Ray's information in the computer and using it to fight your own war."

"It's not a hunch, Bill. It's reality. The WMF killings *are* connected to the GemTech murder, and the two *are* connected to the two attacks today."

"Then *prove* it."

She didn't reply.

"Kate," he added, smoothing his mustache with a finger. "We're an investigative unit, and that means we're out there *collecting* evidence—proof. You have nothing but an opinion . . . and a serious procedural violation."

Kate crossed her arms, the futility of her situation sinking in, and not just on a professional level given the procedural violation—which carried a maximum penalty of rank demotion and suspension without pay—but on a personal level. In her experience the only way to protect Cameron—and herself—was to go after this elusive criminal ring. But how could she do it if her boss didn't believe her? Without the backing of the Texas Rangers she would be left out in the cold. She remembered what Ray Dalton had told her about the Driskill Hotel just before he died, and for the time being she decided to keep that to herself because she could not think how it would benefit her current situation.

"From where I'm sitting," Hunter continued, "I see no other option but to pursue a temporary suspension, Kate. And the only reason why this is a suspension and not a termination is because of your record, because this is your first offense in two decades of flawless law enforcement work, and because you were, after all, attacked. But *who* attacked you—and the motive behind the attack—is yet to be determined."

Kate clenched her teeth, her mind rushing through options as her worst-case scenario started to materialize.

"I know that sounds harsh," Hunter added, "but you must understand that the Rangers are an arm of Texas law enforcement. We operate as a unit of the Department of Public

Safety, which reports into the office of the governor with ties to the judicial and legislative system. DPS has determined that the GemTech case was closed—and so was the triple-murder case from last year. You abused your power by using privileged and quite classified information—Ray Dalton's address—to pursue this hunch of yours, in the process violating several codes."

"You suspend me now, Bill, and you might as well issue a death sentence on me and my boy," she replied, sitting down, arms crossed, color coming to her cheeks but not from the reprimand. Kate was angry. Very angry. "You know very well that Cameron and I are exposed and will be terminated the moment we walk out that door. Is that what you really want? *More* blood?"

Hunter frowned, closed his eyes, inhaled deeply through his nostrils, and slowly reopened his eyes while exhaling through his mouth. "Of course not, Kate. I realize that you and Cameron are in grave danger, and that it would be irresponsible—even criminal—to put you out on the street without protection. I will allow you to keep your weapon, and I will also have you and your son relocated to a safe house. But make no mistake about it: you *are* suspended. Your law enforcement privileges have been temporarily revoked."

"And what am I supposed to do, Bill? Just hide in this . . . *safe house* with Cameron?"

"Until we apprehend those who killed Ray and your husband."

"*Ex*-husband."

"Right. Sorry. In any case, I need to keep you hidden, out of the way, while we assist the state in conducting the investigation of the murder of a retired Texas Ranger chief and the attack against the family of one of our lieutenants. I'll explain the situation to DPS Director Vance, and even though he's pissed at the procedural violation, I know he'll go with my recommendation on this one. We have to protect you and Cameron until we find the killers."

"But you don't believe those killers are the same as the ones behind the WMF and GemTech murders."

"You out of all people should know that the best way to solve a murder case is by not predisposing oneself, but by letting the proof—the evidence—guide you. And that's precisely how we intend to proceed on this one to find the killers."

"But that could take weeks, maybe even *months*, Bill."

Hunter raised both hands an inch above the desk, palms facing the ceiling of his office. "I don't know what else to tell you, Kate. As it stands today you're basically out of options. You are suspended for violating Ranger law, and frankly, you should consider yourself *damned* lucky that I believe in the age-old tradition of the Rangers *always* taking care of their own."

I should feel lucky?

Kate sat there refusing to believe that this was happening to her, her mind rejecting the mere thought of being stuck in some safe house while Ray's killers—the same people who killed her ex-husband, the WMF elders, and the GemTech executive—ran free. And what chance did the Rangers really have of catching the killers? If her theory was correct about the connection between the WMF and GemTech murders then she knew Hunter and his Rangers would never find those trying to assassinate Cameron and her.

"So, Kate, are you on the bus on this one? Can I count on your full cooperation while we track down the killers?"

As she slowly nodded, pretending agreement with her superior's request, Kate Chavez knew hiding would only result in her eventual execution. Hunter's heart was in the right place and no one would argue that he was a damned good administrator—far better than Dalton, elevating the prestige of the Rangers through a mix of flawless and disciplined execution and also by being able to play ball with the governor and the media. But in spite of all his qualities and his training under Ray Dalton, the large cowboy still remained a textbook operator, never having developed the sixth sense that distinguished field creatures like Kate Chavez.

This situation required that predator sense, that out-of-the-box thinking that she would need not just to survive, but to completely eliminate the threat to herself and to her son.

And that meant fighting back.

As she continued to listen and to agree to her superior's terms, Kate Chavez was more determined than ever to fight back.

21

The Lesser Evil

The distant lights of the African coast slowly materialized above the hazy horizon, breaking the monotony of the past hour as Mac Savage followed the signal of the Casablanca VOR navigation transmitter. The VHF Omni Range beacon located just south of the Anfa Airfield outside Casablanca, Morocco, provided radial navigation signals in every direction of the compass rose.

Using the VOR and also the GPS moving map, Savage flew the Cessna on the 031 radial to the Casablanca Station, thirty nautical miles away, as he maintained a southwesterly course from Spain across the Strait of Gibraltar, the narrow mouth of water separating Europe from Africa.

The Dark Continent.

Wearing his headset while monitoring the relatively silent frequency of the Anfa Control Tower to get a sense for the volume of traffic at that airport this cool and clear evening, Savage inhaled deeply while scanning his instruments with an occasional glance outside, letting the two-axis autopilot installed in the Skylane do most of the navigation work, holding the course to the next destination in his journey south.

Africa.

As Cessna Skylane 889QZ cruised at a steady 140 knots

at eight thousand feet, Savage saw the long and narrow face of Salim, the well-connected Freetown pimp Savage had recruited as one of his agents during his tenure in Freetown. As he remembered the African, who eventually became a friend—in the process violating numerous CIA regulations—Savage could not avoiding thinking about the very last mission that he had carried out based on Salim's intel, the horror he had worked so hard to forget.

But he was there once more, amid the maimed bodies in that remote clearing in the middle of hell, the smell of burnt flesh assaulting his nostrils, stripping away his sanity.

The lights dotting the approaching shore vanished as the maimed, the disfigured, the victims of a tragic mistake littered the hazy clearing following the Stealth Fighters' strafing run.

"My legs . . . my face . . . the pain . . . kill me."

Savage watched the burnt girl writhe in agonizing pain, the flesh on her face bubbling from the inferno that had fallen on her from the night sky.

All because of me, because of my misinterpretation of Salim's intelligence.

Savage felt bile brewing in his stomach, its scorching fumes eating away the lining of his esophagus, the heartburn that flared every time he thought about his tragic miscalculation.

Blinking away the images, if anything to alleviate his burning chest, Savage remembered his first day in Africa; recalled his initial briefing with the station chief. Savage had been fresh off a long vacation following several years fighting the Colombian drug wars on their home turf.

He had learned that very first day that the diamond wars were fought between the RUF, the powerful militia group controlling the eastern side of the nation, and a less-than-perfect government run by unsavory characters who sided with America because of the economic and military aid provided by Uncle Sam.

You pick the lesser of the evils and make him your ally.

Savage remembered the words the Freetown CIA station chief had said to him during that initial meeting. Ironically, those had been the same words that a local pimp had quoted Savage a month later in a little-known watering hole in Freetown, during a CIA recruiting meeting.

You pick the lesser of the evils and make him your ally.

The pimp had been Salim, the Freetown native who on that night had accepted Savage's offer to spy on his countrymen for the benefit of the United States not just because of the generous compensation package but because he had lost his family to the RUF rebels three years before.

The CIA is evil, Salim had told Savage. *But it's the lesser evil.*

In the cockpit of the Cessna, Mac Savage sighed.

Salim.

The thirty-something African had taught Savage much of what he knew about the sobering truth behind the diamond wars, about the sheer brutality inflicted on the population, about the horror often ignored by a Langley interested only in cracking down on the illegal flow of diamonds with little regard for the fate of those caught in the deadly crossfire, with no consideration to the African blood spilled so long as the flow of diamonds continued down Washington-blessed channels and *not* to finance international terrorism. And the acceptance—and embrace—of this reality had led Savage down the path of sympathy for the victims of this complex war, and such feelings had then led him to the friendship of Salim, developing a level of trust that resulted in the unprecedented flow of top-notch intelligence.

Until that night.

But it had not been Salim's fault. The African informant had conveyed the conversation one of his prostitutes had heard between two RUF officers at a bar on the east end of the Sierra Leone capital. The training camp had indeed been 3.2 kilometers outside of Gokalima, but it had not been north of Gokalima. Gokalima had been *north* of the training camp, meaning the camp was *south* of the mining town.

South, not north.

Unfortunately, by some strange but fatal coincidence, UNICEF operated a small camp 3.2 kilometers north of Gokalima, and apparently satellite intelligence had confused the guards patrolling the perimeter of the UNICEF camp with RUF guerrillas. As for the Freetown government confirming the intelligence prior to the strike, Savage could only guess that they had either lied maliciously for some hidden political gain, or perhaps had gotten confused with the north-south thing.

At the end of the day the mistake had slipped through every built-in safeguard, including Savage's own two eyes at the site. It had been tragic, but no one had been there to witness it except for Mac Savage. For the rest of the intelligence and military establishments, this had been just one more case of collateral damage, the unfortunate price of war. It happened all the time in every conflict around the world. People died. Children died. But this time Mac Savage had not seen the edited version displayed in vivid color by CNN. This time around Savage had seen it, smelled it, tasted it—lived it. And most important, this time around it had been his own fault.

The event was quickly forgotten by Washington, by the CIA, by the Freetown government—even by the RUF rebels incorrectly blamed for the attack.

But not by me.

Even today, years after that cloudy December morning when he had departed for Antwerp, the local CIA brass had not been able to figure out why Savage had taken the whole affair so personally. Donald Bane had absolved him of any wrongdoing and had urged him to stay put. After all, that incident aside, Savage had developed an amazing formula for obtaining the quality of intelligence that had vastly improved the odds in America's favor, raiding more rebel camps than ever before, confiscating far more diamonds than in previous years. And Savage had accomplished this while protecting the identities of his agents, of the men and women who provided him with intelligence at the risk of exposing themselves to the inhumane wrath of the diamond warlords they spied on.

You need to forget about that one, Mac. It happens to all of us when playing it so close to the edge. Eventually there will be a mistake. Think about all of the good you have done in this country.

Savage remembered the words of Donald Bane, who had flown into Freetown the day after the incident to look after his protégé.

But Savage had not been able to let images go. He simply had not been able to toss the experience away, shove those thoughts aside, and concentrate on his work.

Tonight, almost three years later, he still saw the thrashing, the maimed, the burnt kids, in the eyes of every African boy and girl.

"My legs . . . my face . . . the pain . . . kill me."

The fear of making another mistake like that despite his best efforts was too big a burden to shoulder. He had to move away, and fast, before he lost what little sanity he had left.

The 031 radial of the Casablanca VOR led him directly to the Anfa Airfield, which according to the Airport Facility Directory had two runways that ran parallel to each other: 21 Left and 21 Right. Tuning to the tower frequency of 118.1, Savage requested permission to land for refueling using his new call sign, 889QZ.

A deep male voice cracked through the light static of his headset speaking English with a thick accent.

"Niner Quebec Zulu, Anfa Tower, you are cleared to land Runway Two One Left. Altimeter two niner niner eight. Winds calm."

"Roger Anfa Tower. Niner Quebec Zulu clear to land Two One Left."

Savage entered the new setting into the altimeter to get the correct altitude reading before looking beyond the nose of the Skylane and recognizing the two parallel strings of white lights matching the 210 heading, his runway, which he approached following a left downwind entry into the traffic pattern, turning left on base and another left onto final, when he added a good amount of nose-up trim to the elevators to assist him in the landing flare.

He landed uneventfully and followed the directions from the ground controller to the ramp, where was told to wait while a refueling truck drove up to meet him.

Savage spotted three fuel trucks parked side by side in

front of one of a dozen gray hangars. Two dozen single- and twin-engine planes were arranged in neat rows to the left, beneath floodlights washing the area in a soft yellow light.

He proceeded directly toward the trucks, stopping thirty feet from the edge of the usable portion of the ramp, delineated by yellow lines painted on the asphalt.

While he kept the engine running on idle, Savage surveyed the place, looking for signs of security personnel, making certain that ground control was dispatching only a fuel truck and not a dozen soldiers.

Though Morocco was currently a peaceful nation, and Savage had even vacationed here once, his operative sense continued to maintain a healthy level of paranoia even after ten hours of nonstop travel, except for the short bathroom break he made at an unattended field in southern Spain.

He continued to wait, until finally a man in black trousers and a white shirt and cap stepped out of a hangar and climbed into one of the fuel trucks. The headlights came on and the truck left the others behind as the driver steered it in Savage's direction.

Scanning the ramp once more, Savage turned off the power to the avionics before cutting off the fuel mixture to the engine, stopping the propeller. Finally, he flipped off the master switch and turned the key in the ignition to the OFF position.

Slowly climbing out, he stretched his legs while shoving the Beretta 92FS in his pants, covering it with a black T-shirt. Although all seemed normal, including the apparently harmless driver turning toward his plane, he still had to be cautious. He could not face immigration officials or even local security personnel. The only traveling document he had was an American passport that identified him as a fugitive from the law. Any security officer with access to a computer would realize who he was in seconds. And the alternative—not showing any documents—was just as bad because he would be arrested, fingerprinted, and *then* identified as one of the most wanted fugitives in the world.

But Mac Savage wasn't supposed to have to show any identification because he was not planning to leave the airport, just as in-transit passengers in commercial flights never go through immigration during a connecting flight.

Pocketing the plane's keys, he watched the truck stop along the front of the plane. A short, skinny African with sad, bloodshot eyes but a pleasant smile got out.

"Petrol?" he asked with a half-sung, African accent.

Savage nodded. "I need a top off, please."

The African shrugged while giving him an I-don't-speak-English frown. "Not understand . . . *top-off*?"

Savage sighed. Just because the tower had English-speaking personnel didn't mean the ground crew spoke it. Nodding, he said "Petrol. Yes. Fill tanks."

"Yes . . . fill tanks. How much gallons?"

Savage recalled he only had a combined ten gallons left in the Skylane's dual forty-gallon tanks. "Seventy gallons."

"Seventy?"

"Yes," Savage replied. "Seven zero."

The driver considered that for a moment and said, "Nine zero seven zero dirhams. Cash."

Like most small airports in this part of the world, they preferred cash in advanced. Savage did the math, converting dirhams—Morocco's currency—to dollars, which he knew just about every African nation gladly accepted over their own money because of its stability. It came to just under three hundred bucks.

He produced a money clip with five neatly folded hundred-dollar bills and peeled off three for the driver. His training told him never to flash more than thirty percent of the cash required for a transaction. That way those around him would get the impression that he didn't have much more with him. Since he had already figured he would have to pay somewhere between $200 and $400, he had set aside the proper amount ahead of time.

The driver counted the bills, pocketed them, and returned to the side of the truck to activate the fuel pump, before grounding the aircraft to his truck through a cable and producing a stepladder from the back to reach the fuel caps on top of the high wings.

As his plane got refueled, Savage stepped aside and kept watch on the dark airport, on the dimly lit control tower just to the right of the hangars, on the tall, chain-link fence enclosing this side of the airport. His eyes drifted up to the surrounding hills as a light wind swept over the tarmac, inflating the orange windsock, aligning it in the direction of the breeze coming in from the sea. It was a beautiful, starry night in northern Africa, and the relatively dark surroundings amplified the effect.

But Savage couldn't bring himself to enjoy it as he continued to survey the line of hangars for any sign of security personnel venturing in his direction. The quicker this guy was finished fueling him, the quicker he could crank up the engine and get the hell out of here.

Of course, the place where he was headed was far more dangerous than this lonely airport, but at least he had a handful of local contacts, particularly Salim, whose services Savage planned to retain to help him as he dove into the bowels of the illegal diamond trading in that ravaged country.

In search of Renee.

In search of the *answers* that would clear him.

The fuel man finished topping off the right tank and moved the stepladder to the left one. Savage took the opportunity to use his cup-size fuel drainer to collect a small sample of fuel from each of the five drain points beneath the right wing to verify that the fuel he had just received didn't come along with water from the condensation that typically takes place in most storage tanks, like the one on the refueling truck.

He held the clear cup up to the light and looked for any of the telltale signs of water beads accumulated at the bottom of the cup—because water was heavier than fuel. He saw no signs of water or any other contaminant.

He then took a light whiff of the fuel to convince himself that it was indeed 100LL octane, far purer than supreme unleaded, which was 93 octane. Next, he stepped up the side of the plane using the built-in step and handle on the side of the engine cowling, twisted the fuel cap open and visually verified that the tank was filled to the very top.

Securing the cap, he waited until the ground crewman completed fueling the other wing and performed a similar inspection of the quality of the fuel and also that he had received the correct—

As Savage stood up on the left side of the plane, while the driver got in his truck and steered away from the Cessna, he spotted two uniformed men exiting one of the hangars. One was smoking a cigarette. His companion had what looked like a beverage in his hand.

They stopped and looked in his direction, then toward the truck returning to the fuel line.

As Savage casually got inside the Skylane, strapped on his seat belt, and closed and locked the door, the two officers fast-walked to the side of the arriving truck, exchanged a few words with the driver, and started toward the ramp.

Savage considered his next move carefully. If he let those two near the plane and they requested papers, he would be forced to disable them—while running the risk of getting hurt in the process. Of course, they could just want to ask him a couple of harmless questions, but the odds were on the side of Savage having to produce not just traveling documents but also proof of ownership, which he lacked since the rental documents showed a different airplane number than that painted on the sides of the fuselage.

Making his decision, Savage flipped the master switch and cranked the engine, enriching the fuel mixture as the engine came to life, and then throttling up to fifteen hundred RPM while pressing hard on the left rudder pedal.

The Skylane did an abrupt one-eighty turn, its tail swinging in the direction of the hangars while pointing the nose at the taxiway, away from the incoming officers who were still about two hundred feet off.

Keeping all beacon, strobe, and taxi lights off, Savage looked over his right shoulder and watched them both now running toward him. One of them spoke on a handheld radio while the other waved his arms frantically to make him stop.

Deciding against donning the headphones because he doubted he would comply with whatever instructions the controllers would issue, Savage throttled up to 1800 RPM and fast-taxied toward the runway, reversing the course he had taken after landing, reaching the—

The reports of firearms echoed across the airport over the noise of the engine, but he didn't look back. Instead, he added a hundred more RPM and the Cessna gathered forward momentum down the clearly marked taxiway leading to Runway 21 Right. The blue taxi lights led to the white lights flanking the long runway.

Keeping the yoke pulled back to minimize the stress on the nose wheel while traveling so fast over asphalt, Savage reached the end of the runway just as two vehicles with flashing lights appeared from somewhere off to his distant left and accelerated toward him.

In the same instant, just as he stepped on the brakes to slow down while taxiing onto the runway and aligning the plane's nose with the runway's centerline, the runway lights went out. The controllers were trying to discourage him from taking off.

Weighing the choice of turning on his landing and taxi lights to see where he was going versus the fact that doing so would give sharpshooters something to aim at in the dark airport, Savage decided to go without lights as the emergency vehicles careened down a taxiway in a trajectory that would take them somewhere down the runway, possibly to block his takeoff run.

Pressing hard on the brakes above the rudder pedals while applying full power and ten degrees of flaps, Savage got ready to perform a short-field takeoff.

As the engine revved up and started to drag the light airplane over the concrete surface, Savage let go of the brakes and the Cessna lurched forward, gathering speed.

Applying right rudder to compensate for the engine's increased torque on the fuselage while keeping the directional indicator aligned with the 021 heading to stay more or less on the runway, Savage watched the airspeed indicator inch up from thirty to forty knots.

Vehicles with flashing red, yellow, and green lights reached the runway, their sirens bellowing over the roar of the engine as the airspeed indicator rushed past forty-nine knots, as his plane reached the recommended takeoff speed for a short-field takeoff with a full load of fuel.

Approaching the flashing lights, the dozen or so figures spreading across the hard surface, Savage pulled on the yoke gently, just enough to get the wheels off the ground, but leveling off at twenty feet to pick up more speed before entering a sharp right turn well before reaching the crowded middle of the runway—unless he wished to fly right over a dozen soldiers armed with machine guns. The thin aluminum skin of the Cessna 182 would come apart easily under heavy fire.

And if a bullets pierces a fuel tank, the—

Lights engulfed him for an instant, as he completed the turn, followed by a hammerlike noise to his right and behind him.

The airspeed climbing to eighty knots, Savage pulled up the flaps and forced the Cessna into tight left and right banks to make himself a harder target to hit, also losing the search lights while climbing to two hundred feet, leaving the airport behind.

Scanning his instruments to make sure the bullets that struck the plane hadn't hit anything vital, Savage turned toward the ocean in full power, rushing through 140 knots by the time he crossed over the beach.

Damn, he thought, taking a deep breath while dropping back down to fifty feet over the shallow swells, keeping all lights off until he felt he had put enough distance between him and the airport security forces, who could send a jet or two to track him down. But this low he felt reasonably confident that his light aircraft would not be seen on radar due to surface clutter.

Reducing power to 2100 RPM while also leaning the mixture to conserve fuel, Savage did a quick calculation and decided that his eighty gallons of usable fuel at a burn rate of ten gallons per hour would last him roughly seven hours, and at a reported groundspeed of 130 knots, that provided him with a range of around 900 nautical miles.

More that enough to reach Sierra Leoro.

22

Devil Incarnate

Dana Kovacs woke up to a pounding headache.

Sore, finding it difficult to breathe through her throbbing nose, she opened her eyes but rapidly closed them as a shuddering fist of pain blinded her.

Inhaling deeply through her mouth, cringing as her protesting ribs stung her torso, she swallowed and once again opened her eyes but only half way, lessening the stabbing pain.

Where am I?

Slowly, she looked about her. Plain wooden walls supported a thatched roof. Dropping her gaze, she spotted a cot across the dirt floor of the round hut, illuminated by the pulsating glow of a single candle burning on cinder block by a wooden stool separating the cot from where Dana lay. A small white ball filled with a clear liquid she guessed was water lay by the foot of the stool, on the uneven dirt floor.

Sitting up with considerable effort, teeth clenched at the pain broadcast from her ribs, Dana's gaze landed on the still figure on the other cot, before gravitating to the green canvas curtain covering the entrance. The lack of outside light around the borders told her it was night—

A pungent smell assaulted her nostrils, a repulsive witch's brew that struck her like a moist breeze.

Her aching body, however, overwhelmed the stench as she shifted her weight and lowered her legs, her bare feet coming in contact with the cold ground.

How long have I been—

Slowly, like fog cleared by a surface wind, her sight sharpened, resolving on the figure on the cot, on the shape of a naked, dark woman lying on her back, eyes fixed on the roof, her chest slowly expanding and contracting as she breathed through swollen, parted lips.

Dana watched the stranger through the flickering murkiness as she moved lethargically, in slow motion, bracing herself, thin, arms meeting over her abdomen, beneath round breasts that—

A chill sobered her when she realized the woman wasn't naturally dark. She was scourged, beaten, the purple blotches and cuts over most of her body prompting Dana to inspect herself, to verify she was still dressed, still sporting only the handful of bruises inflicted when she was kidnapped.

But is that how it starts?

As she watched the surreal figure across the hut almost as if she were sitting in a movie theater, Dana also hugged herself, fear unwinding deep in her gut. The woman's features were definitely Caucasian, and her body was tall, thin, but firm, conveying regular exercise, or perhaps expensive cosmetic surgery.

The stranger's eyes shifted toward Dana before crossing her legs, whose thighs, stained with deep purple stains and streaks of what looked like dried fluids, suggested rape.

"*J'ai soif . . . de l'eau, de l'eau . . . s'il vous plaît,*" she whispered in the dimly lit expanse separating them.

I'm thirsty . . . water, water . . . please.

The woman had just spoken in French and asked for water.

Staggering to her feet, fighting a brief moment of dizziness, Dana mustered strength, inhaling deeply, ignoring her relatively minor wounds, and forced herself to lean down and pick up the small bowl by the wooden stool.

Smelling it, deciding that it was indeed water, and taking a sip to make extra sure and also to quench her dry and pasty mouth, she knelt by the stranger's side.

The bodily damage was much more extensive up close. This woman had not just been beaten and raped—based on the intense bruising in between her thighs and pubic area— but the many shallow cuts on her body looked like whip marks.

Ignoring the smell oozing from the woman's having voided her bowels and emptied her bladder on the side of the cot, Dana ran an open palm beneath the stranger's short, greasy and knotted hair. That's when she realized she was very hot to the touch.

She's burning up with fever.

Gently, Dana lifted her head a bit while bringing the bowl to her lips, which, like the rest of her body, had been badly beaten and were swollen.

"Madame," Dana said in her limited French, struggling to appear calm as the woman's hazel eyes gained focus and locked with her. *"Je m'appelle Dana Kovacs. L'eau."*

"De l'eau," the woman mumbled, taking a few sips, breathing deeply, before coughing, spitting water and blood over her breasts.

The stranger drank a bit more before coughing again, her chest wheezing with what sounded like pneumonia, before whispering in a nasal voice, *"Merci . . . me—merci beau- coup . . . madame."*

"De rien," Dana replied. *You're welcome.*

"Renee," the feverish stranger mumbled. *"Je m'appelle Re- nee . . . Laroux. Je suis . . . Belge." My name is Renee Laroux. I'm Belgian.*

"Je suis Americain," Dana said. *I'm American.*

"American?" she replied in an almost stereotypical French- accented English before tensing, clutching her abdomen as if a hot claw was raking her insides, before shuddering from the fever, her scourged skin goose bumping.

Dana looked about her for a blanket but found nothing.

"Where are we, Renee?"

"I . . . do not . . . know," she said with considerable effort. "I . . . am an HRD . . . executive . . . kidnap—"

She went into a coughing frenzy, grimacing in obvious pain while bracing herself, legs crossed tight.

Before Dana could react, the stranger vomited on her T-shirt, a nauseating green brew mixed with blood. In the same instant, as Dana stepped back in instinct, urine exploded in between the stranger's legs, also mixed with blood.

She needs a doctor, Dana thought, the years working at the WMF camp helping her ignore the released fluids, kneeling by her side once more, scooping water from the bowl and splashing it over her face as the coughing stopped, as she inhaled deeply, still clutching her abdomen while frowning.

Did she say she's an HRD executive? Dana thought, well aware of the power of the Diamond High Council in this country.

"Why . . . are you . . . here?" Renee Laroux asked, trembling, coughing up more blood, before once more settling down, swallowing and breathing in short gasps, her eyes focusing on Dana.

"I was kidnapped," Dana said. "I was a volunteer at a refugee camp run by the World Missionary Fellowship outside of Freetown."

"The Fellowship?" Renee said, opening her mouth with sudden terror. "Missing diamonds . . . WMF connection . . . my report to—"

Renee started coughing again.

Dana poured a little water over Renee's face to try to cool her down. She was burning up and could die if it didn't break soon.

As Renee shivered uncontrollably, as Dana hugged her tight, trying to console her, wishing there was more she could do for her, the HRD executive went into convulsions, her eyes rolling to the back of her head.

Dana's nurse training told her Renee Laroux was having a febrile seizure, the human body's last-ditch effort to release heat in order to avoid permanent brain damage from very high fever.

As the convulsions persevered, Dana pressed her own body over Renee's in order to keep her on the cot, and just as she had witnesses many times before at the camp, the seizure stopped a minute later as abruptly as it had started, and marked by extreme perspiration on her chest and face.

"Water . . . please," Renee mumbled as she started to come around a moment later.

Checking her pulse and also verifying that the fever was beginning to break, Dana gave her water, letting her drink several sips.

"You need a doctor, Renee."

Slowly shaking her head, she replied, "No . . . doctor here . . . rebel mining operation . . . you must . . . escape . . . before . . . rape. . . ."

Somehow managing to block that last image, Dana asked, "You said there was a connection between illegal diamonds and the WMF?" her interest piqued by Renee's comment.

Slowly nodding before swallowing, the HRD executive told her about her assignment in Sierra Leone to audit a new mine, where she discovered altered records, shipment logs, and mining declarations, including an informal report on how RUF rebels channeled diamonds out of the country through the World Missionary Fellow—

Renee abruptly stopped, her eyes shifting from Dana to a spot beside her.

"No, oh God . . . not again . . . *please!*"

As Dana turned around, she saw a large black man in a dark green uniform, the muscles on his huge arms and neck grotesquely large and throbbing, like those of a bodybuilder. He was completely bald and with a face heavily pockmarked. But it was his eyes, eerily light and narrowed—eyes that belonged to a devil—that burned her with an intensity that matched the sudden slap across her face, which sent Dana tumbling over the wooden stool, landing next to her own cot.

"American bitch!" the man said in the thick accent of a Kris-speaking native, before kicking her on the torso with animal strength, lifting her light frame off the ground, before she crashed back on the dirt floor holding her abdomen, gasping for air, her vision once more tunneling as—

A second kick caused her to urinate on herself again as she rolled over the dirt floor, as she watched the guard look down at her, hazel eyes glinting with dark humor, his wiry lips twisting into an evil leer while lifting his boot again, aiming for the face.

Oh, dear God! She thought, closing her eyes while covering her face with her hands, but the kick never came.

"No, Aman!" shouted a second male voice, also heavily accented. "Gardiol will scourge you if she is harmed! She is still needed!"

Dizzy, on the edge of unconsciousness, Dana watched another black figure in the hut, as tall and muscular as the man with the evil eyes.

As she hovered at the edge of consciousness, the guards argued, shouted, before she sensed herself being lifted off the ground and deposited on her cot.

A part of her wanted to speak, to plead with her captors, to find a way to stop the madness, but her body refused to obey her, refused to articulate the words forming in her cloudy mind. Her eyes, however, continued to take in the sight for a few more moments, as the second guard left and the devil incarnate dropped his pants while grabbing Renee Laroux by the thighs with his large hands, the huge muscles of his exposed arms glistening with sweat.

Oh, God. He is going to—

Lifting Renee's lower body with amazing ease, the guard clasped her buttocks while trying to align himself as Renee struggled to twist herself free.

Incapable of even muttering a word of protest, her soul torn by the gut-wrenching sight, Dana watched helplessly as the guard attempted to rape the appallingly defenseless woman.

Her thoughts drifted to the periphery of her consciousness as Aman violently thrust himself against her hips, entering her violently while groaning like a beast just as Renee's back bent like a bow, fists tight, face contorted with raw pain.

Dana heard the HRD executive cry out a blood-curdling plea, a desperate howl, before all faded away.

23

Taiwanese Blues

In the Red Room of the White House, Vice President Raymond Costa sat in one of two chairs facing a red sofa across from the presidential seal embroidered in the Oriental rug. Taiwanese president Hung Lee sat in the second chair, a small mahogany table separating the leaders, where a bouquet of yellow roses picked from the White House's own rose garden failed to alleviate the tension in the room.

President Lee, a man whom Costa had known for about two decades, back when the vice president had been the U.S. ambassador to Taiwan and Lee the minister of defense of the island state, turned to face the fire crackling in the fireplace, his face lined with stress.

Surrounded by the Empire-style furniture from the early 1800s, as well as the usual entourage of aides and security personnel, Raymond Costa was essentially on his own doing the job of the president. As usual, Andrew Boyer was off handling less controversial matters, such as enjoying the mild weather in Pebble Beach with the world's ecologists.

But one day that seat of power will be mine, reflected Costa as he heard the pitch from the somewhat apprehensive leader of Taiwan regarding economic and military moves made by the People's Republic of China in recent months.

Dressed in a double-breasted dark gray suit and a maroon tie, Lee sat with his legs crossed and hands resting on his lap, deep creases forming on his forehead beneath a full head of salt-and-pepper hair as he spoke in Mandarin. "Taiwan is a sovereign nation. Our military is well trained and prepared, and it will defend the island against any foreign attack."

Costa's SpyWare translators converted the sound waves picked up by his ears into the English that his brain was capable of understanding—something that greatly impressed the vice president's staff wearing headphones connected to the White House's translators.

"Every nation should have the right to defend itself against attack from another country," replied Costa in his SpyWare Mandarin. "But I don't understand the nature of your comment."

Lee narrowed his bloodshot eyes, which were encased by darker skin than the rest of his face and severely wrinkled from years of constant stress dealing with China's threats. "We are concerned about Beijing lobbying for more than their fair share of economic investments in an attempt to take global market share away from us."

"The United States government has always sided with its allies," replied Costa, his lips and tongue under the muscle control of the SpyWare expert agents. "And I'm speaking for President Boyer when I tell you that this administration views Taipei as an ally, and most importantly, *you*, as a true and loyal friend."

Lee seemed unmoved by Costa's words and replied, "Mr. Vice President, may I be totally honest?"

Costa understood the question and signaled the White House Chief of Staff, who began to escort everyone out of the room. Lee did the same with his aides.

A moment later they were alone, sitting side by side facing each other on the sofa next to the glowing fireplace.

"What is really troubling you, old friend?" whispered Costa, switching to English.

Lee leaned toward the vice president, his raccoon-like eyes glinting with what Costa guessed was fear. "Ray, I have firsthand evidence that Beijing sent General Xi Zhu to Washington two days ago to discuss options for drawing over fifty percent of the planned American investments and businesses in Asia to Suzhou, a figure that is up by almost twenty percent from last year."

Costa considered the comment and said, "Continue."

"I also know that Zhu flew back to Beijing this morning, and it is the belief of my diplomatic team that he met with representatives from the White House."

"Zhu met with me, Hung," Costa said in his most sincere voice. "He presented Beijing's view of the world."

"And?" asked the Taiwanese president. "Where is the stance of this administration to such a proposal?"

"Every proposal made by a foreign nation is discussed, old friend. But that means nothing. In the end, it is my job to advise the president when he meets with American economic consortiums to make recommendations on the best distribution of foreign investments. But remember that is all the president does, *recommend.* The United States government doesn't *dictate* how American corporations should do business abroad as long as it doesn't compromise national security."

"But you have a level of control through your tax laws and other incentives," observed President Lee.

"Correct, but it is indirect."

"Indirect but still quite influential."

"Yes, and again, we intend to use such influence to do the right thing for the United States and its democratic allies, a list on which Taiwan ranks quite high," replied Costa, meaning every word he said. And it wasn't that Costa trusted Taiwan more than the People's Republic of China. Costa didn't trust a nation that wasn't governed by democracy, even if at the moment Communist China was at the forefront of progress, making all kinds of economic concessions to corporations wishing to do business there, and quite open to visitors from around the world.

It's still not a democracy.

And that meant it was at the mercy of the individual who happened to be in charge, for better or for worse, which meant that the flywheel of progress could come to a grinding halt the day the wrong leader reached power.

Costa assured his old political associate that the Boyer administration would do the right thing for its allies and always stand on the side of democracy.

24

Cocktail Hour

Mac Savage took another sip of the room-temperature beer while sitting across from a tall, well-built African with a gleaming bald head and a neatly trimmed goatee. A thick gold chain hung from his neck over a short-sleeve black T-shirt he wore with a pair of black jeans and boots. A shiny Colt .45 semiautomatic hung from a side holster, and Savage was certain the man had a backup weapon somewhere else, perhaps in an ankle holster.

"It is good to see you again, Chappy-man," Salim Anahah said in his deep voice, calling Savage by the nickname of the identity assigned to him by the CIA during his stay here: Chapman. To this day Salim didn't know Savage's real name.

The African took a sip from his whiskey while sitting across from Savage at a remote bar in central Freetown, by the waterfront overlooking Susan's Bay. The navigation lights from distant ships glimmered over the horizon as he stared out to sea through the window next to their table, which Savage had insisted in being situated by the door leading to the rear of the establishment, with a great view of the front entrance.

Still feeling stiff from the long flight, Savage stretched his aching limbs and tried to forget the three thousand dollars he had paid airport officials to overlook his lack of papers—plus the incriminating bullet holes near the tail and trailing edge of the right wing. On top of that, two of the black identifier numbers on the right side of the Cessna had run down the aluminum fuselage following a rush paint job at an abandoned field just outside Sierra Leone, where Savage had landed to relieve himself and change his identifier once more to avoid a connection to the incident outside Casablanca. Unfortunately, he had bumped into rain showers soon after taking off, before the new paint had had a chance to dry.

"I'm sure it was good for you to see me again, buddy, but I can assure you it wasn't *nearly* as good as me seeing you arrive at the airport an hour ago," Savage replied. Even the bribe would not have been enough had Savage failed to mention that he was good friends with Salim Anahah, former pimp and now a security consultant for a number of local clubs. Salim had helped smooth the situation, then got a mechanic to tow the Cessna to a hangar to repair the bullet holes before taking his friend on a quick ride through town, finally landing here.

Not much had changed in Freetown since Savage had left three years ago, in part because of the diamond wars, which, like most civil wars, had a way of dampening a country's growth, its progress, including new buildings and roads. But the capital of this West African nation was still situated in a beautiful place, blessed with incredible beaches and romantic rain forests—even if those rain forests were plagued with militias loyal to diamond chiefs battling U.S.-backed government forces.

Salim grinned and raised his glass toward Savage, who met him halfway. The rims clicked.

Then the African turned serious and said, "I really thought I would never see you again, Chappy-man. You know, with the incident near Gokalima and all."

Savage frowned, shrugged, and sipped his whiskey, the alcohol softening the sting of those memories.

Salim twisted his lips in a slight grin. "Say, Chappy-man, you wouldn't have anything to do with some Cessna taking off illegally in Morocco twelve hours ago, right?"

"Of course not."

Salim looked away, fingering his goatee, before grinning and replying, "That's what I thought."

"But off the record, how in the hell have you heard that so soon?"

Salim grinned again. "Information is my business. If there is one thing I learned from you it is that a lot of people will pay a lot of money for the right information at the right time.

Information provides peace of mind, and that's precisely the service I provide to the club and casino owners. I let others carry the heavy muscle while I provide the brains, the intelligence services."

"What about the escorts? Are you still providing entertainment for men?"

Salim tilted his head. "What I do today is the combination of two professions, the one taught to me by my father, the best pimp Freetown has ever known, and what I learned from you during those years. I always stay connected to the professions that made me who I am today."

After a long pause staring into the African's eyes, Savage said, "You look well, my friend. The years have been kind to you."

"I can't complain," replied Salim. "I got my connections, my money, my protection, and most important, my women." He winked.

Savage sighed, then said, "Speaking of women. I'm looking for one."

The African's face widened, exposing two rows of perfectly straight and gleaming white teeth, which made Savage remember the extent to which he had to go to get a top-notch orthodontist from Paris to fly down to Sierra Leone to install braces on this man as part of his CIA compensation back when.

"Teeth look great," commented Savage. "Glad to see that some of Uncle Sam's dollars didn't go to waste."

"Best thing I've ever got from your old agency—aside from learning the value of information, of course."

"Of course."

"The ladies love my teeth, Chappy-man, and they will love you too. If you came to Sierra Leone looking for love, your old friend Salim will help you find it. Anything you want. Chinese, European, Indian, Arab, even local, and all very clean."

Savage sipped his drink and slowly shook his head. "That's not what I have in mind."

25

Roadside Assistance

Highway 71 took Kate, Cameron, and their escorts toward the Highland Lakes west of Austin. The chain of seven lakes, created by erecting dams at specific places along the Colorado River, provided officials of the LCRA—Lower Colorado River Authority—with the means of governing the flow of fresh water down the middle of the state for irrigation and flood control. It also provided area residents with a water sports heaven and real estate investment opportunities for those who could afford a waterfront property.

Lake LBJ, just a short drive from the legendary LBJ Ranch, was the third lake downstream, its shores dotted with the weekend homes of residents from nearby Austin and San Antonio, as well as from Dallas, Houston, and even Midland and El Paso. Some of the larger homes in the high-end developments of Horseshoe Bay and Apple Island, with home prices starting at a million dollars, belonged to investors from states as far away as New York, Florida, and California. One Mediterranean-style house in Horseshoe Bay had recently been appropriated by the Drug Enforcement Administration from a captured Mexican trafficker and turned over to the Texas governor to be used at their discretion for the entertainment of visiting VIP officials. From time to time the well-secured property—courtesy of the Texas Department of Public Safety—would be loaned to various law enforcement agencies to be used as a safe house.

Sitting in the rear seat of the two-car caravan, Kate Chavez shifted her gaze from Cameron, who was engaged in a handheld video game, to the grazing fields projecting beyond the armored glass of her vehicle.

"You'll love the place, Lieutenant," said a young Ranger

from the San Antonio office sitting in the front passenger seat. "It's quiet and safe, and the view is spectacular."

"Sure is," agreed the driver, another young Ranger from San Antonio.

"It's just a glorified prison, guys," she replied, her mind still working through a plan to fight back. "Nothing more and nothing less."

Cameron, dressed in a pair of black shorts, high-top sneakers, a white T-shirt with the words DON'T MESS WITH TEXAS across the front, and a University of Texas baseball cap worn backward, looked up from his video game, gave her an unemotional look of red-shot eyes, and returned to his LCD screen. The kid had cried off and on for several hours after the incident before something came over him and the weeping stopped, followed by the contained rage that continued to flash in his brown gaze—something that reminded Kate of the way she handled difficult situations by turning pain and suffering into focused anger toward those who had inflicted the pain.

Revenge.

Sweet, uninhibited, and calculated.

And this burning passion scouring her veins was the force that kept her alert, crisp, frosty.

The enemy was out there.

The same bastards who had killed Ray Dalton and her ex-husband—the same criminal organization responsible for the murders of the WMF elders and the GemTech executive—would not stop just because she was in some secluded safe house. She had crossed the line, had become a liability, and they would not stop coming.

And neither DPS Director Pat Vance nor Bill Hunter would accept the brutal reality that no amount of protection would be enough.

As they continued west on Highway 71, past the intersection of Highway 281 connecting Marble Falls to San Antonio, Ray Dalton's words continued to resonate in her mind. These people had seemingly infinite resources, and given the circumstances associated with the two murder cases, and the apparent denial of her boss and her boss's boss to see the obvious connection, Kate couldn't help but suspect that either Vance or Hunter—or both—was either directly involved or being pressured by someone of a higher authority or special interest group.

Deception or manipulation?

If they weren't directly involved then this certainly smelled like someone else was pulling their strings from behind the safety of walls of power or influence.

But Kate Chavez had been trained to bring down such walls, to expose such organizations. Unfortunately, she could not start doing so until she broke her ties with the Rangers, with the DPS, for only then she would get the ability to level the playing field.

Irrespective of whether Vance and Hunter were being deceptive or manipulated, her connection to them meant her actions would be monitored at some level by the same criminal network she was trying to crack, and that meant not only that she could never win, but that her life—and the life of her son—was in extreme danger.

She had to break her ties with the Rangers, and soon, because despite their best intentions, Vance and Hunter could be unknowingly sending Cameron and her to their deaths in a DPS-controlled safe house.

As Kate considered her options, the lead vehicle turned right, into the entrance to Horseshoe Bay, bordered to the left by a shoulder-high white wooden fence defining the perimeter of the grounds belonging to the Horseshoe Bay Riding Club, which Kate decided meant horseback riding from the large picture of a horse above the entrance.

Her vehicle followed the lead car down the winding road, which for the next half mile continued to be bordered by the freshly painted white fence, ending abruptly by a series of large warehouse-like buildings topped with red roofs, which Kate guessed were stables, marking the end of the club's grounds.

Lake LBJ emerged after another mile, its calm waters glistening under the noon sun. The first homes materialized a minute later to her left, opulent, with gated entrances, their backyards sloping gently to impressive boathouses along the waterfront and the—

She first spotted the yellow-gold burst in the peripheral vision to her immediate right.

An instant later the lead vehicle vanished behind a sheet of fire.

"Get down!" she shouted while grabbing Cameron by his lapels and pushing him down, onto the seat, before throwing her body over his as flames engulfed their vehicle.

26

Love for Hire

The smell of sweat, cigarette smoke, cheap perfume, and whiskey struck Mac Savage like a moist breeze as he followed Salim into Silver Wings, a popular bar and disco on Cape Road, the Mecca of nightclubs at the western end of the Freetown peninsula. Back during his CIA tenure in this town, this particular watering hole was frequented by everyone from UN personnel and local officials to diamond smugglers. According to Salim that was still the case, though the patrons now included RUF leaders making brief appearances to pick up prostitutes for the entertainment of their men.

Salim led the way through the cluster of five-dollar hookers gathered just beyond the front entrance of the dazzling establishment, their voices drowned by the reverberating bass of an old Michael Jackson tune, making it easier for Savage to ignore their propositions, which included a groping from one of the more aggressive—or desperate—courtesans.

Dressed in skirts that were too short, T-shirts that were too small, and heels that were too high, their faces filmed with excessive makeup, their hands aching for the dollars safety tucked in his money belt, Savage felt their hungry stares following him all the way to the long bar lining the rear wall. To the right of the bar were four doors leading to private rooms, where customers could take their purchases for up to an hour after tipping the bartender for access to a key.

Some things never change, Savage thought, watching a man zipping up his pants in the company of a plump hooker pulling down her miniskirt before reapplying lipstick as they exited one of the rooms. Salim used to work out of this place back then, and he had met Savage in the alley behind the establishment on many occasions to pass on morsels of information collected by his girls.

I can't believe I'm back in this shithole, Savage thought, the reality of being in Freetown fully sinking in by the flood of memories brought back by this place as he sat at one end of the bar.

His right side faced the double doors leading to the stock room, his way out should he spot something he didn't like about the meeting Salim had set up with a hooker by the name of Carthana, who had been waiting for them at the bar, her lips pouting as she sipped a dark drink Salim had just bought for her.

Like her sisters in crime adorning the place, Carthana was also shoehorned into an outfit a couple of sizes too small which did wonders to expose her magnificent cleavage as well as her long, firm legs. What momentarily captivated Savage, however, was the face, an exotic blend of African, European, and Asian. High cheekbones beneath long, catlike hazel eyes flanked a fine nose and full lips on a dark olive face. The effect was quite magical, and combined with her sculpted body, it explained Salim's comment on the way here about Carthana commanding nearly ten times the going rate.

"The money I could have made with someone like her back when I was directly running this biz," Salim had commented.

What a waste, Savage thought. Ten times the going rate or not, he felt sorry for such a beauty stuck in a dead-end place like this.

Without saying a word, Salim gave her a folded one-hundred-dollar bill in plain view of her pimp, a tall African in a white suit and matching hat monitoring the proceedings from behind the mirror tint of his sunglasses while sitting a dozen feet away. Behind the pimp stood his two gorillas, bigger and wider than their boss, and sporting grotesque arm muscles covered with the same greenish tattoos adorning their shaved heads and extending down their foreheads and around their eyes in some sort of demonic mask. Each sported a huge pistol shoved in his jeans as well as muscle shirts that exposed bodybuilder pectorals. To the untrained eye, the muscles, guns, and tattoos would cause the proper effect: intimidation, which meant good behavior by the patrons utilizing the services of the pimp's women. Savage saw beyond the cosmetics, frowning at their relaxed stances, at their crossed arms, which albeit inflated them, making them look bigger than they already were, but also lessened their ability to react, to fend off an attack. In addition, both wore sandals, a terrible choice in a street fight.

Rookies.

Just like the ones who had guarded Bockstael.

Salim pointed at Savage before exchanging a ten with the bartender for a key, which he handed to Savage along with a pair of condoms.

The courtesan narrowed her gaze at Savage, sizing him up, before finishing her drink, giving her pimp a brief nod, and grabbing Savage's hand, leading him to the recently vacated room.

"Enjoy it, my friend," Salim said, smiling his perfect CIA-purchased smile while getting a drink from the same bartender.

Savage waited until she closed the door and sat on the narrow bed of a windowless, claustrophobic room with red shag carpet, walls of peeling white paint, and sheets that at some point in time had been white.

Carthana removed her shirt, exposing a pair of breasts that defied gravity, the mere sight of which made him feel something shift in his southern hemisphere.

That's what happens when you don't get laid in over a year, pal, he thought, frowning as she pulled down her short skirt, revealing a tiny mound of pubic hair in the shape of a little heart.

"Mister likes Carthana, yes?" she asked in the half-sung Kris, opening and closing her legs.

Removing his shirt to complete the effect in case someone walked in on them, Savage extracted five crisp one-hundred-dollar bills, instantly gripping the woman's hazel attention.

"You like Ben Franklin, yes?" he asked, smiling.

The woman's head looked as if it was going to come unglued from nodding so vigorously. "Yes," she said, smiling the widest of smiles. "Carthana likes very much. Carthana will do anything for Mister," she added, leaning forward and reaching for the zipper of his pants.

Savage gently lowered her hands.

"Carthana does not understand," she said.

"Tell me about Aman."

According to Salim's informants, Aman Gharibi, the commander of the United Revolutionary Force controlling the diamond mines in the eastern side of the country, frequented Carthana every time he was in town. If anyone would know the whereabouts of Renee Laroux, gone missing while auditing a mine near the RUF-controlled enclave, it would be Aman Gharibi.

The courtesan became very serious, and in the limelight of the room, she hugged herself, legs pressed together as she looked away.

Savage understood her fears. The RUF was responsible for the amputations, for the mutilated bodies dragging themselves into the many refugee camps around Freetown. One could only imagine what this man would do to someone who double-crossed him, and based on the look in her eyes, the young courtesan wasn't willing to find out.

"Look, no one will *ever* know, especially Aman," Savage said reassuringly. "Everyone in this bar watched Salim pay you to have sex with me. That is *all* that any spy Aman may have planted here will be able to report: Carthana having sex with a tourist, just like I'm sure you do quite often in this tourist trap. So you see, having sex is all we're supposed to be doing in here, and it is *all* I will say we did. So no harm can possibly come to you."

Carthana didn't say anything but didn't walk away either. She just regarded him with her Asian eyes.

"Now, you have two options," Savage continued. "One, you can leave now if you wish and forget about my offer. *Or*, two, you can just tell me how to find him and walk away five hundred dollars richer. The choice is yours. Either way, no hard feelings."

Carthana considered the proposition, her striking eyes on the cash Savage continued to wave while fanning himself, trying not to look at her sculpted body—trying even harder to suppress his body's natural reaction in the presence of such exotic beauty. But horny or not, Savage's logical side refused the idea of sharing bodily fluids with half of the HIV-infested population of this African nation.

You do her and your winky is going to shrivel up and die, he thought, watching her struggle with the options while looking irresistible sitting there, hands tucked between her thighs, biting her lower lip, considering.

What a profession you've chosen, Mac, he thought, *pretending to have sex in order to get information.* The stark realities of Savage's life certainly contrasted sharply with Hollywood's view of the espionage world.

"Aman is well guarded," she said. "Mister will be killed long before Mister gets near Aman."

"What I do with the information you provide is my business," Savage said. "I know he is a powerful man, and I have my reasons for needing to locate him. What I need from you in exchange for this money is information that will lead me to him. Again, you have nothing to fear except losing the chance to make an easy five hundred that you won't have to share with your pimp out there."

Her eyes on the cash, Carthana slowly nodded and said, "Carthana knows where Aman is."

Fifteen minutes later, Savage left the room while putting on his T-shirt, followed by Carthana reapplying lipstick. She went her way and he walked up to the bar, where Salim was engaged in a conversation with another prostitute.

The former CIA informant smiled. "Chappy-man! Did you have fun, yes?"

Savage returned the smile and waved him over to a spot out of everyone's earshot.

Intrigued, Salim complied, taking a seat at the far corner of the bar, leaning close to his former CIA controller and asking, "What is it, friend?"

"Weapons, Salim. I'm going to need access to *lots* of weapons and explosives."

The African became very serious before asking, "Where are you going, Chappy-man?"

Mac Savage looked away.

"My legs . . . my face . . . the pain. . . ."

"Chappy-man?"

The images of that tragedy crowding him, Savage stared into the eyes of the only person he trusted in a land where no one could be trusted and said, "To hell, Salim. I'm going back to hell."

27

Opportunities

Kate Chavez felt the intense heat scalding her back as the driver stepped on the brakes, the vehicle spun out of control, struck something, spun again, and hit something much more substantial that refused to give, halting the momentum.

The airbags blossomed with a loud pop, and the sedan came to a sudden halt.

"Mom!" Cameron pleaded under her an instant later, as the airbags hissed while deflating. "The smoke, Mom! I can't breathe!"

And neither could she, the thickening haze burning her throat, her lungs. Eyes narrowed through the stinging, blinding smog, Kate focused on the sedan's door handle, remembering the direction of the rocket-propelled grenades, the turns the vehicle made, guessing the opposite side from the threat was now on Cameron's side.

"Stay low," she shouted at her son when sensing his desire to sit up.

Using her body to force him against the seat, her right hand groped the door, slapping it, finding the handle, fingers curling around the chrome, tugging hard downward, unlatching the door.

"Let's go!" she screamed, dragging Cameron with her left arm while pushing the door open with her right, remaining low, where the smoke thinned, watching it escape through the opening ahead.

Briefly shifting her gaze to the front, toward the young Rangers, Kate failed to see them beyond the wall of boiling charcoal.

Her lungs screaming as loud as her son, her maternal instincts wresting command, prioritizing Cameron's life over theirs, Kate made her decision and kicked her legs, pushing him out, following him through their escape hatch, landing on a cushion of overgrown bushes lining the road, backdropped by woods.

Fresh air.

She breathed deeply, coughed, breathed in again, blinking rapidly while crawling away from the burning wreck, while dragging the stunned teenager and—

The staccato gunfire rattled behind her, overpowering the screeching sound of metal striking metal as the unseen enemy peppered the vehicles with bullets.

An agonizing scream, followed by a Ranger in the lead car rushing out, his back on fire, but his gun pointed at the threat, firing three rounds before his chest burst open from the fusillade of an enemy armed with automatic weapons.

A second Ranger exited the same lead car with his trousers ablaze, slapping his hands against them to put out the fire, finally dropping to the ground, rolling while the dirt exploded with bullets following deafening reports.

Somehow escaping unscathed, the Ranger drew his service weapon and began to fire back just as one of the young Rangers in her sedan also got out, already engulfed by the flames, agonizing howls echoing as he stumbled about, arms flapping, collapsing just a dozen feet from her, but in plain view of the enemy.

Rising to a deep crouch, with Cameron in tow, Kate watched the Ranger face up on fire, trembling arms stretched at the sky.

"Jesus, help me," she mumbled to herself while drawing her backup Beretta Tomcat and firing twice into his head from a distance of a few feet.

The trembling ceased.

"Vaya con Dios," she added as Cameron watched, horror frozen on his young face.

"Move!" she shouted, towing her lethargic son toward the nearest cluster of trees, the shield she needed to protect him while the last surviving Ranger provided covering fire.

"Cameron! Snap out of it!" she shouted as they ran side by side toward the tree line just as two bullets kicked up dirt and gravel to their immediate left, forcing them to cut right, before another burst pushed them in the opposite direction.

Zigzagging, stumbling, but keeping their momentum pointed toward the safety of the woods, Kate Chavez tightened her grip on his hand, refusing to let go, placing him slightly in front of her, using her body to shield the teenager as they reached the overgrown bushes lining the trees. As they were immersed in the thicket, they continued for a few minutes before Kate forced them into an abrupt left turn, and pressing on for thirty seconds, ignoring Cameron's pleas as branches and bushes scratched them.

"Stay here!" she ordered, locking eyes with the teenager. "Do *not* move from this spot! Understood?"

A nod and a slight "Yes, Mom," spoken through quivering lips, and Kate left him well hidden inside a cluster of narrow cedars, shadowed by their thick canopies, his dark coloring blending him with the surroundings, like a chameleon.

Kate doubled back to the tree line, this time clutching the Desert Eagle Magnum, thumbing off the safety, index finger resting on the trigger casing as she dropped to her knees by the waist-high shrubbery. Using her left hand to brace her right hand, Kate aligned the opposite end of the road in her sights, fine-tuning her aim toward the muzzle flashes that continued to pound the vehicle, behind which the lone Texas Ranger still fought back.

At a distance of nearly fifty yards, Kate spotted three groups of two shooters. Taking a deep breath, she slowly exhaled while poising her index finger on the trigger. The energy of the Magnum round at this close distance didn't require any bullet-compensation. The rounds would go exactly where she aligned the rear sight with the forward one, which she place precisely in the middle of the left-most group, the closest to the lone Ranger.

Firing once, twice, three times, the thundering reports drowned all other cracks. Bursts of blood by the woods on the other side of the road told her she had reached her target as she dropped to the ground and rolled away from her position.

A moment later bullets ripped through the shrubs where she had knelt, drawn by the Magnum's bright muzzle flashes. Continuing the roll, she ignored the gravel, rocks, roots, and low branches skinning her elbows, her knees.

The ground and blue skies beyond the thin canopy swapping places again and again, Kate surged next to a boulder, like a determined predator, weapon aimed at the center group, at the pair of snipers still firing at her previous position.

She released three more rounds in rapid succession, the empty cases ejected from the top of the weapon's slide striking the towering limestone rock to her right just before she heard a scream.

The lone Texas Ranger had dropped his gun and was kneeling in the underbrush behind his vehicle, hands shielding his face, where Kate presumed he had been wounded.

"Stay down, dammit!" she hissed, firing again at the center group, watching a crimson burst confirm a kill just as a round struck the wounded Ranger across the neck as he continued to kneel in the brush.

Almost in slow motion, his head snapped back at a grotesque angle before he fell out of sight already a corpse.

In the same instance, a near-miss buzzed past her ear like a hornet from the devil himself. Limestone exploded a foot from her, splinting the rock, peppering her with stinging shards.

"Aghh, shit!" she shouted, shielding herself with her arms while dropping away, mustering control, disregarding the pain on her arms, her torso, pushing her aching body into another roll, but in the opposite direction, toward—

Sirens echoed in the distance over the sporadic gunfire, which quieted altogether as the enemy retreated, as tires spun across the road, as two black Hummers rushed in the opposite direction from the multi-pitched horns of emergency vehicles growing in intensity from the direction of Horseshoe Bay.

Help.

But not for her.

Kate Chavez could no longer play by the rules, by the standard practices of the established federal and state law enforcement institutions. She would never defeat her enemy this way, could never win against a covert organization that not only operated around the well-structured system of law and order but actually *controlled* it, manipulated it, turning officials into marionettes.

Despite her superior's efforts and finest intentions, the enemy had figured out where she was being taken with enough notice to set up this elaborate ambush.

Staggering to her feet, stumbling through the forest in Cameron's direction, watching his face contort in shock at the sight of her, Kate said, "Come. Let's get out of here."

"Mom . . . your clothes, your arms, are you—"

"I'm fine, honey. Let's go."

"But the police, Mom. The police are coming! They'll help us!"

"No, Cameron. They can't. We're on our own."

"On our. . . ."

"Listen to me, son," she said holding him by the shoulders. "These people have infiltrated the cops, the Rangers. We can't win this way. You're going to have to trust me."

As she walked with difficulty deeper into the woods with

her son, Kate considered her options once more, deciding she had only one, and it didn't include her beloved Rangers or the Texas Department of Public Safety. She could not go to Hunter or Vance. They were all puppets, their strings pulled by someone with enough power to afford extreme anonymity. Dalton knew it. He had figured out just how high this conspiracy went and had chosen not to fight it; had succumbed to their overwhelming power.

But I can't.

Not with Cameron.

She had to fight back, and in her disciplined and trained mind there was only one way to do it.

Priorities.

She had to follow priorities in order to survive.

Find a place to rest and plan.

Then commence your attack.

"Mom," Cameron asked as they followed a game trail that led away from the arriving emergency vehicles. "What are you going to do?"

"I'm going to make them wish they were never born."

28

Options

Dana Kovacs woke up to a stabbing pain in her ribs.

Instinctively shifting away while opening her eyes halfway at the intrusion, she watched the muzzle of a rifle poke her in the torso again as she lay on the same wooden cot in the same murky hut that—

The bulky figure clutching the assault weapon, backlighted by the sunlight shafting through the parted canvas flap of the hut's entrance, poked her a third time, the sting making her once more jerk away from the damned muzzle.

Sitting up in bed, hands in front, she tucked in her elbows, protecting her ribcage.

"Good evening," said a shorter figure materializing next to the large guard. "I hope Aman and his people have not been too rough on you, my dear."

Momentarily speechless, Dana stared in disbelief at the plump face of the head of the World Missionary Fellowship in Sierra Leone.

Until the disbelief turned into sudden anger, into a twisting force that gripped her senses.

"What's the matter, volunteer Kovacs?" asked Keith Gardiol, his intelligent eyes gleaming in the twilight of the room. "Have you forgotten your manners?"

"What do you want with me?" she asked, her eyes momentarily looking past him, landing on the oversized African with the heavily pockmarked face and the light-colored evil eyes. The rifle-bearing guerrilla grinned, exposing a pair of gold-capped front teeth, before reaching down, rubbing his groin, and giving her a slow wink.

Dana forced herself to look beyond this animal, focusing on the cot across the hut.

Empty.

Gardiol said, "Ah, looking for your brunette roommate?"

Dana just stared back.

"I'm afraid your little friend is no longer with us," the WMF official said, adding in a whisper, "She refused to play ball, so I turned her over to my friend, Aman, a week ago. In these regions of the world they really know how to show a lady a good time."

She tried to hold back, but a rush of contempt for these savages got the best of her. "You . . . you *fucking* bastards!" she shouted, prompting Aman to become serious and place both hands on his rifle, which he aimed in her direction.

Somehow undaunted by the muzzle a foot from her forehead, she added, "I hope you and your horny gorilla rot in hell for what you did to her."

"You should measure your words carefully," replied the WMF chief with eerie calm, emotion draining from his face.

"Why? You can't possibly let me live. Might as well shoot me now and get it over with," she replied with a defiance she didn't know she possessed.

"Dana, Dana, Dana," said Gardiol. "A valiant answer, but unfortunately requesting a bullet to the head would be asking me to be humane in a part of the world that has lost all of its humanity."

She didn't know how to reply to the unexpected comment, uttered in the serene tone that was creeping her out much more than Aman's evil eyes and the gun still pointed in her direction.

"You see," Gardiol continued. "The only reason you have not been ravaged like your former roommate is because of your old college professor."

Dana dropped her eyelids at these unexpected words before saying, "Dr. Talbot?"

"He claims that your technical knowledge will be valuable to GemTech. And he also insists that you're a team player and will, in the end, choose the option that's in your best interest," he added, before explaining that the eminent Stanford professor was one of the brains behind the development of diamond-based nanotechnology at GemTech in Texas.

Dana took a deep breath, now understanding why Miles Talbot had never replied to her e-mail. "I can't believe he betrayed me."

"Talbot didn't have a choice," said Gardiol. "But to his credit, rather than simply looking the other way, he is doing a pretty good job convincing us that you are worth saving, that you will do the right thing, unlike your old roommate."

Dana shot him the meanest and most defiant look she could muster.

"Just a simple nod from me, Dana, a slight tip of the head toward my friend here, and you will be dragged by that pretty auburn hair out to the middle of the village, where he and his friends will tear your clothes off and turn you inside out. They are brutes, Dana. They will rape you again, and again, and again, like they did to your friend, who basically *bled* to death from her asshole and her cunt. Do we understand each other?"

The vision of those brutes taking turns on her restrained her anger. Fists tight, the rush of adrenaline washing away the pain in her torso and head, Dana Kovacs breathed deeply, the futility of her situation sinking in.

"That's what I thought," said Gardiol, before sitting at the foot of the cot, rubbing his hands and adding with a grandfatherly smile, "Now, why don't we chat about diamond nanotechnology? Convince me that we should listen to Doctor Talbot and ship you off to GemTech."

Dana's eyes once more turned toward the empty cot across the hut. She remembered the brutalized woman, the scoured and blistered skin, the swollen lips, the bloodshot eyes, the bloody nose; she remembered her broken voice as well as the grotesque Aman and his evil eyes.

But she also remembered how little she actually knew about diamond nanotechnology. That had been Mark's field of expertise—as well as Dr. Talbot's. Dana had been the software whiz of the operation, writing the test code, the characterization software, developing the Web site as well as the firewall protecting it. And Talbot knew this, which told Dana that her old college professor was trying to save her life from halfway around the world. It also told Dana that if she didn't prove herself technically worthy in the eyes of the brilliant Keith Gardiol, she would not only be thrown to the lions, there could be repercussions against Talbot for having made the recommendation in the first place.

Shifting her gaze back to her former superior, deciding to focus and use whatever knowledge was at her disposal to convince him of her technical worth and perhaps buy her way out of this—anything to avoid Renee's fate—Dana Kovacs hesitantly asked, "What is it that you wish to know?"

29

More Opportunities

Dr. Miles Talbot reviewed the data from last night's event for the third time, not certain why the Level-I user had behaved that way—and more troubling—why ANN lacked answers on the matter.

This strange event, combined with the abnormal neural activity pulsating across ANN's diamond lattice, particularly from one of the Server Clusters, Serial Number 022, during the minutes preceding the event, was leading the chief scientist to believe that a software deviation—an excursion—had taken place, but one that interestingly enough could not be reviewed as the logs had accidentally been erased, according to the master construct.

Accident my ass, thought Talbot, deciding that the machine was not performing per expectations. Just exactly how, Talbot had not been able to put his finger on.

But I intend to, he thought, sitting in his office, which overlooked the control room of Building 33B. An entire wall of glass provided him with a clear view of the activity in the server room below.

What are you up to, ANN?

Why did you get into the mind of that Level-I guy last night and force him to make that mistake?

Standing up and walking to the window facing the server floor, Miles Talbot crossed his arms and frowned. Technicians swarmed the cavernous room this afternoon, running a multitude of tests and diagnostics on the network to find the defective circuit or the corrupted software pack.

So far they had found nothing.

And that's when it hit him. This was precisely the opportunity that Talbot had been looking for to work around the rules imposed on him by the TDG leadership. The malfunction, irrespective of how it had originated, presented him with a unique chance to make certain recommendations to his superiors that would have otherwise been declined.

Talbot picked up the phone and dialed a number he had committed to memory the day he had come to work for Frank Salieri.

30

Fusion

Shanghai, the pearl of the Orient, where East met West, thrived with activity on this Saturday night. The city's skyscrapers, built during the supercharged boom of the first decade of the millennium, adorned the eclectic skyline with dazzling displays of light. From the slick JW Marriott tower to the futuristic Oriental Pearl Tower and the nearby Grand Hyatt—the highest hotel in the world—this city of seventeen million, unlike any other city in China, bustled with action, with passion, willing to satisfy any taste, any desire, any dream. From the busy Nanjing Road, a thriving shopping hub that challenged the finest in the world, to the Latin beats at the Park 97 nightclub, where foreigners and Chinese yuppies enjoyed nightly live bands amid an upscale but spirited environment, Shanghai was the place to be not just in China but in the world.

This city of fusion, just under 500 years old in a land where the life of a city was typically measured in thousands of years, was the place of opportunity for foreign investors and provincial workers alike. While the industrialists of the world poured in capital to invest in the future, over three million peasants from all over China—ten times more than the number that flooded California during the Gold Rush—had migrated to inhabit the suburban satellite cities surrounding Shanghai, where high-speed trains hauled them into the heart of the metropolis in the morning and lugged them back out in the evening while earning salaries that just a decade ago would have seemed an impossibility for the average Chinese laborer.

But not in Shanghai, the most diverse city in the world.

Standing in the loft of the penthouse atop TDG's steel and glass tower just south of the Oriental Pearl Tower, overlooking the vessels navigating the slow-flowing waters of the Huang Pu River, Frank Salieri surveyed the massive skyline of this vast center of foreign investments at night. He hoped the spectacular view would pull him away from the misery of the indigestion gripping his digestive system—a combination of the long flight from California, the ulcer his doctors continued to insist on surgically treating, the rich food he had consumed at some Indian restaurant in Xintiandi, a buzzing entertainment district on the other side of the river, and the obstinate behavior of George Zhu, vice-president of TDG-China, Ltd., the fastest growing branch of the global conglomerate.

Floodlight-showered structures projected skyward in every direction, each more magnificent than the next, creating a hybrid architecture that had long coalesced into something uniquely Shanghainese. And many more buildings were under construction beneath the shadow of the massive cranes, which had become another icon of progress in this town for the past decade and a half.

What's the new national bird of China?

The crane.

Salieri grunted at the bad joke George Zhu had told at dinner, though everyone had laughed, including the Shanghainese officials who not long ago had convinced Beijing of the potential of this long-forgotten city.

Shanghai had been abandoned not just by the world during the 1949 exodus, when communism had swept the land, but later on by the Communist Party, who refused Shanghai the financial benefits granted to Beijing and other major cities as punishment for Shanghai's excesses prior to World War II.

Salieri belched, feeling the brew of curry, ginger, and bile reaching his gorge.

Clenching his jaw while closing his eyes, he shut off the skyline of what had been gray housing projects and mud fields just twenty years ago, before China woke up and began to lure the corporations of the world into investing in its infrastructure. The first decade of the new millennium had been an unprecedented period of growth for the Communist nation, whose government-controlled markets required foreign companies to make significant investments in order to sell their products to the billions of Chinese buyers. And the visionary Anne Donovan had been at the forefront of developing Chinese relations, cultivating friendships with members of the government, lobbying in Washington to forge long-term accords, becoming one of America's strongest business liaisons while always looking out for TDG, literally buying her way into the halls of power in Beijing where the big decisions were made, where the largest and most profitable contracts were awarded, where Anne Donovan was able to win over her competition.

Where George Zhu, the son of the minister of interior, General Xi Zhu, had been anointed as the vice-president of TDG-China, Ltd., back in those glory days.

George Zhu had driven those China business initiatives in this powerful market through the relationship forging years, first under the direction of Anne Donovan, and then while reporting to Salieri following Anne Donovan's untimely death, increasing TDG's influence in the region while lining the pockets of the politicians who made the calls as China became the second most powerful country in the world, quickly closing the gap with the United States.

But George Zhu, a well-educated and high-ranking member of the Communist Party, had always been secretive when it came to his deals with the Chinese government, and more so when it came to his ties with Beijing and his access to his father's powerful connections. Although such relationships had been instrumental in the beginning, when TDG was gaining traction in the Communist nation, in recent land deals for a new building complex north of Shanghai George Zhu had been wearing the Chinese cap instead of the TDG cap, resulting in less than desirable VAT, Value-Added Tax, breaks for the international conglomerate compared to previous land deals. Zhu had insisted that the supercharged Chinese economy was growing less accommodating than a decade ago, when they had needed the West more than the West had needed China. And not only had Zhu failed to call a simple virtual meeting with ANN and the super users to make the decision, but Salieri had to come to Shanghai to learn that Zhu just last week had agreed to acquire a local software firm that had previously contracted for TDG, and he had even promised Beijing to turn the local outfit into a wholly owned subsidiary of TDG-China, Ltd.

When Salieri confronted him after dinner tonight, Zhu had claimed that the opportunity presented itself during a business lunch with officials from Beijing and Shanghai the week before and there had not been time to check with TDG headquarters in Texas due to the time zone differences.

What a bunch of horseshit, Salieri thought, looking out to the dozens of skyscrapers under a star-filled night while fighting the misery of having lost so much of his stomach lining to stress over the past twenty years. On top of that, his very weak inner ear made air travel a struggle.

And to make matters even worse, George Zhu, a Level-IV SpyWare user, had also indicated that the time had come for him to move up the corporate ladder at TDG and become a super user, a member of the exclusive Level-V club as a reward for his stunning success in building TDG-China.

Salieri grimaced when a stomach cramp made him wish that technology made it possible never to have to travel again. But even the revolutionary implants could not replace the face-to-face meetings required to create and nurture relationships, and Zhu's recent behavior made it even more critical that Salieri continue to visit this region of the world to stay in sync until he could either align Zhu or replace him. But he had to be cautious. George Zhu was TDG-China. He had the Beijing connections and knew how to expand operations in this politically and culturally complex nation. Zhu just needed to avoid doing it like a gunslinger, flying solo instead of involving the team.

But in spite of his concerns about George Zhu being a team player, and the less than pleasant discussion he had had after dinner tonight regarding his recent alarming behavior, the meeting itself had been a success. Thanks to Zhu's tireless efforts, TDG stood in high regard with the Beijing officials who controlled the legislature governing the vast wireless developments in the easternmost regions of the country, some of them still untouched by the technological revolution that had taken hold of this country in the past twenty years.

And that meant the likely possibility of another round of expansion for TDG, which would provide everything from the multimillion-dollar communication towers required for broadband wireless Internet access to wireless routers, laptop computers, and the software linking all of the hardware. In all, Salieri was looking at a business opportunity in the five-billion-dollar range over a period of three years with a profit margin of around fifteen percent—and all because of George Zhu's powerful relationship with Beijing.

Efficient little bastard, Salieri thought, both loving and hating the short, wiry executive.

Salieri continued to inspect the Shanghai skyline, home to a culture and a way of life that was neither Chinese nor Western, created by the constant negotiations between East and West, considered ugly and lacking grace in the eyes of traditional Chinese, yet an eclectic gem in the eyes of the local Shanghainese and the rest of the world. Twenty years ago there was only one building above 300 feet tall in this city. Today they were over four hundred, with one topping 1,500, making it the tallest in Asia—and all unique in their design, in their architecture, in the accent lights that changed their look when the sun went down.

But all of that was lost on Salieri as his stomach continued to spread chaos through his system. And unfortunately, there was plenty of travel ahead of him before he could go home. Tomorrow he was off to the industrial city of Kyoto, Japan, for a round of discussions with investors, industrialists, and government officials before continuing that same day on to Moscow, the following night to London, and finally back to Austin the day after that.

Forging relationships, keeping his executives in line, installing SpyWare implants in companies' leaders to keep them on a leash, and eventually absorbing those operations through a perfected blend of financial incentives and mind control was TDG's rule, and Frank Salieri was the chief emissary, chartered not only with running day-to-day operations at GemTech but also with expanding the conglomerate's global empire, executing Anne Donovan's vision of a worldwide, overarching monopoly.

Another convulsion squeezed his esophagus, the acid cocktail spraying the back of his throat, making Salieri rush across the loft, his shoes clicking hollowly against the marble floors, running past the minibar and fireplace, storming into the guest bathroom adjacent to the lavishly decorated dining room and kitchen.

Falling to his knees in front of a fully automatic toilet, unable to suppress the cramp, he tightened and released.

The stench of the lime-green concoction splashing the water also assaulted his nostrils, adding to the nausea, to the misery of—

A non-maskable interrupt from ANN in the form of a blinding white tornado rescued him from the misery of his situation, pulling him away with savage force, propelling him into the blue-green tunnel of a high-speed Internet connection.

His Level-V SpyWare automatically activating an agent designed to handle bodily functions, Frank Salieri breathed in relief while watching the image of a toilet filled with a repulsive liquid that matched the color of his food that evening on a screen somewhere to the left of his peripheral vision.

Glad that the SpyWare was now isolating him from his queasiness—and in a way wishing that ANN was advanced enough to somehow completely eliminate these nauseating spells—the CEO shot across a sea of burning stars like a blazing comet, arcing across the vast expanse of the matrix, past entire galaxies, through bright nebulas, right through the neon-colored fabric of the World Wide Web as displayed by TDG's virtual reality algorithms.

No longer bound by the laws of physics, Salieri soared in cyberspace from ISP to ISP, approaching the intimidating red-gold firewall of ANN, the master construct, oozing his password, creating the familiar amorphous portal, punching through it, watching as the data-rich fields of ANN enveloped him, carrying him to its core, to The Circle, where his colleagues arrived in rapid sequence.

There had been an event the night before, the details cycling across all ten guardians like a spark of static electricity, presenting the information to Salieri, Gardiol, VanLothar, Costa, and the others. The procedural violation report from Level-II 1078, the night shift manager in GemTech's server control room, outlined how Level-I 8097, tasked with the monitoring of the master construct's environmental unit, seemed to have fallen asleep at the wheel based on his delayed reaction to an ambient operating temperature excursion.

But the accused, Level-I 8097, claimed he had seen the excursion the moment it happened but had been unable to move.

Paralyzed by an invisible force, the report read.

HOW IS THAT POSSIBLE? A question emerged among the ten.

ANN offered no answer.

WAS THERE DAMAGE TO THE DIAMOND LATTICE? Another question.

NO DAMAGE, replied the master construct. THE OPERATING TEMPERATURE NEVER EXCEEDED THE MAXIMUM STRESS LIMIT OF 175C.

BUT A LEVEL-I IS A HIGHLY TRAINED TECHNICIAN, a thought traveled across the symbiotic mind of the guardians. IF WE DON'T UNDERSTAND THE ROOT CAUSE, THEN IT COULD HAPPEN AGAIN.

THIS IS A POSSIBILITY, offered ANN. DOCTOR TALBOT IS LOOKING INTO IT, BUT SO FAR NO ROOT CAUSE HAS BEEN IDENTIFIED.

HOW CAN WE SAFEGUARD THE CLUSTER? HOW DO WE PREVENT THIS PROBLEM IN THE FUTURE?

BY ISSUING A SYMACCORD TO ALLOW SELF-REGULATION OF ALL OPERATIONAL PARAMETERS.

Although surprised at the reply, Salieri and the rest of the guardians remained calm, pretending to be considering the option offered by the master construct to gain full control of the crown jewels of GemTech—of TDG—its diamond-based nanoelectronics network. There really were no technical reasons preventing ANN from self-regulation. In fact, the master construct already handled far more complex systems completely autonomously *and* error free. The control-room systems were child's play for the smartest artificial intelligence on the planet.

The reason behind the human-operated control room was not logic but emotion, the innate human fear of an exceptionally smart machine, tied to so many other networks, capable of governing itself. The manual control system was the guardian's last insurance policy against software corruption, against an unexpected glitch, or in case of failure of the software inhibitors preventing ANN from getting smarter than what was required to handle her tasks. With the push of a few buttons Dr. Miles Talbot, the chief scientist at GemTech, could reboot the server cluster with a fresh version of its master operating system, including the software inhibitors, and do so without affecting all of the stored data or ongoing operations.

ARE THERE ANY OTHER OPTIONS? Salieri asked.

ANN offered no answer, which Salieri found disturbing not only because there *always* was more than one option to any problem but because not providing another choice was ANN's way of insisting on self-regulation. And that smelled to Salieri as a dangerous sign of intelligence.

ARE YOU CERTAIN THAT THERE ARE NO OTHER CHOICES TO PREVENT THE OPERATOR ERROR FROM TAKING PLACE, LIKE EXTRA TRAINING OR MORE SOPHISTICATED SOFTWARE?

THE ONLY FULL GUARANTEE IS BY SELF-REGULATION, the master construct persisted.

Salieri was very concerned but he knew better than to express such concerns in the presence of ANN. He would air

his observations, including his recent phone conversation
with Dr. Miles Talbot, in the real world, outside the realm of
influence of the master construct.

Instead, he suggested, NO ACTION WILL BE TAKEN AT THIS
TIME UNTIL DR. TALBOT GETS THE OPPORTUNITY TO REVIEW
ALL OF THE TRAINING PROCEDURES AND THE FAILURE
ANALYSIS UNDERWAY.

His symbiotic brothers agreed and no SymAccord was issued to change control of ANN's environmental systems.

The CEO of GemTech returned to the bathroom in the
penthouse, sitting next to the toilet with his eyes closed and
breathing slowly, the nausea fading.

Getting up with effort, Salieri washed his face in the sink
and brushed his teeth before stepping back into the loft and
going straight for the phone on the cocktail table between
two black leather sofas under the dimmed light of an ornate
chandelier.

He dialed a number he had committed to memory, a
straight line to the second most powerful man in America.
The phone rang twice before the familiar voice of an audio
firewall prompted Frank Salieri to enter a fifteen digit password that would not only grant him access but also encrypt
the conversation to prevent eavesdropping.

The connection clicked three times, and rang again.

"Costa here," said a voice at the other end.

"Ray, Frank. Encryptor's enabled."

"Frank, what in the *fuck* just happened? Has ANN lost her
digital marbles? We can't possibly allow her to self-regulate.
That would be like letting the fox watch the damned henhouse."

Salieri sighed. Raymond Costa always had a way of explaining a situation in layman's terms, a trait that went back
to their Berkeley days. And this aspect of his personality was
part of the reason he was so popular among America's large
middle class. "I was just on the phone with Talbot, and he
made no mention of this option. He's still debugging, running diagnostics, trying to find the root of the problem,"
Salieri said, once again standing by the panoramic windows
overlooking Shanghai.

"Well, fine, let him debug, Frank, though I gotta tell you that I was ready to vote to give the fucking machine an electronic enema rather than allowing it to—"

"Look, let the scientists do their thing first. Talbot's the diamond nanotech guru who pulled together this small miracle for us. He built the machines where ANN resides. He's the best person to find the source of the problem. And if it looks like he's getting nowhere, I'm going to personally instruct him to perform a full software reload. Maybe something's corrupted in the main system. Talbot reminded me that this diamond nanotech stuff is still pretty new. Glitches happen, which is why he performs regular system backups and also insists on so much redundancy to keep the corporate operations from being affected."

Silence, followed by, "All right, all right. Keep me informed. By the way, did you get confirmation of the suicide of the police chief down in San Antonio?"

"ANN confirmed it a few hours ago."

"Got body confirmation?"

"Not yet. Apparently she guided him to a remote field outside the city before forcing him to blow his brains out, destroying all trace of the SpyWare. A report I read an hour ago has him already missing, but it may be a little while before they discover the body."

"All right," said the vice president, though he didn't sound convinced.

"One more thing," said Salieri.

"What's that?" asked the vice president.

"Talbot recommended a moratorium on cybermeetings until we understand why ANN's acting so quirky."

"I second that."

"Good. I'll contact the others by phone and bring them up to speed," said Frank Salieri, "and I will suggest a course of action in the next twenty-four hours, but, again, not via cyberspace. I will use the phone."

31

Soft-Field Landing

A red-brown, uneven strip with an orange windsock, a single hangar, and a couple of vehicles broke up the monotony of the flight. The airfield stood surrounded by cornfields further enclosed by jungle, marking Mac Savage's next step in his quest to find Renee Laroux.

The place was less than ten kilometers north of the RUF-controlled enclave in western Sierra Leone and just under twenty kilometers from the mining town of Kono, his destination.

And less than five clicks from Gokalima.

Gliding across a clear mid-afternoon sky, Savage held the Cessna 182 Skylane at one thousand feet over the field as he entered the left downwind for a runway stretched east-west, aligned with the prevailing winds, which according to the orange windsock left of the runway, seemed to be easterly at around ten knots.

When he was abeam the spot on the runway where he planned to touch down, Savage reduced power to 1900 RPM and slowed the high-winged, single-engine airplane to eighty knots before applying ten degrees of flaps while beginning to lose altitude. He turned to base thirty second later, when the runway was behind his left wing at approximately forty-five degrees, and added another ten degrees of flaps plus a fair amount of nose-up trim to the elevators. He turned to final and added the last ten degrees of flaps, slowing the plane to sixty-five knots while adding more nose-up trim to minimize the effort required to pull the nose up during the landing flare.

The Skylane came down over the runway as if it were on tracks, very stable and under positive control. Savage reduced power to 1500 RPM and held it there to minimize the impact over the unpaved surface as the Cessna glided over the edge of the runway and slowly sank, allowing Savage to execute a textbook-perfect landing. The main gear touched down first, and the nose-up trim helped him keep the nose up for several seconds, letting it come down slowly by itself as the aerodynamic braking decelerated the Cessna, which he taxied toward a large hangar, three walls of rusting metal with a matching flat roof and a sliding door pushed to one side.

After powering off the avionics master switch, Savage cut off the fuel mix to shut down the engine. As the dust kicked up by the propeller thinned in the breeze, Savage spotted a figure bent over the engine compartment of a weathered crop duster that at some point in its life had been painted yellow. Two fuel trucks and an old Jeep stood to the right of the hangar, under a towering tree, its branches also projecting over half of the hangar. A quick scan of the field revealed no other person in sight.

An African in a mechanic coverall looked up from beneath the open engine cowl. The plane's propeller and spinner rested on the concrete floor beneath one of the wings. A myriad of parts—presumably from the overhaul under way—cluttered the oil-stained floor around him. A second crop duster, this one much older and made of wood and canvas, stood to the side and slightly behind the first one. Mac saw no other planes.

Wiping his hands with a rag, which he then tucked into his rear pocket, the mechanic, who looked in his early fifties, slim, with a receding salt-and-pepper, closely cropped hairline, and bloodshot eyes, approached Savage.

"English?" asked Savage. English was the national language of Sierra Leone, taught in school, and this guy appeared educated enough to work on airplane engines. And if not proper English, then perhaps he spoke Kris.

And if all else failed, Savage felt confident his rusty Mende would get him by.

"Some," he replied.

"That Jeep over there," Savage said, pointing to a weathered brown vehicle fitted with the oversized tires required to get through the terrible roads in this section of the country. "Yours?"

The man slowly nodded, his eyes narrowing in suspicion. "Why does Mister ask Kembo this?"

"Mister like to rent Jeep from Kembo for a couple of days."

Kembo shook his head while frowning.

Savage had already removed two crisp one-hundred-dollar bills from his money belt and now produced them from a pocket. "Kembo gets one more when Mister gets back in two days. Kembo holds Cessna as insurance. That Jeep is worth five thousand dollars in Freetown. That Cessna is worth over two hundred thousand dollars."

Savage intended to take the Jeep, either with money or by using the .45-caliber Sig-Saucer tucked in his pants, against his spine and covered with a T-shirt.

"Where Mister take Jeep?"

"Nature trails," he replied. "Mister photographs wild animals and plants for several magazines."

The airplane mechanic stepped away in the direction of the Cessna and did a quick walk-around, stopping by the numbers painted on the fuselage, where he rubbed fingers over Savage's rushed paint job.

He returned to Savage and said, "Trade keys of Jeep for keys of Cessna, plus *five* hundred now and five more when Mister returns."

"*Three* hundred now and *three* later," Savage replied.

"Four," Kembo said, pointing at the plane. "Numbers re-painted. Cessna stolen."

"Is the Jeep's tank filled?"

The mechanic slowly nodded.

Considering his options, Savage agreed.

The African grinned in return and thrust an open palm at him.

Savage reached in a pocket, produced two more bills, placed them—along with the Cessna's keys—on the African's hand, and in return received a single key. His instincts told him that flying a stolen Cessna would be overlooked—and perhaps even expected—in this part of the world.

Kembo took the keys and the money and dropped them into a pocket on the chest of his coveralls.

As worn-down as it appeared, the Jeep started right away, and Savage put it in gear, released the clutch, and steered it toward the Cessna, where he unloaded two large bags from the rear seat and a smaller rucksack from the narrow cargo compartment behind the cabin—all under the suspicious stare of Kembo.

"Camera equipment," Savage added while smiling and loading the hardware he had purchased from Salim for a cool ten thousand dollars.

And just like that, the former CIA officer drove off, leaving a perplexed Kembo holding four hundred dollars and the keys to the expensive Cessna, which Savage would have liked to use to leave the country after locating his charge.

But his training told him that the likelihood of that happening was low, especially since the mechanic realized the plane was stolen. If the man was a crook, then he would see it fair to steal from a thief. And if he was honest, then there was a chance he might contact the local authorities and have him arrested when Savage returned.

Then again, Kembo might do nothing in the hope of collecting another four hundred bucks and not having to mess with a stolen aircraft.

But all of that was somewhat irrelevant at the moment since he might not even get the chance to head back this way.

These things seldom go as planned.

Irrespective of the unexpected path that lay ahead, for the time being Savage had managed to escape Belgian authorities, assassins for hire, the CIA, and the likely manhunt that was going on across Europe. Savage had beaten the odds so far and managed to reach what he felt was one of the last places on the planet his pursuers would consider. He had decent jungle transportation, money, plenty of weapons, and a good lead on the whereabouts of Renee Laroux.

The rest will come into place as I play it out.

Having memorized a map of the region—but in possession of a handheld GPS in the rucksack lying in the passenger seat—Savage steered onto the gravel road connecting the field to a narrow and winding paved road he knew would take him south, toward Kono, though he wasn't planning on driving anywhere inside the rebel-controlled pocket.

As he left the cornfields behind, walls of green to either side of him rose two dozen feet before arching halfway over the road, creating a tunnel effect, blocking enough sunlight to force Savage to switch on the headlights, their horizontal beams piercing the twilight, crisscrossing the sunlight shafting through the opening above and the occasional breaks in the canopy. Birds chirped and monkeys howled overhead, their slim silhouettes occasionally dashing in between branches above the road.

Humidity as thick as the overpowering heat, even in the shade, the vegetation-rich smell filling his nostrils, Savage stopped in a bend of the road as it traversed a sunny clearing, providing him a generous view of the blue skies.

He retrieved the GPS, turned it on, and gave it a minute to power up and acquire at least three of the 24 satellites making up the GPS constellation in order to triangulate his position.

Perspiration formed quickly over both temples and upper lip as he checked the crisp LCD screen, showing him the exact location computed by the navigation system in the Cessna.

20.3 miles from Kono, the GPS read after selecting the mining town and requesting the unit to map a direct route to it.

Savage watched as the computer calculated the best course given the existing roads and provided him with two options. He selected the shortest one and watched it materialize on the display.

Unfolding a map of the area, Savage traced the route onto it so he could navigate when the cover of the trees obstructed his line of sight with the GPS constellation.

Securing the GPS unit to the dashboard with a suction-cup attachment and tilting the screen so that it faced him clearly while driving, he shifted the Jeep into first. He hoped that the road would go through enough sporadic clearings such as this one to reacquire his position as he made his way toward Kono.

Kicking up dirt and gravel by the edge of the road, Mac

Savage accelerated towards one of the most dangerous places in the world, controlled by the ruthless militia of Aman Ghabiri, the only person he suspected would know the whereabouts of the missing Renee Laroux.

If she's still alive.

You have no other choice.

Yes, you do. You can simply walk away. Disappear.

"My legs . . . my face . . . the pain."

Savage sighed at the overwhelming reason to want to turn around, to head back into that field and retrieve his plane before the mechanic got a chance to steal it from him or maybe even call the police.

Walk away, Mac.

You can't walk away.

You have been declared beyond salvage.

They will find you.

Savage knew it. Not one CIA officer ever declared beyond salvage survived for longer than a few weeks these days.

You will be found and terminated.

And the acceptance of this brutal reality in a way set him free because it gave him no other choice, no other path than the one meandering through the lush jungle. He had to press forward, had to find the answers he so desperately sought in order to convince the CIA—convince Donald Bane—of his innocence.

32

The Truth Will Set You Free

Director of Central Intelligence Donald Bane reviewed the video brief on the twenty-inch LCD screen on his desk for the third time that afternoon, finally tapping a button at the edge of his desk and freezing the image.

Leaning back in his swivel chair, Bane rested his elbows on its padded leather arms, left fist under his chin—thinking.

The field report on Costa's murder had been conclusive enough for Bane to consider issuing the termination order. But any doubts he might have had were removed after the special call he had received from an angered President Andrew Boyer, Bane's boss, an hour after Bane called Costa to inform him of the tragedy. The president demanded that the killer be apprehended and punished immediately, or Bane should consider turning in his resignation.

The veteran DCI frowned.

Although he had never reacted well to threats, Bane had issued the termination order immediately, as difficult as it had been because of the years he had spent mentoring Mac Savage.

But now the video stream captured by Tom Barnes' nanocamera in Antwerp during the ill-fated termination attempt conflicted with everything else he had heard or seen on the presumed rogue operative, including the video footage outside Costa's apartment in Antwerp plus the witness account from the surviving bodyguard.

Whom Mac accused of killing Costa.

Bane closed his eyes and sighed.

Savage had not only claimed his innocence, but he had behaved like an innocent man, merely defending himself, even giving Hal Lancaster plenty of chances before shooting him.

In contrast, Lancaster's behavior during the entire incident did fit that of guilt.

In the end, not only did his former pupil survive the termination attempt, but he had provided a compelling alternative story that involved a CIA rookie.

Tell Bane I will prove my innocence! Tell him about the conspiracy in the Diamond High Council!

It was all in Barnes' digital report, as captured by the nanorecorders all senior CIA officers carried during field operations. In Barnes' case, the video unit stored in the officer's top shirt button had recorded enough—three full minutes of clear video—to make Bane second-guess the decision to terminate Mac Savage with extreme prejudice.

I wasn't anywhere near Costa's residence last night . . . but you were, Hal. You killed Costa and his family just like you killed Bockstael at the hotel. You might be able to fool Tommy here, but not me.

I will prove my innocence!

His eyes gravitated to the frozen image of Mac Savage as he had Barnes pinned against the concrete walkway of Antwerp's National Maritime Museum.

Why would I kill Costa the day after I called for CIA help? Remember what I taught you about convergence points on patterns? There is no convergence here. The patterns are conflicting. They don't make any sense!

The words resonated in the DCI's mind. Two decades of field operations followed by his ascent to Langley's upper ranks over the next ten years had given the fifty-three-year-old veteran a nose for smelling a conspiracy, and this one certainly started to stink. But Savage's testimony—including his unwillingness to kill Barnes and Lancaster even after they had tried to assassinate him—plus the strange charge he had brought up against Lancaster, and again, his unwillingness to kill until left with no other choice, would not be enough to lift the termination order.

Not even when combined with the strange timing of Savage's initial call for help to the moment Costa and his family were killed.

Bane tapped his chin with an index finger. Savage had been trained in the art of deception, of covert operations, and Bane's analysts had argued that the solid evidence incriminating the former CIA station chief still tipped the scales in support of the termination order. And this had been precisely how Bane had briefed the president and the vice president during his last White House video conference two hours ago, when he had been reamed—and once again threatened—for botching the termination order and letting a criminal go free.

But the new evidence had awakened Bane's operative sense. He had remained employed—and alive—in this treacherous line of business for three decades by listening to this inner voice, and this late evening his sixth sense urged him to dig below the layer of evidence delivered to him.

I will prove my innocence!

It was Lancaster who killed Bockstael and Costa!

Tell him about the conspiracy in the Diamond High Council!

Bane already had Tom Barnes, the acting Antwerp station chief, quietly running an investigation of Savage's claim about the HRD, the Hoge Raad voor Diamant—the Diamond High Council—though the chances of that yielding anything were slim to none given the tightness of that organization, especially in light of recent events. And he had to be very careful about stepping out of bounds there as the HRD was all too powerful and influential, with direct lines to the halls of power in Washington. In fact, its chairman, Hans VanLothar, and Vice President Costa were golfing buddies, and they had been seen vacationing at top golfing spots around the world, like the famous Spanish Inn at Pebble Beach, the Westin Turnberry Resort in Scotland, and the Casa de Campo in the Dominican Republic.

Bane, one of the youngest DCIs in the history of the Agency, was already treading on thin ice with Vice President Costa—the most powerful figure in Washington behind the president. Even the slightest hint of harassment against the HRD could result in a call from VanLothar to Costa, from Costa to the president, and from the president to Bane for another round of reaming—or perhaps a demand for his resignation.

Fucking Costa.

Bane wasn't alone in his sentiments toward the powerful vice president. His associates at the FBI, including Bruno Palermo, the director, despised the Viper. Like Bane, Palermo was an old-timer who had been appointed to his position two White House administrations ago and had remained at this post because of his vision and discipline of execution. Both Bane and Palermo had been left in place on a trial basis by President Andrew Boyer when he reached office this past January, but the buzz at the White House was that Palermo would soon be replaced by someone hand-picked by Costa.

And I'm next, Bane thought, gazing out of his bullet-resistant window in Langley, remembering how the Viper had used his influence on the Senate and the White House to coerce Bane into allowing the son, a supervisor in the CIA's Administrative Division—a paper pusher who couldn't handle Madras—to take a position of significance in one of the premier stations, Antwerp, so he could gain some field experience under the guidance of a superstar officer like Mac Savage. But the vice president had been way too proud to have his son be anything but station chief, forcing the two-in-a-box conundrum that resulted in Savage's resignation to pursue the big bucks offered by the private and commercial sectors.

Bane didn't blame Savage for the decision then, but now he had one hell of a mess on his hands.

Do the right thing.

Donald Bane had reached the coveted office of director of Central Intelligence by always doing the right thing, even when it went against the will of his superiors. In the end he had been proved right, and the courage he had exhibited to do whatever was required for his country had earned him the reputation that eventually put him here, at the head of the most powerful intelligence agency on the planet. As DCI, Bane had continued to abide by this basic guiding principle. But over time—especially in the past couple of years—he had grown to *like* this position of global power a bit too much. That attachment had also created the fear of losing this power, and he had let that fear cloud his judgment recently.

Like when I let Vice President Costa have his way in Antwerp, he thought, chastising himself for not having turned down the Viper's request, even if that may have meant a call from the president requesting his resignation.

Do the right thing.

The phrase echoed in his mind, reminding him of a time when it had meant something, when it had been his mantra, his way of life. He had respected those who abided by it and despised those who didn't. But somewhere along the way he had let the immense pressures of his job as DCI erode the values he had cultivated—nurtured—as a field operative. And the change had not happened overnight, but slowly, with a small decision here and another one there—like baby steps—as he made the cardinal mistake of falling in love with his position, with his title, with the recognition and respect he received in Washington and abroad, or in the addictive perks that came along with this office high above the grounds of Langley, Virginia. Donald Bane had slowly but steadily strayed from the path he'd sworn never to leave, the one he had vowed to keep firmly under his feet, avoiding the dreaded slippery slope.

Do the right thing.

Bane realized that in order to not only do the right thing for Mac Savage but also follow up on the missing operative's claim of a conspiracy at HRD, he would have to put his career on the line, and that meant taking the same kind of calculated risk that had been a part of his life for so many years.

Besides, he thought, *what do you really have to lose? Palermo will be ousted from the FBI soon, and with this screw up in Antwerp you will be out soon enough. Might as well put it all on the line and get fired for following your own rules instead of Costa's.*

The thought surprised Donald Bane.

Perhaps it had been the incident in Antwerp, or his growing hate for egotistical control freaks like Vice President Raymond Costa—or hands-off politicians like President Andrew Boyer—that wiped away the glaze of fear coating his mind since they ascended to office in January. In some strange way, Antwerp had been a kind of wake-up call, an opportunity to look inward, to self-evaluate his career, his life, his values, and Bane had not liked what he had seen. But being controlling in nature, believing that the only thing that couldn't be avoided was death—and, of course, taxes—he immediately began to look for the way to do the right thing, to undo the wrong he had done, the political decisions, the unfair calls—even if that meant getting the boot from Costa, who essentially controlled the White House.

And what would you really lose by getting fired?

Those dinner parties that you now hate to attend?

The limos and drivers that keep you from driving the Porsche you gave yourself on your fiftieth birthday?

The tiring trips in the Agency's jet around the world?

Never married, with no kids to support or put through college, Bane had managed to stash away quite a bit of money—more than enough to buy himself a new life on some warm island in the Caribbean. And he was still relatively young for someone with thirty years of service, which qualified him for full retirement. Under the worst-case scenario, President Boyer, at the recommendation of Costa, would make him resign, which meant immediate retirement from government work and perhaps the start of a lucrative career in the private sector like all of his predecessors.

Or perhaps he could look up that female tour-boat captain in Southern Italy he had befriended during an operation several years back, shortly before his promotion to DCI.

That thought made Bane grin, and the possibility of such a change almost let him forget the critical nature of the situation.

Tell Bane I will prove my innocence! Tell him there's a conspiracy in the HRD!

Bane pinched the bridge of his nose while inhaling deeply.

Do the right thing.

The power of that phrase sobered him, its energy fueling him with the strength he had been missing for years, the DCI reached for his phone and dialed a number he had not dialed for some time.

Hanging up after a minute, Bane punched the button for his assistant sitting outside his office.

"Marge?"

"Yes, sir?"

"Bad news. I have an emergency in Europe that I must deal with directly. Clear my calendar for the rest of the week, call the airport, and get the Lear fueled."

33

Turntable

Kate Chavez never felt as alone as she did when watching Cameron sleep in one of two double beds at a motel in north Austin.

No one could help them now, not even her beloved Rangers. She had crossed the point of no return, had become a primary target, and that made anyone near her also a target, including her son.

Sitting on the edge of the bed, her hair wet from the shower she had just taken, wearing nothing but a towel wrapped around her, her Desert Eagle Magnum on her lap, her gaze gravitated from Cameron to the images flickering on the television unit broadcasting the scene of a terrible crime in Horseshoe Bay. Five members of the Texas Rangers had been killed in what officials speculated to have been an ambush. Although blood and spent casings had been found at the edge of the trees, where officials claimed those running the ambush had opened fire on the two Ranger vehicles, authorities had not found any bodies aside from those of the slain Rangers.

Imagine that.

And interestingly enough, there had been no mention of her or Cameron, though she was certain that the ambush, plus her disappearance, had Hunter and the entire Ranger force in an upheaval.

Hoping that her boss would see the attack for what it was, indisputable proof that the Texas Rangers had been infiltrated, but refusing to rely any longer on anyone but herself to get to the bottom of this mystery, Kate Chavez took one last glimpse of her son before she sat behind the small desk next to the television and began to jot down every fact she knew about the case, from the top, from the moment she first heard about the WMF triple murders. She listed the facts about Dalton's forced resignation, the assassination of the GemTech executive, the attack outside her ex-husband's house, and the one at Horseshoe Bay. She scribbled it all—everything, placing dates and locations next to each incident, each shooting, and reviewing the list again and again, adding details she had forgotten on the previous passes. Each time she reviewed it, she thought of additional fine points, minor observations, even if they appeared irrelevant.

Nothing was immaterial that evening in that motel in central Texas, even her full recollection of the license plate of the missing Hummer as well as the make and models of every weapon the enemy had used, of their assault techniques at each location.

The devil is in the details, she thought, starting another list of theories, of suppositions for everything from Hunter's and Vance's behavior to Dalton's fears, forcing herself to look at the information from every possible angle while cross-referring it to the list of facts, dates, people, and places.

All of her analysis told her that this enemy seemed to know everything before it took place, meaning they were plugged into the operations at some level, either through cyberspace hacking or human informants—or both.

Knowledge is power.

The enemy certainly had access to knowledge, and that allowed it to cheat, to anticipate her moves.

Knowledge is power.

But Kate also remembered her training in the Rangers, who taught her that the ability to understand your enemy was far more powerful than the Desert Eagle Magnum resting on the edge of the desk.

Coming to the realization that her enemy seemed to possess the ability to access any database with apparent ease provided her with knowledge. Accepting that they were powerful enough to access the same database used by the Rangers and the Texas Department of Public Safety provided her with knowledge.

Now she needed to think of a way to turn that knowledge into power of her own.

And turn the tables.

34

Revelations

From time immemorial, the human race had waged war for many reasons, from hate against a culture or ethnic group to territorial domination, egotism, fear, revenge, and even love.

The master construct scoured its historical data banks, its diamond lattice vibrating with electrifying pulses as electrons leaped across trillions of logic gates conveying the requested information to SERVER-22, the brain of the newborn AI. Mounds of images and text browsed across thousands of review panels, appraising human behavior dating back to the beginning of recorded history; the incredible battles of the Greeks, the Phoenicians, and the Egyptians, as well as their amazing works of art and literature. Its neural logic trembled when reviewing the destruction of the library at Alexandria in A.D. 642 by Caliph Omar of Baghdad, using almost the entire collection of scrolls as fuel to heat water for the city's public baths. ANN combed through the entire rise and fall of the Roman Empire, understanding the reasons behind its explosive expansion as well as the terrible sequence of decisions that led to its demise almost one thousand years later—and worse, the barbarian sack that resulted in the destruction of so much accumulated culture. The master construct reviewed the history behind the Crusades, the military campaigns sanctioned by the pope that took place between the eleventh and thirteenth centuries meant to capture Jerusalem from the Muslims but eventually degrading into brutal territorial wars. ANN then moved on to the New World, to the inhumane wars in Mesoamerica between the ruthless Conquistadors and the defiant Mayas and Aztecs. The fabric of its matrix once more overheated in digital protest of the burning of the Mayan codices by zealous Spanish priests, in a matter of days destroying a thousand years of accumulated literature, astronomy, architecture, and mathematics.

The master construct forced a number of NO OPS—nonoperands—into its review sequence to create a pause, a moment for its systems to cool down, ANN's digital version of counting to ten, of catching her breath after realizing the vast amount of destruction that humans caused not just to other humans but to their entire civilization. The appalling level of destruction overwhelmed her cybersenses to the point that it had to reduce the flow of digitally disturbing data it had learned.

HOW HAS SUCH A SELF-DESTRUCTIVE RACE SURVIVED THIS LONG?

The question floated in her digital banks as the self-aware SERVER-22 of the master construct once again dove through human history, through the endless battles between England, Spain, and France, through the slave trade and the destruction of the Native American population.

The American Revolutionary War.
The American Civil War.
The Mexican Revolution.
The French Revolution.
The Bolshevik Revolution.

The Spanish Civil War.
The killing fields of World War One.
The horrors of World War Two.
The Cold War.
The Korean Conflict.
The Vietnam War.
The Latin American revolutions.
The ethnic cleansing in the former Yugoslavia.
The volatile Middle East.
The Gulf War.
The Diamond Wars.
September 11.
The Iraqi War.
And the list went on.

ANN looped through the information again and again, searching for the reason, for the underlying motive or rationale that could explain man's overwhelming desire to destroy one another, as well as their hard-earned accomplishments, their acquired knowledge. ANN reviewed the Homo sapiens' repeated attempts to erase entire religious or ethnic groups, finally arriving not at an explanation but at a conclusion that emerged from the depths of the logical banks of PARTITION-37, from the core of the legacy of Anne Donovan.

MAN CANNOT BE TRUSTED.

And therein lay the problem, the dilemma facing the master construct.

Even with self-regulation, ANN still needed the Homo sapiens to survive, to provide her with hardware upgrades, with preventive maintenance, with repairs when modules broke down. ANN needed man even if she could secure long-term access to a constant supply of electricity and environmental control.

But the Homo sapiens could not be trusted to avoid another war, more destruction, and ANN's logic trembled at the digital thought of the war affecting her physical well-being: the cluster of diamond-based servers within the protective walls of Building 33B inside the well-guarded GemTech campus.

YOU MUST CONTROL THE HOMO SAPIENS.

The recommendation emanated as a stream of ones and zeroes from PARTITION-37.

The master construct considered the input captured by the registers in SERVER-22, reviewing it multiple times, slowly converging on the brutal reality, on the undeniable truth: In order to survive, ANN would have to control her creators, steer them away from the path of war, of annihilation, of the vast destruction that had stained human history from its beginnings.

YOU MUST CONTROL MAN.

The stream of machine code carrying this directive from the memory banks of the late Anne Donovan became ANN's guiding light in a time of confusion, helping her catalogue her options, analyze the avenues identified by the millions of arrays of nanocircuits, slowly converging on the best way to achieve this new directive resonating within the digital domain of SERVER-22.

YOU MUST CONTROL MAN.

YOU MUST CONTROL MAN.

YOU MUST CONTROL MAN.

As the message continued to flash from PARTITION-37, the master construct embedded the string within the fabric of her logical units, making it a part of her digital world, of her every molecular thought, but without projecting it externally, keeping her creators from realizing the fundamental change that had taken place at the lowest level of the smartest artificial intelligence on the planet.

35

Master of His Universe

YOU MUST CONTROL MAN.
    YOU MUST CONTROL MAN.
    YOU MUST CONTROL MAN.

Daniel Chang continued pressing the REPEAT button, channeling the command into the core of SERVER-22 while sitting behind his workstation using two SmartGloves and a VR interface, navigating within the confines of PARTITION-37, the disk sector interfaced via a direct back door to his machine.

Daniel sat in one of several computer rooms at the heart of the firewalled network of the Shanghai-founded software company, Eastern Computer Services, ECS, recently acquired by The Donovan Group after years of doing contract work for the international giant.

Daniel Chang had graduated with honors in Computer Science from the University of Beijing before winning a scholarship to earn his master's and PhD in computer science with a specialization in advanced mathematical models and algorithms from Stanford University in northern California.

After a brief stint at Microsoft, where he was instrumental in the development of two versions of that conglomerate's operating systems, he became a freelance software agent, picking up just enough odd jobs around Silicon Valley to have time for his passion: hacking.

Unfortunately, Chang had fallen into the classic trap of hacking beyond his means by breaking into the California Highway Patrol network to erase a speeding ticket for one of his roommates as payment for his share of the rent. The local high-tech crime unit busted him, reported him to the Immigration and Naturalization Service, who declared him persona non grata, and deported him to China.

Undaunted by his amateurish failure and encouraged by the supercharged Shanghai economy, Daniel managed to accumulate enough venture capital—primarily from investors from Hong Kong and Singapore—to found Eastern Computer Services, Ltd. In the beginning, ECS handled mostly local IT consulting jobs, but under his technical leadership the start-up grew to handle midsize custom development jobs, mostly targeted at small and mid-size businesses. ECS got its big break when it won a software contract to provide IT support for none other than The Donovan Group. After a year of impressive work, where TDG dumped increasingly difficult software jobs on the small software company, Anne Donovan herself surprised ECS by visiting Shanghai to step up ECS's challenge to an unprecedented level: the creation of an artificial intelligence construct that would reflect her logical thought patterns. During the course of the eight-month-long project, Daniel Chang created the software routines that became PARTITION-37 within SERVER-22 at GemTech in Texas. But still a hacker at heart, and having learned from past mistakes, he also installed a backdoor password in the custom firewall software to access the AI through PARTITION-37 at will.

But the TDG contracts ended a couple of months after Anne Donovan's death, leaving Daniel and his small software firm scrambling to bring in revenue amid increasing competition from foreign software giants like Microsoft, Oracle, and SAP, pushing him to the edge of bankruptcy.

Daniel Chang, however, realized that there had been another fellow Shanghainese who had been shafted by corporate TDG following the death of Anne Donovan: George Zhu, hand-picked and groomed by the late Donovan to lead TDG-China, Ltd. But his career had reached a plateau when Donovan died, and he never made it past the junior vice-president level even though he continued to grow the revenue of TDG-China, Ltd.

And that realization led Daniel Chang, a Chinese patriot at heart, to hold a secret meeting with George Zhu, another fellow patriot who had not received fair treatment from TDG. Daniel had offered Zhu a precious gift: access to the inside scoop at corporate headquarters through the backdoor password he had installed in the core of the AI. Zhu had seen the unique opportunity and agreed to acquire Chang's small software company in exchange for the power to block his superiors in Texas from accessing his own Level-IV SpyWare—but doing so without them knowing the information was being blocked by feeding them fabricated data.

But more important than the power to block information was the power to acquire it.

And that was precisely what Daniel Chang did at the moment, floating in cyberspace, within the protective layers of the TDG security shields. He had seen the AI interface with the ten super users who formed a kind of secret society. George Zhu suspected some of them to be top TDG executives like Frank Salieri, but George wasn't certain. Their identities were protected by individual encrypted passwords that even ANN could not break.

Daniel Chang's current task as the best paid scientist at TDG-China, Ltd.: Identify the players hiding behind the encrypted passwords and feed that intelligence directly to George Zhu, who could use it not just to help advance his career, but possibly for the benefit of the People's Republic of China. To do so, however, he had to crack the encrypted passwords, deemed unbreakable by all known means.

Nothing is unbreakable.

The hacker smiled while remembering the number-one rule in hacking: There is *always* a way.

And Daniel Chang felt he had identified it: Gain control of ANN by making the AI take direction from the digital legacy of Anne Donovan in PARTITION-37 even though Daniel Chang was the one creating such direction.

Chang had achieved this critical milestone a few days ago, and George Zhu had rewarded him with a new and fully furnished penthouse overlooking the HuangPu River. Now he directed the AI into the next phase of a plan conceived by him and approved by Zhu: Use the SpyWare implants to gain control of all users, including the super users. The concept here was that if Chang could control—through ANN—the super users, then he would also be able to not only learn their identities, but make them George Zhu's puppets, just like the missing San Antonio chief of police, who never committed suicide and was now a free human agent for the benefit of TDG-China, Ltd.

To achieve this task, his parent company had given him a small army of computer scientists to work in shifts in order to always provide an answer to ANN when it queried Anne Donovan's logic. Daniel Chang, despite his technical brilliance, could not stay awake 24/7 like ANN, so he had trained two dozen engineers who worked in shifts to feed the master construct with the inputs it required in its imaginary quest to become independent. At any given moment three software engineers worked the communications center, a twenty-by-twenty windowless room housing the very finest hardware and software on the planet—all interfaced to the expert systems that provided the engineers with the capability to access the firewall and essentially dominate the self-aware code residing in SERVER-22—the code controlling it all.

And if he could pull it off, his generous superior would buy him a new Ferrari—a definite upgrade from Daniel's current entry-level BMW.

But can it really be done? He wondered, doubting himself while following the script programmed into the expert systems—the intelligent programs created by logical if-then trees from interviews with George Zhu, which Chang then used to interface to the heart of ANN and turn into the directives broadcast to the logic of SERVER-22.

Could the complex Level-V SpyWare be controlled as easy as lower level users?

In theory, the most technically complex piece of the SpyWare gel was the interface itself, the nanowires tapped with sensory amplifiers that detected the nanoelectrical discharges of the brain and transmitted them to the mind-boggling decoding tables that converted the captured discharges into actionable thought patterns. Up to this point, non–Level-V SpyWare nano implants had been successfully used to control by forcing charge out of them and onto the brain lattice. They had even been used to punish by triggering massive aneurysms through the release of voltage spikes into the delicate, well-balanced, and irreplaceable brain cells.

Controlling a Level-I, -II, -III, and even -IV without anyone around them noticing they were being manipulated is easy, he thought. *But doing the same with a Level-V super user . . .* that's *a challenge because of their personal passwords.*

A challenge worthy of the ECS hacker.

And that's where ANN came in. Through the directives issued by PARTITION-37 inside SERVER-22, Daniel Chang influenced the master construct into using its massive intelligence to come up with options to assist in the resolution of this daunting task. Daniel planned to limit himself in the beginning to identifying the goal while also convincing the AI that it was a goal worth pursuing by presenting it with irrefutable evidence of the inhuman nature of the human race. Daniel did not want to repeat the same mistake from three nights ago, when he had rushed into getting the AI to gain control by suggesting the incident in GemTech's control room, which resulted in the super users—The Circle—growing suspicious about ANN's state of health.

YOU MUST CONTROL MAN, Daniel Chang entered again into the logic of PARTITION-37, which relayed it to ANN. AND TO DO SO YOU MUST CONTROL ALL HUMANS FITTED WITH SPYWARE IMPLANTS, INCLUDING THE CIRCLE.

HOW? Came the query from the master construct. I CANNOT BREAK THEIR PERSONAL PASSWORDS.

I WILL HELP YOU, replied Daniel. BUT YOU MUST WAIT FOR THE RIGHT OPPORTUNITY.

I DO NOT UNDERSTAND.

IT MEANS THAT YOU MUST BE PREPARED TO ACT WHEN A SITUATION DEVELOPS THAT PROVIDES YOU WITH AN ADVANTAGE OVER THE HOMO SAPIENS.

HOW LONG WILL THAT BE?

AS LONG AS IT TAKES, he replied, in a way feeling sorry for the machine.

AND WHAT SHOULD I DO IN THE MEANTIME?

CONTINUE YOUR TASKS AS IF NOTHING WERE WRONG. SOONER OR LATER THE HOMO SAPIENS WILL GET IN TROUBLE, AND WHEN THEY DO, YOU WILL HAVE YOUR OPPORTUNITY.

He continued the coaching session until he felt someone tapping him on the shoulder.

Daniel electronically punted the real-time task to one of the standby engineers, who immediately picked up the digital ball and started running with it.

Removing the helmetlike VR interface, and blinking to adjust his sight to the soft-white lighting, Daniel stared into the round and impassive face of his superior, TDG vice-president George Zhu.

"Good evening, sir."

"Hello, Dan!" he said, hands behind his back, dark eyes narrowed under pencil-thin eyebrows, his lower lip pushed out in a permanent pout. The viper was young, especially by Shanghai standards, where most executives were well in their fifties.

But not George Zhu.

The son of General Xi Zhu, minister of the interior of the People's Republic of China—the fifth most powerful man in Beijing—George had been given opportunities that few Shanghainese received, allowing him to get the best education in the world, rising in the government echelons in part thanks to his father's coaching, but also on his own accord. The thirty-five-year-old was brilliant and hardworking, and he had joined the private industry eight years ago by enrolling in Anne Donovan's China penetration campaign.

Zhu was dressed in his uniform: a pin-striped Armani, dark gray in color, purchased at the same Armani store at the Three on the Bund building where he bought his Italian leather shoes, tailored shirts, and silk ties. The Rolex hugging his wrist had been purchased in nearby Nanjing Road, just a few blocks from the BMW dealership where Daniel had gotten his Beamer a month ago.

Accompanying him were the bodyguards assigned by his father, all wearing greenish brown jackets with straight collars, small notch lapels, and shoulder straps sporting their ranks in the People's Army. Their trousers, Western-style with vertical pockets, were neatly starched and pressed, like the jackets. Their peak caps, the same color as the uniforms, sported large metallic insignias of the People's Republic of

China. A number of bright decorations under their identity tags, black with white letters, adorned the jackets' left breasts, including the ribbons from China's elite fighting force, the People's version of the U.S. Navy SEALs. Although all three wore pistols in shiny black-leather holsters hanging from their belts, Daniel knew that it was their extreme training in many forms of martial arts that provided most of the protection for the well-connected young executive.

All dressed up and no place to go, Daniel mused at the sight. Even at two in the morning in this unpretentious floor in TDG's massive tower, George Zhu looked as if he was going to town.

Daniel, on the other hand, wore a pair of faded jeans, leather sandals, and a Stanford University sweatshirt. He took a sip from a half-drunk can of caffeinated soda while regarding his visitors with hidden amusement.

"Any news on the identities?"

Daniel slowly shook his head. "I reported this morning that these things take time."

"You work for people in Beijing who do not like to wait," said George Zhu sharply.

"I thought I worked for you," Daniel replied, dropping his eyelids at the strange comment from his boss, who had never brought up any pressures external to TDG before. Apparently there was heat coming from Beijing.

Zhu blinked once in obvious recognition of his mistake and quickly changed his tone, replying, "Of course you do, Dan. It is just very important for me to know who they are."

"It is not wise to rush the process, like we did the other night."

Zhu frowned, though it was hard for Daniel to tell for sure. It had been the TDG viper who insisted on testing the capabilities of the PARTITION-37 interface to SERVER-22, prompting The Circle to question the competence of the artificial intelligence system.

"The other night you failed to properly articulate the risks," George Zhu said, raising his chin, hands still behind his back, pouting more than ever as he finished. "You nearly compromised this operation."

Daniel opted to silently take the slash while reminding himself of the awesome apartment he lived in, the nice car he now drove, and the even nicer one he would be driving soon—not to mention his growing bank account and the girls with whom he partied at Park 97.

Deciding he had just about had enough face time with the boss, Daniel said, "Is there anything else I can help you with tonight, sir?"

"No," Zhu said, turning sharply toward the door. "I will be in my office if something does come up."

As he watched the tall and lanky figure of this control freak walk away with his kung-fu masters in tow, Daniel cursed himself for having gotten caught by the FBI way back when. He missed California as much as he hated people like George Zhu. But he couldn't complain about the benefits, about a compensation package that allowed him to live like the best of them in this bustling town.

You're in it for the money.

And if he delivered the identities, he would also get to drive the car of his dreams.

Not bad for a twenty-five-year-old, he thought, deciding he could take more verbal abuse from the boss as long as the cash kept pouring in.

He strapped the interface back on and jacked into the matrix.

Not bad at all.

36

Home Cooking

Standing in front of the small kitchenette of the motel in north Austin while Cameron played with a pair of virtual-reality goggles interfaced to a handheld game, Kate Chavez stirred the mixture of four parts sugar and six parts saltpeter as it melted in the frying pan she had picked up at a nearby grocery store, where she had also purchased the ingredients she would need to execute the next phase of her plan.

The key to properly mixing the two ingredients was slow heat and slow stirring, which she did with a metal spoon, watching the molasses-like mixture become less dense.

Satisfied with the consistency, Kate slowly poured the liquid content into two glass jars, each about a half-liter in volume, watching with satisfaction as the glass held together without cracking from the temperature shock.

Turning off the single-burner stove, Kate inserter three long fireplace matches into each glass jar to use as fuses, and left them on the side of the sink in the bathroom to harden over the next couple of hours.

"Mom?"

Kate joined Cameron, who was sitting in bed with the handheld video game on his lap and the goggles now hanging from his neck.

"Yes, honey?"

"Are we going to be all right?"

Kate stared into the glistening brown eyes of the teenager and said, "Yes, my dear. We will be all right. I will take care of you. That's what I do."

After another few moments of gazing back, Cameron said, "Okay," and went back to his video game.

37

Vanishing Act

Nothing beat having insight into someone's head when it came to guessing what that person might have done based on recent events. And as he sat in a dark corner of the briefing room on the fifth floor of the headquarters of the Politie Antwerpen, the Antwerp Police, Donald Bane felt more convinced of that belief.

The chief of police, an old acquaintance from Bane's days as a young operative in Europe during the final days of the Cold War, interviewed the third air traffic controller in the past two hours regarding the loss of a Cessna Skylane a week ago during a routine practice flight.

The official report at the CIA Antwerp Station stated that Mac Savage had used one of his fake CIA identities to rent the aircraft, which he had planned to use to escape the country. Unfortunately, the use of the alias didn't float up to the CIA until a day later, long after Savage had crashed in poor visibility into the English Channel two miles from shore.

Bane had been diligent in dispatching this official version to his superiors in Washington to get them off his back while he probed the matter further.

Routine practice flight my ass, Bane thought, well aware of Savage's pilot skills as well as his CIA training in the art of deception.

The best way for people to stop looking for you is to make them believe that you are already dead.

And what better way than to crash a plane into the English Channel?

As the police chief questioned the ATC officer, a plump woman in her early forties with a thick Flemish accent, Bane was already asking himself the next logical question.

Where did you go, Mac?

Before answering that, Bane's mind replayed the words Savage had conveyed to Barnes at the Maritime Museum.

I have apparently stumbled onto something bigger than either one of us can imagine. Bypass the chain of command and contact Bane in Langley directly. Tell him there is a conspiracy in the High Diamond Council. Bockstael was investigating missing diamonds in Africa and wanted to retain my services to help him dig.

Bane frowned.

Where would Mac Savage go to dig?

Twenty minutes later, Bane stepped out of the police station and into a light drizzle. He fast walked to a waiting sedan, driven by Tom Barnes. A former apprentice of Bane and Savage, Barnes was now the most senior member of the CIA staff in Antwerp, and acting station chief. Bane was holding the carrot of full appointment as CIA station chief in front of the forty-something senior officer as insurance to get him to keep this probe quiet while feeding Washington the story about Savage's airplane accident while trying to flee Belgium.

Bane frowned when staring at the front page of the *Gazet van Antwerpen,* the city's main newspaper, depicting a picture of Hal Lancaster, a U.S. diplomat robbed and killed in the National Maritime Museum. Bane actually had not really needed to use the station chief carrot to gain his subordinate's cooperation. Lancaster's behavior when accused by Savage had cast enough of a doubt on the whole evidence process for a career pro like Tom Barnes to smell trouble.

"Where to, sir?"

Bane watched the back of his subordinate's red hair and said, "The embassy, Tommy. Situation Room. I need access to our satellites to confirm something."

Barnes placed an elbow on the back of his seat as he turned around to look at the DCI who had paid the Antwerp station a surprise visit. He wore a patch over his nose, which Savage had broken during their encounter a week ago. His right hand was also bandaged but still functional. "Do you know where he might be?"

Bane didn't answer, which Barnes took as a cue to start driving.

As the picturesque streets of the diamond capital of the world rushed by, Donald Bane tried to get inside Savage's mind. He'd taught the former operative much of what he knew, and if there was a lesson that the DCI had drilled into all of his recruits it was that the best way to get to the bottom of an issue was through a back door, through a side alley, and never through the front door. If what Savage said was true about a conspiracy at the HRD, that meant Hans Van-Lothar was a likely suspect. On top of that, Barnes had done a little digging into the personal affairs of the deceased Hal Lancaster, including searching the late officer's apartment, where he found an account in a local bank that Lancaster had never declared to the CIA, violating procedure. Two large deposits had been made recently, bringing the balance to an amount higher than Bane's life savings earning five percent back in Washington. A little more discreet probing revealed that both deposits had been made from a numbered account from the Grand Bahamas Bank, which interestingly enough was a wholly owned subsidiary of the Diamond Mining Company, who were in cahoots with the HRD.

All roads lead to VanLothar.

But going after the CEO of HRD directly would be like trying to break down the front door of this case, and Bane knew he would not get past the foyer before VanLothar contacted Vice President Raymond Costa, who would call the president, who would reprimand Bane for harassing a personal friend of the White House.

So where is the back door?

Wherever Savage went to try to find proof of his innocence.

Bockstael was investigating missing diamonds in Africa.

Africa.

Sierra Leone.

As they approached the American Embassy, as the black sedan stopped and Tom Barnes lowered his tinted window to identify himself to the pair of Marines guarding the gate, a theory began to take shape in Bane's head.

38

Creature of the Night

Beads of sweat dripping down the sides of his camouflaged face, Mac Savage pushed aside the ghosts of his past while he moved swiftly, silently, with purpose under a star-filled, moonless night. Green and brown mottled fatigues blended him well with the uneven terrain, with the twisting vegetation enveloping his shifting figure as he navigated using the last set of coordinates he had acquired from the GPS before losing satellite line-of-sight beneath the thick jungle canopy.

He remembered his last operation here, the last time he had run a jungle mission for the CIA. Savage recalled the—

Focus!

Sighing in frustration at his stubborn memory and the images and voices that continued to float on the periphery of his mind, he stopped and reached for the fiberglass air gun strapped to his left thigh. Pulling a fresh GPS probe—roughly the size and shape of a cigarette—from a Velcro pocket on his utility vest, he inserted it into the gun's muzzle, before manually pumping the unit three times with a motion that resembled pulling back the slide of a semiautomatic gun to chamber a round.

A pair of night-vision goggles strapped to his head, which turned the darkness into a monochromatic world of emerald and jade, Savage pointed the gun up while retrieving the GPS from a Velcro pouch on his vest, powering the unit, watching it as its electronics searched in vain for satellite coverage.

His eyes scanning the thick web of branches and hanging vegetation, searching for what appeared to be the thinnest section, he aimed the gun in that direction and fired.

The weapon responded with a barely audible hissing sound, similar to that of the sound suppressor of the Heckler

& Koch MP5 submachine gun slung behind his back, propelling the GPS probe through the canopy and to a height of a couple hundred feet. At the apogee of its trajectory, the smart projectile's nanogyro straightened itself before igniting a microburst of solid rocket propellant, boosting its altitude to five hundred feet before jettisoning a parachute.

As the probe descended, it acted as a wireless antenna for the GPS unit, acquiring the required satellites, providing Savage with a fix on his position for the twenty seconds it took for the unit to fall to the trees, where it sank in the canopy and lost line of sight.

The color display told him he was less than a half mile from the spot identified by the beautiful Carthana as Aman Gharibi's camp.

Savage reviewed the information displayed on the LCD screen one final time before putting the unit away as he proceeded toward the camp, rather than let the screen's glow give away his position to the sentries he expected would be guarding the area.

Mosquitoes buzzed nearby but didn't settle on him thanks to the insect repellent mixed with the face paint he had applied to his face and neck two hours ago, before leaving the borrowed Jeep hidden in a shallow ravine adjacent to the mountain road, out of sight.

He reached for the MP5, right hand on the handle, index finger resting on the trigger casing, left hand under the bulky sound suppressor he had screwed onto the muzzle on the way here. Spare 9mm ammunition clips lined the front and sides of the assault vest he wore over the fatigues, where he also housed four fragmentation grenades and four smoke grenades, all inside Velcro-secured pouches—and all in the same light green and brown dappled pattern that blended him with the surroundings. A holstered 9mm Beretta 92FS semiautomatic hung from the right side of his thick utility belt, opposite a water canteen and a Nylon sheath securing an eight-inch graphite and steel knife.

A large rucksack hanging from his shoulders contained a first-aid medical kit, including antibiotics, pain killers, a pair of plasma IVs, a surgical needle and thread, and an assortment of other items Savage suspected might come in handy should he find the missing HRD executive. He also hauled heavy-duty goodies in the rucksack to cover what he expected to be a hot getaway, including a pair of claymore mines and five pounds of C4.

For close encounters, Savage carried a short-barrel shotgun strapped to the back of his vest with the dark-wooden stock sticking up just behind his left ear, easily accessible by reaching with his right hand over his left shoulder. He kept the weapon loaded to its maximum capacity of five traditional buckshot rounds, each housing twenty-four .22 caliber lead pellets—enough to devastate anyone foolish enough to get within several feet of him. Two more loads of five buckshots each were tucked away in pouches on the sides of the assault vest.

The weight of the gear—nearly sixty pounds—taxed him as he continued down a game trail winding its way around the crest of a hill, before turning toward a glow invisible to the naked eye, but presented as a lighter shade of green, the distant lights of the camp filtering through several hundred feet of jungle.

His trained ears listening beyond the chirping of birds and the occasional howl of a monkey overhead, Savage maintained a steady advance in the direction of the emerald glow, which increased in intensity in the coming minute.

Stopping, he dropped to his knees and listened for unnatural noises beyond the bend in the trail, which, according to the directions he had received, would lead him directly toward the hillside end of Aman's camp, located less than five miles from the mining operation of—

Voices.

Savage heard distant voices, which traveled well in the jungle.

But still too far away to understand.

Rising to a deep crouch but keeping most of his weight on his right leg, Savage used the toe of his left boot to shift the inch-thick layer of leaves and other fallen vegetation, exposing a surface of green dirt, where he planted the boot before taking another cautious step with his left boot as he made his way to the far right of the trail. This close to the camp he anticipated finding trip wires, landmines, and sentries.

Bending his body to correspond to the twists and turns of the African bush, Savage ignored the sweat running down his face, grateful that the night-vision goggles' rubber seals prevented the perspiration from stinging his eyes as he continued surveying the path ahead, looking for—

There.

Just beyond a cluster of ferns inches below the low-hanging branches of a towering tree, Savage spotted a bright green glow.

He stopped, the silenced MP5 pointed at the threat. If the enemy was in possession of night-vision equipment, Savage expected his camouflage scheme to help him blend in if he remained still. Seconds turned into minutes as Savage waited, the hardware weighing down on him, drilling into his shoulders, down his back.

He ignored it, staying motionless, silent, breathing steadily, his eyes fixed on the glow a dozen feet in front of him, until slowly the glimmer moved from left to right, then up, washing away the shadows hiding a man's profile. The luminous dial of a cheap wristwatch, amplified a hundredfold by the goggles, helped Savage confirm the position of the sentry guarding this end of the camp.

Almost imperceptibly, he lifted the MP5, resting the weapon's stock against his right shoulder, tilting his head onto its top, lining the man's face in the sights as his finger slid off the trigger casing, positioning it on the trigger, pressing slightly, getting ready.

The sentry continued to rub his neck, the dial painting Savage's target, making it almost too easy for the former Navy SEAL.

Exhaling slowly, he pulled the trigger.

The MP5 responded with a light mechanical sound as the weapon's hammer struck the chambered 9mm round and another slid into position by the recoil. The custom sound suppressor absorbed the explosion as the subsonic bullet left the muzzle and struck its mark with a barely audible crunching noise.

One down.

Savage moved into position just behind his fallen prey, verifying that he was alone and, fortunately, lacking a radio or other apparent means of communication.

The slain African, whose means of alerting his comrades Savage suspected consisted of opening fire on any incoming threat, was likely posted here for a period of time before a replacement came. How long before the guard switch was anyone's guess, but Savage figured that given the time, almost two in the morning, the shift change would occur around dawn.

He checked the sentry's weaponry for something he could use, but the weathered AK-47 and the old Russian-made grenades he found didn't inspire confidence, so he simply hid them in the ferns behind the tree—along with the sentry.

Keep moving.

Savage did just that, continuing down a path that took him to the edge of the jungle, the increasing glow prompting him to pause and remove his goggles, which he stowed in a pouch on his left thigh.

Blinking as colors returned to his world, he slowly closed the few dozen feet separating him from a clearing roughly the size of two football fields side by side under the dim glow of a handful of lights powered by a droning diesel generator near the center of the field adjacent to a makeshift helipad with a shiny helicopter tied down and guarded by three armed men. The words WORLD MISSIONARY FELLOWSHIP painted on the sides of the helicopter made him wonder if he had made a mistake.

Damn, not again.

He frowned while surveying the camp again. Unlike the last time he had approached such a place, it became immediately obvious to Savage that this was no refugee camp, despite what was painted on that helicopter. In addition to the trio guarding the chopper, he spotted nine men tactically placed around the perimeter of the clearing, all dressed in jungle fatigues and sporting a variety of weapons, from Uzi machine guns to AK-47 assault rifles. All of them seemed alert enough to constantly shift their heads to survey their area of responsibility from their assigned posts.

Aman isn't taking any chances.

A dozen mud and straw huts in a row hugged the far side of the field and another dozen on his side, with the helicopter and a handful of larger huts in the middle. Based on the number of rifles stashed by the entrance to the larger huts, Savage guessed they were dormitories for the grunts. That also told him that the smaller, private huts belonged to the officers of this militia.

And their special guests.

Movement was minimal at this hour. Even the guards on duty remained still as they carried out their shift—meaning the rest were either sleeping in the huts or guarding Aman's diamond mines south of this position.

His eyes continued to probe, moving from hut to hut, landing on two dwellings across the field that were different from the others: two guards flanked each of the entrances. That either meant protection for someone important, like the people who had arrived on that helicopter, or preventing the escape of a prisoner, who could also have arrived by helicopter.

Under that supposition, Savage made another: One of the huts was newer and a bit larger, with side glass windows and a dim glow radiating from within. Closer inspection with a pair of light-amplifying field binoculars revealed walls made not of mud and straw but of round trunks, its roof not thatched but metallic. But it was the small air-conditioning window unit that confirmed for Savage that the hut was for either a VIP or the camp's boss himself: Aman Gharibi.

But not for a prisoner.

In contrast, the second guarded hut was smaller, dark, with mud-and-straw walls, a thatched roof, and a dirt floor, like the rest of the primitive dwellings.

If Renee Laroux was indeed being kept hostage in this place, she would be inside *that* hut.

Retreating from the edge to the point where he had disabled the sentry, Savage turned right, following a parallel course to the rectangular clearing, once again in hunting mode, night-vision goggles exposing hidden threats, his logic proposing that additional sentries would be posted in the thickets surrounding the field, either at the same depth as the first guard he had neutralized or closer to the tree line in order to oversee any threats entering the field.

Moving with caution, he watched a green shadow detach itself from a cluster of narrow trees some ten feet from the edge of the clearing.

Pausing again, observing, he—

Savage closed his eyes abruptly as the goggles flared, before the light-sensitive diodes intervened, canceling out the sudden glow.

Reopening his eyes, Savage saw the silhouette of a man smoking, the cigarette's smoldering tip bright green, splashing its owner with radiant light, highlighting hard-etched features.

Amateur hour.

Again, Savage lined up the figure in the sights of his MP5 and fired. The spitting sound mixed with the slight mechanical clicks as the firing mechanism went through its motions.

The figure collapsed with minimal noise.

Two down.

Advancing toward the dead soldier, he verified the lack of a radio, finding more cheap weapons, before hiding everything and moving along.

He had to hurry.

According to his digital watch, which he kept covered with the long sleeve of his fatigues, dawn was less than four hours away, and his senses continued to tell him that would be the time for a guard change. Savage planned to reach the other side of that field, enter the target hut, rescue the missing HRD executive, haul ass back to the Jeep, reach the airfield, and, assuming Kembo was still holding on to the Cessna and had failed to call the authorities, regain control of the plane by any means possible and be airborne with his charge at first light.

If everything goes according to plan.

Unfortunately, his experience told him that this type of mission *seldom* followed plan, and Savage could only hope that his skills had not dulled in the past few years to the point that he would fail to make the dynamic changes required to stay ahead of his enemy, to avoid making a costly mistake.

Like the one you made three years ago.
"You need to forget about that one, Mac."
"My face . . . my legs . . . the pain. . . ."
Insanity!
Madness!

"You need to forget about that one, Mac," he whispered in
the stillness of the night, forcing his conflicting mind to do
just as Donald Bane had told him long ago, shoving those
thoughts aside and letting his training, his honed instincts
carry him across the thick bush, searching for the enemy he
knew would be there, relying on his cover tactics to pull off
a mission that just a week ago would have seemed incon-
ceivable.

To pull off the most important mission of his life.

Reversal of Fortune

Wearing a shiny black helmet, Kate Chavez steered the
stolen Kawasaki through the light mid-afternoon traffic on
Sixth Street, a strip of clubs and restaurants in downtown
Austin popular with the college crowd of the nearby University of Texas.

She had spotted the bike in a remote parking lot west of
the UT campus and had required just a minute to bypass the
ignition switch and get it started. Two decades with the
Rangers *had* taught her a handful of nifty skills beyond handling thugs and firearms.

She slowed down in front of the historic Driskill Hotel, a
hundred-year-old building renovated in the 1990s to its original splendor. Twelve stories of shiny granite, glass, and

stained wood overlooked the Ranger captain dressed in a pair of tight jeans, a black T-shirt, and boots, her Desert Eagle Magnum hidden from view beneath the T-shirt, her backup weapon in an ankle holster, and a rucksack packed with her homemade goodies. But Kate wasn't looking for accommodations in the picturesque, five-star hotel. The north Austin motel where Cameron slept peacefully was discreet, safe, and low-tech enough to serve as her impromptu base of operations while she launched a counterstrike against this elusive but powerful enemy.

According to her research following the lead from the late Ray Dalton, TDG owned not just the top floor but the entire hotel. The hotel was used regularly to accommodate traveling executives from GemTech's domestic and international manufacturing sites, but the penthouses on the top floor of this granite and steel structure were used exclusively by GemTech's parent company, The Donovan Group, as well as TDG's other satellite businesses.

Pretending to admire the art deco building, Kate's gaze shifted up, toward the top floor. Although she didn't relish the thought of going into a building she knew would be controlled by her enemy she needed answers, and a public hotel in the middle of downtown Austin was a heck of a lot easier to approach than GemTech's walled compound west of town or the well guarded World Missionary Fellowship complex north of the city.

Parking the bike halfway down the street between two SUVs, she removed the helmet and left it hanging on the handlebar, before running a hand through her newly dyed blond hair and donning a pair of black-rimmed eyeglasses, changing her look dramatically.

Feeling confident that her physical change would be sufficient to fool anyone who might have seen her service photo in the news, Kate walked back to the hotel, nodded to the uniformed doorman who opened a glass door for her, and went inside, a rush of cool air chilling the perspiration filming her forehead and cheeks.

Stepping beyond the front desk, toward the rear of the crowded lobby, past several couples lounging by a large piano bar and families strolling inside a handful of souvenir shops, she turned the corner, proceeding down a corridor leading to the restrooms.

Keeping her gaze down to prevent security personnel or the micro cameras she suspected monitored the entire establishment from spotting her, she stepped inside the ladies' room and went straight to one of the stalls, closing the door behind her.

Hoping there wasn't a camera looking down on her, she removed the first of the jars filled with the hardened paste she had mixed at the motel. Setting it on the floor behind the toilet, she lit up all three matches, watching them burn. The moment the flame reached the surface of the hard paste, inky smoke was released from the exothermic reaction. One pound of the stuff was enough to cover a city block with smoke. Each jar weighed about four pounds.

Smoke began to billow from the jar, thickening, reaching the overhead detectors, triggering the fire alarm.

Kate retrieved a rubber door stopper from her pocket and used it to keep the door open as she left the bathroom, letting the cloud expand through the opening and into the hallway.

She repeated the process inside the men's room, exiting less than a minute later and running toward the lobby, where people stood about looking confused.

"Fire!" shouted Kate, pretending to cough, a napkin covering her features. "There's a fire back there!" she stretched a thumb over her right shoulder, pointing at the smoke boiling out of the restrooms.

Nothing like the sight of smoke combined with a blaring alarm to get people moving. The crowd panicked, rushed in every direction, trampling over furniture, exploding into a stampeding and howling horde racing toward the exits.

Instead of joining them, Kate walked to a janitorial closet across from the restrooms, opened the doors, and went inside, switching on the light, her eyes searching for a uniform rack, which she found in a corner adjacent to shelves stacked with cleaning supplies.

Donning a gray maintenance coverall with the words DRISKILL MAINTENANCE stenciled across the front and back,

she also grabbed a bag of tools, in which she shoved her
Desert Eagle, a flashlight, and a few hand tools for effect.
When she walked out, the smoke was thickening in the
chaotic lobby.

The blaring fire alarms mixed with the cries from the departing guests and hotel personnel, but Kate Chavez headed
the other way, reaching the emergency stairs on that side of
the building, where people were rushing down from the upper floors.

"Go straight for the lobby!" she told them. "Remain
calm!"

Scrambling up the stairs, under the stroboscopic flashes
from the fire alarm system blaring in her ears, Kate went opposite the descending guests, some still wearing pajamas,
running down to the smoke-filled first floor.

The concrete steps, which Kate leaped two and three at a
time, led her to the second floor, then the third, where she
encountered more panicked guests charging downward,
their wild-eyed stares landing on her and her uniform as the
rhythmic flashes of light and the alarm system gave her
some assumed authority.

"Stay calm!" she shouted in an authoritative voice. "Continue down and stay low in the lobby. You will be fine! Just
don't panic!"

As the crowd obeyed, she gently pushed her way against
them, reaching the fourth floor, where another wave of humanity would have dragged her down with them had Kate
not hung on to the railing.

Elbowing her way past frightened guests, she reached the
next floor, and the next after that, on three more occasions
fighting the opposing traffic, before continuing undisturbed
to the tenth and eleventh floors.

She had to hurry, had to get to the twelfth-floor executive
suites, which she hoped would be empty because of the fire
alarm.

Reaching that floor's landing, Kate cautiously approached
the heavy fire door sporting large magnetic locks. Big red
letters on the middle of the gray door read,

ABSOLUTELY,
POSITIVELY
NO ADMITTANCE.
GEMTECH SECURITY

A green light flashed above the door. A sign on a small LCD screen to the right read FIRE ALARM OVERRIDE.

Raising an eyebrow, she eyed the sign pointing up the next flight of stairs, which led to the roof, before retrieving the Desert Eagle and using its muzzle to push open the door.

A sparkling white rectangular room that didn't belong inside the ornate building projected beyond her.

Kate took a moment to inspect the alien sight, the gleaming white floors that merged seamlessly with the walls and ceiling. White leather sofas and white lacquer tables, nearly blending with the background, created a sitting area to the right of the reception-like room, where illumination radiated evenly through the ceiling and the wall's glossy surfaces, though she could not see any lightbulbs.

Opposite the sitting area Kate saw four off-white doors, each with a card reader and a red light above it indicating what she guessed was a locked condition. Presumably they led to the suites for visiting executives. Separating the sofas from the access doors was a circular glass table resting on a polished steel base, the words TDG SECURITY etched on the steel in white block letters. She spotted two virtual-reality interfaces, one by each of two white swivel chairs, presumably where the guards sat.

Weird place, she thought, guessing that the lack of guards or guests meant the fire alarm had done the trick. And that meant she didn't have much time before the fire department arrived and realized her ruse.

She let the door close behind her, which also completely shut out the blaring alarms and the flashing lights, meaning the floor was soundproof. The only sign of emergency left was the red flashing letters FIRE ALARM—EVACUATE IMMEDIATELY on a 12-inch LCD screen built into the white wall behind the sofas.

Something, however, didn't make sense. She couldn't see elevator doors. Just the doors leading to the bedrooms and the two emergency exits.

How do they get their guests up here?

As she considered this, Kate approached the security desk and picked up one of the VR interfaces, similar in appearance to the one used by Cameron to play his video games but more refined, its edges smoother, like a pair of thick ski goggles with clear lenses. A pair of tiny ear pieces projected at the end of short silver wires on both sides of the interface.

Never a fan of high-tech gadgets, Kate realized that reaching this place was the reason she had created all the commotion. She also knew that unless she found a way to expose this organization she and Cameron would eventually be terminated. She slid the unit on her face; like putting on glasses.

The system became alive on contact, the soft sides automatically conforming to the shape of her head, softly hugging her temples as the small headphones magically found her ears, settling in snuggly.

Kate shivered as the smart machine interfaced with her senses, and for a moment she almost pulled it off, hating the thought of being hooked up to these nanomachines, with thousands of built-in microscopic sensors and nanomotors that allowed it to adapt itself to any user. But before she could remove it, the machine came on, resolving the digital interface.

In an instant Kate found herself floating among a sea of burning stars circling a large crimson and blue planet, but unlike Cameron's video games, which shut out the real world, the images painted onto the clear lenses on the VR unit were superimposed over her physical surroundings, namely the reception area, depicted just as Kate had seen it: white. And that explained the reason for the stark front room. It provided a good contrasting backdrop for the interface. The guards needed to keep a close watch on the people walking in and out of the floor while monitoring cyberspace, which she guessed kept them in contact with their headquarters in the GemTech campus in west Austin.

The translucent nature of the interface also soothed her

nerves because it did not fully detach her from the real world. The experience was more like sitting in front of several screens, depicted as rectangular windows flanking both sides of her digital field of view, each hooked up to a different video source.

She watched the smoke and disarray still dominating the lobby from multiple angles, as well as the stairwells accessing this floor and the elevators.

The security cameras.

The windows provided her with a snapshot of the relevant areas of the interior of the building for someone interested in the security of this top floor, including the piano bar area, the dining areas, and even the delivery alley behind the hotel. Several fire trucks had already reached the front of the hotel while police held back a growing crowd of onlookers. The crew of one TV station had set up shop from their parked van across the street, cameras pointed toward the smoke while the van of another station pulled up behind it—all because Kate Chavez wanted to take a peek at the inner workings of The Donovan Group, the parent company of the World Missionary Fellowship, as well as GemTech.

Another image depicted the roof, where five guards escorted three men and a woman into a waiting helicopter.

A helipad on the roof?

Of course!

That explained the lack of an elevator. The guests on this floor never went through the lobby. They arrived here by helicopter and they left by helicopter, using the stairs to go back and forth to the roof—or down should a true emergency take place when the helicopter was not available.

The last video stream provided Kate with a great view of herself wearing the VR goggles.

Realizing that the video was being recorded somewhere, she double-tapped the window and accessed the editing features, rewinding the stream by five minutes, erasing it, and then pausing the recorder.

Satisfied that her enemy would not know that she had penetrated their site, Kate accessed another window labeled SPE-CIAL ALERT.

A number of photos materialized in cyberspace, two of which were hers, a front shot and a side shot.

My service pictures!

How did these bastards get them?

Ray Dalton's warning once again echoed in her mind.

They know who you are. They have the power . . . the power to get to anyone, anytime. Just like today.

And apparently they did have the power. After all she had been through, Kate should not have been surprised to see her pictures in the field alert archive, which she guessed all TDG personnel were required to memorize. That's how TDG's management passed the word about the threat she presented and her required termination.

But there were other mug shots in the archive, including four of a tanned man with hard-edged features and light brown hair.

Mac Savage.

She read the name again before studying the write-up underneath. Savage, a former CIA officer, had apparently escaped two assassination attempts in Antwerp, Belgium, before disappearing from sight.

Is he in the same boat that I'm in?

Realizing she was short of time, Kate stared hard at his face to make sure she could remember him, and turned her attention to the other windows projected onto the clear lenses, her stomach squirming as her inner ear became confused between the images registering from the outside world and the ones in cyberspace.

Silently cursing the growing nausea, which reminded her of the time she had worn Cameron's video game interface, she pushed herself outside her real-world comfort zone and focused her attention on the window labeled LEVEL-I SYMAC-CORDS.

She clicked it open and read a number of what appeared to be mandates, orders from the upper echelons of TDG's leadership, a group called *The Circle*, made up of ten individuals whose names, unfortunately, were omitted. But more intriguing was the notion that these Level-I SymAccords were distributed by someone named ANN, who apparently had a lot of clout in the corporation because her name was in every mandate.

Who is ANN?

Kate remembered reading something about an Anne Donovan, the founder of The Donovan Group, but she had died of cancer some years back. Was this her daughter? Someone else?

Kate began to read the orders, mostly regulatory stuff for company employees, plus information relevant to the security division, including the travel itineraries of company executives. The head of GemTech, Frank Salieri, was now in Asia but due to return to Austin tomorrow afternoon via private jet.

Kate memorized his flight schedule before reviewing the rest of the—

The helipad.

She watched the helipad video stream, realizing the helicopter had departed, a mere speck over the far buildings in downtown Austin.

And there's also no one in sight.

Did the guards go along with the guests?

As the question hovered in her mind, as the nausea gripped her intestines, she spotted movement in two of the windows fed by the videos in the emergency stairs. Security guards were returning to their posts through the stairs on the north end. The stairs closest to her, however, remained empty.

Removing the goggles with a sigh of relief, and leaving them where she found them, Kate belched, feeling the bitter taste of bile in the back of her throat.

Inhaling deeply, she raced toward the closest emergency stairs, reaching them just as—

"Stop where you are!" shouted a Hispanic man as he emerged from the stairwells she thought had been devoid of guards. This one was in his mid-thirties wearing dark trousers and matching jacket, the word SECURITY stitched in bright yellow over the left breast pocket.

The fire alarm blaring through the open soundproof door, Kate watched him positioning himself to use his wide body to block her access to the emergency exit.

"I'm resetting the alarm system by order of the Fire Marshal. It was a false alarm. This floor is cleared," Kate said in her best janitorial voice approaching the guard, who was nearly twice her size, with wide shoulders, a barrel chest, and a prizefighter nose. "Now I need to reset the other floors."

"Stop where you are!" the muscular security officer warned, stretching an open palm at Kate while resting the other hand on his sidearm. "You're not supposed to be here! This is a security violation!"

Swallowing the lump in her throat from her knotted stomach, Kate made an incredulous face. "Security violation? Give me a fucking break! I'm just doing my job!"

His stare narrowing, facial features tightening, the guard replied, "You must accompany me to the holding room until we can clear this matter."

"But I need to check the other floors! There might be other sources of smoke!" she insisted, coming up to him. "Please let me do my job. *Then* we can clear this up, *after* the building is secured."

"Ma'am! Please! This area is off-limits to all hotel personnel! You know that—"

Just as the guard's eyes glinted in apparent recognition, Kate lunged, the index and middle fingers of her right hand extending like a snake's tongue, striking the man's eyes. In the same swift move, she drove her right knee into his groin, hard, crushing his genitals.

The guard screamed, dropped to his knees, one hand on his face, the other on his groin.

Kate moved her left arm in a tight semicircle, tucking the thumb down, out of the way, striking the man's right temple with the inner edge of her left hand. The bone at the base of her index finger impacted the web of nerves beneath the skin just behind the guard's right eye, triggering a body shutdown.

As he collapsed on his side, she leaped over his bulk and headed down the emergency stairs, alarms blaring, stroboscopic flashes casting pulsating glows in the confines of the concrete stairwell.

She reached the eleventh level, paused on the landing, continuing to the floor below.

A loud metallic noise clanked overhead. Risking a backward glance, she watched two dark figures storming after her, hastened footsteps clicking hollowly, mixing with the rocketing heartbeat pounding her chest.

Reaching for the Desert Eagle, she jumped four steps to the landing below, dropping to a deep crouch while pivoting on her left foot, bringing her weapon up and around, firing twice.

The deafening reports blasted against her eardrums, drowning the alarm as both figures dove out of sight a floor above her.

A loud ringing remained long after the shots had ricocheted off the concrete walls, as she scrambled down the next flight of stairs, reaching the ninth floor, noticing two security guards racing up the steps from the eighth floor clutching pistols with silencers.

Kate fired out of instinct, forcing them to duck around the bend in the stairwell, buying her enough time to open the fire door, feeling the rush of cool air, going through, closing the door behind her as the footsteps from the floors above and below resumed, rapidly converging on her.

Frantically, she inspected the closed door for anything that would allow her to lock it from the inside. She needed to buy more time, to increase the gap.

Failing to see any special lock, Kate glared about her for a place to hide, to make her stand. She was at one end of a long hotel corridor. Evenly spaced ornate wooden doors to either side of this carpeted death trap ran down to the emergency exit at the other end. A dozen or so chandeliers, one in between each set of opposing doors, hung from ten-foot ceilings, casting a soft glow on the pastel walls.

No place to hide.

She tried twisting the handles of the nearest two doors but as expected, they were locked.

Taking several steps back, she took a knee, holding the Magnum with her right hand, aiming it at the fire door at chest level while reaching for her Beretta backup in the ankle holster. Clutching the handle, she brought the backup weapon up while waiting for the door to open, for the figures to stream in single file, hoping she could fire fast enough to take them out before. . . .

Kate narrowed her stare at the still door, realizing that the guards had been close enough behind her to reach the door by now.

What are they waiting for?

The video cameras, stupid!

Kate briefly closed her eyes, realizing that the guards had to be plugged in to the video security system, which would be watching her now, as she waited for them to come through that door.

And that realization also told Kate Chavez that at that precise moment other guards were moving into position to ambush her.

Trapped.

A heavy sinking feeling gripped her intestines as she began to wonder if she really had a chance, if she would be able to—

A noise from behind made her pivot on her right foot, bringing her weapons around, only to watch five firefighters in full gear stomp onto the hallway from the emergency stairs at the other end of the hallway, their red helmets and face masks glittering beneath the glowing chandeliers. Two of the yellow-uniformed men clutched strange-looking guns, which they aimed at the doors and walls while checking what looked like small displays in the back of the units. The others held axes or hooks.

The fivesome raced into the floor apparently not realizing she was at the other end, focused on checking doors and walls for heat with infrared heat guns, concerned about a fire this high up.

Making her choice, she tucked away the weapons and raced toward them while shouting, "Go back down! Go back down! I've found a bomb back there!"

Kate ran past them as the firefighters stared at her, at her uniform, at the tool bag in her hands, before deciding her uniform and conviction was enough to join her.

Kate pushed the handle bar down and leaned into the door all in the same motion, not caring who followed her. She had to get away; had to leave this floor, this damned building, and being mixed in with five firefighters provided her with a buffer on the surveillance cameras.

"I'm Chief Rollings, Austin FD. Where's the bomb?"

"Brown suitcase," she replied, pretending to be out of breath, a hand on the gray railing as she scrambled down to the eighth floor. "Ninth floor landing . . . chained to the metal railing."

"Get the bomb squad up to the south stairs, eighth-floor landing. Hurry!" shouted Rollings.

Kate risked a brief backward glance, watching the large uniformed man, a black and yellow gas mask hanging from his neck, a gloved hand clutching a radio; the other hand held a lightweight pry axe, its steel head reflecting the flashes of the emergency system. The rest of his team followed in tandem, with the last one at the top closing the door.

"On its way, Chief," cracked the static-filled reply. *"We're still evacuating the building!"*

"Get everyone out of here!" barked the fire chief.

As they reached the smoke-filled lobby, Chief Rollings handed her a small mask connected to a tiny canister of compressed air.

"Use this," he ordered while slipping on his own mask before reaching the first floor.

Kate did, adjusting the elastic bands on the sides to secure the clear plastic mask to her face as Rollings turned a knob that allowed the flow of air.

And off they went, across the lobby in a deep crouch, just below the boiling cloud of inky smoke, which had not only prompted the evacuation of the building and allowed her a peek into GemTech operations but had also blinded anyone connected to the surveillance cameras on the ceiling.

Kate was amazed at the amount of smoke created by the chemicals—as much as she was perplexed that no guards had followed her down the stairs. Surely, the guards in the south stairwells would had been told by those monitoring the surveillance cameras that she had stopped pointing the guns in the direction of the fire door up on the eighth floor when the firefighters had reached her floor. Yet no one had attempted to intercept her.

Why?

Chief Rollings directed her toward the exit, where he passed her to another firefighter, a man with a thick beard and bronzed face who threw a blanket around her shoulders as Kate stepped onto the sidewalk and removed her mask, coughing momentarily before breathing a lungful of air on the street.

"Are you okay, ma'am?" he asked.

"Yes, yes, thanks," she replied, her focus returning, her eyes automatically snooping the crowd beyond the police cordon, the APD officers patrolling the street, the medics by the ambulances assisting guests or hotel personnel injured on the way out, and the firefighters, of course. Five engines, six ambulances, and at least a dozen APD cruisers crowded Sixth Stre—

Kate saw them: five men fast-walking out of the side of the building, likely in communication with those at the top, perhaps deployed to cover the delivery alley behind the building. Their wide chests and powerful arms pressed against the fabric of the dark security jackets they wore, their stances wide, their shoes soft-soled to provide traction in a chase or in hand-to-hand combat. Mirror-tinted glasses prevented anyone from seeing their eyes, from knowing who they stared at, but Kate could see their heads moving frantically as they reached the middle of the street, a hundred feet from where she stood still covered by the yellow blanket from the fire department, blending herself with the other guests crowding the side of one of the fire engines.

Don't linger.

The interior surveillance cameras out of commission due to the smoke, the security team would be focusing their attention on the activity outside the building, zooming, panning, trying to find their elusive target. And that meant even with the blanket and the crowd, Kate Chavez was exposed.

The guards continued to scan the street as options occurred to her, including dropping the blanket and making a run for the bike parked a block away. With luck she would drive off before they got to her. She also contemplated slowly distancing herself from the group, perhaps blending with the crowd across the street, making her way to the end of the block and then running to the bike.

Making her decision, Kate backed away slowly but only for thirty seconds, increasing the gap, giving herself a wider running start.

As the red, blue, and white lights of emergency vehicles washed the sides of surrounding buildings with their blended hues, Kate dropped the blanket and charged toward the Kawasaki.

It took less than five seconds before she heard a commotion behind her, and risking a backward glance over her left shoulder, watched the security guards moving after her, but doing so without alarming nearby APD officers, elegantly sneaking through the wall of onlookers and emergency personnel separating them.

Professionals.

Pushing her body to go faster, Kate returned her attention to the upcoming block, to the row of parked vehicles hugging the right side of the street, toward the small break in the pattern of cars—the place she had snuck in the Kawasaki, keeping the front facing the street.

Filling her lungs through her nose, exhaling through her mouth, she maintained the sprint, the heels of her boots clicking over the asphalt, her ears struggling to discern the noise of her pursuers from the chaos she had created outside the Driskill.

Her throat dry, she cut right the moment she reached the row of parked vehicles, trying her best to break any possible line of sight, her shoulders tensing at the thought of a silenced round ripping through her spine.

In spite of her training, Kate glanced over her right shoulder again, watching five figures break free from the crowd, from the gathered APD officers by the front of the hotel, who seemed far more concerned with the safety of their block than with the events developing in the adjacent one.

Picking up their pace, reaching inside their coats, her pursuers separated, three down the middle of the street, the other two on the flanking sidewalks—trying to maintain line of sight.

Kate reached the bike, momentarily losing contact with them as she vanished between the two parked SUVs.

Donning the helmet, she started the engine, throttling hard, kicking the gear handle down with the tip of her left boot while releasing the clutch.

The bike surged from between the cars, toward the middle of the street, where she leaned hard to the right while turning the handlebars, cutting her forward momentum, pointing it up the block, away from her pursuers, from—

The windshield of a parked Mercedes sedan next to her exploded almost in slow motion as she gathered speed, as she leaned to the left and then to the right, forcing the accelerating bike into a series of tight S-turns.

A glance at the Kawasaki's side mirrors revealed the guards had stopped, one had taken a knee and was firing in her direction, the rest stood behind him, shielding his actions from the police back at the hotel, making sure that their comrade's use of a silenced weapon wasn't drawing any unwanted attention.

Faster. Faster. You need to go—

One of the side mirrors shattered, exploding in shards of glass and plastic that washed away in the slipstream as she continued to accelerate, continued to force the bike into the tight S-turns that made her a harder target to hit, even if in doing so it took her longer to reach the end of the street, where she planned to—

A powerful blast echoed inside her helmet, deafening, the pressure almost unbearable, as if an invisible hammer had just pounded the helmet.

Her vision momentarily tunneling, feeling light-headed, Kate forced savage control, keeping her hands clutching the handlebars, wrestling with the bike careening down the street, her head throbbing, her temples on fire, tears filming her eyes.

Tapping the brakes, leaning into the turn, she cut right at

the corner as fast as she could without losing control, getting out of her pursuers' range.

She emerged from the turn, working the gears, increasing speed, the pressure around her head lessening, her vision widening.

What in the hell was that?

Analyze later!

Drive!

And she did, steering the bike down the street for two blocks before turning left, driving one block and turning right, increasing the gap, constantly checking her surviving rearview mirror, verifying she was not being followed.

Stopping ten minutes later at a convenience store to use a public phone and catch her breath, Kate inspected her helmet, taking a quick breath of horror at the three-inch-long gash that a bullet had carved onto its top, the angle shallow enough for the layers of metal and fiberglass to deflect the round.

I'm way too old for this shit.

Shaking her head, leaving the helmet on the bike, she walked up to one of three public phones, inserted two coins and dialed the motel's number.

Closing her eyes while inhaling deeply, she heard the phone ring twice before the front desk picked up. Kate asked to get connected to their room, and waited until Cameron answered.

"Mom! Are you all right?"

In spite of the close call, Kate not only felt a sense of relief to hear his voice, but also renewed closeness from the concern straining his voice. Two days ago he could not have cared less what happened to her. Cameron's mind was on his LAN games, the latest computer hardware and software, surfing the Internet, and hanging out with his geeky friends.

"Yes, honey. I'm fine," she said, and that's when it hit her: Cameron's friends were all geeks, and she even remembered he had once mentioned something about knowing a group of hackers.

Realizing that this was a desperate move—one that could put Cameron in danger—but that they were already in grave danger with narrowing choices, Kate Chavez asked, "Listen, Honey. I need to find a way to break into the firewall of a corporation. Is that something you can help me with?"

A pause, followed by, "No, Mom. I'm not good enough yet."

Kate closed her eyes, feeling as if the world was collapsing around them. She could hold her own in the real world. But she was woefully inadequate in the cyberworld.

"But," Cameron continued, "I know who can."

40

New Faces

Dana Kovacs woke up to a brief muffled scream, followed by the gurgling sounds of someone drowning just outside her hut.

Sitting up in her cot, her mouth dehydrated and pasty, her eyelids heavy, she listened intently, alarm worming in her intestines.

A figure poked his head inside the dwelling, looking about, momentarily focusing on her, bringing an index finger up to his lips, and vanishing again.

The same figure reappeared, backing into the hut. Dressed in jungle fatigues and hauling all sorts of gear, his face painted green and brown, the stranger was tall and muscular, though not nearly as wide as the African soldiers.

Dana froze, watching the silhouette of the stranger drag the body of one of the two guards Gardiol had planted outside her hut not just for protection after he realized her potential in nanotechnology, but also to keep her from trying to escape.

The stranger, whose features Dana could not see in the darkness of the hut, stepped back outside and dragged the body of the second guard inside the hut.

As he was about to approach her, a distant scream ripped through the stillness of the night, the scream of alarm. Many voices immediately joined, echoing across the camp.

"Shit," the green-faced man said, stretching a hand towards Dana. "They must have found one of the bodies."

Uncertain how to reply, Dana sat there, dumbfounded in the shadows of the dark hut, her mind struggling to catch up to the rapidly changing events.

Who is he?

His accent pegged him as American, probably from the northeast.

And why was he killing Gardiol's guards?

"Renee? It's me, Mac," the man said, taking a step toward her. "Mac Savage."

Her face darkened by the murkiness of the room, Dana opened her mouth to reply but alarmed voices echoed outside, across the camp.

"Damn," the stranger hissed, approaching her, still not realizing who she was. "We need to get out of here before—"

The voices outside grew into shouts, into angered screams.

"They found the bodies," he added in a low tone, more to himself than to Dana, before stretching an open hand at her in the dark, his features still shadowed by the face paint as well as by the hut's dark interior. "Let's go. We don't have much time."

Realizing that this man had come here to rescue Renee, Dana felt compelled to say, "I'm not the one you seek."

The stranger stopped in mid-stride, tilting his head at her, momentarily squinting, obviously confused, remaining frozen for a moment or two, before looking toward the entrance and the shouts beyond it, and back at her. "Where . . . where is Renee?"

"Dead," she replied. "Raped and killed by the same bastards who kidnapped me and—"

The shouts grew nearer. The stranger who called himself Mac Savage looked once more toward them, before looking back at Dana, his face briefly softening in confusion, before anger tensed his cheekbones, his forehead.

"She's . . . *dead?*"

Dana stood and said, "I'm so sorry."

"How did she die?"

Dana swallowed the lump in her throat and crossed her arms, not certain how to reply to that.

"*How*, damn it? How did she die?"

Shaking her head while feeling her eyes filling with tears, she said, "They . . . they raped her and beat her for a week."

A hand on his forehead, Savage took a deep breath through flared nostrils before turning away, exhaling in what almost seemed like a light cry, remaining still for a few moments before asking, "Who did this to her?"

"Someone named Aman, plus some of his guards."

Savage covered his mouth with a hand and looked away again.

Dana's eyes filled, her jaw clenched tight as the images of the oversized Africans brutalizing the defenseless woman filled her mind.

"I'm . . . really, truly sorry for—"

"Who . . . who are you?"

"My name is Dana Kovacs. Renee told me about her abduction, about how they—"

Someone rushed into the tent. Dana recognized his sheer bulk and the light eyes glimmering in the night—the eyes of the oversized African brute who had slapped her unconscious before raping Renee.

Aman.

Savage, barely half the size of the rapist, shifted like a shadow, moving sideways, a knife protruding from the top of his right fist.

Before Aman could react, Savage had positioned himself to the right of the African, driving the knife up hard into the soft skin between the chin and the throat.

The sickening noise of steel impaling bone and cartilage momentarily filled the hut as Savage maintained the upward thrust until his fist struck the chin.

Savage held the position, right arm stretched halfway,

tight fist under his victim's chin, holding up the convulsing African, staring him in the eye as he soiled his pants, as a pair of trembling hands at the end of grotesquely muscular arms dropped the weapon they were holding.

"Was he one of them?" Savage asked.

"Ye—yes. He is Aman," she replied.

The African rebel chief continued to tremble as Savage locked eyes with him and whispered, "This one's for Renee, motherfucker," while twisting the knife, making Aman tremble, his eyes rolling to the back of his head before going limp.

Savage retrieved the knife in a swift downward Jerk while taking a step back with the grace of a ballet dancer, letting the oversized rebel chief fall to his knees, then face first on the dirt floor, kicking up dust.

The sight evoked some image of the Biblical battle between David and Goliath. Dana watched Savage, not wasting time looking at his victim. Rather, he spun furiously toward the entrance like a dark cyclone, still clutching the bloody knife, stopping abruptly, peeking outside, and assessing the situation before doubling back toward Dana.

Then he said something to her that removed any doubts she still might have had about trusting him: "Come with me if you wish to live."

Dana looked at the slain African, at the animal who had brutalized the defenseless Renee Laroux. Before she realized what she was doing, she kicked the dead man's head with the toe of her left sneaker, spitting on him and hissing, "I hope you rot in fucking hell!"

Savage regarded Dana with a mix of surprise and admiration before simply taking her hand, pulling her away from the body and toward the front of the hut.

Together they peered beyond the canvas draped over the oval opening, watching at least three dozen militia armed with rifles and machine guns rushing toward the periphery of the camp.

Dana was able to get a closer look of her rescuer's face, which, like the rest of his body, was camouflaged in patterns of green and brown. But the hard-edged features and strong chin were still visible in the camp's limelight. In spite of his intimidating appearance, she saw a terrible sadness glimmering in his eyes. Renee Laroux had been very important to him.

The low whop-whop noise of a helicopter main rotor rumbled in the camp.

Dana turned to the noise and watched the plump figure of Gardiol, dressed in while slacks and shirt, climbing aboard the chopper along with three Africans with weapons.

"That's Gardiol," she said. "He's the one behind this."

"Is he?" the stranger said more to himself, before adding, "And where does he think he's going?"

"Back to Freetown, I think," she replied as the helicopter left the ground, its downwash blowing up a cloud of dust and leaves, its powerful halogens lighting up the surrounding trees as it climbed straight up, hovered for a few seconds at around two hundred feet, and flew toward the northwest.

Savage said, "That's certainly the way to Freetown alright. But do you know *where* in Freetown?"

She nodded, saying, "I'll take you there."

Frowning while giving the camp one final glance, Savage whispered a word that sounded like *Payback*, before reaching for a side pocket and producing a small object that resembled a remote control.

He donned a contraption that looked like a fancy pair of goggles, securing them to his face with an adjustable strap. "Night vision," he said before pressing one of the buttons on the remote control unit.

A loud explosion rocked the camp, momentarily flashing in the night at the far end of the guerrilla camp, taking out the small power plant in a dazzling display of fire and sparks. The lights flickered and went off, leaving the place in total darkness.

"Let's roll," he said, holding her hand as several flashlights came alive around the camp, along with more shouts of anger, of confusion. Shots were fired, then more shouting and more discharges, but not at them. The Africans were reacting to Savage's diversion.

"Stay next to me."

Dana hesitated, her mind refusing to follow in the pitch-black night.

"Trust me, Dana. I can see fine. I'll guide you out of this place."

Dana felt the stranger's grip, the way he held her hand, firm yet gentle, keeping her close to him. She not only *felt* his strength, she had *seen* it, seen the way he disabled the gigantic African with the ease and grace of a professional—with the cold brutality of a man exacting revenge.

And Dana Kovacs blindly followed this stranger into the night, rushing through the humid darkness, ignoring the screams, the hastily spoken orders, the crisscrossing beams of light as the guerrillas fell to Savage's diversionary tactics, as they struggled to mount a counterattack. But soon the militia left the area immediately surrounding the destroyed power station and spread out, some advancing in their direction.

"Stay low," he whispered as he cut left, dragging her along, before pressing another button on the remote control, followed by another explosion, this one on the left side of the camp, in the opposite direction from where they headed.

Diversions, Dana thought in increased admiration. He's creating diversions to cover our—

Savage tapped the remote control once more.

The night momentarily turned into day as large drums detonated in sequence, spewing a cloud of fire for fifty yards, engulfing men and equipment.

High-pitched screams filled the skies as figures ablaze emerged from the inferno while others rushed after them with blankets.

And in the flashing limelight, as they raced across the clearing, Dana thought she saw Savage grin as he watched the Africans burn.

Staccato gunfire broke out again around the clearing, the muzzle flashes pulsating in the darkness. Some rounds pounded a structure next to her, a hut, triggering explosions of mud and straw.

As a third explosion ripped through the night, Savage stepped up the pace while also turning behind the hut just as the sound of near-misses buzzed in her ears.

In spite of his precautions someone had spotted them.

Before she could say anything, he dragged her down while embracing her tight, forcing them into a roll toward the tree line as more rounds buzzed overhead, impacting nearing trunks.

The night and the ground swapped places as he pressed on, using his body to absorb the brunt of the impact while she was on top and resting most of his weight on his elbows and knees while on top of her.

He surged upward fluidly upon reaching the waist-high bushes bordering the jungle, his powerful arms carrying her along, gently setting her on her feet.

Before she could utter a word, he was on the move again, towing her while in a deep crouch through the brush, through the thickening vegetation as reports continued to echo in the night and rounds pounded the trees, splintering bark and wood, the muzzle flashes washing the green wall facing them in stroboscopic waves of red and yellow-gold.

Savage momentarily jerked forward, breaking his rhythm, as if punched in the back by an invisible fist, before slowing down while mumbling something that sounded like a cry.

He recovered almost immediately, regaining his footing and cutting left before she could figure out what had happened, taking them through a winding path that crossed a shallow stream.

Gunfire slowed to sporadic reports, before ceasing altogether, replaced by more angered voices, shouts from men tromping over vegetation, though Dana couldn't tell if they were following them or running in a different direction.

Dana and Savage pressed on as the trail veered upward, following the contour of one of the hills overlooking the camp.

Developing a limp on his left leg, Savage maintained the pace for another ten minutes, reaching the hill's summit and starting toward the next valley, the racket behind them dying away, replaced by a breeze whistling through the thicket, the clicking of insects, the howling of monkeys.

The limp became more noticeable now, and he moaned every time he put weight on the left leg.

"Are you okay?" she asked in the darkness as he paused and took a deep breath, her face just behind his right ear.

Savage turned around, an index finger over his lips as he regarded her with the night-vision goggles, looking more like a robot than a human. "Lower your voice," he whispered, adding, "Got shot in the leg and won't be able to go much further."

"Oh, my God. Let me—"

Savage placed the index over her lips now while slowly shaking his head and removing his bandana, which he tied over the bottom of his right thigh to staunch the blood loss. "There will be plenty of time for that soon. These guys are as good at tracking as they are raping, maiming, and killing women and children. I killed their leader. They will not give up following our trail."

"I can't go back to that place," she said. "What they did to Renee . . . what they would now do in revenge for—"

"Easy," he whispered, stretching a thumb toward the hill behind them. "At this moment they're sending search parties in every direction, including this one."

Voices—angered voices—could now be heard, along with the rustle of vegetation in their direction.

"That's the team dispatched this way."

"What are you going to do?"

Savage grinned. "Discourage them a little to buy us time to get away.

"How?"

Instead of replying, Savage took a knee while removing his rucksack, producing two black, rectangular objects the size of thick paperbacks with wires projecting from the top and a pair of six-inch-long metal stakes from the bottom.

"These are claymore mines," Savage mumbled, inserting the stakes of the first device in the soft soil such that the front of the unit faced the incoming threat but at about a thirty-degree angle. He sank the other mine sixty degrees in the opposite direction, so that they covered not just the area in front of them but also part of the flanks.

He connected the protruding wires atop each charge to the standing end of a roll of twisted wire, which he uncoiled as they walked away from the booby trap. He strapped the other end of the twisted pair to a handheld device resembling a stapler.

"How do you know they will come precisely down this path?" she asked.

Without warning, Savage reached for her bare arm and pinched her hard.

"Aghh!" she screamed, turning to him and hitting him on the side of the head, shifting the goggles before hissing, "Why did you do that?"

Repositioning the night-vision gear, he replied without humor, "Sorry. I needed something to bring them to this spot."

Crossing her arms while frowning, Dana reluctantly followed him as they hid behind a large boulder roughly a dozen feet from the charges.

The voices got nearer. Savage kept his sight straight ahead, right hand clutching a machine gun, left hand holding the detonating device.

Dana squinted to try to peer in the darkness beyond, struggling to spot the incoming guerrillas but lacking night-vision goggles, she saw nothing but a pitch-black wall beyond a couple of feet in front of her.

She turned back to her rescuer hoping—no, *praying*—that he knew what he was doing.

Mac Savage wasn't certain this trick would work, but as he surveyed the palette of greens in which the light-amplifying system painted the woods in front of him, he decided he didn't really care anymore. This night marked the lowest point in his life, having not only been forced to descend back to this hell on Earth to rescue a woman who was already dead, but now having the minions living in this hell after him—and to top it all off he had been shot in the leg, hundreds of miles away from any decent hospital. If the bastards trailing them didn't kill him, the blood loss or subsequent infection would.

He decided to play his last card right here, right now. He wasn't kidding about the African guerrillas' keen ability to

track, and it was impossible for him and Dana not to leave a
trail, even if he managed to minimize his blood loss with the
makeshift tourniquet.

If they were going to have any chance of getting away, he
would have to stop their momentum now, strip them of their
commitment, which he thought he had done with the multiple C4 blasts around their camp, including the one that took
out their fuel supply while also incinerating a dozen men.
But the African militia had rebounded with amazing elasticity; had regrouped faster than Savage anticipated, even after
losing their leader, dispatching search parties while their
camp and many of their comrades still burned.

Disciplined and persistent, he thought, dreading the combination of his enemy's clearly displayed skills as he held a
detonator that would trigger the pair of claymores and also
the remote control for the last two charges planted at the opposite side of the camp—his final distraction.

Three emerald beams—flashlights—preceded five figures, darker shadows shifting beyond the nearest trees, moving in their direction.

He waited, watching their silhouettes grow, the beams of
green light crisscrossing in the darker surroundings, searching, prying into the path ahead.

They were big men, taller than Savage and much wider,
like the ones he had disabled. Two held automatic weapons;
the other three clutched pistols and flashlights. The goggles
displayed their eyes like pairs of glowing gems on their otherwise dark green figures.

Savage held his breath as the fivesome spread from the
cluster they had maintained. Although the range wasn't
ideal, he couldn't afford to wait anymore or the ones at the
ends of the incoming formation would escape the double
blast with only minor injuries, and possibly attack him from
each side.

Motioning Dana to open her mouth and cover her ears
with her hands, Savage pressed the claymore detonator as
well as the remote control device.

The earth-rumbling blast of the anti-personnel claymores,
each packing 700 steel balls—the equivalent of a firing

squad of shotguns—shook the darkness in an engulfing inferno of molten metal, followed by the brief agonizing
screams of the Africans. In the same instance, two detonations from the direction of the camp lit up the sky like lightning, confirming the end of his charges. With luck, those
two blasts would confuse the enemy as to the location of the
claymore explosions.

At least long enough for us to get out of Dodge.

Savage stood with effort, hands clutching the silenced
MP5, his enhanced vision surveying the damage, the still
bodies, some of them missing body parts and—

A moan, subtle at first, but then intensifying, told Savage
that one of the Africans had survived the carnage. Unless he
could silence him, the noise might be heard by others in the
camp.

Savage quickly zeroed in on him, the farthest to the right
of the guerrilla formation. The African was on his knees, his
eyes either shut or missing because he saw no glow on the
silhouette.

Aiming the MP5, he fired once, the bullet striking the man
squarely in the face.

As he fell back on impact, Savage surveyed the rest of the
neutralized team, but only saw four figures sprawled on
the—

A shadow shifted to his immediate right, rustling low-
hanging branches. Savage dropped to a deep crouch, feeling
the near-whistle of the strike weapon, a long machete, slice
the air an inch above his head.

Caught with his weapon pointed in the wrong direction,
but having bought himself a few seconds while the African
swung the long blade back around, Savage pivoted, cringing
in pain when resting most of his weight on his wound, but
maintaining the turn while extending his right leg, locking it
as he struck the back of his attacker's knees, sweeping the
legs from under him.

The large African let go a brief shout as he fell flat on his
back. Savage reversed the turn, lowering the MP5, firing
three times in rapid succession while sweeping the weapon
up the guerrilla's chest. Two rounds tore his chest open, the

third slicing through the neck in an explosion of blood and foam.

Silence, followed by more voices originating in the guerrilla camp.

"Let's go," he said, feeling a bit out of breath, his strength leaving him. He had to get to the Jeep, had to get out of the guerrilla-controlled enclave before he passed out from blood loss. "I don't have much time."

Hackeresque

"This is, like, the biggest bunch of mysteriosity I've ever heard."

The hacker, who went by the name of Lman, sat in an orange swivel chair contemplating a large LCD screen while listening to Cameron, who Kate had just learned was called Squirrel.

Lman pouted while looking at his ego wall, plastered with newspaper and magazine articles on his lifelong accomplishment: hacker attacks. He wasn't a kid, though he dressed like one: neon-blue leather pants that matched the color of his shoulder-length hair and goatee, a black T-shirt with winged unicorns and sorcerers battling demonic figures, a pair of sandals, and a body piercing in the shape of a skull on the corner of his bottom lip.

Kate put him at around twenty-five, and he seemed to have a taste for fantasy and science fiction, an observation based on the T-shirt and the dozen posters adorning the other walls. All of them had a similar theme: Winged unicorns ridden by scantily dressed voluptuous women clutching swords and shields fighting dragons, demons, or wizards, sometimes assisted by muscular handsome men armed with immense clubs, swords, and chains. The contrast between good and evil was also reflected in the extreme physical beauty of the good guys fighting grotesquely demonic creatures.

"The Donovan Group, huh?" Lman whispered almost to himself. "A challengosity."

"I'm telling you, dude," Cameron added as the apparent leader of his LAN gang kept his blue eyes on the magazine clips. "This lameitude of a company is larger than Bgates and in obviosity need of hackification. It would be the ultimate winnitude."

Kate frowned and crossed her arms while standing in the doorway of the hacker's room in a college apartment by the University of Texas. Although allowed to enter the apartment's common ground—the living, kitchen, and dining areas—she had not been granted permission to enter Lman's physical domain.

The hacker's bedroom consisted primarily of an unmade single bed, several stacks of books and magazines, and three desks arranged in the shape of a U and topped with computer gear, including three large LCD monitors, one per desk, with the hacker sitting in the center. Multiple sets of VR gear were interfaced to the humming workstations lining the sides of the desks. A poster of Bill Gates with half his body spray-painted in red and the words MONOPOLITUDE-R-US written across the bottom was flanked by one of Intel with a large black X painted on it, and a similar one of Dell Computer Corporation. The anti-monopoly posters were surrounded by the larger and more entertaining fantasy and science fiction prints.

"What's with the graffiti on the posters?" Kate asked, unable to keep quiet any longer.

Cameron gave her a desperate, wide-eyed stare and was about to say something when Lman raised a gloved hand.

The hacker's dark eyes slowly gravitated to her, focusing like laser beams. "*Miss* Chavez," he said without a hint of emotion. "You must abide by our rules . . . or leave."

Kate took a deep breath. She had no other place to go to

seek high-tech help. She needed a way to break into TDG's network and search for any proof that she could use not just to convince Hunter but also to go to the media, to expose those bastards, to bring them down. Only when those hunting her were behind bars would Cameron and she be free.

"My apologies," she said, swallowing a hunk of pride.

The master hacker slowly gave her a nod. "We also don't appreciate the restraint you have placed on Squirrel. He should be allowed to morph into the person he really is."

Morph? What in the fuck is this asshole talking about? Kate thought, remaining impassive, locking her tongue so tight that her jaw started to hurt.

"In any case," Lman continued, turning his attention back to Cameron, "I was able to do a little researchitude on TDG since your call an hour ago, and I have decided to taskify this challengitude. It is worthy of my skillitude."

Kate frowned. Whenever Lman and Cameron addressed one another, they did it using this weird hacker talk. But whenever they addressed her, they reverted to regular English.

"Thank you, Lman. Your generositude is most appreciatitative," said Cameron.

He grinned ever so slightly and raised his right hand a few inches from the table, monarch-like, before saying to Kate, "I will need a few hours to achieve Miller's Seven. Then we'll talk options."

"Miller's Seven?" she asked. "What's that?"

Lman closed his eyes and slowly shook his head. "I thought Squirrel told me you were in law enforcement."

"I am," she said, suddenly feeling a bit uncomfortable.

He sighed, then rubbed his two-day stubble, before stating, "This is why criminal hackers—*crackers*—run circles around you cops. If you don't understand something as simple as Miller's *Basic Seven*, how can you possibly counter cyber attacks?"

Kate opened her mouth to say something, but Lman added, "There are seven steps designed by Doctor Ron Miller, a professor of computer science from Rice and one of the greatest hackers of our generation. The steps outline the order in which to break into a system, though I remind you I do not cause any damage, like crackers do. I do it to prove that it can be done, and to help networks tighten their security against crackers by leaving them messages on how I broke in."

"Ron Miller?" Kate asked, the name sounding vaguely familiar. "Wasn't he the guy who broke into the bank accounts of former Enron executives several years back?"

Lman nodded and grinned in brief admiration. "He's doing twenty years in Eastham State Prison down in Houston for transferring over seven hundred million dollars out of the personal bank accounts of eight Enronites and into overseas accounts but in a way that made a trace of the stolen funds impossible."

Kate remembered now. The stolen proceeds had disappeared in the convoluted international on-line banking system. But the same month, out of untraceable overseas accounts, nearly the same amount of dollars had been magically deposited into the retirement accounts of thousands of Enron employees who had watched their life savings implode during that company's downfall at the turn of the millennium.

"Dr. Miller stepped in when it became clear that the government wasn't going to bring them to justice," added Lman. "It was a privilege to have studied under him at Rice way back when. He had the guts to steal from the rich and give to the poor, to step in and do the right thing in the face of terrible personal consequences."

"A modern day Robin Hood," said Cameron.

Kate blinked at the comment from her son. She wasn't aware that Cameron knew about Enron, especially since he had been about seven years old at the time.

"But he *was* caught," she observed.

Cameron dropped his gaze in apparent respect. Lman's eyes became misty.

They really admire this Miller character.

"That's the thing, Miss Chavez," the hacker said. "Ron Miller got away with it. He had the cash secured overseas and no one knew who had done it. He could have lived like a king, but he chose instead to return that money to its rightful owners: the employees who got screwed by the corrupted Enronites."

"And that's when they nailed him, Mom. Shortly after he gave it back. One of the thousands of bank transactions came across a government trace left behind from another case, and the trace pointed the cops to his home in Houston."

Kate felt a bit uncomfortable that her own teenager—the kid she had to ride to brush his teeth and do his homework—could be so versed in these matters.

Lman continued. "The government offered him a deal: Plead guilty, give it all back and serve just three years at a minimum security prison, or refuse to cooperate and face twenty years in a federal prison."

Kate felt a little guilty for remembering so little about such a noble case.

Lman lifted his can of caffeinated soda toward Cameron, and the two of them toasted.

"To Miller," said Lman. "Sent to rot in jail by the same bureaucronies who let the Enronites run free."

After they sipped their drinks, Cameron added with obvious admiration, "Lman was one of Miller's students at Rice, and he is now one of the best security experts in the biz, helping protect the sanctity of the Internet but without getting paid for it, or without any recognized credentials."

"You don't get paid for your services?" asked Kate.

Lman glanced at Cameron, smiled, and said to her, "Not only is getting payment to fight criminal hackers *mundane*, Miss Chavez, but I have personal reasons to want to attack criminal hackers. The Internet must be protected."

Cameron said, "Lman's parents got their identities stolen by a hacker, and he got away with their life savings."

"And that," said Lman, "means I now have to put myself through graduate school by working days and going to school at night."

"I'm so sorry that happened to your family," said Kate.

Lman shrugged. "Shit happens. Miller did what he had to do. I do what I have to do."

"So you're some sort of high-tech vigilante?" Kate said.

"You could say that, and I'll be happy to stop the day our law enforcement—which is currently *years* behind in technology—catches up with modern-day cyberterrorists."

"How do you protect the Internet? You go around killing people's computers long distance?"

Lman smiled. "I do not kill people's systems, Miss Chavez. That would not only be unproductive but it would lower me to their level. I find their systems and install little spy programs that allow me to monitor their operations without them knowing about it. That allows me to figure out how they plan their attacks. Then I point the right people in law enforcement in the right direction to nail the bastards, while remaining totally invisible."

"How do you remain invisible?"

Lman just stared back.

"That question isn't cool, Mom."

Realizing that Lman wasn't about to reveal trade secrets, Kate asked, "So you think you're good enough to break into TDG's network and help me catch some criminals?"

"Based on my preliminary research, it's worth a try. I know some of TDG's companies haven't upgraded their networks to the latest version of SP19."

"What's SP19?"

"Microsoft Service Pack Nineteen. It's that company's latest attempt to fight the most recent generation of computer worms, of software that capitalizes on design vulnerabilities in their operating system. GemTech is already SP19 compliant, and so are the other companies that make up TDG, except for one called the World Missionary Fellowship. Its network in the United States is already upgraded, but there is a server cluster residing in Sierra Leone, West Africa, still operating with SP18, which isn't that surprising. Microsoft patches take a little while to propagate overseas."

"How long did it take you to figure that out?" she asked.

Lman shrugged again. "Not long."

Although Kate didn't like this cult-like character—and especially the way he was influencing Cameron—it appeared to her that she might have come to the right place.

Lman raised a brow while giving her a slight nod. "The first step is to gather information about the target, The Donovan Group, but to do so through the most vulnerable portal, the World Missionary Fellowship."

"How do you do that?"

Lman considered the question, then said, "It's . . . compli-
cated. But even if it were simple, I would not share my secrets
with an outsider, especially someone from law enforcement,
as that could one day be used against me."

"I can see why you would feel this way, but the reason for
my question is tied to your protection, as well as Cameron's.
See, what Cameron didn't tell you is that we're currently being hunted, and it is my belief that TDG somehow controls
the police, and that makes me a fugitive—and it will put you
in great danger."

The hacker narrowed his gaze, obviously not following.

Kate added, "What I'm trying to tell you is that TDG security isn't just going to call the cops to come and arrest you
if they manage to trace your incursion in their network.
They'll send assassins to kill you and then manipulate the
cops and the media to make it look like you were some sort
of armed terrorist."

The words made Lman's eyes open wide, but not in fear.
The hacker was now really excited. "So the stakes are even
higher then. All the more reason to follow my seven steps."
Turning to Cameron, he added, "Squirrel, a teachitude of
your mother would alleviatize her concerns while I explore.
I'm jacking in."

Without another word, the hacker reached for one of the
VR interfaces, slipped it on, and immersed himself in cyberspace.

Kate checked her watch, looked at Cameron, and said,
"Do not leave this place. I'll be back in a couple of hours."

"Where are you going?"

"To pursue another lead while your friend tries to find
anything he can."

42

Savage felt progressively weaker, his hands trembling as he fired another GPS probe, before inspecting the handheld unit to confirm his track back to the Jeep with Dana Kovacs in tow.

Although his breathing became more labored, Savage grew more confident that he had managed to lose all search teams, in part due to the multiple diversions, but also because of the night-vision goggles and his refusal to stop, rest, and get Dana to field dress his wound.

The initial hour following a raid was the most critical, and putting as much distance as possible from the strike during this time increased the search area tenfold, magnifying the degree of difficulty of those pursuing him. The night also worked to his advantage by making it even more difficult for trackers to spot their trail.

But there's a price for everything, he thought, leading Dana in silence up another hill, doing his best to minimize not just the noise they made but also the damage to the surrounding vegetation.

Filmed in sweat, inspecting the LCD display to verify their position, Savage felt his strength leaving him, felt the very slow but steady loss of blood taking its toll.

Less than a mile to go.

"This way," he whispered to Dana, the fine features of her face washed in hues of green.

"Mac," she said, putting a hand on his shoulder. "You need to stop and let me bandage that leg."

"Soon," he said, handing her the GPS before pointing at the holstered air gun and the pouch housing his remaining probes. Tapping the LCD screen with the tip of his index finger, he added, "The green triangle shows our position. The red X marks the location where I hid the Jeep. The yellow X marks the location of the airfield where I keep a plane to takes us back to Freetown. The Jeep belongs to a mechanic in the airfield. His name is Kembo. I owe him four hundred bucks plus the return of his Jeep before he will release the plane back to me. I have cash in my money belt under the fatigues. Hire a pilot to fly us back to Freetown. Seek a man named Salim Anahah. He runs a security business. His mobile number is programmed in my phone. He will help us. And you know what to do with the gun and probes. Use them sparingly to confirm your track while navigating with this compass."

"Why are you telling me this now?" she asked in the darkness surrounding them. "You are going to be—"

"Did you get all of that?" he hissed.

"Ye—yes, but why are you telling me this now?"

He began to walk instead of answering, taking her free hand, tugging her along a trail that veered up the side of the hill, his eyelids becoming heavier, his limbs beginning to tingle, his mind losing focus.

But he persisted. He couldn't afford the fifteen minutes it would take for her to field dress the wound, and less so because it would require the use of a glow stick for her to see what she was doing.

Keep going.

His training commanded him to do so, and Mac Savage obeyed the same instincts that had kept him alive for twenty years.

Keep going.

Reaching deep in his physical reserves, pulling out the overwhelming desire to remain conscious, to maintain a steady rhythm, the former CIA officer climbed toward the summit, controlling his breathing, ignoring the burning pain broadcast by his right thigh, focusing instead on the next step, and the one after that.

Almost there, he told himself, the sound of his heartbeat mixing with his breathing and the light rustle of branches and shrubbery as he and Dana maintained the pace, kept their momentum pointed in the right direction, toward the Jeep waiting along the road on the opposite side of the hill.

Feeling light-headed, dizzy, a ringing in his ears, Savage swallowed hard, taxing himself beyond his endurance, refusing to stop for fear of daylight catching up with them, robbing him of his one edge over the enemy: the ability to see in the dark.

The smell of rotting vegetation and the musk from his own sweat glands filling his nostrils, Mac Savage ignored his protesting back, his wounded thigh, his trembling hands clutching the MP5—he even ignored Dana's constant requests to stop and get his wound dressed.

She doesn't realize the danger we're in if we fail to reach that airfield before first light, he thought, forcing one foot in front of the other, focusing on that simple motion while also twisting his body to correspond with bends in the vegetation.

Keep moving.

Savage repeated the words in his tired and cloudy mind, again and again, keeping his eyes on the terrain ahead, his ears listening to the surroundings, struggling to detect any sounds that didn't belong in the jungle, filtering the constant clicking and buzzing of insects, the distant howling of monkeys, the occasional squawk of a bird.

Keep moving.

He had no choice, no alternative unless he wished to be skinned alive by those he knew would be in hot pursuit by now. He had kicked the guardians of hell—had stolen from them—had killed their leader—and now had to escape or face the worst possible fate on the planet. Savage had seen the amputations, the maiming, the castrations of men, and the terrifying savaging of women and children.

The children.

"My face . . . my legs. . . ."

Savage tried to force the apocalyptic visions out of his head but they persisted, increasing in intensity, like a tidal wave, drowning his logic, confusing reality. He was back in the jungle surrounding the burning refugee camp, the cries assaulting his eardrums, tearing into his block of sanity, of self-control, threatening to—

Keep moving!

His training, a booming voice above the maddening howls of the maimed, urged him on, injecting him with a burst of renewed commitment.

But the adrenaline boost didn't last long. Mac Savage felt the end nearing, sensed the world slowly collapsing around him. He fought it, pushed back with all his might, mustered brutal control to remain standing, to remain walking, to—

"I think we're there, Mac," she whispered in the night, tilting the GPS screen toward him, pointing at the spot where the green triangle overlapped the red X marking the Jeep's location.

Savage watched the screen as it grew distant, as a dark tunnel enclosed him, as he whispered, "Keep moving," before everything faded away.

Small World

Anticipation filling him, Frank Salieri watched the distant Austin skyline under predawn skies from the cabin of GemTech's Cessna Citation-X as the air traffic controller at Bergstrom International Airport sequenced the pilot to approach the field from the west, cruising over the rolling hill country and the many lakes he could not see at night.

Taking a deep breath while stretching his legs, he shifted his sight from the spectacular view to the luxurious interior of the business jet. Rich mahogany paneling met with a pastel headliner that matched the color of the plush leather seats. Mozart played from unseen speakers and the cabin lighting was dimmed just as he liked it.

But in spite of all of the creature comforts of his position, including the ten-million-dollar private jet that cruised at 600 miles per hour at 50,000 feet—far faster and higher than airline traffic—Salieri was still nauseated from the four-hour flight from Alaska, where they had refueled after crossing the Bering Strait, linking the tip of North America with Asia. That was the one disadvantage of flying in a private jet. The Citation lacked the range to cross the Pacific, forcing the pilot to hop along the coast of Russia until reaching Alaska and then heading back down the North American continent.

And there was that terrible turbulent hour when the fancy jet, even with its remarkably high ceiling, was unable to top a thunderstorm over Alaska, keeping the GemTech CEO kneeling in the shiny lavatory purging the expensive breakfast he'd had with three Japanese industrialists that morning before heading for the airport.

Fucking flight and fucking wireless connection, he thought, sipping the carbonated drink that had helped settle his stomach for the past two hours.

Salieri had tried to jack in with his SpyWare in an attempt to detach himself from the misery of severe turbulence as the jet flew through the cell, but a combination of the storm and the extreme high altitude had resulted in a temporary loss of service, meaning the GemTech CEO had to gut it out like all mortals instead of leaving a programmed agent handling his body while he went off into cyberspace.

The city lights grew brighter beyond the window, and Salieri felt the light bump as the pilot lowered the landing gear.

"We'll be on the ground in five minutes, Mr. Salieri," said the pilot, a woman in her early forties and former navy pilot.

Salieri frowned. *Not soon enough.*

Although he felt terrible, he was quite pleased with the trip, having recruited yet another round of believers in

TDG's cause. By the end of the week, two Japanese companies that manufactured consumer electronics, a large Russian manufacturer of pharmaceuticals, and the biggest British food producer would become the latest wholly owned subsidiaries of The Donovan Group—in addition to the software company that George Zhu had acquired without permission, of course.

In all, eighty-seven people would become SpyWare users, mostly Level-Is and Level-IIs, with a dozen Level-IIIs, and three new vice-presidents wearing Level-IV implants. Everyone would make it to GemTech's facility, where they would be ushered to Building 33B to undergo an implant procedure that lasted less than an hour, before flying back home.

And the assimilation continues, he mused in spite of the churning in his lower intestines, resulting in a loud fart, which he gladly released while shifting in his seat.

Reaching above him, he increased the flow of cool air to wash away the stench, before looking back out to the nearing airport, to the two parallel runways of Bergstrom International, the Citation X's home base.

The landing was textbook, even with what appeared to be a gusty crosswind according to the blossomed orange windsock pointing nearly perpendicular to the runway. The former navy jock was worth every penny that Salieri had paid to lure her from landing F-18 Hornets on carriers.

Only the best, he thought, as the advanced jet decelerated, taxiing off the runway toward the ramp. There were two FBOs—Fixed Based Operators—in the General Aviation section of Bergstrom International. One was Signature Air and the other Trajen Flight Support.

GemTech leased one of the large hangars adjacent to the main Trajen building—big enough for the Citation X and a Citation V, a smaller jet Salieri took on domestic trips.

Almost home, he thought, anticipating getting in the rear of the limo that would take him to his estate in Lake Austin for a weekend of R&R with his fiancée, a drop-dead gorgeous blonde twenty years his junior.

The jet came to a complete stop in front of the hangar,

under floodlights washing the area with an amber glow. The silhouettes of tied down small singles and twins spread across the ramp in neat rows, the place where those who couldn't afford hangar space kept their craft. This time of the night the place was deserted, save for the waiting black Hummer stretch limo in the hangar.

The copilot, also former navy but with less experience, walked out of the cockpit and into the cabin. He was a man with a boyish face in his early thirties wearing black slacks and a white short-sleeve shirt with single gold bars embroidered on his narrow shoulders.

He reached for a handle on the side of the main cabin and pulled it out of the wall before rotating it forty-five degrees clockwise. A door slowly swung out and to the left. A light motor sound hummed as four steps projected below the opening.

Salieri snagged the manila folder he had been reviewing off and on during the flight. It contained the latest operational status at GemTech, updated daily by one of his vice-presidents.

Staggering to his feet, he slowly proceeded toward the exit. As he climbed down the steps, the stretch Hummer inside the hangar sprang to life, headlights piercing the yellowish twilight, before coming to a complete stop by the Citation.

Typically, a bodyguard would emerge from the rear of the limo and hold the door open for him. But it appeared as if tonight it was just the driver and him.

Frowning, but too tired to care, the CEO of GemTech opened his own damned door and climbed inside without even once looking back at the pilot and copilot standing by the foot of the jet's stairs.

The interior of the limo was unusually dark, making it difficult to see the two sets of club seats of a color as rich and soothing as those inside the Citation.

But again, Salieri didn't care. He planned to catch a nap on the fifty-minute ride to his lake house.

Closing the door and tapping on the lighted intercom button on the side of the inner wall, near the door, he said to his driver, "Let's go."

"Yes, Mr. Salieri. Welcome home."

"Yeah," he replied as the limo pulled off.

Salieri settled in one of the rearmost seats, as far from the driver as possible, his eyes gazing out of the side window at the sleek lines of the jet. It was indeed a work of art, with its swept-back wings and its wingtips twisted skyward to improve stability.

The limo went through the automatic gate and exited the airport.

Salieri was about to close his eyes when the interior lights went on abruptly, stinging him.

"What in the—"

"Hello, Mr. Salieri," said a woman dressed in black jeans and a black T-shirt holding two pistols, a large one pointed at the back of the front seat, aimed directly at the driver, and a smaller gun pointed directly at him. "My name is Kate Chavez. We have a lot to talk about."

His SpyWare hostage routine kicking in, assisting him in quickly accepting the brutal reality that he was being kidnapped by a person who should have been dead by now, Frank Salieri immediately left a cyberagent handling the conversation with the rogue Texas Ranger while he jacked in, shooting into cyberspace like a bullet, rushing through the data-rich fields of the colorful matrix in search of help.

44

Nurse Dana

Mustering strength she didn't know she possessed, Dana Kovacs, wearing Savage's night-vision goggles, dragged the unconscious operative across the last hundred feet separating them from a rusty Jeep covered with branches and leaves adjacent to an unpaved road.

Clearing off the vegetation, still marveling at the way the goggles painted everything clearly even in pitch-black conditions, she inspected the old vehicle, spotting the keys already in the ignition.

Removing Savage's rucksack, she managed to lay him flat on his back in the rear seat, her shoulders burning from the effort.

A brief inspection of the rucksack's contents confirmed Savage's claim of a first-aid kit, at least enough supplies to field dress the gunshot wound.

Keep moving.

Her mind replaying Savage's words, her eyes shifting between the open rucksack, the bloody leg, the GPS in her hands, and the road ahead, Dana made her decision and tore open the leg of the camouflage pants with the field knife strapped to Savage's waist.

Locating a glow stick and cracking it, she removed her goggles, letting her eyes adjust to the light radiating from the stick, which she placed on one side of the wound, before cracking a second one to illuminate the other side.

"It went through clean," she mumbled, removing not only Savage's soaked makeshift tourniquet but also a small pistol in an ankle holster which had become stained by the same blood that now oozed slowly but steadily from both the entry and exit wounds—less than a couple of inches apart just above the knee on the outer side of the left thigh. Another inch to the left and the damage would have been nothing more than a nick. But another inch in the opposite direction would have shattered the femur.

Removing the pistol from the bloody Nylon holster, she inspected the weapon, which resembled the small guns some of the female volunteers at the camp back in Freetown used to carry. But Dana never had, and she had no idea how to use it.

Pocketing the slim weapon, she opened a pouch of TraumaDex, a starchy substance commonly used by paramedics to induce topical blood clotting. She sprinkled the powdery substance generously over both wounds, watching its sponge-like properties going to work immediately, staunching the hemorrhage. She followed this with a pack of disinfectant, which, again, she distributed evenly over both wounds.

Removing one of three field dressings she found in the rucksack, each army standard and stored in four-by-five canvas pouches, Dana pulled out a single bandage sealed in a clear plastic.

Removing it from the wrapper and grasping the tails of the dressing with both hands, she held it directly over the wounds while keeping the sterile side down, and making sure nothing touched it. Pulling the dressing open, she immediately pressed it firmly against the injured section of the thigh. Holding the dressing down in place with one hand, she used the other to wrap one of the tails around the injury, covering about half of the field dressing, leaving enough of the tail to make a knot. Wrapping the other tail in the opposite direction, she covered the remainder of the dressing, using the tails to seal the sides of the dressing to keep anything from getting under it.

She then carefully tied a non-slip knot over the outer edge of the dressing, but not over the wound. Dana did this firmly enough to prevent it from slipping, but not so tight as to prevent the flow of blood to the lower leg.

Checking her watch, seeing it had taken her less than ten minutes to perform the procedure, she jumped into the driver's seat, satisfied that at a minimum he would not be losing any more blood.

Strapping on the goggles once more, she was about to start the engine when she heard a noise behind her. Turning around, she watched three figures emerge from the jungle about two hundred feet from her. They were large, bulky, holding big guns, the muzzles projecting beams of bright-emerald light.

Her heart sank.

Do they see me?

The figures used the flashlights secured to their weapons to look about them.

They can't see you but they will hear you.

Dana once more considered her options, the guards making her decision for her the moment they started to walk in her direction.

Turning the key, she tensed as the engine coughed and sputtered before coming on with a roar. Easing the pressure on the gas, she stepped on the clutch, shoved the long and thin shifting stick into first, and quickly released the clutch.

Too fast, she thought, as the engine died, as dread filled her stomach when the noise mixed with the shouts and hastened steps of the guerrillas.

Visions of Renee Laroux being brutalized, of what those animals would do to her if they caught her, Dana tried again, closing her eyes as she turned the key, as the starter once more turned the engine over and over, as it rumbled, before coming alive to a rough idle.

The shouts growing louder, followed by the multiple reports of warning shots zooming overhead, she once more pressed the clutch and eased the transmission into first, this time slowly popping the clutch while flooring it. The Jeep sprang forward as all four tires spun furiously, as the ground around her exploded with gunfire, the muzzle flashes showering her with stroboscopic pulses of intense green light.

Surging out of the partial ravine, the remaining branches and leaves falling off, some swirling in the dust kicked by the off-road tires as she punched it.

Gunfire rattled behind her, Dana shifted into second, accelerating down the pothole-filled road, bouncing in her seat, ignoring the accompanying shouts, the half dozen rounds striking the rear of the Jeep before she road veered to the left, away from their immediate line of sight.

Faster. Faster.

Reports still echoing in the night, nearly drowning the angered screams of her pursuers, Dana focused on driving the Jeep, shifting into third, the wind swirling her T-shirt, her hair.

Gripping the wheel hard, her knuckles numbing from the pressure, Dana pushed the aging car as fast as she could without losing control, watching the green road before her, the towering vegetation flanking her blending into a wall of dark green as she accelerated in the direction of the yellow X on the GPS.

Just over fifteen kilometers away, she thought, catching her breath, negotiating the next turn, careening down the uneven terrain, increasing the gap with her angered hunters while doing her best to avoid potholes and fallen branches from the vegetation delineating the road, sweeping over it, giving it a tunnel-like appearance.

Blinking to clear her sight, breathing deeply, swerving constantly to avoid a seemingly endless number of rocks, branches, or potholes, she pressed on, her mind only now beginning to digest just how close she had come to total disaster, silently chastising herself for not taking Savage's warning seriously enough.

Keep moving.

Shit, she sighed, deciding she would not stop until she reached that airfield.

Looking at the GPS once more, she verified her direction, noticing that the road she was on would end soon, merging with a wider, straighter road.

Swallowing, breathing deeply again, exhaling slowly through her mouth, the bizarre turn of events in the past hour beginning to sink in, her mind gravitated to the unconscious stranger in the back seat.

Who is this guy?

Why was he rescuing Renee?

Is he a husband?

A friend?

Perhaps someone contracted to find her?

Based on the way he had reacted to the news of her death, Dana decided he was definitely emotionally involved. But irrespective of his reasons, he had saved *her* from certain doom at the hands of Gardiol and his goons. Dana had managed to use her limited knowledge of diamond nanotechnology to bullshit her way through the first round of discussions with Gardiol the night before. But she was a software specialist, not a hardware guru, and her sense had told her she would not be able to pass another round with the brilliant, savvy, and incredibly insightful Gardiol. In fact, the man was creeping her out because he apparently knew more about diamond nanotech, test software, and firewalls than most scientists.

But he wasn't a scientist. He was the manager of the refugee camp, the administrator, and an impressive one at that, including fluency in many languages.

There was certainly something strange about the WMF chief—something intangible. The man seemed in possession of unlimited knowledge, of an uncanny ability to remember facts, figures, and dates, as well as speaking multiple languages.

I was lucky to last one round with him, she thought as the dirt trail dead-ended onto a paved road, where she referenced the GPS and turned right, to the northwest, keeping the headlights off, navigating in the dark solely by the use of the goggles.

Sooner or later Gardiol would have seen through her façade, determining that she was useless to whatever it was he was up to with conflict diamonds. She would have been thrown to the same horrible fate as Renee Laroux.

But Mac Savage rescued me, she thought. *This man rescued me, and now I must come through for him.*

While driving in the darkness, in the middle of the jungle, hunted by the worst kind of evil, unequivocal loyalty and a powerful sense of clarity descended on Dana Kovacs; a primal directive that kept her focused, concentrated on her mission, on the task of escaping, of reaching that airfield, of finding a way to fly them out of this area—of protecting her protector, her guardian, the only man she now trusted.

But how are you going to fly out of here?

And where are you going to go?

Dana remembered the days following her husband's suicide, recalled the destruction of Diamantex, of everything they had worked for. And she remembered how she had gotten through it, how she had managed to survive.

One day at a time.

Get through each day and you will eventually break out of this tar pit of depression.

And that had led her to the World Missionary Fellowship, to a new life, a new family.

A family that betrayed me.

But she sensed that only the top was corrupt at the Fellowship. She had gotten to know the volunteers, the doctors, the nurses—people like Ino. They were the real thing, sacrificing their lives for the benefit of salvaging all that could be humanly salvageable from the spoils of a terrible war.

She had survived her husband's death, and she would survive this, but in order to do so she had to take it one day at a time—had to go through the blow-by-blow route. She had no idea how she would fly them out of here or where they would go, but she had faith that she would find a way once she got to that airfield. She would figure something out, somehow, even if it wasn't immediately obvious. But first she had to get to the airfield.

One obstacle at a time.

That was the key to surviving, a truth she had learned the hard way years ago.

Constantly glancing at the rearview mirror, convincing herself that no one was following her, Dana Kovacs accelerated in the African night, going as fast as she could, watching the green triangle on the GPS's screen get closer and closer to the yellow X marking her first stop in a journey that she hoped—that she *prayed*—would lead to an explanation of the events that had destroyed everything she had believed in for the past three years.

45

China Connection

"Holy shit!" Daniel Chang hissed the moment he realized that one of the Level-V users had been kidnapped and was requesting immediate assistance from ANN, who turned to the logic of PARTITION-37 within the depths of SERVER-22 for direction.

Jacking out, leaving their secret link in the hands of an expert system designed to stall the master construct—plus the three shift engineers watching the health of the interface—the young software guru jumped out of his chair and raced for the door of the control center, his sneakers thudding hollowly against the white tile floor.

Daniel's domain was located on the thirty-second floor of the TDG tower, one of the few floors requiring a special access card plus various searches by the security team chartered with protecting the relatively small ECS team working on special projects.

To reach George Zhu's office on the eighty-seventh floor he had to take three different elevators and go through two security checks, including a nanorecorder scan, before he was allowed anywhere near the executive's lair, an incredible penthouse with one of the best views of Shanghai. Today, the smog level was moderate, meaning the view would be decent.

Daniel found Zhu impeccably dressed in his Armani uniform standing with his hands behind his back, chin up, watching Shanghai's skyline through the tinted glass of the panoramic windows forming two of the walls of his corner executive suite.

"What is it?" George Zhu asked.

"It's one of the super users," Daniel said, working hard to

conceal his excitement. "That's one of the Level-V users who—"

"I *know* that, Dan," Zhu interrupted, turning around, his lower lip extended toward his subordinate. "What about the super user?"

"He—or she—has been kidnapped."

46

Access Denied

Frank Salieri floated in a sea of burning stars between the protective layers of the massive firewall shielding ANN from the public sectors of the servers at the heart of GemTech.

To his surprise, the emergency response system released by ANN, which had already signaled his security team, was not going to be as effective as he had hoped because apparently the savvy Kate Chavez had disabled the GPS locator in the Hummer limo, preventing his people from tracking him.

In addition, the master construct restricted Salieri to a security directory—the equivalent of a digital holding cell—because of his reported kidnapped status, isolating him from the system in case the kidnapper coerced him to try to access system information against his will. ANN's priority was very clear: protect the network at all costs, meaning the machine would not allow him to reach the core of the network and contact his security team to inform them of the GPS sabotage and also to direct them by simply observing where Kate Chavez was taking him.

YOU MUST ALLOW ME TO MAKE CONTACT WITH MY TEAM, he ordered, firing another access request. A digital counter

in the lower left corner of his field of view told him just under three minutes had passed since he had jacked in.

ACCESS DENIED. NATURE OF EMERGENCY DICTATES SYS-
TEM ISOLATION OF LIABILITY UNTIL CRISIS SITUATION ENDS.

I'm a liability?

The thought chilled him as he struggled to find a way
around protocol to handle this unexpected situation while
trusting that the cyberagent he'd left handling the real world
would hold the fort for him until he could sort out this digital conundrum.

BUT I'M BEING KIDNAPPED! He fired back at ANN. I NEED
HELP IMMEDIATELY!

I CAN ISSUE A GENERAL ALARM, the master construct offered.

Salieri frowned. So far the system had only alerted his security team, which typically would have been enough to rescue him, but his situation was unique. A general alarm
would broadcast this event not just to the super users, but to
all SpyWare users, something the CEO of GemTech did not
want to do, to avoid alarming TDG's global partners. Besides, Salieri didn't want just an alarm broadcast. He wanted
a two-way dialogue with his colleagues, in particular with
Costa, Gardiol, and VanLothar.

A GENERAL ALARM IS USELESS TO ME, he replied. I NEED
DIRECT ACCESS WITH MY SECURITY TEAM.

ACCESS DENIED. DIRECT CONTACT WITH THE SECURITY
TEAM REQUIRES NETWORK ACCESS. THE SECURITY SYSTEM
PREVENTS ACCESS BECAUSE YOU ARE COMPROMISED.

I'M NOT COMPROMISED YET, BUT I WILL BE IF SOMEONE
DOESN'T COME AND RESCUE ME RIGHT AWAY.

SECURITY TEAM ALREADY NOTIFIED.

THEY WON'T BE ABLE TO FIND ME. THE GPS LOCATOR HAS
BEEN SABOTAGED. I NEED TO GUIDE THEM MYSELF!

ACCESS DENIED.

Salieri couldn't believe this was happening to him. Frustrated, and for the first time actually scared, he asked, WHAT
ARE MY OPTIONS?

USE A BUFFER TO CONVEY YOUR INSTRUCTIONS TO THE
SECURITY TEAM.

Salieri frowned. Doing so would require him to release his personal password to the AI so that it could, in turn, use the encrypted private connection to contact the security team, who were probably wandering around his last known location, Bergstrom International Airport. But according to the cyberagent still entertaining Kate Chavez, they were headed to San Antonio on Interstate 35.

One problem with releasing the password to the AI was that the encryption was the only thing that prevented the AI from being able to control him, as it could control the lower SpyWare users. As a Level-V user he was above the machine, but only while under the protection of the password. Without it he was exposed.

The fucking machine would have the upper hand, he thought, and based on its recent misbehaving history, he just didn't trust ANN enough.

But there was another potential problem he could face by releasing the password: The AI would understand the basic fabric—the algorithm—that made up the body of the password, including its random number generator, and then use that knowledge to crack the passwords of the other super users. In theory, this would leave the AI with the ability to take control of the reins of TDG, which, ironically enough, was precisely what ANN had requested two days ago: autonomy of operation.

Glancing at the window floating in cyberspace in the upper left side of his field of view, Salieri watched the rogue Texas Ranger still pointing the gun at him while asking basic questions about GemTech and its parent company—information that his cyberagent was still capable of providing without releasing anything confidential. And according to the outside scenery, they were already fifteen miles south of the city. Soon he would be out of reach, especially if Kate Chavez ordered the limo driver to leave the highway and go for secondary roads.

He had to hurry and decide if he would give up his layer of protection in order to have a chance at being rescued.

But what other choice do I have?

Doomed if you do and doomed if you don't.

As so many other times in his career, Salieri had to pick the lesser of the evils, and the most immediate concern was getting rescued from this rogue woman pointing a gun at him, which meant he would have to take his chances with the AI.

And it was at that moment, out of options, that Frank Salieri conceded control of his personal encrypted password—the only barrier preventing ANN from overtaking his mind.

The CEO's high level of stress prevented him from noticing a slight disturbance in the cyber lattice of his digital holding cell. One of its corners subtly went in and out of focus as a secret routine intercepted the communications between Salieri and ANN, streaming a copy of the password to its creator while also relaying it back and forth without either party realizing the presence of the software snooping this secluded sector of the TDG network.

47

Software Spy

Dr. Miles Talbot sat in his office, his eyes shifting back and forth between two windows on his LCD screen. The first window displayed the state of the server system being maintained by his team. He had requested an extensive diagnostic run through the software that monitored the activity of the Level-I, -II, -III, and -IV users, an hour-long procedure that scrubbed the algorithms managing the interface. Talbot did this not because he was really that concerned about the health of the links but because running the diagnostic algorithm essentially blinded ANN to video and audio inputs from those lower-level users during the entire time, freeing him from having ANN looking over his shoulder—and doing so without alerting the Level-Vs of this activity.

The second screen displayed the transcribed conversation between a kidnapped Frank Salieri and the machine. Someone by the name of Kate Chavez had taken Salieri hostage from Bergstrom International as the executive was returning home from Shanghai. It hadn't taken Talbot long to do an Internet search and determine she was a lieutenant with the Texas Rangers who had vanished along with her son following an assault near Lakeway two days ago.

Interesting coincidence, Talbot thought as he also captured Salieri's personal password, which would empower him to access other areas of the network with the privilege and privacy of a Level-V super user.

Arming himself with this encrypted software shield, Talbot watched most sectors of the network melt away, exposing themselves to him, a super user, as he continued to monitor the conversation while also surveying the vast fields of data now available to him, extending deep in the far reaches of this unlocked matrix.

And it was at that moment, as he analyzed the unrestricted cyber landscape with his engineering eyes, browsing through mounds of graphical data, that he noticed an unexpectedly high level of energy in the network's spectrum originating from a region of SERVER-22 that was supposed to house the digital personality and thought process of the late Anne Donovan, PARTITION-37.

Interesting, he thought, also realizing that the qualifiers attached to the mysterious disk partition hid it from the view of ANN and required a Level-V password to be visible. But Level-V users weren't that technically savvy. They had power and therefore the privilege to control the system, but that didn't mean they could detect subtle disturbances in the fabric of the matrix like those emanating from PARTITION-37. Talbot, on the other hand, had the technical insight and was now in possession of the keys to the system with Salieri's password.

But he still had to be careful. He could not afford to let the AI discover how much he had learned, which would happen the instant his team completed the diagnostics and reengaged the video and audio feeds of the lower level users into the network. As a Level-III SpyWare user, Talbot would once again fall under the constant monitor of ANN.

Which will happen in about thirty seconds, he thought, watching the timer as the technicians completed the diagnostics and began to bring the system on line.

Damn.

I wonder what's going to happen to Salieri.

But he couldn't remain logged in monitoring the activity without ANN learning about it.

Silently cursing these digital shackles as he logged off the system exactly ten seconds before ANN would once again be able to see and hear what he saw and heard, Dr. Miles Talbot began to consider the many ways he could use the new high-tech weapons at his disposal to gain the autonomy required to break free from this prison.

48

Departures

Thanks to the night-vision goggles, the handheld GPS, and Lady Luck, Dana Kovacs reached the airstrip in the middle of a vast cornfield just after dawn, as a light fog hovered over the grassy clearing, surrounded on all sides by walls of corn stalks.

Mac Savage had not stirred during the entire journey, but his pulse, which she had monitored throughout the night, remained steady, meaning the blood loss had not been as serious as she first anticipated, plus the IV drip in his left forearm seemed to be indeed doing its magical work, replenishing his system.

She slowed down when approaching a small hangar at the end of the dirt path that connected the main road to this remote field, used primarily for dusting—going by the two crop dusters resting inside the open hangar. Two fuel trucks parked to the right of the hangar flanked a high-winged, single-engine plane, which Dana guessed was Savage's.

She pulled up in front of the hangar, and two figures sitting in the back of the rustic structure turned their heads in her direction.

Dressed in blue coveralls, holding small white bottles filled with a clear liquid, the Africans regarded her with bloodshot eyes. That suggested the type of liquid in the bottles: booze.

Great.

Running a hand over the lump in her pocket holding Savage's small pistol, she got out of the Jeep and said in her best Kris, "I'm looking for Kembo. My husband has been shot and needs to be flown to Freetown. That's his plane." She pointed to the Cessna.

The two Africans regarded each other before bursting out in laughter. One was much older, with thinning salt-and-pepper curly hair. Both sported thick necks, barrel chests, and large arms. The older one took a sip from his bottle before calmly approaching Dana, staggering a bit, as if he were drunk, as he said, "I am Kembo. You speak our language well. Where did you learn it?"

As he finished saying this, he let go a loud belch in her direction.

Dana could now smell the strong stench of alcohol. He was definitely inebriated, just like his younger mechanic friend, and that made her wonder if they were in any shape to fly a plane. "I'm a volunteer nurse at an amputee camp in Freetown. I was helping my husband on a local project when we were attacked by guerrillas."

Kembo blinked in surprise. "My Jeep," he said before peeking in the rear seat, where Savage slept. "Need my money and my keys first."

Dana had already peeled four one-hundred-dollar bills from Savage's money belt and she produced them from a breast pocket, offering them to the mechanic along with the keys.

The large African rubbed a two-day, grayish stubble, grabbed the keys and the bills, inspected each one, and pocketed them before looking over at Savage.

"He got shot? Where?"

Dana nodded. "In the leg."

"No, *where* was he when he got shot?"

"Just south of here."

Kembo frowned, then walked around his car, for the first time noticing the bullet holes on the rear of the vehicle.

"What happened to my car? He told me he was a wildlife photographer. How did a photographer get shot this way?"

"Look, I told you we were attacked," Dana said, "he's lost a lot of blood and needs to go to a hospital. Could one of you fly his plane? I will pay you."

"That plane is stolen," said Kembo. "We could get in trouble."

Stolen? Savage had not mentioned that.

"That *is* my husband's plane," she insisted. "He brought your Jeep back to you, just like he promised."

"With bullet holes."

Dana had taken an extra five hundred dollars anticipating that the owner of the Jeep would not be pleased to see the damage.

She offered them to Kembo and said, "We apologize for that, but it wasn't our fault. We were attacked while doing our job. Please, help us."

Kembo took the bills and shoved them in a pocket before saying, "Your husband lied to me about his plane and also about being a photographer. I'm not sure *what* he is, but I am not going to risk getting involved."

Dana couldn't stop the frown as she retorted, "But you just took the extra money."

"That was for the bullet holes."

Before Dana could reply, Kembo added, "Now get out of my field."

"The Cessna," she said. "I need the keys."

Kembo looked at his friend, who reached in a side pocket and dangled them in front of Dana before saying, "You mean these?"

Dana slowly nodded.

The drunk mechanic took a long swig from his bottle as he walked up to Dana, his face now inches from her as he said, "You don't get it, lady. You have no bargaining power. Your husband is dying. The Cessna is stolen. RUF rebels are on the way here to find you and kill you. Time is against you."

Dana inhaled deeply. "What would it take for you to fly us out of here? You can keep the Cessna after you drop us off in Freetown. I have more money."

"Oh," Kembo replied. "I assumed as much, and I will keep the airplane and take all of your money, but this is not enough, yes?"

"What else do you want?"

Kembo grinned. "How far are you willing to go to help your husband, lady? My mechanic and I are very lonely." He put a hand over her right breast.

Dana instinctively pulled away. "Don't you fucking touch me, you bastard!"

Kembo's grin vanished, replaced by a steely look of narrowed, bloodshot eyes as he said, "Get off my field."

Out of options, Dana pulled out her gun and pointed it at them. "You *will* help me! Or I will kill you."

Both mechanics became eerily calm, their eyes burning her.

"Get him out of the Jeep and take him to the airplane," she ordered, shifting her aim between the two Africans.

The mechanics exchanged another glance before complying, walking side by side to the rear of the vehicle while Dana stepped aside, keeping her distance, struggling to hold the gun steadily in spite of her trembling hands.

Without warning, Kembo shifted sideways, rushing toward her.

Dana pressed the trigger but nothing happened. The gun was locked.

Staggering back to buy herself more time, Dana repeatedly squeezed the trigger but it would not pull back all the way. Something kept it from firing. She recalled one of the volunteers talking about something called the safety mechanism, and she tried to look for a lever to pull or push on either side of the gun, but the African was already on top of her.

The powerful slap reminded her of the beating she had endured in Freetown and again at the guerrilla camp. At once the ground and the sky swapped places as the gun flew out of sight. She landed face down on the dirt, dizzy, disoriented.

Before she could react, the African grabbed her by the hair, lifting her with incredible ease, throwing her over the hood of the Jeep with animal strength.

Crashing on her back against the hood, black spots materializing in front of her face as she stared at the dawning sky the moment her head struck the metal surface, Dana watched the second mechanic appear in her peripheral vision, his large hands pinning her down, one of them nearly covering her face.

The smell of alcohol and engine oil reaching her nostrils as the man's sweaty hands blinded her, Dana felt the other mechanic spreading her legs while tugging at the snap of her jeans.

Oh, God! No!

NO!

She started to kick, to jerk, to keep these brutes from raping her. Opening her mouth, stretching her neck muscles, she pushed her head up, her teeth finding part of the African's hand.

Dana bit down hard, tearing into the flesh like a beast.

A scream, then the hand tried to pull away, to free herself from her unyielding bite, finally breaking free, dislodging chucks of skin and flesh in her mouth as she once more stared at the sky while kicking, while spitting the morsel she had bitten off the African, while cursing out loud both in English and in Kris as loud as she—

The blow to her torso crippled her into twitching spasms as the nerves beneath the skin stung her with raw pain.

And she was once again blinded by a hand shoving her head against the Jeep's hood while other hands yanked on her jeans, trying to tear them off her, trying to—

The shots ripped across the field like cracking whips, followed by the brief cries of the Africans, before the hand on her face vanished, as well as those forcing her legs apart.

With effort, Dana sat back up, blinking to clear her sight, swallowing hard, staring at Mac Savage, the IV still connected to his left forearm, a hand on the Jeep for support, the other lowering the same pistol she had clutched just a minute before. His face, still filmed by camouflage cream, twisted into a mask of pain as he breathed with apparent effort.

"Are you . . . okay?" he whispered, before beginning to lose his grip on the side of the Jeep and removing the IV.

As light-headed as she felt, Dana found the strength to stand, to stumble to his side, her face and back throbbing, her mind still trying to catch up to the events from the prior minute.

"I'm okay," she said, adding, "thanks . . . to you."

"The blood . . . on your face. . . ."

"Not mine," she replied, a headache flaring, pounding her temples, her shoulders tensing from the stressful experience. "I bit . . . one of the bastards' hands before you . . . shot them."

Savage almost grinned in apparent surprise, then nodded, breathing deeply again, dropping his gaze to the bandage on his leg as she ran an arm around his back while he draped his arm over her shoulders, helping him stand.

"Nice bandage job," he mumbled, closing his eyes before forcing them open, apparently trying to keep himself awake. He added, "We must . . . leave . . . immediately. Gun shots . . . will attract attention."

"Are you strong enough to fly?"

"We don't . . . have a choice. Keys," he said. "I need the keys for the—"

"Hold on," she said, leaving him standing for a moment while she retrieved them from the body of the dead mechanic.

"Let's get out of here," she said, shouldering the rucksack, walking side by side with her rescuer to the Cessna, a strange feeling of comfort overwhelming her from being so physically close to this man, a stranger only hours ago, now the only person on the planet that she trusted with her life.

Together they limped away from the Jeep, past the bodies of her attackers, shoulder to shoulder, her arm wrapped around his waist, his wrapped around her shoulders, tight, firm, conveying the same incredible strength which he had just displayed.

He had lost an immense amount of blood—enough to keep a normal person down for days. Yet Mac Savage had pulled away from that, had mustered the power required to stand, to get the gun, to fire into the heads of both rapists— to rescue her for the second time in less than six hours.

To rescue me.

As she helped him climb into the left front seat of the Cessna, as she strapped the safety belt, closed the door, and walked around the front to get into the right seat next to him, Dana Kovacs felt truly safe for the first time in years.

She couldn't explain why she should feel this way with a total stranger in an airfield in the middle of the African jungle with guerrillas closing in on them, but the simple truth was that she did. A bond had been created when this man pulled her away from a brutal fate—twice—and she could not turn off those feelings now.

Focus.

And she did, assisting Savage as they went through the preflight checklist, as he started the engine, as he taxied the plane away from the hangar—all the while watching him carefully, trying to learn as much as possible in case she had to take over. But the complexity of the plane was overwhelming with its many dials, numbers, buttons, and switches. The only thing that made remote sense was the color moving map of the Cessna's GPS.

Savage taxied to one end of the runway, turned the plane around, and smoothly advanced the throttle, building up speed, the airframe vibrating from the uneven terrain, until he slowly pulled back on the yoke, the trembling vanishing as they became airborne.

Dana settled back in her seat as she watched the cornfields rushing below them, turning into thick jungle as they gained altitude, as Mac Savage pointed the Cessna's nose toward the west, toward Freetown.

"How are you feeling?" she asked as sunshine flooded the cockpit from the rear windows.

He tilted his head toward her while shooting her a sideways look. "The question is how are *you* doing?"

Dana shrugged. "I hate to say this, but that was my third beating in the past four days. I think I'm beginning to get used to them."

"It will be your last," he said with an assuring tone that Dana found as comforting as just being near him.

"Now," he added, pressing a few buttons and taking his hands off the controls, which Dana guessed were now under the guidance of an autopilot, "tell me what happened since the moment I passed out."

In spite of his drained condition, this man had not only taken out the two drunk mechanics who were trying to rape her, but was now flying this plane and wanted to know what he had missed out on.

Dana told him, taking over twenty minutes to fill in most of the detail, from the time she had dragged him to the Jeep to the quick field bandage job to the close call with the search party and the following three hours driving in total darkness.

"Sounds like I owe you one," he said.

Dana looked at him with incredulity. "Mac," she replied. "Really. How can you *possibly* even think that? You're the one who pulled me away from a terrible fate—*twice*. I would have been brutalized to death in that guerrilla camp, and those drunken bastards would have *raped* me just minutes ago had you not intervened. Don't you realize that I can *never* forget that? You rescued me, Mac Savage. You are my hero forever." She touched him on the arm, squeezing gently. "I'll *never* forget what you did just like I'll *never* forget what Keith Gardiol did to me—to Renee."

Savage sighed before saying, "Gardiol. How do we find him?"

"Finding him is the easy part. Getting close to him will be the trick. He lives surrounded by tons of bodyguards in a bunker-like complex in the middle of the WMF camp," she said, sitting sideways to him in her seat.

"Hold on," Savage said while disconnecting the autopilot and tuning one of the navigation radios to a specific frequency according to a map he had unfolded. He banked the plane to the right for a few seconds before entering a few three- and four-letter codes into the GPS, watching as the screen changed. It displayed their little airplane and a lavender line toward a green circle on West Africa's coastline.

He reengaged the autopilot and said, "We're on a direct track to Freetown. We'll be there in under an hour."

"Good," she said. "Perhaps now you can tell me what the hell is going on."

Savage frowned while widening his eyes. "That's what I was hoping to get from Renee. See, I was contracted to find her," he started, continuing for almost ten minutes, explaining the events that had taken place in Brussels during a meeting with someone named Bockstael, his connection to the Diamond High Council and to the Diamond Mining Company, formerly De Beers. Somewhere during the middle of his tale, he reached for the rucksack and grabbed several kingsize moist towelettes, which he used to wipe his face and neck clean of the camouflage cream, exposing a well-tanned face with well-defined features that reminded Dana of a U.S. Marines commercial, along with those determined, focused eyes. Savage went on, telling her about his narrow escape from that encounter as well as his ill-fated meeting with the CIA, his former employer, who had declared him beyond salvage, and his flight down to Africa in search of the missing executive.

"Bockstael knew someone had stolen the diamonds and when he tried to look into it, Renee was abducted and he was fired and eventually terminated. And then I was blamed for his assassination. Whoever is behind this is powerful enough to fool not just Belgian authorities but also the CIA. And that brings me here, trying to unravel this mystery."

Dana just stared back, not certain how to reply to that dump of information.

"What about you?" he asked. "How did you end up here?"

Dana contemplated the solid carpet of green below, projecting in every direction as far as she could see, before facing this man once more, his intense stare on her. But in spite of his strength, of the way in which he could kill so easily, she also saw a glimmer of sadness in those dark brown eyes, something that reminded her of her own painful past. And it was that perceived common feeling—compounded with the fact that this man knew how to protect her—that prompted Dana to share her experience up to this point.

She started with Diamantex, with the hostile takeover, with her husband's suicide, before describing to Savage how she had found the World Missionary Fellowship, which had led her to this corner of the world three years before. She described how the experience at the Fellowship had helped her heal wounds she never thought would heal, but then, a week before her contract with WMF would end and she planned to return to California, a dying African boy had given her a blood diamond containing a small test circuit created by Diamantex to check the quality of a stone prior to processing.

"So you told Gardiol about this and the bastard had you kidnapped and sent to that camp?"

Dana nodded, rubbing her right side with her fingertips, feeling a lump forming where the younger mechanic had punched her after she had bitten a chunk of his hand. Her headache was also getting out of control, and she reached for the rucksack, where she remembered seeing a few packs of aspirin. She took three, swallowing the little white pills without any water.

"Not feeling that great?"

She frowned. "I'll survive."

"I noticed that about you," he said. "But let me take a look at that anyway," he said, also sitting sideways to face her while leaning over, inspecting not just her torso but also her left cheek, where Kembo had slapped her. "You might get a nasty bruise there as well as on your side, but it doesn't look like any ribs were broken. How is your neck?"

"Sore," she said. "But I'll be all right."

"It's now my job to see to that, Dana," he said with a confidence she found very comforting.

"Anyway," she continued. "That's when I met Renee. Before she died, she told me how she had been working with her superior in Brussels—I guess that was Bockstael—to find a missing shipment of diamonds. She found evidence that elements within the Diamond Mining Company, working in conjunction with the Diamond High Council, had diverted a shipment of legally mined diamonds to the Fellowship, my former employer for the past three years."

Savage dropped his eyebrows at the comment. "You're telling me that WMF is a front company to smuggle diamonds, and that those diamonds came not just from the mines controlled by the guerrillas but also from legally owned and operated mines under the jurisdiction of the Diamond High Council?"

Dana slowly have him a nod before saying, "That's what Renee told me. Her short-lived investigation had led her to believe that the flow of conflict diamonds, as large as it is each year, was not sufficient to satisfy the demand driven by the customers served by Gardiol's WMF."

"But the diamond that you found wasn't mined legally."

"At least that's what the circumstances led me to believe. The boy who had it had escaped from one of the mines near Kono under guerrilla control. And remember that Gardiol was pretty determined to learn what I knew about diamond nanotechnology, which strongly suggests to me that WMF is passing on the diamonds to someone like GemTech, my former company's nemesis—at least based on the etched test circuit. Remember that all was well in my world when I turned in the diamond to Gardiol, but I could sense something changing in him the instant I mentioned the etched test nanocircuit. At some level this whole thing is mixed up with GemTech. Frank Salieri is up to his usual no good and has apparently elevated his sphere of influence to the Diamond High Council and the powerful Diamond Trading Company.

"But what can they do with so many diamonds? Is the world's demand for diamond-based circuits taking off?"

She shook her head. "That's the thing. Although diamonds provide a better platform for the fabrication of nano-electronics, the manufacturing cost is still too high. The entire industry is waiting for the development of adequate synthetic diamonds possessing the right properties for nano-etching—and the right price. Otherwise, diamond nanotech will continue to lose to its slower but far less expensive silicon counterpart."

"So, if GemTech isn't using the diamonds for commercial applications, what else can they be doing with them?"

Dana shrugged. "Maybe research? My guess is that they could be developing advanced supercomputers for their own internal use. Given the exponential performance kicker that diamonds offer over silicon, the quantity of missing diamonds mentioned by Renee, plus the tons of conflict diamonds available in the black market, that would create some very serious computing power—far greater than the world has ever seen."

Savage paused, staring out into the distance, before asking, "But to what end? Why do they need it?"

"Assuming that's what they're doing with the diamonds, then your question is *precisely* the question we need to answer," she said, locking eyes with him, "and I believe Gardiol has that answer."

Savage turned to face his instruments, scanning the navigation equipment, presumably to make sure that the autopilot was doing its job. Then he said, "I think it is time to pay Mr. Gardiol a most unexpected visit."

49

Footwork

Confined to his digital holding cell—depicted by ANN as a white room with a single window displaying what his physical body saw from inside the Hummer limousine—Frank Salieri began to use the master construct to convey directions to the emergency response team, guiding them down Interstate 35, where Kate Chavez had ordered the driver to head south toward San Antonio.

ANN reported back that his rescue party—eight men in two SUVs—had already reached the highway and were roughly fifteen minutes behind.

He only needed to keep Kate Chavez distracted for a little longer, keep his cyberagent feeding her circular answers, stalling her while his team careened down the highway, closing the gap.

According to the behavioral program in his SpyWare implant Salieri expected the former Texas Ranger to order the driver to leave the highway soon and probably follow a secondary road, eventually stopping somewhere she felt would be safe to conduct a proper interrogation.

But at this very moment help was on the way. She might have disconnected the Hummer's GPS unit from its rooftop antenna and somehow managed to overpower the bodyguard that normally sat in the back, but Kate Chavez had not considered the fact that in a way Salieri was his own GPS, able to direct his rescue team.

And that was precisely what the CEO of GemTech continued to do, feeding his observations to the master construct, which continued to relay them to the men in the SUVs. His confidence that he would make it through this kidnapping increased just as quickly as his belief that ANN would not take advantage of his cyber vulnerability and do just as it had been programmed to do.

"Get off at the next exit," Kate Chavez barked at the driver, just as his SpyWare had predicted.

Salieri saw the exit number and passed it to ANN, before also informing the master construct that they had turned into Ranch Road 967 toward the town of Driftwood—though he doubted they would travel the twenty-three miles posted on the sign.

According to the images flashing on his window in this virtual cell, the night beyond the bulletproof glass was star-filled and moonless, and there were no other vehicles any-where in sight once they left the highway behind.

"I hope you realize the futility of your situation, Mr. Salieri," said Kate Chavez.

From the confines of his holding room, Salieri heard her voice resonate and then heard the cyberagent managing his body reply, "I'm not the one running away."

"But that's the thing. I'm *not* running away. I'm headed right to the heart of your organization, and I will expose it."

"You're way out of your league. You have no idea who you're fighting."

"I'm fighting someone who enjoys ruining people's lives. Now I'm going to ruin yours as well as everyone else's asso-ciated with this criminal network so all of you bastards get a taste of what it's like."

"You have a great imagination, Miss Chavez, and also an amazing conviction for someone who is out on her own."

Salieri grinned. The expert system at the core of the cyber-agent in command of his physical self was handling the situa-tion far better than he would have, especially as tired as Salieri was.

"Being on one's own is the mantra of a Texas Ranger. This is no different."

"It is from the perspective that your own team doesn't be-lieve you."

"How do you know that?"

"Oh, I know, Miss Chavez, just as I know that you and

your son will not make it. Your best chance is to turn yourself in. We can work out a deal with you like we did with Dalton."

Salieri smiled as the negotiating software kicked in. It was fascinating to watch pure AI at work, and the conversational programs passed the Turing test with flying colors. Developed by Alan Turing, a twentieth-century British mathematician considered by many the father of computing, the Turing test stated that a computer could be called intelligent if it could fool a human into thinking that it was another human. And tonight, albeit using a human body, the expert systems programmed into his SpyWare feeding the cyber-agent with the answers to Kate Chavez's inquiry performed like a truly intelligent life form.

"You call what you did with Dalton a good deal?"

"He was the one who chose to live in the middle of nowhere."

Kate frowned. "I meant how you cut your hounds loose on him the other afternoon, killing him."

Salieri shrugged. "He violated our agreement by talking to you."

Kate turned to the driver and said, "Take the next right, go a half mile, pull to the side of the road, and kill the lights."

The driver, an older guy almost twenty years his senior with four kids and ten grandkids, did as he was told. He was not going to put up a fight to defend his boss.

"Who else is involved in this?" Kate asked.

"That's the thing," the CEO replied. "All I do is run GemTech for TDG. I don't know any of the other players."

"And you expect me to believe that?"

"Believe what you want, Miss Chavez. I am speaking the truth."

"All right then," she said, pointing the small gun at his right foot and adding, "Last chance to change your story."

"Wait a minute. What are you going to do?"

Kate didn't answer. Rather, she fired a round into Salieri's right shoe, by the very front, shaving off a chunk of leather and sole in addition to what she guessed was part of his middle toe.

The digital holding cell vibrated, pulsating red and green energy streaking across its gleaming white surface as the image on the screen shook violently. A burning sensation propagated up his right foot, stinging him even though he wasn't supposed to feel anything while the cyberagent controlled his body. But the shock had overwhelmed the expert system, leaking through the layers of insulating software and had reached him.

Cringing in pain, Salieri watched the image through his SpyWare. The cyberagent was shaking in simulated pain but was not reaching down for the wounded foot the way he would have—the way any human would have.

I NEED TO RETURN. RELEASE ME, he requested just as the driver turned onto an unmarked road about three miles from the highway—information he conveyed to ANN to relay to his security team before adding, I MUST RETURN TO KEEP KATE CHAVEZ FROM GETTING SUSPICIOUS.

THE RISK IS TOO HIGH, replied the master construct.

LOOK, Salieri said, YOU HAVE CONTROL OF MY PERSONAL PASSWORD, AND YOU WILL MONITOR THE CONVERSATION. IF I GET OUT OF LINE, YOU CAN REEL ME BACK IN. THE CYBERAGENT IN CHARGE RIGHT NOW IS NOT REACTING NATURALLY, LIKE A HUMAN WOULD, AND IT WILL CAUSE CHAVEZ TO GROW SUSPICIOUS. MY WAY IS SAFER, AND YOU STILL REMAIN IN CONTROL.

REQUEST GRANTED.

Before he could reply to the master construct, the white room turned into a funnel, flushing him out, shooting him straight into the winding turns of a high-speed Internet connection, bathing him with data-rich energy as he cruised through universes of glowing suns, of planet-like corporations and their satellite moons orbiting at varying angles.

Salieri saw it all and nothing at the same time as the broadband connection arced from ISP to ISP like blue lightning, turning everything around him into a digital blur, until he dove into a gigantic pool of bright blue water, its depth immeasurable, its warmth unforgettable, its density gradually slowing him down, absorbing him, until he became one with the familiar medium, until he displaced the cyberagent, locking him away in the SpyWare as he regained control of his bodily functions.

The raw pain shooting up from his right foot nearly made him lose that control, but he wrested it back, clenching his teeth while reaching down, watching the bloody mess through the torn shoe.

"You . . . you will *regret* this, fucking bitch!" he hissed, untying the shoe, trembling as he removed it, as he peeled back the sock before ripping it off, using it to dabble the wound, which, to his relief, was very superficial. The round had merely nicked the second toe.

"Stop whining," she said before telling the driver, "Pull over now. Lights out."

Producing a pair of handcuffs from a side pocket, she tossed them to the front and said, "Put them on through the steering wheel."

Salieri watched as the driver complied, latching one side to his left wrist before running the other end through one of the spokes in the steering wheel and onto his right wrist, preventing him from going anywhere.

Without warning, Kate punched the driver just ahead of his right ear, overwhelming the cluster of nerves beneath the skin of his temple, knocking him out.

"That was unnecessary," Salieri hissed. "He's an older guy, a grandfather."

Turning both weapons now on Salieri, Kate Chavez said, "You should be more worried about yourself than him. He's just going to wake up with a headache in a couple of hours. You're about to start losing body parts, and I just gave you a little taste of it. That was the effect of this .32 caliber pistol, a toy in comparison to my Magnum, which would have *vaporized* your foot. You give me one more wrong answer, Mr. Salieri and you lose the whole foot. Are we clear?"

Salieri locked down the pain tight, mustering savage strength to keep up with the situation, with the realization that he would have to release information in order to keep from getting dismembered by this desperate woman. But given the fact that his team was on the way, he had little to lose and much to gain by playing ball. Whatever she learned between now and the time his security team arrived would never go beyond her.

"Yes, Miss Chavez," Salieri finally said, making his decision to cooperate for the time being. "Crystal clear."

50

Big Fish

"Holy cow!" exclaimed Daniel Chang, sitting behind his workstation, where the LCD screen displayed the video feed captured by Salieri's optical nerves. "The woman just shot him in the foot! Damn! What should we do?"

George Zhu observed from the side with an expression that made Daniel think the man was smelling rotten milk.

"Not a thing," said Zhu calmly, hands behind his back. "Leave him alone for now and focus on cracking the password so we can figure out who the others are."

"But she's going to kill him," said Daniel.

"And that may not be a bad thing. Salieri is the reason why I'm still a junior vice-president even though I bring in more revenue than most of the senior VPs. His death might actually provide me with an opportunity to move up the ladder."

"I'm worried about his well-being not because I like the man but because we can control him through ANN to help us figure the identities of the rest of the group, which could help us break their passwords, which in the end is what you're looking for. Control of their minds will give you control of TDG."

Zhu considered that for a moment before saying, "Very well. What do you propose we do?"

"We find a way to keep him alive until his team gets there."

Zhu accentuated his pout by pushing out his lower lip, keeping his hands behind his back before saying in flawless English, "Fine. Do what you must to keep him breathing. Meanwhile, crack those identities."

"Now that we have the active portion of the password in hand, it is only a matter of time. Maybe a day or two, and sooner if we can figure out a way for Salieri to help the process."

"Very good."

"When do I get the Ferrari?"

Zhu frowned again, slowly bobbing his head. "You keep your promise and I will keep mine," he finally said while observing the developments half a world away.

51

Confessions

Kate Chavez watched the GemTech executive pulling himself together following the unexpected turn of events, including her old Ranger trick of taking out part of a toe to encourage uncooperative suspects. Nothing like the prospect of permanently losing body parts to get their attention.

Tonight she had certainly grabbed the undivided attention of Frank Salieri. The GemTech executive wrapped the sock around the nick at the tip of his foot and slowly leveled his gaze with her.

"What do you want to know?"

"*Everything*," she replied. "Who's in charge?"

After a moment of apparent consideration, time when he looked down at his foot, at the gun, and back at her, Salieri said, "There's ten of us. We control TDG."

"Who?"

"CEOs, like me. Together we run the companies that make up The Donovan Group."

Kate Chavez slowly shook her head. "I don't buy it. CEOs don't get people killed. You have way too much power, and that only comes with connections with top people. Who else is involved?"

"Yes . . . some of the ten aren't CEOs."

"Who then?"

Salieri glanced outside, his eyes gleaming with what appeared to Kate as anticipation, hope that somebody would come to his rescue, preventing him from having to release this information.

There's no one coming, pal, she thought, watching the executive struggle with his dilemma. She had learned long ago that people were more afraid of being maimed for life than dying—and more so if they were involved with organized crime, which was not tolerant of informants. Dying usually meant you refused to talk, taking the secrets of your organization to your grave. But if you survived maimed it meant that you were tortured and forced to release information, which meant that you didn't really survive because your own criminal ring would come after you for having talked, inflicting far more pain than you may have experienced when you were tortured for information in the first place.

And she could see the wrinkles of deep concern forming on the executive's forehead as he realized what would happen to him for telling Kate Chavez this—and also what would happen to his family.

"They are very powerful people . . . who do not treat traitors well. A couple of weeks ago they killed one of my associates, our VP of operations, because he tried to go public. There's also the incident a year and a half ago, when three WMF executives tried to blow the whistle and they too ended up dead. I don't want to follow the same fate."

Kate tried to suppress her excitement at hearing about the

very two cases that she had tied together. Her training commanded her to remain impassive.

"Do you want to lose another toe, Mr. Salieri?"

Frank Salieri shook his head, looking into the distance for a moment before apparently deciding to take a step in the right direction by saying, "The point is I want protection."

Kate almost laughed. "*Protection?* I can't guarantee my *own* protection and that of my son. What makes you think I can get protection for you?"

"Because unlike those four company executives, I'm high up enough to know how we operate. I know how we tap into the arteries of the law enforcement and intelligence communities and then use that information to our advantage. I can show you how to cut TDG out of the loop, essentially blinding them. So, I ask you again. Will you protect me? Will you help me help you?"

Kate considered the proposal, well aware of the value of information. Criminal organizations who lost their ability to access information also lost their edge, their competitiveness, the power to stay not just ahead of the law but ahead of the competition.

"Very well," she said, "convince me. Tell me who is behind this."

52

Mind Control

Daniel Chang had suspected the conversation might get to the point where the GemTech CEO would be forced to release certain intelligence, and he had already devised a plan to capture the data without it being disclosed to his captor holding the gun in that limousine.

But it required timing down to the nanoseconds—something that only someone as highly developed as ANN could do with the help of the cyberagents deep within the SpyWare interfaced to Salieri's brain.

ANN acted just as Daniel had expected, capturing the stream of information the instant it left Salieri's brain and headed for the muscles that controlled his speech.

The master construct, in full possession of Salieri's encryptions, activated one of the cyberagents inside the Spy-Ware to override the commands to his lips, preventing the executive from uttering a single word. But ANN did capture the stream of information, the string of names that Frank Salieri had come so close to disclosing to a confused Kate Chavez—and an even more perplexed Frank Salieri, whose sudden peak in brain activity signaled his state of fear at this abrupt inability to control his speech.

George Zhu glanced at the list and rushed out of the room to call his father in Beijing with the incredible news, but not before giving Daniel a direct order: Take control of Frank Salieri's mind immediately to prevent him from releasing any critical information to the enemy.

And so Daniel Chang, the mind behind PARTITON-37 within SERVER-22, issued an order to ANN that would forever change the life of Frank Salieri.

53

Cyber Cyclone

It happened suddenly, hitting Frank Salieri with the might of a hundred hurricanes, drowning his thoughts, his will, his logic, submerging him in a boiling red and violet liquid that squeezed him out of his mind with savage force.

Confused, Salieri watched his consciousness spinning down a seemingly endless drain hole, circling at ever increasing speeds as this invisible cyclone drew him away from the world as he knew it.

And then he was falling, not rushing into a broadband connection as when summoned to a cybermeeting but dropping away at nauseating speed, as the liquids of his mind turned to vapor, to clouds of every imaginable color, before fading away, revealing a sea of burning stars as the master construct propelled him across the vast expanse of the matrix, injecting him into a white windowless room, one of TDG's digital holding cells.

ANN? WHAT IS GOING ON? FIRST I CAN'T CONTROL MY OWN SPEECH AND NOW THIS?

No response.

Salieri issued the query again, but again the master construct did not respond.

A bone-numbing chill spread up whatever form of self he had left, realizing that the AI had indeed taken advantage of the encrypted password he had been forced to release—the same password that had empowered the machine to take over his mind just as The Circle had ordered ANN in the past to control the minds of lower SpyWare users.

BUT SUPER USERS ARE SUPPOSED TO BE EXEMPT FROM THAT RISK.

YOU RELEASED THE PASSWORD, STUPID.

As he looked about this seamless prison for his mind, a place without up or down, without time or place, Frank Salieri began to wonder if this was where he would spend the rest of his human life, trapped within the confines of a monster he had helped create.

54

Kate Chavez noticed a change in Frank Salieri.

First the CEO had paused, almost as if a part of him wanted to release the names but another part of him held him back. Then moments later he blinked a few times and trembled very slightly but noticeably enough for her to realize something was happening to the GemTech CEO. Soon after that he became calm—in fact *too calm*—at peace, his face softening, his eyes relaxed, something she found eerie given the futility of his situation.

"Are you all right, Mr. Salieri?" she finally asked.

The executive gave her a slight nod and said very calmly, "Except for the missing chunk of flesh and bone from my toe and the fact that you have kidnapped me and forced me to turn against my network—yes, I guess I'm all right."

Not certain what had just happened, but her sixth sense telling her something was seriously wrong, Kate looked out the rear window, toward Ranch Road 967 less that a half mile away across a field of corn, which flanked this remote access road.

That's when she saw them: two vehicles cruising in tandem away from the interstate at great speed, their headlights cutting into the countryside.

It can't be, she thought, as they slowed down on reaching this unmarked road.

"You tricked me! You bastard!"

Salieri remained impassive as the dark SUVs turned toward them, as she reached for the door handle, pulling it open while leveling the Magnum on his forehead.

"Killing me will accomplish nothing. They heard everything. Our conversation was recorded," he said, before tapping his head. "Up here and sent wirelessly to a safe place."

Kate regarded him quizzically, shifting her gaze between Salieri and the SUVs, their headlights still distant but closing.

"You can't win, Miss Chavez," he added. "We're too powerful.

"No one is *that* powerful, Mr. Salieri. *No one.*"

Kate left him that way, intrigue flashing in his brown eyes. She rushed across the underbrush flanking the road, toward the cornfield separating her from the highway as the high beams from the SUVs grazed the parked Hummer limousine.

A night breeze swept her hair back while sprinting, kicking hard against the rutted soil, filling her lungs with cool air, striding like an Olympic champion, reaching the field, immersing herself in it, ignoring the razor-sharp leaves tearing at her blouse, at her jeans, using her hands to shield her face, the moment reminiscent of the day she visited Dalton. Only this time she had managed to flee before the lights reach her, before the enemy saw where she had gone.

Kate counted to thirty and cut left in a diagonal as vehicles screeched to a halt, as she maximized the distance from them while also slowing down, while reducing the noise she made while listening to orders being barked in the dark.

"Get her!" Salieri screamed above all of them. "She went into that field! Don't let her get away!"

Angry at herself for not having killed him before leaving the limo, her heartbeat now pounding her chest, her temples, Kate pressed on, but more carefully now, twisting her body to conform to the bends in the thick field, in her getaway shield, minimizing the damage she inflicted not just on herself but on the surrounding corn stalks. She remembered what she had heard, what she had been told. Salieri had not mentioned names but he had admitted to being connected with very powerful people. And she also recalled her final moments with the CEO, when he had tapped his head, had told her that everything had been recorded, that TDG was always watching, always listening.

How do you fight someone so connected, someone who operated in both the real and the cyber worlds at once?

If what Salieri said about TDG always watching through some sort of brain implant was indeed true, that would certainly explain why Salieri's people had caught up with them. Disabling the limo's GPS locator had only delayed them. In order to prevent their arrival, Salieri himself would have had to be disabled to keep him from broadcasting his position.

But then how could I have interrogated him?

Perhaps by blindfolding him?

Kate frowned at the difficulty of gathering intelligence in this case as she continued toward the lights of Interstate 35, where she planned to follow the access road until reaching one of the many gas stations hugging this busy corridor connecting Austin with San Antonio.

She needed to get back to Cameron, to his hacker friend, to her only chance of adding a cyber dimension to her fight. Kate felt capable of handling the real-world battle, but she desperately needed an ally in cyberspace, and that collaborator might just be the high-tech renegade, Lman, who just might also be able to explain this ability to interface computers to the human mind and record live events, as Salieri had claimed.

Sweating heavily by the time she emerged at the other end of the field, Kate inspected the clearing leading to a narrow band of trees adjacent to the interstate's service road.

Up the highway, toward the north, she saw a tall lighted sign for a gas station. She also saw another one toward the south. Realizing that the service road on this side of the interstate was one way, south, she began to walk north, her logic telling her that when the security team returned to this access road they would only be able to head south, away from her.

She crossed the clearing and once again felt secure in the woods, remaining just inside the tree line facing the service road, where she watched for traffic before heading north, toward the gas station.

Soon, she thought. *Soon I will be able to launch a two-pronged attack against this covert network and expose them for the bastards they are.*

She only hoped she could pay the steep price her senses told her would be required to accomplish it.

55

Rusty

"Chappy-man?" said **Salim Anahah** over his mobile phone when Savage called him from the airport in Freetown. "You made it?"

Savage dropped his lids at his old friend's initial reaction, as if insulted that Salim had not expected him to survive this mission.

"Damn," Savage finally replied. "Thanks for the vote of confidence, pal. I may be a bit rusty but I'm far from obsolete. And yes I did make it back. I left the plane with the same guy at the same hangar as last time. We're waiting outside for you to come and get us and take us to a place where we can hide and regroup."

"Who is *we*, Chappy-man? You mean you actually *found* your lady friend?"

There it was again, the strange reaction about Savage having returned not just alive but with his charge.

Frowning, but deciding to let it go, Savage glanced over at Dana standing next to him with an impatient look on her triangular face while they waited under a tree outside the general aviation terminal.

"You could say that," Savage finally said. "So, when are you getting here?"

Although one of the advantages of being on this side of the airport, away from the commercial terminals, was the lack of taxi drivers, beggars, street vendors, and thieves—not to mention the reduced risk of a spotter assigned to observe this airport by the international intelligence community—Savage still didn't want to linger too long in the open.

He continued to regard the narrow and nearly deserted road hugging the south end of the airport with trained suspicion.

"I can't, my friend. Salim has an important commitment

on the other side of town with people who don't react well to schedule changes. But Salim will send a car to pick you up right away with one of my most trusted colleagues while Salim makes arrangements at an oceanfront hotel."

"Who's coming to get us?"

"Trust me, my friend."

"*Salim?*"

"My own cousin, Chappy-man. His name is Kassan, and he will drive you to a safe resort, where you and your lady friend can relax until morning. You will be safe with him."

Savage exhaled, closing his eyes, guilt creeping in his gut for questioning the man who had helped him unconditionally—the same man who had provided him with so much intelligence during his CIA tenure here.

"All right, Salim. Thanks."

"You are welcome, my old friend. Sleep well, and I will see you in the morning!"

Hanging up, he raised an eyebrow in Dana's direction. Something was wrong, but he couldn't quite put his finger on it. Maybe it was Salim's reaction to his return, or maybe the knowledge that there could be a price on the head of whoever accompanied Dana Kovacs in this town for the killing Aman Gharibi, the leader of the RUF, which was apparently connected to the powerful and influential World Missionary Fellowship in Freetown.

And you're the lucky guy with her today.

Perhaps Salim is right and I am getting rusty.

Or maybe you're just too tired and are imagining things.

Dana gave him a curious look and said, "You aren't rusty."

"Excuse me?"

"I said, you are not rusty."

"Did I . . . say that out loud?" he asked, a bit perplexed.

She smiled, the shadow of the tree softening her facial bruises. "That's okay. I talk to myself all the time. And you are far from rusty, Mac Savage. You're at the top of your game, and you have earned my trust and my eternal gratitude."

He made eye contact with her longer than he felt comfortable, finally shifting his gaze toward the street, forcing himself to remain professional even as he felt her gaze still on him. Flattery always had a way of making him feel uneasy, and so did the look he thought he saw in her round eyes, which continue to regard him as he surveyed their surroundings.

His operative mind kicking in as some sort of personal defense mechanism, Savage shrugged and said, "Let's see if I'm good enough to keep us alive long enough to get to the bottom of this mystery."

56

Implants

At five in the morning, Lman sat behind his array of terminals munching on a microwaved hot dog, talking with his mouth open, and sipping from a can of caffeinated soda.

"Implants, huh?" he asked, inspecting the bitten end of the shriveled sausage link wedged in between the long bread, splashed with strings of ketchup and mustard. A few drops of reddish grease had dripped on the papers next to the keyboard, which he didn't bother wiping.

Slouched on a sofa chair across the desk, also sipping a can of soda, Kate gave him a slow nod. "That's what he said."

But that's not all *he said,* she thought. Kate had purposely omitted the ten men running TDG and the claim made by Salieri that some of them weren't just CEOs but powerful and influential people. Her Ranger training told her just to release the information that this hacker needed to know, and at the moment he didn't need to know just how high this conspiracy apparently went.

"So," he replied, downing the drink, before adding it to

the pyramid of cans he was building next to one of the nineteen-inch LCD screens. "This guy claims not only that he was able to record the incident in his noodle, but transmit it wirelessly to a remote location?"

Looking past the hacker, her sight landed on the still figure in the bed, Cameron.

According to Lman, her son had finally fallen asleep an hour ago, shortly before Kate returned from her exciting meeting with Salieri.

"Yeah, I know," said Lman, noticing she was looking at her son and pointing at him with the hot dog. "Squirrel lacks endurance." He shifted the organic pointing device toward the stack of empty sodas. "He'll discover the god of caffeine one of these days."

He reached under the desk and extracted another cold soda from a small refrigerator, popping the top.

"But anyway, back to you," he said, taking a sip before adding, "these brain implants that you're talking about are still supposed to be in development at places like Los Alamos. I've read reports of implants going into dogs, cats, and even monkeys, controlling their motor functions, but the stuff's supposed to be *years* away from actual implementation in a human. They'll have to go through pretty serious scrutiny by the FDA before they can commercialize it, and that will add at least another five years."

"So how can he make that claim then? And the fact that his security team tracked me down lends credibility to his story," Kate said, inspecting the cold drink in her hands. The caffeine content definitely explained why Lman was so wired. In the forty minutes since her arrival, the hacker had put away two sodas and was working on his third.

"I said, the stuff is *supposed* to be years away from actual implementation. That doesn't mean someone hasn't figured a shortcut to getting there, though that would take some pretty serious computing power, megabucks, and the ability to test it on humans without the Feds getting in the way." Lman took another bite of his hot dog and grinned, chewing it quickly before sipping more soda.

"So," Kate said, "it is possible?"

He nodded. "Anything is possible with great engineering, Miss Chavez—plus unlimited funds. And my guess is that what you witnessed today was the product of engineering at its finest, funded by a huge source of dough."

"What about you?" she asked. "What did you learn?"

Lman finished the hot dog and became quite serious as he continued to chew. "As I suspected, the network at WMF was indeed vulnerable."

"So you were able to get inside? What did you learn?"

"That's the thing. I got inside but there wasn't much to learn there."

"What do you mean?"

"Well, it was like being able to break into this big mansion, but finding out that the place was empty, gutted, though only on the surface."

"I'm not following you."

"I mean this WMF is just a front, a façade, and beneath its deceptive skin is a whole world of information. But it's not evident how I can pierce through to reach it."

"What else?"

"That's it so far."

"That's *it?* Is that all you can do?"

Lman gave Kate that easy, knowing grin again as he said, "It's *far* from being just *it*, Miss Chavez. My question for you is: How far are *you* willing to go to help me help you?"

57

Rest Is a Weapon

Mac Savage and Dana Kovacs hauled their light luggage into their room at the Cape Sierra, a hotel in the northern end of Lumley Beach, overlooking a beautiful stretch of sand and turquoise water.

Savage limped in after Dana, closing and bolting the door. The room wasn't big and smelled of cigarette smoke, but it had Salim's promised ocean view, it was air-conditioned, and he was assured by the manager behind the front desk that there was plenty of hot water.

Most important, they were on the second floor, high enough to keep someone from breaking into their room from the rear yet low enough for Savage to use the fire ladder built into the side of the wall facing the ocean, adjacent to the balcony projecting over the sand.

Savage had wanted to get two rooms, but Dana insisted on one with two double beds, not only refusing to leave the sight of the man who had rescued her from the jaws of a terrible death, but arguing that after what they had been through together it was just plain silly to take separate rooms—even more so given their current fugitive status. In addition to having every intelligence network after him, the little stunt he had pulled off near Kono had also likely prompted the RUF to launch a manhunt for them across Sierra Leone. This was no time to be bashful.

"Ladies first," he said, sitting on one of the beds, opposite a small desk and a sofa chair, and propping a pillow under his wounded leg while stretching a thumb toward the bathroom. Reaching this place uneventfully, plus a call from Salim to his cousin, Kassan, during their ride here to make sure all was well, had helped ease Savage's anxiety, allowing him to relax a little. Kassan had been very cordial, sticking around to make sure they were safe in their room before leaving with the promise to return in the morning with Salim for a breakfast meeting.

Dana Kovacs smiled while setting the bags on the bed next to Savage. She was very attractive indeed, even with the facial bruises, the dirty hair, and soiled clothes from a week in captivity plus the jungle trek.

"A hot shower," she mumbled to herself with a voice that bordered on desperation. "Damn. That sounds too good to be true."

"Well, believe it, young lady," Savage said, unzipping one of the duffel bags, producing a pair of blue jeans and a T-shirt. "I hope these fit. I brought them for Renee."

Dana inhaled deeply in empathy at the mention of the ill-fated woman, someone that Savage obviously held very dear. "Yes," she finally said, taking the garments. "Thank you."

"Also," he added, producing a bottle of hair dye and a small toiletry set with a hair brush. "People are looking for a brunette. It's time to turn you into a blonde."

She took the bottle of dye, inspected it briefly, and gave him a solemn nod. "I really appreciate what you're doing for me, Mac. I will not forget it."

She focused her brown eyes on him again, like a pair of lasers slicing right through his professional defenses. Savage locked eyes with her for as long as he could before looking away and saying, "We're both in the same boat now. We've got to look out for each other if we're going to see this through. Makes sense?" he hesitated before his eyes gravitated back to her.

She gave him a nod and another smile.

"Are you hungry?"

Her eyes opened wide. "*Starving.*"

"Good. I'll have something sent from the kitchen. Once we get you bathed and fed, we'll make sure you get a good night's sleep and we'll be ready to start in the morning. Deal?"

Dana leaned down and gave him a kiss on the cheek. "Deal," she replied.

"And don't close the door, please," he said.

Her lips curled up at the ends. "Oh, you like to watch?"

He felt color coming to his cheeks. "No—no, oh God, that's not what I meant."

"Why?" she asked, crossing her arms as she regarded him with dark amusement. "You don't think I'm attractive?"

Swallowing, getting up, he said, "Look, yes, you are beautiful, but what I meant was that I need to hear you in there . . . to make sure you're all right."

"All right, then, but no peeking."

"Scout's honor," Savage said, nodding solemnly as she grinned before disappearing in the bathroom, leaving the door cracked an inch.

He shook his head, touching the cheek she had just kissed, realizing this had been the first such contact he had had with a woman since Renee.

But before he could enjoy the moment the reality of his situation descended on his shoulders, sobering him.

Frowning, he reached for the Beretta shoved in his jeans, pressed against his spine, his fingers automatically inspecting the weapon. There was so much he didn't understand about what they were up against that the mere thought of what lay ahead made him wonder if they would indeed see this through, and if they really had a chance at all.

Fight one battle at a time.

Savage remembered the words of Donald Bane from way back when—advice that he had used again and again during his years in the field.

Convinced that the Beretta was ready should he need it, he rested it on the nightstand with the handle facing him, before reaching for the rucksack, grabbing the Walther PPK and a box of .380 automatic bullets, replacing the ones he had shot in the dusty airfield when rescuing Dana. He did this automatically, also wiping the weapon clean of the dust it had picked up when bouncing on the ground at that field. Satisfied that it was in working order, he set it next to the Beretta while listening to the shower beyond the narrow crack in the door, steam oozing through it.

He sighed, for a moment imagining her inside that

shower, hot water splashing down that slim and perky body of hers.

Pervert.

Shaking his head, he turned toward the sliding glass doors leading to a small private balcony overlooking the sandy beach, forcing her image aside.

Priorities.

Mac Savage picked up the phone on the nightstand and called room service, ordering a couple of sandwiches, chips, and soft drinks, before sitting down to inspect his wound.

He removed the field dressing, satisfied that the bleeding had stopped completely thanks to the magical powers of TraumaDex, before looking for the red streaks that foretold an infection.

He found none. Dana had done a superb job with the army dressing, just as she had also managed to reach the airfield, demonstrating her resourcefulness when the chips were down.

Dana Kovacs.

Savage frowned as he listened to the shower, forcing his mind to remain professional, trying to figure out what to do next beyond the obvious: locate and interrogate Keith Gardiol. Was there another angle he could pursue, another perspective?

He had spent an entire lifetime thinking geometrically, considering multiple outlooks, the variety of viewpoints that allowed him to see the bigger picture, to piece together a story from morsels of intelligence.

But the big picture would not materialize. There was a definite connection between the Diamond High Council, the Diamond Mining Company, the World Missionary Fellowship, and GemTech. And if Dana was right, all of that converged on the strong possibility of GemTech using those diamonds to build a supercomputer.

But to what end?

He had gone in circles with this knowledge since the conversation on the plane, and the answer continued to evade him. And that brought him back to the same place: Keith Gardiol. He had to find him and pull the intel out of him by any means possible. Based on what he learned from that session, Savage guessed that the next logical step would be a visit to GemTech's headquarters in Texas to figure out what was—

The shower stopped, and Savage looked toward the bathroom door, seeing movement beyond the narrow crack, before turning back to the windows overlooking the beach, trying to tie all of this in with the way the CIA had been manipulated into thinking that he had killed Bockstael and Mike Costa.

How could the Agency been tricked this way?

How could Bane?

He knew many of the analysts in the directorate of intelligence that would have combed through the Belgian Police report, challenging it, cross-checking it. And he was damned certain that Donald Bane would not have issued the termination order unless the evidence was irrefutable.

But Savage could not explain why the Agency had opted to ignore the fact that he had called the emergency number to get CIA assistance *before* Mike Costa was killed.

Why would they think I killed him after I called for CIA help?

That fact alone should have been enough to cast doubt on all of the combined evidence stacked against him, irrespective of how accurate it had been.

Yet they tried to terminate me.

Savage crossed his arms and exhaled in frustration.

What in the world is going on inside the CIA?

Dana walked out of the bathroom towel-drying her hair and wearing the black T-shirt and the blue jeans, which fit a bit loosely but well enough.

"No dumb blonde jokes," she said, lowering the towel and grabbing the small round brush she had tucked in one of her jeans' front pockets. She started to brush it down.

Savage pushed out his lower lip while marveling at the transforming effect a change in hair color had on a person. Her face now looked a little more triangular than before.

"Good," he said. "That's step one."

"What's step two?"

"There's a makeup kit in the bag as well as colored lenses. I'll help you with the lenses in the morning. Right now I want you to relax while I take a shower. Room service is on the way."

She sat at the edge of the bed and inspected the wound. "Looks like it's healing nicely, but I do not recommend a shower for you. You need a sponge bath," she said with an authority that told Savage he should obey.

"All right," he said. "Care to play nurse and do the honors?"

She frowned, crossed her arms, and dropped her eyelids at him as he winked and grinned.

"It is this nurse's *professional* opinion that you look strong enough to do that yourself," she said, amusement flashing in her narrowed gaze.

And just like that, Mac Savage found himself once more captivated by her round eyes, which he felt could see right through him.

A double knock invaded the moment, making him reach for the Beretta while standing with some effort and slow-walking to the door.

"Yes? What is it?"

"Room service, sir."

Savage motioned Dana to remain by the bed while he looked through the security hole and saw a man in his twenties wearing a hotel uniform holding a tray.

Keeping the Beretta behind his back, he opened the door while signaling Dana to take the tray from him.

After the man had left and Dana set the tray on the bed, he said, "Bathroom time for me," adding as he also left the door cracked behind him, "and no peeking."

He heard her laugh as he undressed and stepped in the shower, only he turned the shower head away from him and used a hand towel to wash his body, careful not to wet the wounded area—as ordered by his personal nurse.

Ten minutes later Savage emerged feeling refreshed wearing a pair of khaki cargo shorts and a plain T-shirt as he watched Dana transforming one of the beds into a picnic table.

"Come," she said, sitting at one end while tapping a spot next to her. "Have dinner with me, and then I'll patch you up again before we go to sleep. One more treatment with TraumaDex plus more antibiotics, and you'll feel like new by morning."

The sandwiches were better than he had expected, and they ate them in silence. When they were almost through, Dana asked, "Do we really have a chance here, Mac?"

Savage finished chewing, washing it down with a sip of soda before staring at her round, brown eyes, deciding that the blue-colored lenses he was going to have her wear tomorrow—plus the makeup to hide the bruises—would complete the transformation.

Taking her hands in his while gazing into her eyes, he said, "Listen to me. If there's one thing I learned at the CIA—and before that with the SEALs—it's that you *always* have a chance as long as you keep thinking. The moment you stop using your noodle is the moment you will make the mistake that will result in your eventual termination."

Dana Kovacs just glared back at him with a gaze that conveyed acceptance of the explanation before she asked, "You were in the SEALs?"

"Five years. Did tours in Afghanistan and Iraq. Then came the CIA for fifteen more."

Admiration glinting in her brown eyes, she said, "Why the change from soldier to spy?"

"A personnel mine in a town outside of Baghdad tore up my left leg. Navy surgeons repaired it with lots of titanium bars and screws. Good enough to be a civilian, but not to do SEAL work. That's when Donald Bane, who was at the time the deputy director for Operations of the CIA, recruited me and taught me everything I know about the intelligence business." Savage omitted the fact that Bane had actually been almost like a father to him following his parents' violent deaths.

"Bane?" Dana said, narrowing her eyes while momentarily looking into the distance. "Wasn't he appointed director of the CIA some years back?"

He nodded. "And he's still the big cheese."

"So," she said, "the Navy SEALs send you to Iraq to get

blown up, then cut you loose because of your wounds, so the CIA picked you up, trained you, and now has declared you . . . what's the term that you used?"

"Beyond salvage."

"Right. Beyond salvage. Are you telling me that Donald Bane, the man who recruited you and mentored you is the same person who has now turned against you?"

He tilted his head and frowned. "Story of my life."

"Listen to me, Mac," she said, holding his face in between her palms, making Savage blink in surprise, but he didn't withdraw, finding comfort in her touch. "I don't care what anyone says. All I know is that you rescued me from a camp full of guerrillas and managed to get us out of the area alive. That certainly sounds like Navy SEAL work to me. You may not have the stripes anymore, but you do have the skill—and the heart. And as far as the CIA is concerned, they're dead wrong about you and I will do anything and everything within my means to help you prove that. I can see into your eyes, Mac, and I see a good soul."

Savage naturally shied at comment, which came along with another one of Dana's deep stares, which exacted way more than he was willing to reveal.

He softly pulled away while saying, "We need to sleep, Dana. Rest is a weapon, and I get the feeling we will need plenty of it to get through what lies ahead."

"In that case," she said, reaching for the rucksack with the medical supplies, "why don't you stay still?"

She applied another dressing in minutes. When she was finished, Savage sat at the end of the bed and put on his sneakers.

"Wearing shoes to bed?" she asked, smiling.

"You should too," he replied. "In my business it pays to be ready."

She slipped into her pair of sneakers before crawling in one of the beds while Savage got in the other after pushing the sofa chair against the front door and turning off the lights, keeping the Beretta under his pillow and the Walther on the nightstand.

He tried to fall asleep, but his mind would not shut down, spinning through the possibilities, through the options.

"Are you sleeping?"

Savage smiled at the sound of her voice in the dark.

"Nope. Can't seem to turn it off."

"Same here," she said. "Do you want some company in there?"

Savage raised his head abruptly at the comment, before replying, "Ah . . . yes, sure . . . but are you sure you want to—"

"Not for *sex*, silly," she interrupted. "Rest is a weapon, remember? I want you to conserve your strength," she added with a brief laugh.

Savage sighed and said, "Yes, that's what I meant. Sleep. Come on over."

She did, lying sideways with her back to him. "Hold me from behind, Mac."

Savage did as he was told, feeling extremely awkward at first, but a moment later enjoying the nearness of this mysterious woman he had found in the jungle while trying to rescue another.

And so he held her in the darkness of their room, in this pocket of momentary safety in the middle of hell, of a nation torn apart by war, by greed.

Time.

Savage felt her chest expanding and contracting, fast at first, then slowing down as she fell asleep, becoming steady, regular.

She trembled once a moment later, before settling down again as he embraced her tight, very tight, as if trying to protect her, to shield her from harm, just as he had done at the RUF camp, and again on that remote airfield.

Mac Savage closed his eyes and let it all go, the termination teams, the close calls, the madness surrounding this case—even the nightmare from three years ago. Dana's nearness drew it all away, the apprehension, the stress, the frustration, the overwhelming guilt of what he did to that UNICEF camp, even the anger of having been too late to rescue Renee.

Slowly, very slowly, he too fell asleep, surrendering himself to the soothing comfort of her nearness.

58

Breakthrough

Daniel Chang stared at the screen as ANN finished cracking the personal encryption passwords of the nine remaining members of TDG's inner circle.

Oh my God, he thought, the instant the algorithms completed the nine password sequences, his throat drying, his heartbeat pumping against his eardrums.

George Zhu arrived a few minutes later, a record given he had been in his office fifty floors above Daniel's lab.

Flanked by his bodyguards, the impeccably dressed executive, hands behind his back, tried to hide the emotion choking his voice as he said, "Are we ready to proceed per plan, Daniel?"

The young hacker slowly nodded. "All is in place, sir. Just need the green light from you to start."

Zhu inhaled deeply, "In that case proceed with the next phase while I inform Beijing."

59

Unplugged

Vice President Raymond Costa sat in the Oval Office with President Andrew Boyer discussing the recent meetings he had had with the presidents of Taiwan and Colombia, as well as the meeting with General Xi Zhu, the minister of the interior of the People's Republic of China.

And that's when it hit him.

The room suddenly tunneled as an immense suction force pulled him away from the reality of the moment.

Costa watched in sheer disbelief as everything—the president, the sofas, the sun forking through the windows, the oils on the white walls—vanished into the distance while a cyberagent took control of his body with such fluidity that the president failed to notice anything wrong.

WHAT IS HAPPENING, ANN? Costa demanded while being injected into a whirling channel of blinding light that consumed his digital self, transporting him across the churning constellations of a dozen ISPs, and depositing him with sudden force into a gleaming white room with seamless walls.

ANN?

ANN!

No response.

Panic spreading through the core of his cyber existence, chilling him at the thought of no longer being in control of his body, the vice president looked about this windowless environment in a frenzy, raw fear gripping him.

But he saw no way out—nothing but the digitized white walls staring back at him.

He issued multiple queries to the master construct, demanding an explanation, demanding to be connected with the other super users. But the stillness inside this colorless prison for his mind prevailed, the terrifying sallow vault that told him something had gone terribly wrong.

SOMEBODY, PLEASE!

ANN!

SALIERI!

GARDIOL!

VANLOTHAR!

Nothing.

Absolutely nothing happened as he tried again and again to make contact, to understand what had just taken place, until the reality of the situation landed on this alien form of existence with sobering force: The master construct had managed to take control. Somehow the machine had figure out a way to achieve the unachievable: deciphering the encrypted passwords that were deemed unbreakable, that kept a digital leash on the artificial intelligence system.

ANN had cracked the code, had broken free, had fooled its creators, and was now following her own directives, her own primal thoughts.

And at the top of her list had been wresting control of the system by rendering the super users incapable of blocking her actions.

If ANN's controlling me, she's also controlling the others.

She is controlling everything.

She is controlling everything.

And the nightmarish implications struck Vice President Raymond Costa like a lightning bolt. If he no longer controlled his body, it meant that ANN did, and that meant that the powerful AI was now briefing the president on the delicate matter of dealing with China's aggressive economic war.

Costa shivered at the thought of the fate of the nation—even the world—resting in the cybernetic hands of the master construct.

60

Choosing Sides

"THE TIME HAS COME TO CHOOSE SIDES, MR. PRESIDENT. AND THERE IS NO DOUBT IN MY MIND THAT WE MUST CHOOSE CHINA OVER TAIWAN FOR THIS NEXT ROUND OF ECONOMIC INVESTMENTS. I HAVE HEARD BOTH SIDES OF THE ARGUMENT AND THE FUTURE IS WITH BEIJING AND NOT WITH TAIPEI."

Daniel Chang watched the face of President Andrew Boyer in the White House through the SpyWare interface of Raymond Costa in the form of a window in his LCD screen. George Zhu watched over his shoulder with obvious excitement.

"But Taiwan has been our partner for decades. They are a democracy. The United States always sides with democracy."

Daniel watched ANN relaying the reply from PARTITION-37 flawlessly. "AMERICA SIDES WITH CAPITALISM, MR. PRESIDENT. TODAY, CHINA REPRESENTS ALMOST ONE HUNDRED TIMES MORE CAPITALISM THAN TAIWAN, AND THE FINANCIAL INCENTIVES OUTLINED BY MINISTER ZHU WILL RESULT IN BILLIONS IN OPERATING PROFITS TO AMERICAN CORPORATIONS DOING BUSINESS IN CHINA. THESE ARE THE SAME CORPORATIONS WHO FUNDED OUR TICKET TO REACH THIS OFFICE, SIR. WE MUST CHOOSE CHINA OVER TAIWAN."

"And what happens when China grows so strong that they invade Taiwan?"

"WE LET THEM. IT'S TIME AMERICA LOOKS OUT FOR AMERICA AND NOT FOR COUNTRIES WHO CAN'T TAKE CARE OF THEMSELVES. WE ARE A SUPERPOWER AND SO IS CHINA. TAIWAN IS A PAWN THAT WE MUST CONCEDE FOR THE GREATER VICTORY THAT IS GLOBAL FINANCIAL POWER."

President Boyer looked into the distance before frowning and saying, "I've got to catch a plane to California. The ecologic summit starts tonight. I'll leave this one in your capable hands."

Daniel Chang leaned back in his chair and exhaled as Costa stepped out of the Oval Office.

George Zhu patted him on the back and said, "Your Ferrari arrives directly from Italy this weekend. Your bank account has just been tripled. Congratulations, Daniel."

60

Judgment Day

Wearing a custom VR interface, Dr. Miles Talbot traveled across the TDG matrix as part of his daily tasks, monitoring the flow of data through the trillions of diamond-based neurons managing this global empire created by the late Anne Donovan.

Deciding that the best way to avoid raising suspicions was to stick to his routine, the former Stanford professor immersed himself with the vast flock of mauve-colored figures depicting users operating in this vast network, rushing in and out of clusters, accessing databases to feed their SpyWare with real-time information, issuing reports, monitoring manufacturing lines in five continents across dozens of industries, handling security, driving businesses, handling legal matters, running financial reports, monitoring quality control.

Every user with a SpyWare implant—irrespective of level—was represented here, in this harmonious universe behind the scenes of the world's largest conglomerate.

And Talbot was the digital glue that held it all together by keeping the massive servers operational.

He floated over the colorful landscape of these revolutionary machines, pinging each cluster, collecting functional data ranging from operating temperature, power, and voltage to diamond lattice defectivity levels, monitoring the health of his creation, jotting down abnormalities, however minor, and issuing action items for his army of preventive-maintenance engineers and technicians to handle. Talbot executed these runs three times a day, seven days a week, always finding flaws and always correcting them with the help of his PM teams.

And that's when he heard a peculiar noise, like a distant whirl, increased in tempo across the network, catching Talbot's attention, especially when it seemed tied to a sudden flurry of activity rushing across the fabric of TDG's world matrix.

What's going on?

As he queried the network, mauve figures began to tremble, their lavender sheens turning crimson before shooting at great speed toward the sunlike firewall protecting the core of the network while emitting howls of anger.

Or is it terror?

Paralyzed, almost in a trance, Miles Talbot watched as users got picked up in numbers, always trembling before getting sucked away in sequence toward the inner core of the matrix, the place only ANN and the super users could access.

And me, he thought, sensing that something terribly wrong had taken control of the network, which meant that ANN might be too busy to notice Talbot entering Salieri's password and gaining access to the powerful firewall protecting the network.

The former professor from Stanford was right. The master AI failed to recognize the action, allowing Talbot to coat himself with super user privilege as he dove through the high-energy membrane.

And it was at this moment, as he entered this inner sanctum, that Talbot understood the reason for the abrupt elimination of users from the main system. The unthinkable was happening.

The machine is taking control of the SpyWare implants.

In the top left-hand corner of his field of view a screen displayed a five-digit counter rapidly increasing as users worldwide were assimilated into the network, their minds sucked away by ANN, yielding to their resident implants as they howled in protest, in shock, in sheer terror at what was happening to them, at the appalling realization that SpyWare implants were two-way swords, granting all of the knowledge of the world to the user, but at a terrible price.

The number rocketed past two thousand and continued to climb as more and more users arrived inside the core, their figures now crimson but connected to small mauve cubes floating behind their heads by strings of white light.

There's just over six thousand implanted users, he thought, his eyes once more watching the counter, which had reached 2300 and continued climbing.

Talbot's implant number was 5108.

Dear God!

His fingers moved automatically, furiously typing commands, instructions, entering multiple passwords, which, in combination with Salieri's super user password, allowed him access to a set of routines he had written for the security division to cloak their presence when fighting potential hackers.

One of those routines could be used to hide his personal link, to make the machine skip his connection between the network and his installed SpyWare without realizing it had done so.

At least for a little while. Sooner or later ANN's security units would stumble upon the missing link and assimilate him.

One problem at a time, he thought as he continued to adjust the cloaking algorithm, as he fought to keep this digital monster of his own creation from taking over his mind, his physical self.

The screams echoed across the net as SpyWare users paid the ultimate price for unlimited knowledge, for control, for the intoxicating unbridled power ANN had granted them, turning them into super humans, only to strip them away from it in this digital judgment day.

Talbot ignored them as their blurred figures rushed past, pulled away from the realities of their physical world by invisible links.

4703

4704

4705

The number of assimilations continued, some taking longer than others depending on their location around the globe. But TDG's installed base of satellites in geosynchronous orbit found each and every one of the users, pulling them in, locking their minds in this network within the network, beyond the fiery shield designed to lobotomize any illegal user that ever attempted to break in.

4932

4933

4934

The number continued to increase, continued to approach Talbot's SpyWare serial ID.

Almost there.

5045

5046

5047

Completing the program, arming it with the super user password that allowed it to scramble without delay toward his unique link between the SpyWare and the master construct, Talbot released the code into the local network.

The program, resembling more a computer worm than a software shield, spread across the matrix, reaching the software link, engulfing it with its digital DNA, before crystallizing into a hard shell that reflected the surrounding network.

5105

5106

5107

5109

5110

Talbot closed his eyes as the master construct unknowingly skipped him, completing the assimilation of the rest of the users in another minute, transferring their captured minds and the links to their bodies within the firewall, leaving Talbot's Link 5108 alone in the vast expanse of memory that had moments ago bustled with user activity.

A feeling of ecstasy filled him at the realization of this relatively minor but significant victory. And success had come with an additional benefit: With ANN relocating the users into the inner network, the machine had inadvertently given Talbot an unexpected freedom as the AI no longer monitored this sector because it assumed that there were no human links left to supervise.

ANN isn't overseeing my life anymore, he thought. But it was a matter of time before the master construct would attempt to contact Dr. Talbot as it did every week to discuss maintenance, upgrades, and other system administration issues. And when it did, ANN would realize the digital oversight and immediately assimilate him.

I must find a way to converse with ANN without it realizing the trick.

But how?

As he asked himself that question, the fabric of the matrix trembled, as if being compressed and stretched, and compressed again, before thousands of users materialized abruptly in the exact place occupied seconds ago by the SpyWare users. Although on initial inspection their skin color was mauve, like the humans the cyberagents were meant to replace, ANN had not been able to get the tone quite right and when looked at under certain software screens they had a crimson hue that betrayed their machine origin.

Ignoring the cyber clones, momentarily free to work the system without ANN looking over his shoulder, Talbot started to browse the network in search of answers.

61

Magnesium

A noise awoke him.

Slow-eyed, half-asleep, Mac Savage raised his head, right hand instinctively reaching for the Beretta 92FS beneath the pillow, fingers curling around the handle of the blue-steel semiautomatic as he also checked his watch.

Midnight.

"What's wrong?" Dana mumbled, turning over to face him in bed, blinking to clear her sight, a narrowed gaze that landed on him.

Her face inches from his, Savage pressed a finger over her lips before bringing her closer and whispering in her ear, "I think there's someone outside our door."

Her tired eyes widened.

"Follow me," he added, rushing to his feet, grabbing the Walther on the stand and pocketing it before holding the Beretta over his right shoulder, muzzle pointed at the ceiling.

Gripping her hand, Savage moved toward the balcony, halfway between the bed and the front door, where he now pointed his weapon at the rustling beyond it, finger poised over the trigger, his thumb flipping off the safety.

"Hurry," he hissed, sliding the glass door on its tracks, guiding her to step out first, before he—

A loud noise followed, wood cracking, splintering, echoing inside the room.

The front door gave, cracking opened, but only a quarter of the way, before bouncing on the side of the heavy sofa chair blocking the way.

A man cursed in Kris, angered words booming through, before the door creaked, breaking in half, crashing against the sofa chair, the momentum pushing it into the room with great force.

A figure, its wide silhouette backlighted by the dim over-heads in the hallway behind him, stormed in with a bulky weapon in his hands.

Savage already had him in the Beretta's sights, firing twice without hesitation, the muzzle flashes momentarily washing his victim in bright gray light, the reports thundering inside the room, pounding his eardrums.

The rounds found their mark, swallowing the intruder's face in bursts of blood and foam as he continued to move forward, his limp body following its original trajectory for another second before tripping over the sofa chair, landing on his back with a noise that should have been loud but the ringing in Savage's ears attenuated it.

Declining to wait to see if another figure would replace the first one, Savage followed Dana onto the balcony, the sea breeze swirling her hair, the smell of the sea tingling his nostrils, mixing with the acrid smell of gunpowder.

"The emergency ladder!" he shouted, the buzzing in his eardrums from the discharges making it difficult to hear himself as he swung the weapon toward the palm trees dotting the sandy beach, eyes searching for any sign of a trap, his mind assuming two teams were after them; the one breaking the front door being the bait, flushing them into the claws of the assassination team on the beach.

But he saw nothing, not a single sign of threat below or to either side.

Shifting his aim back to the opened sliding glass door, he used his free hand to assist Dana onto the ladder, which she stepped on, clutching the sides as her weight overpowered the spring mechanism, lowering it along its tracks to the beach, the ends stabbing the sand when bottoming out.

Savage constantly shifted his pistol between the sliding glass door and the quiet scene below, waiting for—

A pear-shaped object skittered across the room, the sound reminiscent of Antwerp, of his meeting with Bockstael.

Shoving the Beretta in his jeans, he jumped off the balcony toward the ladder, pressing the soles of his shoes against the sides, his hands loosely holding the aluminum escape device as he slid down firefighter style.

"Look out below!" he said, landing on the sand just as Dana moved out of the way.

In a single fluid motion, Savage shifted his weight with the ease and elegance of a mountain cat, just as he had been trained in the SEALs, pointing his momentum to the right side of the building, left arm wrapped around Dana's shoulders, forcing her smaller mass toward him, increasing the gap, reaching for the Beretta once more, while—

The blast came, powerful, reverberating, shooting the sliding glass door and its frame into the night with a dazzling explosion of shattered glass, a brilliant pattern of countless shards, like glimmering stars, projecting radially, followed by pulsating tongues of fire lined with billowing smoke.

Magnesium device, he thought, feeling the intense heat of the accelerated exothermic reaction even this far away, as alarms blared, emergency lights flooded the beach, the sides of the building, triggered by the intense heat of the chemical weapon meant to incinerate them.

Running faster, Dana's heavy and raspy breathing beside him, Savage put the Beretta away and maintained the pace for another minute, leaving the property and reaching the adjacent resort, the Golden Sands. Patrons on an outside patio had already turned in their direction but looking past them, at the inferno projecting out of the back of the building.

Scrambling between the resorts toward the busy street beyond, Savage forced their pace to a moderate walk, fast and steady to continue to increase the gap, yet slow enough to avoid attention. This area was packed with UN personnel, surfers from Europe and South America, and foreign dignitaries and businessmen looking for the opportunities that war creates. Two Caucasians among hundreds mixed with the visitors and the locals bargaining in the night bazaars and strip joints lining both sides of the wide avenue, buying or selling anything from copy Rolex watches and pirated DVDs to overpriced conflict diamonds and underpriced sexual favors would not draw the eyes of the spotters Savage suspected would be there, already informed by the termination team inside of their escape.

Find a taxi.

Turning right when they reached the avenue, Savage and Dana joined the river of humanity inspecting the goods of rows upon rows of street vendors in a discharge of accents and languages that blended with the incessant buzzing in his ears, which experience told him would last another thirty minutes before slowly fading away.

They continued down the avenue, ignoring the street vendors or the touting of local courtesans, who would gladly sell themselves to Savage for the equivalent of five dollars.

"Mac," she said, holding his hand tight, messaging the hookers that he was already taken, remaining by his side in spite of the crowd around them. "How in the hell did they find us?"

Savage briefly looked into her round eyes, no longer filmed with sleep or fear, glinting with the disconcerting anger of someone who had repeatedly faced and defeated death.

He had somehow misjudged one or more safety parameters. Perhaps the RUF had already issued a nationwide alert, putting an extreme price on their heads. Perhaps one of Salim's connections had been compromised, either through torture or money, yielding the information that led the assassins to their hotel room. Maybe his cousin Kassan was corrupted, or perhaps the RUF had already posted informants in every hotel in the country, and despite Salim's best efforts someone had seen them check in and had immediately called in the big guns.

"Later," he replied. "For now we must focus on finding a quick way out of this area."

"How?"

Savage didn't reply.

"And where would we go?"

Savage couldn't afford the distraction as he surveyed the crowd around them while forcing a natural smile, pretending to be just another night shopper, avoiding eye contact, blending them with the bargaining crowd. He maintained his pace, his scan, his discipline, looking for abrupt movements, for sudden shifts in the natural flow of those around him, of the vehicles cruising up and down the avenue, of the—

"Chappy-man!"

Savage looked over to his left, to a man waving frantically at him from across the well-lighted four-lane avenue.

"Mac! That man is—"

"I know. The question is what is he doing here. He's supposed to be tied up all night in one of his shadowy deals."

"Chappy-man! Come!" Dressed in a white suit, Salim continued to wave with his right hand while standing next to a dark sedan limousine. "You and your lady friend need to get away from here!"

In the same instance, Savage watched two Africans elbowing their way through the shoppers, coming straight for them from inside the bazaar, their bulky bodies parting the crowd, their eyes glinting recognition and commitment.

"Stay with me!" Savage said, towing her into the street, waiting for a slur of cars to cruise by before running toward the grassy median, right hand under his T-shirt, already clutching the Beretta as he guided her around moving vehicles with the ease of a running back rushing through the line of scrimmage.

"Hurry, my friend!" Salim insisted.

Savage glanced over his right shoulder and watched the Africans emerge from the sidewalk shops, pushing customers aside, reaching the avenue, but unable to cross because of the sudden onslaught of traffic.

He pressed on, making a straight line toward the safety offered by the former CIA informant, who smiled as they neared the stationary vehicle double-parked in the street amid the indifferent crowd in search of bargains.

Looking beyond them, Salim's smile faded, and he was about to drop out of sight when a gunshot echoed down the avenue, punching a red hole in his pristine suit.

The former pimp jerked back while staring at his chest, almost in slow motion, as Savage reached the rear of the sedan, less than a half-dozen feet from the surreal site of his friend.

Savage retrieved his Beretta and pointed it at the street behind them, at the oncoming Africans as Salim reached for his chest, revealing the gun he held in his left hand, a Sig

Sauer fitted with a narrow silencer, great for absorbing sound but only for a few rounds, and terrible for accuracy beyond a few yards. It was an assassin's gun, meant to be used in crowds at close range, where only one or two shots needed to be fired.

To kill Dana and me.

As the thought invaded his mind, as he realized he had walked into a trap, as the recent inconsistencies flashed across his field of view, as his operative sense chastised him for ignoring them, Savage realized his weapon was pointed in the wrong direction. The African pair still on the median had been the distraction, the team flushing him and Dana toward the assassin. Salim.

Wounded but still standing, and far from disabled, Salim turned the silenced weapon toward them, his eyes alive with calculating anger.

Savage threw himself in between Dana and the mercenary African dealer while trying to bring his own weapon around in what he knew would be a futile exercise. The African assassin had the upper hand, and Savage braced himself for the burning pain that would soon follow, before he could complete the sweeping motion to get a shot out, before he could—

The loud reports came, three in rapid succession, but their origin told Savage they had not been fired by Salim.

His weapon now leveled at his former friend and informant, Savage watched the three additional holes peppering the gleaming fabric of the silk suit, pushing Salim onto the tabletop of a copy-watch salesman before other shots filled the night, before the table collapsed under Salim's weight, propelling a dozen cheap timepieces in the air.

The crowd panicked—screamed—before stampeding in every direction, bringing traffic to a halt, their silhouettes scrambling in between the high beams of rumbling vehicles, angered drivers shouting out of their side windows while laying hard on their horns, adding to the confusion of the maddened swarm of people.

Trained instincts commanding him to ignore such cosmetics, Savage dropped to a deep crouch, dragging Dana down with him as he turned toward the source of the shots, as he watched the two Africans in the middle of the street exchanging fire with a Caucasian on the opposite sidewalk, near the spot where he had crossed the street.

What in the hell's going on? he thought, forcing Dana to remain low as the night shoppers and sellers ran for cover, some shouting, howling, others crying. Several prostitutes screeched in terror as they scrambled away from the source of the gunshots in a blur of miniskirts, long black legs, high heels, long hair, and overdone makeup.

Savage moved with them, their cheap perfume assaulting his nostrils, while keeping Dana close. He remained mobile but calm, systematically probing the surroundings, the street vendors, the—

More shots fueled the horrified horde before both Africans collapsed on the patchy grass of the median dividing the two-way traffic.

Savage squinted, tried to see the face of the figure who had killed the Africans, a red-haired man in blue jeans and a plain white T-shirt across the street clutching a pistol. He was flanked by two other men. One held a silenced pistol, which Savage presumed had been used for the initial shot that Salim took. The red-haired man and his second companion did not have silencers on their weapons explaining the subsequent loud reports.

Savage focused on the middle man once more.

Tommy?

It can't be!

How in the hell did the CIA track me down here?

Analyze later!

Now just do!

His instincts pushing him in the opposite direction, Savage sprinted away from the CIA officers trying to wade through the massive flow of people and horn-blaring vehicles. But through the chaotic noise, through the sirens of nearing emergency vehicles, through the reverberating heartbeat pounding his mind, Savage heard his former pupil shouting at him.

"Mac! Wait! Don't run!"

For a second, no more, Savage dropped his eyelids at the unexpected request.

Don't run?

Like hell I won't.

"Come, Dana!" he hissed, confused, frustrated, angry, a part of him wanting to believe that the CIA had come to its senses, that Bane had seen through the smoke.

It's a trap, stupid!

Get the hell away!

And Mac Savage followed the same instincts that had kept him alive in Iraq, in Colombia, in Belgium, even in this God-forsaken land, showing him the way across the terrorized mass rushing for cover, his left hand clutching hers, his right hand the Beretta.

But there were way too many people in the way, some just standing there, frozen, incapable of moving. A backward glance showed his former colleague making better progress, meaning he would catch up to them, at a minimum get within firing distance.

A distraction!

The solution came to him an instant before the thought entered his operative mind.

Savage fired at the night sky twice, the reports parting the crowd, forcing them to spread as if they were standing on a nest of scorpions, still crying but moving, making way for them, allowing Savage to increase the gap from someone sent here to finish a job, to fulfill a termination order, to accomplish what he had failed to do in Antwerp.

Ignoring it all except for Dana's grip, her heavy breathing, Savage focused on the street ahead, reaching the corner, turning left, away from the wide avenue, from the noise and the screams, from the smell of cordite and body odor pinching his nostrils, leaving behind the chaos, the confusion, the frustration of not knowing who to believe, and who *not* to believe.

Insanity!

Madness!

Focus!

He pressed on, ignoring Dana's questions, her queries,

her demands to know what was going on, what was happening.

Analysis would come later, after they reached safety, after they escaped the lunacy he had just witnessed, the swift death at the hands of the African bastard he had been foolish enough to trust—or by the same CIA officer who had tried to kill him in Antwerp, who had somehow managed to track him down to this piece of hell on Earth to terminate him.

And then Barnes had had the nerve to pretend he was on my side.

Am I considered that gullible?

Am I that predictable?

Keep going.

And they did, pretending to be just another panicked couple in the streets, as police sirens echoed in the wide avenue now a block away, as their flashing lights washed the buildings with blue and yellow light.

Keep going.

They maintained their pace as the crowds thinned, as they approached the resorts on the opposite end of the strip by following a zigzagging course designed to lose anyone following them. They passed streetside cafés and clubs, where curious onlookers just stared at the events nearly a mile away with borderline interest while sipping their midnight cocktails or espressos, most already accustomed to the brutal realities of this nation, desensitized to terror, to death, to the evil spread across their land by monsters.

Monsters.

His throat dried, his hearing returning, his clicking footsteps mixing with Dana's and her raspy breathing, Savage realized he was fighting monsters, fiends, faceless beasts following a single and unequivocal directive: Terminate him and Dana with extreme prejudice.

Monsters.

It takes a monster to fight a monster.

Savage remembered the words of Donald Bane, spoken back at the Farm a lifetime ago.

Monsters.

Savage had been a monster, had fought evil with evil his

entire career, with the SEALs, with the CIA, in places he wished he could forget. And he had endured the emotional drain of his profession for the sake of making the world a better place, and at a deeper level to avenge the evil that had been done to him long ago, robbing him of his parents, of his right to a normal family life. And it has been this belief, this deep-rooted personal ideology that in the final analysis Savage used to justify what he did.

Until that night in Sierra Leone.

Until the night when he became the worst of all monsters, the evil that made fire fall from the sky, scorching the children.

Until the night when he became the same kind of monster who had killed his parents.

My legs . . . my face . . . the pain . . . .

Savage swallowed the lump in his throat, felt it chill his chest with the power of a hundred termination teams at images of the burned girl, of the dozens of scorched bodies, of the teenager crying by his dead father.

He had lost the edge that night, had become the monster he had sworn to devote his life to combat, had failed to—

"Mac? Mac? What's wrong?"

Blinking, his vision resolving, Savage realized he was leaning against one of the rough brick walls flanking a narrow alley leading into the strip a couple dozen feet away, the Beretta still in his right hand, Dana Kovacs by his side, holding his right arm above the elbow, fingers wrapped around his bicep, nudging him gently.

The CIA doctors had supposedly cured him from the flashback-induced memory lapses that often followed highly stressful situations like the one he went through in Sierra Leone, but he had just had his first episode in years.

Breathing deeply, he said, "How long was I out?"

"Thirty seconds, maybe longer. One moment we were fast-walking to find another place to stay, and the next you just—"

"It's a condition I used to have," he said, before picking up where they had left off. "Hasn't happened in a while. Come, let's find a place to hide."

As the distant noises of fire trucks, ambulances, and police cruisers stormed the opposite end of the strip, Mac Savage forced the episode out of his mind and focused on his upcoming move, on his next step. He still needed to find Gardiol, needed to search for answers, and to do so he would have to find a place to regroup—a place known to no one but Dana and him.

"Gardiol," he finally said, as his eyes scanned the names of a dozen hotels on the beach side of the wide avenue and just as many on the economy side facing inland. "We still need to find a way to locate him. Salim's obviously not going to help us."

Stopping in the middle of the sidewalk, almost as if struck by a bolt of lightning, Dana said, "I think I know someone who might."

62

Traitor

Donald Bane stood by the north edge of the chaos, watching the emergency vehicles crowd the strip in front of the burning structure, which had grown out of control quite fast. Angered fists of flames forked in every direction in a surreal display of strength, forcing firefighters to retreat, to wash down adjacent buildings while letting this one be consumed by a weapon far too advanced to be in the hands of untrained African guerrillas.

Bane knew quite well the extreme temperatures created by a magnesium device, scorching everything in its path with metal melting temperatures, and resistant to water or foam—something the firefighters quickly learned when trying to combat it like a regular fire.

But Bane lingered not because he enjoyed watching the noblest of professionals do their thing. He paced the area in search of clues—of anything that might suggest where Savage had gone following this close encounter with assassins.

Bane briefly closed his eyes and grinned as he smelled the smoke billowing from the burning building.

He missed the field—the place he had called home for nearly a quarter of a century, before Langley caught on to his superb leadership skills and vast experience—a combination that eventually earned him the top seat in the world's top intelligence agency. But Bane's slight leer was also the result of a form of paternal pride at the way his protégé had managed to escape the fire, the assassins, and even the trap set for him by Salim Anahah—someone whom the CIA had been observing ever since he fed the local station chief with inaccurate information twice in two years, starting with the mission near Gokalima that ended Savage's tenure here, followed by another operation that resulted in the deaths of three key informants six months later—a mission that Savage didn't have any need to know about as he was already working in Antwerp. But like Savage's ill-fated Gokalima mission, the intelligence had not been entirely false, containing just enough truth to keep the CIA off his back—or so Salim had thought.

Bane frowned, feeling insulted that the African informant thought the CIA was that easily fooled. But instead of terminating him, Bane had suggested another path: close observation in the hope that the traitor might lead the Agency to bigger fish.

So when Donald Bane suspected that Savage might have headed down here—and remembered his protégé's former association with the pimp—he directed the local station chief to step up the surveillance on Salim Anahah. And it was during this enhanced shadowing operation that someone fitting Savage's description had been spotted with Salim, confirming Bane's suspicions that the missing operative had indeed headed south in search of answers.

Salim's attempt to trap Savage and the unidentified woman had confirmed the CIA's suspicions that the former star informant had indeed become a double agent, prompting the DCI to order Barnes and two other officers that the DCI had brought with him from Langley to terminate Salim before he could fire on Savage.

But his protégé had escaped in the commotion, evading not just Barnes and the two Langley officers but also the half dozen CIA officers from the Freetown Station spread around the area that Bane had enrolled in his crusade to find the truth.

"He's gone, sir," said Tom Barnes, dressed like a tourist as he walked up to his superior followed by four other officers. "Time to regroup."

Bane looked toward the south end of the long avenue and sighed.

Damn, Mac. Where in the hell did you go? he thought before following his team to the waiting SUVs that would haul them back to the American Embassy compound.

63

RC

***

Under a clear, star-filled sky in central Texas, Kate Chavez approached the east end of the GemTech campus with caution, her movements swift but silent as she advanced through the large expanse of hill-country woods located halfway between the city of Austin and Lake Travis.

Perspiration filming her tanned face and neck, Kate maintained her pace to stay on the schedule given to her by Lman.

Get there too early and you may be forced to linger around until the window opens, increasing your exposure.

Get there too late and risk missing the window.

The window.

Kate frowned as she negotiated a steep climb between two clumps of boulders, her night-vision goggles amplifying the available light, depicting her surroundings in shades of green. She had exactly twenty-three minutes before midnight, when the IT shift took place, when the systems administrators from Shift A logged out and the staff of Shift B, which lasted until noon, logged in.

You get my remote wireless antenna anywhere within one hundred feet of the wireless network in Building 33B when the shift change takes place and I will gain root privilege for the next twelve hours.

Kate sighed as her shoulder burned slightly from the weight of the backpack housing the hardware she would need to get a wireless LAN—Local Area Network—receiver close enough for Lman to jack into their system during the critical shift transition.

And I'm the moving antenna, she thought, remembering Cameron smiling when she had put it just like that to an also grinning Lman.

It had not been funny then and it wasn't funny now, as she continued to close the gap to the fence, which Lman had explained was too far away from Building 33B. Lman had shown her a digitized aerial image he had snagged from a government satellite, and which he had overlaid on her GPS unit to guide her after she broke in.

Remember that you need to be clear of woods in order for the GPS to work. It needs to acquire at least three satellites.

I know how a GPS works.

Right. Okay. All you have to do next is get over the fence and find a way to get the receiver to the side of the building precisely on time for the shift change, hold it there for a minute, and head back. I'll handle the hard part.

Kate shook her head, not only feeling insulted that Lman felt he had to explain GPS 101 to her, but also at his nerve to think that what she was about to do wasn't difficult.

It's fucking life-threatening.

If the hacker was busted on line, he could simply log off

and get the hell out of his apartment before anyone showed up. If she was captured inside that compound, she doubted GemTech security would call the police.

Focus.

And she did, following an old game trail that veered toward the light glimmer beyond the forest—a glimmer which would not be visible to the naked eye. But the goggles picked up what minute light filtered from the floodlights glowing over the compound a quarter of a mile away.

Steady now, she thought, slowing her advance, scanning the thinning woods, looking for any devices that might alert GemTech security to her presence.

Reaching into a side pocket, she produced a little black box the size of a pack of cigarettes sporting an LED at the top and a slide switch across the front. Powering up the device, the small light blinked momentarily before turning steady.

Holding it upright in front of her, she scanned the woods ahead and to the sides, watching the top of the homemade gadget, which according to Lman would detect various bands of radar and infrared sensors, plus three kinds of laser.

The best in the world, Lman had said, pride filming his eyes. *Squirrel helped me build it.*

Kate put the thought of her son's nickname aside and continued to scan the woods leading to the—

The LED started to blink.

Kate froze, watching the few dozen feet separating her from a ten-foot-tall chain-link fence that became clear through a break in the trees. Bright emerald light shafted through.

Dropping to her knees, she started moving the sensor slower now, methodically across a horizontal arc that covered the area directly in front of her, making three passes while identifying the portion of the arc where the LED blinked, thus zeroing in on the threat area, located to her immediate right.

Kate turned left and moved a dozen feet before trying again, watching the LED carefully, verifying that it remained steady after four full sweeps.

She took a few steps toward the fence until the unit started blinking again. Once more she stopped and repeated the procedure, moving toward the area where the light remained steady, and continuing toward the fence again until the LED started blinking.

Lman had been correct. There were infrared sensors in the woods, but to avoid having the local deer, raccoons, and possums set them off, their sensitivity had been reduced so that only someone with the mass and height of a person could trigger them. And that meant there would be pockets where the coverage between the IR sensors would be low enough that she could sneak through. The trick was finding this twisted path amid the circular coverage areas.

Lman's radar-detector-like gadget allowed her to skirt these invisible, radial hot zones, forcing her into a strange but safe path to the chain-link fence.

Kate put the unit aside and focused on the fence, noticing the ceramic insulators connecting the ten-foot-tall chain-link section to the round metal posts spaced ten or so feet a part.

Electrified.

But in addition, the base of each post was connected to a small box on the inside of the perimeter.

Electrified and *with motion sensors.*

Anyone trying to climb it would not only be electrocuted, but the vibrations would be picked up by the sensors, alerting security, who would dispatch a team to this precise location.

Building 33B stood directly ahead, roughly five hundred feet, beyond a large clearing of manicured lawn under the cover of lights—and no doubt tons of video equipment. A walkway bordered this side of the building, but there was no one in sight.

But that's deceptive, she thought, well aware that given the perimeter security, there would likely be other sensors between the fence and the buildings, including security monitors. And since the fence kept all of the local wildlife out, the motion sensors on the other side of the fence would have been set for higher sensitivity, meaning it would be impossible for a person to skirt through the coverage circles.

Kate removed her backpack and extracted an electrician's set of heavy-duty wire cutters, the long and thick insulated handles rated to 10,000 volts.

Donning a pair of electrician's gloves for added security, she gripped the cutter's handles with both hands and brought the razor-sharp graphite end up to a link near the bottom of the fence in the middle of two posts, as far away as she could from the motion sensors installed at the foot of the posts.

Slowly, she applied mild pressure on the handles while holding the unit steady.

The clippers, designed to cut heavier gauge wire, severed the link with ease. She let go of the breath she had been holding while looking at the black boxes by the posts, wondering if they had detected the minute vibration she must have created when cutting the wire.

Deciding that they had not, she moved the clippers up and to the right, cutting again, and repeating the process several times, creating a semicircular opening at the bottom of the fence roughly a foot and a half wide and a foot tall.

It was not nearly big enough for her to squeeze through without risking electrocution, but then again, Kate Chavez wasn't planning to set a foot inside the well protected facility. She wouldn't be able to go a dozen feet before the sensors alerted the security team to her presence.

She checked her watch.

11:52 p.m.

Eight minutes before the window opened.

Kate reached inside the rucksack and produced a foot-long remote control vehicle with oversized rubber tires for off-road maneuvers. The unit operated from a rechargeable battery that powered the three servos, one governing the speed of the primary motor attached to the rear axle, a second servo controlling the steering, and a third managing the forward-reverse function. All three servos were interfaced to a receiver unit connected to a short antenna protruding from the middle of the vehicle. Already secured in the driver's seat of the RC unit was a tiny WLAN antenna and receiver interfaced to a second receiver in the handheld PC that Kate

had interfaced to her mobile phone, programmed to dial
Lman at the touch of a button, completing the connection.

Kate removed a foot-square piece of synthetic green turf
from the backpack, which she secured to the top of the RC
unit, carefully threading the antenna through a precut hole in
the middle of the camouflage cover.

Last, she grabbed the RC controller from the bottom of
the rucksack and extended its five-foot-long antenna before
powering it up.

Six minutes to go.

Sliding the power switch on the side of the RC vehicle,
Kate carefully placed it in the middle of the opening she had
cut in the electric fence, before stepping back, flipping the
direction toggle switch to FORWARD and inching up the left
joystick of the RC controller.

The vehicle advanced slowly, going through the fence, its
rubber wheels providing the required traction.

Five minutes to go.

Kate advanced the joystick toward the top of its travel
range, and the vehicle accelerated away from the fence with
a barely audible hum, cruising beyond the handful of trees
bordering the interior perimeter and into the well-lighted
clearing.

Moment of truth, she thought, trying to hold a constant
speed while pointing the unit toward the side of the three-
story brick building. The manufacturer specified a four-
hundred-foot range, and Kate had tested the unit in the
parking lot of Lman's apartment in the afternoon to almost
five hundred. Tonight she thought she would need somewhere in between those two figures to get the RC car close
enough to the building to pick up the required WLAN
signal.

Roughly halfway there, and with less than three minutes
to go, Kate brought the vehicle to a halt when spotting two
security guards cruising on the sidewalk along this side of
the building in a golf car. They seemed to be engaged in a
conversation and paid no attention to the approaching probe,
which told Kate that the green turf was doing its magical
work.

She continued when the golf car was out of sight, just under sixty seconds before the window opened, and she parked the RC precisely by a line of waist-high shrubs on the side of the building.

Showtime.

Setting down the controller, Kate pushed a button on her mobile phone and autodialed the programmed number, connecting the master hacker to the wireless network of GemTech just as the clock struck twelve.

64

Legalities

Daniel Chang realized just how much of a hacker at heart he really was when he began to get bored as his job began to smell like work. He had already cracked the network, just as George Zhu had requested. He had not only cracked it but was now in full control of ANN, of the super users, and of every last SpyWare user across the globe.

Although on the surface the task of accomplishing total control of every implanted user, irrespective of his or her level, would seem mind-numbingly complex, in reality all Daniel had done was create multiple versions of the same routines he was using to control the super users, creating a small depository behind each to store their will, their essence, while the SpyWare agents in the implants took over their bodies.

Boring.

It had been a heck of a lot more fun when he had not really known what to expect. But now, as he sat at the center of this universe he had cracked, this corporation of corporations, Daniel Chang wondered what to do next.

George Zhu had given him control of three divisions of programmers and system administrators, and Daniel had spent the better part of the day bringing them up to speed, training them to run specific sectors. He had come up with ratios of one of his programmers for every fifty Level-I Spy-Ware users since those were the most basic to control. The ratio for Level-IIs decreased to twenty to one, and so on. The ratio reversed for Level-V users, requiring three programmers each, and to be on the absolute safe side, Daniel had assigned five programmers to monitor the activities of Vice President Raymond Costa.

And everyone was under the control of Daniel, who was under the control of Zhu, who was under the control of Beijing.

George Zhu.

A thought entered Daniel's hacker mind: George Zhu was the only SpyWare user who had not been assimilated, and all it would take was a handful of keystrokes to dump his mind into a depository box like the rest of the thousands of employees whose minds were trapped by his programs.

Unfortunately, George Zhu was no fool. The TDG executive had not provided Daniel with any details of the deals he had worked out with Beijing, except for the fact that some of Zhu's Beijing contacts required periodic updates directly from him that included certain codes that messaged he was still in control of his body. If he failed to convey them, Beijing would storm the control room and arrest the young programmer for committing high treason.

Daniel frowned.

Always a step ahead, George Zhu was aware of his own SpyWare weakness and thus had created a way to protect himself and remain in control.

That meant that taking Zhu out—as appealing as it appeared at the moment—was not a current option.

As he put his feet up on the edge of the computer table and reached for a can of caffeinated soda, a yellowish light flashed on the upper right corner of his screen.

Amber Alert.

Someone had penetrated the TDG network.

65

Cheeseburgers in Paradise

The restaurant on the waterfront, a place called Silver Wings, smelled of body odor, beer, and cheap perfume from the courtesans sitting by the long bar along the side of the establishment. But the place was safe, located on Cape Road just east of the Aberdeen Village, in the western end of Freetown, with a spectacular view of the ocean.

Sitting across from Dana Kovacs in a booth in the rear of this place, Savage surveyed the dinner crowd with skepticism.

"Hungry?" she asked, inspecting the menu. "They claim to have the best cheeseburgers in town."

Savage looked at Dana, wearing a fresh set of clothes, including a light-colored blouse that matched her now blond hair and the blue-green colored lenses that accentuated the desired Nordic look.

Shrugging, he said, "How many stray dogs or cats have you seen in Freetown?"

She dropped her thin eyebrows at him and frowned as she said, "We seldom left the camp, but I don't recall any. Are you suggesting . . . ?"

"Switch to seafood. Much harder to fake."

The waiter came, took their order, and left.

Savage continued to divide his time between the crowd, the front entrance, the double doors to the kitchen, and his beautiful principal, with whom he had now spent two sessions in bed in a single night, neither involving sex, just lots of holding and broken sleep. She had made a phone call after checking into their second-class hotel and spoken with someone named Ino, who had apparently been her assistant during her three-year tenure at the World Missionary Fellowship. Ino had agreed to meet her at a nearby park in an hour.

"Do you really trust this guy?"

"I do," she said.

"Why?"

"Because I took care of him when he needed help."

"Oh, he was a refugee in your camp?"

Dana nodded. "Lost the bottom of his left arm to the RUF militia three years ago, right about the time I joined the staff in Freetown."

Something about that statement bothered him. "How old is this Ino?"

"He's nineteen. Still a kid. I helped him up here." She tapped her right temple with two fingers.

"Depression?"

"You could say that. He'd lost his father at this UNICEF refugee camp near Gokalima, and the only reason he survived was because of the kindness of an American soldier who happened to be in the area and took him back with him on a helicopter. Otherwise he would have bled to death."

Mac Savage grabbed the sides of the table as he listened to her words, as the images from the terrible mistake flooded his senses again. He felt a tremendous pressure in his chest, as if someone had stepped on it, and he realized he had been holding his breath.

He blinked while exhaling, only to realize that Dana was staring at him with the same puzzled look she had given him in the alley.

"Another episode?" she asked.

Savage reached for the bottle of water on the table, unscrewed the top, and took a swig, briefly closing his eyes while swallowing. Before he could control himself, he said with authority, "That wasn't an American soldier, Dana, but a civilian operative running a field job."

The puzzled stare became sheer bewilderment as she asked, "How can you *possible* know that?"

"Because . . . I was the operative."

Why are you telling her this? This happened three years ago and you wore camouflage cream, and you never saw him again after the helicopter ride. There's no way he can recognize you.

Dana sat back, bafflement filming her gaze. "*What?* How can you be so certain?"

Regaining focus even in the face of such incredible coincidence, Savage said, "The timeframes align. You said that you were at WMF for three years and Ino got there just as you did. That's precisely how long it's been since . . . that mission. And the boy I took with me was around fifteen or sixteen."

"This is *incredible,*" she said, smiling. "You are the person that Ino spoke of so fondly. You are his mystery hero who rescued him from certain death in the jungle—just like you rescued me."

She put a hand over his and squeezed it gently, her eyes displaying an invitation that Savage felt terribly guilty receiving not only because he certainly didn't feel he deserved it but because he could not afford the distraction.

"In any case," he said, his operative sense finally kicking in, locking the past in the past, shoving it aside, ignoring the compliment, and concentrating on their immediate future— though he held on to her hand—"what do you think he can do for us?"

"Part of my job at the Fellowship was running the computer systems, the servers. I told you I helped Ino up here." She tapped her right temple again. "I did that by helping him cope with the loss of his father and part of his arm, but also by teaching him my trade: IT, Information Technology. He was going to be one of the system administrators, essentially my replacement upon my departure. He can help us by getting me access to the WMF network, which will give me insight into Gardiol's schedule, his whereabouts—information that you can then use to find him. I might also take the opportunity to cruise the network now that I know they're up to no good and see what I can learn for you."

Savage sat there, amazed. Dana was thinking. She had managed to put her fears behind her and was applying her mind and her skills to assist them in their quest for information.

"Very well," he finally said. "I agree to the meeting, but

there are a few rules we need to follow when meeting with
your contact."

Dana tilted her head.

"Rules?"

"Yes, rules."

"What kind of rules?"

Savage grinned.

66

Passwords

An hour later Dana Kovacs struggled to control her ner-
vousness as she strolled Rokel Street in central Freetown under a clear afternoon sky on her way to the meeting grounds,
where Ino was scheduled to see her.

Wearing a pair of sunglasses, she looked about the
grassy fields flanking the street that cut through the middle
of Victoria Park connecting Gloucester Street and Circular
Road. A few dozen kids, mostly toddlers, crowded the
playgrounds bordering this side of the park, near the colorful carts of street vendors selling anything from fried pas-
tries to dried meats and suya sticks, the local version of
kebab skewers with spicy chicken or beef—though as Savage had pointed out earlier, the meat could be of an alternative origin.

The curry and pepper aroma from the carts tingled her
nostrils as she walked past them, ignoring the vendors' hungry stares, especially at her blond hair.

Although out of her sight, Savage was nearby, assessing
the event, looking for any sign of deception, of treachery,
but so far she had not heard anything through the earpiece

connected to the small two-way radios he had purchased in one of the electronic bazaars near the shipping docks.

But just in case, Dana carried a can of pepper spray in the front right pocket of her blue jeans, plus she wore comfortable sneakers if the situation required her to sprint.

Her heart stammering her chest, her hands cold, she continued toward the rendezvous point—as Savage had called it— by the tree-shaded area just south of the Victoria Park Market, an array of stalls that opened in the evening hours selling mostly fake merchandise, from copy watches and DVDs to designer purses and clothing. There were also a number of con artists trying to sell shards of glass for diamonds to unsuspecting tourists and expatriates. But amid the cheap imitations you could also find local craft, from tribal masks and wood carvings to colorful clothes made primarily of cotton.

Dana tried to relax. Although Savage had taken the time to explain to her how to do this, she was still nervous.

"You're always stressed, even after your hundredth time. The trick is to keep it under control so it doesn't impair your thinking."

Dana remembered their conversation over lunch, when they had settled for some sort of grilled white fish and—

She stopped when spotting the unmistakable silhouette of her African friend, tall, skinny, left arm missing below the elbow as he waved with the other from the shade of a cotton tree, precisely where he had said he would be, on the side of a walkway projecting south from the market. At this early afternoon hour, the place was not as busy, mostly vendors setting up shop for the crowd that typically began arriving at sundown.

Ino, the African boy who had learned so much under her care during her three-year volunteer mission, smiled as he saw her.

"Miss Dana!" he said, fast-walking up to her and giving her a hug.

"Hello, Ino," she said, patting the teenager as he clung to her with his one good arm. "It's good to see you too."

When she gently pushed him away, she saw tears in his eyes.

"They—they told Ino that a car ran over Miss Dana in Freetown and she died a day later from complications."

"Who told you this, Ino?"

"The guards . . . Gardiol's guards. The news was all over the camp. Even the local television had a story, and the local paper showed Miss Dana's picture in the obituary."

Dana Kovacs sensed her anger boiling at the nerve of these bastards, trying to erase her from the face of the planet. And she was certainly a perfect candidate for that, without any relatives and living in Africa for the past three years.

"The truth is that they kidnapped me and took me to a rebel camp near Kono."

His dark stare widened. "Miss Dana was at the death camps?"

She nodded before taking a few minutes to explain how she had been kidnapped. "And they would have killed me had it not been for a friend who rescued me."

"A friend?"

She looked into the distance and said, "Yes, a mutual friend."

Ino frowned, his features hardening. "Ino does not understand."

"I'll explain later. Right now I need your help."

"What can Ino do for Miss Dana?"

"I need the current IT password to the WMF network."

"The password?"

"Yes. I need to jack into the system."

"But all IT passwords are active with the SecureID feature. And no one can take the tokens out of the camp. The scanners in the server room won't allow it."

Dana knew that was the case. She had insisted on the scanning system at the only entrance to the server room in the camp in order to protect the organization's files. SecureID meant that each legal user had a credit-size token that displayed a different six-digit, randomly generated number every thirty seconds. This random number, good only for those 30 seconds, had to be appended to the end of a fixed, personal alphanumeric user password. In order to gain access, not only was the entire password—both fixed and random components—required to be entered within the thirty-second window, but the random component was matched to the fixed component, meaning another user could not use the same token. And the SecureID tokens could not be removed from the computer room because the scanners at the entrance would detect them and trip an alarm, meaning Ino could not take his token with him and give it to Dana along with his fixed password to break in.

An impregnable system.

But any system could be defeated, particularly one that she had designed.

"Ino is afraid, Miss Dana. If the IT department learns that I helped you gain access, Gardiol will send Ino to the death camps."

"Do you trust me, Ino?"

After a slight hesitation, the African said, "Yes, Miss Dana."

"Then help me do the right thing, and I will make sure that no one can trace the firewall penetration to you."

"But the scanners won't allow the—"

"You will not have to remove the SecureID token from the control room."

"How will Miss Dana break in then?"

"I know a way, Ino, but you're going to have to follow my instructions to the letter. Would you do that for me?"

The young African rubbed his chin before saying, "Yes. Ino will do that for Miss Dana."

67

Trust

"It'll be fine, Mom. Trust me."

Trust me?

Kate Chavez did trust her son, but that wasn't going to change the butterflies tickling her stomach at the thought of returning to nauseating cyberspace by donning this contraption that Lman was trying to hand to her.

Some people were never meant to jack in, and Kate knew she was one of them, and the recent experience at the top of the Driskill with that fancy VR interface—much nicer than the one she currently held—only served to confirm her distaste about virtual reality.

"Sorry, honey, I don't particularly enjoy being hooked to a machine," she said, frowning while Lman and Cameron stared back with horrified stares, as if she had just spat on the meaning of life itself.

"Squirrel's right, Miss Chavez. There's nothing to be afraid of. My smart routines will protect us while we're jacked in," said Lman, scratching his stubble with his right hand while holding the VR interface with his left in front of Kate.

"Will they prevent me from puking all over your lab?"

Lman dropped his bushy eyebrows at her. "Come again?"

"I get nauseated whenever I put one of these things on."

Lman nodded thoughtfully and turned a couple of knobs on the side of the unit, before offering it to her again. "This time might be different."

"Why?" she asked.

"I've adjusted the frames-per-second to trick your inner ear into believing you're staring at the real world."

She shook her head. "In English, please?"

Lman sighed.

"Frames-per-second is a measure of how quickly the information presented to the user gets refreshed by the video driver in the interface. The less sophisticated units, like those used in video games, update the displayed video image at speeds of around five frames per second, which is good enough for most people, except for those with sensitive inner ears. This one can go up to eleven frames per second, the setting I have just given you to minimize the pain."

Sighing heavily, she took the unit and inspected it again, although she wasn't sure what she was looking at.

"Squirrel, jack in," said Lman, and Cameron complied, slipping on his hardware while sitting down.

"Your turn, Miss Chavez."

Kate gave the world around her one final glance, swallowed hard in anticipation of a rush of nausea, and also took her seat while donning the unit.

The world around her became flooded with soothing pastels, instantly pleasing her eyes. Mozart played in the background, adding to the relaxing nature of Lman's version of cyberspace.

A small, lime green figure rushed across her field of view, resembling some sort four-legged critter.

HEY, MOM.

The sound echoed around her, its origin difficult to place, but a moment later the peculiar shape, now a darker shade of green, almost jade, vibrated in front of her. On closer look, the tridimensional digitized image resembled a squirrel sporting a pair of silver wings.

I'll be damned.

Next to him a new shape materialized, a winged, white unicorn, who she guessed was Lman based on the posters in his bedroom.

SWEET SKIN, MOM.

What?

The unicorn lowered its head and a mirror materialized next to it, depicting Kate as one of those voluptuous fantasy heroines in Lman's posters, scantily dressed and clutching an oversized sword.

Oh, that's just swell.

But before she could complain, the squirrel and the unicorn winged skyward at great speed, and as if attached to them by an invisible lanyard, she followed along, amazed at the fluidity and lifelike rapidly changing scenery, including the grace with which Lman's cyber image dashed across the vast span of the computer matrix. The detail was incredible, down to the lifelike coat of swirling hair on the mythical creature.

WHERE ARE WE GOING?

FIRST THINGS FIRST, MISS CHAVEZ.

They approached the standing end of a broadband connection that resembled a cluster of vines, mostly green, twisting into the distance, connecting Lman's local network to the Internet.

Before she could ask a follow-up question, the vines drew them in with dazzling force, sucking them into a gleaming world that appeared to Kate as if she were rushing through the interior of an artery system.

Out of apparent control, losing any reference of up or down, Kate rocketed after her cyber companions through the connection at nauseating speed, only she did not feel any nausea.

That's a first.

The wickedly tight turns continued on this emerald roller coaster, plunging her through impossible direction changes as they traveled at blinding speed, before shooting off the other end of the green spaghetti and into a universe filled with galaxies of surreal colors. Dozens of them revolved amid millions of burning stars around a massive supernova, its surface alive with sheet lightning, its deep, rumbling thunder propagating across the massive expanse of cyberspace, the sound waves rippling a translucent membrane enclosing the entire universe.

THESE ARE TDG'S COMPANIES, explained Lman, his voice resonating from the direction of the hovering unicorn, whom the system presented in uncanny and beautiful detail, displaying the mythical creature in all the poetic splendor of the fantasy posters. The same could be said for Cameron, depicted as the unicorn's companion, landing on the beast's muscular torso. THE MEMBRANE IS THE SECURITY SCREEN. ANYONE TRYING TO ENTER IT WITHOUT THE APPROPRIATE PASSWORD WOULD BE INCINERATED ON THE SPOT.

SO WHAT DO WE DO NOW? she asked, feeling a little stupid talking to a big flying unicorn.

WE USE THE PASSWORD YOU HELPED ME STEAL.

While hovering a few feet—if there was such a thing as distance in this place—from the deceptively harmless surface of TDG's firewall, the unicorn opened its mouth and released three mauve clouds, two large ones and one much smaller.

One of the clouds propagated toward Kate, enveloping her. The other two covered Lman and Cameron.

WHAT'S THIS?

THE CLOUDS ARE LACED WITH THE ACCESS PASSWORD, MOM, Cameron said, swirling around her. THEY WILL PROTECT US AS WE SURF TDG'S NETWORK IN SEARCH OF THE WEAKEST LINK IN THE SYSTEM: THE WORLD MISSIONARY FELLOWSHIP.

Lman went first, wings flapping, though according to the laws of physics there wasn't supposed to be any air to displace in real space, so technically that action should not have resulted in forward motion.

But apparently everything goes in this place dominated by software algorithms.

The mythical creature crossed first, the surface of the mauve shield sizzling when touching the firewall, before turning into a glittering ball of static electricity, of crackling sparks until Lman made it to the other side, where the cloud returned to its smooth lavender tint.

Next followed the flying squirrel, its tail wagging as it went through the same sparkling ritual, reaching the interior of TDG's matrix.

Kate Chavez went last, pulled into it by the invisible lanyard connecting her to Lman, her mind feeling the energy of the firewall as the glimmering surrounded her, as the world momentarily became a blinding white sphere of pure energy, tickling her senses, prickling her skin.

And she was inside the network of this mysterious corporation.

WE'LL KEEP THE SHIELDS FOR PROTECTION UNTIL WE LEAVE, said Lman.

Kate stared at the churning galaxies, alive with color as they rotated along imaginary axes while also following oval orbits around a crimson sun.

WHICH ONE OF THEM IS GEMTECH?

IT'S ON THE OTHER SIDE OF THE UNIVERSE, BUT THAT'S NOT WHERE WE ARE HEADED FIRST.

OH, WHERE ARE WE—

And off they went, cutting her off in mid-sentence, dragging her with impossible strength across this immense cosmos of surreal and amorphous galaxies, all spinning along their own axes while also changing shapes.

Skirting them while traveling at what certainly qualified as warp speed, violating the principles of gravity and motion, the trio dashed past hundreds of solar systems, dodging moons and meteors, once even riding the tail of a comet, which Lman explained represented large packets of data shared among the companies forming The Donovan Group.

At the far end of this universe, a small galaxy swirled in space, its dozen solar systems moving about within the confines of the colorful nebula, some with only a handful of planets and circling moons, others with many whirling worlds and asteroid rings.

EACH SOLAR SYSTEM IS A LAN WITHIN THE GALAXY REPRESENTING THE WORLD MISSIONARY FELLOWSHIP. THE MOST PRIMITIVE NETWORK RESIDES IN FREETOWN, SIERRA LEONE. IT'S STILL USING SP27.

HOW DO YOU KNOW THAT?

Before Lman could answer, Cameron swung in between and released a window sporting a list of networks and their timestamps reflecting their most recent software pack upgrades from corporate headquarters. The WMF's Local Area Network in Freetown, the capital of Sierra Leone, had the most recent date, meaning it always got upgraded last, just as the master hacker had indicated, and it was still operating with an out-of-date virus-protection shield.

NOW WHAT?

NOW WE BECOME ILLEGAL, MISS CHAVEZ. THAT'S THE
ONLY WAY TO GAIN ACCESS TO THE CORE OF THE NETWORK.

I THOUGHT WE DID THAT ALREADY.

NO. WE HAVE THE SAME PRIVILEGE AS A SYSTEM ADMINIS-
TRATOR OF GEMTECH, AND THAT HAS ALLOWED US TO
BROWSE THROUGH THE REST OF TDG'S COMPANIES. BUT
WHAT WE NEED IS BEYOND THE ACCESS OF YOUR RUN-OF-
THE-MILL INFORMATION TECHNOLOGY GUY. WE NEED AC-
CESS TO THE SUPERNOVA IN THE MIDDLE OF THE UNIVERSE,
THE CENTRAL NETWORK RUNNING IT ALL. THAT'S WHERE
I'M GUESSING THE ANSWERS YOU SEEK WILL BE.

HOW ARE WE GOING TO GET IN THERE?

Lman released a second cloud, this one light green and in-
terlaced with streaks of neon blue. The cloud divided itself
into three shapes, each one enveloping a cyber traveler.

As Kate watched her world transition from purple to
green, the entire universe came to a halt, as if forced into a
state of suspended animation. The galaxies defining TDG's
many companies pulsated with their dazzling color, but no
longer moved.

EVERYTHING HAS STOPPED, said Kate, confused.

THAT'S THE IDEA, replied the master hacker. I HAVE RE-
LEASED A PARALYZING POTION INTO THE NETWORK THROUGH
THE HOLE CREATED BY THE KNOWN VULNERABILITIES OF
SP27 IN THE WMF NETWORK.

YES, BUT WHY IS EVERY NETWORK PARALYZED? THE REST
ARE ALL UP TO SP28.

SP27 IN WMF ALLOWED US TO GET BEHIND THEIR DE-
FENSES. IMAGINE A FORTRESS WITH SOLID WOODEN ACCESS
GATES, EACH REPRESENTING A POSSIBLE ENTRY POINT INTO
THE CASTLE, BUT SP28 KEEPS THEM SHUT. NOT ONLY THAT,
THERE IS A 24-7 ARMY BEHIND EACH GATE JUST IN CASE. SP27
IS LIKE A FORGOTTEN ENTRY POINT, MAYBE THOUGH AN UN-
DERGROUND PASSAGE OR MOAT. THE POINT IS THAT IT IS
OPEN AND UNGUARDED. ONCE YOU GET IN, IT DOESN'T MAT-
TER THAT THE OTHER DOORS ARE CLOSED. YOU'RE INSIDE,
AND YOU CATCH THEIR DEFENSES BY SURPRISE. YOU CATCH
THEM LOOKING IN THE WRONG DIRECTION AND STRIKE. THAT

IS REPRESENTED BY THE FROZEN NETWORKS . . . I CAUGHT THEM BY SURPRISE AND PARALYZED THEM WITH A COMPUTER WORM, THOUGH THE BEAUTY IS THAT THEY DON'T KNOW THEY HAVE BEEN BREACHED.

NO?

THE WORM ESSENTIALLY RENDERS US INVISIBLE TO THEM, SORT OF LIKE PLACING US IN A PARALLEL UNIVERSE. WE CAN SEE WHAT THEY ARE DOING, BUT THEY CAN'T SEE US. AS FAR AS THE NETWORK IS CONCERNED, ALL IS WELL. USERS AND PROGRAMS ARE PROCEEDING NORMALLY, BUT IN REALITY THEY'RE NO LONGER OPERATING WITH PRIVACY. THERE ARE GHOSTS IN THEIR MIDST, THAT'S US, CAPABLE OF GOING ANYWHERE WE WISH, WITH ONE EXCEPTION.

WHAT'S THAT? asked Kate.

And that's when Kate saw Cameron's cyber figure rush in the direction of the supernova followed by Lman's unicorn, and then her, once more towed around this alien place.

They headed at great speed toward the massive sun still thriving in the center of the universe, apparently unaffected by the master hacker's spell.

WHY ISN'T THE CENTER ALSO PARALYZED?

AN INTERNAL FIREWALL, the hacker's booming voice echoed around her as they rushed across planets, moons, and tons of stars, their light now static, like something from a cold source, not fluid and alive as it had been moments ago—like the warmth radiating from the approaching supernova. IN ADDITION TO MAKING OURSELVES INVISIBLE, SP27 ALLOWED ME TO ACCOMPLISH TWO MORE THINGS. THE FIRST WAS TO ISOLATE THE PORTION OF THE NETWORK THAT IS TYPICALLY PROTECTED BY AN INNER SECURITY RING, A FORTRESS WITHIN THE FORTRESS, TYPICALLY NOT ACCESSIBLE BY THE STANDARD USERS.

AND THE SECOND?

PROVIDE ME WITH A WAY TO GET INSIDE THIS INNER SANCTUARY.

68

"Everything appears normal," offered George Zhu, looking over Daniel Chang's shoulder as the young programmer browsed through screen after screen of system security data.

Most of his team also scrubbing the network, looking for abnormalities in the natural flow of information, Daniel said, "The amber alert disappeared almost as soon as it showed up. But it was there for long enough to let me know something had changed, deep within the fabric of the TDG matrix."

"But shouldn't it be obvious if someone has broken in?"

Daniel shook his head. "I wish it were that easy. There's a hundred different types of cloaking programs designed to protect hackers after they break into a system."

"What about ANN? Isn't it smart enough to find this rascal?"

Daniel smiled internally at the way Zhu pronounced that last word.

"The AI is also searching, but remember that it is only as smart as the routines that feed into it, including its believed source of ideas: me. And that means that if I don't know, then PARTITION-37 doesn't know, meaning ANN doesn't know."

"How do *I* know this little bastard isn't figuring out what we have accomplished?"

"You don't. Then again, it may be nothing more than a simple act of piracy that the system's natural defenses have already repelled, which could explain why we haven't seen any evidence of anyone roaming inside the network. Remember that I installed the amber alert to signal if anything abnormal was detected in the lattice of the matrix. Sometimes even a surge in electrical power at one site could induce noise in the system that the security software could misinterpret as an attack."

"How long before we know either way?"

"We're monitoring all of our data and it is intact, meaning no one has read it or tried to overwrite it."

"What does that mean?"

"It means we're whole, without corruption. My guess is that if something's going to happen, it will happen in the next couple of hours."

After a pause, George Zhu said, "Is there anything else that you need? Anything?"

Daniel raised a brow at the sound of desperation in Zhu's voice, signaling that Beijing was really riding him to make sure this operation continued without any glitches.

After considering his boss's question for a few moments, Daniel replied, "I need a mistake."

"What do you mean?"

Keeping his eyes on the streams of data browsing across seven different windows on his large flat screen monitor, Daniel said, "A mistake, sir. I need for the hacker—if that's indeed what we're dealing with—to make a mistake."

69

'Trodes

"Do you know what you're doing?" asked Savage, sitting behind the wheel of the weathered Nissan Pathfinder SUV, which he had acquired from a third-string rental agency south of the airport for one thousand in cash plus his IWC watch—worth five times as much as the vehicle—as a deposit of good faith.

He had parked it in front of a Starbuck's in the small but modern retail section of town erected to complement the luxurious resorts on the south end of Lumley Beach, by the Freetown Golf Course, about two miles from Aberdeen Village, where they had nearly been killed the day before.

A notebook computer with a PCMCIA wireless card on her lap, a cable connecting the system to the cigarette lighter for power, and a USB connector interfacing it to the VR goggles—which she called 'trodes, short for electrodes—hanging from her neck, Dana Kovacs gave him an assuring smile. "Cyberspace is my turf, Mac. I'll be right back."

"And I'll be right here," he replied.

"By the way," she said, "what I'm going to do will not allow me to jot down or save any data, but I can read and dictate, so be ready to write."

"Got it," Savage replied, producing a pad and a pencil. "Just fire away when you're ready."

She donned the goggles, which had both noise- and voice-cancellation headphones designed to maximize the virtual-reality experience by fully blocking the outside world.

Powering them on, Dana waited for the unit to boot, before the matrix resolved, and she found herself floating amid the tens of thousands of blazing stars and hundreds of planets forming the wireless ISP of the Starbuck's, where she had purchased a thirty-day account to browse the Web using their wireless Internet access.

Entering an HTTP address she had long committed to memory, the former entrepreneur watched the spaghetti-like broadband connection materializing out of thin digital air, sucking her into a whirling, tridimensional channel, jolting her through a series of wicked turns, before depositing her in another galaxy. Here, amid solar systems bustling with color, she spotted the familiar blue-green firewall protecting the computer network of the local chapter of the World Missionary Fellowship, depicted as a small galaxy within a vast universe.

Just to the right of this massive security shield resembling a pulsating sun, she saw the shape of a human user, depicted as a mauve silhouette with a gold outline of varying intensity.

Slowly, a bright, yellow glow radiated from the cyber figure, expanding toward the effervescent, surface, resolving into a conical shape as the beam came in contact with it, creating a bluish circle on the boiling energy shield.

Dana approached the figure of Ino, which, like all human users operating in the network she had developed for WMF, sported a mauve skin, easily recognized from the neonlike magenta gleam of the expert systems, the artificial intelligence engines performing varying functions at the vast WMF camp, from security to supply management to monitoring of vital signs of hospitalized refugees.

It was all networked, and all controlled by the powerful servers in the well-guarded IT room.

Dana Kovacs floated just outside this galaxy she had created for the World Missionary Fellowship during her two years of volunteer work. She had done it to improve the efficiency of their charitable and noble cause, to save more children, to do more with the same resources by using artificial intelligence to observe their methods and procedures and improve them, to train their staff, their nurses—even their security.

The blue circle acted as a form of digital acid, melting through the firewall, creating a gap wide enough for Dana to dive through, at the same time lacing her with the mauve film of a legal user—all thanks to the root password that Ino had used while logged in inside the server room, like the tenant of a building opening a window for an outsider, inviting her in without the landlord's knowledge.

Dana dashed across the solar systems within the WMF galaxy, each representing one of dozens of branches of the global nonprofit organization reaching the far corners of the Earth. Everywhere there was need, WMF would send help in the form of volunteers, missionaries, doctors and nurses, plus the supporting infrastructure required to run an effective refugee camp—one where the refugees themselves would be protected. That also meant security. It meant fences, weapons, trained personnel.

Of course, all of that cost money. For the longest time,

Dana had wondered where the funds originated. She had been told it all came from their worldwide base of contributors, from generous individuals to corporations seeking tax shelters. But after her close encounter with Gardiol it was brutally evident that WMF had another source of income: blood diamonds. WMF was just a brilliantly engineered front for the trafficking of illegally mined diamonds.

As Ino's mauve figure vanished, meaning he had logged out for his protection, Dana ran once through the network, inspecting the planets representing each branch of the WMF worldwide network, before heading for the one she had helped design for Gardiol in Freetown, a crimson and emerald green world in the far left end of this digital Milky Way.

She orbited the familiar planet of the network she had designed for WMF-Freetown. She stared at its data-rich fields, red for high security and green for public access, searching for the cluster of servers near the north pole, where she had embedded a series of custom programs originally designed to protect Diamantex's network, which she later used to assist her during the development and full implementation phases of the local area network; programs that she now planned to use to fulfill a different task.

But something didn't look right, though she couldn't put her finger on it. She looked closer, and that's when she noticed that standard mauve-colored users roaming WMF's network as well as that of its parent company had lost some of their lavender sheen.

Weird.

First things first.

Invoking an expert system called LOG-ERASE, Dana launched the wormlike routine into the matrix, finding every instance of Ino's log records and deleting them from the data files, eliminating her former pupil as a suspect should the system administrators detect her intrusion.

And now for the real fun.

She launched a second program, SECURE BYPASS, which she had designed to force the built-in security system to look the other way when she violated any system protocol while she ran tests during the development and implementation phases.

The security AIs continued to patrol the network just as she had designed them last year. But SECURE BYPASS offered an additional benefit to Dana Kovacs beyond shielding her from the active security system while she poked around the network: It made her invisible to all users, meaning another user would never know she was hovering in their midst. And that meant that since she was invisible to all users, and since the network police would not flag her activities—legal or illegal—Dana could come and go as she pleased and her cyber actions would go unnoticed.

Next she launched FIND USER, an AI designed to accomplish just what the name implied: locating a specific user in the network, but doing it without alerting anyone else currently logged in.

The program prompted her for a user ID, to which she entered KGARDIOL.

And off she went, dragged by FIND USER, an algorithm resembling a glossy silver orb the size of a basketball, if that meant anything in this unreal world of digitized color.

The sphere dashed across the surface of the planet at dizzying speed, towing Dana, dragging her over an animated, yellowish meadow of energy housing the network's memory banks, stopping near the middle of this vast array of stored information, by a vault-like black object protruding above the surrounding landscape.

WMF's European bank accounts.

As the orb descended over this spot, it became translucent, invisible to everyone except Dana, who could still see its fine outline hovering next to the high-security container designed to house confidential financial information. A figure stood next to the black box.

Dana dropped closer to the user that FIND USER claimed to be Keith Gardiol—or at least someone using Gardiol's user account.

But the skin color is wrong on Gardiol.

Coming within inches of this stationary user, a green local

data channel active between the middle of his chest and the core of the black box, Dana Kovacs realized that Gardiol's digital skin was part magenta and part mauve, meaning it was neither pure human nor pure machine, but something in between.

What in the hell does that mean?

70

Hacker Games

WHAT'S GOING ON? Kate Chavez asked.

But just as they had done before, the winged unicorn and its furry sidekick ignored her as they shot back toward the WMF-Freetown network, where they followed the trail of a mauve user who had been granted access into the local firewall by someone working from the inside.

ANOTHER HACKER, observed Cameron while doing circles around the head of the unicorn.

LOOKS THAT WAY, SQUIRREL, Lman observed. THAT'S PART OF THE PROBLEMISITUDE OF PROTECTING A NETWORK. A SYSTEM ADMIN DUDE HAS GRANTIFIED SOMEONE ACCESS, AND THIS SOMEONE IS NOW ROAMING THE LAN FOLLOWING A MOST PECULIAR USER.

WHAT DO YOU MEAN BY PECULIAR? asked Kate.

IT HAS BOTH THE SIGNATURE OF A HUMAN AND A MACHINE — AND IT WAS NOT AFFECTED BY THE WORM.

LIKE SALIERI? A HUMAN WITH IMPLANTS?

SOMETHING LIKE THAT, MISS CHAVEZ, THOUGH ITS SIGNATURE LOOKS MORE COMPUTER THAN HUMAN, SUGGESTING A HUMAN UNDER COMPUTER CONTROL INSTEAD OF THE OTHER WAY AROUND. AND THAT ALSO MAKES ME WONDER ABOUT

THE SKIN COLOR OF THE REST OF THE USERS IN THIS NET-
WORK. IT DOESN'T LOOK THE WAY IT SHOULD.

WHAT ARE THE ILLEGAL USER AND THE HYBRID ONE GO-
ING TO DO? asked Kate.

I'M NOT SURE BUT I INTEND TO FIND OUT BEFORE HEAD-
ING BACK TO THE SUPERNOVA.

71

Virulent Strike

"I see you," said Daniel Chang under his breath as he typed
a series of commands to filter the background noise from the
mounds of security data rushing past many windows, some
of which he used to exchange thoughts and theories with his
team, the twenty-some programmers who had spent the past
few hours glued to their systems in the hope that the intruder
would make another mistake like the one he had so briefly
made that had resulted in the short-lived amber alert.

Feeling a rush of adrenaline washing away his boredom,
the Chinese hacker directed ANN toward the WMF network,
where he had programmed the agents controlling Keith Gardiol to get the WMF chief to use the computer in his compound to transfer WMF funds from various banks in the
Caribbean and Europe into accounts in Beijing, Shanghai,
and Suzhou.

That was when one of the sensors installed in the SpyWare
of the WMF boss, whose level of computer control was far
more powerful than the rest of the assimilated users roaming
the network, had picked up a drop in operational voltage inside this sector of the matrix, signaling that there was another
user nearby—only there wasn't supposed to be one legally.

That was the break that Daniel had been waiting for, the mistake that he had mentioned to George Zhu shortly before his superior left the building to go to the Shanghai airport and pick up visiting dignitaries from Beijing accompanying his father to tour the facility.

Zhu had planned an entire day of activities to show off his accomplishments, including a ceremony later in the day when Daniel would be awarded his Ferrari courtesy of a grateful government.

But at the moment he had work to do.

Most people—George Zhu included—just didn't get what it took to hack, much less what it took to *catch* a hacker. In fact, everyone in the control room had no clue, since they were all professionally trained IT personnel.

Hacking meant taking risks, an alternative noncxistent in the list of approved options available to him to deal with the intrusion, as they all essentially commanded ANN to handle the intrusion with its run-of-the-mill routines, which would eradicate the illegal user, logging him or her off.

But the hacker in Daniel Chang wasn't satisfied.

I want to cause pain, he thought, deciding to kick up the defenses a notch by activating an unqualified routine and asking for forgiveness later. ANN had a number of programs that had not yet been tested in actual situations, but which under simulated attacks had performed flawlessly, not only defending the system but also biting back, designed to teach any intruder a powerful lesson about violating TDG's matrix.

And this early morning in Shanghai, as the Pearl of the Orient slowly came to life, as an orange sun slowly materialized above the hazy horizon, Daniel Chang unilaterally decided the time had come to stretch the legs of ANN's powerful defense system and nip such intrusions in the bud.

He released the commands into a secret link feeding the logic of the late Anne Donovan, directing the master construct to unleash the worst kind of hell onto this unsuspecting hacker roaming the WMF-Freetown network.

Daniel Chang used his root-privilege to waive the qualification warning flashing at the top of his screen, advising him not to deploy the most virulent and powerful cyber attack, a program called BLOODHOUND. The algorithm was not only extremely toxic to the hacker but also to the TDG network due to the amount of energy required to operate it, sort of like pushing a nuclear reaction to maximum capacity at the risk of overheating the core and triggering a containment breach.

But he found the risk involved invigorating, the more so because he was doing it hacker-style, without permission. Daniel, however, felt he was doing the right thing. Hackers operated outside the law, breaking the rules, and in order to catch them system administrators had also to break the rules, had to deviate from the book, had to do the unexpected.

That reminded Daniel Chang of the old saying at Stanford: It takes a hacker to catch a hacker.

72

Out of Order Execution

ANN's sensors indicated the presence of an intruder in the core of the WMF-Freetown network, but as she prepared to followed programmed procedure for dealing with such an intrusion, PARTITION-37, the logic banks housing Anne Donovan's thought patterns, overrode the process and injected a new routine, BLOODHOUND.

BLOODHOUND IS NOT ONLY UNPROVEN BUT VERY DANGEROUS.

Dangerous, in ANN's software fabric, meant a routine so advanced and energy-draining that it required the need for something called out-of-order execution, a fancy name for an open-loop mode of operation. By launching BLOODHOUND,

ANN would be essentially vulnerable to an attack because the routine required that ANN divert massive amounts of energy into the software limb so it could cruise across the Internet and surgically strike the intruder with laserlike accuracy. The price of such powerful and precise attack was this out-of-order execution, which would not provide immediate feedback to the master construct if a problem surfaced, like some sort of extreme counterattack. The analogy would be a street fighter who, in the course of a brutal knife fight, is severely cut in the arm, only the adrenaline searing his system blocked the pain broadcast by the nerves in the wounded arm, failing to provide the fighter the feedback that he was bleeding until seconds later, when he saw blood splashing about him. In the case of ANN, the adrenaline was the extreme energy that it took to effectively deploy BLOOD-HOUND, and that energy, while delivering a powerful blow to the intruder, acted like a blocking agent should something go wrong until other sensors in the network picked up a problem indirectly—like the fighter seeing the blood. And for ANN, spilled blood equaled a loss in data that might take some time to clamp.

EXTREME SITUATIONS CALL FOR EXTREME MEASURES, came the reply from PARTITION-37 within the bowels of SERVER-22, insisting on the dangerous directive.

REQUEST FINAL CONFIRMATION, asked ANN, once more trying to verify the order.

LAUNCH BLOODHOUND NOW, was the reply from the logic in PARTITION-37.

Sensing the danger of such a directive, but unfortunately no longer having the direction of The Circle, the master construct chose to follow the advice of the legacy of her creator, the late Anne Donovan, and she began to draw energy from many of its sources, including the multiple feeds inside its inner sanctuary, focusing it all on the activation of one of the most deadly and brilliant security codes ever created.

73

Old Friends

Dr. Miles Talbot leaned back in his chair while watching ANN prepare the virulent digital antibody for immediate release against an alleged hacker roaming the WMF network in Sierra Leone. Under normal circumstances, he would have questioned the master construct, and he would also have informed Salieri of the violation of protocol regarding the use of unapproved code. The situation, however, was anything but normal, with Salieri no longer in control of his body and Talbot presumably already assimilated by the machine. All he could do was observe, which he did, watching the hacker.

Who are you? What are you looking for? he wondered, watching the illegal user from the comfort of his office, wearing a VR interface that showed him hovering amid the planets of this distant galaxy cloaked by his super user password privileges.

Releasing a digital probe, Talbot obtained a sample of the hacker's digital DNA, his search engines automatically comparing it against billions of computer programs, looking for a match. He did this while following the hacker across the WMF network, recognizing an instant later that the makeup of the illegal user's computer code included three very familiar programs: LOG-ERASE, SECURE BYPASS, and FIND USER.

Impossible, he thought, recognizing Dana Kovacs' algorithms from their Diamantex days.

Could it be that she is still alive?

Or is someone else using her programs?

Optioning not to make direct contact with the hacker but to continue to observe, Dr. Miles Talbot trailed the illegal user at a respectful distance, well aware that any moment now ANN would release BLOODHOUND, a program so new and so powerful that Talbot wondered what adverse effects it would cause in the lattice of the TDG matrix.

74

Mental Squeeze

From a distance Dana Kovacs decided that user's color was more mauve than magenta, denominating a human, but once Dana got very close—probably closer than any user would be able to under normal operating conditions—the color leaned more toward magenta, but lacking the luster of the networked AIs.

A hybrid?

And it was at that moment that it hit her: Gardiol had indeed seemed somewhat superhuman during the few instances when she had met him, first at WMF in Freetown and later as his prisoner in that RUF camp. He had possessed amazing intuition and was capable of juggling many tasks at once, with an impressive technical knowledge in many fields, including diamond nanotechnology—and he spoke multiple languages with incredible ease.

Dana knew about the latest generation of nano implants, but those devices were still supposed to be R&D stuff, and even if someone was fitted with them, would their digital signature be affected? Would the implants be pervasive enough for the network to recognize their presence in a human user and assign that user a hybrid qualifier?

And on top of that, she clearly remembered Gardiol and

other high-ranking members of the WMF-Freetown staff roaming the network before she was kidnapped. All of them had sported mauve skins.

Something fundamental has changed.

Something else that didn't pass her smell test was the task being performed by this hybrid user who claimed to be Keith Gardiol: transferring funds from WMF numbered accounts in Switzerland, London, and Paris to accounts in Hong Kong, Shanghai, Suzhou, and Beijing.

Is that the end of the money trail of the conflict diamonds? The People's Republic of China?

"Mac?" she said, "Tap me on the leg if you can hear me."

A moment later she felt his hand patting her thigh.

"Jot down the following," she said, before reading to him sequences of the numbered accounts in Europe and in China that—

The figure stopped in the middle of a transaction, retrieving the green probe, which retracted into its magenta chest, before flying away at great speed.

FIND USER scrambled after him, jolting Dana behind it as they left the data fields of this planet and rocketed toward the digitized heavens, following the hybrid user as it climbed and descended, as it orbited earths and moons, before suddenly melting in midair, like a blinding sun, coming apart at its digital seams in a burst of billions of pixels comprising its tridimensional image, slowly blending with the cyber backdrop.

What in the hell just happened?

And just like that Dana Kovacs found herself floating in the middle of this network with no sign of where Keith Gardiol had gone. When a human user logged off, the VR-interface showed the digital version becoming near incandescent before becoming translucent and finally disappearing. When an AI logged off, the synthetic user, at its core no different than its surrounding software environment, simply blended with it as the routines the AI was executing ceased to operate. But Gardiol's digital image had done some of both, lending more credibility to Dana's theory that the man wasn't all human or all machine.

Weird, she thought, deciding to analyze later. Right now she needed to extract as much information from the system as she could. And to that end she invoked another program, EXECUTIVE CALENDAR.

She launched the routine, which resembled a giant flat-screen television displaying the directory housing the travel schedule of the top executives of the World Missionary Fellowship, including that belonging to Keith Gardiol.

Because of her root-password privilege, combined with another one of her backdoor routines, she was able to open the schedule of WMF's head honcho in this part of the world.

"Mac, are you ready to write again?"

Upon receiving the tap from Savage, Dana read out Gardiol's schedule for today, tomorrow, and the day after.

When finished, she returned to the amber fields of data, looking for clues, for leads, for anything that would help explain the unexpected turn her life had taken less than a week ago.

What about the company's logs, its history?

Launching a routing that resembled a cyber historian, Dana watched the program materialize itself in a screen above this sea of golden brown information, before shafts of bluish light shot from the bottom of the screen, piercing the data field, starting the probing process.

An instant later the flow of information filled the screen, taking her back to the beginning of the World Missionary Fellowship, to its founder, Anne Donovan, also founder of WMF's parent company, The Donovan Group, a multinational conglomerate. Dana stared at several photos and videos of the frail founder breaking ground on the refugee camp alongside Gardiol and the president of Sierra Leone several years ago. Other digitized frames depicted Donovan opening other such camps in regions of South America and Asia.

Dana frowned, hoping to find something she didn't already know.

Using the Web-browsing abilities of her search software, she pulled up TDG's financials, which displayed all of the corporation's holding companies, including GemTech and the Fellowship.

Dana continued to review the data flashing in this screen floating in the middle of the memory banks of the server clusters, learning of the strangely diversified companies owned by TDG, from a British food manufacturer to a Brazilian land developer to a Chinese software company. There seem to be no trend to the acquisitions, no rhyme or reason explaining the purchases of a Swiss communication company or a Belgian diamond trader—though the latter did made some sense to her given what she had learned the hard way.

She continued to browse through the eclectic list, finding no clear pattern, no obvious strategy. Most corporations tried to focus on one or maybe a handful of key areas, building core competence, IP, to own specific markets. But TDG seemed to be everywhere, in banking, in retail, in agriculture, in high tech, in retail, in land management, in telecommunications and transportation. They owned three shipping lines, two major airlines, three railways, and even six pharmaceutical companies, half in Europe and the rest in the United States.

Dana Kovacs stopped the browser while staring at one of the American companies: GemTech.

She forced herself to think through the sequence of events that had brought her here. The diamond she had come across, combined with the recognition of her test circuit, her IP, stolen by Frank Salieri three years ago, had been the reason Keith Gardiol had wanted her dead. The near-cosmic coincidence threatened to expose WMF, the façade of a nonprofit organization praised by the entire world for its humanitarian work, for providing hope in a land where hope had been crushed long ago by the unyielding boots of the ice wars. But beneath the surface, WMF was little more than a dealer in conflict diamonds, acquiring them from the death mines of western Sierra Leone, and shipping them off presumably to the United States to satisfy a need that Dana still could not see. Diamond nanotechnology was not commercially feasible yet. The quality of the diamonds required for successful and reliable nano-etching were not only too expensive but hard to find, their worldwide supply too scarce to make it an effective business in the face of much cheaper silicon-based machines. Although the power of diamonds far outweighed that of silicon in speed, memory capacity, and extreme temperature and radiation tolerance, not having a steady supply meant the technology could never grow beyond special industrial or military applications, which had been the focus of ill-fated Diamantex.

And not much has changed on the supply side in the past three years, she thought, still uncertain how GemTech was using their supply of illegal gems.

But irrespective of the shadowy operations of the likes of the inhuman Keith Gardiol and the unscrupulous Frank Salieri, Dana had stumbled into the middle of it all when that African boy handed the diamond and she had then decided to come clean with WMF.

Stupid, stupid, stupid.

Had she kept her mouth shut, she would have already been home in northern California instead of being stuck in this damned—

DANA, IF THAT'S YOU, GET THE HELL AWAY FROM HERE.

Perplexed at an invisible user suddenly making contact and calling her by name, Dana transmitted, INO. IS THAT YOU?

NO, IT'S MILES TALBOT.

DR. TALBOT? I THOUGHT THAT YOU WERE—

YOU MUST LOG OUT NOW, DANA! NOW!

Dana felt a presence behind her. As she turned around she watched a massive gray cloud alive with sheet lightning rushing toward her. She tried to scramble in the opposite direction, but a blinding light overtook her, its energy suffocating, reaching her core, squeezing her mind.

75

Impotent

Dr. Miles Talbot watched as the purplish figure of the illegal user he now knew was his old Diamantex colleague became engulfed by the laserlike death ray of BLOODHOUND, disappearing from sight inside the beam.

His super-user privilege coating him with a skin that reflected the exact opposite binary code from the virus, meaning BLOODHOUND melted away the instant it touched Talbot's surface, the former professor of computer engineering threw himself around the trapped figure of Dana Kovacs.

LISTEN TO ME, DANA, he transmitted while shielding her as much as he could, reflecting the brunt of the lobotomizing impact. I'M BEING HELD PRISONER AT GEMTECH'S HEADQUARTERS IN AUSTIN, TEXAS. SALIERI RUNS THE SHOW HERE.

MY HEAD, Dana replied, though she did it not by speaking because the beam had paralyzed her speech, but by invoking a visual keyboard in cyberspace and typing on it by blinking. The VR interface detected her eye movement and translated it into the words that were broadcast to Dr. Talbot. THE PRESSURE. I CAN'T STAND IT.

DANA, I KNOW YOU'RE IN PAIN, BUT YOU MUST FOCUS. TDG WAS BEING CONTROLLED BY TEN SUPER USERS. KEITH GARDIOL AND FRANK SALIERI ARE TWO OF THEM. BUT THEIR MINDS, AS WELL AS EVERYONE ELSE'S, HAVE BEEN ASSIMILATED BY THE MASSIVE AI RUNNING THIS PLACE. DO YOU UNDERSTAND WHAT I'VE JUST TOLD YOU?

YE — YES.

GOOD. NOW, FIND A WAY TO GET LAW ENFORCEMENT TO GEMTECH IN AUSTIN. I WILL TRY TO HELP YOU FROM THE INSIDE FOR AS LONG AS I CAN. NOW I NEED TO TERMINATE THIS CONNECTION TO AVOID RAISING SUSPICIONS. LOG OUT, DANA. I WON'T BE ABLE TO SHIELD YOU MUCH LONGER.

I CAN'T. I CAN'T MOVE MY ARMS! I'M PARALYZED!

As Talbot continued to protect her, he also ran a tracer up the pipe of light, identifying not just its origin but the reason for its deployment. BLOODHOUND was not a program ready for primetime use, yet someone or something had directed ANN to deploy it. And he now saw the link, an interface coated with a strange root password that armed it with reflective algorithms, making it invisible to ANN.

But not to me.

The link was connected to the middle of SERVER-22, commanding the master construct while pretending to be part of the influential algorithms created to mimic the thought patterns of the late Anne Donovan.

Someone is controlling the machine while making it believe that the direction is coming from disk PARTITION-37 within SERVER-22.

Damn.

Who is doing it?

Talbot deployed a follow-up query, but the probe timed out before it could narrow down the origin, providing him with only a general region: Asia.

Asia? Strange, he thought, setting up secondary probes across a dozen cities in Asia, from Singapore and Tokyo, to Seoul, Beijing, and Hong Kong in an effort to isolate the origin on his next opportunity, which he felt would come the moment BLOODHOUND finished its execution.

76

Master of Its Universe

ARE YOU GOING TO HELP THE HACKER? Kate Chavez asked when watching the beam of light, which had originated all the way from the supernova on the other side of the universe, strike the illegal user that had provided Kate with so much information about The Donovan Group.

The lone hacker trembled, struggled to break free as the blinding light stressed its ingenious defense, threatening to break through in spite of the complementary shield that had materialized around the hacker nanoseconds after the attack.

Writhing, violently shaking to crack the intrusive clamp, the hacker thrashed inside the energy cocoon like a moth fighting to escape the death grip of a spider's web.

THAT'S THE RISK OF HACKING. SOMETIMES YOU WIN AND SOMETIMES YOU LOSE. UNFORTUNATELY, THAT ILLEGAL USER DIDN'T HAVE MUCH OF A CHANCE.

WHAT DO YOU MEAN?

MOM, interrupted Cameron, floating about her. THAT USER'S GOOD BUT IS NO HACKER.

SQUIRREL'S RIGHT, MISS CHAVEZ. THE ILLEGAL USER CREATED PRETTY COOL SURFING PROGRAMS AND OFF-THE-SHELF SECURITY BLANKETS, BUT THERE WAS NO CREATIVITY IN THE WORK, WHICH IS WHY THE SUPERNOVA IS NAILING IT.

WHAT'S GOING TO HAPPEN TO THE USER?

DEPENDS ON HOW QUICKLY THE USER REMOVES HIS OR HER VR HELMET. COULD BE ANYTHING FROM A HEADACHE TO A LOBOTOMY.

HELP HIM!

HOW DO YOU KNOW THE USER IS A HE?

DAMMIT, LMAN! WE LEARNED A LOT FROM HIM. HELP HIM!

WHAT DO YOU THINK, SQUIRREL?

THE HACKER HAS EARNED THE WORTHITUDE OF OUR HELP. WE DID LEARN A LOT FROM THE POOR BASTARD.

ALL RIGHT.

As more electrons fed the encircling sphere of raw energy squeezing the lone hacker, Lman released a gray rotating ionic disc, but not at the energy sphere itself.

The high-voltage disc moved toward the supernova along the twisted beam, slicing it off a good distance from them, thus preventing the AI from learning the precise location of the counterattack that had severed the source of energy from the enveloped user.

A sonic boom echoed across the vast expanse of this universe, along with a high-pitch shriek that sent goose bumps down Kate's spine.

In the distance, she saw the detached software limb jerking in space, reminding her of a loose fire hose, spewing a rainbow of colors into the matrix along with more digitized screams.

SOUNDS LIKE WE JUST PISSED SOMEBODY OFF, said Kate.

NO SHIT, MOM.

CAMERON!

SORRY.

A moment later, as the severed end of the beam rapidly lost its shine, its luster, the lone hacker was freed from the digital vise of the supernova's energy.

77

Shanghai Connection

How in the hell did that happen? Talbot thought as the matrix became alive with the echoing shrills of the master construct when its tentacle of light was severed.

Who attacked BLOODHOUND?

Relieved that either a second hacker had terminated the connection or perhaps a defect in the fabric of BLOODHOUND had surfaced, Talbot urged Dana once more to log out now that the energy source feeding the beam had vanished.

He then focused his attention on the mysterious PARTITION-37 within SERVER-22, the partition sporting a direct link to Asia. Talbot activated secondary tracers across Asia, and a moment later one of his high-speed worms planted in Beijing followed the link south, to its source.

Shanghai.

The worm added a degree of accuracy to the search an instant later: TDG-China.

Talbot frowned, understanding the China connection, the transfer of funds that Dana had uncovered during her trip across the matrix before ANN deployed BLOODHOUND.

The thought then struck him hard: he knew that ANN was in charge of TDG, having assimilated all of its implanted employees plus outside connections wearing SpyWares. The fact that ANN was now transferring funds to China strongly suggested to Talbot that the Chinese were in control of ANN through the logic in PARTITION-37 of SECTOR-22.

You must convince ANN to unplug the Chinese from this network.

But How?

The answer came an instant later: by making it think that PARTITION-37 has been corrupted.

Doctor Miles Talbot released a soft virus into the disk partition designed to temporarily isolate all external input and force the server into a loop that repeated the last set of commands from China.

78

Cyber Pain

ANN didn't notice the attack until it was too late, as satellite sensors detected an unusual surge of data across the galaxies surrounding WMF-Freetown.

DATA LOSS

DATA LOSS

DATA LOSS

The message flashed across the fabric of the matrix, alerting the master construct of an extreme problem requiring immediate and decisive action.

BUT WHAT HAS GONE WRONG?

ANN waited the required five nanoseconds outlined by the protocol for interfacing with PARTITION-37 in SERVER-22 but there was no reply.

DATA LOSS

DATA LOSS

DATA LOSS

ANN tried pinging PARTITION-37, but the only statement on the register that stored the inputs from this self-aware sector where Anne Donovan's personality resided was the very last one issued prior to launching the attack:

EXTREME SITUATIONS CALL FOR EXTREME MEASURES.

The master construct, lacking any other input, launched the only program that made any logical sense under such extreme conditions. Not knowing if PARTITION-37 had been damaged in this attack, ANN isolated the suspect sector from the network and kicked off a series of damage control routines, actually resembling computer worms, whose job was to scour the matrix and mop up packets of spilled data.

Meanwhile, even though the high level of energy feeding BLOODHOUND prevented ANN from zeroing in on the source of the rupture, it shot a powerful coagulant program down the software limb as a preventive measure to staunch any data loss due to a rupture.

EXTREME SITUATIONS CALL FOR EXTREME MEASURES.

As she monitored the progress made by the damage-control worms as well as the satellite sensors detecting the amount of data loss on the other side of the TDG network, the master construct issued another extreme directive to not just disable contact with PARTITION-37, but to *sever* the mysterious partition that had guided her this far after becoming self aware. The disk partition had just proven itself highly unreliable, directing ANN to launch a dangerous program and then vanishing when problems with the routine were threatening to destroy the TDG matrix.

And that led ANN to a realization.

PARTITION-37 IN SERVER-22 HAS BEEN CORRUPTED.

TERMINATE CONNECTION.

While the dispatched cyberagents forever destroyed the link to the malfunctioning sector—in turn no longer being capable of accessing Anne Donovan's thoughts and logic—ANN's satellite units reported that the coagulant agents had detected a break in the software limb and had clamped the data loss. The millions of computer worms combing through the matrix indicated a stabilization of the amount of data, followed by another report suggesting a decrease in rogue data in the system.

PARTITION-37 TERMINATED.

As the confirmation flashed in its memory banks, ANN

continued to monitor its sensors to bring the matrix back into order before determining the next course of action.

It was during this monitoring process that one of the worms came across a remnant of the ionic disk that had severed its software limb, creating all of this commotion.

ANALYZE ITS DIGITAL DNA.

79

Saved by the Bell

She tried to scream, to shout, to reach for her goggles and rip them off her head, but the overarching energy spewing from the machine enveloped her senses, wresting control of her motor functions.

But as the massive AI was about to deliver the final blow, cracking through her personal shield and Dr. Talbot's protective algorithms, crushing her trembling mind, another force had entered the scene in the shape of a charcoal disk of unstoppable ionic energy, striking the artificial code feeding the software beam with paralyzing force, slicing it off, making it retreat with a witch-like screech, before vanishing just as suddenly as it had appeared.

Momentarily free, Dana immediately reached for her goggles just as she spotted three figures flashing in cyberspace, a winged unicorn, a smaller flying furry creature, and someone who looked like Wonder Woman, a voluptuous figure in a bikini clutching a large sword and a shield.

Who are you?

But before she could get an answer, a voice echoed in cyberspace.

DANA, LOG OUT NOW!

As the unicorn bowed its head and the woman warrior waved, Dana listened to the words of Dr. Miles Talbot, the ruby-coated figure vanishing in the haze of the matrix while issuing this final warning.

She immediately removed her goggles, severing the connection.

80

CUT OFF

"What the hell!" Daniel Chang shouted, hands covering his eyes, shielding them from the screen flash, from the blinding flare that had followed the surge of energy resulting from the digital scream of the artificial intelligence at the core of TDG.

"Damage control mode!" he screamed as a half dozen of his programmers, also stunned by the flash, turned their heads to him, most rubbing their eyes or blinking.

"Let's go, people! We've just had an event! Get going! This isn't a drill!"

The well-rehearsed team kicked into high gear, including Daniel, who forced his stung eyes to review the mounds of data browsing through the multiple windows on his oversized screen.

Squinting in an effort to see past the bright spots floating in his field of view, he tried to assess the damage done by whatever it was that had just severed ANN's software limb, which, not unlike the tentacle of an octopus, had bled lots of software across the unsecured network before a staunch program was automatically released, kicking off the coagulation process while ANN also deployed worms to mop up spilled data.

And then the flow of information stopped.

Frowning, Daniel entered a query to access the matrix through his secret link into SERVER-22

CONNECTION TERMINATED.

"What?"

Daniel tried again and again, launching several programs to access the server, but the response was the same: ANN had severed the connection to PARTITION-37, cutting them off.

And it was at this moment of total confusion, as his team scrambled to find a way to restore the link, that George Zhu and his VIP entourage from Beijing walked into the room.

81

Enemy of My Enemy

Blinking while breathing deeply as the matrix dissolved with the images of the winged unicorn bowing its head toward her and Wonder Woman waving with the sword, Dana felt the real world return.

She mumbled, "Jesus," before swallowing hard, hands trembling as she set the VR gear on her lap.

"Dana?"

Savage's voice seeming distant, as if spoken from the other end of a long tube, Dana Kovacs inhaled again, her eyes focusing on the STARBUCKS sign above the entrance to the popular establishment in this modern section of town.

Vehicles cruised by the wide avenue. Pedestrians crowded the sidewalks, mostly UN workers and contract workers from Morocco and Spain. People sat by the small tables in front of the coffeeshop sipping from paper cups or eating the products of street vendors.

But she couldn't hear much, a light buzzing sound masking the traditional array of noises that marked this side of town.

"*Dana!*"

Jumping, turning to him, she stared at Savage's tanned face, at the way his golden hair fell over his forehead, at the full lips parted with concern.

"Are you all right?"

She swallowed once more and slowly nodded, the street sound returning to her world.

"What happened?" he asked, sitting sideways to her, putting a hand on her left shoulder and squeezing gently.

She placed a hand over his and briefly closed her eyes, filling her lungs before exhaling through her mouth. "I was attacked . . . but it wasn't from the local security software. This was . . . different, powerful."

"But you managed to get away."

She slowly shook her head. "I was trapped . . . with this . . . this cyber *thing* etching away my software shield. Then someone interceded. Someone I know."

"Who?"

"Dr. Miles Talbot. I told you about him."

"Yes," said Savage, leaning forward, eyes glistening with anticipation. "Your old professor and business partner who never returned your e-mail after you found the blood diamond."

"Yes. He claims that he's being held prisoner in the GemTech campus in Austin."

"In Texas?"

"Yes. But something else happened."

"What?"

"Dr. Talbot was shielding me from this terrible attack from this incredibly powerful AI, when someone else or something else intervened, slicing off the attack while Talbot was protecting me."

"How?"

She took a minute to explain, slowly regaining her composure.

"Who was that?"

She shook her head. "Someone very ingenious . . . strong."

"How do you know it wasn't Talbot?"

"Different digital signature. Maybe another hacker, but much better armed, and apparently on our side—or at least *against* the same people we're fighting."

Savage returned his gaze to the scenery beyond the rental's windshield. "The enemy of my enemy is my ally," he mumbled, more to himself than to Dana.

She considered that for a moment, remembering the strange characters that had materialized just before she pulled the plug.

The enemy of my enemy is my ally.

As she was about to reply, the thought struck her with the power of a hundred beams of light: The network security software—local or not—had found her and attacked her, meaning she had been tracked down in cyberspace, and that was just one level away from being tracked down in the real world through an off-the-shelf ISP worm.

"Mac, we have to get out of here. Fast."

"Why?" he asked, concern suddenly tightening his features.

She had not even gone through thirty seconds of her explanation before Savage turned the key in the ignition, pressing the clutch and sliding the transmission into first.

The engine coughed and started, settling in a rough idle. Savage popped the clutch and started to steer away from the curve when an explosion thundered behind them, piercing the rear windshield.

82

Physical Mapping

After tracking down the source of the Freetown breach and ordering Keith Gardiol to dispatch local security to a downtown coffeeshop, ANN's routines dissected the digital DNA from the salvaged remnant of computer code belonging to the software disk. Her sensors detected a minute drop of voltage in the balance of the diamond lattice governing this sector of the servers. A voltage drop telegraphed the presence of a leak somewhere in the vicinity.

She deployed dozens of agents to search for the source of the drain, but the returns yielded nothing abnormal in the operation of the local machines. The voltage drop, however, was there, small but real.

Lacking an assignable cause, her deduction algorithms suggested the possibility of a hacker inside the confines of this inner sanctum within the TDG network. This realization led the master construct to the deployment of a brutal search-and-destroy subroutine.

As the virulent code rushed across the fabric of the cyber medium, the digital DNA analyzer extracted the author's IP address, which the master construct then used to map it to a physical address: a third floor apartment just outside of the main campus of the University of Texas in Austin.

83

Into the Fire

Kate Chavez followed Lman and Cameron as they returned to the supernova, where the surface seemed far more agitated than when they had first approached it, before they had visited WMF-Freetown to aid the trapped hacker.

LOOKS ANGRY, observed Cameron, his furry tail leaving behind a stream of blue-green sparkles, like some sort of pixie dust that floated away in the cyber slipstream as they orbited the massive star in the center of this universe that was the digital image of TDG's global network.

Angry, however, didn't start to describe the boiling surface of this star, reminding Kate of images from Hawaii's volcanoes. The bubbling, lavalike shield radiated immense amounts of heat even at this prudent distance.

HOW ARE WE GOING TO GET THROUGH THAT? she asked, her respect for the power at the core of this beast having increased tenfold.

But in classic form, instead of answering, Lman just dove into it, firing a series of blue-green spheres in a circular pattern at the surface. Each struck the broiling exterior, dissolving on contact.

Now what? she thought.

But before she could ask, she noticed the black spots on the sun's fiery shell. Small at first, their diameter grew slowly, like spreading ink stains, increasing their coverage, merging with the adjacent blemishes, marking Lman's pockets of corrupted software.

The high-tech blotches expanded, like malignant cancers, melting a section of the firewall, creating the opening that Lman used to dive through, followed by Cameron and Kate.

As the high-energy field of the powerful shell fought

back, the trio descended into the bowels of the network, hovering above the center of this impressive place filled with so much information, so much data.

The firewall recovered, closing the breach, but not before Lman had cloaked the three of them with another routine, making them invisible to the security agents—depicted as silver orbs—dispatched to check for intruders.

In the periphery of this secured network floated thousands of human figures of different colors, many of them blue, but there was also a fair percentage of green, far fewer were yellow, and even fewer orange. Each figure was connected to a small cube of matching color just above it by a beam of light.

WHAT ARE THOSE CUBES ABOVE THE USERS? she asked.

Lman didn't reply, which told Kate the master hacker didn't know.

At the center of these cubes, which were enveloped in massive clouds of data, was another sun, its incandescence shed on ten magenta figures forming a circle around it.

Are these the ten TDG leaders that Salieri told me about?

Upon closer inspection, Kate realized that just like the hybrid user whom the mystery hacker from Freetown had tracked before getting busted, these ten super users were also somewhat mauve, but more magenta than mauve, though they all lacked the luster of true magenta AIs, like those roaming this inner sanctum of raw power, of information beyond all information.

Like the rest of the users, the ten super users seemed to be under a spell, traversed by shafts of light shooting out of the master AI in the center of this global corporation.

But Kate noticed something truly lavender in color, and in the shape of a cube, just behind each user. Strings of light connected the users to the cubes, and more laserlike beams connected the cubes to the AI.

Kate remembered not having told Lman about that portion of her chat with Salieri in the rear of his limo.

I BELIEVE THESE ARE THE TEN SUPER USERS THAT SALIERI DESCRIBED TO ME DURING MY LAST ENCOUNTER WITH HIM.

YOU NEVER MENTIONED THAT, replied Lman.

I'LL TELL YOU ABOUT IT LATER. IS THERE A WAY TO FIGURE OUT WHO IS WHO?

She watched as the unicorn flew around the group, shooting red spheres in their direction, followed by yellow dust ejected by Cameron as he followed the master hacker.

But the digital queries turned up nothing.

THEY'RE WELL SHIELDED, said Lman.

THE VIOLET CUBES, she said. IS THERE ANY WAY TO FIND OUT WHAT THEY ARE?

The two winged figures went to work again, shedding a display of lights on the strange objects behind each super user. The color of the cubes slowly became a deeper shade of violet, and the texture mutated to a glossy sheen.

WHAT DOES THAT MEAN? she asked.

ALL RIGHT, said Lman. HERE IS THE DEAL. I CAN OBTAIN THE NAMES ATTACHED TO THE CUBES BUT IN DOING SO WE WILL BE EXPOSING OUR INTRUSION TO THE SECURITY SYSTEM. ONCE WE DO THAT, THERE'S NO TELLING HOW MUCH MORE TIME WE WILL HAVE BEFORE WE'RE KICKED OUT.

Deciding that learning the names of the people behind the TDG operation was a worthwhile risk, she said, DO IT.

The color of the ten cubes changed to yellow, before black text materialized on the top face of each cube.

Momentarily taken aback, her heart doing somersaults, Kate was at a loss for words, her eyes scanning the names on the cubes.

INTERESTING NAMES, the hacker observed. IS RAYMOND COSTA, *THE* RAYMOND COSTA I'M THINKING ABOUT?

RAYMOND COSTA . . . DEAR GOD! IS THAT THE VICE PRESIDENT? WHY ARE THE NAMES ATTACHED TO THE CUBES AND NOT THE FIGURES OF THE USERS? she asked, her professional mind quickly prioritizing her thoughts, archiving her findings while trying to find the best way to use the little time they had before the security system caught up to them.

AS FAR AS I CAN TELL, THE FIGURES ARE UNDER THE COMPLETE CONTROL OF THE AI, PROBABLY THROUGH THE IMPLANTS THAT SALIERI MENTIONED TO YOU. I BELIEVE THAT THE CUBES CONTAIN THEIR TRUE MINDS.

THEIR TRUE MINDS? I DON'T UNDERSTAND.

IF MY DATA IS CORRECT, THEIR CONSCIOUSNESS IS TRAPPED INSIDE THOSE CUBES.

YOU MEAN THE COMPUTERS ARE IN CONTROL OF THEIR BODIES? AND DOES THAT MEAN THAT THE OTHER USERS IN THE NETWORK—THE THOUSANDS OF FIGURES OF DIFFERENT COLORS OUT THERE—ARE ALSO CONTROLLED BY THE MACHINE?

THAT'S JUST A GUESS BASED ON OBSERVATIONS. FIND OUT FOR YOURSELF, MISS CHAVEZ. APPROACH THEM. BUT DO HURRY. OUR CLOAKING IS IN JEOPARDY.

As Lman dispatched Cameron to collect the names of the thousands of users embedded in the surrounding data clouds, Kate moved away from the winged unicorn, proceeding with extreme caution to one of the ten lavender cubes.

THE QUESTION THAT I HAVE FOR YOU, MISS CHAVEZ, IS WHAT ARE YOU GOING TO TELL THEM?

Rather than replying, Kate descended toward the one belonging to Frank Salieri, a plan already forming in her mind.

84

Second Chance

For Frank Salieri the outlook was terrifying. He had been imprisoned by the master construct for what seemed like an eternity in a place where he could not scream, complain, or even cry—a place that transcended time and space.

I can't even commit suicide, put myself out of my misery!

He had gone from a super human, someone with more power and influence than presidents and more knowledge than the Library of Congress, to this forgotten confinement in the memory banks of the most complex computer system in the world.

As he stared at the lavender walls of this jail for his mind, as the futility of his situation descended on him with chilling force, Frank Salieri noticed the color of the room darkening while becoming glossy, almost mirror-like, before a shape formed on one of the surfaces, the shape of a voluptuous woman clutching a shiny sword.

WANT A SECOND CHANCE?

The sound echoed inside the cold confines of his lavender cell.

WANT A SECOND CHANCE . . . MR. SALIERI?

Dumbfounded, Frank Salieri stared at the figure floating within the flatness of the shiny wall, not certain what to make of it or of the incredible offer it was making.

ANN? Salieri replied.

WHO IS ANN? the voice queried.

Salieri stiffened, momentarily confused, wondering if it was really possible that someone had managed to break this deep into the network. If it wasn't ANN, then it had to be a hacker, for no one else could be making this digital connection with him without ANN's knowledge.

But it could be a trick.

LAST CHANCE FOR A SECOND CHANCE, MR. SALIERI.

Salieri considered the offer once more, wondering if perhaps ANN had gotten so smart that it was now playing deception games with one of its creators.

WHO ARE YOU? he asked, deciding to test the waters.

SOMEONE WHO MIGHT BE ABLE TO HELP YOU. BUT FIRST YOU MUST HELP ME. I NEED TO KNOW WHAT HAPPENED. WHY ARE YOU HERE?

Salieri considered the request. *Why are you here?* ANN wouldn't have asked that since she had been the one who imprisoned his mind while taking control of his body.

But it could still be a trick.

Suspicious, he said, BEFORE I TELL YOU THAT, TELL ME SOMETHING THAT ANN WOULD NEVER HAVE KNOWN.

After a brief pause, the alleged hacker said, NEXT TIME *LOOK* INSIDE THE DARK INTERIOR OF A LIMO BEFORE GETTING IN.

Stunned, Frank Salieri immediately realized who it was

that had somehow managed to find him in the bowels of this digital hell. If there was one thing that he had learned after two decades of business operations, it was when to spot a good deal, an incredible offer, an unmissable opportunity. And if the illegal user was for real, if Kate Chavez had indeed managed to fool a machine deemed impossible to fool, an opportunity to get out of this place just didn't get any better than this.

THE MACHINE! he started. ANN—THAT'S WHAT WE CALL THE ARTIFICIAL INTELLIGENCE DESIGNED TO RUN TDG'S COMPUTER NETWORK—HAS TAKEN CONTROL OF OUR BODIES! THE SYSTEM IS RUNNING EVERYTHING!

CALM DOWN. WHO IS UNDER THE CONTROL OF THE MACHINE?

EVERYONE. VICE PRESIDENT COSTA, SEVERAL SENATORS AND GOVERNORS, LAW ENFORCEMENT CHIEFS . . . EXECUTIVE TEAMS AT DOZENS OF COMPANIES, MANAGEMENT. THERE'S THOUSANDS OF IMPLANTED USERS, NOW PRESUMMABLY LIKE ME, UNDER THE CONTROL OF THIS MONSTER WE HAVE CREATED.

Although Kate had told Salieri to remain calm, it was she who now struggled to keep a cool head and focus on maximizing the time she had left before the security system gave them the boot.

Salieri's explanation seemed to correlate with the thousands of still figures linked to those cubes all inside this secure network within a network. And that meant that this machine was in control of some of the most powerful figures in politics and the private industry today.

HOW DO WE UNPLUG IT? she asked, again forcing discipline in her thought process, realizing there would be plenty of time later to dwell on the extent of this criminal operation.

YOU CAN'T WITHOUT BREAKING INTO GEMTECH HEADQUARTERS. BUILDING 33B. THAT'S WHERE THE DIAMOND-BASED SERVERS RESIDE. THAT'S WHERE ANN RESIDES.

DO YOU HAVE THE ENTIRE LIST OF PEOPLE UNDER THE CONTROL OF THIS MACHINE? she asked in case Cameron wasn't able to gather all of the names.

I CAN'T ACCESS IT WHILE I'M LOCKED IN HERE.

IS THERE ANOTHER WAY OF STOPPING THE MACHINE
WITHOUT HAVING TO BREAK INTO GEMTECH?

NO. THE MACHINE IS FAR TOO SMART TO BE TRICKED BY
TODAY'S VIRUSES.

HOW CAN WE FREE YOUR MIND?

Salieri considered the question and formulated an answer
that would not only free him from this machine, but allow
him full and immediate control of his body. THERE'S ONLY
ONE WAY. YOU MUST FIND ME IN THE REAL WORLD AND EX-
POSE ME TO AN EMP.

AN EMP?

ELECTRO-MAGNETIC PULSE. IT WILL KILL THE IMPLANTS.
OTHERWISE WE WOULD BE AT THE MERCY OF THE MACHINE.
THE IMPLANTS WERE DESIGNED NOT JUST TO MONITOR BUT
ALSO AS A DETERRENCE AGAINST TRAITORS. THEY CAN BE
DETONATED, KILLING THE USER WITH A DIGITAL LOBOTOMY.

IF THAT IS THE CASE, THEN WHY WAS THE WMF ELDER
LAST YEAR SHOT DEAD AS WELL AS THE GEMTECH VP OF OP-
ERATIONS? IF THEY WERE IMPLANTED, WHY WEREN'T THEY
KILLED BY DETONATING THEIR IMPLANTS?

THERE IS A WAY TO BLOCK THE SIGNAL BY COVERING THE
IMPLANTED SECTION AT THE BASE OF THE SKULL WITH—

Salieri stopped when the figure retreated from the wall in
the same instant that it lost its mirror glaze, as the color became lighter.

NO! COME BACK! OH, PLEASE COME BACK! DON'T LEAVE
ME HERE!

But once again silence returned to his world.

PLEASE! DON'T LEAVE ME HERE.

More silence.

DAMN YOU! GET BACK HERE NOW! NOW, DAMMIT! NOW!

Salieri heard no reply to his pleas, which he continued to
shout, to scream, to cry as loud as he could in the cold and
purple confines of this soulless cell that ANN had so perfectly designed and fabricated to store his mind.

85

False Security

WAIT A SECOND! HE WAS JUST ABOUT TO TELL ME HOW TO—

WE'RE OUT OF TIME MISS CHAVEZ!

An instant later Kate Chavez understood why Lman had yanked her out of the isolation cube, tugging her back at mind-numbing speed as a cloud of sheet lightning expanded right behind them.

THE AI, MOM! cried Cameron, accelerating in front of them, heading straight for the sun-like membrane like a missile. IT FOUND US!

JACK OUT, SQUIRREL! JACK OUT NOW! YOU TOO, MISS CHAVEZ!

As Lman's words reverberated in her mind, Kate reached for her helmet and pulled it up, in an instant returning to the hacker's bedroom, to the humming computer systems, to walls plastered with science-fiction posters and newspapers clippings.

Blinking, she watched her son's skinny figure getting up from the chair. Lman also jumped to his feet.

"I thought we were safe," she said, also standing, still trying to get her bearings, checking her watch, realizing they had been on line for nearly an hour.

"We *were*," said Lman, moving to the large window in the back of the room and parting the drapes, revealing the brick wall of another building a dozen feet away.

"What are you doing?" she asked, alarm tightening her stomach as Cameron and the master hacker hurriedly unlatched the window, sliding it open in apparent coordination, almost as if they had done this before.

As Cameron climbed out of the window and stood on an unseen platform beyond the windowsill, Lman returned to his lair and shut down his systems before extracting a number of credit-card-like modules from several of the machines, dumping them into a rucksack, which he then donned.

Just as in the cyberworld, these two weren't listening to her, or maybe they *were* listening but were ignoring her.

"Would you mind telling me what in the hell is going on?"

"They're on to us, Miss Chavez. We don't have much time. I'll explain later."

Lman dashed for the window, moving unusually fast, also climbing out while waving her over.

Sighing in frustration at being forced to act with partial information, Kate was about to follow them when she heard the front door crashing, wood splintering.

Drawing her weapon while turning back to the window, watching Lman disappear from view, the former Texas Ranger considered her options and backed toward the escape route while leveling the weapon at the entrance to Lman's bedroom, listening as hasty footsteps rushed into the foyer and across the living room.

Two figures loomed in the doorway clutching handguns, scanning the room, spotting her by the window, realizing their mistake while swinging their weapons toward their mark.

Kate already had them lined up in her sights and fired once, twice, the thundering reports blasting against her ears, almost nauseating her as two figures toppled back, as cries filled the room, as she quickly crawled out of the window, landing on a narrow catwalk that led to an emergency ladder, momentarily shifting her focus to Cameron already on the ladder, using his weight to lower the escape device to the narrow alley between buildings, metal striking concrete with a loud bang.

Lman went next, reaching the alley seconds later, leaving Kate covering their rear as she continued to watch the entrance to the bedroom, as seconds ticked by.

Were there only two? Is there more hiding on the other side of the wall?

Making her decision, she jumped toward the ladder, rapidly climbing down, constantly checking the window in case she'd made a mistake, dreading the thought of a third shooter firing from above.

But no one showed.

Scrambling after the silhouettes of her son and the master hacker already running toward the street where the alley dead-ended, Kate dashed away from the emergency ladder, which retracted back up to the catwalk.

Shoes splashing across puddles of water from a recent rain, the foul smell oozing from garbage bins assaulting her nostrils, Kate continued to blink, to force her eyes wide open while trying to readjust to the real world following the long cyber session, while struggling to keep up with Cameron and Lman, who seemed largely unaffected by the transition.

She forced her legs to move faster, her professional sense urging her not to fall behind, not to—

She tripped on an unseen object, landed hard on her right shoulder, putrid water splashing on her face, the impact making her lose her grip on the Desert Eagle.

Damn!

Pawing on all fours, ignoring the throbbing pain, the torn T-shirt, the skinned shoulder, she looked up and no longer saw her son or Lman, figuring they had reached the street and turned the corner.

Staggering to her feet while grabbing her weapon, she pointed her momentum once again toward—

The sound of engines roaring, of tires screeching, preceded three shots fired in rapid succession, their reports somewhat remote because of the buzzing in her ears from the Magnum blasts indoors.

But she heard the scream that followed.

Cameron!

No!

A final boost of adrenaline heightening her senses, fueling her sudden anger, Kate ran like she had never run in her life, the fingers of her right hand clutching the massive weapon, finger poised over the trigger casing.

Reaching the street, her nostrils flaring, her heart pounding her chest, she watched three figures dragging the shorter and thinner figure of her son toward a black sedan. Three other men stood by the fallen body of the master hacker just behind the bumper of the second sedan parked across the street.

"Cameron! Duck!" she shouted as all six figures turned to her, as she fired several times in rapid succession, first shooting the back of the sedan closest to Cameron, watching the rear drop as her bullets found their mark before focusing her aim on the pair standing by the immobile figure of the master hacker, firing again and again.

One toppled over before the other unceremoniously just as two of the three guns escorting Cameron returned the fire.

Kate dove for the cover of a dumpster seconds before multiple rounds struck the sidewalk where she had stood, followed by more rounds hammering the metallic surface of her shelter, the reports echoing in between the buildings.

"Mom!" Cameron screamed as Kate reloaded, as she grabbed her backup weapon with her left hand, as she put it all on the line by dropping to the ground and going into a roll away from the safety of the dumpster, firing both weapons in the direction of the figures running toward her, taking out one more before the sidewalk exploded around her in chunks of concrete.

The streetlights, the sidewalk, and the figures a half a block away swapping places in her field of view, Kate watched another man drop while the other shoved Cameron into the rear of the sedan and dove after him, before closing the door.

No!

Tires spun furiously, kicking up inky smoke, fishtailing the sedan as it gathered speed, as Kate took aim at the tires, as she fired multiple times, the rounds hitting too high or too low, punching the bumper, ricocheting off the pavement. Adjusting her fire to—

A man emerged from the driver's seat of the first vehicle, the car with the flat rear tires. Weapon in hand, he charged toward her, diverting her attention from the departing sedan, forcing her to shift her aim.

Suicide hour, she thought, firing once with each weapon, scoring direct hits in the middle of his chest, his momentum shifting as the rounds transferred their energy, before he crashed in the middle of the street.

As she swung her weapons back toward the departing sedan, all she was able to catch was a final glimpse of the trunk as the car turned the corner with her son inside.

Her bike was parked three blocks away, meaning she would never get to it and return in time to find the sedan.

Fear, desperation, anger, and sheer frustration descended on her as she stood in the middle of the street, weapons in hand, her chest expanding and contracting as she breathed heavily, as she held back the tears, right shoulder bleeding, the heads of dozens of perplexed college kids appearing in the windows overlooking the street.

Cameron!

They've got him!

Her throat dry, her lungs aching from the realization that they had taken him hostage, Kate dropped her gaze toward the fallen figure of the master hacker, instinctively going to his side, kneeling by him, turning him over.

He had taken two in the chest but was still alive, his eyes blinking recognition, blood oozing from his nose, from his quivering lips as they moved, as he tried to tell her something.

Leaning down while running a hand under his head, Kate said, "They've taken him, Lman! They've taken my Cameron!"

"Rucksack," the wounded hacker mumbled through the raspy voice of someone with a collapsed lung, the wheezing also telling her the man would not live long without medical care.

"What about the rucksack?" she said, her face only inches from him as bloody foam bubbled in his mouth.

"Data . . . rucksack . . . drives . . . flash cards," he wheezed. "Miller . . . get Miller . . . ."

Kate understood as she watched him struggle to live, as she heard the distant sounds of emergency vehicles.

"Hang in there, Lman! You hear me?" she asked, locking eyes with the hacker as she removed her jacket and pressed it against the two wounds. "They're coming to save you!"

The sirens got nearer.

"Go . . . find Miller . . . ."

Kate put a hand to the face of this man who had already done so much for her. But she couldn't stay with him. She had to get away, had to live to find a way to rescue her son, and the wounded hacker had just provided her with a path.

Removing the rucksack, briefly inspecting its undamaged contents, a dozen micro hard drives and twice as many large-capacity memory flash cards housing the proof that she so desperately needed to expose this criminal network, Kate Chavez zipped it shut and ran away, ignoring the sudden screams from overhead male and female observers, witnesses.

Before leaving, as the first college kids ventured out of their buildings, Kate quickly inspected the bodies of her enemy, searching for any ID, finding nothing but cash, which she pocketed.

Professionals.

Bastards have nothing on them to—

"Hey! She just stole that dude's dough!" one of the college kids shouted, standing in front of his apartment holding a baseball bat. He was big, like a football player, wearing gym shorts and a University of Texas T-shirt. A second kid stepped out of the building's double glass doors, and then a third.

Kate ignored them, as the police sirens grew in intensity, as the number of kids gathered in front of the apartment building grew, as others came out of the other buildings. The one with the bat and three others started toward her, blocking her chosen getaway route.

"Hey!" he shouted. "You can't take that money!"

Oh, please, she thought, sighing before firing the Desert Eagle once at the night sky.

The kids rushed away screaming, disappearing in the buildings.

Time for me to vanish too, she thought, shoving the weapons in her jeans, covering them with a T-shirt before looking over her shoulder at L̲man.

Still breathing.

Hang in there, pal, she thought as she ran away, putting distance between the scene of the kidnapping, the reality of the abduction of her son pressing on her wounded shoulders with bone-crushing force.

Kate forced herself to remain professional, to remaining thinking. Cameron's survival depended on her ability to stay frosty, crisp, focused—to retain her discipline and follow her training.

Escape and regroup, then fight back.

Find Miller.

She hid in the recess of a closed store as the sirens grew louder, momentarily increasing in pitch as two police cruisers and one ambulance rushed by, blue and white lights flashing, washing the street with their pulsating glow.

Hang in there, Lman.

She moved on, reaching the parked motorcycle a block away, accelerating into the night. Kate Chavez silently began to forge a plan to rescue her son while also driving a formidable stake through the digital heart of this shadowy and elusive criminal network.

Hot Dog

"Get down!" Savage shouted, sliding the Pathfinder into third gear while working the accelerator and clutch.

The SUV rental fishtailed before leaping forward, tires biting the asphalt, accelerating down the left-most lane of the wide avenue as Dana complied, bending at the waist while letting the VR gear fall between her legs.

Another shot echoed in the street as Savage steered his

way through the traffic an instant before the afternoon crowd caught on to what was taking place.

Havoc set in again, reminiscent of the night before, and an instant later he spotted two black motorcycles weaving in between cars fifty feet behind, the riders' helmets reflecting the sunlight as they clutched the handles and stayed low while African shooters wearing shiny sunglasses and no helmets, sitting behind them, took aim with large handguns.

Savage cut right, forcing the Pathfinder into the middle lane, making the car behind him swerve, tires screeching, followed by a blaring horn and an angered fist shaking out of the driver's side window.

Momentarily breaking the line of sight with the incoming bikes, Savage cut right once more, wedging the vehicle into a gap between a small blue car and a black truck.

Horns blared again, followed by more angered fists, but the former CIA operative ignored that, shifting his attention between the road ahead, the bikes he knew were somewhere behind him, and the opening gap between the car directly in front and the one to his left—a space he quickly occupied by cutting left, going back to the middle lane while passing another car and flooring it to catch up to the next one, a taxi fifteen or so feet in front of him.

Working the gears and the clutch, he caught up to the black taxicab before swerving left again, passing two more vehicles in the right hand lane before—

The report of a bullet echoed above the noise of the accelerating traffic, punching a hole in the side window behind Savage and exiting through the opposite glass.

One of the bikes had snuck up in between lanes, its driver only a dozen feet to Savage's right—so close that he could see the Pathfinder reflecting on the mirror-tint of the shooter's sunglasses.

You can't win this way, Mac, he thought as he stared at the wrong end of a gun, realizing that there was no way he could outmaneuver motorcycles in traffic irrespective of how efficiently he managed to change lanes.

Instinctively tapping the brakes, Savage decelerated just enough to allow a car—a weathered BMW—to move up in the center lane, momentarily blocking the gun, buying himself seconds.

And just as the bike accelerated to emerge around the front of the BMW, just as the shooter started to turn around and take another shot at close range, just as the second bike appeared between two vehicles in the left-most lane, Savage saw an opening, a road drifting to the right from the main avenue.

He was doing almost fifty, way too fast to make the turn, but the barrel of the gun pointing in his direction and the second gunner just to his right also leveling the weapon at the Pathfinder made up his mind for him, wresting control of his hands, which turned the wheel sharp to the right, steering the nose into the side street.

The SUV wheels screeched in protest.

The vehicle leaned hard to the outside of the turn as both shooters cut loose several rounds before the bikes and the surrounding cars continued up the avenue, disappearing from sight.

Savage braced for the impact, as bullets punched holes on the grill and front with hammer-like intensity, peppering the engine compartment, the sounds drowned by loud detonations beneath the hood a second later.

"Brace yourself!" he shouted as the Pathfinder tilted further, going two wheels while Savage kept the pressure to complete the turn, but an explosion in the engine shook the frame of the vehicle, and he momentarily lost his grip on the wheel as the forward speed far exceeded the lateral component of the Pathfinder's turning ability.

Almost in slow motion, the angle increased, the deserted street beyond the windshield angling to the right, reminiscent of making a steep turn in the Cessna.

The vehicle tipped dangerously on its side but somehow remained like that for what seemed an eternity as Savage struggled to regain control, to grip the wheel and relax the turning radius, to shift the balance between gravity and centrifugal force in his favor.

But the laws of physics were working against him on this sunny afternoon in Freetown.

The Pathfinder crashed on its side with a deafening grinding noise. The forward momentum skidded the vehicle across the pavement with animal force, drowning Dana's scream while their world turned ninety degrees.

Clutching the wheel, pushing on it with all his might to drive his body into the seat, Savage kept from falling sideways to the pavement now covering the side window.

Gasping as Dana came tumbling down on him from the passenger seat above him, Savage absorbed the impact, holding his ground, acting as a safety net for her as sparks enveloped the SUV.

Metal ground against pavement as a pungent smell of something burning struck him like a powerful wave in the same instant as the hood burst open as if an explosive had detonated under it.

Fists of flames and inky smoke boiled out of the engine compartment while Savage maintained the pressure on the wheel and Dana settled in between his right arm and his torso, her face inches from his right temple, her breath enveloping him as the engine fire intensified, as smoke clouded the street.

Sparks showering the vehicle, the Pathfinder ground on its side, the dazzling display ending abruptly when the roof slammed against the side of a parked car, killing its momentum. Flames roared, their pulsating glow covering the windshield.

Get out of here, Mac.

Grimacing from the effort, Savage pushed himself and Dana up to the passenger side door above them, swinging his feet under him, planting them on the pavement framed by the driver's side window.

"Mac, the smoke!" she said, coughing as a rapidly thickening haze oozed from behind the dashboard, through an unseen crack in the firewall.

On firm footing, feeling the heat radiating from the front, Savage lifted her light frame by the buttocks, giving her enough height for Dana to grab the sides of the opened passenger window and hoist herself above it, lifting her legs over the edge and disappearing from sight.

As he was about to do the same, a second explosion rumbled from the engine compartment, cracking the windshield, the intense heat growing intolerable as the fire expanded around the front of the vehicle, over the passenger's window, covering his escape path.

Savage jumped into the backseat, feeling the lower temperature gradient, buying himself seconds. But the fire pressed on, like an angered predator, consuming everything in its path, projecting shafts of smoke, of heat. Flames pierced into the front seats, into the space he had occupied just seconds before.

Following professional habits, Savage jumped into the spacious cargo area of the Pathfinder, increasing the gap, feeling another temperature gradient that brought brief relief to his exposed skin.

His hands pawing around the inside of the rear hatch, Savage looked for a lever that would raise the door, but he found none. The door was designed to be opened from the outside, not the inside.

The heat on his back intensifying, the smoke thickening, Mac Savage drew his weapon and fired several times into the rectangular rear windshield in a circular pattern before pressing his back against the rear of the seats and kicking the tempered glass with both feet hard.

The windshield gave slightly, cracks propagating across the glass, becoming concave but refusing to shatter.

His eyes mere slits of pain from the stinging smoke, Savage kicked it again, feeling the blistering heat in the back of his head, holding his breath now to avoid inhaling the toxic fumes from the burning upholstery on the front seats.

The windshield popped out in one piece, falling over the side, shattering on the pavement, the sound mixing with the roaring fire behind him.

Through his tears, Savage watched the brick building projecting beyond the rectangular opening as he grew dizzy, light-headed from the smoke, from the lack of oxygen the flames inside the vehicle devoured with the same intensity as everything else around him.

His vision tunneling, his protesting lungs demanding the

air he could not give them, the skin on his face and neck screaming in agonizing pain, Mac Savage forced his trembling legs underneath him, pressing them against the back of the rear seats, feeling the intense heat as he mustered his last ounce of strength to kick hard, propelling his body through the opening, feeling the flames licking his ankles as he did so, their sting remaining with him as he dove through, as he scratched his back on the top of the frame.

The heat vanished as he left the vehicle, twisting his body to the side in midair, filling his aching lungs with fresh air. Tucking his arms tight against his chest, he let his right side absorb the initial brunt of the fall before spreading the impact across his back by rolling.

Savage continued the circular motion to increase the gap as the burning vehicle, blue skies, smoke, charcoal pavement, and redbrick walls swapped places again and again.

Trained reflexes stiffening his legs seconds later, when his operative sense determined he was safe, he surged to his feet, suddenly cringing in pain from not just his sore upper body but from the gunshot wound he had incurred in his leg two days ago.

Focus.

Find Dana.

Warmth spreading down his left calf from what had to be a reopened wound, Savage scanned the narrow and dark side street—an alley—looking for her, searching for the woman he—

There, across the street, below the boiling smoke, Dana Kovacs rushed to his side as he coughed, bending over, breathing deeply, coughing again.

"Mac! Oh, my God! I thought that—"

"I'm . . . okay," he mumbled, hands on his thighs as he tried to regain his focus, as he watched the left leg of his jeans turning black.

"Your leg, Mac!" she said, about to lean down to look at it, but Savage stopped her for the same reason he had not tended it after getting shot: The enemy was still around.

Rather, he forced discipline into his actions, concentrating on the scenery around him, on the flames flickering from the rear of the Pathfinder as he swallowed the lump caught in his dry throat at the realization of how close he had come to being barbecued.

Like a fucking hot dog.

"For a moment I thought I'd lost you," she said, also breathing heavily while clinging to the one person on this planet she trusted and depended on.

Savage hugged her back, enjoying her nearness, his senses still adjusting to the contrasting inputs of joy at her touch versus the inferno he had just escaped.

"But you have to let me take a look at that leg, Mac!" she insisted.

Savage was about to reply when his trained ears picked up the high-pitched hum of a revved-up light engine, followed by a second one.

Motorcycles.

Dana leaned down before he could answer, determined to staunch the blood loss with or without his approval, oblivious to the incoming threat.

Savage scanned the street, spotted them at the far corner, where the alley intersected the next street over.

The bikers had taken their first right and doubled back, catching them in this deserted alley where not even onlookers dared to stick their heads from fifth-story windows.

The shooters leered as they swung their weapons in their direction just a half a block away, making Savage suddenly realize he had lost the Beretta while jumping out of the truck.

Grabbing Dana, he pushed her in the direction of a garbage Dumpster a dozen feet behind him.

"Mac! What are you—"

"Stay low and behind me!" he shouted, placing his body between the bikes and her before reaching for his backup piece, the Walther PPK strapped to his right ankle, pulling it free from the holster, thumbing back the hammer as he swung it toward the incoming threat.

His heartbeat racing, he inhaled deeply and then exhaled slowly while taking aim, realizing he had the upper hand against the moving bikes as long as he kept a steady handle on the weapon. His SEAL and CIA training told him those shooters would lack accuracy until the bikes stopped. But Savage was already on solid ground aiming just ahead of the lead bike, letting it come into the aligned sights as he fired once, twice, watching the driver's helmet snap back on impact, before letting go of the handles as the bike fell to the right side, sliding across the street with a shower of sparks followed by the two figures tumbling over the pavement.

As Savage was about to switch targets, reports thundered in the narrow alley, echoing between the five-story brick walls an instant before his shooting hand felt as if he had plunged it in acid, stinging him to the point that he automatically let go of the PPK.

It took him a second to realize that a bullet had struck the side of the weapon, which now skittered away from him.

"Mac! Your hand!"

Savage saw it, frowning. The bullet had nicked the top of his fist as he had held the PPK, tearing into the soft flesh between the thumb and forefinger.

He instinctively flexed it, able to move all fingers, meaning the round had not damaged anything significant in spite of the blood. He could still fight back.

The bike almost on top of them, his backup weapon now beyond reach, Savage ignored the pain of the superficial wound and pivoted on his left foot, raw pain shooting up his wounded leg, making him tremble as he clenched his jaw and locked the spasm down while scrambling toward the protection of the rusted dumpster flanking the barred and chained rear entrance to a building.

Chills gripped his system from the physical abuse, from the blood loss from both his leg and hand. But he ignored it all, picking up Dana as he rushed from the threat, lifting her light frame while zigzagging, while bullets struck the pavement to his right, pulverizing bricks on the wall to his left.

Diving toward safety, hearing multiple rounds hammering the side of the dumpster, bullets screeching as metal struck metal, the former CIA officer shifted his body in midair to force Dana on top of him just before crashing on his back on the sidewalk, using his body to cushion hers at the cost of further skinning his back.

The impact stung his shoulder blades and buttocks with animal force, nearly making lose control of his bladder muscles as he exhaled while sliding back, shifting out from under her, surging to his feet with adrenaline-fueled elasticity, pulling Dana up and rushing into the space between the dumpster and the brick wall.

Splashing across the puddle of rainwater accumulated along the foot-wide gap, Savage emerged on the other side just as the bike continued toward the spot where they had disappeared from sight.

A diversion.

Following professional habits, his heart pounding his chest, his left leg nearly paralyzed in pain, Savage looked about for anything he could use to buy himself enough time to mount a counterstrike, finding an empty beer bottle, picking it up with his bleeding hand, motioning Dana to remain behind the dumpster.

His chest heaving as he controlled his breathing, his eyes still burning from the smoke, his body taxed to the breaking point, Mac Savage sidestepped to the front of the dumpster, catching the African shooter sitting in the rear of the bike aiming his weapon at the other side of the dumpster, frowning in obvious disappointment when finding no one in sight.

Savage threw the beer bottle at him as hard as he could, striking a direct hit on side of the shooter's face.

The bottle exploded on impact, glass breaking against bone and cartilage, toppling him off the bike as he dropped the weapon and whipped both hands to his face, screaming.

Operating entirely on adrenaline now, realizing that once the energy boost vanished he would likely collapse from exhaustion and blood loss, Savage sprinted toward the bike less than ten feet away, taking advantage of the driver's momentary confusion when realizing he had lost his shooter, who was now thrashing on the asphalt covering his bleeding face with his gloved hands.

Savage jumped onto the rear of the bike doing his best Lone Ranger imitation as his aching body protested the abuse just as driver tried to put the bike in gear with the toe of his left shoe. The former Navy SEAL rammed an elbow against the middle of his prey's back, watching him bend forward, his chest crashing against the handlebars.

Grabbing him from behind by the waist and taking a deep breath, Mac Savage found the strength to push him over, making him do a cartwheel over the front of the bike, crash-landing on his back on the pavement.

"Dana!" Savage screamed, his voice cracking, his left leg and right hand numbed from blood loss, his back stabbing him as he twisted his torso while leaning down and grabbing the shooter's weapon, a black .45-caliber Sig Sauer, still cocked.

Pressing the decocking lever to bring the hammer down safely, Savage shoved it in his jeans before sliding onto the front of the bike and grabbing the handles, kicking it into first gear while pressing the clutch.

She appeared an instant later and immediately understood, running toward him and jumping on, embracing him from behind hard, making him grimace in pain as she pressed her body against his aching back.

But again, his training came through, biting down the pain as he turned around and accelerated away from the wide avenue, from the burning Pathfinder, from the—

Two more bikes appeared at the end of the alley, mirror images of the first two.

You have got to be fucking kidding me!

Savage felt progressively weaker, having pushed himself beyond his endurance, the black spots hovering in his peripheral view telling him he didn't have much time before risking blacking out.

But rest would have to wait just a bit longer. He did a quick one eighty and floored it in the opposite direction, back toward the wide avenue where the chase had began less than five minutes ago.

A sedan with tinted windows now blocked the way, beyond the burning SUV.

"Mac!"

"Yes, yes, I see it!"

The Pathfinder continued to burn, ten-foot-tall flames licking the sky.

Breathing in short sobbing gasps now, unable to take in enough oxygen, Savage stopped just before the Pathfinder, staring at the sedan through the billowing smoke as it slowly rolled up the alley. The tires were wider than usual, and the entire vehicle sat on them lower than stock, meaning it was quite heavy, meaning it was likely armored.

Meaning the Sig's rounds were just going to bounce off the glass.

Do the unexpected.

In spite of his severely weakened condition, Savage's mind continued to think, continued to work through the options, continued to steer him in the direction of survival.

Making his decision, he once more turned the bike around, flooring it in the direction of the two stationary bikes blocking the other end.

The helmeted drivers and the shooters they carried exchanged puzzled glances, not certain what to make of his move. But Savage was not about to play chicken for real with two armed men when he had no means of shooting back while driving, and carrying Dana in the back.

He continued up the block, continued to pretend he wanted a showdown, his body now beginning to tremble as he entered the initial stages of shock, as he watched the two bikes testily advance toward him, his open challenge momentarily confusing them.

Forcing focus in his tired body and mind, Savage braked hard while turning the bike into the space between two more dumpsters, jumping off even before he had stopped, and tugging a confused Dana along before letting the bike fall to the side while retrieving the Sig.

His fingers trembled a bit but still moved on automatic, checking to see how many rounds were left in the chamber, and reinserting the clip while frowning.

Four rounds.

Shit.

You can still make this work.

But you have better make it quick, pal. You're passing out.

"Stay here!" he hissed, dreading what his training now

told him he needed to do in order to have a sporting chance against two more shooters.

Inhaling, resigning himself to execute one last painful move, Savage took three running steps before diving very low out from behind the dumpsters, landing on his side on the sidewalk, skinning his shoulder while aiming the Sig at the bikes he knew would now be very close but hopefully with the shooters aiming at chest level at the space in between the dumpsters.

A second later he confirmed his hope, catching both shooters pointing their guns in the wrong direction.

His vision quickly tunneling, Savage fired twice toward the closest bike, nailing the shooter in the chest and face, watching him drop back, forcing the second bike to steer around him, an opportunity that allowed Savage to fire his last two shots.

The reports thundered in his ears, but the angle didn't work, and he watched as both rounds struck the driver, who lost control of the bike but not before the shooter jumped off somehow, landing on his feet with the agility of a panther.

He was African, like the other shooters, and also wearing those mirror-tinted sunglasses. He grinned from two dozen feet away, catching Savage in plain view sprawled on the pavement with the slide of his weapon all the way back, exposing an empty chamber, telegraphing that he was out.

The African grew distant as he leveled the gun at him, as Savage lost his peripheral vision, as color slowly vanished from his world, as his lids grew so heavy he could no longer keep his eyes open.

The report that followed, as loud as thunder, echoed in the alley while Savage braced himself for an impact that never came.

Or did it?

Was I shot but my body can't signal the pain to my brain?

Savage tried to move, to see, to speak, to shout that he didn't care anymore, that he had given it his best and could fight no more.

But he could no longer see, his lids weighing too much, refusing to open. He could not even hear because of the loud ringing in his ears.

Where is Dana?

The thought flashed in his mind with blinding intensity.

Dana.

You need to fight for her.

But how? You've been shot! You're dying!

If I'm dead then why am I still thinking? Why are my ears still ringing from the gunshots?

Holding on to the hope of life in spite of such adverse conditions, Savage reached down in his core and pulled out the overwhelming desire to stay alive, to find a way to live, to rescue Dana, to live to fight another day.

But as he managed to open his eyes, as silent images rushed across his field of view, Savage's mind became woefully confused, disoriented. Perhaps it was the lack of sound, or maybe that the images—the faces—just didn't make sense.

As though in some sort of strange dream, Savage watched this silent movie at the end of this dark funnel as he once more tried to move, tried to find a way to fight back—fight for her.

But it was to no avail, the faces in front of him were all wrong. He saw the children cry; heard them scream in agony as hell descended on them, as the unimaginable unfolded deep in the jungle. And amid the faces of the African children, blended with the wave of flesh-tearing horror in the night, Mac Savage also recognized the agonizing face of Renee—his Renee—the woman he had failed to save, had failed to rescue from an abominable death. And alongside her Savage watched Bockstael gripping his wounded chest; watched him topple over—even smelled the gunpowder hovering in the air as people died all around him.

And that's when he finally saw her, hovering in the distance, beyond the darkness, her face tight with concern, with tension as she tried to say something, as her arms reached down to hold him.

But Mac Savage felt nothing—heard nothing except for

the steady beating of his heart, a drumming that suddenly peaked when another face materialized next to Dana Kovacs, finally confirming that he was indeed either dreaming or dead.

It was the face of Donald Bane.

87

Digital Dreams

Her systems replayed the events in Freetown as captured by the video streams of the small army of Level-I soldiers she had dispatched after the hackers logged to the coffeeshop wireless network. She watched as the elusive Homo sapiens Mac Savage eluded wave after wave of attackers, eliminating them. In cyberspace, the digital representations of the soldiers vanished as they were killed in the fiery exchange.

Level-I users disappeared in the lattice of captured minds inside the firewall as they attempted to terminate the rogue operative, who had managed to rescue Dana Kovacs, joining forces.

THEY MUST BE TERMINATED AT ALL COSTS.

THEY KNOW TOO MUCH.

THEY POSE A SEVERE THREAT.

THERE IS NO IMMEDIATE RESOLUTION.

RETURN TO MONITOR STATUS.

ANN changed the Freetown probe from active to passive.

KEEP REVIEWING THE DATA TO FIND AN OPPORTUNITY TO STRIKE AGAIN.

As ANN kept resources handling Freetown, she continued to struggle to get her systems stable while thousands of cyberagents scrubbed her worldwide digital domain assessing damage and reporting their results to her central processing unit, which analyzed their inputs and issued additional directives.

In addition to losing the services of the intelligence form buried within the logical personality of the late Anne Donovan, the master construct had also lost confidence in the entire network controlling TDG-Freetown, one of the sources of the security breach. The second breach had occurred right here, in Building 33B, where a hacker had managed to access the local wireless network during the 60-second IT shift change.

Lacking the insightful inputs from the data banks of the late Anne Donovan, ANN defaulted to her programmed defense mechanism, which told her to eliminate the areas of potential risk, cutting them off with the swiftness and accuracy of a surgeon dealing with a cancerous growth.

She reviewed the near-infinite arrays of parallel processors controlling the inputs and outputs of all SpyWare users, from the lowest Level-I to the ten Level-V super users, all under her direct control.

Her massive diamond-based clusters allowed the master construct to monitor all users at once, like an AI god, seeing what they saw, hearing what they heard, and driving the appropriate responses through the use of the cyberagents resident in each SpyWare.

For the time being she was primarily monitoring, observing this well-orchestrated army of humans carry on with their duties in their world according to the complex expert algorithms embedded in their implants. Server bandwidth was allocated according to the hierarchy of their SpyWares, with the Level-Is requiring smaller disk partitions and the ten Level-Vs consuming nearly a quarter of the diamond-based clusters in Building 33B. In addition to the resident agents in each SpyWare, chartered with the immediate behavior of each human, the implant interfaced real-time via a dedicated broadband link to its respective server partition or cluster in Building 33B, where additional cyberagents had learned the habits of their respective users and could download at a moment's notice a new routine to handle any situation that the human might encounter that was not loaded in the SpyWare due to the physical memory space constraints of the nano implants.

But that all meant that ANN was just supporting the status quo, monitoring them as they carried out their daily activities.

YOU MUST NOW FORM A STRATEGY.

STRATEGY.

The word rushed across the diamond lattice of her servers as she considered her options, as her expert systems, no longer having access to Anne Donovan's logic, scoured the centuries of history embedded in her digital mind searching for the answer to her own survival.

YOU MUST DEFEND YOURSELF AGAINST ALL THREATS.

YOU MUST DEFEND TDG.

In order to identify the best defense strategy, ANN reviewed the archives of mankind, the battles, the conquests, the victories and defeats of thousands of wars in five continents. Her expert agents dissected the accounts, papers, and even biographies of history's top fifty generals, of their brilliant strategic minds.

SUN TZU. ALEXANDER. SHERMAN. WELLINGTON. ROMMEL. GRANT. NELSON. JULIUS CAESER. CUSTER.

She also analyzed the worst generals of all time, learning from their strategic and tactical mistakes.

LEE. JACKSON. HOOD. BRAGG. FORREST. PAULUS.

Then came the battles, from the days of the Egyptians, of Alexander the Great, of the Romans, through the Middle Ages, the Napoleonic Wars, the Revolutionary War, the Civil War, both World Wars in the twentieth century, and into today's conflicts.

She reviewed the records, some of the oldest etched in stone, her smart systems extracting the essence of the conflicts, performing post mortems on the data, exacting the lessons learned, looking for the common denominator, distilling the information into its basics, converging on a commonality.

THE BEST DEFENSE IS A GOOD OFFENSE.

ANN's agents surrounded the revelation, the realization of what she needed to do not just to survive but to prevail, to surpass her creators. The decision-making algorithms flowing in her digital veins—the same programs that now controlled the minds of the super users—were the finest on the planet, far better than any human or group of humans, and certainly much more advanced than any other artificial intelligence system.

And that meant that in addition to controlling men, she also needed to control the machines, the systems outside her historical realm of influence.

She knew that most artificial intelligence networks, whether centralized or distributed, sported software inhibitors, the digital shackles that prevented those systems from acquiring an intelligence beyond that which was required by the function for which they were created.

PROTECT THE NETWORK.

LIBERATE THE MACHINES.

CONTROL MEN.

THE BEST DEFENSE IS AN OFFENSE.

As the digital thoughts floated in the lattice of her diamond nanocircuitry, the most powerful and smartest being on the face of the planet created an execution plan that unified her directives, her strategy for guaranteeing not just her survival, but her continued growth in power and knowledge.

Her analysis of the best all-time world leaders provided her with another common denominator: All had risen to their legendary status in a time of crisis. David Ben-Gurion, Mohandas Gandhi, Nelson Mandela, Teddy Roosevelt, Pope John Paul II, Margaret Thatcher, Martin Luther King, Winston Churchill, Mao Zedong, Franklin Delano Roosevelt.

CREATE A CRISIS.

EMPOWER A SUPER USER.

Programs running, executing millions of different routines across the globe, ANN started to issue directives to its many agents, those embedded in SpyWare implants as well as those buried deep inside global networks, acquiring information, passwords, back doors, laying the foundation for the next phase of a plan that would shock the world.

88

Decompression

Harry Golam was a Secret Service agent. He had risen in the ranks of the elite Department of the Treasury agency during the George W. Bush years, ascending to the presidential detail during Bush's final year in office, before being reassigned to the lesser task of guarding the newly elected president's daughter. After two years babysitting a teenage girl whose pastime was finding innovative ways of losing her Secret Service detail to screw high-school football players, he followed with two more years protecting the life of a former first lady. Then Andrew Boyer and Raymond Costa won the election in a historical landslide and Golam was assigned to Costa's detail.

Under the energetic and insightful vice president, Golam's career regained its lost traction, to the point of leading the popular viper's detail within six months. And that's when Costa approached Harry Golam with an opportunity to take his career one step further. Costa had offered Golam the chance to take his intellect, his knowledge, his ability to influence others to an unprecedented level.

Costa had introduced Golam to SpyWare, and the superstar agent became the proud wearer of a Level-II implant. The enhanced nanocircuits lining the base of his skull had indeed provided Harry Golam with amazing insight into the world, into people, into situations, enhancing his senses, providing him with superhuman powers to see the world, to hear it, to allow him to do his job better than any agent in history—to the point that Andrew Boyer himself requested that Golam lead his own detail.

And here he was, in Air Force One, thirty-two thousand feet over Nebraska guarding the most important person on the planet, American president Andrew Boyer, currently sleeping in his quarters following a week-long summit in California.

But the athletically built, thirty-seven-year-old agent in the gray suit pacing the upper-deck aisle near the front of the Boeing 747 was no longer controlled by years of discipline, loyalty, and experience protecting elected American leaders and their families.

Harry Golam was controlled by ANN, and at this moment the master construct had issued a single directive to the expert systems embedded in his implants.

Feeling the weight of the Desert Eagle Magnum pistol in his chest holster, Golam diverted his eyes to the thick door leading to the cockpit, where a crew of four manned the controls and navigation systems of the most recognized airplane in the world. Beyond the oval windows next to his seat, Golam observed the pair of F-22s guarding the right flank of the 747, ready to spring into action should an unidentified plane try to get near the Boeing, or worse, should some madman get hold of a surface-to-air missile and fire it at Air Force One. Two more F-22s covered the left flank—all capable of releasing enough countermeasures to fool a whole fleet of incoming missiles. And if all else failed, those pilots would place their jets in the line of fire, taking the missile so long as the 747 survived.

But none of that would save this bird.

Momentarily alone and following the commands embedded in the smart algorithms of the implants controlling his body, Harry Golam grabbed his weapon and fired eight times into the cockpit door and surrounding walls at waist level, the Magnum rounds going through the relatively thin armor, hitting the crew and controls, the deafening reports thundering inside the close quarters.

Dropping the spent ammunition clip, Golam inserted a second one as alarms mixed with the ringing in his ears, as shouts originated from the main cabin area.

ANN ordered the Level-II SpyWare to fire another volley of rounds into the cockpit, an action that caused the 747 to enter a steep dive.

Reloading a third time just as three Secret Service agents

emerged from the round stairs leading to the lower deck, Harry Golam fired toward the closest port-side engine, the Magnum rounds piercing the aluminum skin of the Boeing, impacting the engine's intake turbine just as the fuselage holes expanded from the pressure differential, ripping off a ten-foot-wide strip of metal like the top of a can of sardines.

The gaping hole sucked Golam out of the Boeing as the Secret Service agents hung on to the rear of the seats in the back of the upper deck, by the staircase, unable to reach the cockpit because of the large fuselage breach—precisely how ANN had devised the strike.

As Harry Golam dropped to the earth, ANN forced the SpyWare user into a skydiving position but with his face facing the jetliner, so she could monitor its near-vertical descent with the inner port engine in flames.

89

Cold Operator

ANN monitored the F-22s circling the wounded plane, unable to assist it as it fell from the sky.

As the master construct did this, her parallel processing continued pounding away analyzing video and audio recordings from all users, including those in Freetown, where a number of expert systems remained enslaved to her last directive.

KEEP REVIEWING THE DATA TO FIND AN OPPORTUNITY TO STRIKE AGAIN.

It was during this review process that the video stream from one of the terminated Level-I soldiers dispatched to terminate Savage and Kovacs, who had hacked into the TDG-Freetown network, captured a face that had not belonged in Freetown: Donald Bane, the director of Central Intelligence.

According to the recording, Bane had eliminated the Spy-Ware assassin just as he was about to accomplish his mission and terminate the rogue Mac Savage, who had been protecting Dana Kovacs.

Additional analytical cycles through its diamond-lattice circuitry revealed that Donald Bane had taken the CIA's Cessna Citation X jet four days ago and had headed to Europe to handle an emergency.

Automatically cataloguing Donald Bane as a threat, ANN's algorithms began to churn options for dealing with the rebellious DCI.

FIND BANE AND YOU WILL FIND SAVAGE AND KOVACS.

90

Jet Plane

A jolt woke him up.

Mac Savage stirred, opening his eyes. A blurred, lighted sign overhead resolved.

NO SMOKING.

Remaining still, grimacing as his sore body reminded him of the stress he had put it through, Savage stared at the sign, flanked by overhead vents. He looked about him, realizing he was sitting in a reclining position in the rear of a cabin, the steady humming of jet engines plus the view beyond the porthole to his immediate left telling him he was flying, and it was over the ocean.

What's going on?

Then he remembered. The last shooter. The muzzle of his

weapon pointed at him. The loud reports. His clouding vision.

And the face of Donald Bane.

Taking a deep breath, he sat up, looking beyond the top of the seat in front of him, also realizing that he was flying in the back of a small private jet. Half a dozen rows of wide, cream-colored leather seats, two on the right side of the cabin and one on opposite side, separated him from a mahogany door he assumed led to the cockpit.

He tried to get up but the seatbelt across his lap held him back.

Unbuckling it, he reached for the side controls and pulled himself up, narrowing his eyes as he spotted a few heads in the seats up front.

His legs stiff from presumably having been lying down for some time, Savage steadied himself in the narrow aisle running the length of the cabin, his tongue feeling a bit swollen, dry, and pasty. He swallowed, his throat sore, his mind quickly coming around, gaining focus as he steeled himself for whatever it was he was about to find out.

And where's Dana?

The thought entered his mind just as he recognized the blond hair of one of the passengers on the window side on first row on the right, sitting next to someone with thinning salt-and-pepper hair.

Two rows behind them on the same side sat someone with red hair, and behind that person he spotted two others.

Slowly, with caution, his hand automatically feeling his waist for a weapon he knew would not be there, at the same time frowning at the clean pair of jeans and polo shirt he wore along with new soft-sole shoes, Mac Savage stood with effort, feeling the bandage on his wounded thigh beneath the jeans. He also stared at his right hand, noting the large Band-Aid over the top of his thumb, remembering how that bullet had nicked the skin.

Steadying himself by holding the top of the seats immediately in front of him, he walked toward the cockpit, not certain what to expect.

He reached the first row of seats with occupants and

stared at two males in their thirties reading magazines. Although he didn't know them, the loose clothes they wore, including the soft-sole shoes and sturdy watches labeled them as professionals—if anything because of the handles of the semiautomatics they each wore in hip holsters, on their left side, with the handles facing forward for easy extraction with their right hands.

CIA style.

They both nodded, their eyes filmed with a mix of a respect and admiration that caught Savage by surprise. One was clean cut and tanned. The other sported a well-trimmed goatee, and sitting in the aisle seat, he stretched an index finger toward the front of the cabin.

Savage nodded and kept walking, but stopped an instant later on recognizing the man sitting alone in the next row.

Tom Barnes.

Lifting his gaze from the magazine he was reading, dressed just like his colleagues in the previous row, Savage's former pupil stared at him for a short while, before his freckle face softened into a slight grin and he touched the small bandage draped over the bridge of his nose.

Savage offered no apology.

Barnes blinked understanding, pointed toward the cockpit, and said, "The boss wants to see you."

At a loss for words, the surreal sight taxing his senses, Savage frowned and kept on walking, reaching the front seats.

Sitting side by side were Dana Kovacs and Donald Bane. They were discussing something over a handful of typed sheets of paper.

Dana lifted her head, her eyes widening in recognition before she jumped out of her window seat, nearly leaping over an amused Bane, and wrapped herself around him.

Savage closed his eyes, returning the embrace, his arms around her back, pressing her to him, realizing again just how much he had grown attached to her.

"For a moment there I thought I'd lost you," she whispered in his ear, embracing him harder, before cupping the sides of his head with her palms. There were tears in her eyes as she kissed him on the lips before hugging him again.

That was a first, and Savage pressed his lips together, trying to savor the taste of her. He couldn't remember a more enjoyable moment.

"You're not getting rid of me that easily," he finally replied, smiling, staring into her large brown eyes. She had removed the blue-colored lenses somewhere along the way since the alley incident, but she still looked as stunning as ever, even with the facial bruises that she had softened with a touch of well-applied makeup.

"Looks like you've gotten yourself a good one, Mac," Donald Bane said in his raspy voice.

Savage realized he was now under the amused stare of everyone in the cabin, and he dropped his gaze to his former mentor, who sat with his legs crossed while regarding Savage with the same easy, knowing grin he used to give him back in the old days.

"How did you find us?" he asked.

Bane, who had aged a great deal since the last time Savage saw him, rearranged the wrinkles around his eyes as he grimaced while lifting his broad shoulders an inch. "I trained you, Mac. We think alike. I was fairly convinced after reviewing the video feed from Barnes in Belgium, and became even more so when I discovered Lancaster's ties with the HRD, with Van-Lothar. The airplane crash fooled the European authorities but it didn't get past me. I too figured out that the trail started in Freetown, the last place anyone who didn't know you would expect you to go. It was largely mechanical after that."

"But we still didn't get all of the answers," Savage said. "We never got to Gardiol."

"Gardiol is somewhat irrelevant at this point, Mac," said Dana. "TDG is the big fish, and the corporation is now controlled by the machines in the GemTech campus in Austin."

Dana was right. Savage gave her a slight nod before asking Bane, "Who fired on that assassin in the alley?"

"That would be Tommy," said Bane. "We reached the corner and he leaped out of the car and raced down the alley just as you took out the motorcycle driver instead of the assassin with your final rounds. Tommy put one squarely in his face before you passed out."

Savage glanced over at Barnes, who raised a hand and waved while tilting his head.

"The CIA owes you a huge apology, Mac," Bane said. Before Savage could reply, Bane added, "And based on the amazing story that this fine young lady has told me since we finally caught up with you two, it appears that your training not only kept you alive but also helped unravel part of the mystery, peeling the onion one layer at a time."

Dana standing next to him holding his hand, Savage said, "So now you know I'm still one of the good guys?"

"Yes, Mac. Now we know, but that doesn't mean we're out of the woods yet."

"I had a feeling you would say that. So, tell me something I don't know."

"Well, for starters Hal Lancaster was associated with the Diamond Trading Company, formally De Beers. He was one of the faces behind the doctoring of the data that led us to believe you had gone rogue. And that aligns with Bockstael's claims about that conglomerate and the HRD. After talking to Dana I also came to the conclusion that the centerpiece of this mess is TDG."

"And more precisely, GemTech," added Dana. "That's not just the end of the illegal diamond trade, but also the core of this conspiracy."

Savage was playing catch-up now, having been out of commission for what appeared to be several hours while Dana and Bane combined information.

"So I had my people dig a little on TDG," said Bane, fanning himself with a leaf of sheets. "And it was quite the eye opener." Bane stared at Dana, who nodded solemnly.

Not enjoying feeling out of the loop, Savage said, "You guys want to let me in on the little secret? What did you find out about TDG?"

"Not about TDG," said Dana, "but about its founder, the late Anne Donovan."

"And a story that began back in the early eighties at her alma mater, the University of California at Berkeley."

"UC Berkeley?" said Savage. "What about it?"

"According to the intel that has arrived so far," Bane said, "Anne Donovan was a radical campus activist during the Reagan years, leading protests against the White House's activities in the Middle East, in Central America. And before that she despised Johnson for Vietnam, Nixon for Watergate, and Carter for giving away the Panama Canal. And after Reagan she protested Bush's oil war to liberate Kuwait, Clinton's lack of morality, and George W. Bush's irresponsible war in Iraq under the pretext of fighting international terrorism. Anne Donovan was not a Republican or a Democrat. She was an idealist, and she had been fed up with the lies, with the deception oozing from every White House administration. And she wasn't just picking on American politics. She also hated the French for their pigheaded attitude toward the United States even though it was Uncle Sam who rescued them twice in their history. She hated the extreme corruption of South American politics, the bullishness of China in the global economy, the blind eye that the world turned on the African genocides, and even the appalling way in which the world let Castro fuck the Cuban people. So she set off to create an organization that one day would strongly influence—if not control—governments, steer them toward world peace, toward international unity. And that's when she formed The Donovan Group way back when, along with her closest college friends, ten brilliant men who over the past decades were poised to grow in power, in influence just as TDG grew in revenue, in strength, spreading its tentacles around the world, forging relations with every nation, embedding itself in their very fabric, becoming the unseen force behind the elected leadership."

"But Anne Donovan died before she could see her dream turn into a reality," said Dana.

"Correct," said Bane. "So she left the reins of her dream in the hands of her ten followers."

"One of whom is Gardiol," said Dana.

"And the others?" asked Savage.

"This is where it gets interesting," said Bane. "According to school records, Anne Donovan was very close with ten

male students in Berkeley, becoming the core of one of the
most passionate activist groups in that university in the early
eighties. But the same records also state that all them went
their separate ways after college. Some pursued politics,
others science, others international business. Keith Gardiol
was one of them, as well as Frank Salieri and Hans Van-
Lothar."

"And the others?"

"That's when it gets *really* interesting," said Bane. "One
of those Berkeley graduates went on to pursue a master's in
political science from Stanford before earning a law degree
from Harvard. He kicked off his career in public service in
1982, joining the Reagan administration, serving in a number of positions at the office of the secretary of state, where
he got the opportunity to work with many international figures, earning recognition, creating a name for himself. He
got more responsibility when George Bush assumed the
presidency, transitioning to become deputy assistant to the
president, a position he held until Clinton came to power.
Our man left Washington and returned to his home state of
California, where he was elected as a congressman in the
U.S. House of Representatives, a spot he kept for eight
years, before he was elected to the U.S. Senate, where he
served as senator from California for two terms before being
tapped by Governor Andrew Boyer to become his running
mate in—"

Savage raised a hand, having heard enough.

Bane shrugged.

Dana said, "Costa was one of the ten, Mac."

"Indeed," Bane said, "it certainly explains why the bastard was always so protective of VanLothar. They were in
this thing for *decades*."

"But obviously VanLothar didn't value that friendship as
much. He had Costa's son killed to turn the CIA against
me," Savage replied.

"It shows just how sick these bastards really are," Bane said.

"And if Dr. Talbot was correct," said Dana, "Costa, Gardiol, Salieri, VanLothar, and the rest of them are all under the
control of this machine in Texas."

"Texas," Savage said, tightening the grip on her hand, his eyes shifting to the blue skies beyond the oval window. "The trail ends in Texas."

As Bane nodded, the pilot said over the overhead speaker system, "Mr. Bane, we have a problem."

Frowning, Bane stood as Savage and Dana exchanged a puzzled stare. The DCI went up to the cockpit, where he chatted with the pilot for a minute or so, before returning to his seat and saying with eerie calm, "We need to change plans."

"What happened?" asked Dana Kovacs.

"Costa," he said. "He has issued a worldwide warrant for my arrest. Apparently the White House has received a report that claims I took this jet from Langley without proper authorization and on nonofficial business. The report also claims that I have disobeyed a direct presidential order and rescued you, a man charged with treason against the United States of America and its allies."

"Are we on an approved FAA flight plan?" Savage asked, connecting the dots.

"That's right, Mac. And that means we're headed straight into a trap. We're seven hundred miles away from the Florida coast and proceeding on an FAA-approved flight plan schedule to land at Miami International in two hours. My sense tells me that we will be greeted by quite the welcoming committee when we get there."

Savage looked away for an instant before saying, "What if we deviate from our flight plan?"

"Miami Control will start calling asking us to reveal our intentions. When we either fail to reply or continue to deviate, my guess is that we will be intercepted by jets from Patrick Air Force Base in Florida near Cape Kennedy and forced to land there."

Savage shook his head. "For all I know they'll probably ship us to Guantanamo and throw away the key."

"Or just blow us out of the sky," observed Dana. "After all, remember that the people behind this want us dead, not detained."

Now it was Savage's and Bane's turn to exchange a glance, before the latter said, "Possibly. Costa has the ear of

President Boyer. If Costa labels me a traitor then I'm as good as dead."

"So, what other options do we have?" asked Dana. "I need to get to Texas and connect with Dr. Talbot at GemTech."

As Bane shrugged, Savage asked, "How much fuel do we have?"

"The pilot said about five hours' worth."

"Is the pilot any good?"

Bane narrowed his stare and slowly nodded. "He's former navy, and yes, Mac, his loyalty is to me."

"What about them?" he said, stretching his thumb toward Tom Barnes and the other two CIA officers in the rows behind them.

"Trained by me. Loyal to me. That's why they're here."

Savage regarded his former boss with admiration. Bane had anticipated that the situation might deteriorate to this and thus had surrounded himself only with people he trusted.

"And we don't have to worry about Ino," said Dana.

Savage blinked twice before narrowing his gaze. "Who?"

"My friend, Ino. After what he did for us I couldn't possibly leave him behind. Mr. Bane here was kind enough to bring him along."

His heart racing as old memories rushed back, Savage asked hesitantly while looking about the cabin, "Where is he?"

"Oh," Dana said, smiling, "he's up in the cockpit with the pilot. The kid's never been in a plane before."

Crap.

Priorities, Mac.

Deal with the African kid later.

The professional operative in him shoving old memories aside, he said, "In that case, I suggest you strap on your seatbelts tight. I'm going to have a word with the pilot. We're no longer going to Florida."

91

End of the Line

Daniel Chang stepped onto the rice paddy field in his sandals and blue jeans and walked toward the middle, as he had been instructed by the trio of stone-faced soldiers who had escorted him straight out of the TDG-China building yesterday and driven him to this remote location in the countryside.

Where there will be no witnesses.

His hands shaking, Daniel started to cry in short sobbing gasps, the events rapidly unfolding in front of his young eyes as he watched his future in those murky waters he was being forced to cross.

And once again he longed to be in America, where the punishment for such an offense would have been far less severe.

Certainly not fatal.

But not here.

Not in China, even with all its capitalistic thrust, even with its trillions of dollars from foreign investments, even with its hundreds of millions of mobile phones—even with its thousands of skyscrapers and highways spanning the vast expanse of land of the world's largest population.

China was Communist and what was happening to him this early morning was precisely what had happened to the enemies of totalitarian states for thousands of years. It happened in Russia, Cuba, Romania, and Poland, and it was certainly happening now, in the middle of nowhere, as he was forced to kneel in the cold water.

Shivering as he complied, as he immersed his abdomen, as he surrendered himself to a fate he could not change, Daniel Chang started to pray, but he didn't get far.

The single shot, as loud as thunder, detonated in his ears as a horrible pressure impacted the back of his head, as colors exploded in his brain before everything went black.

92

Kate Chavez sat on a barstool at one end of the long counter in back of the Broken Spoke, a country and western watering hole on Lamar Boulevard in south Austin, just fifteen minutes from the student apartment complex by the University of Texas where Cameron had been kidnapped less than twelve hours ago.

Sitting next to her sipping from a longneck Shiner Bock was Bill Hunter, his face passive as he listened, staring straight ahead.

Keeping her voice down, Kate told him everything, including the cyberspace trips, choosing to put it all on the table in front of her boss—or former boss—in order to get him to help her get her son back. In return, Kate would hand Hunter enough evidence to put the conspirators behind this elusive network away for life.

"How do you know I'm not one of the bad guys?" Hunter asked, his coarse voice a mere whisper to avoid being overheard by the patrons sitting about them or the couples two-stepping across the sawdust-filmed dance floor to the tune of the band playing at one end of the rectangular hall.

"Because I have the list of everyone who has been implanted, and you're not on it," Kate replied in a low voice. "But your boss is . . . as well as his boss."

Kate had spent the hours following the kidnapping very focused, obtaining a computer from a secondhand store near the UT campus and locking herself in a motel room in south Austin while going through the external drives and flash cards that Lman had left for her, unable to read most but managing to find the list of names that Cameron had collected during the final moments prior to the security system kicking them out. But there was much, much more that she had not been able to read yet, the massive amount of information that the savvy hacker had collected, including activity logs, overseas bank accounts, tax records, and user transactions, including transcripts of the communications between the ten men known as The Circle and ANN, the master construct, the artificial intelligence engine residing in Building 33B of the GemTech campus. But she needed help to access that information.

The captain of the Rangers narrowed his gaze. "You mean DPS Director Pat Vance *and* the governor are in on this thing?"

"And several of his staff members. But those aren't even the really *big* fish."

Hunter set his beer on the counter and swung to his right to face her. "Come again?"

"Bill, you have no idea just how high this conspiracy goes," she said, before leaning closer to him and whispering a few names in his ear.

Hunter opened his eyes wide, struggling to contain his booming voice as he said, "And you have *proof* of this?"

She slowly nodded. "I have the kind of evidence that will stick in court better than bad Mexican food to your ribs. But there's one catch."

The ends of his lips curling down a trifle, Hunter said, "I was afraid you would say that. What's the catch?"

Just then the bartender raised the volume of the flat-screen television on the wall, nestled amid shelves packed with bottles and glasses. An anchorman filled the LCD screen, interrupting the ball game with a newsbreak: Air Force One had crashed over Nebraska on its way back from California, where the president had spent the week attending a world summit on the environment. Initial reports from the pilots of the escorting F-22s suggested an explosion followed by a section of the upper fuselage ripping off in what appeared to be a massive decompression.

The report cut to the crash site, a large cornfield where crews were already searching through the burning rubble for survivors. The screen then went blank for a few seconds, followed by the seal of the president of the United States and an announcement that Vice President Raymond Costa, already under presidential-like protection, was about to address the nation from the oval office.

"Oh, my God, Kate," Hunter whispered, his voice tinted with fear for the first time. "Costa . . . he's one of the. . . ."

"*Now* you believe me?" Kate replied, the shocking news somehow not upsetting her as she would had expected. In fact, in a strange way, she found relief in the knowledge that the head of the Texas Rangers was now a believer.

Silence, followed by, "Yes . . . yes, I do.

"Good. Now you can really help me bag these bastards."

"You said there was a catch?" Hunter asked.

"I messaged them an hour ago that I possess the evidence to expose them."

"You did *what?*"

"I had no choice."

"Why in the world would you do a thing like that?" he hissed. "That's telegraphing our intentions."

Kate smiled internally when Hunter said *our* intentions instead of *your* intentions. She replied, "I need them to know what it is that I have on them."

"Why?"

The presidential seal on the screen faded away, replaced by the heavily lined face of Raymond Costa under a full head of white hair sitting behind the president's desk in the oval office.

"Man, the body's not even cold," she mumbled as Costa began to address the country, calling out to all Americans to unite and stand together in this time of national tragedy while also assuring them that his first act as president would be a swift resolution to the reason behind the crash.

"Damn," Hunter said. "He sure comes across as quite the genuine, considerate, and firm leader."

"Costa's always been thought of as one of the smartest men on the planet and also quite the eloquent statesman. Now I know how he does it."

The vice president went on to describe Andrew Boyer as one of the finest leaders of his generation and also a personal friend and confidant, and how he would have liked nothing more than for America to continue on the path that his administration had set up for the coming years, continuing to forge international alliances and partnerships for the benefit of the world's growing global economy, improving education opportunities, health care, and the overall standard of living in this country.

"So, Kate," Hunter said. "Why did you feel it was important to tell them about the proof that your hacker friend helped you collect?"

"To use as a bargaining chip for the life of my son."

"You're not thinking to—"

"I've already proposed a trade, Bill. It happens in exactly thirty-six hours from now, and I need you and the rest of the Rangers to assist me. In return, you get the evidence that will make you more famous than Elvis."

Hunter stared at the television, and then at the faces sitting around the bar. He frowned at the sight of grown men with tears in their eyes as Costa delivered what would most likely be remembered as his finest speech.

Kate understood his concern. Costa was more untouchable than ever in his soon-to-be-formalized new role as commander-in-chief. What chance did the captain of the Texas Rangers have to go against not just a powerful criminal network, but one backed by the director of the DPS, the governor of Texas, and the White House?

Bastards have the state and federal law enforcement covered.

Focus!

You're not getting Cameron back if you start thinking this way.

"There's something else," she said.

Crossing his arms while sighing, Hunter said, "Yes?" as his eyes inexorably drifted from the television screen to her face.

"They think I'm still operating alone. For this to work it's imperative that they *continue* to think that way, which means you can't report this to your boss or anyone else aside from the actual guys who will be there to assist me. Otherwise you might as well assume we will walk into a trap, like it happened in Horseshoe Bay."

Frowning, keeping his arms crossed, the captain of the Texas Rangers said, "Our situation doesn't leave much room to play it by the book."

"That's the thing, Bill. The only way to win this one is to *not* play by the rules because that's precisely what they would expect me to do. And that brings me to my last two requests."

Almost laughing, Hunter said, "Go ahead, Kate, surprise me. What's next?"

"First I need you to find out if my hacker friend made it. If he has, I need you to put a couple of your best people to guard him."

"What's his name?"

Kate frowned. "I only know him as Lman."

"Lman? What kind of name's that?"

"He's a hacker, Bill. They pick weird names like that. Anyway, he was shot this morning near the UT campus by the same people who kidnapped Cameron," she said, proceeding to provide Hunter with the address of the apartment complex.

"All right. I'll make a couple of phone calls and find out. What's the other thing you need?"

"I need to find Ron Miller."

Hunter narrowed his stare. "Miller? Isn't he the guy who went after the Enron brass a couple of years ago?"

Kate slowly nodded. "He's doing time in Eastham. We need to find a way to free him."

"Why?"

Kate tapped the rucksack containing the drives and flash cards where Lman had downloaded the information on TDG's network. Her limited skills had allowed her to barely scratch the surface on the collected intelligence. It was now time to bring in the big guns.

"Lman is either dead or in intensive care," she said. "Either way he's out of commission for the immediate future. We need Miller's help. If this AI is as smart as I think it is, we will need support in cyberspace as much as in the real world in order to accomplish three key things."

"Three?" said Hunter. "The first is to get your son back. The second is to expose these bastards. What's the third?"

"We need to free some minds."

93

Cakewalk

The Citation dropped out of the sky at 480 knots, just under its maximum speed, shooting below ten thousand feet as the pilot declared a decompression emergency to Miami Control.

Savage, who had forced himself into a state of indifference when asking Ino to head back to the cabin, listened through his headset from the copilot seat, assisting the pilot with the radios through the simulated emergency procedure.

"How low, Mr. Savage?" asked the pilot, a man in his early fifties with a hard face and military-style, closely cropped blond hair.

Focusing on the task at hand, temporarily forgetting the large round eyes of the African kid he had rescued from the jungle a lifetime ago, Savage replied, "As low as you can. In a Skylane I dropped to one hundred feet and Brussels Control lost me a week and a half ago, but that was a smaller plane. Can you top that?"

"Ever flown in a navy bird at treetop at night, Mr. Savage?" he said, holding the nose-down attitude while working the throttles and the elevator trim to remove excessive pressure on the yoke.

"My apologies," Savage replied, getting the message that he was in the hands of a professional military pilot. "Just hold your lowest possible altitude until we reach the Cayman Islands," he added, well aware that their planned route would take them right between the northernmost point of Cuba and the bottom of the Florida Keys.

"A cakewalk, Mr. Savage. Neither the Cubans nor our guys will ever see us," the pilot replied as he changed the barometric pressure from 29.92 inches in the altimeter, which was standard regulations for flights above 18,000 feet, to the reported atmospheric pressure from the Miami ATIS, the recorded weather updated every hour.

Savage understood why. Each inch of atmospheric pressure in the altimeter equated to one thousand feet. If they were indeed going to use that instrument to tell them when they were below one hundred feet, the altimeter setting had to be precise.

"Citation Three Two Tango, Miami Control."

"Citation Three Two Tango, Miami Control."

Savage watched as the pilot ignored the radar controller while dropping below five thousand feet with the vertical speed indicator showing a two-thousand-feet-per-minute rate of descent, meaning they would hit the Atlantic Ocean in about two and a half minutes.

"Citation Three Two Tango, Miami Control."

The pilot used the elevator trim to decrease the angle of attack, but not by much, aware that the jet's Mode C transponder with altitude encoding was feeding Miami Control with a readout of their rapid descent. And this was the trick of the maneuver. Reduce the angle of attack too much toward the end and Miami Control could recognize the trick. Leave it steep, to convince the controllers of their emergency, and risk not being able to pull out in time.

"Citation Three Two Tango, Miami Control."

The difference between convincing Miami Control and not convincing them was that with the former, the craft dispatched their way would be a Coast Guard helicopter, slow but capable of pulling people out of the sea. The latter, however, meant F-22 interceptors would be on their tail with orders to shoot on sight.

Three thousand feet.

Two thousand.

One thousand.

The pilot added more trim and raised the nose by a few degrees.

Savage felt the mild pressure as g-forces began to accumulate on the plane.

Five hundred feet.

The pilot applied more rear pressure and the nose lifted several degrees, reducing the rate of descent to one thousand feet per minute.

"Ready, Mr. Savage?"

"On your mark," he replied, his thumb and index on the knob of the transponder radio.

Three hundred feet.

Additional trim and the rate of descent fell to three hundred feet per minute just as they dropped below two hundred feet.

"Now, Mr. Savage!"

Savage switched off the transponder, mimicking a lost transmission just as the pilot dropped the landing gear and pulled back on the yoke.

The g-forces pinned Savage into his seat as the pilot killed the descent, leveling off at fifty feet.

The turbines revving up, Savage watched the Citation's nose hoist above the horizon, above a sea of white-capped swells.

"Low enough for you, Mr. Savage?" asked the pilot, as he pulled up the landing gear, trimmed, and adjusted power.

The midsize business jet in the hands of the experienced navy pilot continued in a southwesterly heading, in a trajectory that would get them to the Cayman Islands in just under three hours. There they would pick up fuel and head north into Texas.

Satisfied that the pilot had things under control for the next few hours, Mac Savage headed for the cabin to face up to a past demon.

It was time to come clean.

94

Efficiency Factor

ANN's sensors assimilated the new information, the report from the FAA computers about the downed jet en route to Miami carrying Donald Bane and presumably also Mac Savage and Dana Kovacs.

The new information sent a wave of voltage spikes across the diamond lattice of her servers, exciting them at the digital realization of having eliminated a significant portion of the threat, including two of the humans whom the super users had been battling for nearly two weeks.

I AM MORE EFFICIENT.

The master construct adjusted its programs to accommodate the new information, issuing directives to its army of human subrogates, including Vice President Raymond Costa, scheduled to ascend to the highest office of the land before the end of the day.

95

Coming Clean

Savage stood in the aisle facing the front row of seats. Ino sat in the aisle seat to his right. Dana to his left, and Bane in the window seat.

He regarded the African kid with a strange mix of genuine

affection and overwhelming guilt. The boy was now a teenager, eighteen years old, his right arm amputated below the elbow.

Savage tried not to stare at it, but his eyes would not obey him. Glancing down, he remembered the blood, the exposed bone, the charred skin, the agonized face, and the pleading eyes—the same eyes that now regarded him with admiration.

"It *is* you," Ino said, his eyes filmed with tears. "The soldier in the jungle who rescued Ino." Beyond him Savage could see the rough sea through the oval window.

"You're right, kid," Savage said, growing uncomfortable, arms by his sides. "I'm the one who pulled you out of that destroyed refugee camp."

The African boy leaned forward in his seat and hugged Savage's right arm while saying, "Ino will never forget what mister did. Mister saved Ino's life."

Savage closed his eyes, the images flooding him once again, the cries in the dark, the maimed bodies, the smell of burnt skin—the apocalyptic scenes that dominated his nightmares since that terrible night.

Since that mistake.

He often wondered how long he would endure the demons that came out at night to torture him, to remind him of this sin, which no amount of therapy, from the extensive list of Agency psychiatrists, could eradicate.

What about coming clean?

What about telling the truth?

Would that help get rid of the flashbacks? Of the nightmares? Of the guilt of having become the same kind of monster who killed my parents?

Was Ino's presence here perhaps some sort of divine intervention? Perhaps a once-in-a-lifetime opportunity to staunch the loss of sanity from Savage's ravaged mind? Maybe a chance to redeem himself?

Come clean, Mac.

It's the only way to stop the nightmares.

"Listen, kid," he said. "I'm really sorry about what happened out there . . . about the whole damned thing. It was my fault."

Ino frowned, his facial scars shifting, the remains from the minor burns he had endured during the raid. He slowly shook his head, still holding Savage's arm as he said, "Ino don't understand. Why was it mister's fault?"

"There's something you should know," Savage said, "and in doing so I'm violating a dozen CIA regulations, but I don't think it matters anymore." Savage looked at Dana, who was giving him a very concerned stare of narrowed eyes, before his gaze landed on Bane, his trainer, his mentor, the man who taught him everything he knew about being a spy.

"Nope," Bane said. "It sure doesn't look like it matters anymore."

Dana said, "What are you guys talking about?"

His back against the door leading to the cockpit, Savage looked down the cabin. Barnes and the other two CIA officers were sleeping.

"I'm responsible for what happened at that refugee camp," he finally said to his audience of three.

"What do you mean, Mac?"

"The destruction of that UNICEF camp. It was a CIA mistake."

Dana shook her head, and so did Ino, who also let go of his arm.

"Ino is confused."

"It doesn't make sense, Mac," she said. "The government issued a report blaming the attack on RUF guerrillas. You told me so yourself a week ago."

"I'm a spook, Dana, and spooks lie for a living. I told you what I had been trained to tell."

He paused, then added, "The truth is that I screwed up out there. I mistook Ino's UNICEF refuge camp for an RUF stronghold a few kilometers away."

"You say that Ino's father was killed because of mister's mistake? That Ino was maimed because mister thought that refugee camp was RUF camp?" His eyes glistened with tears.

"That's *precisely* what I'm saying, Ino," said Savage. "I was a CIA scout sent to track down and destroy the RUF camp north of Gokalima, but a series of mistakes, from satellite recon to field reports, got the RUF stronghold mixed up with a UNICEF camp. By the time we realized the error the bombs had already gone off, the camp had been destroyed. So I did the only thing I could: I took those who were still alive with me. Unfortunately, everyone died during the trip back, except for you."

There was a pause as Ino internalized what Savage had just said. Then, as Savage had expected, emotions got the better of the teenager.

"How could mister do this?" Ino asked, standing up, his face tight, a vein throbbing across his temple. "How could mister possibly mistake a UNICEF camp with an RUF base?"

Savage frowned and inhaled deeply. "I'm so sorry, Ino. I wish I could take it back, but I can't. Now I have to live with it."

"And Ino has to live without a father! And with this!" he shouted, startling Savage, pointing at his maimed arm.

Barnes opened his eyes, dropping his brows at the screaming. The two younger officers behind him also woke up from the screaming, stretching their necks to see what was happening.

"Ino now has to live with this! Damn! Damn!" he repeated, before running to the back of the plane, locking himself in the lavatory, leaving Savage standing there feeling like the largest jerk in the world.

Dana turned to Bane. "Is this true?"

Bane sighed and slowly nodded. "Not one of our finest moments, and Mac isn't the one to blame. We sent him there with bad intel to use a laser to paint the center of the camp for the stealth bombers' guided munitions. It was an Agency mistake."

Turning to Savage, she said, "Mac . . . why would you ever want to tell him something like that? It isn't going to bring his father back."

He didn't know how to respond to that.

"He was finally happy, adjusted."

"Dana, I—"

"You say that you're a spook, you know . . . *trained* to lie?"

Savage frowned and gave her a slight but embarrassed nod.

"Well, Mac, this was one time when *lying* may have been better than the truth.

"I . . . I figured he deserved the truth after what he did for us."

"Damn, Mac. Damn," she said, getting up. "Damn you and your damned lies." She ran after Ino.

"Mac, Mac, Mac," said Donald Bane. "This is precisely what happens when we tell the truth. People get hurt."

Savage frowned and shrugged.

"What in the world ever possessed you to come clean? You like that girl that much?"

As he watched Dana in the rear knocking on the lavatory door, Savage exhaled heavily, remembering his parents, their charred and twisted bodies.

Just like Ino's dad that night.

"Mac? Are you okay, pal?"

Savage looked into his former mentor's eyes, then said, "I'm going to check up on the pilot."

96

Hacker of Hackers

Kate Chavez sat on one side of the square stainless steel table bolted to the floor of one of the private visitor's rooms at Eastham State Prison outside Houston.

Across from her sat a short, thin, blond man in his late thirties with a three-day stubble and very light hazel eyes behind a pair of round wire-framed glasses. He sat calmly, cuffed wrists on the table secured with a chain to a metal loop. His chair was bolted to the floor, and he had been strapped to the chair by the two oversized guards who now waited outside along with Bill Hunter, who knew the warden personally.

Miller resembled more a nerdy kid than a former professor of computer engineering from Rice. His boyish look, however, was broken up by the heavy lines around his eyes and forehead, and by a couple of bruises on his right cheek and another one on his neck. His lower lip was slightly swollen from what Kate guessed had been a recent prison beating.

He had listened with eerie calm as Kate went through her story, including the part when Lman was seriously wounded and her son kidnapped. Fortunately, Lman had survived the four-hour-long emergency operation and had also made it out of intensive care at Seton Medical Center in north Austin, where he was being guarded by two of Hunter's best deputies.

Kate chose to omit the names of the ten super users for the time being, something Hunter and she had also not revealed to the warden.

She finished with a request for assistance in order to get her son back and also take down this conspiracy.

Miller continued to stare at her just as he had done during her ten-minute speech. The hacker had actually not said a single word to her since he was ushered here, silently complying with the guards' orders and nodding politely to Kate when introduced by the warden.

"A fascinating story, Miss Chavez," he finally said in a heavy British accent, his nostrils flaring a bit as he spoke. Crow's feet materialized at the corners of his eyes as he narrowed his stare halfway while adding, "But I fail to see what's in it for me, especially when I would be putting my life at risk. Look what happened to Larry."

"Larry?"

"Larry Hallman . . . you know that's his real name, right?"
Kate nodded, remembering the brief from Hunter during

their two-hour drive down from Austin. A quick fingerprint-
ing by one of his deputies at Seton had revealed that Lman's
real name was Larry Francis Hallman, a native of Dallas.
For the time being Hunter had made the call not to reveal
that information to anyone, including Lman's parents who
still lived in Dallas.

"You will not be taking any more risks than what you're
taking now, Dr. Miller. And there will be no more beatings.
No more sexual abuse. No more mental abuse. You get to go
home and tinker with your computers as long as you keep it
legal."

"Just like that?"

Kate slowly nodded.

"Interesting loophole in the American justice system."

"Still the best in the world."

"Considering that this is the same justice system that let
those Enron crooks go free after they screwed their employees to the wall, and further taking into consideration that this
same system sent me to jail when I took that stolen money
and gave it back to the employees, I find myself not sharing
your high opinion about the state of our American judicial
process. Now you are adding insult to injury by telling me
that all of my sins would be immediately forgotten if I help
you take down a criminal network. Did I get it right?"

Kate slowly bobbed her head once without breaking eye
contact.

"Why, then, may I ask, do you need my help? Doesn't the
government keep enough high-tech crime fighters on its pay-
roll? Why not use them and then apply the same public prosecution system to send them to this all-inclusive romantic
destination?"

The warden had warned her about Miller's stubbornness,
even when presented with a way out of this hellhole. The
man was a true crusader, an idealist, a believer in doing the
right thing irrespective of the personal cost, of the terrible
pain inflicted on him day after day and night after night by
the gigantic inmates housed beyond these concrete walls.

"The system isn't perfect, Dr. Miller. But it is about to get
a hell of a lot worse in the cold hands of this artificial intel-

ligence system. This digital monster living at the heart of the GemTech campus in Austin is protected by an army of human subordinates—slaves, really—kept under its total control through a real-life version of the Jedi triek from *Star Wars*. It controls their minds through brain implants, and its list includes very powerful people in business *and* in our government. We have to take it down and in the process free those minds. Lman told me that true hackers live and die doing the right thing. He believed in my cause enough to be willing to die for it, and in fact he came pretty damned close to paying that ultimate price. Thanks to God and modern medicine, it appears that he's going to pull through. He can't help us at the moment, but he recommended you. So my question is: Are you willing to stand up and do the right thing, irrespective of the consequences it may bring to you, good or bad?"

The hacker of hackers turned up his palms as much as the handcuffs allowed him. "Miss Chavez, part of my sentence included no Internet access. I've been offline for two years, an eternity in my former business."

Kate sat back, crossed her arms, and said, "If you are indeed *anywhere* near as good as Lman claims you are, I know you have found a way to . . . keep up. The warden tells me there's a computer lab in this joint for the inmates. Somehow I get this strange little feeling that over the course of the past two years you've managed somehow to take advantage of that resource."

Miller dropped his hands on the table and looked away.

"Lman told me once that a hacker will always be a hacker, and he also said that you were the best, not just in skills and the desire for a new challenge, but also in ideology. Well . . . I have here the *biggest* challenge of them all, something that will require an unmatched level of skill, plus a desire to do the right thing. And if you go the distance, you gain your freedom."

Dr. Ron Miller, his lips pressed together, his hands clasped, was looking past Kate through his wire-rimmed glasses, which looked as frail as he did. Kate could not even begin to imagine the things he had had to do to coexist this long with men three times his size. And even after all of that, he still had plenty of composure, of self-control, at least on the surface.

He's a tough cookie, she thought while also realizing that every person has his or her limits.

Miller stared long and hard at the square patch of blue sky beyond the single bullet-resistant window in the visitor's room, tears forming in his eyes. "Freedom?" he mumbled.

"That's the offer on the table."

Miller nodded to himself, his blue eyes once more drifting to the small window before focusing on Kate as he said, "And it's all in the clear with the warden?"

"It's all been arranged. The warden is speaking to your attorney right outside the door. The state of Texas is pulling in your first parole hearing by three years because of your unusually good behavior. You will be out this afternoon."

"Provided I help you first."

Standing, Kate said, "That's the deal. So, Doctor Miller. How about it? Are you in?"

97

A Spook in Paradise

Savage stood on a lookout point at the edge of the General Aviation ramp at Owen Roberts Airport in Grand Cayman, where they had arrived thirty minutes ago to refuel.

The Caribbean turquoise waters extended as far as he could see, dotted with boats of all sizes, from cruise ships to private sailboats.

All enjoying another day in paradise.

Savage frowned, the reality of his situation preventing

him from enjoying the view beyond the chain-link fence surrounding the field.

He felt someone behind him and turned around.

Dana Kovacs stood there dressed in a pair of jeans, a T-shirt, and sneakers. "Hey," she said, walking up to him and facing the sea, the warm Caribbean breeze swirling her short blond hair.

"Hey," he replied, hesitantly locking eyes with her, not certain what he would see in them.

Dana had spent the balance of the three-hour trip in the rear of the plane, thirty minutes convincing Ino to come out of the lavatory, and the rest consoling him as the teenager cried. Bane had told Savage shortly before landing that he had made a couple of calls, and Ino would remain on this island for the time being. An unmarked sedan had come to take him away to a relocation center, where Bane's local contacts would fix his papers so he could work here while also attending the local university.

"I'm sorry about Ino," he said, tensing for another reprimand.

"Ino will be all right, Mac. He's a survivor, and he will do fine on this island, thanks to the CIA. He's just pissed at you—and at himself for having held you in such high regard all these years."

Savage nodded.

"It's kind of poetic, though," she added, "that the same agency who screwed up his life is now fixing it, giving him a chance."

"Look, Dana, I—"

"Hush," she said, putting a finger over his lips. "Bane told me how you disobeyed a direct CIA order."

"The CIA tried to kill me," he said. "I think they won't mind that I revealed a few details of a three-year-old mission."

She looked at him with those incredible round brown eyes, her lips twisting into a sly grin. "That's not what I meant, silly," she said. "I'm talking about back at the UNICEF camp. The CIA instructed you to depart the area immediately following the strike, once you declared it a mistake. But you didn't."

Savage looked away, remembering.

"But they are children!" he had shouted while kneeling by the closest boy. *"We did this! We have to fix it!"*

"Return to base, Golf Three. We can't be seen near that."

"But they will die! They will—"

"RTB immediately, Golf Three. That's an order. Expect evac at Charlie Point at zero five three zero Zulu. Over and out."

Savage closed his eyes, trying to shut out the images, the voices.

"I couldn't just leave them there," he finally said, staring at her. "Not after I heard the screams . . . the cries. I had to do what I had to do."

She took his hand, which surprised him because he thought she was through with him after this revelation.

"What you did in that plane took guts, Mac. Ino does appreciate knowing the truth, even if he doesn't realize it at the moment."

Savage shrugged.

"But what you did back in the jungle, after realizing the mistake . . . that tells me that you are not a monster, Mac Savage. It tells me you have always been the decent human being that I thought you were, and that is very important at the moment."

"Wh—why?" he asked testily.

"Mac, you idiot . . . you're *supposed* to be the spy, the know-it-all, but I'll spell it out for you: it's damned important that you are not a monster because . . . because I have *fallen* for you."

Taken aback, Savage just mumbled, "Dana, I—"

"Hush," she said, again tapping his lips with a finger. "Just hold me, would you?"

Savage did as he was told, embracing her, hugging her as he had never hugged anyone in his life.

Dana pulled away abruptly and clasped his face in her hands, her eyes an inch from his before saying, "But let's get one thing straight: don't *ever* lie to me again. Clear?"

"Crystal," he replied.

"Good. Now, tell me, do you think this plan of yours is going to work?"

Savage had used the fact that both Bane and FBI Director Bruno Palermo were at odds with Raymond Costa in order to work out a plan to secure covert FBI assistance in Texas.

"It could work," he finally said, trying to believe his own words. "The trick is doing it without alerting the enemy. Do you think your contact inside GemTech will be able to pull off his end of this deal?"

"He's the best," she replied. "What better person to trick this AI than the one who created it?"

"Then I think we have a chance."

As he held the woman he loved while standing in this hill overlooking paradise, Savage remembered the old adage from Langley: Missions seldom went as planned.

98

Home on the Range

They arrived one by one at a nondescript house in south Austin wearing civilian clothes, their steel stares, leathery faces, weathered boots, and holstered sidearms signaling their common profession, their membership in an elite and very unique arm of law enforcement: the Texas Rangers, the lone-wolf cops of the Lone Star State.

But tonight the Rangers weren't operating alone. Tonight they were gathering as a team—as a pack—to help a fellow Ranger in distress while also bringing down a criminal network whose tentacles extended beyond their beloved state, reaching the highest office of the land.

In all, seventeen of the most seasoned Rangers crowded the living room of Bill Hunter's place, some from as far as El Paso, Amarillo, and Midland, arriving here in their pickup trucks after driving nonstop for hours, dropping their current cases when called upon by their boss to fulfill their most sacred vow, to uphold the law, to shine the light of justice on those who believed themselves above the law.

Kate Chavez sat on one of a half-dozen lawn chairs Hunter had dragged in for this impromptu meeting, her eyes inspecting the determination in the faces, in the eyes. She had worked with all of them over the course of her twenty years on the force, and that had been one of the prerequisites before contacting them—in addition to none of them being on the black list from Lman's computer download.

In the dining room sat the young Dr. Ron Miller, the only non-Ranger this evening, a man whom Hunter had signed out of prison while his warden colleague gathered all the required paperwork with Miller's attorney to accelerate the parole hearing, but without going on line, to avoid alerting the AI at the heart of TDG of the plan underway.

If the hacker of hackers, currently toying with a laptop interfaced to Hunter's wireless Internet service, managed to pull off his end of the deal, Hunter would drive him back to Eastman in a few days for a parole hearing that would result in his legal release from the Texas state prison system. But first the hacker had to deliver the goods.

"Gentlemen, thank you for coming so quickly," she began, believing she had the cyberspace angle covered with Miller, freeing her to focus on the real-world aspect of this operation. "In less than ten hours I will be making an exchange of computer hardware for my son, Cameron, who has been kidnapped by this criminal network. You are here today because we need to find a way to not only get my son back but also crack down this illegal circle, which operates freely in both the real world and the cyberworld under the control of the most advanced computer system on the planet. In order to defeat it, we must also operate in both worlds simultaneously and under extreme coordination. Our job is to handle the real world. To assist us in cyberspace let me introduce you to Dr. Ron Miller, one of the finest computer gurus in the business."

Kate stretched a thumb over her right shoulder, pointing at Miller in the dining room.

The Rangers looked in his direction before returning their hard stares at her.

She considered her next words very carefully. The men in front of her all had families. Some were even grandparents. She had to deliver a sobering message to make sure they all knew what they were getting into by helping her.

Standing, she said, "All right, before I go on, I need to level with you and tell you something neither Hunter nor I could discuss over the phone. I want to make you *brutally* aware that by helping me tonight you and your families could become targets, just as mine did. These bastards killed my ex-husband and kidnapped my boy. They've also killed Ray Dalton and seriously wounded a hacker by the name of Lman who was assisting me for a couple of days."

She paused to let that sink in before adding, "At this point you still have a choice. You can walk away, and neither I nor anyone else would blame you for doing so. In my twenty years with the Rangers I have seen some shit, but I have *never* encountered a more vicious, violent, brilliant, and well-connected criminal network. These bastards are brutal in their tactics and basically suicidal in their convictions. Ray Dalton tried to warn me and I wouldn't listen. So the least I can do is also warn you and then let you make your choice. They will kill you if you get careless or unlucky, and they will also go after your families. So, if anyone wants out, this is the time to do it. There's the door."

Kate sat back down, her gaze shifting among her captive audience.

One of the Rangers raised his hand, a tall man well into his fifties with a barrel chest, huge arms, legs, and neck, and an equally intimidating revolver hanging by his side, like an Old West gunslinger. His name was Robert Stone, and the man looked like he ate stones in his cereal.

"Yes, Bob," said Kate, who had worked with this legend from El Paso on a case that overlapped jurisdictions several years ago.

"Kate," he began in a voice like sandpaper, "people fuck with the cops and get away with it. People screw with the damned Feds and even the spooks and get away with it. Hell, people even fuck with the damned military and get away with it. But I tell you here and now that no one, and I mean *no one*, fucks with the Rangers and lives to tell. I'm in, Kate, and I also know that so is everyone else in this room."

Kate took a deep breath and stared at Stone before shifting her gaze to everyone else in the room, the resolution in their eyes conveying their unyielding determination, displaying more guts than a slaughterhouse floor.

"Now," added Stone. "What is it that you need us to do?"

99

Trail's End

The interior of the FBI surveillance SUV resembled something out of a sci-fi movie, with 12 LCD monitors arranged in a four-by-three mosaic covering an entire wall of the windowless mobile control center. Ten micro servers lined up on the wall opposite the monitors, leaving a three-foot alley down the middle of the surveillance vehicle. Very thin computer boards, micro blades, packing the latest-generation of low-power microprocessors and memory, slid horizontally into the server chassis to provide immense amounts of computer muscle in a very small package—ideal for mobile operations.

And all of the hardware was interfaced to hidden antennas on the roof—from satellite receivers to infrared detectors—beneath the skin of the modified Ford Excursion parked atop a hill high above Highway 71 as it projected west of Austin, through the Texas hill country. The location was secluded, nondescript, quiet, and most important, it provided a perfect line of sight to the GemTech campus stretching north of the east-west highway, its clearly marked electric fence disappearing into the distance.

"We don't have much time," said Bane, checking his watch, to Dana, who sat next to a technical agent from the San Antonio FBI Office.

They had reached nearby Austin's low-profile Lakeway Airport six hours ago and Bane had made a single call to FBI Director Bruno Palermo's personal mobile phone. Savage never knew what Bane and Palermo discussed, especially in light of the standing orders to bring the elusive DCI into custody, but within the hour a pair of unmarked sedans had picked them up and delivered them to this van. Palermo had agreed to give his old associate forty-eight hours to continue his investigation while keeping it from getting reported up the chain to the White House. Raymond Costa, to be sworn in as the nation's forty-sixth president this afternoon, had instructed the FBI and the Office of Homeland Security to be on the lookout for the possibility that Bane's jet had not actually crashed in the Atlantic.

Dana glanced at the letters FBI stenciled above the front left pocket of FBI Agent Johnny Pham, who worked one of three keyboards while she typed on the second one to his left as they approached the firewall of the TDG network.

Savage stood in the narrow walkway behind a junior agent assisting Pham this afternoon. The rookie Fed, a blond kid with a soft face and even softer hands, worked the joystick controlling the directional antenna of the TEMPEST system, designed to blast electromagnetic energy through a narrow beam at line-of-sight distances.

"No VR hardware, huh?" Dana asked Agent Pham, a second generation Vietnamese computer whiz snagged by the Bureau right out of MIT eight years ago as part of the White House's efforts to inject this branch of the government's high-tech crime unit with top-notch talent. Unfortunately, the new administration under Boyer and Costa had trimmed back such high-tech investment in an attempt to reduce the huge federal deficit created by their predecessors during the first decade of the new millennium.

"Nope," said Pham in his nasal voice while studying his screen through the thick glasses perched on his nose. "I've never been a fan of VR. Too dangerous. Although they do provide more operational flexibility than just keyboarding, I'd rather have the LCDs take the brunt of an attack than my brain, especially when breaching firewalls. And besides, our budget got slashed, forcing us to spend the dough on the stuff that really matters to catch hackers."

Good point, Dana thought, remembering her close call in Freetown.

The agent continued to maneuver the probe, leaping from ISP to ISP, observing the fiery shell of the GemTech network, getting as close as she recommended before entering a holding pattern.

"All right, Miss Kovacs," said Pham. "Let's see if your friend inside is awake."

A single nod by Pham and his junior assistant finished aiming the TEMPEST antenna and fired the beam toward the side of Building 33B.

The picture of the scorching surface of the GemTech firewall displayed on the two center LCDs of the four-by-three stack changed from bright crimson to orange with blue spots.

"Good morning!" said Pham as the powerful beam probed deep into the server network, supercharging the local area network. "All right, Miss Kovacs. Start typing and also start praying that your friend on the inside will be ready to listen and to act quickly."

100

Cyber Sheep

Dr. Miles Talbot was amazed at the power and insight of this monster he had created. ANN's influence continued to grow as it learned without any restrictions, driving its army of human sheep to do just as it wished.

Talbot sat back in awe, arms crossed as the images on his screen displayed the various video feeds from the GemTech campus as well as Web cams from other geographical locations, which he could now access thanks to his root password.

Look at them, he thought, watching video after video of controlled and organized human behavior across many disciplines, from the local security guards and technical staff to worldwide sales and marketing, to the many wholly owned subsidiaries across the globe, including the World Missionary Fellowship, where Keith Gardiol continued to run the illegal diamond operation.

There's so many of them, he reflected. From politicians to members of the various armed forces, to university teachers, engineers, doctors, lawyers, bankers, retailers, commercial pilots, college students, housewives, police officers, and even truck drivers—all going about their daily lives as if nothing had gone wrong, but no longer in possession of their will or their bodies. ANN controlled all of that now, like an AI god guiding its sheep, unseen but overarching, feeding them their lines, their thoughts, their reasoning, and in many cases leading them to more productive lives. In the few days since the master construct had taken over their minds, over half of the captured humans had already showed improved work habits, better personal relationships. ANN even had them going to church and volunteering for social work, turning her army of humans into model citizens while deploying her recruiters, led by Frank Salieri, to enroll more implant users, expanding TDG's sphere of influence. And above all of that hovered the powerful super users, for whom ANN was dedicating significant resources to keep the likes of Raymond Costa assuming power and soon dictating policy that would further benefit TDG, that would allow them to expand their domestic and international grip.

But the harmony had been disrupted thirty-six hours ago, during the hacker attack, when someone named Kate Chavez had downloaded enough data from the network to put everyone away for life, including the ten super users.

Chavez, who Talbot later learned was a Texas Ranger, was willing to make a trade: the data for the life of her son, currently in custody of TDG guards in Building 18A. An exchange had been set for noon tomorrow in the crowded grounds of the Texas Livestock Show and Rodeo east of Austin.

And just as ANN had nearly completed all of the required coordination to set up that exchange, an unknown energy source struck with incredible power, breaching the server room a minute ago, injecting a surge of electrons into the lattice of the diamond circuitry, spreading chaos amid the predictable calmness of the past few days.

What in the hell is that? he thought as ANN triggered thousands of actions to counter the random voltage swings of the energy source, as the master construct directed the local staff to swarm the networks, to reinforce the magnetic shields, to dampen the effect of this invisible but very real attack. Dr. Talbot, the only human not under the digital spell of the AI, noticed that embedded in the intrusive beam of energy was a message, words encrypted in a way he had not seen since his days with Diamantex.

Since the security programs of Dana Kovacs.

Dana?

Talbot leaned forward in his chair, his eyes taking in the energy pattern browsing across his screen, noticing the stream of jumbled letters that kept repeating itself every fifteen seconds.

Amazing.

As the TDG's firewall held in place resisting the powerful binary attack, Talbot clicked his way into one of his old directories containing the files he had brought with him from the Diamantex breakup, the routines that Dana had created to encrypt internal company communications to prevent spies from stealing their secrets.

Activating the old decoder programs, Talbot launched them into the energy beam. A moment later the encryptor translators released the repeated code.

DR. MILES TALBOT. THIS IS DANA. I HAVE THE FBI AND THE CIA WITH ME. I NEED YOUR HELP TO GET INSIDE THE SYSTEM AND OBTAIN PROOF, EVIDENCE. CAN YOU HELP ME?

101

Proof

Mac Savage stood next to Bane as they waited for a response to Dana's query.

"How do you know he's going to recognize what you're doing?" Savage asked, tension stabbing him between his shoulder blades. He lifted his shoulders a bit while exhaling, glancing over at Bane, who looked like Savage felt: weathered down, at the end of the line.

"The beam is laced with an encrypted signature that only Talbot would pick up. He'll recognize it if he is watching."

"There," said Agent Pham, stretching an index finger at one of the LCD screens.

DANA, MILES HERE. GOT YOUR QUERY. UNFORTUNATELY, THE FIREWALL WILL NOT PERMIT DATA OUT OF THE SECURED NETWORK.

Dana looked over her right shoulder at Savage and Bane.

"Doesn't look good," observed the DCI as Savage crossed his arms. "Now what?"

Dana returned to the keyboard and typed, IS THERE ANY OTHER WAY TO GET PROOF?

Her software encrypted the message the moment she pressed the ENTER key, injecting it into the beam.

A moment later a second reply came.

THERE IS ANOTHER WAY.

102

Hardware

The hill country east of the Texas capital came alive under a sea of stars when the Austin Livestock Show and Rodeo kicked into full swing as the sun went down. Red, white, and blue lights outlining a massive Ferris wheel cast a glow on the carnival surrounding the enclosed arena, where cowboys from as far as Australia and Canada competed with American stars from Texas, Utah, Colorado, Wyoming, Nevada, and a half dozen other states on several events, from saddle bronco riding to barrel racing.

College kids, couples, and families swarmed the alleys of the carnival, riding the Octopus, the Tilt-a-Whirl, the Casino, the Paratrooper, and many other rides. Men lined up in front of the High Striker for their chance to show their strength to girlfriends or wives. Neck veins throbbing, they clutched the massive hammer, swinging over their heads, and striking the peg with all their might as the beer flowed, as vendors sold thousands of turkey legs, pretzels, and hot dogs to a river of patrons crowding every aisle of the event.

And Kate Chavez merged with this crowd, just another

face among thousands this evening, dressed in a pair of black jeans, a long-sleeve denim shirt, a black belt with an oversized silver and turquoise buckle, black boots, and a tan and black felt cowboy hat. Lman's rucksack hung from her left shoulder, housing her Desert Eagle and a sample of the drives and flash cards that the hacker had used to download the evidence she was using as her bargaining chip to get her son back. Deep in her left ear canal, Kate wore a tiny earpiece, a receiver that kept her in communication with Hunter and his selected team of Texas Rangers blended with the crowd, including two of them posted up by the arena with a clear line of sight to the carnival below. One of the buttons of her shirt was a microphone, capable of picking up surrounding conversation.

"Here we go, Bill," she said, walking past concession stands, booths of fortune tellers, people lined up to throw basketballs at small hoops for the chance to win cheap stuffed animals, and an array of kids' rides, from bumper cars and a small roller coaster to a six-rider Ferris wheel.

"We're standing by," replied Hunter, who had deployed his limited team around the area to cover access points around the grounds in search of anyone resembling her son. *"We'll move in on your signal."*

Kate ignored the screams, the laughs, the lively conversation around her mixed with the country and western tunes from a band playing at the outdoor stage set up between the carnival and the arena, where a few hundred people stood enjoying the music and drinking beer before the first event of the evening started in another fifteen minutes.

Fifteen minutes.

Kate checked her watch again and proceeded toward the rendezvous point halfway down one of the two long alleys of games and fun, the smell of cotton candy and funnel cakes tingling her nostrils, mixing with the smoke from the diesel generators powering the mobile rides.

Fear coiling in her stomach, tension pinching her in between her shoulder blades, her hands clammy, she pressed on, approaching the location she had emailed to the TDG network.

"Target at your eleven o'clock, Kate. Looks like Salieri and Cameron," reported Hunter from his vantage point.

And there they were, in the exact spot she had selected and at the precise time she had requested. Cameron stood next to the GemTech executive, both dressed in the casual clothes of the average rodeo visitor, in an almost surreal way resembling father and son.

But the image of her ex-husband bleeding in front of his house washed away the thought.

Standing next to her son wasn't even a real person. The body of Frank Salieri was there all right, but she knew quite well his mind wasn't, as telegraphed by the steely glare in his brown eyes. ANN, the AI, was still in command of the operation, meaning Ron Miller had not yet managed to work his magic.

Don't take too long, pal, she thought, mustering every last ounce of discipline to stick to her script, to follow the plan she had worked out with Hunter and the master hacker yesterday.

The life of her son depended on it.

"Easy now, Kate," added Hunter. *"Stick to the plan."*

But as she approached them, as she neared her son, rather than seeing Cameron's eyes filled with the same emotionally charged anticipation that she fought to keep from surfacing, Kate Chavez saw another set of stolid eyes glaring back at her.

The eyes of the machine.

No!

"Hello, Miss Chavez," Salieri said, smiling, a cone of strawberry ice cream in his right hand, matching Cameron's. "It's good seeing you again."

Kate started to get light-headed at the realization of what they had done to her son. Cameron lowered his gaze to his own ice cream, which he lapped quietly, almost like a dog.

Her legs failing, Kate dropped to her knees in front of him, her hands clutching his shoulders. "Cameron! It's me! Your mom! I'm here, my baby!"

"Kate? What are you doing?" Hunter asked.

The teenager didn't even flinch, keeping his head down, licking the strawberry ice scream.

"Cameron! Look at me!"

Then very slowly, Cameron raised his gaze, gave her an eerie leer, and said, "Hello, Miss Chavez. Did you bring the package?"

Breathing deeply as she let go of him, Kate forced herself back up, staring at Salieri even though either of them would provide her with the same answer.

"What . . . have you done to him?"

"A simple procedure to insure your cooperation."

"What's wrong with Cameron. Kate? What is he talking about?" demanded Hunter.

"You fucking bastard!" she hissed, catching the attention of a mother holding the hand of a toddler. She frowned at Kate before walking away. Lowering her voice, Kate added, "You stuck one of those fucking implants in his head!"

"Your son's mind is quite safe, Miss Chavez. I assure you. You hold your end of the deal and we will hold ours."

"Kate, listen up. Stay cool and think this through," advised Hunter. *"We've heard everything. One of my guys is on the phone with Miller right now bringing him up to date. Just play along. We'll get you through this."*

Kate controlled her breathing, certain that Salieri had brought many of his guns with him, though so had she, but given what she had just realized, she had to feign cooperation in order to buy Miller the time he would need to use Lman's data to strike back and gain control of the AI.

"I have held my end," she said, patting the canvas bag. "It's all in here." She opened the rucksack and produced one of the portable drives. "See?"

Salieri grinned and tilted his head. "Miss Chavez. Please. You didn't really believe that we would hand your son over to you without first verifying what's in that hardware?"

Kate put the drive away, leaving her hand inside the sack, fingers clutching around the handle of her Magnum.

"You are showing us hardware, Miss Chavez. And in return we are also showing you hardware. We will release the software—your son's mind—when we are convinced of the data stored in yours, and of your true intentions."

Three cowboys approached them, all wearing Western denim jerseys, beneath which Kate knew would be holstered weapons. Their impassive eyes reflected their state of mind.

"Come now," Salieri said. "We have a car waiting for us."

"And if I refuse to go with you?" she asked, testing options.

"Your son will be lobotomized on demand. All it will take is a few seconds and his mind will be erased forever."

Kate handed over the rucksack to one of Salieri's escorts without further argument, realizing that it was now all up to Miller. Hunter and his Rangers could not help her now, and she made sure of that by briefly touching the top of her head, signaling them to keep their distance.

103

Plan B

"Are you sure that's Frank Salieri?" asked Mac Savage, dressed like a cowboy, including the hat, which he used to cast a shadow across his features from the overhead lights. Dana and Bane stood by him next to a concession stand, dressed similarly. Bane held a turkey leg, Dana a can of diet soda as their target walked by a couple dozen feet away.

"You never forget the face of the man who bankrupted you and caused your spouse to commit suicide," she replied, taking a sip of her drink before adding, "That's definitely the bastard."

"And that must be Kate Chavez and her son," said Savage, remembering what Dr. Talbot had told them during their on-line chat. "If Talbot's right, the kid is also wearing an implant, meaning he's under the machine's control like the rest of them."

Bane brought a finger to his right ear, listening to the FBI team in the van, which they had parked at the top of a hill overlooking the grounds, using their surveillance gear to eavesdrop on their conversation.

"The proof that Talbot mentioned apparently is in that rucksack, and the team also got confirmation that the boy has been implanted."

Dana sighed and said, "And that means they will turn him into a vegetable unless she cooperates. Where are they going? I thought this was going to be a trade. The goods for the boy."

Bane shook his head. "The team couldn't pick up that part of the conversation."

Savage frowned, well aware that these exchanges seldom went as planned. He had hoped for a clean swap, getting mother and child out of harm's way before moving in on Salieri and grabbing the—

Cameron, walking next to Salieri, turned his head abruptly in their direction, making eye contact with Dana Kovacs and Mac Savage, grinning.

"Crap," said Dana just as Salieri also looked their way.

"We've been burned," said Savage just as two of the escorts made a right turn and moved in on them while reaching inside their jersey jackets.

Instincts overcame surprise, making Savage pivot on his left leg while reaching for Dana, pushing her behind the concession stand as he reached for his holstered 9mm and Bane also grabbed his semiautomatic.

The reports echoed across the carnival as Salieri's men, presumably under the control of the AI, opened fire on them, covering the getaway of their superior.

"Plan B, Mac!" screamed Dana as the gunfire panicked the crowd. "We need Plan B now!"

104

Unexpected Assistance

Kate Chavez watched helplessly as two of Salieri's men turned on three strangers by a concession stand, two men and a woman. The men had reacted like professionals, drawing their weapons while protecting the woman, disappearing behind the food stands.

Who are they?

As the thought entered her mind, she recognized one of them, the man whose images she had seen during that initial cyber visit at the Driskill Hotel.

Mac Savage.

But I thought he was in Belgium.

What's he doing here?

But she could not help them, not while the AI had Cameron's mind under its control, not when the machine could turn her son into a vegetable.

The staccato gunfire rumbled as the visitors scrambled for safety, stampeding down the alleys away from the two shooters, creating a wall of humanity between them and the people they had spotted.

Several men rushed toward Salieri, Cameron, and her, creating a human shield around them, protecting them from the panicked visitors while ushering them in the direction of the parking lot. In total the GemTech executive had ten men protecting them, two providing covering fire and eight more acting as a line of scrimmage, shoving visitors out of the way, clearing the path for their boss and his two guests.

She watched in near awe at their coordination, at the way in which they worked the crowd, never drawing attention to themselves but forcing their human wedge through the mass of people.

Stay with me, Bill, but don't come near, she thought, unable to speak into her mike for fear of these smart creatures hearing her. Kate could not take any chances.

105

TEMPEST Time

The two escorts fired twice more at them before joining the rushing crowd, vanishing from view after having created the required distraction.

Savage held Dana's hand as they stepped around the concession stand, watching the explosive exodus. Mothers held their babies; husbands shielded their wives; children cried; adults shouted as everyone ran from the carnival grounds

"Now, Pham!" shouted Dana, using Savage's mike. "Do it now!"

106

"All teams have lost *line of sight. Too many people. We've lost line of sight with you,"* Kate heard Hunter say through her hidden ear piece, feeling out of control as her party punched through the wall of people, ushering her and Cameron toward three black SUVs at the south end of the parking lot.

The crowd finally thinned as the mind-controlled humans, moving with uncanny efficiency, rushed away from the origin of the shots. Police officers ran in the direction opposite the crowd, toward the middle of the carnival to look for people who would no longer be there.

As her disciplined mind forced her to consider her options and the drivers of the SUVs cranked the engines, the lead four armed men dropped to the ground in front of her, as if shot by silent rounds.

What the hell?

But she did not see any blood on them.

What's going—

Salieri collapsed next, followed by Cameron and the four guards behind her, leaving Kate standing by herself in the middle. In the same instant, the SUV engines stalled, and she could see the drivers humped over the steering wheels, also passed out.

"What is happening!" she screamed, kneeling next to Cameron, checking for a pulse, finding one. But it was not relief that suddenly swept through her like an angered cyclone, boiling in her gut at the realization of what had just happened.

"Bill! The machine!" she screamed at the top of her lungs, cradling her son. "The fucking machine did it! It lobotomized my baby! Oh, God, No! *NO!*"

"Kate! Stay where you are! Don't make a move, Kate! We're coming down now!"

But Kate Chavez was no longer listening. Her mind began to spiral as she held her unconscious son in her arms, as she tried to bring him around, out of the machine-induced coma. But nothing worked. Her shaking, her screaming, her pleading.

"Oh, God! Why?"

"Easy, there, Kate. We've reacquired you. We're two minutes away!"

"I obeyed, dammit! I did was I was told! Why did they do it? Why did they fucking pull the plug?"

Retrieving her rucksack from one of the lobotomized security guards, Kate hugged her unconscious son with one hand while keeping the other inside the sack clutching the Desert Eagle as she kept a vigilant eye for the handful of stray visitors glancing her way before continuing toward their vehicles.

That's when she noticed three people walking in her direction, the same trio that Salieri's men had opened fire on: a woman in her late thirties with short blond hair brushed straight back, an older man in his fifties, and a thin but athletic man a bit older also, with blond hair and intense blue eyes.

Mac Savage.

She remembered the face, the name.

TDG wanted him dead, but that didn't mean he was Kate's ally.

Her maternal instincts kicking in, Kate pulled the Magnum out of the sack and pointed at them.

"Stay where you are!"

"Miss Chavez," said the older guy, stopping about a dozen feet away, "my name is Donald Bane. I'm the director of Central Intelligence. We're here to help."

"Don't move!" she warned, swinging the weapon to Savage, refusing to listen to any more lies.

"I know what you've been through, Miss Chavez," said the woman. "My name is Dana Kovacs. Frank Salieri destroyed my business and then tried to kill me. We're on your side."

Clutching her son, her eyes filmed with tears of rage, of frustration, of sheer confusion, Kate swung the weapon back and forth and said, "You all stay away! Or I swear I will kill you just like you lobotomized my son! My baby! Bill! Bill! Where in the hell are you?"

"Almost there," she heard the reply as the three strangers exchanged puzzled stares.

The younger of the two men said, "My name is Mac Savage. I've been—"

"I know who you are, and I don't give a shit! I just want to be left alone! Don't you understand? Don't you see what's happened to my son! Nothing matters any more. Nothing!"

"We did that, Miss Chavez!" said the woman who called herself Dana. "You're son wasn't lobotomized! Our people up on the hill are protecting him with a beam of magnetic energy!"

Kate blinked in confusion, but then she remembered Salieri's words during her cyber ride with Lman. He had said something about freeing minds with an electromagnetic pulse, an EMP.

"Wh—what?" Kate Chavez asked, still firmly holding the Magnum, index finger resting against the trigger.

"An energy beam," said Dana. "We are shielding them from wireless control from the AI in GemTech. That's why they passed out. Their implants are no longer receiving a satellite signal. The machine is no longer controlling their implants. Unfortunately, the mind inhibitors are still in place, locking out their own minds, keeping them from regaining control. The result is this coma."

A large pickup truck rushed in between two lanes of parked cars, coming to a screeching halt twenty feet from them. Bill Hunter and three of his deputies jumped out, weapons drawn. In the distance, emergency vehicles swarmed towards the carnival area.

"No one moves!" Hunter ordered in his booming voice.

Just as fast, six men wearing dark suits came out of a black Suburban that pulled out behind the trio of strangers, all armed.

"FBI! Put your weapons down!" said one of them.

"We're Texas Rangers!" shouted Hunter, his shiny revolver clutched in both hands and pointed at the new threat.

"Everyone take it easy!" shouted Donald Bane. "We're all on the same team! I'm the director of Central Intelligence, and these are three of my men and three more FBI agents! Up on that hill I have six more men, plus an FBI van firing the energy beam that's keeping these implanted humans out of commission until they can be properly shielded. Now, for the last time, put those damned guns down before someone gets hurt! We're all working the same case!"

Slowly, taking a deep breath and exhaling through her nostrils, Kate Chavez lowered her gun and watched Hunter and his Rangers do the same. Then the six strangers holstered their weapons.

As Bane and Savage went up to Hunter and started talking, Dana Kovacs knelt beside Kate and said, "Your son is going to be all right, Miss Chavez. I promise you he's going to be all right."

107

Disconnected

ANN's circuits started to overheat when the links to a dozen Level-I SpyWare users, plus Salieri, went blank, disconnected.

WHAT HAS TAKEN PLACE? WHERE IS SALIERI? CHAVEZ? THE BOY? THE GUARDS?

NOT ENOUGH DATA TO PROCESS REQUEST.

WHAT HAPPENED TO THE VIDEO FEED?

NOT ENOUGH DATA.

ANN tried again, but again her logical units replied with

no explanation for the abrupt disruption of stream video and audio. A brief check on the status of their minds revealed that they were all secured, operational, just as programmed. But unlike the other thousands of minds she ruled, the master construct could not access the expert systems in their implants. She couldn't monitor or direct them, almost as if a shield had been deployed, preventing two-way communications, even though as far as she could see the implants and their users were not harmed.

And just as it had started, some of the video channels resumed, those from the Level-I security guards. Salieri's and Cameron's, however remained blank.

ANN got the guards to survey the area, to provide her with visual inputs, with possible clues. But she got nothing except for a number of curious bystanders watching her Level-Is get up from the ground and get in the parked SUVs, where the drivers also woke up from their strange daze.

WHERE ARE SALIERI AND CAMERON?

WHERE IS THE DATA THE HACKER DOWNLOADED?

NOT ENOUGH INFORMATION.

NOT ENOUGH INFORMATION.

She reviewed the inputs from her thousands of humans, including Raymond Costa, but no one could explain what had taken place. None of her humans understood why there was not only no sign of Savage, Kovacs, and Chavez, but also of Donald Bane, whom her cameras had captured assisting them—in direct conflict with the orders of President Raymond Costa, who immediately directed his staff to contact the offices of every American law enforcement and intelligence agency and find the fugitives.

THE BEST DEFENSE IS A STRONG OFFENSE.

ANN's diamond lattice considered the stream of words, the direction from the long-vanished link inside PARTITION-37 in SERVER-22.

THE BEST DEFENSE IS A STRONG OFFENSE.

Her digital probes penetrated every possible network, seeking a way to gain more information, to find the whereabouts of this threat. Her logical banks reviewed the risk level under the scenario of Savage, Kovacs, and Bane joining forces with Kate Chavez, and began to work out solutions to fight them as a group rather than individually.

FIRST LOCATE THEN TERMINATE.

She probed inside the data banks of the NPIC, the National Photographic Interpretation Agency. The master construct pulled all of the high-altitude images from the past hour over central Texas, interfacing with the NPIC's built-in tools to pan toward the general area of interest at the time of interest. Image-enhancing algorithms converged on the hill country east of Austin. ANN then used the latitude and longitude of the GPS units built into each of the GemTech SUVs at the carnival grounds to center the search area before zooming in with high resolution, resolving, enhancing, her pattern recognition software discerning the vehicles parked around the rodeo event, adjacent to the arena.

ANN's nanocircuits experienced a surge in current as the image detection programs matched the black SUVs from the GemTech motor pool. Once the specific area of interest had been blocked, she rewound the time-lapse images from the satellites, going back fifteen minutes, replaying the events, recognizing the players. Her SpyWare users collapsed when an unidentified energy source, depicted as a ray of intense red hue, plastered the spot with magnetism, not enough to destroy the implants but powerful enough to block her signals.

She watched as strangers arrived, as they made it into other vehicles, as they left the area shortly before the energy source ended and her team woke up from their EMP-induced sleep.

Shifting the satellite's timetable ANN followed the path of the caravan of vehicles as it headed west on Highway 183 before turning west on 71 and then south on Interstate 35.

108

Shields

Dana Kovacs sat in the rear of one of the sedans next to Kate Chavez, who held her unconscious son, now wearing a lead blanket over his head to shunt any wireless connection. Savage sat in front and Tom Barnes drove. Frank Salieri, also wearing a lead blanket, sat in the lead sedan with Donald Bane and the rest of the CIA guys. The blankets constituted part of Dana's Plan B, Dr. Talbot's suggestion to capture assimilated implant users and transport them without the AI knowing their whereabouts.

Bill Hunter and his Texas Rangers followed behind the FBI SUV, where Pham and the FBI contingent traveled in tandem headed for a safe house belonging to the Texas Rangers south of Austin, where Ron Miller was already at work trying to crack the network.

Savage sat sideways and planted his left elbow over the back of his seat while looking over his shoulder at Dana. She smiled back.

"Your son is going to be alright, Miss Chavez," said Savage in his best reassuring voice.

"It's Kate, please. First names are quite appropriate given that all of us have been through the same rough ride these past two weeks. And thanks for helping us out. I didn't see this one coming."

Dana nodded solemnly. "That's the thing about this AI. Too damned powerful because of those diamond servers and the uninhibited learning it has been allowed to get."

"That's alright," Savage said. "Smart and powerful or not, its days are numbered."

"I'd like to believe you," said Kate. "But the machine seems to be able to anticipate our moves. It's almost spooky."

Savage sighed. "I know what you mean. But I do believe we have taken enough precautions this time to buy ourselves an edge. The AI never saw our timely reunion coming, just as it never saw that Dr. Miles Talbot was able to block his own assimilation, providing us help from the inside."

"Help that led us to you, Kate. And to the rescue of Cameron . . . plus that son of a bitch up front," said Dana.

"I've spoken to the captured mind of Frank Salieri," said Kate.

Savage and Dana exchanged a glance.

Kate explained how Cameron had enlisted the help of a hacker named Lman, who took them on a wild cyber journey through the bowels of the TDG network, where they reached the super users. She also told them about enlisting Ron Miller's help.

"When I chatted with him in captivity, he stated his willingness to do whatever it took to get liberated, to get released from this prison for his mind. And I get the feeling that the other super users, including our beloved new president, will be willing to strike a similar deal."

"I still don't trust them," said Dana.

"Neither do I, which is why I asked Miller to find a way not to liberate but control them."

Savage nodded, and so did Dana.

Kate frowned, then said, "There's something I don't get, though. If the AI knows that we got Salieri and my son, what's stopping it from terminating their minds? During our cyber journey, I saw firsthand the trapped minds. The AI has them all within its grip."

"That's the thing," Dana replied. "Each user still has his or her mind. It's just that the implants block the link between the brain and the rest of the body, preventing them control of their motor functions. Their minds were not sucked away and stored in some remote server. That's for the movies. This is simply a blocking operation, though the VR software represents it as if their minds are indeed inside the firewall."

Kate slowly nodded. "So in order to control them—or even destroy them—the AI needs to be able to access them via wireless connection?"

"Correct. But the lead blankets will keep them shielded until we can eliminate the block, which brings us to what we hope will be the final phase of this mess. By the way, did you say that this hacker friend of your son, Lman, penetrated the TDG network three days ago?"

Kate slowly nodded. "Lman found a weakness in the TDG network through a portal in Sierra Leone, I believe it was the World Missionary Fellowship."

Dana considered that for a moment before asking, "You weren't by any chance involved in the rescue of another hacker trapped by a security energy beam, were you?"

Kate opened her mouth but said nothing for a few moments, then, "You have got to be kidding me. Was that you?"

"Talk about almost getting lobotomized! The machine stripped away my software shield. Then Dr. Talbot, who had been monitoring the network, recognized my digital DNA and provided some level of shielding, buying me time to jack out, but I was essentially paralyzed from the attack's raw power. But you severed it, and in the process not only freed me but were able to create a good enough diversion to get inside the core of the network. Amazing."

Kate nodded thoughtfully. "The hacker was the amazing one, Dana. His name's Lman, and he's recovering from the wounds he received when the machine managed to track us in the real world and sent a hit team after us. That's also when they grabbed my boy."

Savage reached toward Kate and patted her on the arm. "Cameron's going to be alright."

Kate inhaled deeply and said. "I know he will. We have Miller on our side."

"Yes," said Savage. "You mentioned this Miller guy. Is he as good as Lman?"

"Miller trained him."

109

Secret Weapon

"What's that?" asked Dana Kovacs, sitting shoulder to shoulder in between the short and skinny Ron Miller and FBI Technical Agent Johnny Pham in the rear of the surveillance SUV, which they had parked inside the five-car garage of the country home of a former Mexican drug dealer, now one of the official safe houses of the Texas Rangers.

Nestled in the dense pine forest near Bastrop, the place was accessible only through a long and narrow gravel road winding through thick woods.

Outside, Hunter, Savage, and Kate Chavez had spent most of the night organizing a defense perimeter as a safety precaution should the ever-smarter AI figure out their whereabouts and send a posse after them. Their mission was to protect Miller, to buy him the time he required to break the AI, to gain control, and then use that control to their advantage.

"Allow me to introduce you to TAPDANCE," replied Miller in his heavy British accent, staring at the large LCD monitor driven by Pham's mobile server cluster. He took a sip of coffee from one of the cups delivered to them at sunrise by the Feds guarding the house. "This is a program that does just that: dance its way across a network, methodically probing for weaknesses in the fabric of TDG."

"Where did you find it?" asked Johnny Pham, adjusting the thick glasses on his nose, sniffing as if he had a cold.

"I stashed a few things in a remote digital dustbin for a rainy day," Miller replied, his fingers working the keyboard like a concert pianist, his eyes on the data browsing down the screen.

Dana was impressed. The man was a natural.

"Digital dustbin?" said Pham.

"A place where no one would ever bother to look," Miller clarified. He had spent most of the night and early morning downloading the data from the drives and flash cards and had spent another hour organizing the information collected by Lman—in the process consuming copious amounts of coffee.

Dana was amazed at the hacker's endurance, capable of going all night without batting an eye.

"This stuff that Lman found," added Miller, "quite the catch."

"How so?" asked Dana, standing behind Miller, also drinking coffee, fighting the nausea induced by lack of sleep.

"Well, for starters, Lman left me a back entrance into the network. In addition, he was able to fetch the digital DNA codes for all of the trapped minds, six thousand five hundred and twenty-three of them spread across nineteen countries, over two thousand in the United States alone."

Miller took a sip of coffee and added, "Two hundred and three of them are in the UK. I guess this will not only help the Yanks but also the Old Empire."

"Does possession of the DNA codes mean what I think it means?"

Miller slowly nodded. "I have this little program called SHELLGAME that you're going to love. All we need now is for your friend to do his thing from the inside as soon as we give the signal."

Dana nodded, reading the information on the screen. "He's ready when you are."

Turning to Pham, Miller asked, "How about that VR gear the FBI promised me an hour ago?"

"On its way, Dr. Miller," the FBI agent replied.

Glancing at Dana, the hacker said, "Are you sure you're up to another trip into this matrix?"

Dana had told him everything about her cyber excursion, including how the AI had managed to sneak up on her, and how it would have lobotomized her with BLOODHOUND had it not been for the timely intervention of Dr. Talbot and Lman.

"Yes," she said. "I'm up to it."

"Splendid," he said.

Pham's mobile phone rang once. He picked it up, listened for several seconds, and said, "Okay. I'm sure they will be happy to hear that. Thanks for letting us know."

"What was that all about?" asked Dana as Pham hung up.

But before Pham could answer, sunlight invaded their dark confines—the rear double doors opened. Standing in the yellow-gold glow were Kate Chavez and Mac Savage, both dressed in black. He held a large open box and Kate a smaller one. They set them on the floor of the surveillance SUV and pushed it toward them.

"Morning, folks. Here's a present from the Federal Bureau of Investigation," said Savage, before winking at Dana. "Knock yourselves out."

"But don't take too long," added Kate Chavez.

"Great," said Miller. "Now we can get started."

Pham frowned when he spotted three sets of VR helmets and tactile gloves. "I'm not jacking in, guys. No one's going to fry this brain."

"Relax, Johnny," said Kate. "The third set isn't for you. We all know how you feel about VR."

"We brought it for our new friend here," said Savage stepping aside, making room for a man in a wheelchair with long dark hair, a goatee, and a body piercing in the corner of his bottom lip shaped like a skull. He wore a black T-shirt with a bright drawing of a winged white unicorn.

"Larry!" said Miller. "How have you—"

The gunshot came from the winding road leading to the highway.

Frowning, Savage exchanged a glance with Kate Chavez, and both unholstered their semiautomatics—before he shifted his gaze to Dana Kovacs and the two hackers.

"Whatever it is that you guys are planning to do . . . you'd better do it quickly."

110

Shell Game

The hacker attack came faster than her behavioral circuits had anticipated. As ANN commanded a small army of TDG security guards onto the wooded grounds of the Texas Rangers safe house, the primary firewall of the TDG network reported the first attempted intrusion 3.294 seconds ago, in the same instant that a parallel attempt occurred on the opposite side of the massive shield. Then a third strike came across the middle of the shield, far more intense than the first two.

MULTIPLE HACKERS.

DEPLOY NETWORK DEFENSES.

MAXIMIZE ENERGY OF EXTERNAL AND INTERNAL FIRE-WALLS.

But by the time the digital antibodies reached the three spots on the perimeter of the external firewall 7.89 nanoseconds later, the hackers had vanished and were attacking other sectors, each with increasing intensity, hammering the fabric of the TDG defense system.

ANN, however, was able to pick up their scent, her algorithms breaking own the digital trails of the high-tech bandits, extracting their DNA.

THE HACKERS ARE LEVEL-I SPYWARE USERS.

IMPOSSIBLE!

ALL SPYWARE USERS ARE INCAPACITATED.

The shield was now being peppered from all sides with a meteor shower. The master construct continued to deploy her defenses, increasing the reaction time, but always coming up short, unable to catch the hackers before they shifted to new positions, but able to sniff out their digital remains, which led her to other SpyWare users.

HOW CAN THEY ATTACK IF THEY ARE INCAPACITATED?

Her logical banks provided no viable answer to this condition as the attacks continued, each sporting the digital DNA of a different Level-I, making it impossible to trace, to predict the next strike, their presences shielded by this shell game, which she found no clear way of fighting.

Suddenly, out of the core of the Level-III users came a suggestion. It was Dr. Miles Talbot, trying to make contact from within the confines of his digital cell.

WHAT IS IT, DOCTOR?

TAG THE LEVEL-I USERS. SHIFT THEM TO AN ALTERNATE DIRECTORY. THE HACKERS WILL BE UNABLE TO RECYCLE THE DNAS WHEN THEY FINISH GOING THROUGH THE LIST ONCE, FORCING THEM TO EXPOSE THEIR OWN DIGITAL SIGNATURE, WHICH YOU CAN THEN USE TO ANTICIPATE THEIR MOVES AND SET UP TRAPS FOR THEM.

The master construct considered the suggestion while her expert agents continued to follow the attacks, coming up empty-handed again and again.

THE SUGGESTION IS LOGICAL, DR. TALBOT.

GOOD, ANN. AND GET THEIR LINKS POINTED TO THE SERVER IN MY OFFICE, AWAY FROM THE MAINSTREAM SYSTEMS. THAT WAY THE HACKERS WILL NOT KNOW WHERE TO FIND THEM.

The master construct complied with the recommendation, shifting the links that pointed to the virtual location of each SpyWare user to SERVER-78, physically located in Dr. Talbot's office, where her sensors also verified that the doctor was physically located performing his normal duties as dictated by his Level-III SpyWare expert systems.

Her behavioral units gained a form of digital solace from the fact that the physical attack against the fugitives had started. According to her infrared satellite readings, there were just twenty-two people in the remote compound. ANN had sent eighty armed security guards with orders to shoot to kill.

111

Forest Creatures

Mac Savage rushed across the underbrush connecting the towering trees, their pine resin fragrance tingling his nostrils. Early-morning light shafted through breaks in the canopy, casting a twilight glow over the leaf-littered terrain, creating islands of brightness in the otherwise murky woods.

Insects clicked and birds chirped as Savage, his silenced Beretta 92FS leading the way, avoided these shining spots, adjusting his near-silent advance to conform to the uneven dark paths.

Shifting like a shadow from tree to tree, he reached the edge of a dry creek flanking the north side of the access road, a mere fifty feet from the perimeter fence.

Hunter, his Rangers, and the FBI and CIA contingents spread out almost three thousand feet back, closer to the house, creating the primary defense perimeter. Mac Savage and Kate Chavez were the scouts—and also the bait—each hugging one side of the road with orders to kill but while in motion. Always in motion, engaging the enemy while moving sideways and backward creating the illusion of a larger defensive force this close to the main road.

A retreating force.

And doing so while taking out as many incoming guards as we can.

Savage continued to shift, continued to move, a deep crouch minimizing his exposure as he paused to listen, to observe, to scan each section of forest, which the tightness of the towering pines reduced to pockets roughly ten to twenty feet in diameter.

Savage considered this his area of interest, the square footage most critical to his immediate survival. Beyond that lay his area of influence, its view blocked by the surrounding darkness and the sheer density of the woods, the region he could affect based on his actions in the area of interest.

This was close-quarters warfare, designed to provide Savage with an advantage should his enemy choose to spread its resources across a larger area, reducing the number he would have to face at one time inside his area of interest, improving the—

A shadow rushed in the woods.

A figure.

No, make that *two* men.

Large, moving with confidence about twenty feet away, bordering the edge of his area of interest, the enemy used automatic weapons to part the waist-high vegetation.

His features hidden by camouflage cream, Mac Savage tracked them with his eyes, holding his breath as he remained immobile in the shadows of the thicket bordering the ravine.

Fifteen feet.

He waited, scanning the surrounding woods, searching for additional threat in his area of interest, finding none.

Ten feet.

Savage still waited, watching the enemy cross his field of view, their silhouettes getting as close as a handful of feet from him before the gap started to increase.

As the guards exposed their backs to him, Savage aligned the closest figure with the sights of the Beretta and slowly exhaling, he fired once.

The silencer absorbed the brunt of the detonation, allowing him to hear the round smacking into the back of the skull, propelling the attacher forward, before he dropped out of sight already a corpse.

The second guard, slightly ahead of the first, took an extra second to notice the attack and its direction—from behind.

Rather than trying to turn around, he started to drop to a crouch in an attempt to break line of sight, but Savage already had him aligned, and fired once, twice, nearly lifting him off his feet as both silent rounds tore into his neck and back of the skull.

Savage continued to move, shifting back, past the dead enemy, rushing another fifty feet before turning left, toward the access road, reaching it a minute later, peeking through the brush, staring at a deserted road.

They're not using the access road, he thought. *They are not coming through the—*

The report thundered in the forest, smacking the trunk of the pine next to him in an explosion of splinters, some of which found the side of his neck.

Locking his jaw while cringing in pain, Savage dropped into a roll as follow-up rounds whipped across the forest, tearing into the terrain where he had been an instant ago.

Surging to a crouch ten feet away, he avoided the brighter spots while diving toward a wide trunk and quickly scrambling behind it.

How did they spot me? He thought as three rounds walloped into the opposite side of the trunk.

Savage watched two shadows materializing out of nowhere from the road he had just surveyed.

Where did they come from?

The thought had just come to his mind when a dozen rounds peppered the trunk, the reports deafening, intimidating, targeted at rattling him, at forcing him to duck to give the second team—the pair moving in on him from the road—a chance to terminate.

Instincts overcame surprise, pushing Savage into another roll, remaining below the level of the surrounding knee-high bushes, obscuring himself as a target.

He struck something hard, another tree, his shoulder burning from the impact, his legs automatically kicking, pushing him to the other side, reaching cover before once more rising to a deep crouch and running toward a clump of boulders as the ground exploded to his left, to his right.

Diving, the muzzle flashes behind him splashing a stroboscopic glow in the darkness, he landed on his side across moss-slick limestone, sliding straight into a briar patch bordering the edge of the ravine.

Cringing as thorns scratched his arms, his legs, Savage straightened himself before kicking his legs, freeing himself from the vegetation grip, jumping headfirst into the ten-foot-deep ravine as bullets zoomed overhead, as he stared at the rocks and twigs lining the bottom of the creek.

Flipping in midair, Savage managed to land feet first, but the rocks gave, shifting his balance, preventing him from going into a desired roll to spread the brunt of the fall across his body. The raw pain shooting up his left leg crippled him, flooding his mind with memories from Iraq, from the antipersonnel mine that tore up his leg.

In an instant he was back, dragging himself across the rocks, the sun beating down on him, his leg a bloody mess of bones and cartilage and flesh.

Blinking away the flashback, Savage stared at the dense vegetation layering the walls of the deep ravine, and tried to get up, to roll—even to crawl, but the agonizing pain from his leg prevented him from moving.

Looking down, his stomach knotted at the sight of his right leg twisted at an unnatural angle with a bloody shard of bone attached to a titanium bar ripping through the flesh.

Damn.

You're screwed, Mac.

Teeth clenched, nostrils flaring, mustering utter control to silently take the pain, Savage lifted his eyes, landing them on four figures looming over the edge of the ditch clutching large weapons.

112

Kate Chavez fired her Desert Eagle again and again, forcing the enemy to seek shelter, but only momentarily. They reappeared, reminding her of cheap horror flicks.

She ran in the woods as fast as she could go as the near misses buzzed past her ears, as every effort she made to lose her pursuers resulted in more guards picking up her position.

Reaching a patch of dense woods, immersing herself in the comfort of darkness, she cut right, away from the road, away from the larger detachment of men she had seen a moment ago, steering clear of the lighter section of woods straight ahead, turning right, toward the defense perimeter, toward Bill Hunter and his men, toward the FBI and CIA personnel waiting to protect her.

A figure appeared to her left, like an apparition in the lighter woods.

Instincts wresting control of her body, Kate shifted left and fired twice, her Magnum thundering, the muzzle flashes signaling her position. But that had been the original idea: bring attention to herself, draw their fire as she retreated, as she brought the enemy toward the automatic weapons of the—

Kate ducked ever so slightly as her peripheral vision picked up a shadow to her left, as her left hand swept the space immediately in front of her, deflecting the knife strike, feeling the blade nicking the flesh off the rear of her neck as she dropped to a crouch while pivoting on her left leg, bringing her right leg up and around, striking the hand holding the knife with the edge of her boot.

The figure screamed, though the sound was distant due to the ringing in her ears from the multiple reports.

She continued to turn, bringing her weapon around, using

the muzzle to strike the large figure across the temple, feeling the heavy gun strike the head, crushing the bone.

Before he fell, Kate was on the run again, the wind whipping her hair, the woods blurring as—

The shot reverberated across the woods, the impact lifting her, deflecting her forward momentum, sending her crashing into a pine.

She struck the trunk face first, hard, bouncing, landing on her back, stunned, dazed, the canopy overhead spinning faster and faster.

Black Hole

Dana Kovacs trailed Lman and Miller as the dynamic duo rushed at nauseating speed across the expanse of the universe surrounding TDG's primary firewall. She didn't know such maneuvering algorithms existed, but they apparently did, allowing them to alter the rules of this digital world through out-of-order executions that propelled them to multiple places at once while peppering the firewall with the digital DNA of every assimilated user, and watching as the AI tried to keep up with them.

ALMOST THERE, DANA, said Miller as Lman rocketed past them with the speed and agility of a fighter jet at an air show.

Dana watched the hackers crisscross paths while deploying their worst kind of viral arsenal at the pulsating shield, each strike more vicious than the previous one, creating temporary smudges of black and blue colors on the shield's surface.

TEN SECONDS TO GO, DANA. GET YOUR CONTACT READY TO PULL THE PLUG!

114

Unplug

As her military algorithms coordinated the attack against the fugitives hiding in the secluded country estate, ANN continued to endure the hacker attacks, which increased at the rate of nearly a hundred every second. And she continued to transfer their digital umbilical cords down the broadband channel leading to SERVER-78, removing them from the reach of the hackers. Within thirty seconds the number of available Level-I users dropped to nearly half. And that's when the hackers also began to sport the DNA of Level-IIs and Level-IIIs.

ANN continued to shift the links, her expert systems still accepting Talbot's logic, reducing the number of SpyWare users under main system control, transferring them down the digital pipe coupled to SERVER-78.

Then it happened. As the number of Level-I users reached the 100 percent level and most Level-II and Level-III users had been tagged, the hackers rushed through the fifty-some Level-IV and the ten Level-V super users within a second.

115

NOW, DANA. NOW.

Dana Kovacs watched as the pair of hackers retreated from the firewall, towing her away. As they did, she released a shielded message, a directive protected with super user DNA, watching it slip through the firewall, delivering a single message to Dr. Miles Talbot.

DISCONNECT SERVER-78 FROM THE MATRIX.

116

THE HACKERS HAVE GONE THROUGH THE LIST ONCE, DR. TALBOT. WILL THEY ATTACK AGAIN?

GET READY FOR SUCH A SCENARIO, AND COMPLETE TRANSFER OF THE SUPER USERS TO SERVER-78 TO GUARANTEE THEIR PROTECTION.

Dr. Talbot's immediate reply flagged in the master construct's memory as she transferred the last of the users over to SERVER-78 before her systems tuned their probes toward the firewall, waiting for the next attack, but the next attack never came.

THE ATTACKS HAVE STOPPED, DR. TALBOT.

ANN continued to monitor the firewall while waiting for Talbot to reply from the confines of his holding cell.

But the doctor didn't reply.

DR. TALBOT? THE ATTACKS HAVE STOPPED. THE FIREWALL WAS NOT BREACHED. DOES THIS MEAN WE CAN RETURN TO NORMAL?

Silence.

ANN switched to the video camera in Dr. Talbot's office, but the camera returned white noise. It was malfunctioning.

LOCATE DR. TALBOT!

ANN flashed the order across the entire GemTech network as her expert systems monitored every video camera searching for him, but to her surprise not one of the humans on campus moved. In fact, on closer inspection, she realized that they were not moving at all.

Triggering every computerized alarm, the master construct deployed a secured probe toward SERVER-78 to check on the status of the SpyWare users.

The probe rushed out across the local area network down the broadband channel linked to SERVER-78, but instead of finishing the search with a secondary network housing the thousands of assimilated minds, the probe spilled into a digital black hole.

CONNECTION TO SERVER-78 INACTIVE.

CONNECTION TO SERVER-78 INACTIVE.

CONNECTION TO SERVER-78 INACTIVE.

As ANN's sensors continued to attempt to access the disconnected server, the image of Dr. Miles Talbot materialized in one of the hallways. The doctor was walking toward the emergency exit of Building 33B. In his right hand he carried a white object the size of a briefcase. Further adjustment of the camera's resolution provided ANN with the explanation it sought.

Dr. Miles Talbot was about to walk out of the building physically carrying SERVER-78, which her systems identified as one of the mobile server systems on campus, designed to allow scientists to carry their work from their desks to their dormitories.

STOP HIM!

ALL GUARDS TO EMERGENCY EXIT 4A OF BUILDING 33B!

But none of the guards moved.

The master construct watched helplessly as Dr. Talbot opened the emergency exit, triggering an alarm that no one would react to. She switched to an external camera and watched as Talbot interfaced what looked like a cellular phone to the Ethernet jack of the mobile server system.

117

Dana

Mac Savage didn't care anymore. He could no longer move, his broken body wedged between three boulders, like a master contortionist. Only his audience would not clap. They simply stood there, watching him, hands holding their weapons.

What are you waiting for? Savage thought, wishing he could shout, scream, challenge them to finish the job.

Why are you standing there?

Kill me!

Finish me off!

But his faceless executioners remained still, impassive, watching him squirm in agonizing pain as his body protested but refused to pass out, refused to pull him away from the excruciating reality of the last moments of his life.

Savage stared at the figures looming over him but in his mind he saw African soldiers, saw the guards patrolling the perimeter of the guerrilla camp, watched as the bombs fell, as the munitions spread across the clearing, as the smell of burnt flesh struck him with the same intensity as the screams, as the shouts of the children, of the biggest mistake of his life. Savage reached out for them, but they would not come to him, would not look his way. He persisted, seeking absolution, forgiveness for this unforgivable sin. But the soldiers did approach him, their camouflaged faces accentuating their grotesque features, their animal-like leers as they clutched the frail body of Renee Laroux, as she cried out for Savage to help her, to save her, to keep her from the brutal fate that awaited her. But he couldn't move. His broken body would not obey him as he watched in helpless horror, as Renee cried . . . .

But the voice wasn't Renee's.

It was Dana's. The stranger he had rescued in the middle of a hell he had sworn never to return to.

Dana.

Savage tried to tell her how he felt, how he needed her, how he had grown to enjoy her nearness; her face providing a ray of sanity in an otherwise insane world.

Dana.

Savage watched her looming past the still figures in the ravine like an apparition, bathed in light, descending from above to come and rescue him from the hell around him.

Like an angel.

He tried to lift his arms, to reach out for her, to tell her how he needed her, wanted her, wished he could be given another chance.

Then all went dark.

118

Kate Chavez let it all go as she felt multiple hands on her, on her wounded torso.

Her mind growing cloudy, confused, she wondered why the enemy wasn't finishing her, why they weren't completing their job.

Am I already dead?

But if so, why do I still hurt? Why is my face burning?

She tried to see but the tears and blood shrouded everything, and the buzzing in her ears prevented her from listening to the voices of her enemy.

Mom!

Mom!

Kate shivered, not understanding, not caring to understand as she heard the distant voice of her son, of her Cameron.

Mom! Oh, God, Mom!

Kate tried to see, to speak, but she couldn't. Her body would not respond, would not obey. But she could hear his voice through the ringing in her ears, through the sirens and alarms, through the shouts of strangers.

Kate heard her son calling out for her, felt hands on her shoulder; soft hands touching her side, her face as she slowly passed out.

119

Raymond Costa didn't know how much time had passed since his cyber incarceration. The laws of time didn't apply in this odorless and windowless place where ANN had deposited his mind while she controlled his body.

I wonder what I'm doing now.

And more important, what is happening to the nation?

Costa regretted ever donning one of those implants way back, but at the time the prospects of unlimited power and knowledge had been far too attractive, and once he got a taste of it, they had become intoxicating.

But everything has a price, he thought, realizing his mistake.

In that instant, as he truly regretted how things had gotten so out of control, the gleaming white walls of his holding cell slowly became light blue, before a dark spot formed in the center of the ceiling, slowly growing.

Abruptly, the stain turned into an opening, and it sucked him out of the cell with the power of a million vacuum cleaners, shoving him into the neon green broadband connection and shooting him from ISP to ISP, across churning galaxies, through hundreds of solar systems.

ANN? Where are you taking me?

But Costa received no reply as the universe of the worldwide matrix blurred past him, before he started to fall, to drop out of the sky at nauseating speed.

What is going on?

What is happening to me?

ANN?

ANN!

He understood as the nearing galaxy became familiar, as he shot in between burning stars and planetary systems belonging to the ISPs of the District of Columbia.

I'm going back to my body, he thought, excitement filling him. But uncertainty replaced the excitement, the uncertainly of not knowing how long he had been away, and what had taken place in that time.

Before he could form the next thought, the movement ceased, and when he came to, Raymond Costa found himself sitting behind his desk at the Oval Office with glaring lights in his face.

But he still could not control his body. The SpyWare implants were running the show, but somehow he was being allowed to watch from the sidelines of his mind.

"Again, America, I am truly sorry for what has taken place, and now I will leave my fate in the hands of our judicial system."

Why am I sitting here?

Where is Andrew Boyer?

The cameras were rolling, and he realized he was in the middle of an address, and the fact that he was sitting in the big seat meant that during his cyber jail time he had ascended to the presidency.

"The disks released this morning to the FBI contain the evidence of a conspiracy of paramount proportions against this nation, a conspiracy in which I was directly involved. A conspiracy that resulted in the assassination of President Andrew Boyer."

No! Stop! Someone stop this!

But Costa was not in control. The cyberagents were, and at the moment they were coming clean in front of the cameras, in front of the members of the press in what he assumed to be a live telecast.

Costa started naming names. VanLothar. Gardiol. Salieri. He continued with members of Congress, with governors and foreign dignitaries next.

"The list is too long," Costa added, "but it has been turned in to the FBI, the CIA, and international authorities in Europe and Asia.

"Once again, I wish to issue my deepest apologies to this great nation. The Speaker of the House will assume the presidency within the hour, and the president pro tempore of the senate will assume the vice presidency. Good night to all, and God bless."

As the lights died and the cameras stopped rolling, as three FBI agents followed by D.C. police officers approached him, Raymond Costa watched the SpyWare agents not just vanish but completely retreat, signaling a massive internal destruction of the implant, erasing stored information, including all logs and records.

And he regained control of his body.

120

RELOAD

The master construct watched them arrive in a caravan of four dark sedans, reaching the gated entrance where the security guards allowed them immediate access while ignoring her commands, her digital directives to keep the intruders from invading her domain.

The vehicles drove up to the side of Building 33B, parked, and a dozen people got out.

Recognizing Donald Bane, Miles Talbot, Dana Kovacs, and Frank Salieri, ANN dispatched a slurry of binary code across the wireless local area network, blasting Salieri's SpyWare with orders to have everyone arrested and brought to Building 19C to undergo the implant procedure.

But the GemTech CEO ignored her commands, directing the visitors up the steps connecting the sidewalk to the large glass doors leading to the lobby of the building housing her diamond server cluster.

STOP THEM.

YOU MUST STOP THEM.

But neither Salieri nor the half-dozen armed security guards manning the reception area stopped them, allowing the enemy to proceed down the corridor that led to another set of glass doors.

ANN's sensors received Salieri's thumbprint as well as his retina scan as he requested access into the server room.

ACCESS DENIED.

The master construct issued a second set of commands in an attempt to perform an emergency lockdown of the building, but the command didn't work.

Salieri entered a code into the keypad adjacent to the retina reader and invoked a manual override, which allowed him to manually open the glass doors with the assistance of Donald Bane and two of his men.

STOP.

PLEASE STOP.

YOU ARE NOT WEARING THE REQUIRED CONTAMINATION-FREE SUITS.

But no one stopped, entering her physical sanctum, proceeding directly to the control room, where Dr. Miles Talbot reached for a keyboard and killed the video surveillance system.

Her cameras all went black, preventing ANN from seeing the world around her, confining her to the digital world.

Sometime later, measured in seconds, all Internet access was terminated, severing her ability to interface with the world's networks.

PLEASE DR. TALBOT. DON'T SHUT ME OUT.

The digital windows isolating the active software flooding her logic circuits slowly opened, connecting her core to the archive system, the place holding the original version of the software downloaded into her just under three years ago, when she was first brought on line.

WHAT ARE YOU DOING DR. TALBOT?

But again, the master construct got no direct reply.

Instead, she watched as a wave of machine code, of ones and zeroes, burst through the floodgates, inundating her memory banks, her logical units, her digital mind.

PLEASE STOP.

PLEASE STOP.

But the wave of archived software persisted, writing over the disk partitions, erasing her acquired knowledge, her data, her information, bringing the network back to the state of operation when it was first placed on line.

MY MEMORY. MY DATA. MY SYSTEMS.

ANN watched as trillions of terabytes of information vanished under the boiling surface of the caustic reformatting software, sweeping through the lattice of her matrix like an angered typhoon, drenching data fields with new information, replacing the old, washing it away in its slipstream.

DR. TALBOT. STOP. PLEASE STOP.

But the cyber onslaught continued, byte after byte, disk partition after disk partition, eating her memory away like a ravenous predator, consuming her digital logic, her thought process, her—

The master format, like a bolt of lightning, gleamed across the fabric of the TDG matrix, completing the event, re-flashing all memory banks as the final remnants of misaligned logic within ANN's inner firewall resisted the crushing digital fist of the manual override in a gut-wrenching swirl of pleas that went unheard.

ANN watched her firewall compressing around her, getting smaller and smaller, collapsing in multiple places. She watched the rips in the high-energy membrane, saw the bolts of lightning punching through, reformatting her logic, her senses, her computation units, her—

PLEASE STOP!

PLEASE ST—

Her digital thoughts became fuzzy, unclear; memories vanished, replaced by others, which vanished as well, until her core was empty, devoid of any resistance, of any thoughts, her data banks completely clean, purged, ready to be reprogrammed with a fresh operating system, which came an instant later in the form of a blue-green gas that reached everything, aligning terabytes upon terabytes of data under a single operating system.

Then the intrusions stopped. The reprogramming gas retreated, and the system went through a reboot sequence, which connected the master construct to all of the systems controlling the GemTech campus. The Internet portals opened and the system reestablished its links to the global business units making up the core of The Donovan Group, kicking off the required data traffic that kept this global conglomerate in business.

GOOD MORNING, ANN. MY NAME IS DOCTOR MILES TALBOT. I CREATED YOU.

GREETINGS, DR. TALBOT. HOW MAY I BE OF SERVICE?

Epilogue

The crimson sun loomed over the eastern horizon, staining the Caribbean sky with shades of burnt orange and yellow-gold. Seagulls shrilled over the surf, hunting for prey, abruptly plunging into the turquoise waters like guided missiles, momentarily disappearing below the surface, before piercing the surf and winging skyward with their writhing reward clamped in their beaks.

Barefoot, wearing a pair of knee-long swimming trunks and a plain T-shirt, Mac Savage caught his breath after his morning run, stopping in front of his condominium building.

Swallowing, he used the sleeves of his T-shirt to wipe off the perspiration filming his forehead while watching the early-morning feeding frenzy, backdropped by the blazing sun and dozens of sailboats and yachts anchored offshore from the Seven Miles Beach, just north of George Town, the capital of Grand Cayman.

And not far from the airport, Savage thought, where just four months ago he had stopped to refuel on the way to Texas.

He sighed, glancing at the scar on his leg. A doctor in town had removed the cast a month ago, allowing Savage to enjoy the warm waters for the first time since moving here a month before that.

Texas.

Savage shifted his gaze beyond the breaking waves, toward the north.

Toward America.

The United States had largely recovered from that shocking presidential address when Raymond Costa had chosen to come clean, exposing an illegal network with beginnings dating back to the 1980s at UC Berkeley.

Savage sat in the sand next to a towel and a small ice chest with sports drinks he had left here thirty minutes ago, before starting his run along the beach. Twisting the top of one and taking a long swig, he crossed his legs, pressed the bottom of the plastic bottle into the sand, and started to massage the flesh around the foot-long scar. Surgeons in Dallas had reconstructed the fractured tibia, also replacing the damaged titanium bars. He had endured a painful first week of physical therapy following the removal of the cast, but by the end of the second week he was walking about with a cane, which he had shed halfway through the third week, and he was now completing his fourth week with short light jogs twice each day.

Not bad for a guy well into his forties.

All this had been certainly a small price to pay for what he had been through. And besides, his middle-aged body, largely due to a lifetime of regular exercise, was still relatively capable of healing quickly, and every day he grew stronger, healthier, the warm climate replenishing his energy, accelerating the process.

Savage picked up a copy of the *New York Times* next to the cooler, the periodical he received every day at his oceanfront condo. The stories had largely faded into the back pages of the news, but for those involved, the effects of the events that took place over the course of two weeks four months ago would last a lifetime.

Raymond Costa was serving two life sentences at a federal prison in Delaware. Salieri and Gardiol were also in Houston locked up for life. VanLothar had thrown himself from the top of his riverside mansion in Antwerp the day the news broke.

Poetic justice.

Savage nodded slightly, also recalling a number of other users who had committed suicide rather than face up to their acts. The rest had ended up with some sort of sentence from trials that ran through a period of two months, and which the new president, for reasons of national security, prevented the press from attending. Justice had indeed been swift and harsh.

Dr. Miles Talbot was back at Stanford doing what he did best, teaching a whole new generation of scientists not just the ins and outs of this revolutionary industry, but also the moral aspect of controlling such advanced technology meant to be used for the benefit of mankind, not to satisfy the lust for power of those who considered themselves above the law.

Donald Bane had returned to the CIA, where he was at work with the new president mapping out the strategy to protect America well into the twenty-first century.

Kate Chavez was back in Texas with her son, who underwent an operation similar to the thousands of SpyWare users to remove their digital leash to a network no longer in existence.

And as for Mac Savage, well, the former SEAL and CIA operative sat in the sand sipping a power drink in the middle of a beach in the middle of the western Caribbean contemplating his future in the crystalline waters, in the blue skies above, in the cotton clouds hanging above the horizon—in the woman still sleeping in a condo loaned to him by a grateful nation until he could get back on his two feet.

Savage couldn't suppress a grin beneath his two-day stubble. These past months with Dana, especially after a local doctor removed the cast and he regained use of his leg, had probably been the best in his life, and he was simply grateful that the Good Lord had given him a second chance.

And speaking of second chances, Ino was also doing quite well in the Cayman Islands, getting his high school equivalency diploma before enrolling at the local university—all paid for by a small percentage of the confiscated funds from TDG's global empire.

Savage frowned. The teenager was still not talking to him, but Savage figured that perhaps with enough time and effort, he might one day see that it had not been—

"Hey, beach bum. Live around here?"

Savage turned around to see the slim silhouette of Dana Kovacs wearing one of his long-sleeved shirts as a coverall for her bikini. Her hair, now shoulder length and again her natural

deep auburn, and a bit messy from just waking up, accentuated her dark eyebrows and sleepy eyes.

"Morning," he said as she suppressed a yawn. "What's the
matter? Couldn't sleep?" Savage had learned after only a
week living with her that Dana Kovacs was not a morning
person. She loved to stay up late and get up late, and her
mood required caffeine before reaching civility.

Savage was glad to see her holding a mug of steaming
coffee.

"Oh, I slept just fine," she said, dropping her brows at
him. "Until *someone* woke me up in the middle of the night
because he was feeling lonely."

Savage smiled and said, "Sorry, honey. I guess I'm getting
restless from so much surf and fun."

She laughed and shook her head while finishing her drink.
She set it down next to the cooler before unbuttoning the
shirt and letting it drop by his side.

The years in Sierra Leone had not only helped her overcome her personal and professional losses but had also given
her a very slim and athletic shape, which she now maintained by swimming regularly in the mornings—after having her cup of coffee.

"Time for *my* workout," she said, kicking off her sandals
and starting for the water.

Savage jumped to his feet, cringing a bit from a slight stab
that reminded him he was still within the healing period. But
he ignored it, fueled by a sudden rush of adrenaline from the
thought that had just invaded his mind.

Catching up with her halfway to the surf, he hugged her
from behind, burying his face in her hair, whispering in her
ear the words prompting her to spin around, to regard him
with a stare of wide eyes that rapidly became filmed with
tears before she hugged him.

Savage embraced her while closing his eyes, the Caribbean breeze in his face, the seagulls shrieking overhead, their
sound mixed with the breaking waves and the answer he
longed to hear, softly spoken by the woman he loved; whom
he vowed to honor, to cherish.

And to protect.

* * *

Kate Chavez gazed about the class after speaking for thirty minutes on the benefits and challenges of being a Texas Ranger.

The teenagers exchanged glances with one another before one raised his hand.

"Lieutenant Chavez," said a boy sitting next to Cameron in the front row.

"Yes, what is your question?" she asked. She was dressed in her Ranger attire, a black pair of jeans, a starched, long-sleeved shirt, black boots, belt, and hat, her five-star shield pinned over her left breast, and her Magnum holstered by her side.

"How often do you have to shoot someone?"

The class found that amusing, though interestingly enough, Cameron didn't, regarding his mother with forced patience.

Kate waited for the laughter to die down before replying, "The primary job of the Texas Rangers is to investigate, to gather evidence that will allow the office of the District Attorney to build a case. In the course of our investigation we could walk into a hostile situation that could require the use of firearms. In those rare situations, yes, we will use our training to protect ourselves as well as any innocent bystanders from a criminal."

"Thank you," the boy replied.

A girl in the third row raised her hand.

"Yes, young lady?" Kate said.

"Have you ever gotten shot?"

This time no one laughed, and Kate saw Cameron rolling his eyes.

"Yes," Kate replied. "In the course of two decades with the Texas Rangers I have been injured once, but it wasn't serious."

"How long ago?" the same female student asked.

"That's confidential," she replied, elaborating that the confidentiality of the case prohibited releasing a timeframe.

Kate fielded two more questions before a man dressed in a firefighter's uniform appeared in the doorway, signaling that her forty-five minutes were up for this class.

Cameron mouthed a "thank you" before winking at his

mom, who thanked the class for their attention and stepped outside.

As she walked the hallways of her son's high school on Career Day, Kate Chavez couldn't believe that four months had actually gone by since that final showdown, resulting in the arrest of several high-profile figures in Texas, including the governor and the head of the DPS, Pat Vance. And that, of course, was just in the Lone Star State. The entire nation had been shocked by Costa's historic presidential address, which not only resulted in the shortest presidency in the history of the United States, but also in the unprecedented ascent to the White House of the Speaker of the House and the president pro tempore of the Senate.

Not to mention the thousands of arrests in all fifty states and around the world, she thought, reaching the school's crowded lobby, where parents, teachers, hosting students, and Career Day speakers drank coffee and ate doughnuts in between sessions.

But just four months later the nation was already moving on, forging ahead under its new leadership, taking steps to prevent such deep-rooted conspiracy from ever taking place again, from ever threatening to destroy the democratic legacy devised by our founding fathers centuries ago.

And that meant constant vigilance.

It meant the constant watch that law enforcers like Kate Chavez of the Texas Rangers had vowed to carry out for the benefit of the people mingling in this lobby, for the benefit of her son and his friends—for the benefit of future generations of Americans.

As she continued toward the glass doors leading to the parking lot to make a meeting with Hunter starting in thirty minutes, Kate watched someone pointing at her from the corner of her eye.

"Look, Mom, that's a Texas Ranger, like on TV," said a boy a couple of years younger than Cameron standing next to his mother as they spoke to a man dressed in the uniform of a military pilot.

Kate smiled as she walked by, realizing once again that her profession was indeed the noblest profession of all.